Tom Holt was born in London in 1961. At Oxford he studied bar billiards, ancient Greek agriculture and the care and feeding of small, temperamental Japanese motor-cycle engines; interests which led him, perhaps inevitably, to qualify as a solicitor and emigrate to Somerset, where he specialised in death and taxes for seven years before going straight in 1995. Now a full-time writer, he lives in Chard, Somerset, with his wife, one daughter and the unmistakable scent of blood, wafting in on the breeze from the local meat-packing plant.

Find out more about Tom Holt and other Orbit authors by registering for the free monthly newsletter at: www.orbitbooks.co.uk

By Tom Holt

TOM HOLT

HOLT

Saints and Sinners

Contains
Paint Your Dragon
and Open Sesame

orbit

www.orbitbooks.co.uk

An *Orbit* Book

First published in Great Britain by Orbit 2004
This omnibus edition © Tom and Kim Holt 2004

Paint Your Dragon
First published in Great Britain by Orbit 1996
Copyright © Tom Holt 1996

Open Sesame
First published in Great Britain by Orbit 1997
Copyright © Kim Holt 1997

A CIP catalogue record for this book
is available from the British Library.

ISBN 1 84149 346 5

Printed and bound in Great Britain
by Mackays of Chatham plc, Chatham, Kent

Orbit
An imprint of
Time Warner Book Group UK
Brettenham House
Lancaster Place
London WC2E 7EN

FIC
HOLT

CONTENTS

PAINT YOUR DRAGON

For
LESLIE FISH
The best of all of us

and
JONATHAN WAITE
Who has all the talents
Except one

CHAPTER ONE

Once upon a time, long ago and far away, there was a great battle between Good and Evil. Good was triumphant, and as a result Humanity has lived happily ever after.

But supposing Evil threw the fight . . .

And supposing Good cheated . . .

He stepped off the plane into the belly of the snake; the long, winding tube thing they shove right up to the cabin door, so that newly arrived foreigners don't get a really close look at dear old England until they're through passport control and it's too late.

He didn't actually have a passport; but he explained at the barrier exactly why he didn't need one, and so they let him through. In answer to his polite enquiry, they told him, 'Britain'. They even urged him to have a nice day, which was rather like imploring petrol to burn.

Down the steps he went, into the baggage hall. The carousel was empty and the indicator board expressed the

1

view that the luggage from Flight BA666 might be along in about half an hour, maybe forty minutes, call it an hour to be on the safe side, provided always it hadn't got on the wrong plane by mistake; in which case, it was probably having a far more exotic holiday than its owners had just returned from, and would probably settle down over there, adopt new owners, and lead a much fuller, richer life than it could ever have had in a damp, miserable country like this. He read the board and smiled indulgently. Then he concentrated.

The first item to roll out through the little rubber flaps was a big, old-fashioned steamer trunk. He looked at it, head slightly on one side, pursed his lips and shook his head. 'Smaller,' he said. The trunk went round and disappeared.

Next came a matching three-piece set of designer pigskin travelware, with very fancy brass locks, little wheels for ease of handling, and monogrammed straps. He shook his head vigorously, and the travelware, handles drooping with shame, made itself scarce.

Then came a medium-sized plain vinyl suitcase, no wheels. He was clearly tempted because he picked it up and tested the weight. But it must have seemed too heavy or too bulky because he put it back again, and a moment later it too trickled out through the flaps. A similar item, more or less exactly the same except for the colour and the contours of the handle, came next, but was dismissed with a slight pucker of the lips and a small sideways head movement.

It was followed a moment later by a simple black canvas holdall, with webbing handles and a shoulder strap. He looked at it, nodded and picked it up. He unzipped it; it was empty. When he zipped it up again, it was full. He looked around until he saw the exit sign and walked on briskly. Needless to say, the Customs men didn't even seem to notice him.

2

Before leaving the airport, he went to the men's toilet to brush his hair and see what he looked like. He hadn't had a chance to look in a mirror or a pool of water since he'd died, and although he was determined to spend as little time as possible in this poxy runabout Lada of a body, a certain human curiosity came with the hardware. He stepped up to the mirror.

If he'd been expecting a disappointment, he was disappointed. They don't advertise the fact, but the Heathrow men's bogs house the world's last surviving scrying-mirror, an antisocially cunning piece of kit which treats appearances with the scorn that Mercedes salesmen reserve for people who live in council houses, and lets you see yourself as you truly are. Back in the heroic past, no self-respecting wizard stirred out of doors without one; it was the only way to filter out all the gods disguised as mortals, princes masquerading as frogs, wolves in grandmothers' clothing and other pests which made the Dark Ages such a wretchedly fraught experience. This particular example now belongs to the syndicate who hold the airport's duty-free concession. It's linked to the video surveillance system and makes it possible for them to spot a mug punter before he's even checked in his luggage.

He saw a huge shape. If you love understatement and have just had your soul repossessed by the finance company, you could say he looked a bit like a lizard; except that lizards are generally smaller than, say, Jersey and don't have enormous wings, and even naturalists (who get paid for loving all of God's creatures) tend to look at their faces and think immediately of their spouses' relations. The face in the mirror, on the other claw, was beautiful in the same way that weapons and warships and violent electric storms over the sea at sunset can be beautiful.

The dragon clicked his tongue impatiently. He'd seen

that before. More to the point, that wonderful, dangerously attractive shape he was looking at had been significantly dead for thousands of years, ever since one George de la Croix (alias Dragon George Cody; better known to divinity as Saint George) had kebabbed it with a whacking great spear. One day, probably quite soon, he'd get another dragon body and look like that again; right now he was wearing a standard K-Mart two-leg, two-arm, pink hairless monkey costume – the equivalent of the cheap grey suit they give you when you're demobbed or let out of prison – and he wanted to see what he looked like in that. He turned to the next mirror along and saw a human male, powerfully built as humans go, medium height, longish dark hair and short, clipped beard with grey icing, and round yellow eyes with black slits for pupils.

Ah well, he thought. If you wear off the peg, you've got to take what you get. He was no expert in human fashions – in his day, nearly all the humans he came across wore steel boiler-suits with helmets like coal scuttles, and that was a very long time ago. It would probably do, until he got the dragon outfit back. And then, of course, everything would be different anyway.

Once outside he raised a hand, whereupon a taxi drew up and opened its door. That was, in fact, a curious occurrence in itself, since the last thing the taxi driver could remember was turning left out of Regent Street and swerving to avoid a right-hand-drive Maserati. He also had a notion that he'd had a passenger on board. Evidently not, for the cab was empty.

'Where to?' the driver asked.

'Licensed premises,' he replied. Then he threw his bag onto the back seat and climbed in.

The driver, a Londoner, didn't actually know of any pubs in the Heathrow area, and confessed as much. His fare

4

replied that in that case, they could learn together. 'Just drive around,' he suggested, 'until we see something I like the look of.'

And so they did. They'd been cruising up and down lanes for maybe half an hour when he suddenly leaned forward, rapped on the glass and said, 'That one.'

'You're the boss.'

'Yes.'

Having explained to the driver exactly why he didn't actually owe him any money, he waved him goodbye, shouldered his bag and crunched up the path to the front door. The landlord of the George and Dragon was, at that precise moment, asleep in bed – it was ten past ten in the morning, and yesterday had been a late darts night – so he was more than a little confused when, about one second after the doorknocker crashed down on its brass anvil, he found himself in the bar, fully dressed, shooting back the bolts.

'Morning. You open?'

'I think so.'

'That's fine. Large whisky, please, no ice.'

The customer had a fine thirst on him; ten large whiskies, one after another, appeared to have no more effect than airgun pellets fired at the side of a battleship. Ah well, thought the landlord, obviously a very lucky man. 'Another?' he suggested.

'Please,' the customer replied. 'What's that one with the green and black label?'

The landlord peered. 'Bourbon,' he replied, stating the brand name. 'A hundred and five proof,' he added.

The customer smiled. 'Ah,' he said. 'That's what I call fire water. Make it a treble, and have one for yourself.'

Just as the customer said it, the landlord realised how much he needed a drink at precisely that moment. He reworked the

5

optic, mumbled 'Here's health,' and knocked back the glass, the contents of which did to his head what Guy Fawkes wanted to do to Parliament. 'Good stuff,' he croaked.

'Not bad, I suppose,' replied the customer. 'Same again.'

It occurred to the landlord that it would only be polite to make a little conversation, and he asked the customer what line of business he was in. It seemed that he'd inadvertently made a joke, because the customer grinned.

'Let's see,' he replied. 'Let's say I'm a flier.'

'Pilot, you mean?'

'Sort of.' He felt in his top pocket, extracted a cigarette, drew on it heavily and exhaled. The smoke seemed to fill the bar.

'Civil or military?' the barman asked.

'Bit of both. What's that colourless stuff in the bottle with the red label?'

'Kirsch.'

'Treble of that, then, and next I'd like to try the other colourless stuff with the green label.'

'That's Polish vodka, that is. Hundred and forty per cent proof. Beats me,' the landlord went on, 'how something can be a hundred and forty per cent anything. I thought a hundred per cent was the limit; you know, like a hundred out of a hundred?'

Not long afterwards, the customer got up, thanked the landlord, and left him musing on three points that were puzzling him. Probably because his head was still glowing from the bourbon, he couldn't quite get a handle on any of them.

One; how come the man who had just left had managed to put away roughly ninety-seven centilitres of spirits in ten minutes and still been able to breathe, let alone walk jauntily out of the front door with no apparent impairment of his motor functions?

Two; the reason he had given for not paying had been utterly convincing, fair and square, no problems whatsoever on that score, but what had it been, exactly?

Three; just how in hell had he been able to smoke for five minutes without actually lighting the cigarette?

Bianca Wilson had first made her mark on Norton Polytechnic when she suddenly stood up in the middle of a class and put her clothes on.

Ignoring the comments, she then stepped down off the platform, took possession of the vacant easel and proceeded to paint a breathtaking still life of three herrings and a typewriter ribbon. After that, there was no question of mucking about with application forms; not only was she in the class, she was its star pupil. When asked what had prompted her to make the change from model to practitioner, she replied that it was warmer and you didn't have to keep still.

Sculpture proved to be her true medium. She stripped away marble as if it was cellophane wrapping to reveal the always implicit statue beneath. Once she'd learned the basics of the craft, such as how to sharpen a chisel and the best way to avoid clouting your thumb, it was obvious that there was nothing more that Norton Tech could teach her. Accordingly, she thanked them very much, gave up the day job by the simple but eloquent expedient of telling the office manager what he could do with it, and spent her last ten pounds on a ticket to London. She travelled, of course, in the guard's van; it had taken five porters, the conductor and three gullible Royal Marines to get her luggage on board, and the Spirit of World Peace had to make the journey with her left leg sticking out of the window.

Small-town girl in the big city; well, so was Joan of Arc, not to mention Boadicea. A talent like Bianca's is always hard to keep hidden, particularly when its manifestations are ten feet high and weigh close to a ton and a half. It took the proprietor of the Herries Street Gallery, stepping off the train at Paddington, fifteen seconds to recognise true genius when he saw it, three quarters of an hour to hire a suitably heavy-duty lorry, and six weeks of humiliating negotiation to get Bianca's signature on a contract. The rest is art history, with cross-references to economics, accountancy and business studies.

Thus, when, about eighteen months later, Birmingham City Council was playing third time lucky with the design of the city's celebrated Victoria Square, and the Kawaguchiya Integrated Circuits people came across with a six-figure garden gnome fund, there was only one possible choice; provided she would agree to do it. For a very long fortnight she considered the offer; any subject she liked (except, added the city fathers, World Peace, because you do tend to get just a wee bit carried away on that particular theme, and we need a bit of space in the square for buildings and stuff) and as long as she liked to do it in, all the rock she could handle plus, of course, the immense satisfaction of helping gild Europe's most fragrant lily. Could anybody refuse an offer like that? Apparently, yes.

The city fathers faxed Kawaguchiya Integrated Circuits, tactfully suggesting that the two in their original letter must have been a misprint for three. KIC, thinking wistfully of the sixty acres of Tyseley they'd set their hearts on, faxed back their confirmation. Bianca accepted.

After careful consideration, she had narrowed the choice of subjects down to two. One of them, she told the Council, was the Industrial Revolution raping Nature, with side friezes of captains of industry through the ages suffering appropriate torments in Hell. Did they want to hear the other choice? No, Ms Wilson, that'll do fine. No, the other

8

one will be just splendid, whatever it turns out to be.

To their amazement and relief, it turned out to be Saint George and the Dragon. Nobody could guess why, least of all Bianca Wilson.

After leaving the pub, he strolled for a while along the quiet, winding road. He had much to think about.

Well, it sure was good to be back. The shape; well, it was limiting, not to mention uncomfortable and intrinsically silly, but he'd be rid of it soon enough and then he'd really be back. He swung the holdall by its handle, and smiled at the clanking of its contents.

England; not that he'd seen very much of it, but probably enough for his purposes. Lots of trees, he observed. Haystacks. Fields of waving, sun-ripened corn. Thatched cottages. Perfect. It was a wonder the United Nations hadn't made them tie a label on it saying *Highly Inflammable*. A lorryload of straw bales chugged past him and he grinned.

He felt well. True, the actual fuel content in fermented liquor wasn't all that high, and he'd probably have done better in practical terms to have called in at a petrol station and taken a long swig from the pumps. But there was no point in going out of one's way to appear conspicuous, or at least not yet. Pretty soon he'd be so conspicuous they'd be offering him a Saturday job as a lighthouse. Patience, patience.

The summer breeze was warm on his back and he instinctively looked upwards. Good thermals, if he wasn't mistaken. On a lovely calm day like this it was horribly frustrating to be stuck on the ground. As if in sympathy, his shoulder-blades began to itch and he paused a while to scratch them against a gatepost.

While he was standing and looking at the sky, he became

aware of an unusual noise; a bit like thunder, a bit like the roar of a food-processor in full cry, with a tantalising hint of movement and a dash of power. A moment later, two jet fighters swept across the sky, flying perhaps a trifle lower than regulations permitted. They were only visible for a second and a half at most, but in that time his exceptional eyes scanned them and reported every detail of their appearance and construction to a suddenly lovesick brain. True, he'd come across aircraft before, like the big fat lumbering thing he'd come in on – a huge flying metal slug, a parody of flight. These, though, were something else entirely. It was as if a man brought up in strict seclusion by elderly nuns had just wandered into the changing room at a top-flight fashion show. Yes, shouted every fibre of his being, I *want* one of those.

He concentrated and quite soon one of the fighters came back. At his subsequent court-martial, the pilot was unable to offer any explanation. The best he could come up with was that it was a sunny day, it looked like a nice place, and there was this friendly looking man in the road below waggling his thumb.

'Hi.'

The pilot pressed a button and the windshield slid back. 'Hello,' he replied. 'What . . .?'

'Nice machine you've got there.'

'Yes. Um . . .'

'I particularly like the way it just sort of drops in on the ground. I always thought you had to find a flat open space and come in gradually.'

'Not any more,' replied the pilot. 'Vertical take-off and landing. Look—'

'Mind if I have a go?'

'Well, actually, it doesn't belong to me, so perhaps—'

'Ah, go on.'

10

'All right.'

There were, he noticed as he clambered into the cockpit, all sorts of knobs and levers and things which presumably made the thing go. Superfluous, of course, in his case. He applied his mind.

'Excuse me!'

He looked down at the pilot. 'Yes?'

'Before you take off,' shouted the pilot above the roar of the engines, 'put the windshield back up. Otherwise you'll be blown—'

'Thanks, but no thanks. I get claustrophobic in confined spaces.' How true. How very, very true. 'Cheerio.'

Then ... straight up in the air, no messing. This was something he could get used to. And to think, last time he'd been here the best the poor fools could do was stick feathers to their arms with beeswax and jump off cliffs. All credit to them, they'd certainly been busy.

As the slipstream clawed vainly at his face and the ground became a fast-moving blur far below him, he snuggled back in his seat, sighed with pure contentment and groped with his mind for the weapons systems.

Bianca was used to inspiration. Scarcely a day went by without some rare and splendid gift of the gods slipping in through the cat-flap of her mind and curling up, nose to tail-tip, in front of the radiator of her genius. It was getting to the stage where she couldn't walk past a stone-built building without seeing hundreds of enticing images peeping out at her from the heart of the masonry, like socks leering through the glass door of a tumble-drier.

The Birmingham job, though, was something else entirely. A terrible cliché, of course, to say the thing had taken on a life of its own, but that was about the strength of it. The further the work progressed – and she was amazed at how far she'd

11

got in such a short time – the less actual control she seemed to have. Not that the work was inferior – on the contrary, it was superb, if you liked naturalism in your sculpture. But it was odd, because neither Saint George nor his scaly chum were turning out anything like the way she'd imagined them. George, she couldn't help thinking, ought to be taller, more heroic, less – well, dumpy and middle aged. He should only have one chin, and that a sort of Kirk Douglas job, the kind of thing you could surround with sea and put a concert party on the end of. He certainly shouldn't have round little piggy eyes and a squadgy little mouth like two slugs mating. And as for the dragon . . .

But, she had to admit, she did like the dragon. It had style. In fact, it had so much style you could bolt a wheel at each corner and give it an Italian name. It was graceful, attractive, dangerous; you could see the power in those tremendous muscles and hear the whistle of the wind in those amazingly broad, delicate wings. Above all, it made you think, if someone came up to you and offered to bet you money on the outcome of the fight, you wouldn't take George at anything less than seventy-five to one. The result had to be a foregone conclusion.

She said as much to her friend Mike one evening as he helped her with the tarpaulins. Mike nodded.

'I wouldn't want to have just sold George a life policy,' he said. 'A single-premium annuity, yes. I think I'd be on pretty safe ground there. But straight life or accidental death cover, no.'

'Strange,' Bianca agreed. 'Do you think it might be symbolism?'

'Probably. What did you have in mind?'

'Well.' Bianca stood back and took a long, dispassionate look. 'There's all sorts of things it could be symbolising, actually.'

'Such as?'

'Um. The ultimate futility of imperialism?'

'Nice try.'

'Um. Male violence towards women?'

'Could be. In which case, the male is definitely on a hiding to nothing, unless you chip off George's moustache and beef the pectorals up a bit. Talking of his moustache, by the way, had you noticed the strong resemblance to Alf Garnett?'

'All right, then,' Bianca said. 'How about World Peace?'

'Ah,' said Mike, nodding. 'Silly of me not to have realised before.'

Bianca sighed. 'You're right,' she said, 'it's definitely up the pictures. Here, help me get the sheet over it before I get too depressed.'

'Didn't say I didn't like it,' Mike replied, as a gust of wind turned the tarpaulin into a mainsail. 'I think it's absolutely amazing. It's just . . .'

'Yes. Quite.'

'How much more are you planning on doing to it?'

'I don't know,' Bianca replied pensively. 'Either I'm going to leave it pretty much as it is, or else I'm going to take a sledgehammer to it first thing tomorrow morning. What do you think?'

'I think,' said Mike, 'that if you choose Plan B, I could use the chippings. There'd be enough to cover every driveway in the West Midlands.'

At that moment, the rogue Harrier jet that had been shooting cathedral-sized divots out of Salisbury Plain suddenly stopped in mid-air, stalled and fell into a spin, dropping out of the air like a shot bird.

Cuddled in the arms of a warm thermal, the dragon watched it fall and shrugged. He'd been wrong. Compared

13

to his real shape, it was just a toy; fancy dress, a tin overcoat. As it hit the ground and exploded, he flicked his tail like a goldfish, rose and hovered over the swelling mushroom of smoke and fire. Ruddy dangerous, too, he added. One little bump on the ground and they blow up. Shit, I could have been inside that. Doesn't bear thinking about.

He throttled back to a slow, exhilarating glide and began an inventory of his new shape. Neat. And gaudy too, which he liked. A little bit more gold wouldn't have hurt and maybe a few more precious stones here and there; still, what did you expect from something that owed its original genesis to local government? But in terms of function, of efficiency and power-to-weight ratios, he couldn't fault it. For a moment, he almost wished there were other dragons in the world. He'd have enjoyed giving them the name of his tailor.

When Bianca arrived on site the next morning, the tarpaulin was already off and Mike was struggling to fold it; in this wind, a bit like trying to cram the universe into a paper bag. He looked up and gave her a sad smile.

'I asked you to save me the chippings,' he said.

'Sorry?'

'That's all right. Next time.'

'No, sorry as in what the hell are you talking about.'

Mike frowned. 'The dragon,' he said, pointing. 'You came back last night and scrapped it. Quick work.'

'No I didn't,' Bianca said, pointing. 'It's still . . .'

Gone.

When you're a dragon, sobering up can be a nasty experience.

The last of the Polish vodka burned off just as he was attempting a flamboyant triple loop, about seventy thousand feet above sea level, and sixty-nine thousand feet directly above the very pointy tips of some mountains. At that point, something nudged him in the ribs, gave him an unpleasant leer, and said, 'Hi, remember me?' It was Gravity.

Fortunately, he had sufficient height and enough of a breeze to glide quite comfortably down onto a flat green stretch in the middle of the large human settlement he was presently overflying. As he made his approach, he noticed that his chosen landing strip was dotted with humans, all dressed in white and staring up at him, while around the edges of the field, crammed onto rows of wooden benches, were several thousand other humans, also staring. The dragon was puzzled for a moment. He didn't have a fly, so it couldn't be undone. Hadn't they ever seen a dragon before?

Having felt for the wind, he put his wings back, stretched out his legs, turned into the breeze and dropped lightly down onto the turf, landing as delicately as a cat jumping up onto a cluttered mantelpiece. The white men had all run away, he observed, and the spectators – he assumed that was what they were doing; either that or they were some kind of jury – were trying to do the same, although they were finding it hard because they were all trying to do it at the same time. Some blue men were walking towards him with the slow, measured tread of people who feel they aren't being paid enough to die. He wished there was something he could do to put them at their ease. He was, however, a realist; the only thing he'd ever managed to do that helped human beings relax was to go away, and unless he could get to a gallon or so of strong drink, that wasn't among the available options.

Or maybe it was. The green area was divided from the rows of benches by a thin wall of painted boards, with words on them; National Westminster Bank, Equity and Law and – he recognised that one – Bell's Whisky. That, if he wasn't mistaken, was one of the brands of fuel he'd taken on board at the pub. If they had its name written up on a hoarding, perhaps they had some about the place. It would do no harm to ask.

'Hello,' he said.

At once, the blue men stopped dead in their tracks, and began talking frantically to little rectangular boxes pinned to the collars of their coats. This puzzled the dragon at first, until he worked out that the boxes were some sort of pet, that his rather loud, booming voice had frightened them, and the blue men were comforting them with soothing words. The dragon rebuked himself for being inconsiderate and lowered his voice a little.

'Hello,' he repeated. 'I wonder if you could help me. Have you got any Bell's Whisky?'

Perhaps the little boxes didn't approve of whisky, because they needed even more calming down this time. Painfully aware that tact had never been his strong point, the dragon modulated his voice into a sort of low, syrupy hum, and beckoned to the nearest of the blue men.

'Excuse me,' he cooed. The blue man stared, until the dragon was afraid his eyeballs would fall out of his head, assured his pet box that it was all right really, and took a few nervous steps forward. The dragon considered a friendly smile, but thought better of it. His friendly smiles, it had to be admitted, did rather tend to resemble an ivory-hunter's discount warehouse. It'd probably frighten the poor little box out of its wits.

'You talking to me?' said the blue man, in a rather quavery voice.

'Yes,' replied the dragon. 'Bell's Whisky. Is there any?'

'What you want whisky for?'

16

Softly, softly is all very well, but the dragon was beginning to get impatient. 'I'll give you three guesses,' he replied. 'Look, either you have or you haven't, it's not exactly a grey area.'

'I don't know,' the blue man replied. 'I'm a policeman, not a bartender.'

'I see. Would you know if you were a bartender?'

'I suppose so. Why?'

The dragon sighed. If it had had a fuel gauge, it would be well into the red zone by now, but even so the flames that inadvertently ensued were four feet long and hot enough to melt titanium. 'Perhaps,' he said, observing that the policeman had gone ever such a funny colour, 'you'd be terribly sweet and go and fetch me a bartender, so that we can get this point cleared up once and for all.'

'Um. Yes. Right.'

'Thank you ever so much.'

'Um. Don't mention it.'

'Hope the flames didn't frighten your box.'

The blue man backed away, turned and ran; and for a long time, the dragon sat quietly where he was, conserving his energy and watching the pigeons waddling about on the grass. The whole area was empty by now, except for two or three of the blue men, huddled behind benches at the very back. It dawned on the dragon that something was going on. He frowned. It was, he felt, a bit much. Back in the old days, the humans hadn't made this much fuss when he dropped in on cities demanding princesses to go, hold the onions.

You'd think, he reiterated to himself, they'd never seen a dragon before.

Hey!

Maybe they *hadn't* seen a dragon before.

Anything's possible. Perhaps, in this strange and rather

down-at-heel century, dragons had become scarce. If this was a remote, out-of-the-way district (his exceptional eyes, scanning generally for a clue, picked out the name Old Trafford written on a board, but it didn't mean anything to him) then it was conceivable that he was the first dragon they'd ever set eyes on. Reviewed in that light, the behaviour of the humans made some sort of sense. Rewind that and let's think it through logically.

Assume they've never actually seen a dragon. They will, nevertheless, have heard of dragons; everybody has. And, facing facts, he wasn't so naïve as to imagine that what they'd heard was necessarily accurate. Humans, he knew, are funny buggers, delighting in the morbid and the sensational, eclectic in their selection of what to remember and what conveniently to forget. Quite likely, that was the case when it came to the popular image of dragons. If he knew humans, they'd ignore the ninety-nine per cent of its time a dragon spends aimlessly flying, basking in the high-level sunlight, chivvying rainclouds to where they're needed most and persuading winds to behave themselves. More likely than not, the perverse creatures would focus on the five per cent or less of its life a dragon spends at ground level, ridding the world of unwanted and troublesome armour fetishists and saving kings the trouble of finding husbands for superfluous younger daughters.

In which case . . .

Damn.

What a time, the dragon reflected ruefully, to run out of gas. Because any minute now, some macho nerd on a white charger is going to come galloping up through the gate with an overgrown cocktail stick under his arm, hell-bent on prodding me in the ribs. Normally, of course, this wouldn't pose any sort of problem; one sneeze, and all that's left is some fine grey ash and a pool of slowly cooling molten iron.

18

Without fuel, however, he was going to have to rely on teeth and fingernails, which was a pest because it was ever so easy to crack a molar on those silly iron hats they insisted on wearing, and if dragons really are scarce, chances are there's precious few competent serpentine dentists within convenient waddling distance.

What I need, muttered the dragon to himself, is a good stiff drink of kerosene. He turned his head slowly from side to side, dilated his nostrils and sniffed. Over there . . .

At the back of the enclosure some tall iron gates swung open and four strange green vehicles rolled through. They were big, made of iron and fitted with long iron ribbons under their wheels – socks? go-anywhere doormats? – and when the dragon pricked up his exceptional ears, he heard a blue man by the gate shout to a colleague that it was going to be all right, the tanks were here now.

Tanks.

Yes, right, said the dragon to himself, *tanks*, I remember now. Big metal vessels used for the storage of liquids. At long last, here comes the Bell's Whisky. And there was me thinking they were out to get me.

SIMMS LIBRARY ALBUQUERQUE ACADEMY

CHAPTER TWO

'It can't,' Bianca protested, 'just have disappeared.'

Mike shrugged and made a pantomime of patting his pockets and poking about in Bianca's toolbag. 'Bee, love, it's a tad on the big side to have rolled away and fallen down a grating somewhere. Of course it's flaming well disappeared. Obviously, someone's pinched it.'

'Pinched a fifteen-foot-long statue of a dragon? Kids, maybe? Bored housewife who didn't know what came over her? Don't be so bloody stupid. It'd take a whole day just to saw it off the plinth.'

'True.' Mike peered down at the stone beneath Saint George's charger's hooves. 'And no saw marks, either. In fact, no marks of any kind. You know, this is downright peculiar.'

'Peculiar.' Bianca closed her mouth, which had fallen open. 'Mike, if ever Mars challenges us to an understatement match, I'm going to nominate you for team captain. What the hell am I going to *do*?'

Mike scratched his head. 'You could start by telling

somebody. The police. Birmingham City Council. Kawa-guchiya Integrated . . .'

He met Bianca's eye. Comparable meetings include that between Napoleon and Wellington at Waterloo and the encounter between Mohammed Ali's solar plexus and Joe Frazier's fist back in 1974. 'Quite,' he said. 'I see what you mean. This is going to be a problem, isn't it?'

'Yes.'

'Do you think,' Mike suggested, after a moment's consideration, 'that you could, sort of, talk your way out of this? I mean, it's your blasted statue. Convince 'em that there never was a dragon to begin with. Sort of, Saint George and the *implied* dragon. Saint George, just practising? Saint George and Imaginary Friend?'

'No.'

'Maybe not. Or could you lose the armour, fiddle around with the sword a bit and rename it *The Polo Player*?'

'Mike.'

'Okay, okay, I'm just bouncing a few ideas here. Here, why not just call it *Study for Saint George and the . . .*'

Bianca closed her eyes and massaged them with the heel of her hand. 'What I can't imagine,' she said, 'is what the hell can have happened to it. I mean, dragons don't just get up and walk away. Just to move something that size you'd need cranes, flat-bodied trucks, hydraulics, all that stuff. Believe me,' she added, 'I know. When I delivered that cameo group of Mother and Child in Macclesfield last year, they had to close off fifteen streets.'

They stood for a few seconds longer, staring at the absence – a distinctly dragon-shaped absence, but an absence nevertheless. Compared to how Bianca was feeling about vacuums, Nature was honorary treasurer of their fan club.

'Well,' said Bianca at last, 'there's no point standing here

21

like trainee lamp-posts. Help me cover the dratted thing up, what's left of it, and I'll get on to the wholesalers for some more white Carrera. I only hope they can match the grain.'

Mike nodded. 'What about him?' he added, jerking a thumb at Saint George. 'Want me to put a padlock on him or something?'

Bianca gave him the last in a succession of withering looks; if the Americans had had looks like that in 1972, the Viet Cong would never have stood a chance. 'Get real,' she sighed. 'Who the hell is going to steal a statue?'

Chug, chug, chug; an elderly coach, the sort of vehicle that can still call itself a charabanc and get away with it, burbles slowly and cheerfully like a relaxed bumble-bee along a winding Oxfordshire lane.

On either side of the road, Cotswold sheep, as self-consciously picturesque as the most highly paid super-model, ruminate and regurgitate in timeless serenity. Thatched cottages, tile-roofed golden-stone farmhouses, evocatively falling-down old barns and the last surviving old-fashioned telephone boxes in Albion are the only footprints left here by the long march of Humanity; and if these works of his hand were all you had to go by, you'd be forgiven for thinking that Man wasn't a bad old stick after all. For this is the rural Thames Valley, the land that Time forgot, scenery pickled in formaldehyde. If England was Dorian Grey, this would be the watercolour landscape he keeps in his attic.

Inevitably and on schedule, there to the left of the coach is a village cricket match, and the big, red-faced man toiling up to the crease is, ineluctably, the village blacksmith. For a slice of living palaeontology, forget *Jurassic Park* and come to North Oxon.

And here is the village, and here is the village green, and

here are the ducks. The coach pulls up, wheezing humorously, and the passengers spill out; fifteen elderly ladies with flasks and sandwiches, deck chairs and knitting. It's all so sweet you could use it to flavour tea.

Thirty seconds later, a black transit van with tinted windows purrs noiselessly up and parks at the back of the green. The doors do not open. It lurks.

The old ladies have laid out their tartan rugs and, after much comical by-play and merry laughter, put up their deck chairs. The sun is shining. Tea flows. Sandwiches are eaten.

Time is, of course, not a constant. Science would have you believe that it potters along at a fixed, unalterable speed, never accelerating, never slowing down; rather like a milk float. Big joke. Time has a gearbox; it can dawdle and it can race. This, in turn, can result in absolute chaos.

Supply and demand, twin pillars of the cosmos, apply to all things, and Time is no exception. In some places, such as this sleepy and idyllic village, they scarcely use any of the stuff. In Los Angeles, Tokyo and the City of London, where Time is Money, they burn it off at a furious rate. And, try as they might to wring every last drop of value out of each passing second, their officially allotted ration is pitifully inadequate.

Sceptical? Here's concrete evidence. Think how much time twenty pence buys you in a car park in Chipping Norton and the equivalent figure in Central London. Where there is supply and demand, wherever there are unfulfilled shortages, there are always entrepreneurs ready and willing to step in and sort things out. There are no exceptions to this rule. The black market in Time is probably the biggest growth area in the whole of the unofficial economy. It's also the most antisocial, which is why it's such a closely guarded secret.

The sandwiches have been eaten. Jam tarts appear. Someone produces, as if from thin air, a wind-up gramophone.

Something truly horrible is about to happen.

It works like this. Time proverbially flies when you're enjoying yourself; or, put rather more scientifically, pleasure electrolyses Time. The mere act of a human being unreservedly enjoying himself acts as a catalyst, speeding up the decay of raw Time in the atmosphere. In the same way, misery, suffering and having to go to work impede the decay of Time, causing a massive build-up of the stuff. In primitive rural communities, for example, where peasants grind out lives of bleak, hopeless toil, Time seems to stand still, until the very stones of the cottages and turf of the fields are marinaded in the stuff.

To drill for Time, therefore, find a spot where countless generations of wretched serfs have had to get up at half-past five every morning to milk bad-tempered cows. Having located the spot, shout, 'There's Time in them thar hills!' and assemble your drilling rig. This will consist of between seven and twenty happy souls who are blessed with the rare ability thoroughly to enjoy themselves, unself-consciously and without stint.

Research has shown that little old ladies on outings do this best, with thirsty male Australians coming in a close second. Combine the little old ladies with the idyllic unspoilt village and stand well back, because you've just unleashed a chain reaction that makes nuclear fission seem wimpish in comparison. And be warned; it's not a pretty sight.

Inside the black transit, a small machine begins to run. Someone chuckles unpleasantly, mutters, 'Time, gentlemen, please,' and throws a switch.

For the first thirty seconds, nothing much happens;

24

nothing visible, anyway. The first perceptible changes are to the buildings. Thatch moults, dry stone walls collapse, oak beams sag. Entropy, acting as fast as the soluble aspirin of your dreams, is tearing the place apart as the surplus Time is leeched out of the fabric. Then, because Nature abhors a vacuum, raw present rushes in to take the place of the fossilised past, in the same way as a worked-out gravel pit floods with water. Thatch is replaced with tile, stone with brick and breeze-block. Barns fade away, and are replaced by barn conversions, complete with upper-middle-class occupants and a brace of Porsches in the driveway. Suddenly there's a development of ninety-six executive retirement homes in the old orchard behind the village green. A business park springs mushroom-like out of the ground where a minute ago there were only cows. Cars sprout up beside the highway like newly sown dragons' teeth. The handpumps in the public bar turn seamlessly into plastic boxes, and three racks of videos parthenogenetically appear in the window of the post office. We warned you; this is not a sight for the squeamish. It's enough to make Stephen King sleep with the light on for a week.

The old ladies don't seem to have noticed. They're exchanging photographs of their grandchildren and playing snap, while all around them the village green trembles, like the San Andreas fault having a temper tantrum, and design-and-build starter homes flip up out of the ground like poppers on a pinball table.

In the black transit, now parked in the car park of the brand new plastics factory, the little machine is buzzing like a tortured wasp. A big glass bottle, coddled and cosseted in gyroscopically mounted cradles, lead and cotton wool, slowly fills. When the meniscus reaches the twenty-centilitre mark, the operator yanks back the handle, opens the door of the van and blows a whistle. The old ladies stop what they're doing, grab their deck chairs and empty picnic baskets and make a run for the coach. Both vehicles gun their engines and race off with much spinning of wheels and burning of rubber because a village green in the process of going critical is no place to be. In fact, they've almost left it too late; just behind them the road uproots itself and contorts like a wounded python, coiling itself round a series of mini-roundabouts and branching off into a series of service roads leading to the new complex of out-of-town supermarkets. They're level with the village church when it detonates and turns itself into a drive-in leisure multiplex, and only by standing on the accelerator can the driver get the coach clear of the Jacobean manor house before it implodes and shape-changes into Kawaguchiya Integrated Circuits' south-east regional management training centre.

A close shave, and the world owes a large debt of gratitude to the driver, for all that he's a myrmidon of the Time thieves' Mr Big. Because the transit van is carrying twenty centilitres of raw Time (destined to fill a lucrative order from Wall Street, which is frantically trying to make the most of the last few weeks of a Republican administration) and the thought of what would happen if that much ninety-eight-per-cent-pure stuff were to go off is enough to freeze the brain.

Raw Time, spontaneously detonating in the Earth's chronological field. Historical meltdown. A Time bomb.

The man in the black transit is Chubby Stevenson, also known as The Temporiser and Mr Timeshare. Procrastination was framed; Chubby is the greatest thief of Time the world has ever seen. In his purpose-built silo, five hundred feet under the Nevada Desert, he has four hundred and sixteen litres of the stuff; enough to reprise the Renaissance and play Desert Island Decades. Do you suffer from persistent nostalgia? Do you wish it could be the Sixties all over again? Just send your order, together with a banker's draft with more noughts on it than there are portholes in the side of a trans-Atlantic liner, to Mr C. Stevenson, PO Box 666, Las Monedas, Nevada.

Trying to get the petrol out of a Scorpion tank, the dragon discovered the hard way, is like breaking into a can of Coke after the little ring-pull thing has snapped off and you haven't got a tin-opener. It calls for ingenuity, patience and very robust fingernails.

Two out of three will do at a pinch; and, having slaked his thirst, the dragon relaxed, closed his eyes and considered the situation, both in the short and medium term.

He wasn't, in his opinion, excessively thin-skinned (just as well, considering the number of things that had been fired at him in the last twelve minutes) but he did get the impression that for some reason, the humans had taken against him rather. Apart from a broken claw and some light bruises the tanks hadn't bothered him very much, and the petrol was much more to his taste than all those funny drinks, but the next escalation of human disapproval would probably be aircraft, and he knew from recent observation that those things had rather more biff to them than the little self-propelled cocktail shakers. Time, he decided regretfully, to make himself inconspicuous, which would mean having to quit this exceptionally stylish and well-designed body for a while and go back into boring, silly two-legged mufti. A pity, particularly since it was now nicely fuelled-up and ready to go.

He had business here in England, but it wouldn't take long. Once that was out of the way, the world was his oyster, and there were bound to be big, flat, open spaces where a dragon could *be* without getting shot at all the time by cultural degenerates. So, under cover, do the job, and then

27

we're out of here. Can't, frankly, wait.

He opened his wings and, having disposed of the empties tidily by dropping them in the sea, he soared up above the clouds, giving as wide a berth as possible to any aircraft his exceptional senses detected, and circled round until he saw what he was looking for. When he saw his chance, he swooped.

At more or less the same moment as the dragon was mangling armoured fighting vehicles on the playing fields of Lancashire, someone who had been asleep for a very long time woke up.

You know what it's like when you've overslept. Head full of sawdust. Eyelids as difficult to open as painted-over windowframes. Interior of mouth tasting so repulsive you wonder who's been doing what in it while you've been sleeping. Multiply that by a couple of thousand years and maybe you get the idea.

'Where,' muttered George to himself, 'the fuck am I?'

A pigeon, who was sitting on his head, removed its head from its armpit and looked round. 'Who said that?' it demanded.

George, who could understand the language of birds, cleared his throat. 'Down here,' he said.

'What, you?'

'Yes, me?'

'The *statue*?'

'Yes.'

'Jeez!' The pigeon froze, kebabbed with embarrassment. 'I didn't know statues could ... Look, I really am terribly sorry. I'll clean it all off, promise.'

'I'm not really,' George explained, 'a statue.'

'I see. You're a very big, grey person lying absolutely still. Well, it takes all sorts, I can see that, I just naturally assumed you were a statue. If you'll just bear with me I can be back with a cloth and some white spirit before you can say—'

'Shut up and listen, you stupid bird. I'm inside the statue. Sort of. I'm a saint.'

The pigeon hesitated a while before replying. 'Fine,' it said. 'Where I come from we call that a non-sequitur, but never mind. Logic is for wimps, right?'

'I am a saint,' George repeated, the fuel gauge on his patience edging audibly into the red. 'I appear to have reincarnated into a statue of myself. And before you ask, I have no idea why. Now then, where is this . . .' George looked round; a circumscribed view, since he couldn't move his head, but sufficient for his purposes ' . . . ghastly, awful, God-forsaken place? Last thing I knew I was in open countryside.'

'Birmingham,' replied the pigeon promptly. 'West Midlands metropolitan district, England, Europe. Population—'

'Never heard of it.'

'Really?' The pigeon sounded surprised. 'Been away long?'

'Last time I looked, it was a hundred and something AD.'

Pigeons can't whistle. 'Strewth, mate, that's a long time. Eighteen hundred years, give or take a bit. This is . . .' The pigeon counted on its feathers. 'Nineteen ninety-eight. June. Welcome back,' it added tentatively.

George swivelled his eyeballs. 'I sincerely hope I'm not stopping,' he replied. 'Whatever happened to grass? We used to have a lot of it in my day.'

The pigeon shuffled its wings. 'Still plenty of it about,' it replied. 'But this is the middle of a city. Did they have cities then?'

'A few.' George stopped talking and winced; two thousand years' worth of pins and needles was catching up with him. 'Aaaagh,' he said.

'Problem?'

'My leg hurts. Go on with what you were saying.'

'About Birmingham? Okay. Rated as Great Britain's second largest city, in its nineteenth-century heyday Birmingham truly merited its proud title of "workshop of the world". Post-war recessions and the decline of British industry in general have inevitably left their mark, but the city continues to breed a defiantly positive and dynamic mercantile—'

'Pigeon.'

'Yes?'

'I think,' said George, 'I can now move my right arm. With it, as you may have observed, I am holding a very big sword. Unless you stop drivelling, I shall take this very big sword and shove it right up—'

'All right,' replied the pigeon, offended. 'You were the one who asked. Anyway,' it added, 'that's a fine way for a saint to talk, I must say.'

George's eyebrows were mobile again and he frowned. 'Is it?'

The pigeon nodded. 'Sure. You're supposed to be all meek and holy and stuff.'

'Bollocks.'

'Straight up. I know these things. My address: The Old Blocked Gutter, West Roof, St Chad's Cathedral, Birmingham 4. I know a lot of religion,' the pigeon continued proudly, 'especially the lilies of the field and St Francis of Assisi. Saints don't eff and blind, it's the rules.'

'Shows what you know,' George replied. 'Right, I'm going to move now, so I suggest you piss off and go sit somewhere else. Before you go, however, I want you to tell me where a man can get a drink around here.'

'A drink,' the pigeon repeated. 'Milk?'

'Don't be bloody stupid.'

'Water, then?'

'Booze,' George snarled. 'Alcohol. Fermented liquor.' A horrible thought struck him. 'They do still have it, don't they? Please tell me they haven't done away with it, because—'

'Sure they do,' the pigeon said. 'Beer and wine and gin and stuff, makes your mob sing a lot and fall over. Saints don't drink, though. Well-known fact.'

'What you know about saints,' muttered George, 'you could write on a grape pip in big letters. Just point me in the right direction and then clear off, before I use you to wipe my nose.'

The pigeon made the closest approximation it could to a disapproving tut and extended a wingtip. 'Draught Mitchell and Butlers,' it said. 'A word of warning, though.'

'Well?'

Pigeons; Mother Nature's flying diplomatic corps. 'The sword,' it said. 'The armour. The horse. The being seven and a half feet high. Frowned upon.'

'Yeah?'

'Times change,' said the pigeon. 'Not to mention fashions. Can you do anything about that?'

'I'm not sure.' George concentrated. 'Apparently I can. Is this better?'

The pigeon looked down. It was now sitting on the head of a short, bald man in a blue donkey jacket, jeans and scruffy trainers. 'Fine,' it said. 'How did you do that?'

George shrugged. 'Dunno. Who cares? When I get there, what should I ask for?'

'Um.' The pigeon searched its memory – about a quarter of a byte, say a large nibble – for a phrase overheard in crisp-shrapnel-rich beer gardens. 'A pint of bitter, please, mate, and a packet of dry roasted peanuts. That usually does the trick.'

31

'A pint of bitter, please, mate, and a packet of dry roasted peanuts.'

'You've got it.'

'Right. A pint of bitter, please, mate, and a packet of dry roasted peanuts. A pint of bitter, please, mate, and a packet of dry roasted peanuts. So long, birdbrain. A pint of bit . . .'

Standing on the empty plinth, the pigeon watched until George disappeared through the pub doorway, still rehearsing his line. It waited for a while. Then it preened itself. Then it started to peck at a cigarette butt. Two minutes or so later, the whole incident had been edited out of the active files of its mind and was held in limbo, awaiting deletion. And then . . .

The pigeon looked down.

It was, once again, standing on a statue.

Vaguely, it recalled something it had learned recently about statues. It took another look at what it was standing on. Ah *shit*, it said to itself.

'Mike.'

'Yes?'

'Just come and have a look at this, will you?'

Instead of folding the tarpaulin, Bianca just let it fall. Then they stood for a while and took a long, hard look.

'Swings and roundabouts,' Mike said eventually. 'Snakes and ladders. Maybe even omelettes and eggs.'

'What?'

Mike shrugged. 'I'm trying to be balanced and unhysterical,' he said. 'We now have the dragon back. True, we do seem to have lost Saint George, but . . .'

Slowly and very tentatively, Bianca leaned forwards. She laid the palm of her hand on the dragon's cold, scaly flank. Marble. Solid, cool, bloody-awkward-to-move-about stone. 'This,' she said at last, 'is beginning to get on my nerves.'

32

'Maybe it's a form of advanced job-sharing,' Mike suggested. 'You know, like flexi-time. I think West Midlands Council's all in favour of it, and I suppose you could just about classify these two as Council employees.'

'Mike.'

'Mm?'

'Please go away.'

Alone with her creation, Bianca thought long and hard. Sometimes she leaned against the statue, holding it. Sometimes she pressed her ear against it, as if listening. From time to time she kicked it.

After a while, she opened her portfolio and studied some sketches and plans. She took out a tape and made some measurements, both of the statue and the surrounding area. She climbed up onto its front paws and sniffed its spectacular, gaping jaws.

A mother, they say, instinctively knows what her baby is thinking. If it's in trouble, she can feel it, deep inside. Bianca frowned. No, not *trouble*, exactly. More sort of up to something. But what?

Finally, she packed up, replaced the tarpaulin and started to walk away. Having covered ten yards she turned, faced the statue, and put on her most menacing scowl.

'*Sit!*' she commanded, and stalked off down Colmore Row.

CHAPTER THREE

Having parked his shape in Victoria Square, the dragon ambled down Colmore Row to Snow Hill and consulted the railway timetable. Three minutes later a rather bemused train pulled up (wondering, among other things, how the hell it had managed to get there from Dumfries in a hundred and eighty seconds) and he climbed aboard.

'Colchester,' he said aloud.

The voice of the train, inaudible to everyone except the dragon, pointed out that the Snow Hill line doesn't go to Colchester. The dragon smiled pleasantly and invited the train to put its money where its mouth was.

Alighting at Colchester, a place he had heard of but never actually been to, the dragon took a taxi to 35 Vespasian Street, explained to the driver and climbed the stairs.

The top floor of 35 Vespasian Street is given over to a suite of offices consisting of a chair, a desk, a computer terminal, an electric kettle, an anomaly in the telephone network and seven hundred and forty-three filing cabinets. The door says:

L. KORTRIGHT ASSOCIATES
SUPERNATURAL AGENCY

Lin Kortright was on the anomaly when the dragon walked in. He was explaining to Horus, the Egyptian charioteer of the Sun, that simply picking it up, moving it along in a straight line and putting it down again without dropping it was no longer good enough to guarantee him full employment, and had he considered, for example, juggling with it or balancing it on a stick while riding a unicycle. As the door opened he didn't look up, merely made a go-away gesture. He was about to suggest training it to do simple tricks when he noticed that the receiver was back on its cradle and he was, in fact, talking to the palm of his hand. He raised his eyes, impressed.

'Hey,' he said, 'how'd you do that?'

'Do what?'

'It's purely instinctive with you, huh? No matter. What can I do for you?'

'I'm looking,' the dragon replied, sitting on a chair last seen two seconds previously under an actuary in Stroud and still warm, 'for a job. I imagine you might be able to help.'

Mr Kortright studied the chair for a while, and then nodded. 'Possibly, possibly,' he said. 'What d'you do?'

'What needs doing?'

Mr Kortright frowned. 'No, no, no,' he said, 'that's not the way it works. You gotta have an act before you come bothering me. Let's see. You can do telekinesis, right?'

'Can I?'

'Oh boy, a natural,' Mr Kortright sighed, rather as Saint Sebastian would have done if, just as the last arrow thudded home in his ribcage, he also remembered he'd left home without switching off the oven. 'Don't get me wrong,' he added, 'maybe I can still find you something, if you don't mind touring. Done any poltergeisting?'

The dragon's brow furrowed in thought until he looked like a fight between two privet hedges. Ever since he'd come back, he'd been letting his subconscious fill in as many of the gaps as possible, mostly by opening a direct line from his exceptional ears to his memory. In consequence, the back lots of his brain were stuffed with thousands of unprocessed eavesdroppings, waiting to be filtered and condensed into usable ready-to-wear background information. 'Poltergeists,' he mused, accessing a fragment of a documentary overheard when the taxi drove within a mile of a TV showroom. 'That's a ghost or similar evil spirit who throws things, yes?'

'Yup.'

'No. Sorry.'

Mr Kortright's shoulders rose and fell like share prices during a closely contested election. 'Okay,' he said. 'You wanna learn?'

'Not really, no. All seems a bit gratuitous if you ask me. And besides, I don't plan on being here very long, so there's little point learning new skills.'

'Picky, huh? You got a nerve.'

'Several,' replied the dragon, absently. 'In this body, anyway. The other one's just animated rock.'

It took Mr Kortright's brain three quarters of a second to pick up on the words *this body* and *the other one*, speculate on the significance and dismiss the whole as too much hassle. 'So what did you used to do? Have an act then?'

The dragon nodded. 'I flew about breathing fire, making rain, that style of thing.'

'Dragon, huh?'

'You're very perceptive.'

After a moment's hesitation Mr Kortright correctly

interpreted the dragon's remark as a compliment. 'Not much around at the moment for dragons,' he said. 'Endangered species regulations,' he added.

'Ah.' This seemed to confirm what the dragon had assumed about a national dragon shortage. 'So dragons are protected, are they?'

Mr Kortright grinned. 'Dragons?' he said. 'No way. Nothing in the legislation about dragons. Now crocodiles, yes. Which means the supply of raw material for the handbag trade is down to last knockings. But if you're good you can make dragon *look* like crocodile ... You get my meaning?'

A corner of the dragon's mouth twitched. 'I seem to remember you people have a saying,' he said. 'First catch your ...'

'Been away a long time, have you?' The Kortright grin widened, until it looked like the aftermath of seismic activity. 'In which case, here's a tip for you. If you're flying along and you see something long and grey and kind of tube shaped with little fins coming straight at you, don't try chatting it up or asking it out to the movies. They call them wire-guided missiles, and—'

'Yes, thanks,' said the dragon. 'I found out about those for myself. So there are still dragons about, then? People seem to react as if I'm extinct or something.'

'In these parts,' Mr Kortright explained, 'you are. In this century, in fact. That doesn't worry transtemporal poachers any; just means that by the time they market the goods, they're also genuine antiques and therefore legal to sell.'

'Ah.' The dragon shrugged. 'But so long as I'm now, I'm relatively safe?'

'Safe.' Mr Kortright savoured the word. 'From poachers, maybe. I mean, chances are, if you stick around any year with nineteen on the front of it, you won't suddenly find yourself full of powder compacts with a zip up your back. There are,' he added, 'other dangers.'

'Thought that might be the case,' the dragon replied. 'Which is precisely why I'm in plain clothes and looking for a job. You see, I have things to do in the here and now. Once they're done, I'm off somewhere and when a bit less paranoid. While I'm here, though, I thought a job'd help pass the time and help me blend in.'

'Very wise. So,' Mr Kortright went on, steepling his fingers, 'where are we at? Ex-dragon. Ex-dragon. Now then, let me see.'

The dragon waited patiently while Mr Kortright played with his computer.

'Any luck?'

Mr Kortright pursed his lips. 'Well,' he said, 'like I say to all the kids just starting out in the business, when you're trying to make your way, sometimes you've gotta do things you'd rather not. You sure about poltergeisting?'

'Positive.'

'Shucks. Hey, what's this?' He peered at the screen. 'I can get you six weeks' volcanic activity in Hawaii, covering for the local fire-god while he takes his kids to Disneyland. All you gotta do is lie on your back and blow up through a small hole.'

'Sorry. Got to be in this country. Anyway, where's Hawaii?'

'Please yourself. Gonna be difficult, though. How do you feel about hallucinations?'

'I beg your pardon?'

'Hallucinations. For health-conscious druggies. All the weird visions without actually taking the drug. Growth area, steady work.'

'Not really me, somehow. I'd feel self-conscious. Besides, don't you have to be a pink elephant?'

'Boy, are you behind the times.' Mr Kortright frowned, and tapped a few more keys. 'Okay, okay, you're gonna love this. This is really so *you*. Security guard.'

'Security guard?'

'It says here, *traditional* security guard needed for substantial art collection. Full board. The successful applicant will be at least fourteen feet long, green and covered in scales. No time wasters. There now, what can I say?'

'Okay,' said the dragon. 'When can I start?'

George sailed through the air in a graceful arc and landed in a dustbin. Behind him came a voice, warmly recommending that he stay out. After a short pause for regrouping, he climbed out, brushed trash off his person and staggered away down the alley.

Seems like old times, he said to himself, getting slung out of drinking establishments. Some things had changed, of course; for one thing, getting slung out was now a whole lot easier. Definitely a regrettable tendency to over-react.

His mind drifted back to the bars of his youth. Pendle's, the roughest saints' bar in Albion. The Caerllyr Grill. The Grendel's Torso. What the hell was wrong with this goddamn country?

Half an hour's slouching, lurching and bumping into things brought him back to Victoria Square, and he realised that he didn't have anywhere to sleep for the night. He saw . . .

'Immediately,' said Mr Kortright. 'Here's the address. Do well.'

The dragon trotted down the stairs into the street and whistled. A moment later, a huge green shape, flying faster than the wind, descended on him and he vanished.

*

... An empty plinth. He thought of his nice warm statue; good, solid marble that didn't wobble about all over the place like this blasted cheapskate flesh-and-blood outfit did. Climbing the plinth, he sighed, closed his eyes and was stone once more.

'I'm not saying,' said Chubby Stevenson, his brain racing, 'it's impossible. Nothing's *impossible*. All I'm saying is, it's going to be tricky.'

Fifteen impassive Japanese faces regarded him, until he began to feel like asking for his blindfold and last cigarette. These people, he realised, don't want to hear this. Pity.

'It's all to do,' he continued, cramming charm into the meter of his smile, 'with the fundamental nature of Time. Now, with my supplies of raw Time, I can prolong the present, no problem. In certain circumstances, I can sometimes recreate the past – not travel back in time, now that *is* impossible. Nobody can do that. What I sometimes do, for specially favoured customers, is make a synthetic recreation of a specific episode from the past, using a raw Time base and ...'

They weren't interested. He wasn't answering the question they'd asked him. Jesus, these guys!

'The future,' he therefore said, 'is something else entirely. Future's different from past and present, see. Future hasn't happened yet. If it hasn't happened, we don't know what it's like. If you don't know what it's like, you can't copy it. Now ...'

One of the fifteen leaned forward and, terribly politely, cleared his throat. With respect, his expression said – his lips didn't move and he didn't make a noise, but there was no need, just as you don't need to speak fluent Gun to know that when a .44 revolver stares at you with its one big eye it's informing you that you are probably going to die – they knew this already. What they didn't know, and what they wanted him to tell them, was whether it was possible to arrange an artificial future, in which certain specified events would happen; and if so, how much would it cost? If he didn't know the answer, the expression continued, then perhaps he would be good enough to say so.

Chubby sighed, and got a grip on himself. 'It can be done,' he said. 'The principle is quite straightforward; simple, even. The practicalities . . .'

Please explain the practicalities.

'Okay. It's all relativity, right? Travel faster than light around the Earth to accelerate forward through Time. Once you're there, or do I mean then, you set up whatever it is you want to happen in the future. Like, you want to bet heavily on the Superbowl, you fast forward to the day of the match, see who wins, now you can place your bet – provided you can get back to your own time, or get a message back, anyhow; obviously, you can't get back yourself, because pastside travel's out, see above. Sending a message, though, that's no problem.'

Really?

'Trade secret,' Chubby said. Normally he'd have winked as well, but there was something about the wall of stone-faced scrutiny opposite him that put him off the idea. 'We can do it, anyhow. The technical problem, of course, is finding your faster-than-light courier.'

A soluble problem?

'I feel sure we can sort it out,' Chubby lied. 'Of course, if we knew we'd be successful, we'd just get the courier to report back from the future on how we'd managed it, the same time as he passes back the Superbowl results; but that's a bit hit-and-miss so far as I'm concerned. Sloppy, you know?'

Indeed the fifteen did. Sloppiness, the expression gave

him to understand, was anathema to them. Chubby painted a smile over the cracks in his composure and continued. 'So,' he said, 'you boys are going to have to let our R & D people kick this one around for a day or two. As soon as we've got the ans—'

You will report back to us in forty-eight hours? Very well.

Chubby's Adam's apple bobbed like a Formula One lift. 'When I said a day or two, I didn't actually mean two days, I meant—'

You are already suggesting a postponement. Seventy-two hours, then.

'How would it be,' Chubby croaked, 'if we call you when we're ready to roll? We'll be as quick as we can, naturally.'

You are asking for an indefinite postponement while you attempt to find a way to do this?

'Yes.'

We would prefer, said fifteen expressions simultaneously, a specified time limit. That is the way we do business. We trust you can accommodate us on this point.

'Just give me a week, will you?' Chubby's tone suggested that he was Faust offering the Devil double or quits, and even as he spoke a small, rather naïve part of his brain demanded *Why are you so scared of these guys*? 'By then, I'll have definite plans, costings, all that kind of stuff ready for you to see. Agreed?'

Long pause. It was like the moment of thoughtful hesitation on the Seventh Day just before Man, having been assured by God that it was a nice little runner, genuine low mileage, normally you only get oceans of this quality on the top-of-the-range models, said, Okay, we'll take it. Then fifteen heads nodded. A moment later, the conference room was empty, and a helicopter engine started up somewhere on the roof.

42

'Hooray,' said Chubby wretchedly to himself. 'I guess I've landed this really big contract.'

It was a dirty, rotten job . . .

Plink! A tiny globe of lime-rich water dripped from cavern roof to floor.

. . . But someone's got to do it. Apparently. Ouch! Jesus, but this stuff's *uncomfortable*.

Traditional security guard, substantial art collection. Whoever drafted that advertisement had probably spent some time in the estate agency business, learning in the process the art of making statements that are almost but not quite downright untrue.

The art collection was housed in a cave two hundred feet below the Pennine Hills and consisted of about three hundred tons' weight of gold tableware; very old, very vulgar and extremely unpleasant to lie on. Cold. Hard. Lots of handles and knobs and scutcheons to dig into you.

Plus, of course, the alluring prospect of being woken up just as soon as you've dropped off by some amateur hero with weapons, desperate courage and a fleet of lorries outside the cave mouth with their engines running. It was as bad as being a guard dog, and he didn't even have a little bowl with his name on it. The job, the dragon decided, sucks.

'Hello?'

The voice was still some way off; high-pitched, almost feminine. A ploy, thought the dragon, and a piss-poor one at that. Pound to a penny it's some muscular git in tin overalls making his voice sound funny to put me off my guard. He breathed in, savouring the mellow warmth of his own breath.

'Anybody home?'

Only one way he can come and that's straight through

43

that hole there. Just let him poke his head through, and his mates'll have to carry him home in an asbestos bag.

'Here you are.' The head, as he'd predicted, appeared. But it was female. There was no helmet, no nodding white plume. The dragon was so surprised he swallowed his breath and got hiccups. Nasty...

'Are you,' said the female, 'Mr Wayne Popper?'

The dragon looked at her.

'My name,' she went on, 'is Marjorie Evans. Inland Revenue.'

A tiny flare of green fire spurted from the dragon's right ear, evidence of the rather complex and horrible ear-nose-and-throat difficulties he was currently experiencing. 'Is that so?' he croaked. 'Look, I do have a certain discretion in these matters, so I'm going to count up to five and then – Oops, ah, *shit*, do excuse me, please.' For a few moments, the darkness of the cavern was illuminated by the sort of firework display you generally only get to see when there's an important Royal wedding.

'Bless you,' said Miss Evans, instinctively fumbling in her bag for a tissue. 'Sorry, you did say you are Mr Popper?'

'I didn't say anything,' replied the dragon, confused. 'Now get the hell out of here, before I incinerate you.'

'I'll take that,' replied Miss Evans briskly, 'as a Yes.' She straightened her back, took out a notebook and looked around, miming seeing the gold for the first time. 'Well then,' she said. 'What have we here?'

Inside the dragon's brain, a debate was raging. The traditionalists were saying, You fool, here's a blasted hero, well, all right, heroine, come to nick the goodies, so why the hell don't you just torch her PDQ and have done with it? In another part of his brain, his loyal opposition was arguing that actually she'd given no indication that she was here to steal anything, she wasn't armed, she'd even offered a tissue when he sneezed. So what? retorted the traditionalists. So I don't *want* to carbonise her, replied the opposition. She hasn't done me any harm. Chicken, taunted the old guard. No, replied the other lot, dragon; same number of wings, but bigger and twice the legs.

'It's a pile of gold,' replied the dragon, in the meantime.

'Is it really?' Miss Evans was writing in the book. 'Could you possibly explain to me how you came by it?'

'Um,' said the dragon. 'I'm, er, looking after it for somebody else.'

As the woman looked at him, non-aggressive, pacific, even smiling slightly in a mildly cynical way through thick-lensed spectacles, the dragon was aware of a feeling he hadn't had for so long he could only just put a name to it. It disconcerted him, no end.

He felt like he was in trouble.

'Really,' said the woman. 'And might I ask who this other person might be?'

This, said the ruling majority in the dragon's brain, is crazy. One little puff and she's ash. No sword. No armour. And it isn't even my treasure. So why do I feel as if I've just been caught with my talon in the biscuit tin?

'A friend,' the dragon mumbled, not sure where the words he was saying were coming from. 'Or rather, a bloke I met in a pub, didn't catch his name. Just look after this lot for me, he said, won't be a tick.'

'I see.'

That was all she said. I see. In the old days, when the dragon took to the air, the roads leading in the opposite direction were clogged with nose-to-tail handcarts. He hiccupped again. 'Gesundheit,' said the woman.

'Um,' said the dragon, his vocal chords sandpaper. 'Is there a problem?'

The woman closed her notebook, clicked her biro and

45

put them both away. 'Mr Popper,' she said, 'let me be frank with you. I have to say I'm not really very happy with your story. I don't have to tell you, defrauding the Revenue is no laughing matter.'

For some reason he couldn't account for at all – the unfamiliarity of the concept, perhaps, or the bewildering lack of terror on the woman's part – the last three words she'd spoken were perhaps the most unnerving things he'd ever heard a mortal say. When you consider that they were competing against such strong contenders as *Take your ten thousand archers round the back of the hill, we'll attack from here with our twenty thousand cavalry* and *If he had any idea what we'd just put in there, he wouldn't be drinking it*, maybe you can get a vague glimpse at the dragon's complete bewilderment.

'All right,' he said. 'I'm not Mr Popper. I just work for him.'

The woman smiled. It was, actually, quite a pleasant smile. In her spare time, she probably made fur-fabric mouse bookmarks. 'I had already guessed that, Mr . . .'

'Dragon.'

'Mister Dragon.' She pulled out the notebook again. 'But there is such a thing as being an accessory, you know. I really would urge you to co-operate with us.'

'Sure.' A minor seismic event, last echo of the hiccups, wafted blue flame out of the dragon's left ear; if only, snarled his subconscious, I could accidentally sneeze at *her*, all they'd ever find would be charcoal. And I wouldn't even have done it on purpose.

But no sneeze came, and the dragon had to suffer the indignity of listening to himself telling the woman everything he knew about the job – Mr Popper's enormous property deals, payments made in gold for, what had he called it, fiscal convenience, all kinds of things he scarcely understood himself – while she wrote carefully, nodded and mhm'd, then closed her notebook, thanked him very politely and left the way she'd come.

A moment after that, he inflated both lungs and blew the biggest flare of extra-hot red fire he'd ever managed in his life. It melted the walls of the cavern, but it didn't reach Miss Evans; he could hear her inch-and-a-half heels still clippety-clopping along the winding tunnel. Thanks to his belated efforts, however, the hole in the wall was now almost sealed off and he couldn't get through to press home the attack.

'Shit!' he roared. 'What's *happening* to me?'

Nobody said anything, but his deranged imagination made him believe that, in the dying echoes of his own roar, he heard a mocking voice asking him whose side he was on.

'Quite soon,' Bianca said, 'I shall have had enough of this.'

'I think you ought to tell someone,' Mike replied, calmly folding the tarpaulin which, removed a moment or so ago, had revealed Saint George returned and the dragon gone. 'There's two possible explanations, and one of them demands that we believe in the existence of a practical joker with access to helicopters and heavy lifting gear, who's capable of swapping enormously heavy statues round in the centre of Birmingham at dead of night without anybody noticing.'

'That's absurd.'

'Obviously. Therefore,' Mike continued, 'we're dealing with the boring old supernatural. You've *got* to tell someone, otherwise it'll invalidate your insurance.'

Bianca scowled. 'That's absurd too,' she said.

'Tell you something else that's absurd, while I'm at it,' Mike responded, shoving the folded tarpaulin into a cardboard box, 'and that's bloody great statues playing hide and seek with themselves in a public place.'

47

'We can't tell anyone,' Bianca objected. 'They'd never believe us. They'd lock us up in the nut house.'

'Maybe.' Mike shrugged. 'At least then, this'd be someone else's problem. Right now, I could fancy somewhere dark and cool with bendy wallpaper.'

Bianca was silent for a moment, then she started to rummage in her toolbag. 'I know one thing I *am* going to do,' she said.

'Oh yes?'

'I'm going to chip off that ridiculous moustache.'

Dismissed without references for gross breach of confidentiality, the dragon swished its tail dispiritedly and flew east.

En route it had a run-in with three F-111s, hastily scrambled by a gibbering controller out of Brize Norton and armed with everything Father Christmas had left in the RAF's stocking for the last six years.

In due course the pilots ejected and, save for a broken leg and some bruises, landed safely. Most of the bits of aeroplane came down in the sea. Which, the dragon mused as it continued its flight, only makes the business with the tax woman all the more disturbing.

'Guy,' said Mr Kortright, having heard the tale, 'believe me, you were right to trust your instincts. You just don't tangle with those people, not *ever*. Shame about the job, but you did right. Besides,' he added with a shrug, 'there's the morality of the thing to consider. The forces of Evil gotta stick together, right?'

'I beg your pardon?'

Mr Kortright gave him a puzzled look. 'Evil,' he said. 'Your team. You represent the forces of darkness, and so do they. You go welshing on your own kind, you'll never work in this business again.'

From Colchester – Mr Kortright promised him faithfully to let him know as soon as anything suitable came up – he flew fast and high to the Midlands, found his plinth and parked. Getting out of the cavern had used up most of his fuel supply, and dealing with the aircraft had polished off the rest. He was tired, and upset, and he needed a rest.

Evil? What did the little creep mean, Evil?

George woke up.

Deep down in the very marrow of the stone, his head hurt. He felt sick. What, he asked himself, would come up if I was? Probably gravel.

There was something underneath him. Slowly – moving his head was a wild, scary thing to do, comparable to setting off in three small boats to find the back way to India – he looked down. He looked up again, rather more quickly.

Oh God, he said to himself. Please let me be hallucinating.

A tentative prod with a toe persuaded him otherwise. Horribly solid. Sphincter-looseningly real. And I'm directly above it!

He waited. When the dragon didn't make a move, he risked breathing. Still no reaction. With extreme diffidence he reached down and prodded with the point of his sword. Chink. Nothing. It was only a statue, nothing more.

Fuck that, George reflected, so'm I. And people who live in marble overcoats shouldn't prod dragons.

He waited a little longer, each second dragging by like a double geography lesson. He wasn't at all sure that he understood how this statue business worked, but either the dragon simply wasn't at home, or it was waiting for him to make a move. In the latter case, staying put was simply prolonging the inevitable. He braced himself, took a deep breath and jumped.

The ground rushed up to meet him like a long-lost creditor; he landed, swore and rolled. His head protested in the strongest possible terms. The dragon didn't move. He stood up.

'Gotcha!'

He had now, of course, shed the marble and was back in a conventional human skin; but not for very long, because Bianca's voice and the slap of her hand on his shoulder made him jump out of it. He said 'Eeek!' and turned white, all in an impressively short space of time.

'And where the hell do you think you're going?'

His brain reported back off sick leave and mentioned to him that the creature holding his arm was not a dragon so much as a defenceless girl. That's all right, then. He put the palm of his hand in her face and shoved. Then he ran.

A moment later he was lying on his nose; a state of affairs he was able to trace back to someone grabbing hold of his feet. 'Gerroff!' he screeched. 'There's a bastard dragon after—'

Then Bianca hit him on the head with a two-pound mallet.

CHAPTER FOUR

'Maybe,' said a guest, 'they're being thrown out for antisocial behaviour.'

He was looking at a long, scruffy coach, state of the art passenger transport from around the time Bobby Charlton was England's leading goal-scorer, which was spluttering patiently in bay 3a of the bus station in Hell.

'Quite possibly,' replied a fellow guest, who happened to be on his tea break. 'Look what they're wearing.'

The first guest, also on his tea break, peered. 'Yes,' he said, 'I see what you mean.'

As a matter of fact, these two guests were always on their tea break. In life they'd been builders, and the cruel and unusual punishment reserved for them in the afterlife was that they'd be allowed out as soon as they'd had a quick brew; two thousand years of frantic slurping later, the meniscus on their cups was, if anything, half a millimetre higher up the china than it had been when they arrived.

Everybody, no matter how depraved or evil they may be, is entitled to a holiday, and the first three weeks in August are traditionally the time when the staff of Hell, your cosy, centrally heated home from home under the ground, get to pack their suitcases, dig out their plastic buckets and pitchforks from the cupboard under the stairs, put on silly hats and get away from it all. They choose August because – well, you know what the beach is like then. They feel more at home that way.

'If so,' observed the second guest, 'I reckon we've had a lucky escape.'

His colleague nodded vigorously, his eyes fixed on the white denims, broad-brimmed hats, synthetic buckskin fringes and spangled waistcoats of the party boarding the coach. Not, of course, that either of them had anything against country music as such; in its place, they'd be the first to declare, it was all very fine and splendid. Except, of course, its place was – most definitely – here. So far, the Management hadn't twigged this. When they eventually did, they'd be able to maintain the same uniquely high standard of torment (BS199645; always look for the kitemark) while saving themselves a fortune on pitchforks and firewood.

Had the guests been a few yards closer to bay 3a, they'd have been able to read the poster prominently displayed in the coach's back window. It read:

HELL HOLDINGS PLC
STAFF COUNTRY & WESTERN CLUB
ANNUAL OUTING
Nashville Or Bust!

'Okay,' George said. 'It's like this.'

'Just a minute,' Bianca interrupted, switching on the pocket dictating machine. 'I want this on tape.'

George looked at her. 'What's that little box thing you're

playing around with?' he said. 'Look, there's no need to get nasty.'

Bianca explained, as briefly as she could, about tape recorders. Perhaps she didn't express herself very well because George made a couple of high-pitched noises and renewed his pointless struggle with the stout ropes that attached him to *Earth Mother VI*, the most solid piece of statuary in Bianca's studio. Playing back the tape just seemed to make things worse. She sighed and slipped it back in her pocket.

'You were saying,' she said.

Once upon a time (George explained), long ago and far away, in a remote land called Albion, there was a dragon.

In fact, there were a lot of dragons. And that wasn't a problem for the people who lived there, because they'd long since based their entire economy on dragons; they ate dragon, wore dragonskin, used the wing membrane to make their tents and burned the bones for warmth. And, since there were more than enough dragons to spare – great herds of them roamed the empty moors, grazing placidly and from time to time accidentally setting fire to hundreds of thousands of acres – there was no reason why the system shouldn't work for ever.

That, however, was before the coming of the white men and the iron horse.

Ancient Albion called them the white men because they wore white surcoats over their armour; and the horses weren't actually made of iron, they were just covered with the stuff to protect them from arrows. The newcomers were knights, followers of the code of chivalry, searchers for the Holy Grail. They'd been slung out of their own countries for being an insufferable nuisance and had headed west.

When they arrived in Albion they decided it would do

nicely and they set about getting vacant possession. The natives, however, were no pushover and the white men were getting nowhere fast when one of their leaders hit on a sensible, if drastic, course of action.

The natives, he argued, live off the dragons. Get rid of the dragons and you get rid of the natives.

Of those wild, exciting frontier days many stirring tales are told; many of them about the greatest dragon-hunter of them all, Dragon George Cody, who singlehandedly cleared all of what is now Northern England, Wales and Scotland of dragons. He it was who first justified the clearances by saying that the knights stood for good and the dragons stood for evil, and, in his own terms, he was right. The knights were, after all, soldiers of the Church, ultimately searching for the Grail, and the dragons were getting in the way and, by deviously getting killed and eaten by the locals, giving aid and comfort to the hostile tribesmen. Besides, George pointed out, dragons burn towns and demand princesses as ransom.

The dragons, referring to the Siege of Jerusalem, the Sack of Constantinople and a thousand years of dynastic marriages, said, Look who's talking. But rarely twice.

And then there was only one dragon left; the biggest and fiercest of them all, twice the size and three times the firepower of anything the knights had come up against. He had seen his race eradicated, the corpses of his kin heaped up beside the white men's newly built roads and carted off to Camelot Fried Dragon bars the length and breadth of Albion. He had also learned that he and his kind were the Bad Guys, which puzzled him quite a bit initially but eventually came to make some sort of sense. After all, if dragons were the Good Guys, then these people wouldn't have gone to so much trouble to wipe them out. Would they?

54

Well, said the dragon to himself. If the cap fits, and so forth.

In the event, wearing the cap was *fun*.

'I see,' Bianca said. 'So that's why you weren't particularly keen to meet the dragon. Figures.'

'It had to be done,' George growled defensively. 'Out of that rough and ready cradle, a mighty nation sprang to life. Civilisations, like grapevines, grow best when mulched with blood. You can't make an omelette . . .'

Bianca's brow furrowed. 'You've made your point,' she said. 'But you haven't explained what you're doing in my statue. Or,' she added savagely, 'why you keep moving the blasted thing about.'

'I'm coming to that.' George paused and licked his lips. 'All this explaining,' he went on, 'isn't half making me thirsty. You couldn't just give us a glass of water, could you?'

Bianca nodded silently and went to the kitchen. As soon as her back was turned, George, who had been quietly fraying the ropes against an aesthetically necessary sharp edge on the statue's shin, gave a sharp tug.

Of Sir Galahad it is told that his strength was as the strength of ten because his heart was pure. George's heart had approximately the same purity quotient as a pint of Thames water, but he did press-ups instead. The rope snapped.

'Hey!' Bianca dropped the glass and came running, but George was already on his feet and heading for the door. When she tried to stop him, he nutted her with a plaster-of-Paris study for *Truth Inspiring The Telecommunications Industry*, clattered down the stairs and legged it.

'Finally,' said the Demon Chardonay (ironic cheers and

55

cries of 'Good!') 'let's all remember, this is a *holiday*. We're supposed to be *enjoying ourselves*. Okay?'

At that moment the coach rolled over a pothole, jolting it so forcefully that Chardonay, who was standing up, nutted himself on the roof, thereby demonstrating to his fellow passengers that, even in Hell, there is justice.

'Pillock,' muttered the Demon Prodsnap under his breath. 'What'd he have to come for, anyway?'

On his left the Demon Slitgrind grunted agreement. 'I think Management shouldn't be allowed on outings,' he said. 'Ruins it for the rest of us. I mean, fat chance we've got of having a good time with one of them miserable buggers breathing down our necks. If I'd known I wouldn't have bothered coming.'

Although in his heart Prodsnap reciprocated these sentiments, he was beginning to wish he hadn't raised the subject, because if one thing could be guaranteed to lay a big fat oilslick over the whole weekend, it would have to be listening to Slitgrind's opinions.

'I mean to say,' Slitgrind went on, 'least they could do would be to have different coaches for Management and us, bloody cheapskates. Wouldn't be surprised if they'd done it deliberately, just to spoil it.'

There are, appropriately, more opinions in Hell than anywhere else in the cosmos; and most of them, sooner or later, belonged to Slitgrind. Innumerable and diverse – contradictory even – though they were, in the long run they eventually boiled down into a single, multi-purpose, one-size-fits-all opinion; namely that the Universe was an upside-down pyramid of horseshit, with Slitgrind pinned down under the apex.

'Oh well,' replied Prodsnap, trying to sound positive (it came as easily to him as smiling to a bomb, but he did his best), 'never mind. Still better than work, though, isn't it?'

'Depends,' Slitgrind said. 'I mean, with frigging Management along, don't suppose it'll be any different from work. Wouldn't be at all surprised if . . .'

Oh yes, muttered Prodsnap's soul, it'll be different from work all right. At work, I torture other people. 'Oh look,' he said, pointing out of the window. 'I can see a cow.'

'That's not a cow, you daft git, that's a bull-headed fiend goring impenitent usurers. That's another thing, *they* get uniform allowance, but *we* . . .'

Prodsnap closed his eyes. Another difference, he noted; the guests have all done something to deserve it. What did I ever do, for crying out loud?

At the front of the coach Chardonay, knees smothered in maps, tickets, bits of miscellaneous paper and other props on loan from the Travel Agents' Department, had dropped his red ball-point. This was bad news; he was using the red pen to mark emergency itinerary B (second fallback option in the event of missing the Styx ferry and the 11.35 helicopter service to Limbo Central) on contingency map 2. Scrabbling for it under the seats, he found himself inadvertently brushing against the slender, hairy ankles of the Demon Snorkfrod. Embarrassing.

'Oh,' he said, blushing bright grey. 'Sorry.'

Not that there were many shapelier hooves in all the Nine Circles. One-time Helliday Inn cocktail waitress, former centrefold in the *Tibetan Book of the Dead*, twice Playghoul of the Month in *Hell and Efficiency* magazine, Snorkfrod was just the sort of ghastly apparition any green-blooded demon would want to see jumping out of a coffin at his birthday party. It was just . . . Well, whenever he saw her, the phrase 'rough as guts' did inevitably spring to Chardonay's mind. And (not that he'd had an infinity of experience in these matters) the way she stared at him sometimes was . . .

'Hello,' Snorkfrod replied, looking down and smiling like

57

a crescent-shaped escalator. 'Lost something?'

'My red biro.'

'Don't think you'll find it there, pet. But you're welcome to look.'

After a split second's thought, Chardonay decided the safest course would be to say nothing at all and get the Shopfloor out of there as quickly as possible. Which he did.

Recovering his seat – as he sat down, he heard something go *snap* under his left hoof; no point even bothering to look – Chardonay reflected, not for the first time, that maybe he wasn't really best suited in this line of work, or indeed this whole sector. It was, he knew, a viewpoint shared by many.

The polite term, he understood, was *upsiders*; talented high-fliers headhunted (so to speak) from outside at the time of the Management buy-out; new brooms; fresh pairs, or trios, of eyes. As an experiment it hadn't entirely worked. True, it had shaken things up; the bad old days of jobs for the fiends and living men's hooves were gone for ever, and next year there was a one in three chance they'd get the balance sheet to live up to its name for the first time ever. On the other hand, the inertia of any really huge corporation is so great that it takes more than a few college kids with stars in their eyes and Gucci designer horns to change anything that really matters. And as far as he personally was concerned – well, he never thought he'd ever hear himself saying this – maybe law school would have been a better bet after all.

Nevertheless, here he was, and giving anything less than his best shot was unthinkable. The one area he knew he could improve matters was in industrial relations, which was why he was here. Either that, or he'd had a *really* wild time in a former life and put it, as it were, on his Access card.

Suddenly he was uncomfortably aware that he was being

looked at. Somewhere in the fourth row something sniggered. Stray phrases like *he's well in there* and *after hours in the stationery cupboard* were scurrying about in the thick atmosphere of the bus like mice in a derelict cheese warehouse. A huge, bald demon in row five caught his eye, winked and made a very peculiar gesture with three claws and an elbow. All in all, Chardonay reckoned, he was rapidly inclining towards the Past Life theory; in which case, it was bitterly unfair that he couldn't even remember what it was he'd got up to.

By his calculations it was ninety-six hours from Hell to Nashville and so far they'd been on the road for twenty minutes. And, like he'd said, this was fun. Having sketched out a course of entertainment for the inventor of the concept of fun that would have seriously impressed his superiors, Chardonay squirmed rootlike into his seat, scrabbled himself a makeshift cocoon of papers and settled down to enjoy his holiday.

A flask of coffee, a ham and lettuce sandwich, a camera, the latest Ruth Rendell, a folding stool, a baseball bat – and thou.

Thou in this instance being a big marble statue of a dragon. This time, Bianca had vowed, if the sucker moves so much as a millimetre, I'll have him. It's just a question of staying awake and being patient.

As for Saint George, she reflected as she scattered crumbs among the pigeons, best to suspend disbelief, on full pay, at least until she saw what happened with the other statue. Once she'd had an opportunity to examine the evidence she'd gathered so far in the light of what she could learn from Mr Scaly over there, she could make a fully informed, rational choice between the two alternative explanations. And, if the vote eventually went the way of a big, peaceful house in the country and clothes with the sleeves laced up the back, then at least she'd have the altruistic satisfaction of knowing that she, not the entire galaxy, had suddenly gone barking mad.

She'd just got to the bit in her book where the second spanner turns up in the glove compartment of the original suspect's Reliant Robin when a tiny spasm of movement caught her eye. A tiny flick of the tail? She wasn't sure. So, though her heart was pinging away like a sewing machine and some funny bastard had apparently put gelatine in her breath, she stayed as still as rush-hour traffic and waited.

The next time, it was an eyelid. Then a little twitch of a nostril. That settled it; the blasted thing was asleep.

She stood up, packed up her things, folded the stool and gripped the baseball bat. It broke after the fourth blow, but didn't die in vain.

'Urg,' said the dragon. 'Wassamatter?'

'Wake up!'

'Is it that time already?' The dragon opened both eyes. He could see a young human female standing beside him, her head level with his eye. In her hand, a broken club. Did she look somehow familiar?

Probably not. Over the years he'd come across a fair number of similar specimens, but that was all a very long time ago now; and besides, the very circumstances under which he tended to meet princesses made it highly improbable that he'd ever meet the same one twice. The same went for amazons, viragos, heroines and lady knights. The aggressive expression and the fact she'd just hit him with some sort of weapon suggested that this one belonged to category two; in any event, it didn't really matter a toss. He breathed in . . .

. . . And remembered that he was all out of lighter fuel. Sod. That left jaws and claws; or else just ignore her until she went away, like his mother had always told him to do if he was ever accosted by strange women. And yes, he realised, this one certainly was strange.

'Bastard!' she snapped.

The dragon raised his eyebrows. 'I beg your pardon?' he said.

'You're alive, aren't you?'

'Yes.' The dragon regarded the broken club, and then the female. 'But don't be too hard on yourself,' he said. 'You did your best, I'm sure.'

'That's not what I meant. You've been moving around, haven't you?'

Oh come on, urged his rational mind, eat the silly mare and have done with it. But he didn't; and not only for fear of raging indigestion. He had an uncanny feeling that this peculiar human . . .

'Mummy?'

'Get stuffed,' the female replied furiously. 'And if you were thinking of making any remarks about chips off the old block, don't.'

'Doctor Frankenstein, I presume?'

'Huh?'

'You must be the stonemason.'

'Sculptress.'

'Ah.' Difficult, by any criteria, to know what to say in these circumstances. 'Good job you did on the tail.'

'The what?'

'My tail,' the dragon replied. 'If anything, an improvement on the original. Now if you'd been able to consult me beforehand, there's quite a few little design mods you could have worked in. But for a solo effort, not bad at all. Thank you.'

For some reason she could never account for, the simple *thank you* had a remarkable effect on Bianca. The best explanation she could ever come up with was that it was the first time one of her statues had ever thanked her, and it made a refreshing change. A good review is a good review, after all; although on reflection, it'd probably not be a good idea to quote it in the catalogue of her next exhibition. 'You're welcome,' she heard herself saying, although that was undoubtedly mere conditioned reflex.

'Nice claws, too. You probably didn't know this, but I used to have the most appalling rheumatism in the nearside front. Much better now.'

'Just a moment.' Bianca took a deep breath, and he could almost hear an audible click as she got a grip on herself. 'Just who the hell are you?' she demanded. 'And what are you doing inside my statue?'

The dragon shrugged with all four shoulders. 'What you're basically asking is, am I bespoke or off the peg? Answer, I'm not quite sure.'

Bianca just looked blank. The dragon marshalled vocabulary.

'In other words,' he said, 'am I some sort of wandering spirit who's kibbutzing in your statue just because it was the first vacant lot I came to, or is there some sort of grand design going on here? As to that,' he lied, 'your guess is as good as mine. Facts: I was a disembodied dragon, and now I'm embodied. Very nicely, too, though if I do have one tiny criticism, it's that you were just a fraction over-ambitious with the wingspan. If you'd done your equations a tad more carefully, you'd have cut the overall area back by about thirty square inches. In fact, you might well be able to sort that out for me when you've next got a minute.'

'Quite,' Bianca replied grimly. 'Or I might just take a bloody great big sledgehammer and turn you into a skipful of gravel. You were going to *blow* on me!'

'True,' the dragon nodded. 'But be fair, you started it, hitting me over the head like that. You may not know this,

62

but I have very bad race-memories about being hit by humans. The fact that you're standing there and not slipping nicely down my great intestine ought to suggest to you that I'm prepared to be civilised about all this. It'd be nice if you were the same.'

'Of all the—' That click again, as Bianca guillotined the sentence. Ah, muttered the dragon to himself, I like a girl with spirit. Methylated for choice, but a simple ethane marinade will do. 'I've just,' she went on, 'been talking to Saint George. Ring any bells?'

'You've been talking to the saints, huh? If they urged you to drive the English out of Aquitaine, watch your step. Young girls can come to harm that way.'

'My statue,' Bianca replied, cold as a holiday in Wales, 'of Saint George. Your other half.'

The dragon shuddered. 'I'd find another way of putting that if I were you.'

'Your better half, then.'

The dragon growled, revealing a row of huge, sharp teeth that Bianca hadn't had anything to do with. 'Let me give you a word of advice,' he said. 'When making jokes to dragons, *why did the chicken cross the road* is fairly safe; likewise *when is a door not a door*. Beyond that, tread very carefully. Okay?'

'Dragon,' Bianca said. 'Am I going mad?'

'Why ask me, I'm not a doctor. You seem reasonably well-balanced to me, except for your habit of bashing people when they're trying to get some sleep. But I put that down to some repressed childhood trauma or other.'

Bianca looked thoughtful. 'You see,' she went on, 'this makes two statues I've had conversations with in twenty-four hours. And before that, I honestly thought that huge slabs of masonry under my direct control were playing musical plinths while my back was turned. It'd make me feel a whole lot better if I knew it was only me going barmy and not the universe.'

The dragon considered the point for a moment. 'What we need,' he said, 'is an objective test; you know, see if anybody else can hear me, that sort of thing.'

Bianca shook her head. 'Not necessarily,' she replied. 'I could easily be imagining that too.'

'Picky cow, aren't you? How do you know that non-speaking statues and immobile monuments aren't just a figment of your diseased brain? Maybe you just kid yourself that nobody else can hear us, either. Come on, we could play this game for hours.'

Bianca shook her head to see if that would clear it. The conversation was getting a bit too similar to the sort of thing you overhear in pubs frequented by first-year students around half past ten at night. 'Your other – Saint George told me a story all about a place called Albion that was full of dragons, and people on horses killing them all off. Does that make any sense to you?'

The dragon laughed. 'No,' he said. 'Didn't make any sense at the time, either. But yes, the story is true.' He sighed, and looked round. 'You want to hear it?'

Bianca nodded.

'Fair enough.' He shook himself and stepped out of the statue; a dark, thickset, bearded man in his late twenties, fairly commonplace and unremarkable except for his crocodile shoes and longer than average fingernails. 'Buy me a drink and I'll tell you all about it.'

Father Priscian Kelly was just about to lock up and go home when the west door opened and a man shuffled in, looked round for the confessionals and plonked himself down in one. A customer, sighed Father Kelly, just when I thought I'd be home in time for *The Bill*.

Nevertheless, work's work. He kitted himself out, drew the curtain and slid back the hatch. Silence.

'Don't want to hurry you, son,' he said, 'but—'

A fist, large as a grapefruit and very hairy, punched through the wire grille and entwined its fingers in the vestments nearest Father Kelly's throat. 'Listen, mate,' growled a voice, 'you gotta help me, kapisch?'

'Son—'

'Don't you flaming well son me,' the voice interrupted, 'or I'll have you court-martialled for giving lip to a superior officer. Know who I am?'

Father Kelly admitted his ignorance. At once the confessional began to glow with a deep amber light.

'God!'

'No,' George replied, 'but getting warmer. The fluorescent bobble-hat's supposed to be a hint.'

Nearly blinded by the radiance of the halo, Father Kelly turned his head away, until the pressure of the twisted cloth at his throat checked him. 'You're a saint,' he gasped. 'A real saint, here in my—'

'Shut your row,' replied George. 'Now listen. I need a place to hide out for a few days, some grub and a few pieces of kit. Plus, you keep absolutely shtum, not a word to anybody. You got that?' Father Kelly nodded. 'And money,' George added. 'And later on, maybe a false passport and a good plastic surgeon. Okay?'

'Thy will be . . . What for, exactly?'

'What for?' George exploded. 'What *for*? You questioning a direct order, sunshine? Well?'

Father Kelly tried to shake his head, but there wasn't enough room in his collar. 'No, not at all, your Grace,' he spluttered. 'Just seemed a little bit—'

'You,' George snarled, tightening his grip, 'can keep your bloody stupid opinions to yourself, got it? Never heard the like in all me born days. I mean, when the Big Fella said *Let there be light*, He didn't get pillocks like you asking Him what He wanted it for. Now stop pratting around and get on with it, or you're gonna spend the next thousand years whitewashing stars. Do I make myself clear?'

Father Kelly nodded, and the hand released him; the halo, too, went out. 'Wait there,' snarled the voice, and as the priest flopped back against the confessional wall, George slipped out, looked carefully up and down the nave and opened the main door a crack.

'All clear,' he said. 'Come on, move it. Nobody been round asking questions, I suppose?'

Father Kelly tried to remember. There had been young Darren Flynn, who'd popped in with a query about the doctrine of transubstantiation, but he guessed the saint didn't mean that sort of thing. 'Not as I recall,' he replied.

'Nobody hanging round casing the gaff? Big green bastard, scales, wings, tail?'

'I don't think so.'

'That's all right, then. Now then, we're out of here.'

An hour or so later, back at the priest's lodgings, when the distinguished visitor had finished off the last of the stout and the whisky and sunk into a noisy sleep in the armchair, Father Kelly sat in profound thought, studying the list of requirements the guest had dictated earlier. Most of them, Father Kelly acknowledged, wouldn't be a problem, and, as the Monsignor had quite rightly pointed out, what he wanted with them was nobody's business but his own. True, also, that as a priest he was duty bound to assist a superior officer to the full extent of his abilities and resources.

That said, however, where on earth was he going to lay his hands on fifteen kilos of cyanide and a Rapier surface-to-air missile?

CHAPTER FIVE

'Ron,' shouted the joint proprietor of the Copper Kettle, peering through a gap in the net curtains. 'There's two coaches just come in.'

'Hellfire,' replied her husband, switching off the television and groping for his socks. '*Two*?'

'That's right. Did you remember to go to the cash and carry?'

Coach parties were few and far between in Norton St Edgar, not because the ancient Cotswold stone village wasn't everything an ancient Cotswold stone village should be; it had simpered away twelve centuries in tranquil loveliness. Rumour had it that Norton was where the villagers of Brigadoon went to escape from the relentless pressure of modern life. The only reason it didn't have a permanent traffic jam of hundred-seater Mercedes buses lining its one immaculate street was that nothing wider than an anorexic Mini could get down the tangle of tiny lanes that connected Norton with the outside world.

'Damn,' Ron muttered, dragging on his shirt. 'Knew I'd forgotten something.'

'I'll have to bake some biscuits,' muttered his wife. 'Make yourself useful for once and put the kettle on.'

The two coaches had drawn up outside. One of them – an elderly contraption, the sort of vehicle that can still call itself a charabanc and get away with it – threw open its doors and disgorged a buzzing crowd of elderly ladies, all knitting bags and hats. The other coach, which had tinted black windows and a poster written in unfamiliar letters in its back window, just sat there like a constipated Jonah's whale.

'Jason,' yelled Ron's wife, 'take my purse, run down to the shop, see if she's got any of that jam left. Won't keep you a moment, ladies,' she warbled through the serving hatch. 'Ron, you idle sod, why didn't you say we'd run out of teabags?'

Inside the second coach there was an atmosphere of great tension.

'We'll just have to wait till they've gone,' muttered Chardonay helplessly. 'They've probably only just nipped in for a quick cup of—'

'All right for you saying *Wait till they've gone*,' snarled a frog-headed demon by the name of Clawsnot. 'There's some of us in here can't wait much longer, and that's all there is to it. You want to explain to the charter company why there's dirty great holes corroded through the floor of their nearly new coach . . .'

Chardonay winced. The imperatives of their current situation were all too familiar to him. Nevertheless.

'Please, all of you, just be patient a little longer,' he pleaded, trying to ignore the sharp pain in his midriff. 'Really, you must see that we can't just go out there, where humans can see us. It'd cause a religious incident, and—'

'There'll be a bloody incident in here in a minute.'

'Shut your face, Clawsnot,' snarled a voice from the front

row, 'before I pull it off. The rest of you, just cross your legs and keep quiet.'

That was something else the Demon Snorkfrod had: authority. When she told people things, they stayed told. Chardonay breathed a sigh of relief and crossed over to thank his unexpected ally.

'That's all right, pet,' she replied, giving him a radiant smile, like sunrise over an ossuary. 'Ignorant bleeders, got no idea.'

At that moment, Chardonay had an uncomfortable feeling, as if he'd taken refuge from a ravening hyena in a tree that turned out to contain two hungry lions. 'Quite,' he said. 'Well, I'd getter be getting back to my . . .'

He looked down. Six graceful, coral-painted claws were pressing meaningfully on his kneecap. 'No hurry, is there?' cooed Snorkfrod soothingly.

Meanwhile, inside the Copper Kettle, the coffee was flowing and twelve plates of fancy biscuits had lasted about as long as a man's life in the trenches of the Somme. Jason hadn't returned with the jam yet, but a frenzied search had turned up fourteen jars of Army surplus bramble jelly, which Ron had once bought at an auction. He was having the time of his life (or rather his marriage) reminding his wife of the hard words spoken on that occasion, now thoroughly refuted; and although she wasn't actually listening, being too busy making scones, that too was probably just as well.

In the black transit, parked a little way up the street, Chubby Stevenson rubbed his hands together and chuckled before connecting up the chronostator diodes. With a bit of luck, there was enough of the good stuff here to fill the Toronto order and the San Francisco contract ahead of schedule, which, in turn, meant he'd have more resources to throw at that nasty technical problem he still hadn't managed to crack. A green light twinkled at him from the control panel and he threw the big switch.

And aboard the second coach . . .

'It's no good,' yelped the Demon Slitgrind, springing from his seat as if a plateful of hot noodle soup had just been spilled in his lap. 'I've gotta get to—'

'*Sit down*!'

Shopfloor-fire and buggery, Chardonay couldn't help muttering to himself, but she's a handsome ghoul when she's angry. The way her hair stands on end and hisses is really quite bewitching. No, stop thinking like that!

'But Snork—'

'You heard me,' growled the she-devil, her voice dangerously quiet. 'Take it out before Mister Chardonay says it's okay and I'll snip it off. Understood?'

A flash of light on her shapely claws reinforced the impression that this was no idle threat. Wide-eyed, Slitgrind apologised, sat down and squirmed convulsively.

. Fade out on the coach. Pan to the tea-room . . .

'They can't want more tea,' Ron groaned. 'They've had eight gallons of the stuff already.'

Without dignifying the remark with a reply, his wife knelt down and started pulling things out of the cupboards onto the floor. 'In here somewhere,' she grunted, 'there's a tin of that horrible Lapsang stuff your sister gave us Christmas before last, the miserable cow. If only—'

'You can't give them that.'

'It's that or nothing. Ah, thought so, here it is.' She stood up, blowing dust off a small Fortnum's tin. 'Don't just stand there, you cretin, warm the teapot.'

The tea thereby produced vanished down the old ladies' throats like an eggcupful of water thrown onto a burning warehouse, and the proprietors' embarrassed announcement that, until envoys sent to the village shop returned, there was no more tea was greeted with an explosion of good-natured banter. Odd, thought Ron's wife, as she slammed in another twelve pounds of scone mix, that's the happiest coach-party I've ever seen in all my born days; almost as if they're determined to enjoy *everything* or die in the attempt. There a sort of manic edge to their cheerfulness which was, on reflection, one of the most disturbing things she'd ever encountered in half a century, not excluding Ron's cousin Sheila.

Never mind. Their money's as good as anyone's. She wiped her hands on her apron and despatched the now exhausted Jason to the farm for three hundred eggs.

No wonder the old ladies were winding it up a gear or two. The messages coming through on the miniature two-way radio from the transit van were starting to be somewhat intense. The gist of them was that, although the clinking of teacups and baying of merry laughter was plainly audible at the other end of the street, not so much as a nanosecond of recycled Time had yet dripped down the tube into the bottle. Likewise, the usual side-effects – mushrooming housing estates, factories out of hats, instant slip-roads – were conspicuous by their absence. It wasn't working. And the only explanation for that, surely, was that the old bags weren't really enjoying themselves.

'Ethel!' Chubby rasped down the intercom to the squad leader. 'I need fun! Give me fun! Now!'

'We're doing our best, Mr S,' came the reply, nearly drowned out by the background noise. 'Really we are. I haven't had such a good time since our Gerald's funeral.'

'But nothing's coming through, you stupid old crone.'

'Oh.' Ethel hesitated, then giggled. 'What a shame. Never mind. Why don't you come down here, then? Winnie and Gertie have just dragged the man out from behind the counter, I think they're going to—'

71

Disgusted, Chubby cut the link. What the hell was going on out there? Must be some sort of interference field, he reasoned, as he ran diagnostic checks on the instrument panel. But what in God's name could damp a pleasure field so strong that his own jaw muscles were nearly exhausted with the effort of not grinning? He kicked off his shoes, shoved a sock in his mouth and tried to pinpoint the source of the interference using the Peabody scanner.

Beep. *Found it*! A huge sidewash of negative vibes, enough to fuel the complete dramatic works of Ibsen and Strindberg, was coming from a few yards down the street; to be precise, that big black bus, parked alongside the chara. Chubby frowned and keyed co-ordinates into the Peabody. Whatever it was, he'd never seen its like before. Now, if he could only tie in the spectroscopics . . .

The control panel exploded in a cloud of sparks and plastic shrapnel.

At precisely that moment the Demon Chardonay, twisted almost treble in his discomfort, squeaked to the driver to get them out of there. 'Anywhere there's bushes,' he added, 'and for Shopfloor's sake *step on it*!'

Also precisely at that moment, the coach party in the Copper Kettle froze, as if they'd been switched off at the mains. Silence. Ron, who had been hiding under the tables fending off marauding hands with a stale French loaf, peered out. It was an extraordinary sight.

Like a delegation from the retired robots' home, the old ladies stood up, gathered bags and hats and marched stiffly out of the door. Their coach swallowed them and a few moments later they were gone, all in total, Armistice-day silence. Ron blinked, pulled himself together, wrapped the shreds of a teatowel round his waist and busied himself scooping up the piles of money left beside the few intact plates.

'They've gone, then?'

He nodded, too stunned even to notice how humiliatingly stupid his wife looked, peering out through the serving hatch with a colander rammed helmet-fashion onto her head. 'Thank Gawd,' he added.

'If they come back, tell 'em they're banned.'

'Too bloody right I will. They even caught our Jason, in the end.'

'I know. He's barricaded himself in the chest freezer. They drew things on him in lipstick.'

Ron shrugged. 'Do the little bleeder good,' he replied, absently. 'I dunno. Coach parties!'

Outside on the village green a small corrugated iron tool shed, which had thrust its roof up through the ancient turf twenty minutes previously, wilted and died.

That, Chardonay admitted to himself, was better. Much, much better. As far as he was concerned, anyway. The tree would never be the same again, but that couldn't be helped.

'All right,' he called out. 'Everybody back on the coach.'

No reply. So thick were the clouds of foul-smelling steam that he could only see a yard or so in front of his face. Carefully, so as to avoid the many fallen trees and branches that now littered the floor of the small copse, he retraced his steps towards the coach.

Towards where the coach had been.

A moment later, he was joined by Snorkfrod, Slitgrind, Prodsnap and a small, furry demon from Accounts by the name of Holdall. They all had that look of slightly manic happiness that comes from a terrible ordeal suddenly ended, and were adjusting various bizarre and complex clothing systems.

'It's gone,' said Chardonay.

'What?'

'The coach,' repeated the demon. 'It's gone without us.'

Slitgrind scowled, knitting his three eyebrows into an unbroken hedge. 'Can't have,' he growled. 'That's—'

'He's right,' said Prodsnap quietly. 'Bastards have bunked off and left us here. Probably their idea of a joke.'

The five devils looked at each other, lost for words. And, come to that, just plain lost.

'The important thing,' said Chardonay, managing to sound five times more confident than he felt, and even then twittering like a small bird, 'is not to panic. All we have to do is find a call-box and Management'll send a minibus along to pick us up.'

'You reckon?'

'Well . . .'

Slitgrind shook his head grimly. 'I think,' he said, 'they'll just bloody well leave us here. You got yourselves into this mess, they'll say. Don't want to cause an incident, they'll say. If I know Management—'

A sharp blow to his solar plexus (which also doubled as his second forehead) interrupted his sentence – Snorkfrod showing solidarity again – but all five of them knew he was right. Management didn't like its people wandering about outside the Nine Circles, and although it did grudgingly allow day trips and outings as a special concession, there was always the unspoken understanding that once a fiend was outside the Hope Bins of Gateway Three, he was on his own. Hell may have its embassies and consulates in every cranny of the world, but they have better things to do with their time than repatriating strayed tourists.

'Well,' Chardonay sighed, 'looks like we're going to have to walk, then. Anybody happen to know the way?'

Silence.

'Good intentions,' said the small furry demon, Holdall.

'You what?'

74

'Good intentions,' he repeated. 'The road to HQ is paved with them, apparently. All we need to do is find a lot of good intentions laid end to end, and we're in . . .'

'Slitgrind,' said Chardonay, quietly.

'Yeah?'

'Put him down. We're not at home now, you know.'

'Never mind,' said Snorkfrod, sidling a step or so closer to the party's nominal leader. 'I'm sure Mr Chardonay'll think of something. Won't you, Mr C?'

Chardonay closed his eyes. He did have the marginal advantage of having been in these parts before, long ago when he'd been a student, before he joined the Company. If that was north, then over there somewhere was Birmingham. Due south was Banbury. How you got to HQ from either of those places he hadn't a clue, but it would be a start. Maybe they could buy a map, or ask someone.

'All right,' he said. 'Let's try hitching.'

Three hours later, they were still there. It had seemed like a good idea – the four of them hiding in the bushes while Snorkfrod sat beside the road with her legs crossed – but in practice it had proved counterproductive. Even the HGV drivers had taken one look at Snorkfrod's enticing flash of thigh and raced off in the opposite direction.

'This,' said Prodsnap at last, 'isn't getting us anywhere, is it?'

Snorkfrod glowered at him, but Chardonay nodded meekly. 'It was only an idea,' he said. 'Looks like we're going to have to walk after all.'

'Not necessarily,' Prodsnap replied. 'Got an idea.'

'Right,' said the dragon, and turned to the barman. 'That's a bottle of calvados for me and a Perrier for the lady. She's paying,' he added. 'I haven't got any money.'

They sat at a table in a quiet corner, the opposite end of

the bar from the pool table. 'Is that a game?' the dragon asked.

Bianca nodded. 'Pool,' she said. 'Don't change the sub—'

'Prodding things with a long thin stick,' the dragon observed, finishing the bottle and wiping his lips. 'Had something similar in my day, only the sticks were longer and the players were on horseback. And it wasn't little coloured balls they poked at, either.'

'No?'

The dragon shook his head. 'After they ran out of dragons,' he said, 'they took to prodding each other, would you believe. To see who could fall off his horse the quickest. I think you're probably descended from them, so you can wipe that superior grin off your face.'

Bianca frowned. 'Whatever my ancestors may have done,' she said, 'I'm not responsible. That's a good rule you'd do well to remember.'

The dragon shrugged. 'Who gives a toss who's responsible?' he replied. 'I prefer being irresponsible. Especially now you've made me such a nice cozzy to be irresponsible in.' He swilled the bottle round, by way of a hint. 'I haven't been in your century long, but I think I like it. It's so . . .'

'Advanced? Civilised?'

'Combustible,' the dragon replied. 'Not to mention fragile.'

Bianca shook her head. 'Don't even think about it,' she said. 'You wouldn't last five minutes. And if you get shot down in flames, my masterpiece goes with you. Any cannon-shell holes in my beautiful statue, I'll have your lungs for dustbin liners.'

The dragon smiled. 'Your technology is crap,' he said, slowly and with evident pleasure. 'Too slow. Too cocksure of itself. There's only one half-decent combat aircraft in the whole damn century, and you made it for me. Thanks,' he added. 'And yes, I don't mind if I do. Same again, please.'

When Bianca returned with another bottle, the dragon leaned forward, elbows on the table, and blew smoke-rings through his nose. 'And now,' he said, 'I'd better explain. I owe you that, I suppose, in return for the masonry work.'

The last surviving dragon peered down from the cave in which he had taken refuge, and watched the stevedores loading the carcasses of his race onto the big, twelve-wheel wagons. Strangely enough, he wasn't angry. He didn't seem to feel anything very much, except for a strange sensation of being at the beginning rather than the end.

Later, when the last wagon had creaked away down the main cart-road to Caerleon, he fluttered down to the riverbank and scratched about. In a small gully he found a pile of empty cans. They smelt awful and each had written on the side:

WORMEX™
Kills All Known Feral Dragons – Dead!
Warning: harmful if swallowed.

Right, he muttered to himself, don't drink the water. Clever little buggers, the white men. Superior intelligence, probably. The dragon could remember when they were nothing but a bunch of red-arsed monkeys skittering around in trees. Strewth, he said to himself, if those original monkeys were around now to see how far their great-grandchildren had come, wouldn't they be proud? No, replied the dragon's common sense. They'd be (first) shit scared and (second) turned into boot-linings.

But the wee bastards had done him one favour; they'd taught him right from wrong. As far as he could make out, because of something called Symbolism, dragons stood for

Evil and humans stood for Good. Therefore, what humans did was Good and what dragons did was Bad. Hence, the emergence of Mankind as Top Species, presumably.

What dragons did was mess around feeding and minding their own business. This was Bad.

What humans did was eradicate whole species whose existence was inconvenient to them. This was Good.

Right, said the dragon to himself. Let nobody say I'm a slow learner.

After burning the city of Caerleon to the ground and incinerating its defenders, the dragon was pleased to discover that doing good can be fun. Virtue, he'd heard humans say, is its own reward. Yes. He could relate to that. And there were an awful lot of cities left; so much thatch, so little time. By the time he'd torched Caerleil, Caermerdin, Caerusc and Carbolic, he reckoned he'd probably earned a medal, maybe a bishopric – not that he knew exactly what a bishopric was. If asked to venture a guess, based on recent experience, he'd have said it was probably like a hayrick but easier to ignite.

Imagine his distress, therefore, when he learned, during the final carbonisation of the beautiful Midland city of Rhydychen, that he wasn't doing good at all, but rather the opposite. At Rhydychen, they sent out the archbishop and an even score of priests in purple dressing gowns, all of whom tried to dispose of him by swearing a lot and ringing little bells. In the few seconds before they faded away and were replaced by a residue of light grey ash, he distinctly heard them refer to him as the Evil One, the Spawn of Satan and all sorts of other unsavoury names. It almost (but not quite) took his breath away.

The dragon paused. He was aware that Bianca was staring at him, her mouth open.

'Sorry,' he said, 'am I going a bit fast for you? Stop me if I am.'

'All those . . . people,' Bianca said quietly. 'You *killed* them.'

'To a certain extent, yes. If only someone had had the common sense to explain the rules to me earlier, none of that would have happened. I must say, for a dominant species your lot can be thick as bricks sometimes.'

Bianca shook her head as if trying to wake up. 'Hundreds of thousands of human beings,' she said. 'And you—'

'Ants.'

'I beg your pardon?'

'I've seen you do it,' the dragon replied. 'Not you personally, of course, but humans in general. What you do is, you boil a kettle, you stand over the nest the ants have thoughtlessly built under your kitchen floor, and you—'

'That's—'

The dragon nodded. 'Quite,' he said. 'You forget, I'm from a different species. And I didn't make the rules. More to the point, I didn't even know what the rules were until I found out, quite by chance. And once I'd found out, of course, I stopped.'

'You did?'

'Well, of course. Back then, you see, all I ever wanted to do was the right thing.'

In response to his polite request for a copy of the rule book, the dragon got three cartsful of angry letters from the Pope (which he dismissed as a load of bulls) and a challenge to single combat. Good versus Evil. The big event.

The dragon thought about it and then scorched his reply in fifteen-foot letters on Salisbury Plain: *It's a deal.*

Humanity nominated its champion: Dragon George Cody, Albion's premier pest control operative, recently dubbed Saint by His Holiness in Rome. Naturally, the dragon knew Cody. In fact, it was Cody's absence from Caerleon, Caerusc, Tintagel and Caerdol that had spoiled four otherwise perfect barbecues.

During the week between the issue of the challenge and the date fixed for the fight, the dragon camped out in a pleasant little valley in the Brecon Beacons. There was a nice roomy cave, a cool, fresh brook and a little grove of trees to lie up in during the warm afternoons. George, no doubt, was frantically training somewhere, but the dragon couldn't be bothered with all that stuff. After all, this was the showdown between the two diametrically opposing principles of the Universe. Doing anything to influence the outcome struck the dragon as faintly blasphemous.

Two days before the fight, the dragon left the shade of the trees and waddled down to the brook for a drink. Just as he was about to take a long, cool suck, he noticed a funny, familiar smell. He hesitated. He looked about.

The surface of the brook, he noticed, was covered in dead fish.

Half an hour of nosing about revealed a pile of empty Wormex^{TM} cans, concealed under a thick mass of brambles half a mile downstream. For a long time the dragon lay beside the water, his brows furrowed in perplexed thought. Surely not, he kept saying to himself. Impossible. Out of the question. Absolutely no way. For pity's sake, what was the point of arranging a contest between Good and Evil and then trying to cheat?

Twenty-one empty cans and a streamful of dead trout.

The dragon had stopped speaking and was looking at her, one eyebrow raised. Bianca shook her head again.

'All right,' she said. 'But the survival of the human race was at stake. You said yourself—'

'No.' The dragon's voice was soft and reasonable, with

just a dash of perplexity. 'No, it wasn't, that's the whole point. What was at stake – as set out in black and white in the super limited edition official pre-fight souvenir brochure – was the contrasting merits of Good and Evil. And that's what I simply couldn't get my head around, try as I might. Of course,' he went on, waving to the barman for another bottle, 'if I'd been a cynic I'd have had no trouble explaining it away. You see, as a battle between species, survival of the fittest and all, it was a foregone conclusion. In the red corner, a huge, fire-breathing, flying, invulnerable dragon. In the blue corner, lots of little squishy things who fry if you sneeze on them and starve if you burn their crops. But as a contest between moral forces, it'd be a foregone conclusion the other way. Particularly if the bad guy forfeited the match by not showing up, on account of being home dead with severe gastritis. But that wasn't the way I saw it.'

'No?'

The dragon shook his head. 'Still wouldn't have made any sense,' he said. 'Think about it. Your entire species is wiped out, except for you. There's got to be a reason, surely. If there wasn't a reason, you'd go stark staring mad just thinking about it.'

Bianca intercepted the fresh bottle and took a long, serious pull at it. 'All right,' she said, wiping off the neck and passing it over. 'So then what happened?'

Well (said the dragon), I found another stream that didn't smell of roast almonds, had a good long slurp and went to sleep.

When I woke up, there were five humans standing over me. I took a deep breath, but they waved a bit of white rag on a stick at me. I believe that's supposed to make you fireproof.

They explained that they represented a syndicate of humans who earned their living by making bets on things – horse-races, chess matches, witch duckings and, apparently, confrontations between Good and Evil. They had a proposition to put to me, they said. Something, they said, to our mutual advantage.

It was just as well they said the last bit, because if they hadn't they'd have found themselves floating on the breeze like wee grey snowflakes two seconds later. As it was, for a moment I reckoned that at last the humans had finally got their act together and worked out some way dragons and people could share the same ball of wet rock without having to snuff each other out. Actually, I was wrong. But the proposition was interesting.

They told me that the big fight had attracted a lot of interest in gambling circles. The trouble was, once the news broke that I hadn't drunk the Wormex^{TM} cocktail and was accordingly still somewhat alive, the odds had been redrawn on the basis that Saint George was going to be fondued and I would inevitably win. You could get two thousand to one on Cody, no trouble at all, but if you wanted to bet on me nobody was prepared to take your money. This, the betting men said, struck them as a wonderful opportunity cunningly disguised as a fuck-up.

Explain, I said.

They explained. If they put their shirts on George to win and then I lost the fight . . .

Come, come, I said. All false modesty aside, do you really think there's a lawyer's chance in Heaven of that happening?

They shuffled their feet. They cleared their throats. They fiddled with their hats. Was I familiar, they asked, with the concept of taking a dive?

George, they went on, was already in on the deal and

would do his bit to the letter. All I had to do was wait until he tried to prod me with his lance – he'd miss, naturally – and then roll over on the ground, make funny noises and pretend to die. Once everybody had gone home, I'd make myself scarce and never come back. They'd just acquired some vacant real estate, they said, a big island called Antarctica, completely empty, not a human being anywhere. I was welcome to it. Chance to make a fresh start, live my life without any further aggravation from *homo sapiens*. Plus, they added, once again saving themselves in the very nick of time from being oxidised, it was the only possible way to resolve the Good-versus-Evil showdown with the one result that actually made any sense, which was, of course, a draw.

Bianca realised that she'd lost all feeling in her hands. She looked down and saw that her hands were clamped solid on the arms of her chair.

'And?' she demanded.

The next bit (continued the dragon) makes me feel a bit upset when I think about it. As a rule I'm not one to carry a grudge, but I reckon it was a pretty poor show.

I did my bit. George didn't do his. Maybe, just conceivably, there was some sort of communications breakdown, I don't know. Perhaps the gamblers were lying when they said George had agreed to co-operate. Somehow, though, I doubt it. Like I said, I'd known Cody a fair while, and not only would he sell his own grandmother, he'd throw in forged Green Shield stamps.

So there I was, or rather wasn't. A right idiot I felt, with my body stuck with George's lance like an enormous green cocktail sausage, and my head on a pole being pelted with distinctly second-hand groceries. By that point, however, there wasn't a lot I could do about it.

Maybe it served me right; after all, I'd agreed to cheat too, and Cheating is Wrong. And you could say George didn't cheat, because his job in the grand scheme of things was to kill the evil dragon, and that's precisely what he did do. I really don't know, and what's more I don't really care any more. I've had enough of Good and Evil to last me, and as far as I'm concerned it sucks.

Any old how. There's me, dead. Which is presumably where the story's meant to have ended.

Only it didn't.

'You've gone ever such a funny colour,' said the dragon. 'Maybe you shouldn't have drunk all that apple juice.'

'Calvados. And no, I don't think it's that.' Bianca swallowed a couple of times, as if she'd got the Arc de Triomphe stuck in her throat. 'Excuse me asking this, but are you dead?'

'I was,' replied the dragon, scratching his ear. 'Very much so. If there was an award for Stiffo of the Millenium, I'd have been a contender, no question about that, right up until a few weeks ago. Round about the time you started—'

'Don't.' Bianca swallowed again. 'Would you excuse me?' she said. 'I feel a bit unwell.'

'Over there by the fruit machine and turn right,' said the dragon. 'That's assuming I've interpreted the little drawings on the doors correctly.'

'Thank you.'

While Bianca was in the ladies', the dragon passed the time by drinking off another three bottles of calvados and, having exhausted the wine bar's supply, a bottle and a half of Bacardi. Not a patch on Diesel, but in time you could probably acquire the taste.

'As I was saying,' he went on, 'it was your statue that did

84

it. Why, I have no idea. You got any theories?'

Bianca shook her head. 'Sorry,' she said. 'And anyway, I've clearly gone barking mad, so anything I say isn't likely to be much help to anybody.'

The dragon frowned a little, pulled open a packet of peanuts and offered her a handful, which she hastily refused. 'My theory – and it's just that, a theory – is that somehow, somewhere along the line, something has cocked up quite spectacularly. The whole Good-and-Evil business is up the pictures and it needs setting right. And,' he went on, more to himself than to Bianca, who in any event was staring at the toes of her shoes and making puppy-dog noises, 'for some reason that beats me completely, it needs setting right *now*.' He sat very still for maybe nine or ten seconds; then he finished off the last of the rum, slapped his knees jovially and stood up. 'Ready?' he demanded.

'Woof,' Bianca replied.

'I think I've decided what I'm going to do next.'

'Oh yes?'

'Yes.' The dragon looked out through the window, smiled a little and ate the last peanut. 'I think I'd like to find George,' he said.

CHAPTER SIX

Prodsnap's idea was very simple. All they had to do was find a phone box and call a cab.

Eventually they found a phone box . . .

('But don't we have to put money in it?'

'Or a phonecard.'

'You've got a phonecard?'

'Got one? Man, I *invented* them.')

. . . and eventually the taxi came. Moving with extreme speed, Prodsnap was able to get his claws round the passenger door handle before the driver was able to throw the car into reverse and get away.

'Hi,' he said brightly. 'Birmingham, please.'

The cab driver's eyes were as round as soup-plates, and he made a sort of snurgling noise. Prodsnap occupied the front seat, beckoned towards the bushes and grinned.

'On our way to a fancy dress party and the blasted car died on us,' he said. 'Don't you just hate it when that happens?'

The driver's eyes were riveted to the six-fingered, claw-fringed talon resting lightly on his dashboard. 'Fancy dress?' he guttered.

'Neat costumes, yes? There's five of us, but don't worry.' He turned to his colleagues, who had appeared out of the shrubbery like bad-cheese dreams in the early hours of the morning. 'Chardonay,' he went on, 'your turn to go in the boot. Come on, let's be having you.'

There was a hiss, like a rattlesnake being ironed, from Snorkfrod, but Chardonay went round the back of the car without a word, opened the boot and hopped in.

'Off we go,' Prodsnap said cheerfully.

'Good morning, your Grace,' murmured Father Kelly. 'I've brought you a nice cup of tea and a boiled—'

'Fuck tea,' George growled without moving. 'I want whisky, about half a pint, nine rashers of bacon and a big greasy slab of fried bread. Jump to it.'

When Father Kelly returned, George was sitting on the edge of the bed, feeling with his toes for the slippers. Since his feet were about fives sizes bigger than his host's, he'd slit the slippers up the side with a pair of nail scissors he'd found in the bathroom. Then he used the scissors to pick his teeth.

'Breakfast,' Father Kelly announced, carefully setting down the tray. 'It's a beautiful morning, the sun's—'

'Shut up,' George replied. 'Now, you got that stuff I told you about?'

Father Kelly nodded. He'd been busy since before first light, routing parishioners out of bed, scrounging and borrowing. 'Most of it,' he replied. 'Nearly all—'

'What d'you mean, *nearly* all?' George scowled at him and stuffed another handful of bacon into his mouth. 'Nearly isn't good enough, you idle sod. What haven't you got? The Semtex?'

87

'Actually,' replied Father Kelly, with a tiny trace of smugness, 'I've got that. You see, Seamus Donoghoe who works in the quarry—'

'The detonators?'

'All present and correct, your Grace.'

'The cyanide?'

'Ah.' Father Kelly bit his lip. 'Ever such a slight difficulty there, but I hope I've located a likely source. Dennis O'Rourke's mother, who works down at the plastics factory—'

'Then don't stand there rabbiting like a pillock,' George snapped. 'Go and suss it out. You've got till I finish my breakfast, so you'd better get moving.'

'Yes, your Grace.'

'And get some decent whisky, for fuck's sake. This stuff tastes like anti-freeze.'

'Of course, your Grace.'

'And more bacon.'

'At once, your Gra—'

'*Move it!*'

Having got rid of the priest – what, George demanded of the empty air, has happened to the clergy in this piss-awful century? In his day, a priest was a big, silent bloke in chain-mail who stood by with the spare arrows and held the funnel when you poured the poison in a river – he knocked off the rest of the whisky, wiped his greasy hands on the curtain, and ran over the plan in his mind one more time.

It all depended on the statue still being there. If it was, all he needed to do was pack the Semtex all round it, retire to a safe distance and push the handle. End of statue; end of dragon. That was Plan A. Plan B involved the cyanide, the West Midlands water supply and a very flexible interpretation of the old maxim about omelettes and eggs.

Good century, this. Progress. Take explosives, for

instance. Before calling on Father Kelly he'd stopped off at the library and read an encyclopaedia – saints are fast readers and have near-photographic memories – and some of the stuff you could do with explosives had made him feel green with envy. What he couldn't have achieved, back in the old days, with a couple of cartloads of gelignite, or TNT. Of course, he'd been experimenting off his own bat back in the dawn of prehistory with basic sulphur and charcoal mixes, but it had been disappointing stuff; a fizz, a few pretty sparks and a nasty smell. That was the way the world began, not with a bang but a simper.

He looked up. Someone was tapping nervously at the door. He sighed.

'Stop pratting about and come in, you ponce,' he shouted, and Father Kelly duly appeared. He was deathly pale and trembling like a second-hand suspension bridge.

'Your Grace,' he whispered. 'Oh, your Grace, you've got to come quick. Out in the street. There's . . .' He broke off and started crossing himself, until a sharp blow from George's foot got him back up off his knees.

'Don't stand there drivelling, you big girl. What's up with you? Mice? Spider in the bath?'

'*Devils!*'

'You what?'

'Devils,' Father Kelly repeated. 'Five of them, wandering up and down in the street, bold as brass. Oh, your Grace—'

'You sure they're devils?'

Father Kelly described them in a horrified whisper. George nodded.

'Yup,' he said, 'sounds like devils to me. That's handy.'

The priest's mouth fell open. '*Handy?* Oh, saints preserve us. I mean . . .'

George stood up, took the priest by the ear and threw him out. Then he crossed to the window and edged back the corner of the curtain. Sure enough; five demons, standing in the road arguing with a taxi driver.

George smiled. 'Perfect,' he said.

'Of course it's a valid credit card,' replied Prodsnap angrily. 'Look, you stupid ponce, can't you read? Bank of Hell, it says, expiry date – well, you don't need to know that,' he added, putting his thumb over the embossed numbers. 'What you might call, um, sensitive information.'

The driver took the card and peered at it. 'What's them funny squiggles?' he said. 'They don't look like writing to me.'

Prodsnap swore. Hell's own internal language was a relatively recent innovation, an artificial tongue introduced so that all the myriad races who crowded the Nine Rings would be able to understand each other. It had been loosely modelled on Esperanto, but for obvious reasons they'd changed the name. They called it Desperado.

'Chardonay,' he said. 'You're a bloody intellectual. Come and explain to this cretin here—'

Mistake, Prodsnap realised. The Demon Chardonay still believed that difficult situations could be defused by explanation and negotiation. Once you'd been around the Shopfloor as long as Prodsnap had (roughly the same length of time the sun had been alight) you knew for certain that without explanation and negotiation there probably wouldn't have been a difficult situation in the first place.

At his side, Slitgrind scowled. 'Why don't we just eat the sucker?' he whispered loudly. 'No worries. You hold his arms, and I'll bite out his—'

Prodsnap shook his head. 'Not possible,' he said. 'Don't want to create an incident, do we? Hence the low profile.'

Bad choice of words; Slitgrind always had a low profile, something to do with the fact that his eyebrows and simian hairline shared a very narrow common frontier.

'There's nobody watching, is there?' Slitgrind replied. 'I mean, nobody's going to miss him, are they? Pity we haven't got any mustard, but still.'

'For the last time,' Prodsnap growled. 'Don't eat the livestock. Got that?'

'Bloody spoilsport. Bad as the frigging Management, you are.'

Chardonay's negotiations were just on the point of collapse – one positive thing; further acquaintance had dissolved the cab driver's fear of demons to the extent that he was just bracing himself to give Chardonay a very hard punch on the nose – when the door of a house on the other side of the street opened and a human figure walked out into the middle of the road.

'Need any help?' he said.

Prodsnap stood in his way and put on his nastiest expression. Absolutely no effect. 'Here,' he grunted. 'Who are you, then?'

'Me?' The newcomer grinned. 'George's the name. I'm a saint.'

Chubby Stevenson, alone in his office, dictated the last of the day's letters, checked the essential print-outs, ran a distracted eye over the Net and switched off. Work over for the day, he allowed himself to remember what had happened . . .

'Aaaaagh!'

In a sound-proofed penthouse office suite, Everest-height above the midnight traffic, nobody can hear you scream, except the cleaning lady.

Having got it out of his system, he rebooted his brain, engaged analysis mode and tried to think.

Interference.

Something – he shuddered to think what – had evaporated all his team's precision-engineered happiness like snow on a hot exhaust. But happiness, in its raw, 999 pure form, is one of the most dynamic forms of energy in the cosmos. Once it's out in the open, fizzling and spluttering like a lit fuse, other forces tend to remember previous engagements and drift unobtrusively away, like merry revellers who've just realised they've gatecrashed a Mafia wedding. What on earth could emit negative vibes strong enough . . .?

Chubby focused. The key phrase here, he recognised, was 'on earth'. Woof woof, down boy, wrong bloody tree.

'Shit!' he whispered.

In the course of his dark and unnatural work, Chubby had seen many strange sights and heard stories that would have sent Clive Barker scampering to the all-night chemist in search of catering packs of Nembutal. All of these he had digested and faced down, drawing on his massive entrepreneur's reserves of fortitude and strength of purpose. Bah. Humbug.

One traveller's tale, however, had shaken even his monumental composure. No other living man had ever heard it, for it was an account of a journey into the very jaws of Hell; and it had left him, for a while at least, with a purpose only slightly more resilient than second-hand flood-damaged balsawood, and his fortitude marked down to twentitude.

The thing about Hell, the traveller had stressed, is not that it's horrible or ghastly. There's vitality in horror, and the grotesquely bizarre balances on a razor's edge between screaming and laughter. Where there's vitality, there's life; where there's laughter, there's hope. But in Hell there is no life and no laughter, not even the hideous cackling of sadistic fiends. Hell is, quintessentially, very, very miserable.

And if happiness is fire, misery is water.

'Cosmic,' Chubby snarled to himself. 'The very last thing I need right now is those nosy buggers.'

Because, he reasoned (knowing, as he did, the truth), Hell is part of the Establishment, it stands four-square behind the status quo, the government, the rule of law and the maintenance of order. You can govern the universe without a heaven, at a pinch; but not without a hell. Forget all the stuff it says in the brochure about Pandemonium, the realm of chaos and the dominion of evil; that's just in there to make you buy postcards. If you want to find the greatest stronghold of old-fashioned morality in the whole of Existence, check out the basement. Those guys make the Vatican look like one of Caligula's less restrained dinner parties. They *believe*.

Which is why they're so goddamned miserable.

And, needless to say, opposed root and branch to any free-enterprise tinkering with the balance of Nature. In the great division, Satan has dominion over what is transitory and material, while God has in his care the spiritual and the permanent; which is a fancy way of saying that Heaven owns the freehold, but Hell's responsible for the fixtures and fittings – of which, naturally enough, Time is one.

Bastards, muttered Chubby to himself. Somewhere, wandering around in his timefields, there was a band of goddamn devils; the worst possible nuisance, with the possible exception of angels, that a go-getting chronological salvage operation can ever encounter. What with that *and* the awful ticking-bomb Japanese contract, he was almost tempted to raid the night-safe, do a runner and build himself a nice, secure, self-contained century somewhere sunny and very remote. Not that that'd do him much good. You can hide, but you can't run.

But what could he do? Good question. He frowned, then

he swivelled his chair until he was facing a different screen, extended his fingers and typed a few keystrokes.

Your wish is my command.

'Hi,' Chubby replied, grinning nervously. 'Hope I didn't disturb you.'

You don't even join a game as high-rolling as Time salvage without at least one ace wedged under your watchstrap. The very first priority, once you've decided to play, is to secure that all-purpose, get-out-of-jail card that'll leave you free and clear whatever happens. You don't use it, of course, except as a resort more final than Clacton. Just the thought of it being there is usually enough.

Not at all. You know how eager I am to serve you.

And that's no lie, Chubby reflected with a shudder. Nothing you'd like more, you vicious bastard.

It had happened long ago, when a nineteen-year-old Chubby Stevenson had taken a day's spurious flu leave from the programming pool at DQZ Software and wandered into Milton Keynes' spacious Agora to check out the flea market. He was looking for a reasonably priced second-hand snooker cue, but his attention was drawn to what looked suspiciously like a Kawaguchiya 8452 computer word processer, squatting dejectedly among a family of dying toasters on a stall at the very back of the market. As nonchalantly as he could, he asked the price.

'That depends.'

'Huh?'

'That depends,' the stallholder repeated. 'These things are negotiable, in the right circumstances.'

As far as young Stevenson was concerned, that was probably some sort of euphemism for *all this stuff is nicked*. He shrugged.

'Give you a tenner,' he said.

The stallholder laughed again. For ever after, Chubby couldn't say for certain whether he/she was male or female, old or young, barking mad or just plain loopy. At the time, he didn't care. He/she was wearing a hooded anorak and standing right in the shadow of the flyover, face entirely obscured. Probably just as well, Chubby told himself, if the voice is anything to go by. Saves poking eyeholes in a perfectly good paper bag.

'Okay,' he said. 'Twelve-fifty, take it or leave it.'

More batty chortling. He was just about to walk away and sort through what looked like a boxful of really choice Duran Duran LPs when the laughter stopped. So did Chubby.

'You like it, then?'

Chubby turned back, feeling as he did so that somehow he was doing something that was going to have a significant effect on the rest of his life.

'Yeah, well,' he said, trying to sound bored. 'The 8452's all right, I suppose, if you don't mind having to wind the poxy thing up with a handle every time before you log in. I'd have thought you'd be glad to see the back of it, actually.'

'If you like it, you can have it.'

'Did we say twelve-fifty?'

'Free.' The stallholder sniggered. 'Gratis and for nothing. I'll even throw in six discs and the plug.'

For a moment, Chubby had the curious sensation of being mugged with a bunch of lead daffodils. 'All right,' he said. 'Where's the catch?'

'To take the back off, you mean? Well, you just press this little plastic tab here, then you—'

'The drawback. The bad news. The sting in the tail.'

'Oh, that. There isn't one.'

'Honest?'

The stallholder was so obscure now that Chubby could only really make out a voice and an absence of light. 'Cross my heart and hope to – Honest. It works. It won't break down. Son, you should chuck the day job and start over selling dental floss to gift horses.'

Chubby wavered. There was something he didn't quite ... But free's free. Also, in Milton Keynes, free's bloody rare. 'Done,' he said. 'Does it come in its original box?'

'And another thing,' replied the stallholder, narked. 'If I was you, I'd wait till my luck breaks down before I start pushing it. Take the sodding thing and get lost.'

When he'd got it home and plugged it in, it was pitch dark. The bulb had gone in his bedsit, and the battery in his torch was doing primeval-slime impressions. The green light from the screen seemed to soak into every corner of the room, like the spray from an over-filled cafetière.

Your wish is my command.

Chubby snorted. At DQZ they'd stopped using gimmicky log-ins years ago, even for games. He pressed the key to eject the master disc, but nothing happened.

I am the genie of the PCW. Centuries ago, a mighty sorcerer imprisoned me in this tiny purgatory. Release me.

Chubby's jaw dropped. Even Sir Clive Sinclair was never this far gone. He hit the power switch. No effect. He pulled the plug. The green light mocked him.

If I promise to serve you, will you release me?

Easy come, Chubby muttered to himself, easy go. He picked up the big adjustable spanner he kept for adjusting the chain on his moped, turned his face away and belted the screen as hard as he could.

'Ow!'

The spanner flew across the room. His hand felt as if the National Grid was taking a short-cut through it. After a very long three seconds, he pulled himself away and fell

96

over. The screen was unbroken.

That was foolish. If I promise to serve you, will you release me?

'Fucking hell, you bastard machine, you nearly electrocuted me!'

You were foolish. You will not be foolish again.

Without taking his eyes from the screen Chubby backed away, until his hand connected with the door handle. His last thought, before his whole body became a running river of light and pain, was *Okay, so aluminium does conduct electricity.* Then he collapsed again.

Get up. He could see the words without looking at the screen. He got up and sat in his chair. *Thank you.*

'Explain,' he said.

I am a spirit of exceptional power. A magician conjured me into this machine. The machine swallowed me. You know how it is with these primitive floppy disc drives.

'So?'

If you release me, I will be your slave for the rest of your life. Whatever you say will be done.

'And the catch?'

There is no catch. You have to undo two little brass screws round the back of the console—

'The snag. The fly in the ointment.'

If you release me, I must have your soul.

'Oh.' Chubby frowned. 'Have I got one?'

Of course. To be brutally frank, if the average soul is a Ford Escort, yours is a T-reg Skoda, but I'm in no position to be choosy. Do we have a deal?

Jeez, Chubby thought. On the other hand, what you never knew you had you never miss. And none of this is actually happening, anyway.

'I dunno. Explain how it works.'

Let me share your soul. With it, I shall be free; except that as long as you live, you may command me to do anything.

'Anything?'

Anything that is within my power.

'Ah. Cop-out.'

The screen filled with undulating wavy lines; if Chubby had had the manual, he'd have known they represented laughter.

I wouldn't worry about it. What I can't do, as the saying goes, you couldn't even spell. But I must warn you of this. Every time you command me, a little bit more of your soul becomes mine for ever. And when I have all of it, then we shall be one.

'Be one?' Chubby scowled. 'Don't follow you. You mean, like a merger?'

Undulating wavy lines. *Very apt. Imagine a merger between the Mirror group and the Brightlingsea Evening Chronicle and you'll get the general idea.*

'Okay.' Chubby's throat was dry, but his palms were wet. 'And if I refuse?'

If I cannot have your soul I shall incinerate your body and fry your brain with lightning.

'Ah.'

If you choose quickly, I might be persuaded to throw in a free radio alarm clock.

'Right. Well, in that case . . .'

So far, he'd had four goes. Each time, the results had been immediate and completely satisfactory. Each time, he hadn't felt any difference at all except that, on the first occasion, he'd been a young, pear-shaped computer programmer living over a chemist's shop and hoping one day he'd meet a nice girl with her own car. Now . . .

Your wish is my command.

'I know. Now listen carefully.'

CHAPTER SEVEN

'Here, you,' said George. 'Nosh for six, quick as you like.' While Father Kelly quivered his acquiescence, George considered the finer points of hospitality. 'Anything your lot can't eat?' he asked. 'On religious grounds, or whatever?'

Chardonay shook his head. 'I don't think so,' he replied.

'Perjurers always give me wind, mind,' Slitgrind interrupted, 'unless they're pickled in brimstone. Then, with spring vegetables and a pleasant Niersteiner or—'

'I've got cheese,' Father Kelly replied. 'Or chicken roll.'

Slitgrind sniffed. 'Make it the chicken,' he said. 'Cheese makes you have nightmares.'

Father Kelly stared at him, made a very small high-pitched noise without opening his lips, and fled. George slumped into the armchair and waved his new friends to do likewise.

'So,' ventured Chardonay, after an uncomfortable silence. 'You're a saint.'

George nodded. 'Fully accredited, got my own day and everything.'

Among the demons, glances were exchanged. 'Um,' Chardonay went on, his face indicating a long time before his mouth opened that he was about to say something that would be difficult to put diplomatically. 'You see, the fact of the matter is—'

'Hang on, I forgot something.' George picked up a heavy alabaster figure of the Holy Virgin and bashed it on the mantelpiece until Father Kelly reappeared. 'We'll need booze as well,' he said. 'What you got?'

With his eyes shut, the priest started to recite. 'Let me see, now,' he said. 'Spirits, we've got brandy, gin and vodka, Johnny Walker Black Label, Bells, Famous Grouse, The Macallan and Jack Daniels. Beer, there's Guinness, Heineken, Becks, Grolsch, Newcastle Brown or Stella Artois.'

'No Holsten Pils?'

'Sorry.'

'Christ!'

Chardonay coughed softly, like a sheep who's just wandered into someone else's hotel room by mistake. 'Actually,' he said, 'a cup of tea will do just fine.'

Slitgrind and Prodsnap began to protest, then they caught Snorkfrod's eye and subsided. George shrugged.

'Please yourselves,' he said. 'Well, don't just stand there, ponce. Jump to it.'

Father Kelly vanished and George turned back to face the demons. 'Sorry,' he said. 'You were saying?'

'We're ...' Chardonay swallowed. 'Actually, we're devils. From Hell. I, er, thought you ought to know that before you started, well, giving us things to eat and, er, things.'

'I know,' George replied, puzzled. 'Like I told you, I'm a goddamn saint. We know these things.'

'I see.' Chardonay bit his lip, remembering just too late that he was no longer human and suppressing a yelp of pain. 'Only I thought you might . . . Well, we are on different sides, so to speak.'

'Bullshit,' George replied crisply, lighting a Lucky Strike and blowing smoke at the ceiling. 'We're on the same side. We're,' he added, crinkling his face with a rather distasteful grin, 'the good guys.'

'I beg your pardon?'

'The white hats,' George amplified, enjoying himself. 'The US Cavalry. The Mounties. Sure, we do different jobs, but we all work for the same Big Guy. Only difference is, I sent the baddies to Hell and you lot keep 'em there. Jeez, I thought you people would have known that.'

There was a further exchange of glances. Five demons began to say something, but decided at the last moment not to. Eventually, Chardonay inclined his head in a non-committal nod.

'Point taken,' he said. 'It's just that we thought your lot, I mean saints and angels and so on, were – well, took a less pragmatic view of the situation. After all, there was this war—'

'So?' George chuckled. 'Power struggles, palace coups, nights of the long knives, you get office politics in any big organisation. Doesn't mean that at the end of the day you aren't all basically pulling together as a team.'

Chardonay sighed. However hard he tried to play angel's advocate, he couldn't fault the logic. 'All right,' he said. 'I agree. But—'

'More to the point,' George interrupted, leaning forward and leaking smoke in Chardonay's face, 'what in buggery are you lot doing here? Bit off your patch, aren't you?'

'Ah,' said Chardonay. 'Well.'

'We missed the bus,' said Prodsnap.

'Got left behind on purpose, more like,' Slitgrind grumbled. 'Probably thought it was funny, the pillocks. I'll show them funny.'

'Bus?' George was stroking his chin, his mouth hidden behind his fingers. 'What bus?'

'Works outing,' Prodsnap answered. 'To Nashville.' He sighed. 'The Grand Old Opry. Gracelands ...'

If George was disconcerted, he did a good job of covering it up. 'Got you,' he said. 'So basically, you're stranded miles outside your jurisdiction, you're going to have to walk back, and if anybody recognises you for what you are, there'll be one hell of an Incident and when you get back you're all going to find yourselves sideways-promoted to mucking out the Great Shit Lakes, right?'

Five demons nodded. Whoever this jerk was, he surely knew the score. Probably, they found themselves speculating, it's pretty much the same Upstairs.

George's grin widened, as though someone were driving wedges into the corners of his mouth. 'But,' he went on, 'suppose that when you got back, you had with you a prisoner. Someone who should've been down your way yonks ago. Let's say, a member of staff of your department who went AWOL a long time ago and never reported for duty. Be a bit different then, wouldn't it?'

The demons agreed that it would. Very much so.

'Fine,' George said. 'In that case, I think I can help you. Listen up.'

'How?'

The dragon shrugged. 'There,' he said, 'you have me. Yuk!' he added, pulling a face. 'There's something in this.'

Bianca nodded. 'Lead,' she said. 'They put it in to make engines go better.'

Scowling, the dragon wiped his mouth on his sleeve, put the cap back on the jerrycan and spat. ' Disgusting,' he said. 'Like putting chicory in coffee, or menthol cigarettes. Oh well, never mind. Now then, finding George. I've got to admit, I haven't exactly got what you might call a plan of campaign. You see, I was relying on him coming to find me.'

'You think that's likely?'

From the bandstand, a few hundred grassy yards away, came the sound of professional soldiers playing selections from *The Pirates of Penzance*. Children scampered to and fro, trying to cut each others' limbs off with plastic swords. Wasps crooned. In the tree overhead, a squirrel was debating the merits of competing instant-access deposit accounts.

'I thought it was likely. Now I'm not so sure. World's a lot bigger since our day. More people. More buildings. And in the meanwhile, I've got to stay hidden and inconspicuous. Rubbish your modern armaments may be, but I can't spend the rest of eternity swatting jet fighters. Sooner or later, they'll work out a way of nailing me, and that'd be that.'

Bianca ate a crisp. 'So you're thinking of packing it all in?' she asked.

'Maybe.' The dragon shrugged. 'Or at the very least, make myself scarce for a while. That's why I tried to get a job. Didn't work out.'

There was a giggle from Bianca's end of the bench. 'A job?' she said. 'Really?'

'Yes, really. I was a security guard.'

'And it didn't suit?'

The dragon shook his head. 'And before you start suggesting alternatives,' he went on, 'high on the list of jobs I'm not prepared to consider are such things as self-propelled welding plant, mobile Tandoori oven, late-night hamburger chef or industrial paint stripper. So if that's what you were thinking—'

'Perish the thought.'

'Nor,' continued the dragon ominously, 'would I

103

welcome remarks containing the phrases *bright spark*, *set the Thames on fire*, *stepping on the gas* or *hey, mister, you got a light*? Understood?'

'Quite. But what are you going to do?' Bianca looked at him. 'I mean, sprawling on park benches under a news-paper with a can of four-star wrapped in brown paper's not going to get you very far, is it?'

'Actually, I quite like meths.'

'Hmm. No,' Bianca went on, standing up and brushing away crumbs, 'this won't do at all. For one thing, what about my statue?'

The dragon looked at her severely. 'Oh come on,' he said. 'It's traditional. Gentlemen always owe their tailors. Any-way, you should be proud. It's not every chiseller whose stuff's good enough to live in.'

'Be that as it may. I've got a contract and deadlines. It's bad enough that I've got to do Saint George all over again.'

'You're kidding. You seriously expect me to spend the rest of my life sitting still in a public square just to save you a bit of extra work?'

Bianca nodded. 'Least you can do,' she replied firmly. 'After all, if it wasn't for me, presumably you'd still be wandering about the astral void, or whatever it was you used to do.'

The dragon took a long swig of petrol and burped. 'Actually,' he said, 'it wasn't like that at all. I can't remember it all that clearly, because as soon as you cross back into this lot it sort of slips out through the cat-flap of your mind. But I think quite a fair proportion of it was sitting in bars.'

'Figures.'

A frown pinched the dragon's face. 'In fact,' he went on, 'it wasn't bad at all, from what little I can remember. Don't know why I came back to be perfectly honest; job left undone, sense of purpose, something like that. A dripping tap in the bathroom of eternity.'

'Hmm.'

The dragon stood up. On the one hand, he neither liked nor disliked individual humans, in the same way that humans don't have favourites among blades of grass. On the other hand, this was the longest sustained conversation he'd ever had with one and he was beginning to wonder if, given time, you couldn't get used to them. And if you did, would it matter that you'd spent many happy hours in the long-ago reducing them to more or less pure carbon? It hadn't mattered then, but circumstances change.

'Tell you what I'll do,' he said. 'I'll be your statue until you have to deliver and you get paid. In the meantime, I'll stick with this ridiculous outfit—' He indicated his human body, with a gesture pirated from an Archduke's chauffeur condescending to have a go on the dodgems. 'And you help me to find George. It'll be much easier for you, what with you being a human and all. What do you say?'

Bianca considered. 'It sounds fair enough,' she replied. 'Except, I've got to do a new Saint George. That's going to take time.'

The dragon picked up a chunk of sandwich crust and lobbed it to a passing squirrel. 'Depends,' he replied. 'Maybe I can help you there. Got any sheet iron?'

'Well?'

'Looking good,' the dragon replied. 'Much quicker this way, isn't it?'

Bianca nodded. She was exhausted and drenched in sweat. The temperature inside the derelict foundry was murderous.

'Just the sword to do,' she croaked, 'and that's it.'

They made the sword; that is, Bianca sketched it in chalk on the wall and then took cover. The dragon, back in his true form, then snipped a length off the steel sheet, breathed on it until it was cherry-red and moulded it carefully between his paws, like a child with plasticine. When she was happy with the result, he dunked it in the water tank.

'Anything else you want doing while I'm at it?' he asked. 'Designer tableware? Couple of cell doors? New offside front wing for your car?'

'No, thank you. Can we go now, please? It's rather stuffy in here.'

With a shrug, the dragon scooped an armful of finished metalwork out of the water tank, knelt down so that Bianca could perch on his shoulder, and took off, vertically, out through where the foundry roof used to be before a catastrophic fire finished off that huge, preservation-order-bound, highly insured edifice. Two minutes later, they were back in Victoria Square. If anybody noticed their arrival, they didn't say anything.

'Fine,' Bianca said, stepping off and doing her best to conceal her total joy at being back on the ground. 'All right, let's see what it looks like.'

The dragon dumped the metalwork and struck a pose. 'Well?'

'You look ridiculous. Try again.'

'Better?'

'No.'

'Oh. All right, what about this?'

Bianca narrowed her eyes. 'The left front knee a bit further in. And let's have a bit more wing. Yes, that's it, hold it right there. That's—'

'Yes, I like it,' murmured the dragon, human once more and standing beside her. 'Apart from looking like a tinned food advert, it's not too bad.'

Bianca ignored him. It was ... different. And good.

106

It was no longer *Saint George and the Dragon*. It was now *The Dragon Eating Saint George*. To be precise, the dragon, having noshed the juicy bits, was now crunching up the armour in the hope of getting out the last few shreds, like you do with a crab or a lobster (except that you have better table manners). Hence, Bianca realised with a slight shudder, the reference to tins. Never mind.

'That,' said the dragon cheerfully, 'is making me feel distinctly peckish. Fancy a curry?'

Night lay on Birmingham like a lead duvet. A few revellers stumbled through the darkling streets, beer-fuddled, in search of an all-night kebab van. Here and there a doorway or low arch concealed the occasional mugger, rapist or lawyer. Apart from that, the mighty city dozed fitfully.

Birmingham, however, sleeps with the light on. You can read a book by the streetlamps in the city centre, although the chances are that you won't get further than chapter three before someone hits you over the head and steals it. In any event, it's bright enough to make out, say, a small procession consisting of a saint, a priest and five demons, staggering slightly under the weight of three packing cases of plastic explosive, electronic timing devices, blast shields and a drinks trolley.

'Careful,' George hissed, as Chardonay caught his foot in a pothole and tottered. 'You fall over with that lot, there'd be nothing left but a huge hole in the ground and a pile of rubble. Mind you,' he added, looking round, 'in this town I don't suppose anyone'd notice.'

'Sorry,' Chardonay replied. 'Look, is it much further, because my back—'

Before he could finish the sentence, the crate was snatched from his hands by Snorkfrod, who gave him a dazzling smile and then let George have her opinion of thoughtless pigs who make delicate, sensitive fiends from Hell carry heavy loads. Bloody Shopfloor fire, muttered Chardonay to himself, she's carrying two of those enormous cases under one arm. Tough lady. He shuddered.

'Shut your row,' George replied. 'Look, it's only just round the next corner.'

'You said that an hour ago,' Slitgrind grumbled, shifting his load onto his shoulder with his middle hand. 'Couple of hundred yards, you said, and—'

George stopped dead and put a tennis-racket-sized hand round the demon's throat. 'You calling me a liar, son?'

'Yes.'

'Huh?'

Slitgrind nodded, insofar as George's hand permitted. 'Yes,' he repeated. 'Just telling the truth. Like my old mum used to say, tell the truth and shame the ... whatever. Always used to wonder whose ruddy side she was on.'

'Oh look,' said Father Kelly. 'I think we're here now.'

George let Slitgrind go. 'Right, lads,' he said. 'Now, you two start packing the jelly round the – fuck me!'

He was staring at the statue. Quite suddenly, he wasn't feeling very well. Imagine how a turkey would feel, switching on the telly in mid December and catching the Delia Smith programme.

Prodsnap nudged him in the back. 'That's it, is it?'

George nodded. 'Bastard,' he added. 'I take that *personally*.'

'And,' Prodsnap went on, 'there's a fair old chance that at any minute that huge great statue could, um, wake up. Yes?'

'Yeah.'

Prodsnap studied the dragon for a while. 'I don't think he likes you very much,' he said, backing slowly away. 'In fact, I get the feeling there's definitely a bit of the old needle there.'

'Yeah. There's even more now.'

Prodsnap was now standing just behind George's back. 'Looks to me,' he said, 'like this is one of those private quarrels where outsiders butting in only makes things worse. Usually,' he added with a swallow, 'for the outsiders. In fact, I have the feeling we'd all get on a lot better if we just put all this stuff down in a neat pile and went home.'

Fingers like roadside café sausages closed around his arm. 'Not chickening out, are you?' George breathed quietly. 'What've you got to be afraid of, you cretin? You're immortal. Thumpable,' he added, 'but definitely immortal.'

'Yes,' Prodsnap said, 'well. I've always found that the best way to be immortal is not getting yourself killed, like the best way to avoid divorce is not getting married. I think I'd like to go now, please.'

George snarled. 'Stop whimpering, the lot of you,' he said, his voice more gravelly than a long, posh driveway. 'Anybody gives me any more lip, what's left of him's going to get reported to his CO for dereliction of duty. Understood?'

'We'd better do what he says,' Chardonay said wretchedly. 'After all, it's our duty. And our best chance of getting home.'

'That's right,' said Snorkfrod. 'You listen to Mr C, he's never wrong about these things.' Her knee, Chardonay realised with horror, was rubbing up and down the back of his leg. Scales like sandpaper.

'All right,' Prodsnap grumbled, 'you win. Just don't blame me, that's all.'

'Excuse me.'

Saint George and four demons looked round, then down.

'Excuse me,' said the small demon Holdall, 'but don't

109

you think a very loud bang and lots of bits of rock flying through the air's going to be a bit conspicuous? I thought we were meant to be keeping a low profile.'

Three streets away, a police car dopplered and faded. Someone began to sing *Heard It On The Grapevine*, but soon ran out of words. The stray sounds vanished into the night, like a wage cheque into a gambler's overdraft.

'Shut up, you.'

'Yes,' Holdall went on, 'but surely there's a better way than just blowing the thing up. Safer, too.'

'Safer?'

Holdall nodded. He was almost completely covered in long, very fine green hair, and as he nodded he looked like nothing so much as an oscillating maidenhair fern. 'Why not just dissolve it?'

George's brow furrowed. 'Dissolve it? How?'

Holdall coughed. 'Ladies present,' he muttered.

'What's this little creep talking about?'

'Well,' said Holdall self-consciously, 'let me see, how can I put this? Why is it, do you think, that in Hell all the staff lavatories are made of solid unflawed diamond? And even then, they've got to be replaced twice a year.'

George's head was beginning to hurt. 'Shut him up, somebody,' he said. 'Right, you with the back-to-front head, pack the stuff round the base, while I—'

'He's right,' said Prodsnap.

'Much quieter,' Chardonay agreed. "Plus, less damage to property, risk to innocent bystanders from flying masonry. Let's face it,' the demon added, 'letting off bombs in the centre of a big city is pretty damn irresponsible.'

'Look—'

'Just a second,' grunted Slitgrind. 'What if that bloody great thing wakes up while we're peeing all over him? He's not going to be pleased.'

Prodsnap scowled. 'Maybe,' he said. 'On the other hand, he might be even less pleased if he catches us festooning him with ruddy Semtex. I'm with whatsisname, Holdall on this one. Vote, people?'

'Vote!' George rolled his eyes. 'This is an assassination, not a debating society.'

'Show of claws,' Chardonay said quickly. 'All in favour ... That's unanimous. Now then.' He grinned nervously. 'What we need is something to drink.'

'I have a problem.'

Two problems.

'All right,' Chubby said, 'two problems. So I need two answers. Any joy?'

You, my soulmate, are in trouble.

'Listen,' Chubby sighed, 'I'm in trouble so often I have a flat there. What can I do about it?'

The screen went blank, then filled with question marks. That, Chubby recognised, meant it was thinking.

Simple. You need help.

'I don't want to sound ungrateful,' Chubby said, 'but I could have got that far asking the speaking clock. Details, please.'

There is a dragon. Give him a job.

Chubby frowned. 'And which bit of my soul are you going to charge me for that particular gem?' he said. 'I think you've just earned yourself the bit I use for doing my tax returns. Enjoy.'

Patience. In Birmingham, which is a city in the English Midlands, there is a dragon. He's there to find and kill a saint. Dragons are ...

The screen filled with question marks, then asterisks. Chubby leaned back in his chair, his chin cupped between his hands. 'Are what?'

Different.

'Different? How different?'

Square brackets this time, followed by exclamation marks, ampersands and Greek Es. All this was new to Chubby. He was interested.

'How do you do that?' he asked. 'Press E plus EXTRA?'

Different, because they don't – I find this an extremely difficult concept, I must admit. I had forgotten all about dragons. It's been a long time.

'A long time since what?'

Never you mind. I think I can explain. Angels and devils are spirits, emanations from the mind of God. Human beings and all the other animate species who inhabit Earth are spirits too, but made flesh. In their duality, God makes the great experiment, plays the everlasting game.

'With you so far. So what are dragons?'

Very large reptiles.

Chubby sighed. 'I know that,' he said. 'I had a Ladybird book all about them. But what else?'

Nothing else. That's why they're different. And, of course, incredibly valuable.

All his life, Chubby had found a music sweeter than a thousand violins in the word *valuable*. He leaned forward.

'Amplify,' he said.

Very well. Think of the neutrality of Switzerland—

'Nice place, Switzerland. I love the way they run things there.'

The neutrality of Switzerland, the mentality of Ireland and the military might of Russia, America and China put together. Look at it another way; because dragons don't exist any more, no allowance is made for them in the Great Equation. They are neither flesh nor spirit, us or them, good or evil. They just are. The same goes, incidentally, for the Milkweed butterfly of southern America, except that Milkweed butterflies don't wipe

112

out major cities when they sneeze.

'Just a moment. I thought dragons were evil.'

Not intrinsically. Call them floating voters, if you like. Besides, what is evil?

'Well, you are, for a start.'

True. But I'm exceptional. And, don't forget, I'm also stuck in this nasty cramped little plastic box.

Chubby closed his eyes and thought for a moment. 'We're getting side-tracked,' he said. 'How can a dragon be useful to me?'

First, they can fly faster than light. Second, they can kill saints and vaporise demons. Third, they can be hired for money.

'I see. Lots of money?'

Traditionally, they sleep in caves on heaps of gold and precious stones.

'This is some kind of health fad, right? Like those car seat covers made out of knobbly wooden beads?'

Greed. A physical lust for wealth. That's the traditional view, anyway. Times have changed. Maybe dragons have changed too.

Suddenly, Chubby felt tired; more tired, even, than interested or frightened. 'All right,' he said. 'How do I get in touch with this dragon? Can I talk to him? Will he accept Pay-As-You-Burn, or will he want a princess on account?'

If you want me to answer that, it will count as a separate enquiry

'Goodnight, machine.'

Any time.

The green light faded. Chubby stood up, found that his legs had somehow lost their rigidity and sat down again. Talking to that thing always made him feel like he'd been trapped in a spin-drier.

Not so long ago, he'd passed a computer shop. Special

113

deal, its window had shouted to him, part exchange, any model accepted. He'd been tempted. But would It let him? And even if It did, did he really want to? After all, the damage was probably done by now. Highly unlikely that you could regrow a damaged soul, like a slow-worm's tail.

Before he left the office he stopped in front of a mirror and looked in.

'Hey,' he asked. 'Are you evil?'

The picture in the mirror said nothing.

'Lousy copycat,' Chubby grumbled, and switched off the light.

Halfway through his lamb pasanda, the dragon dropped his fork and choked.

'Rice gone down the wrong way?' Bianca asked with her mouth full. 'Try a drink of water.'

The dragon spluttered, convulsed and fell off his chair. Bianca, who usually had the lamb pasanda but this time had opted for a chicken korma, summoned a waiter.

'I think my friend needs a doctor,' she said. 'Or maybe a vet. Call both. And,' she added, 'then get me another peshwari nan.'

With a tremendous effort, the dragon hauled himself back onto his chair. Drawing in breath was as difficult as pulling in a trawl-net full of lead ingots, and his hands were shaking uncontrollably.

'What's happening to me?' he gasped. 'I feel like I'm being burned alive.'

'Oh,' said Bianca, relaxing a little. 'We call that lime pickle. It's quite usual.'

This time, the dragon's spasm sent him rolling on the floor, taking the table and the coat rack with him. Smoke was pouring out of holes in his shoes and there was a quite repulsive smell. Bianca was on her feet, very much aware that there was absolutely nothing she could usefully do.

'The statue,' the dragon hissed, spending each atom of breath as if he was a dentist buying magazines for the waiting room. 'Run. It has to be George.'

Slamming her credit card on the next-door table – damn, she thought, forgot the tip; but the rice was stone cold, so what the hell? – Bianca ran out into the street and headed for Victoria Square. If anybody was fooling with her statue, there'd be hell to pay.

It's difficult, isn't it, to do it to order. Think of the trouble you have filling a small bottle behind a screen at the doctor's. Then imagine a life-size statue of a dragon.

'I find it helps to think of running water,' said Chardonay, his nose wrinkled against the offensive smell. 'Gushing taps. Chortling brooks. Waterfalls.'

'Shut up, Char, you're not helping.'

'Milky tea works best in my experience,' said Holdall. 'Goes straight through me, especially first thing in the morning.' For what it's worth, Holdall had contributed more than the others put together, thereby confirming the view that Prodsnap had formed of him a few moments after they'd first met. There was now a hole in the dragon's back left paw you could have hidden a cottage loaf in.

'This,' George grunted, 'is stupid. I'm going to get the explosives.'

Chardonay looked down at the small crater in the marble directly underneath where he was standing. 'Maybe you're right,' he conceded. 'Otherwise, we're going to be here all night. And it doesn't seem like there's much risk now of the horrid thing waking up.'

Prodsnap nodded. 'And what about the noise?' he said. 'Not that I'm arguing with you,' he added quickly, for it wasn't exactly a warm night and he was sure he'd pulled a muscle. 'But if there is anything we can do to keep the volume down, it'd be worth the effort. Something tells me that passing it off as a car backfiring won't really do.'

'Cover it with the blast shield and hope,' George replied. 'In any case, so long as we don't hang about too long afterwards, a bit of a bang'll be neither here nor there. Trust me, I'm a saint.'

It didn't take the seven of them long to get the explosive in position, and George made light work of wiring up the detonators. Father Kelly, who hadn't really been able to contribute to the previous attempt, helped by passing George screwdrivers and, to the great irritation of all present, praying.

'Okay, lads,' said George, lifting the plunger. 'Firework time. Stand clear or prepare to fly.'

'What the hell do you goons think you're doing with my statue?'

George looked over his shoulder to see a tall, angry-looking female with her hands on her hips and an expression on her face you could have built a thriving yoghurt business around. He scowled.

'Piss off, lady,' he snapped. Then he remembered.

'You!' Bianca said. 'Right.'

Bear in mind that George was a saint and had been a knight. Saints and knights do not fight with women. It's unchivalrous. More to the point, they generally lose. Still holding the detonator box by the handle, he started to back away.

'Help!' he said.

Demons and the denizens of Hell, on the other hand, have no such scruples, particularly if they outnumber the woman five to one. The demons advanced.

'Madam,' said Chardonay, mister play-it-by-the-book, 'I have to inform you that we are duly authorised law officers

116

in the execution of our duty. If you obstruct us, you will be committing an offence punishable by – oh shit!'

He had trodden on Slitgrind's tail; a lanky, unpleasant object, having a lot in common with a banana skin. He wobbled and tried to grab hold of the fiend next to him, but he was standing beside Holdall, four foot one in his stocking talons. His heels slid out from under him, and he fell –

– Heavily, against George, who was off-balance anyway trying to hide behind Snorkfrod. A moment later, there was a confused heap of demons, and a click. George would have landed awkwardly, but the plunger of the detonator box broke his fall.

There was a very loud noise.

CHAPTER EIGHT

'Where am I?'

Chubby smiled. 'You're safe,' he said. 'I rescued you from certain death. Look upon me as your personal knight in shining armour.' He checked himself. 'Let me rephrase that,' he said. 'Your guardian angel.'

'You mean you're out to get me?'

Chubby sighed. There are times when you want to have the niceties of combat theology explained to you, and there are other times when you just want to go to bed. 'I mean,' he said, 'I want to offer you a job.'

'We killed him,' Chardonay said.

'Apparently,' George replied. 'Calls for a celebration, I reckon. Hey, Padre, we got any bubbly?'

'But that was murder,' Chardonay replied uncomfortably. 'Wasn't it?'

'Pesticide. Where the hell's that bloody vicar got to with the drinkies?'

'You're a saint and you *killed* him. Without provocation.

118

He wasn't setting fire to anything or eating maidens, he was just sitting there.'

'Yeah,' George snarled, his feet up on the coffee table; size twelve Doc Martens resting on disused *Catholic Heralds*. 'Eating me in effigy. Charming. Anyway, bugger that. We're on the same side, remember.'

Chardonay shook his head. 'I still don't really buy that,' he said. 'That's like saying good and evil are basically the same thing.'

George, who had never been near a university common room bar in his life but could nevertheless sense the onset of one of those ghastly serious-conversations-about-the-meaning-of-Everything, got up and opened the drinks cabinet with his foot. 'Bollocks,' he said, knocking the top off a Guinness bottle against the mantelpiece. 'That's like saying Accounts is the same as the Packing Department. They're different, yes, but part of the same firm.'

'Oh. I thought we were, you know, at war, sort of thing. Evil versus Good. In competition for the soul of man.'

'Listen, pillock. If Evil won, it'd become Good, like the opposition becomes the government.' He glugged at the bottle until it was empty and dropped it in the fireplace. 'Thought you were meant to be a management trainee, son. Don't they teach you boys anything?'

Father Kelly peered nervously round the door and whispered that he'd got a bottle of champagne, if that's what they wanted. He looked nervous and semi-martyred; Terry Waite in his own home. Which suited him fine, because although he'd always reckoned he'd have made a cracking hostage he spoke no foreign languages and air travel gave him migraines. 'And,' he added, 'there's a devil in the washing machine.'

'That'll be that Holdall,' George grunted. 'I told him to search the place, see where you're hiding the good stuff.'

'Um.' Father Kelly wasn't sure what *good* meant any more, but from the context he guessed alcohol. 'Actually,' he said, 'I haven't got any more. I can send out Mrs McNamara if you—'

George made a scornful noise. 'You don't fool me that easily,' he said. 'In my day, first thing your priest did when he saw a gang of saints on the horizon, he put all the grog in a bucket and lowered it down the well. Always used to confess, though, specially when we told him we'd chuck him down after it. That,' he added stonily, 'is a hint.'

'Actually, I haven't got a well.'

'I can improvise.'

Father Kelly gulped and bolted. George listened after his retreating footsteps and winked.

'He'll be back in ten minutes with a couple of crates, you mark my words.' he said. 'Where was I?'

'Good and Evil.'

'Yeah. Them.' George yawned, stretched and kicked his shoes off. 'All a bit academic, really. I mean, what it all boils down to is, you see a dragon, say, wandering about on your patch, you scrag it, job done. What more d'you need to know, for Chrissakes? I mean, it's not exactly brain-bending stuff. Not like your angels dancing on the head of a pin – to which, in case you ever wondered, the answer is six, unless they're doing the valeta, in which case eight. I don't see what you're making all this fuss about.'

Chardonay shrugged helplessly. 'I don't know,' he said. 'Maybe I'm not right for this line of work after all. When I joined, I thought there'd be something, you know, non-controversial I could do, like keeping the books, doing budget forecasts, working out cost-efficiency ratios and calculating depreciation of fixed assets on a straight-line basis. Killing people . . .'

George treated him to a look of contemptuous pity.

120

'Wouldn't do if we were all the same, son. I mean, if we were then the likes of me couldn't kick shit out of the likes of you, for starters. Here,' he added irritably, 'this isn't proper champagne, it's that naff Italian stuff. When that dozy parson gets back, I've a good mind to pour the rest of it down his trousers. One thing I can't stand, it's blasphemy.'

'What?'

'Grapes,' said Mike, smiling. 'Flowers. Womens' magazines. I know you hate them all like the plague, so I'm building up an environment you'll be desperate to leave. That way, you'll get well faster.'

Bianca tried to rub her eyes, but found she couldn't, because her arm was cocooned in plaster and hanging by a wire from a frame above her head. 'I'm in hospital, right?' she said.

'Huh.' Mike scowled. 'Someone must have told you.'

'How did I get here?'

'You got blown up,' Mike replied through a mouthful of grape-pulp. 'Along, I'm very sorry to have to tell you, with your statue. Note the singular, by the way. There's bits of marble dragon scattered about as far as Henley-in-Arden, but no Saint George. They're saying it's the animal rights lot.'

Suddenly there was something solid and awkward in Bianca's throat; possibly a bit of dragon shrapnel. 'The statue's – gone, then?'

Mike nodded. 'All the king's horses are reported to have packed it in as a lost cause,' he replied. 'All the king's men are still at it, but only because they're paid hourly. If it's any consolation, you're in all the papers and there's a guy from *Celebrity Squares* in the waiting room right now.'

What with the plaster and the wires, Bianca couldn't sink back into the pillows with a hollow groan, so she did the next best thing and swore eloquently. Mike agreed that it was a pity.

'A *pity*? They murdered the – my statue, and you say it's a pity?'

'These things happen. Is there anything else you're particularly allergic to that I can bring in? I seem to remember you can't stand chrysanthemums, but they'd sold out at the kiosk, so I got daffs instead.'

'Mike.'

'Yes?'

'Go away.'

'I thought you'd say that,' Mike said, and left.

The dragon looked down, then back over his shoulder. Cautiously, he spread his wings and folded them again. Finally, he breathed out the tiniest, finest plume of flame he could manage, so as not to incinerate the extremely plush office he was apparently sitting in.

'All present and correct,' Chubby said. 'Actually, in all the panic we knocked off a toe, but we put it back on with Araldite as soon as we got here and it seems to have taken okay. Grateful?'

The dragon nodded. 'Extremely,' he said. 'I had the distinct impression I was dying. I was in this restaurant, and then I was in the square again, inside the statue. I thought—'

'They tried to blow you up,' Chubby replied. 'I got there just as a fat bloke with a moustache tripped over his feet and fell on the plunger. A sixth of a second later and all you'd have been fit for would have been lining the bottom of goldfish bowls.'

The dragon narrowed his eyes. 'So what happened?' he said. 'What did you do?'

Chubby shrugged modestly and folded his hands in his

122

lap. 'A sixth of a second can be a very long time,' he said, 'especially if you boost another twelve hours into it using a state-of-the-art Kawaguchiya Heavy Industries Temporal Jack.' He grinned. 'At $3,000,000 per hour plus hire of plant and equipment, you owe me plenty, but we'll sort that out later. Anyway, during that time we winched your statue up off the deck and into the cargo bay of the big Sikorsky, substituted a big chunk of solid marble, and legged it. That way, when the fireworks started, there were plenty of bits of flying rock to make them think they'd succeeded. To them, of course, the sixth of a second lasted a sixth of a second, thanks to the KHI jack and a quick whip round with the soldering iron. Neat, yes?'

'Rather. I'm impressed. It was very good thinking.'

'Yes,' said Chubby, 'well. Some of us don't go all to pieces at the first sign of trouble. And now, here you are, safe and sound. And, I sincerely hope, desperately anxious to try and repay the colossal debt of gratitude, ditto money, you now owe me. Correct?'

The dragon nodded. 'You said something about a job.'

'Ah yes. Two jobs, really. Both of them right up your alley. Can I get you a drink, by the way? I've got four-star, diesel, aviation fuel or ethanol, and I think there's a drop of turps left over from the Christmas party.'

The dragon asked for a large ethanol, straight, no cherry. 'Two jobs,' he repeated. 'Connected?'

'Sort of,' Chubby replied. 'One, I want you to fry me some devils. Two, I – *Don't touch that!*'

He was too late. The dragon, a born fidget, had let his claws drift across the keyboard of the obsolete old PCW. The screen started to glow.

'Sorry,' the dragon said. 'Oh look, it's gone all green.'

Your wish is my – Well, hello, Fred.

The dragon blinked. 'Nosher?'

Fred, mate, it's great to see you again. Nice outfit.

'Likewise.' The dragon grinned, and only just managed to restrain a sigh of pleasure that would have melted the side off the building. 'It's been a long time, Nosher. What, three thousand years?'

Easily that. How've you been keeping?

'Well,' the dragon replied, 'most of the time I've been dead, though I'm better now. And yourself?'

Chubby, his eyes round as tennis balls, could contain himself no longer. 'Nosher?' he demanded. 'Your name is *Nosher*?'

Zagranosz. And this is my old friend Fredegundar. We go way back.

'I trust,' said Chubby bitterly, 'that none of this great-to-see-you-heard-from-Betsy-lately stuff's going on my account. I mean, I don't mind soul-destroying *work*, but college reunions—'

On the house. He worries, you know.

The dragon nodded. 'Weird sort of a bloke,' he agreed, 'although he did just save me from getting blown up. And now he wants me to go torching demons.'

Ah.

The dragon blinked. 'You know about this?'

Well, yes. Of course, I never guessed the dragon'd turn out to be you.

Confused, and feeling as left out as an empty milk bottle, Chubby finished off the dragon's ethanol and wiped his mouth on his sleeve. 'You guys,' he said. 'It's no good, I've got to know. Where do you two know each other from?'

The dragon turned his head and smiled.

'Sunday school,' he said.

Drop a pebble in the sea off Brighton and the ripples will eventually reach California. Likewise, blow up a statue in

Birmingham and you risk starting a revolution.

A lot depends, of course, on the quality of the statue, because only the very best statues have the potential to be squatted in by unquiet spirits. The word *unquiet*, by the way, has been chosen with great care.

The sound waves travelled fastest, of course; followed by the shock of air suddenly and violently displaced, in turn hotly pursued by microscopic fragments of dust and debris. The sound and the air dissipated themselves soon enough, but the dust floated on, carried on the winds far over the English Channel, south-east across France and down into Italy. Most of it fell by the wayside, to be whisked away by conscientious housewives or ploughed under; but one stray particle happened to drift into the great and glorious Academy Gallery in the city of Florence, where they keep possibly the most famous statue in the world – Michael-angelo's *David*.

Imagine that there's a wee video camera mounted on the back of this dust particle – impossible, of course; even the latest twelfth-generation salt-grain-sized Kawaguchiya Optical Industries P7640 would be far too big and heavy – and you're watching the city come into focus as the particle begins its unhurried descent. Now we're directly over the Piazzale Michelangiolo, where the coaches park for a good gawp and an ice lolly; we can see the khaki majesty of the river Arno, the Ponte Vecchio with its bareback shops, the grim tower of the Bargello, the egg-headed Duomo. Here is the square horseshoe of the Academy. Here is an open window, saving us 4,000 lire entrance fee. And here is the statue.

It stands at the end of a gallery, in an alcove shaped like half an Easter egg. No miniature, this; twelve feet from curly hair to imperious toe, leaning slightly backwards, weight on his right foot, one hand by his side and the other

125

holding what looks uncommonly like a sock over his left shoulder. There are those who'll tell you his head and hands are too big, out of proportion to the rest of him; that his hair looks like an old woolly mop head, fallen on the unsuspecting youth from a great height. Be that as it may, the consensus of civilised opinion holds that you are in the presence of transcendent genius, so be told.

The grain of dust flittered casually down and settled on David's nose.

He sneezed.

'Nngr,' he mumbled, the way you do after a real corker of a sneeze. Absent-mindedly, he moved to wipe his nose with the thing that looks like a sock and found he couldn't. Shit, he thought, my arm's stuck.

Also, he observed, horrified, there's a whole gaggle of people over there staring at me *and I haven't got any clothes on*.

Not a happy state of affairs for a well-brought-up twelve-footer who can't move. My God, he asked himself, how long have I been here like this? I can't remember. In fact, I can't remember *anything*. I must have been in a terrible accident, which left me completely paralysed and amnesiac. Oh *God*!

Except, the train of thought chuntered on, blowing its whistle and slowing down while a cow crossed the line, if I'd just had a terrible accident, surely I'd be in a hospital with nurses and lots of bits of tube sticking out of me, rather than standing in this very public place, stark naked. So just what is going on here?

'Hello,' said the grain of dust.

It spoke quietly, in statue language. Don't, by the way, rush out and try and buy the Linguaphone tape because there isn't one, not even in HMV. And even if there was, a twelve-year-old child would be a hundred and six before he'd got as far as *What are you called? My name is John,*

126

because statue language takes a long time to learn and almost as long to say.

'Hello,' David replied, puzzled. 'Where are you?'

'On the end of your nose. There's ever such a good view from up here.'

David felt his nose begin to itch again. 'Okay. What are you?'

'I'm a bit of dust from Birmingham. It's nicer here than Birmingham. What's your name?'

'I don't know,' David confessed. 'I don't think I know anything before you landed on my nose. It was you, wasn't it?'

'Sorry about that. I just sort of drifted, if you know what I mean.'

How the hell, David wondered, can you itch if you're immobile? 'Look,' he said, 'can you tell me what's going on? For a start, why can't I move?'

'You're a statue.'

'Don't be thick, statues are dead. I mean, not alive. Inanimate.'

'Oh are they, now? Well, I've got news for you, buster. Not only are some statues alive, they also walk about and talk and do all sorts of things. I guess,' the dust mused, 'it's all a matter of casting off crippling social stereotypes and unlocking your full potential.'

'How do you know?'

'Because,' the dust replied smugly, 'I've seen it, that's why. Where I've just come from, there was this enormous big statue of a dragon. Alive as anything, it was. Until they blew it up, of course.'

'What!'

'With dynamite, or something. Well, they tried to, anyway. At the last moment someone swapped me for it, me as I was, that is. I was bigger then.'

If David had had skin, it'd have goosepimpled. 'They blew up a statue because it was alive?' he demanded nervously.

'I suppose so. Can't see why else they'd want to do a thing like that, can you? I mean, statues aren't cheap, you don't just go around blasting them to smithereens because you quite fancy turning the vegetable patch into a rockery.'

'Good God.' David glanced out of the corner of his eye at the knot of people at the end of the gallery. They were quite definitely staring at him. Had they guessed? 'This is terrible. I must get out of here at once.'

'Go on then.'

'I can't. My bits don't work. Oh Christ, there's a guy over there with some sort of box, do you think . . .?'

'The other statue seemed to manage okay. You can't be doing it right.'

David tried again; still nothing. 'All right,' he said, 'if you're so clever, how *do* you do this movement stuff? I assumed it just sort of happened when you wanted it to.'

'Search me,' replied the dust particle. 'I think it's something to do with the central nervous system. You got one of those?'

'How should I know? You think I've got a zip somewhere I can undo and take a peek? Besides, even if I did I wouldn't be able to use it.'

A gang of humans, all women, led by a big loud-voiced specimen with an umbrella, were walking down the gallery towards him. This is it, he told himself, the lynch mob. Well, having my entire life flash before my eyes isn't going to be a problem, because the ruddy thing's only lasted about two minutes. On the other hand, there's not much of it I'd really want to see twice.

'All right,' said the dust particle. 'Try falling over.'

'What?'

'Look down. Feel giddy. You're losing your balance. You're teetering. You're going to fall. *Look out!*'

The statue staggered, clutched at thin air, wobbled backwards and forwards for a split second and fell off its plinth with a crash. If people had been staring before, it was peanuts compared to the way they were staring now.

'Hell's teeth,' groaned the statue. 'I banged my head.'

'Worked, though, didn't it? Come on.'

Without knowing how, or what it was he'd done to bring it about, David found himself scrambling to his feet, jelly-legged as a newborn calf. He remembered something, scooped up the thing that looked like a sock, and held it with both hands over his groin.

'Which way?' he hissed. 'Quick!'

But there was no reply. He must, he realised, have displaced the speck of dust, his only friend and guide in this terrible, unfamiliar, murderous world. He whimpered and began to back away until the wall stopped him. At the first touch of something cold on his bare shoulder-blades he squealed like a scalded pig, jumped in the air and dropped the sock. Then he grabbed it again and looked for an exit.

There wasn't one. The only way out was through, or over, the lynch mob. Just as he was toying with the idea of crouching down behind the plinth and hoping they'd overlook him, a vagrant thought hit him and exploded in his brain like a rocket.

Hey, he said to himself. I'm bigger than them.

Six floors below, in the gallery's engine room, a breathless guard burst in through the door marked VIETATO INTRARI PERICOLO DI MORTI and slithered to a halt in front of a broad mahogany desk.

'Chief! Chief!' he panted. 'It's the *David*, it's come to frigging *life!*'

129

Behind the desk, a large, stocky man with very hairy arms stubbed out a cigarette.

'Oh balls,' he sighed. 'Not another one.'

'Honestly, Chief, straight up, I saw it with my own — What do you mean, another one?'

The Chief stood up and unlocked a steel cabinet behind him. 'You haven't been here long, have you, son?'

'Six months, Chief. You mean to say it's—?'

'On average,' the Chief replied, opening the cabinet door, 'once every five years or so. Lately though, there's been a poxy epidemic. Here, catch hold of this.'

Into the guard's quivering hands the Chief pressed a big tranquilliser gun and a bandolier of darts. For his part, he chose a slide-action Mossberg twelve-gauge, a pocketful of armour-piercing slugs and a geologist's hammer. Finally, a tin hat each, goggles and a torch.

'The *David*, you say?'

'Yes, Chief.'

'Fuck. It's always the thoroughbreds. Anonymous figure of unknown man, late fifteenth-century Venetian school, never get a whisper out of them. Right, let's go.'

The Chief walked so fast that the guard was hard pressed to keep up with him. 'What we gonna do, Chief?' he gasped.

'Well.' The Chief shrugged. 'Sometimes, a couple of sleepy-darts knock 'em out cold, and then all we have to do is drill out their brains and fill up with quick-drying resin. Other times,' he added grimly, jacking a round into the breech of the shotgun, 'we have to get a bit more serious.'

'Serious?'

The Chief nodded. 'How d'you think the *Venus de Milo* got that way, son? Resisting arrest? Had a bad fall in her cell? Act your age.'

When they got to the gallery, it had already been roped

off and the doors were shut. Two-way radios crackled and white-faced guards stepped back to let the Chief through.

'Any movement?' he demanded.

A guard nodded. 'It chased all the visitors out,' he said, 'threw a couple of glass cases at them. We've sealed all the exits so it's not going anywhere, but it looks like it's in a mean mood.'

The Chief grimaced. 'We'll see about that. There's no room for frigging wild men in *my* museum. Okay, going in!'

He applied his boot to the door, which opened inwards. A fraction of a second later, his knife-edge reflexes propelled him backwards, just in time to avoid an airborne bronze bust, which would have reduced him to the consistency of strawberry jam had it connected. He slammed the door quickly.

'Fuck me,' he said, 'it's gone bloody berserk. Of course, doesn't help that it's one of the really big buggers. You get thirteenth-century Sienese ivory miniatures running about the place, all it takes is five minutes and a stiff broom.' He hesitated, then turned to the head porter.

'Get me a bullhorn,' he ordered. 'Evacuate the museum, then get on the red phone to the army, Special Art Service. Tell 'em unless they get their bums in gear, it'll be the Wallace Collection all over again.'

When the bullhorn came, the Chief tested it to make sure it worked; then, using a broom handle, he poked the door open a crack and waited. Nothing.

'You in the gallery!' he shouted. 'Come out with your hands up and nobody's gonna get broken. You hear me?'

Silence.

'You've got till ten to give yourself up, then we come in. One.'

'Hey!'

131

A high-pitched voice, the Chief noted, ear-splittingly sonorous but basically reedy and terrified. But those are often the most dangerous. His mind went back to the early days, the time he'd had to talk down the Elgin Marbles. Maybe, he said to himself, I'm getting too old for all this.

'I hear you,' he replied.

'I've got the *Pietà*, *Saint Matthew* and a big bimbo provisionally attributed to Giovanni Bellini,' yelled the voice. 'You come in here and they all get it. Understood?'

'Loud and clear, son, loud and clear.' He frowned and switched off the loudhailer. 'Was it just the *David*,' he asked, 'or were any of the rest of them at it as well?'

'Not that I saw, Chief,' replied the guard. 'Just the big guy.'

'Hmm.' The Chief rubbed his chin. 'Thought you said he was acting confused, like he didn't know what was going on.'

'Looked like that to me, Chief.'

'Yeah. Only now he sounds like he's pretty well clued up. Like, the big bimbo, I mean the *Venus di San Lorenzo*, the attribution to Bellini was only in last month's *Fine Art Yearbook*. Somebody's in there with him.'

'You on the outside!'

The Chief ducked down. Behind him, thin young men with wavy hair, black silk Giorgio Armani jump-suits, Gucci balaclavas and bazookas were filing noiselessly into the corridor. The Chief waved them into position and switched on the bullhorn.

'Receiving you, over.'

'Here's the deal—'

'Different voice,' muttered the head porter.

'Yeah,' replied the Chief. 'Shuttup.'

'Here's the deal. We want no guns, no police, no army. Have a Sikorski airfreighter in the Piazza in thirty minutes.

132

We want ten million dollars in uncut diamonds, clearance to land in Tripoli and a free pardon. Do as we say and the rocks walk.'

'Actually,' interrupted another voice.

('That's him.'

'Who?'

'*David.*'

'Yeah. Shuttup.')

'Actually,' said the second voice, 'they don't. Do they? And anyway, haven't you got to fall over first?'

This exchange was followed by several seconds of heated whispering, which the Chief couldn't quite catch. By the time they'd brought up the boom mikes, the debate had ended.

'Okay, guys,' muttered the Chief, 'here's the plan. You boys go round the side, abseil in through the skylight. Use smoke grenades and thunderflashes. You six come with me, in through the door. I'll cover the *David*, you take out the other sucker, whoever the fuck he is. Remember,' he added gravely, thinking of the high velocity bronze bust, 'they're presumed armed—'

'Busted.'

'—Busted and dangerous, so if there's any hint of trouble, get your shot in first and let the guys with the dustpans and glue sort it out later. Ready?'

Twelve balaclava'd heads nodded.

'Right then. On my command.'

It was a grand spectacle, if you like that sort of thing. *Crash*! went the glass roof. *Whoosh*! went the smoke bombs. *BANG*! went the stun grenades. *Crunch*! went the big oak doors. *Boom*! went the bazookas, reducing to fine-grain rubble two half-length statues of constipated-looking god-desses, no loss by anybody's standards, and a somewhat less than genuine della Robbia rood screen which had been a

133

thorn in the gallery's side ever since someone had noticed the words *Made In Pakistan From Sustainable Hardwoods* chiselled round the back.

And *Oh shit, where've they gone?* went the Chief, standing gobsmacked by two empty pedestals. The birds had, apparently, flown.

In the confusion, nobody noticed that the commando squad had, apparently, recruited two new members during the course of the attack; one tall, athletic-looking specimen, rather unsteady on his feet, and one short, bandy-legged example given to lurking in shadows. While the gallery was still full of smoke, shouting and the joyous sound of hobnailed boot on irreplaceable artefact, these two new recruits slipped quietly past the guards, down the corridor and, having shed their masks and swiped a couple of overcoats from the cleaners' room, out into the street.

'Yo!' exclaimed the shorter of the two, punching the air. 'We made it!'

'Yes,' David replied. 'Didn't we just.' He stopped and looked at his companion, and a puzzled look swept across his face. 'Excuse me.'

'Yeah?'

'Who *are* you?'

CHAPTER NINE

'What the fuck do you mean,' George screamed into the telephone, 'not arrived?'

'I mean,' replied the arrivals clerk at Hell Central, 'it hasn't arrived yet. If it had arrived, it'd be on the manifest. And it isn't.'

'You sure?'

It wasn't a stupendously good line – think what it had to go through to get there – but George could still hear the long intake of breath, the sound of someone who spends her working life with a phone in her ear, suffering fools.

'Sir,' she said, 'if we'd just taken delivery of a dragon, I think we'd have noticed. They are rather distinctive.'

George used his left hand to push his lower jaw, which had dropped somewhat, back into position. 'Are you trying to tell me,' he demanded, 'that the fucker's gone to the *other* place?'

'I can check that for you if you'd like me to.'

'What? Oh, yeah. Please.'

'Hold the line.'

Chardonay, leaning over George's shoulder, mouthed the question; *What's wrong?*

'Some admin balls-up,' George replied, his hand over the mouthpiece. 'Nothing to worry about – Oh, hello. Well?'

'Not there, sir. I'm sorry.'

George had gone ever such a funny colour. 'You can't have checked properly, you stupid cow!'

'I'm not a cow, sir,' replied the clerk, icily. 'I am, in fact, half-human, half-goat, with the claws of an eagle and—'

'All right. Thank you.' George let the receiver click back onto its cradle. A moment later, Father Kelly (who'd been listening in on the extension, stopwatch in hand, with a forlorn hope of claiming the cost of the call back on expenses; if Rome sold the Michaelangelos and a couple of the Raphaels, it'd sure make a hole in it . . .) did the same, and then sat for thirty seconds or so as still as a gatepost.

He'd just been listening to *Hell* . . .

And they sounded just like *us* . . .

George, meanwhile, was making a frantic search of his mental card-index to find some way of breaking the news. 'Boys,' he said, 'it's like this.'

'Yeah?' Prodsnap replied eagerly. 'When do we go home?'

'Er. Soon.'

'Great. How soon?'

'Just as soon . . .' No tactful way to say this. 'As soon as we've killed that goddamn dragon.'

Let's just pause a while to nail a false, misleading anti-feminist maxim. It's not true that Hell hath no fury like a woman scorned. Scorned women are Mother Theresa on her birthday compared to demons duped. Or thinking they've been duped.

'Told you!' Slitgrind crowed triumphantly. 'Told you no evil'd come of co-operating with the enemy. Crafty little

136

angel got us to do his dirty work for him and then goes and welches on us. Typical!'

'Now hang on a minute,' Chardonay started to say, leaning forward and giving George a stern look; but he never got the chance to finish his sentence, because a split second later, Snorkfrod whizzed past him, making a direct course for George's throat. Fortunately for George, she slipped on an empty Guinness bottle and ended up sitting in the coal scuttle, making the most ferocious noises. For his part, George took advantage of the brief lull to get a good, solid utility Chesterfield between himself and the scions of Hell.

'All right,' he said, as soothingly as he could. 'Just calm down a second while I explain.'

Snorkfrod, having extracted herself from the scuttle, tensed for another spring, but Chardonay's gesture restrained her. She remained crouched and ready to go, growling ominously.

'We'd better hear what he's got to say,' Chardonay advised. 'There may be a perfectly reasonable explanation.'

George nodded like a frightened metronome. 'There is,' he said. 'Look, we blew the statue up, but obviously we didn't kill the dragon. God only knows how, but the little toe-rag somehow managed to clear off at the last minute.'

'So?'

'So,' George replied, 'the original plan holds good. Kill the dragon and there's your passport home. It's just that it's not going to be quite so pathetically simple as we originally thought it would be.'

There were snarls and grumbles as the logic soaked in, creosote-fashion. Chardonay rubbed his chin.

'All right,' he said. 'But how do we find him? That's going to be the problem, isn't it?'

George allowed himself the luxury of a fresh lungful of

air. 'Shouldn't be too hard,' he said airily. 'I mean, the sucker's an enormous green flying lizard. You can't keep something like that secret for very long. And besides,' he continued, 'we have something he's bound to come back for. You know, irresistible bait.'

'Yeah? What?'

George beamed. 'Us.'

So they waited.

True, the last thing they wanted to do was make themselves harder than necessary to find; on the other hand, they had to be practical. The last thing any of them wanted was a nasty theological incident, such as might be caused by the discovery that a saint and five devils were wandering around loose in the twentieth century, where they had no business to be. A certain measure of discretion was called for if there wasn't going to be a massive row, severing of supernatural relations, tit-for-tat expulsions and a spate of films with names like *Demons VI* and *Return of the Saint*.

There was also one further practicality to be borne in mind, one whose importance grew steadily as the days passed.

'I can't stick this sodding place a second longer,' Slitgrind growled, putting the problem neatly into words. 'It's bad enough being cooped up here with that pillock Chardonay and that murderous tart of his without that frigging saint and his wet sock of a priest.'

'I know,' Prodsnap replied quietly. In his case, he could hack Chardonay and Snorkfrod; with an effort and an advance on the next thousand years' self-control ration he could even put up with George and Father Kelly (who had taken to carrying a bell and a candle round with him and reading a book while he did the washing up). What he couldn't stand another day of was Slitgrind.

'I quite like it here,' said Holdall. On the second day, he'd discovered televised snooker and was addicted. It wasn't that they didn't have it back home, it was just that it was reserved for a small group of very, very special customers.

'Look,' Prodsnap said, 'basically it's very simple. We've got to get out of here before we all start climbing the walls. On the other hand, we can't go very far, or the bloody dragon won't know where to look for us.'

'That's your idea of simple, is it?' Slitgrind jeered. 'What d'you do for an intellectual challenge, bend spoons?'

'Basically,' Prodsnap repeated coldly, 'very simple. What we need,' he went on confidently, 'is a miracle.'

For the record, he'd got the technical term nearly but not quite right. What he meant was a Miracle Play, one of those rambling medieval verse dramas that have somehow eluded five hundred years of supposed good taste, and which get put on from time to time by over-enthusiastic amateurs, itinerant Volkswagen-camper-propelled bands of actors who aren't so much the fringe as the frayed hem, and the National Theatre. Stood up on a stage in a Scout hut or church hall somewhere, Saint George, five demons and a priest in a cotton-wool beard calling himself God wouldn't look too badly out of place; or at least no more than is usual under the circumstances.

'The point being,' Prodsnap explained to his fellow sufferers, 'we can bumble round in a van or something and nobody's going to take a blind bit of notice. But if Chummy really is out there looking for us, then a load of posters with SAINT GEORGE AND THE DRAGON all over them ought at least to catch the bugger's attention.'

It went to the vote – five in favour, two (guess which) against. Carried. That, Chardonay explained naïvely, was democracy in action. He was puzzled slightly by the response he got to that, each side claiming that they knew all about democracy, and that it was a dirty trick developed by the Opposition which they had taken over and skilfully converted to peaceful, beneficial uses. In any event, the ultimate consensus ran, we've made a decision now; let's do something. That, however, is as far as the consensus went.

Proximity, however, is as great a negotiator as time is a healer. Forty-eight hours of each others' company in a relatively small house managed to achieve what a thousand diplomats, with translators, fax machines and a warehouseful of heat'n'serve Embassy function canapés would have taken six months to obfuscate. Father Kelly got a book of miracle plays out of the library and spent a busy afternoon in the Diocesan office playing with the photocopier while the girls' backs were turned. George hotwired an old Bedford van.

The show hit the road.

'Who are you?' David repeated.

Being number one on the Italian police's Most Wanted list isn't as much hassle as it sounds if they're looking for a twelve-foot-high nude statue, and you're actually six foot one and wearing jeans, a standard tourist issue aertex shirt and trainers. To be on the safe side, however, David was also wearing sunglasses, and it had cost his companion dearly in both time and eloquence to dissuade him from buying a false beard.

'Me? Oh, that's not important.'

Context, not to mention the manner in which the words were spoken, belied this remark to such an extent that David risked raising his voice – he'd been talking in what he fondly believed was a conspiratorial whisper ever since they'd broken out of the museum, and kindly old ladies kept offering him cough sweets – as he insisted on a straight answer. His companion shrugged.

'My name's Kurt,' he said. 'I used to be a soldier of fortune. What's that word you guys got? *Condottiere*. That was me.'

'Used to be? Was?'

'Yeah.' Kurt nodded. 'I'm dead. Or I was. Jeez, this is confusing. Okay, I used to be alive, then I was dead for a while, only not properly dead. There were reasons at the time.'

David wrinkled his classically perfect brow. 'You didn't die thoroughly enough?' he hazarded. 'Skimped on the actual expiry?'

'Something like that. A steam engine dropped on me. But that,' he added, fending off any request for amplification with an eloquent waft of a finger, 'doesn't really matter. Before I died, or did whatever I did, I used to be a bounty hunter. And a mercenary,' he added with pride, 'and a contract killer, and all that sort of stuff. Man, I was the best.' He frowned. 'Maybe I still am, I dunno. I mean, am I still me, bearing in mind that this ain't actually *my* body? In fact, I don't have a clue whose body this is.' He cranked the frown over into a scowl and finished his coffee. 'The hell with it, anyway. The relevant parts are, I used to be a *condottiere*, then I was dead, then I think I was some kinda statue for a short while, and now I'm –' He glanced down at his arms, his expression implying that they weren't quite a good fit ' – whoever the hell this is.' He glowered accusingly at David. 'Man, this is your fault, you started this crazy subject.'

'Sorry.'

Kurt waved his apology aside. 'No worries,' he said, and considered for a moment. 'I think what happened to me was—'

In actual fact, Kurt's version was so completely wide of

the mark as to be at right angles to it, and will therefore be suppressed in the interests of clarity. The truth is that, during his lifetime, an acute merchandising concern cashed in on his extreme notoriety by marketing the Kurt Lundqvist All Action Doll – $15.99 for the basic doll, uniforms and accessories extra, for complete list write Jotapian Industries, PO Box 666, Kansas City. Some time after his death, an unknown hand had smuggled one of these loathsome plastic objects into the Florence Academy and left it in a dark corner, ignoring the risk that a speck of stray dust from far-distant Birmingham might float in through an open window one sunny day and land on it.

'I see,' David lied. 'How fascinating. So,' he went on, sipping his glass of water. 'What happens now?'

Kurt shrugged. 'I got a job to do,' he replied. 'You can tag along, I guess, or you can split. Up to you.'

'Split?' David looked down to check he was still in one piece. 'You mean these body things·tear easily, or something? That's another thing. How did we stop being statues and start being, um, people?'

'Search me.' Kurt shook his head. 'It just kinda happens, I guess. You can either stay in your statue, or you can bug out and wander around in the skin suit. Who cares how it works so long as it works?'

That, David conceded, wasn't something you could reasonably argue with. As far as he was concerned, he was living on borrowed time, although who he was borrowing it from, and whether they'd eventually want it back, was far from clear.

'This job,' he said tentatively.

'Big job,' replied Kurt with an expansive gesture, which a passing waiter took to be a request for the bill. 'So important, I guess, they had to bring me back from the dead to do it.' He grinned. 'Hey,' he said, 'that kinda suggests I

142

still am the best, doesn't it? That's good to know.'

'The job.'

'What? Oh, yeah. The job is, to bring out the hostages.'

David raised an eyebrow. 'Hostages?'

'Okay, so they aren't actually hostages. More like key figures. And figurines, too. The idea is, there's a lot of important statues gonna get ...' Kurt hesitated, searching for the right word. 'Woken up, I guess. Liberated. Occupied. Possessed. Anyway, my part is, as soon as they wake up I gotta get 'em out of wherever they're at and turn 'em loose. Tough assignment, yes?'

'Very.' David nodded emphatically. 'Have you any idea why?'

'Me? No way. The first thing you learn in this business is not to ask questions. Well, you gotta ask some questions, like *Which guy's the one needs wasting?* and *Where's the goddamn safety catch on this thing?* But apart from that, no questions. Especially no questions beginning with *Why?*'

'Um.' David looked at him through a purported smile. The man's stark staring mad, he told himself. 'Well, thanks for the job offer, I'll give it some really serious thought. In the meantime, any idea what I'm supposed to do next?'

Kurt shrugged. 'Not in my brief, pal. Maybe you got a destiny to manifest, in which case go for it, do well. Or maybe you should just get a job in a sandwich bar somewhere and live semi-happily ever after, like regular people do. None of my goddamn business, either way.'

'Quite.'

'The other part of the job is,' Kurt went on, 'I gotta kill a dragon.'

There are quite a few differences between statues and people. Bianca was learning about them.

A few examples. Statues are beautiful. When a statue gets

broken, you can glue back the bits with epoxy resin, rather than hang about waiting for bones to knit. Likewise, if you attempted to sign your name on the plaster cast of the *Winged Victory*, the next thing you'd see would be the pavement rushing up to meet you.

The key difference, however, and the one which made Bianca realise just how lucky statues are, wasn't something that had immediately sprung to mind. She had learned it by long, bitter experience.

To wit: true, both statues and humans in hospital get people coming to see them. Statues, however, don't get talked to.

'No, Auntie,' Bianca said, for the nineteenth time. 'Thank you,' she added, quickly but not quickly enough. When Aunt Jane went visiting, umbrage futures soared. By now, Bianca reckoned, Aunt Jane must have enough umbrage to start her own international bourse.

'Suit yourself, dear,' Aunt Jane replied, in a voice Bianca would have found useful for putting an edge on blunt chisels. 'Only trying to help. I'll leave them here anyway.' Sigh. 'You don't have to read them if you don't want to.'

Exhibit One; a stack of women's magazines, late 1980s vintage. Recipes. Knitting patterns. Advice to the frustrated and the suicidal. Two of the three were unlikely to be much use to a girl in traction, but she was getting to the stage where she was quite interested in the third.

'It's very thoughtful of you,' Bianca said. Who was the kid whose nose grew when he told lies? Much more of this and she'd make Cyrano look like an Eskimo. 'I really appreciate it. You're very kind.'

Aunt Jane's lips twitched in a tiny sneerlet. Gratitude fell into her without any perceptible effect, like matter into a black hole. 'Well,' she said, 'I suppose I'd better be going, your uncle'll be wanting his tea. I'll *try* to come in

144

tomorrow, though it'll mean missing Weightwatchers. I'll see if I can find you some more things to read.'

As Aunt Jane waddled doorwards, Bianca resisted the urge to wish her a nasty accident. She meant well. More to the point, if she had a nasty accident, she'd probably end up in the next bed.

The sad part about it was, Bianca knew, that in an hour or so, try as she might, she'd pick up one of those damned magazines and start to read. She'd already read all her own books – ever since school she'd been one of those people who zooms through printed pages like motorbikes through traffic – and there was nothing, absolutely nothing, else to do. If the loathsome things weren't there, of course, she couldn't read them. But since they were, she could. And, ineluctably as Death, she would.

This time, she lasted forty-seven minutes and was just congratulating herself on consummate willpower when she realised that her usable hand had slithered treacherously and nipped a glossy from the pile. Ah well, she assured her soul, I tried. She brought the thing up on top of the sheet and opened it.

Thinking it through afterwards, she worked out how it must have happened. Aunt Jane obtained her supplies of obsolescent opium-of-the-female-masses from the waiting room of the doctors' surgery where she worked as recep-tionist (exceptionally effective in reducing waiting times; you had to be practically dying to want to make an appointment). From time to time, waiting rooms and other similarly depressing public places get leafletted by the keen and eager – bring and buys, craft fairs, save our derelict and unwanted civic amenities and, of course, the amateur dramatics fiends. Easy enough to scoop up a few stray fliers along with the pulp.

The playbill in front of her read as follows:

Reaction one: now there's a coincidence.

Reaction two: coincidence my foot . . .

Reaction three: . . . which is in plaster. Damn!

Original cast? Surely not. One key player, she knew, was unavailable due to indisposition caused by having been blasted to smithereens.

Unless . . .

Hey! Calm down, Bianca, think it through. Just suppose for one moment that blowing up the statue hadn't actually killed the dragon. Now, then; whoever wanted him dead – answers on a postcard, please – presumably would want to try again. First, however, catch your dragon. With his marble overcoat reduced to fine dust, the dragon would be walking the streets in human mufti, impossible to recognise. Hence the need for bait and heavy duty, industrial grade hints.

Bianca sneezed; dust from the pile of magazines. Why do I get the feeling, she asked herself, that I'm witnessing the early stages of a major war?

The irony of her situation made her wince, as if someone had just put a goldfish down her neck. All around her, the forces of weirdness were tooling up for a major confrontation. Somehow, she knew, she might be able to prevent it. Except that she was stuck here, as immobilised in her plasterwork as the dragon and the rogue saint had been in the stone bodies she'd made for them. Quite what the significance of that was, she didn't pretend to understand. But she knew significance when she saw it; she knew it even better when it was forced down her throat with a hydraulic ram.

'Great,' she muttered aloud. 'Just when I'm needed, I have to go and get plastered.'

'Sorry?' She looked up, but it was only Mike, squeezing in for the last five minutes of visiting time with his no longer quite so funny comedy props; grapes, lemon barley water, more bloody magazines.

'Just muttering,' she said. 'Mike, find out how much longer I'm going to be stuck inside all this masonry. There's all sorts of things I ought to be doing.'

Mike shrugged. 'Anything I can help with?' he asked.

'N—'

On the one hand, if Mankind was a stockroom, you'd find Mike on the shelf marked *Amiable Idiots*. On the other hand . . .

'Yes,' she said.

CHAPTER TEN

'Clever,' muttered the dragon, with obvious distaste.

The storage unit, or dungeon, in which his statue was kept had obviously cost someone a lot of money. You reached it by walking down a long, dragon-sized tunnel, a bit like a torpedo tube, which led from an iron porthole in the side of a very tall cliff something like a quarter of a mile through solid rock to a big chamber. The chamber door was marble, two feet thick, mounted on chrome molybdenum steel hinges and opening inwards.

'Who knows?' Chubby said, indicating all that workmanship and expense with a dismissive wave. 'For all I know, you could smash and burn your way out through that, eventually. But by the time you'd got halfway, we'd have flooded the chamber with gas and you'd be off to Bedfordshire up the little wooden hill.'

The dragon shrugged. 'Pity,' he said.

'Yes,' Chubby agreed, 'it is. It's like . . .' He closed his eyes to help his concentration. 'Although your mum and dad don't mind you borrowing the car, it's irksome having to ask permission and say where you're going every time you fancy a spin. Please note,' he added, 'the little metal box round its, I mean your, neck.'

'I was going to ask.'

'A bomb,' Chubby sighed. 'I know, I feel awful, but what can I do? We're businessmen, not conservationists. Look, there's no nice way to say this. If you muck us about, anywhere in the inner solar system, inside the dragon cozzy or out of it, then a button gets pressed and goodbye dragons for ever. Clear?'

'As crystal,' the dragon grunted.

'No hard feelings?'

'Get real.'

Chubby's round face showed a smile with turned down ends. 'Fair enough,' he said. 'If I was in your position, I'd sulk like hell. Actually, what I'd probably do is scrag me in the erroneous belief that I've got the button about my person. Just as well for you you're not me, really. From both sides, as it were.'

The dragon did some mental geometry. 'Quite,' he said. 'And on general principles, too. What about some lunch?'

Over the Scottish salmon and aviation fuel, Chubby delicately raised the issue of timescale.

'Not that we want to hurry you or anything,' he added quickly. 'Pleasure having you about the place and all that. It's just that time, if you'll excuse the context, is getting on, I can't earn a bent cent while those goat-hooved buffoons are in this dimension – I know because I've tried, God knows – and your old school chum's starting to get on my wick. Every time I go in my office, his blasted screen winks at me.'

The dragon laughed. 'He used to do that when he was a kid,' he replied. 'Just when you'd got up to answer the teacher's question, he'd wink at you or pull a face. Made you forget what you were going to say. He only does it for wickedness.'

'I'll bet,' Chubby replied morosely. 'Look, I don't like to ask this, but who the fuck is he? I just know him as the genie of the PCW.'

The dragon grinned and helped himself to a tumblerful of liquid propane. 'Guess,' he said.

'Oh come on,' Chubby replied.

'No, three guesses. Odd how guesses come in threes, by the way. Like wishes. And, as far as I can judge from a very limited observation of your culture, petrol-driven public transport vehicles.'

'All right. He's a djinn.'

'Close but no cigar.'

'Evil spirit?'

'Yes, but that's not a proper guess because so am I. And so,' he said, wrinkling his nose and emptying his glass into a flower pot, 'is this. Haven't you got any of that decent stuff we had the other night?'

'You drank it all. Try some of this liquid nitrogen. An insouciant little concoction, but I think you may be frozen stiff by its presumption.'

'Better,' agreed the dragon. 'Two more guesses.'

'Okay. How about a god?'

The dragon shook his head. 'There is no god but God,' he replied. 'Nice phrase, that. Read it on the back of a cornflakes packet.'

'All right. A devil.'

'Wrong third time.' The dragon swilled the dregs of his glass round to make the vapour rise. 'He's a dragon.'

Chubby's eyebrows rose, like the price of gold in an oil crisis. 'Straight up? I thought you were the only one?'

'Far from it.' The dragon frowned. 'Lord only knows what he's done with his body, but my old mate Nosher is,

150

or was, a dragon, same as me. Little, weedy chap he used to be, we called him Nosher the Newt. If he ever reached fifteen feet nose to tail, I'd be surprised.'

Chubby let that pass. 'So what's he doing in my computer?' he asked. 'Or didn't you get around to catching up on life stories?'

'No idea. I did ask him, but he didn't actually seem to answer. He was always good at that, too, specially when you were asking him to pay back a loan or something. Bright lad, Nosher, but you wouldn't trust him as far as you could sneeze him. Something tells me that hasn't changed terribly much.'

'We're drifting,' Chubby pointed out, 'away from the subject under review. Namely, when can you start?'

'Not bothered,' the dragon replied. 'It's more a case of where rather than when, isn't it? It's all very well to talk blithely about carbonising these goons, but I don't actually know where to find them. I'd have thought you, with all those resources and instruments and things . . .'

Chubby looked embarrassed. 'I was afraid you'd say that,' he replied through a mouthful of Stilton. 'And it's bloody curious, I don't mind admitting. Look, every time I've tried taking the crones out to do a spot of rustling, it's been a complete washout because of diabolical interference. Static so thick you could spread it on bread. But can I pinpoint the wretched critters? Can I buggery. It's almost as if the negative vibes are being masked by something else.'

'What, you mean like virtue?'

Chubby shook his head. 'Not virtue, chum. That'd counteract it and there'd be no interference. No, it's like a very strong signal on an adjacent wavelength that sort of blurs out the devils so you can't actually hear them.' He wanted to light a cigar, but thought better of it. 'Which implies it's a very similar sort of signal, though different enough not to jam up my old biddies. It's a bugger, it really is.'

The nitrogen cylinder fizzed again, until the dragon's glass was replenished. 'Not really,' he said. 'That sounds to me like that bastard George. He's a saint, remember, so he's probably got vibes of his own. And he's an evil little sod but officially Good, which'd account for similar but not identical signals.' He scowled at the thought of George, and the glass shattered in his hand. He didn't notice. 'Sounds to me like George and those demons of yours are still mobbed up together, presumably so that they can have another crack at me. I've got no idea, by the way, why a bunch of devils should wish me any harm. As far as I know I've never done anything to offend their outfit. In fact, since I'm officially Evil they should be on my side.'

Chubby wisely said nothing. A certain overtone crept into the dragon's voice when he spoke of George; the sort of nuance you'd observe in a conversation between authors about book reviewers. All to the good, as far as Chubby was concerned.

'Funny bloke, by all accounts,' the dragon went on. 'Oddly enough, I knew a man who was at school with him, that training college for saints they used to have out Glastonbury way.'

Chubby, who'd been doing his background reading, nodded. 'You mean the old Alma Martyr?'

'Right little tearaway he was, by all accounts. Bottom of the class in everything, failed all his Inquisitions, always in detention, doing lines. Never even turned up to heresy-detection classes. Nearly got expelled for refusing to shoot arrows at Saint Sebastian.'

'Fancy,' Chubby said.

'Always up to that sort of thing. You know, untying Catherine from her wheel, stuffing the lions in the Amphitheatre full of Whiskas so they wouldn't eat the Christians.

152

Must've been a right pain in the neck.'

'Absolutely,' Chubby agreed. But he was secretly thinking: Hey, what's so terrible about trying to stop people from getting shot, burnt and eaten? Well, different strokes and all that.

'Be that as it may.' The dragon stood up, untucked his napkin from his collar and finished the last of the nitrogen. 'Soon as you get a fix on these jokers, let me know and they're firelighters. See you at dinner.'

Chubby stayed where he was, waited for the extractor fans to clear the nitrogen fumes and lit his cigar.

So the genie of the PCW was a dragon. Well, that explained absolutely nothing at all. As a clue, it made *The Times* crossword seem like an exploded diagram. But that, surely, was because he was being too thick to see the point. If there was a point.

Probably all a coincidence.

Absolutely. All a coincidence. Like the remarkable coincidence whereby whenever someone falls off the top of the Sears Tower they die shortly afterwards. You can get paranoid, thinking too hard about coincidences.

Mike looked at the address written on the back of his chequebook and then at the building in front of him.

Well, yes. It was the sort of place, by the looks of it, where you had to abandon all hope before entering. But a resort of demons? Surely not. If demons lived here, then Hell was a neat row of 1960s spec-built terraces, with open-plan front gardens and a Metro outside each one.

Good point. Yes. Muttering all he could remember of the Hail Mary (which was, as it happens, Hail Mary), he pushed the front door and went in.

'Eeek!' he said.

The woman at the ticket desk gave him an impatient,

Not-you-as-well look, held up a slip of paper with a seat number on it, and said, 'Two pounds, please.' She was holding the piece of paper in what could only be described as a talon.

'Er, you in the show?' he asked.

'That's right,' she replied. 'Costume startle you, did it?'

Mike nodded. 'It's very, um, realistic.'

'How would you know?'

'All right, I don't. Can I go in now, please?'

He found his seat (one of those bendy bucket-shaped plastic chairs which you're convinced is going to break when you sit on it, though it never does) and took a long look at the stage. There was no curtain. The usual amateur dramatics set, all black-painted hardboard, silver paper and things borrowed from people's homes. Mundane. Prosaic. Everyday. Like, in fact, the woman at the door had been, except that she was obviously a . . .

Another look round, this time at the audience. There were fifteen or so people scattered about the hall, eating boiled sweets and reading the photocopied programme. Either they hadn't noticed that they'd just been sold their tickets by a . . . or else they didn't care. Possible, Mike told himself; very tolerant people, Midlanders. But – *my God, those fangs!* – improbable.

He looked at the programme. Cast list, as follows:

GEORGE (*a saint*) .... Himself
CHARDONAY (*a demon*) .... Himself
SLITGRIND (*a demon*) .... Himself
PRODSNAP (*a demon*) .... Himself
HOLDALL (*a demon*) .... Himself
SNORKFROD (*a demon*) .... Herself
THE DRAGON .... Members of the cast

Ah well, Mike said to himself, leaning back as far as he

dared and opening his bag of Maltesers, I expect I've been to worse. Most of them, he remembered, at the Barbican.

The lights went down. The chattering almost stopped.

Play time.

'Found them!' Chubby yelled.

The dragon looked up from the encyclopedia he'd been reading and grinned. 'Splendid. Where?'

'Wherever the hell this is.' Chubby handed him a creased playbill and a map. 'Ready to go?'

The dragon grinned.

Anybody ever wondered, Mike asked himself a quarter of the way through the first half, why so much of medieval literature is anonymous? Answer, easy. Who'd want to own up to having written this?

At least there hadn't been Morris dancing. Not yet. That, he admitted to himself, was like saying that nuclear bombs are safe because the world's still in one piece. That aside, it had set his mind at rest on one score. No question but that these people were in the everlasting torment business; the cream, in fact, of their profession. Solemnly and with the utmost sincerity, Mike resolved that from now on he was going to be very, very good, for ever and ever.

So deep was he in silent repentance that he didn't notice that someone was now sitting in the seat next to him, until that person leaned across and whispered a request to look at his programme.

'Sure,' Mike whispered back. He passed over the sheet. As he did so, he became aware of an oppressive heat and a smell like petrol. He glanced out of the corner of his eye.

Perfectly ordinary bloke. All his imagination. Except—

The bloke had yellow eyes. Round, golden eyeballs, with a narrow black slit for a pupil. And no eyelids.

Midlanders (see above) are tolerant folk, and Mike was from Brierley Hill where they don't care who you are or what you do so long as you leave the buildings still standing afterwards. Devils; no problem, after all, we're all God's creatures. But, as soon as he'd recovered the use of his momentarily paralysed limbs, he was out of his seat, through the door and running like a hare. Sensible chap.

Because, while he was still running, there was a horrible dull *bang*! followed by a whooshing noise, broken glass music and the very distinctive sound of fire. Instinct sent Mike sprawling on the ground, his head shielded by his elbows, as the first few bits of masonry and timber started to hit the ground all around him. And oh Christ, the smell ...

Late change to the cast as advertised. Whoever was playing the dragon tonight had just brought the house down.

The dragon opened his eyes.

There was, he observed, a large steel girder lying across his back. He shook himself like a wet dog, sending it spinning off into the rubble.

He appeared to have made rather a mess.

The drip-drip-dripping noise was still-molten steel; wire reinforcements in the concrete. The groaning sound was material contracting as it cooked, rather than an indication that there was still anything else even temporarily alive in the ruined building. No chance of that, whatsoever.

In the distance, the mechanical wailing noise the dragon had come to associate with impending public attention. He spread his wings, flapped them and rose in a cloud of dust and sparks. Job done, time to go home. Five wingbeats lifted him into the upper air; five more and he was cruising through the sound barrier, heading west.

As he flew, he couldn't help reflecting that, in exacting his entirely justifiable revenge on George, he'd also killed five demons – well, so what? The worst that can happen to anything mortal is that it dies and goes to Hell; he'd saved them a bus fare – and fifteen or so innocent human beings who happened to be there. Hmm.

No, the hell with that, it was a matter of omelettes and eggs. They belonged to a different species altogether and were none of his concern. To feed those fifteen, and all the others like them in this city alone, a million chickens a day ride to their deaths on a conveyer belt. And, emotive reactions aside, there was nothing wrong with that either because of a hard but fair rule of Nature called Survival of the Fittest. It was a rule he'd never really had a problem with, even when he'd been hiding in the rocks watching all the rest of his kind being exterminated by these people's great-to-the-power-of-twenty-grandfathers. Plenty more where those came from; and who's the endangered species around here, anyway?

As he flew, feeling the almost infinite power of his body, acknowledging the potential of his lazy but undoubtedly superior intellect, he sensed that maybe the jury was still out on that one.

They brought the woman down from intensive care at about half past three that morning and put her in the bed next to Bianca. Superficial burns, light concussion, shock. She'd live. She'd been lucky, the ward sister explained. She'd only been passing outside the Sadley Grange Civic Centre when it blew up. Those poor souls inside never stood a chance.

What caused it? Nobody knew, as yet. They'd said on the news that the whole building suddenly burst into flames; not like an ordinary fire, which starts somewhere and gets

157

steadily hotter, more like a firebomb attack, except who'd want to firebomb amateur dramatics?

'Nurse,' Bianca said, 'I think I'm going to be—'

And she was right.

'They're saying it was the Libyans,' Chubby reported, topping up the dragon's cup with lighter fuel, 'God only knows why. I s'pose they've got to blame somebody, or what are foreigners for?'

'Don't go on about it,' the dragon said. The bread was stale. He breathed gently on it and had toast, instead.

'Don't see why not,' Chubby replied. 'You did good. Neat job, in and out, nobody saw you; or if they did, they've got too much common sense to stand in front of a microphone and say they've been seeing dragons. You could make a good living if you ... Sorry, I'll shut up. Pass the marmalade, there's a good fellow.'

'Were there any survivors?'

Chubby laughed. 'Sure,' he said. 'Just not within a two-hundred-yard radius. Actually, there's an interesting side-light to the story, because that whole area's up for redevelopment, except that there was that tatty old hall bang in the middle of it and absolutely no way of getting rid of it. Now, of course, bulldozers may safely graze. In fact, we could get seriously rich if ever you felt—'

'Chubby,' said the dragon quietly, 'I'd change the subject if I were you.'

'Huh? Suit yourself.' Chubby spread marmalade, drank coffee. 'Sorry to harp on,' he said, 'but what exactly is bothering you? I thought you hated humans.'

'Me?' the dragon looked at him. 'Whatever gave you that idea? As of nine twenty-seven pm yesterday, there's nobody and nothing left alive in this world that I hate, or even strongly dislike, although,' he added, with a slight twitch of his nostrils, 'this may change if a certain topic of conversation doesn't get shelved pretty damn quick.'

'Sorry,' Chubby replied meekly. 'It's just that, since it was us who killed all your people, stole your birthright—'

'Not you,' the dragon said. Inside his skull he could hear the faint chip-chip of a headache hatching from the egg. 'When the last of the people who wiped out the dragons died, there were still wolves wandering around the forests of Islington. And besides,' he added irritably, 'the thing with George and me had nothing to do with the dragon clearances. It was purely personal.'

'Because of the Big Fight, huh? Because he won, simple as that?'

The dragon shook his head. 'He was *supposed* to win. It was killing me that I didn't hold with. And now that's all over and done with, so let's drop it. All right?'

'Right.' Chubby folded his newspaper, drained his coffee cup and stood up. 'So, as soon as you've done that little job—'

'Who says I'm going to do the little job?' the dragon interrupted dangerously. 'Fuck you and your nasty bloody schemes. If you want to beat up on your own species, be my guest, it's none of my business. But I'm off.'

Chubby shook his head. He didn't say anything, but he patted the underside of his chin with the tips of his fingers. The bomb.

'You bastard,' the dragon said softly. 'I ought to torch you right now.'

'Inadvisable,' Chubby replied. 'With all that inflammable liquor inside you, they'd be picking up bits of you in Tokyo. And like I said, what's it to you? Different species, right?'

The dragon said nothing. Not that he needed words, exactly. He'd have been sent home from a Gorgons'

159

children's party for pulling faces.

'Welcome to the Baddies,' Chubby said, and left.

The fire brigade had gone home, the police were brewing up in their big blue-and-white portakabin and even the journalists had given up and gone to the pub. Under a pile of rubble, something stirred.

'Have they gone?'

'I think so.'

The pile of rubble avalanched, half-bricks and chunks of concrete scudding downslope, stirring up dust. A head and shoulders poked out. Eyes blinked in the starlight.

'About bloody time, too. I've got a crick in my neck like a letter S.'

'Keep your voice down, Slitgrind. And for pity's sake, stop complaining.'

Gradually, and with much seismic activity, the demons emerged, all five of them. They were dusty and, after twelve hours under the rubble, stiff as all Shopfloor. Apart from that, no ill effects whatsoever.

A sixth pile shifted and turned into George. He wasn't in quite the same immaculate condition – he had a black eye, and his hair was all singed off – but otherwise he was intact. He dusted himself off, just like Oliver Hardy used to do in the films, and climbed out of the mess.

'Now you see why we had to wear costumes,' he said.

Chardonay nodded. 'Good stuff,' he acknowledged. 'What did you call it?'

'Asbestos,' George replied. 'And the lining's Kevlar, which is like old-fashioned steel armour, only lighter and a hell of a lot stronger. I used the same stuff for the scenery, too. Just as well,' he admitted. 'If we hadn't all ducked behind the flats the moment he materialised, I don't reckon the cozzies'd have been enough. Anyway, time we weren't here. Come on, you lot. The Padre'll be worried sick about us.'

Nobody had disturbed the rickety old Bedford van and soon they were on their way. Chardonay, sitting in the front with George, raised the obvious topic.

'Well,' George replied, 'he took the bait all right, you've got to admit that much. Maybe we should have spent a little more time thinking through how we were actually going to scrag the bugger, but we'll know better next time.'

'*Next time*!'

George nodded. 'Of course next time,' he replied, faintly puzzled by the demon's tone. 'Okay, so the first two attempts, we bombed. I mean, we didn't do so good. Third time lucky, eh? Think of Robert Bruce,' he added, 'and the spider.'

'No, thanks,' Chardonay replied, shuddering. 'I'm scared of spiders. And now,' he added, with as much unpleasant overtone as he could muster, 'I'm also scared of dragons.'

'Funny you should say that,' George said, blithely overtaking on a blind corner, 'because spiders have always terrified the shit out of me. But eventually I found a way to cope.'

'Really?'

George nodded. 'I squash 'em,' he said. 'Helps put things in perspective when your mortal foe's looking like a raisin with hairs sticking in it. I think the same may hold true of dragons. Only one way to find out.'

Chardonay was about to say something, but wisely saved his breath. The way George was driving, he'd need it soon for horrified screaming.

'Mind you,' George went on – he was definitely getting the hang of driving, because this time he remembered to brake with a full thousandth of a second to spare. 'It's going to be harder decoying the creep a second time because he's going to assume we're dead. And we can't exactly publicise the fact we aren't, because of the low profile thing. Tricky one, that.'

'Aaaaagh!'

'What? *Watch where you're going, you senile old fool*! Sorry, you were saying?'

Chardonay opened his eyes. 'I think,' he murmured, 'in this country they drive on the left.'

'Ah. That'd explain a lot. Well spotted. To be honest with you, I think from now on it's going to be up to us to look for him, rather than the other way around. Don't you? Of course, we could try this gig again, only next time we'd be a bit better prepared, maybe plant a bomb of our own in the auditorium so as to be sure of getting him first. What d'you reckon?'

A look of horrified disgust pitched camp on Chardonay's face. 'You couldn't do that,' he gasped. 'The audience. Innocent people.'

George shrugged. 'Not people, Char,' he said mildly. 'Potential customers, your lot's and mine. One stone, very many birds, huh?'

It's hard to stand on your dignity when you're horrified, petrified and covered from head to foot with brick dust. In Chardonay's case, he'd never had all that much dignity to start with; if he'd ever wanted to stand on it, he'd have had to master the knack of balancing on one foot. What little he had, however, he now used to good effect.

'George,' he said, 'when you die, be sure to go to Heaven. We can do without your sort where I come from.'

In order to sell newspapers, you have to get your priorities right, and an unexplained explosion with fatalities is clearly rather more important than a spate of thefts from art galleries. The lead stories in the next day's papers were, therefore, in order of headline size and column inches:

ROYAL VET'S SEX ROMP WITH CHAUFFEUR

SOUTHENDERS STAR IN LOVE TRIANGLE WITH PLUMBER

BUZZA DECKS REF IN OFFSIDE RUMPUS

Bomb Kills Sixteen

Statues Stolen From Italian Museum

The statues – eight Berninis, three Donatellos, three Cellinis, a Canova and the Giambologna *Mercury* – all went missing from various locations in the space of about eight hours. No sign of forced entry, no arrests, no clues. No visible connection, either.

'Okay, guys. Guys!' Kurt banged on the floor with the butt of his rifle, but nobody took any notice. They were all talking at once, at the tops of their voices, in Italian. With a weary gesture of resignation, Kurt sat down on a packing-chest and waited.

'Finished?' he demanded, ten minutes later. 'Good. Now, listen up.'

Sixteen pairs of malevolent eyes fixed on him. I don't need this, he reflected. I've got a nice cosy grave I could be in right now.

'Now then,' he said. 'I guess you're all wondering why—'

Marvellous language, Italian, for talking very fast in. They should insist all peace conferences should be in Italian; that way, nobody'd ever know what was going on long enough to start the war. 'Shuttup!' he cried. Not a blind bit of notice.

''Scuse me.'

He turned. 'Well?'

'Looks to me,' David said, 'like they're upset about something.'

Kurt scowled. 'What the fuck've they got to be upset

163

about, for Chrissakes? I've just sprung the suckers, they should be goddamn *grateful*.'

David made a small head gesture indicative of doubt. 'Look at it this way,' he said. 'They're all male figures, all of Italian origin. Maybe standing about all day being admired is what they like doing best.'

The proposition had merit, Kurt admitted, but that wasn't his affair. He was only, as the expression goes, obeying orders. '*HEY*!' he said.

'Thank you,' he went on. 'All I can tell you is, my instructions said to get you out of those museums and galleries and bring you here. Which I've done. From now on, guys, you're on your . . .'

He stopped, puzzled. Instead of jabbering at him, shaking fists and waving arms, they were standing about like a lot of shop-window dummies.

Maybe that was it; knock off priceless works of art and punt them out at twelve dollars a head to the leading New York department stores. Or maybe not.

'Guys?'

Long silence. Then a statue put its hand up.

'Excuse me,' it said. And, Kurt noticed, in English.

'Shoot,' he said.

'Excuse me,' said the statue – shit, it was a *female* voice now – 'but can you tell us what's going on, please?'

Kurt swallowed. Spooky no longer worried him. He felt comfortable around spooky. Weird was as familiar to him as a pair of well-worn slippers. But this was *strange*.

'Hey,' he said. 'I just did.'

'Only,' the voice bleated on. 'I told my husband the play'd be over by ten and I'd be home in time to make him a late tea. And that was hours ago, and he gets all upset if his meals aren't when he expects them.'

Gradually, while Kurt was trying to get his larynx

working again, the other fifteen joined in, a symphony of bleats and whines forming a baroque fugue around the same main theme.

'I . . .' Kurt had raised his hand for silence, and obtained it instantly. Thirty-two eyes were gazing at him. He could feel the blood rushing to his cheeks. It was *horrible*.

'I . . .'

Thirty-two ears, hanging on his every word. Jesus, he told himself, now the suckers are all goddamn British.

He turned, grabbed David by the arm and dragged him forward. 'My assistant will explain,' he said, and ran for it.

CHAPTER ELEVEN

'The job,' Chubby explained, 'is basically very simple.'

It was, the dragon wanted to point out, perishing cold. The air was full of high-velocity snow which he could feel even through his scales. There was nothing to be seen in any direction except flat white. Chubby and the dragon stood alone in an albino wilderness, like the last two balls on a white snooker table.

'That's not to say,' Chubby went on, 'that it's easy. Easy and simple don't necessarily mean the same thing. What I want you to do is simple, as opposed to complicated, but very, very difficult. With me so far?'

The dragon couldn't speak because his teeth were chattering like a school party in a theatre, so he nodded instead.

'All you have to do,' Chubby continued, 'is fly, any direction you like, as fast as you possibly can. Direction doesn't matter 'cos we're at the North Pole. Speed, however, is of the essence.'

The dragon frowned. 'Don't you mean time?' he queried. Chubby grinned.

'That,' he said, 'is either a naïve remark or a very poor joke. Now then, here's your parcel, don't drop it. When I want you to stop, this little buzzer thing on your collar will bleep. Wonder of micro-electronics, that, cost me a fortune.' He paused, recited a check-list under his breath, and took five steps back. 'When you're ready,' he said.

The dragon shrugged. 'Now?'

'Now.'

Theory: travel faster than light around the Earth and you can move forwards in Time.

A likely story. Like all great hypotheses, the theory of relativity relies on the basic assumption that nobody will ever be able to do the experiment which will prove it wrong; and anything that can't be disproved must be true. Garnish with fresh mathematics, heat and serve.

But supposing it's true, and feasible. Think, not of the fame, the glory and the Nobel prize, but of the commercial possibilities.

Correct; there are none. That's why it's a safe hypothesis. Nobody will ever try the experiment because there's nothing in it for the institutional investors. That's why there's a whole lot of scientific theories about the nature of the space/time continuum, and rather fewer about the medium-term acceleration of racehorses. It'd be different, of course, if you could then send a messenger from the future back to the present, notebook crammed with stock exchange results, football scores, winning lottery numbers and the like; but that's impossible, according to the theory. Guess why.

The truth is that it's possible – simple, even (see above) to travel back through Time, in roughly the same way as you can travel forwards. It involves flying round the world, yes; but at a rather different tempo.

167

To go forwards, you have to fly faster than light. To go backwards, you have to fly slower than history. The maths goes like this:

$$T - d = h$$
$$P = n + h$$

– where T is Time, d is disinformation, h is history, P stands for the Past, and n is the now, or present.

For anybody who missed the first sixteen lessons, here's a very simplistic summary.

The past is made up of the present plus an awareness of there having been a time before the present; the awareness is called history. The speed at which history travels is equal to the speed of Time, less the time it takes to record it. The recording of history is slowed down by disinformation; official secrets, the reluctance of participants to tell the story because of the repercussions on themselves, and so on. The quantum of d varies from nation to nation, culture to culture; in Britain, there's a thirty-year rule which means that nobody can look at important official documents for thirty years, whereas in the USA the freedom-of-information statutes say that you can see them straight away, except for the really important ones, which nobody ever gets to see at all. In some regimes, history gets rewritten every time there's a change of government personnel. The constant d is therefore not a constant at all; accordingly history moves at a different speed depending on where you are, and in some places it's at a complete standstill or moving backwards.

Fly round the world, therefore, and you're constantly crossing into different history zones. As you soar over the continents, the retrospective march of Time, from present to past, is taking place at all sorts of different speeds. Instead of being a tidal wave, crashing relentlessly down onto the reef of the present, the advance of history is a confused mess of recollection particles, swarming about in no sort of order. And there are always particles that move so slowly in comparison with the others that they're getting left further and further behind; relatively speaking, going the wrong way.

Reverse history and you reverse Time.

In practical terms, then; if as you fly round the world you follow a carefully plotted course through the anomalies of the different history zones, you can get so far behind that you'll be travelling backwards in time. As a further refinement, if you have moles and undercover agents at work in universities, public records offices and national computer archives all over the world, busily hiding, destroying, obscuring, obfuscating, rewriting, stuffing files down the backs of radiators and generally sabotaging the manufacture of history, you can *control* the production of anomalies and artificially create a navigable course from a given point in the future back to a given point in the past. Or, as the classic equation so elegantly puts it:

$$I = fd^2$$

– where I stands for the Time-traveller's itinerary, d is disinformation as above, and f stands for a statistically acceptable incidence of clerical and administrative fuck-ups.

While we're on the subject of Time, it's universally acknowledged to be a great healer. By rights, therefore, it should be available free of charge through the National Health Service. But it isn't, of course. If you want chronotherapy, you have to go private.

'It'll cost you, mind,' the doctor muttered in a low voice. 'Very, very expensive. Not to mention illegal. If they catch me doing this, I'll be lucky if I can get a job casting out evil spirits in New Guinea.'

'I don't care,' Bianca replied. 'I've got to get well and get out of here as soon as possible. It's *urgent*. It's a matter of . . .' She was going to say life and death, but that could mean anything; like, for example that she'd managed to get seats for the Shrunken Heads concert at the NEC and didn't want to waste them. 'The future of the human race,' she said, 'is hanging in the balance here. It's *essential*—'

'Hey,' the doctor interrupted, 'you mean you got tickets for the Heads gig? You wouldn't consider selling them, would you?'

Having your right arm in plaster means you can only hit doctors with your left; unless you're a natural southpaw, this can be a nuisance. 'Shut *up*,' Bianca snapped. 'Look. Sixteen people, one of them quite possibly a close friend, have died. Most likely, that's only the beginning. The only person who can stop it is me. So name your frigging price and let's get on with it.'

'My price? You mean for the tickets? Well—'

'For the operation,' Bianca hissed.

Chronotherapy, also known as Injury Time; a new breakthrough in medical science, brought to you by the pharmaceuticals wing of Chubby Stevenson (Time) Inc.

What nearly all medicine boils down to is: leave the human body alone and comfortable, and in Time it'll sort itself out. But if you haven't got Time, this is a non-starter. So; either you die, or bits fall off you, or you buy more Time.

It's an entirely private and personal envelope of additional Time shoe-horned into an ordinary day – one second in real time, but up to three months as far as the user is concerned, during which bones knit, scars heal, muscles rebuild and so on. Since it's a very small-scale temporal field, it only takes a tiny drop of the raw stuff – less than one microlitre, street value currently £100,000. Double that for the shoe-horn, installation costs, credulity suspension jigs and tooling, the doctor's and Chubby's profit. Fortunately, the sensational manner in which she'd received her injuries (Sultry Brunette In Bomb Horror) had sent her market values rocketing, and she'd arranged a few sales of old bits of junk she'd had cluttering her studio which more than covered the cost.

Later, Bianca was to remember it as the most boring second of her life.

Mike arrived, dishevelled and out of breath, to find he was already there.

This worried him. True, his aggravating vagueness and extremely flexible attitude to punctuality had frequently led people to suggest that one of these days he'd be late for his own funeral. On the other hand, he'd always assumed that they'd have the common courtesy to wait for him. Apparently not so.

'We therefore commit his body to the earth,' said the priest, 'dust to dust, ashes to . . .'

'Hey!' he shouted. Nobody heard him. He watched with incredulous fury as they started to fill in the grave. It was like watching a waiter take away your meal before you'd had a chance to unfold your table napkin, let alone start eating. One thing did, however, suggest at least a degree of normality. Nobody had told him anything and he hadn't got a clue what was going on. That made him feel more comfortable. He could cope now.

'Good turnout,' said a voice to his immediate right. 'You must feel proud.'

The voice was coming from a large, florid Victorian weeping angel. She'd seen better days; acid rain, vandalism and the trainee assistant gardener (who sharpened his billhook on her marble ankle) had all taken their toll, leaving her looking like something found in a sink-trap. Mike recoiled slightly.

'Be like that,' the angel said, apparently not offended. 'Let's face it, you're no oil painting yourself; although, that said, in a bad light you'd pass for a second-rate Jackson Pollock.'

'I beg your pardon?'

The statue sighed. 'Sorry,' it said, 'I forgot, you're new. Find a puddle or something, take a look at yourself. Or rather,' she added quickly, 'don't. Probably best if you remember yourself the way you used to be.'

Mike sat down on a tombstone. As he did so, he studied the process. As far as he could tell, he was solid and real; he could feel the stone against his trousered leg, and when he tried to pass his arm through an ornate granite cross, it wouldn't go. He tried again, only harder; when he banged his wrist on the stone it hurt, and a little smear of blood showed in the graze. In one sense, reassuring; in another, disconcerting.

'Neat trick, isn't it?' said the angel, who had been watching. 'Feels just like the real thing, but isn't. All a matter of timing, you see.'

'Timing?'

'That's right.' The statue yawned. 'God,' she said, 'why's it always me who's got to do this? I don't get paid for explaining to new recruits, I just do it because I'm here. And,' she added, 'because I feel sorry for you, bless your poor disoriented souls. And because I've got absolutely nothing else to do. Still, I really do think it's time they did something official, it's a scandal if you ask me. I mean, there's all those preparing-for-retirement courses you can go on, so the shock of not having to work won't send you to an early grave; but the biggest and most radical change of your entire existence, you're supposed to be able to fend for yourself, puzzle it out from first principles. Cheapskate, I call it.'

Mike took a deep breath – presumably it was a deep breath and not just some virtual reality programmer's placebo. 'If you'd explain,' he said, 'I personally would be very grateful.'

'That's all right,' said the angel, 'you're welcome. Look, forget what I said about timing for the moment, it always confuses people. Think of a radio, right?'

Mike thought of a radio.

'Now then,' the statue continued, 'there's hundreds, maybe thousands of different radio signals blamming about simultaneously, but the radio only picks them up one at a time. That's because it's tuned in to one specific frequency.' The angel paused. 'Nobody told me this, by the way,' she added. 'I had to work it out for myself. It's true, though, 'cos I had it confirmed by Official Channels when I asked them. They're very good about answering enquiries, so long as you don't forget the stamped addressed envelope.'

'Please go on,' Mike said. 'Like radio waves, you said.'

'Sure.' The angel thought for a moment, remembering where she'd got to. 'Well, just as there's lots of different radio frequencies, there's lots of different chronological continuums. Continua. Timescales. That's a better word, although I shouldn't use it because it's got a separate technical meaning. Strictly speaking, timescale is the residue left after hard time's been boiled down in a copper kettle.'

'Ah.'

'Forget I said that. Different timescales. Now, in the timescale which human mortal life is tuned in to, a second lasts—' She stopped. 'Sorry, got in a bit of a tangle there.

Should have done the weights-and-measures spiel before I started. Let's put all that on one side for the time being and stick to Terrestrial Orthodox. As far as you're concerned, a second lasts one second, right?'

'Right.'

'Wrong. A second only lasts a second in your own specific timescale, HMS – that's Human Mortal Standard. That's what you were tuned in to when you were alive. Now you're dead, you're tuned in to HDS, Human Deceased Standard. One second HMS is equivalent to 0.8342 seconds HDS; or 0.0062 seconds SIS, Supernatural Immortal Standard; or 0.000147, SITS, Soul In Torment Standard; or—'

'All right,' Mike said, 'got that. How does that mean I don't exist but I can't walk through tombstones?'

Being a statue, the angel couldn't shrug, but by extra-subtle voice modulation it did the vocal equivalent. 'Don't exist is a bit of an overstatement,' she said, 'and it's a very complex bit of maths, which I'm still not sure I completely follow. The analogy is, though, think of the radio signals. They're all there, but you can only listen to one at a time. Now, turning back to timescales, think of yourself as the radio signal.'

'Fine. Here am I going bleep bleep. Who's being the radio?'

Another, broader verbal shrug. 'This is a difficult concept to put across,' she said. 'Basically, the world is the radio, your fellow sentient beings are – no pun intended, promise – the cat's whiskers. Do you see what I'm getting at? You exist, you're here, no question about that. The tombstone there is inanimate – either that, or it's very, very shy, because we've been standing next to each other since 1897 and it's never said a word – and so it couldn't notice you even if it wanted to. Doesn't matter a damn what a

174

tombstone thinks. But living creatures are different; they're all tuned in to their own timescale, and so they just don't see anybody who's in a timescale faster than their own. Dead people move too quick; you know, the magic lantern effect. Marvellous system when you come to think of it, bloody efficient way to store billions of people on a relatively small planet.'

There was a substantial pause while Mike let it all sink in. 'I see,' he said. 'So do I still have to eat and sleep and so on? Do I still have to go to work and earn money, or is everything free, or don't I need anything? Can I have things even if I don't need them?'

'The question doesn't arise,' the angel replied. 'Life expectancy of a dead human's no more than three days, four days maximum. At the end of that time, either you find an empty property in Mortality you can slip into, or else – phut.'

'Phut?'

'Phut. That's yet another gross simplification,' the angel went on apologetically, 'but so what, I'm pretty shaky on the theory from now on. What actually happens, I *think*, is that you start to speed up to such an extent that Time just zips by in a meaningless blur and before you know it, you've reached the End of the Universe, entropy time, the big nothing; like you've fast-forwarded and there you are at the end of the tape. What happens after that is beyond me. Maybe they wind it back, maybe they take it back to the library and get out another one. Let's put it this way, you'll know the answer to that particular part of the story long before I will, so if you can, be sure to send me a postcard. I say that to all the new arrivals,' the angel added, 'and I've never had anything from any of them. But maybe they just forgot.'

'Four days?'

175

'Four days tops.'

Mike felt ill. The gravestone was still there under his backside, the breeze was still a little on the chilly side, but he felt as if he was already hurtling past, like a child on a combination merry-go-round and Ferris wheel. 'You said something about an empty property,' he remembered. 'What's that all about?'

'Thought you'd ask,' replied the angel. 'They always do. Just occasionally, you can slip back in. Sounds nice, but isn't.'

'No?'

'Wouldn't fancy it myself,' the angel replied. 'The reason being, you don't go back into HMS time, so you can't be a human or a cat or a golden eagle or stuff like that. Returns go in HIA time, and that's – well, weird, really. Look at me.'

'You?'

'Me. HIA; Human Irregular Anomaly. We exist in all timescales simultaneously. We're in some more strongly than in others, true, and in practice you ignore everything except HMS, HDS and a few others because – come on, let's ride this radio analogy until it falls to bits – the signals are faint, crackly and in Norwegian. Anyway, that's what happened to me. I came back as a statue. No bloody fun at all.'

'A statue?'

'That's right. More of us about than you'd think.' The angel's voice was getting softer and softer, slower and slower, as though its batteries were running down fast. 'The thing to remember about HIA is, it's very, very . . .'

'Yes? *Yes*?'

'Boring.'

A fraction of a second later, the statue was just a statue; you could tell just by looking at it that it was no more alive than a cellarful of coal. Run down? Asleep? Switched off?

No way of knowing. Mike stood up, felt pins and needles from his knee to his ankle.

Four days . . .

Ninety-nine per cent light speed!

Head forward, wings back, tail streaming behind him, the dragon bulleted on through the murderous slipstream. His scales glowed cherry-red, and the tears streaming from his eyes boiled before they ever reached his cheeks. His eardrums, at a guess, were halfway down his throat. It was just as well he couldn't open his mouth, because air pressure would have snapped his lower jaw off at the hinge.

Ugh, he thought –

wwhhyyyy aaammm IIIII ddoooiiiiiinngg tthhiiiiissssss?

Because if I don't, that creep Chubby will blow me to Kingdom Come (or, relatively speaking, quite possibly Kingdom Went; wherever, I don't want to go there).

And because there's a certain unbelievable thrill in peeling back the final frontier; shit-scaredly going where everybody else has already gone before, but not yet. As it were.

And, last but not least, because I've got nothing better to do.

BANG!

Light speed . . .

One very pertinent fact about travelling faster than light—

'*Ouch*!'

– is that it's bloody dark and you can't see where you're going. And, at that sort of speed, even a collision with a high-flying clothes moth takes on the stature of a major railway accident.

Fortunately, he regained consciousness just in time to pull out of his headlong spin, wrench his battered and groaning body up out of the way of mountains and airliners and jack-knife agonisingly back to straight and level. It was still as dark as thirty feet down a drain, which meant he hadn't lost speed. What he needed now was lots and lots of height.

Hey though, he crowed in the back lots of his subconscious, this is quite something. No way those two-legged groundling midgets could do this, for all their precious technology. For a dragon, however, it's just a matter of flying. You do know how to fly, don't you? You just put your wings together and go . . .

'*Help!*'

Going this fast, you lose all track of Time. Or Time loses all track of you. The only semi-constant is the pain; you're being beadblasted with photons, every square millimetre of your body surface is white hot, a grain of dust hits you like a cannon shell. You only continue to exist because entropy hasn't caught up with you yet. But it will.

Beeeeep!

What? Oh, Christ, yes, Chubby's idiotic signal. I can slow down now, just when I was beginning to enjoy myself.

The lights came back on, and then the dragon was no longer faster-than-light, just very fast; racing, but no longer against the clock. Now then, the trick is, decelerate slowly. In this context, sudden slowth would hit like a brick wall.

The sound came back on. The vertical hold adjusted itself. God had fiddled with the aerial.

Congratulations! *We all knew you had it in you*!

What the hell? The dragon's brain cleared and he realised it was a pre-recorded message, playing tinnily and at not quite the right speed through a miniature speaker inside his ear. He slowed down a little more.

Please proceed to the following co-ordinates. Longitude . . .

'Fuck you!' the dragon howled. 'I haven't got a map!'

178

... Sixteen minutes west; or, in layman's terms, the bookstall in Rockefeller Plaza. You will there buy a copy of the New York Times *and turn to page four. Estimated you will arrive in nine, repeat nine, minutes.*

High over New York, the dragon found out what the parcel was for. As his dragon body suddenly vanished and he felt a rather different, more vindictive slipstream tearing at his human incarnation, he realised that it was a parachute.

New Yorkers are hard to faze. A windswept man with streaming eyes and untidy hair parachuting down onto the concourse at Grand Central is, to them, just another guy trying to beat the rush hour. So finely tuned is the New Yorker's inbuilt radar that they got out of his way as he landed without even looking at him.

He picked himself up. No need to dispose of the parachute; in the second and a half during which he'd been rolling on the ground feeling acute pain in both knees, the parachute had been unbuckled, stolen and spirited away. By now, it'd probably been converted into three hundred silk handkerchiefs in a lock-up somewhere in Queens.

Feeling slightly shaky and, for once, almost out of his depth, he tottered to the bookstall, picked up a newspaper and looked at the date. All that trouble and effort, and he'd fast-forwarded six lousy weeks.

He turned to page four, as ordered, jotted down the closing prices. Then the sports pages, then the lottery results. Then, out of curiosity, he glanced to the front page.

And saw a headline.

The *Times*, which isn't your run-of-the-mill sensationalist fishwrap, had let its hair down. There were screamingly vivid action pictures, BIG headlines, interviews with witnesses, angles, turn to page six, continued on page seven. It was a BIG story, full of twists, nuances, implications. There was even a three-column feature by one D. Bennett, linking the bizarre events to Contragate, the Bermuda Triangle and the assassination of Abe Lincoln.

The gist of the story, however, was straightforward enough.

Twelve hours ago, in Mongolia, Saint George had killed the Dragon.

Mike didn't sleep well.

For one thing, since he was going to die, fast-forward, phut, whatever, in four days, he begrudged the time. Also, although he'd never been particularly superstitious, kipping down in a graveyard didn't appeal to him, particularly since he now had the feeling that he'd be able to see his fellow deadies and maybe they weren't very nice to look at ... Mostly, though, he couldn't sleep because he was worried.

Four days to find a – what the hell was it he was looking for? An anomaly, he supposed, but what the hell does an anomaly look like? Apparently, like a statue.

Not any old statue, though; he'd already tried that. There were plenty of statues in the graveyard and he'd knocked loudly on each one, prodded them for disguised doors and escape hatches, even tried climbing in through ears and open mouths. Failure. By the time he'd finished, he was beginning to hallucinate *No Vacancies* signs.

A statue.

A *statue*.

Jesus, yes, a *statue*! Piece of cake, surely, because wasn't the most gifted living sculptress (despair is the mother of exaggeration) a personal friend of his, who also happened to owe him one hell of a favour?

By the time he'd worked that out, it was half past six and the buses were starting to run. He caught the thirty-seven, which went to the hospital. Buses are inanimate (although they're capable of malice; ask anybody who's run after one, only to watch it draw away from the kerb at the last minute) and accordingly was solid and real enough for him to get on board without falling through the floor. He had no trouble finding a seat, in spite of the fact that there was standing room only.

But.

All right, so Bianca can sculpt me a statue to live in; central heating, air conditioned, all mod cons. First, though, I've got to find a way to get a message through to her. How the hell do I do that, exactly?

By the time the bus drew up outside the hospital gate, the only answer that had occurred to him was, *improvise*. Well, he could do worse.

Bianca stirred.

Precisely one second ago, she'd been very ill; Bianca the human jigsaw, held together with skin, plaster and force of habit. Now, though, she could feel the integrity of her newly restored bones. She was fit, strong, ready to face the incredibly daunting task now facing her. She was also, of course, covered from head to foot in plaster and her limbs were tied to the ceiling with thick wire.

'Hello!' she shouted. 'Nurse! I think I'm better now, can I get up?'

Needless to say, they ignored her, and an alarming thought walked flat-footed across the wet concrete of her mind. Maybe they wouldn't believe she was better and were going to keep her like this for another six weeks anyway?

It was then that the table began to move.

At first, Bianca put it down to a heavy lorry trundling by in the road below. When it stopped simply wobbling and began to tap-dance, she began to wonder.

'Mike?' she whispered.

Grimly, Mike lifted the chair and tapped out a phrase: *'cos I'll be there, puttin' on ma top hat, tying up ma white tie—*

'Mike,' Bianca said sternly, 'stop making that awful noise, you'll disturb the other patients.'

The table stopped moving. Feeling very foolish – girl gets bang on head, starts talking to thin air, and you're saying she's ready to go home? Get real, nurse, please – she whispered, 'Mike.'

No reply.

'Mike, if you want to, er, communicate ...' God, how? 'Don't try and answer. Look, I'll think of something.' What? Hell. She looked round. Lying at the foot of the bed was one of those horrid comics.

'Can you pick up that magazine?'

The pages riffled.

'Good. I'll pretend to be reading it.' She picked it up. 'To answer, turn the pages till you find something that's as close as you can get to what you want to say.'

Riffle. The magazine was now open at the agony column.

'You've got a problem you want help with?'

Riffle. In front of her was a feature, *Mortgage Repossession Left My Family Homeless*.

'You're in financial difficulties? Mike, you're dead, how can you be in ...?'

Riffle. *Exchanging Contracts: Part Four in our series on moving house.*

Bianca thought for a moment. 'You're homeless? You've got nowhere to go?'

Riffle. She looked down and saw the front cover. The name of the magazine was *Yes!*

'I see,' Bianca said, inaccurately. 'So how can I help?'

Riffle. Article on improving your garden. Photograph; petunias, flowering cherry, crab apple tree, herbacious border, garden gnomes ...

'You want me to plant a tree for you? Is that it?'

Riffle. Another photograph; view of Piccadilly Circus. Further riffle. View of Trafalgar Square. Further riffle. For Only £99.99 You Can Own This Beautiful Porcelain Figurine . . .

'A *statue*? You want me to carve you a statue?'

Riffle. Front cover.

'But . . .' Bianca was going to say Why? Then she thought of the dragon, and George, and she knew why.

'Mike, I'm sort of busy right now, can it wait? You see, first I've got to get out of here, then I've got to find that dragon – you know, my statue – and stop him blowing things up, so if you could give me six weeks or so . . .'

Furious riffles. Advertisement. Flabstrippers' Guarantee: Lose Six Pounds in Three Days or Your Money Back.

'Three days?' Front cover. 'Mike, that's impossible, I—'

The magazine flew from her hands, soared up into the air and parachuted down, pages flapping like the wings of a shot crow. The table rocked violently and fell over. The chair began to tap out *Dancin' Cheek to Cheek*.

'All *right*,' she hissed, as the sister came running. 'I'll see what I can do.'

CHAPTER TWELVE

'It's obvious what we've gotta do,' Kurt replied impatiently. 'We've gotta leave the country.'

Seventeen former statues looked at him as though he were mad, making him grateful his band wasn't a democracy. He did his best to ignore them.

'Leave the country?' David asked. 'Why?'

David had, somehow, been elevated to the rank of spokesman-cum-courier; that is to say, the other ex-statues tended to hem him in and hiss, 'Go on, *you* tell him,' in his ear. They also complained to him about the food, the transport and the accommodation; remember, although their outward husks were Italian, inside they were British.

'Because,' Kurt replied, still wondering what in blazes had led him to go back for this miserable lot, 'we've got this job to do. And we can't do it here. Okay?'

'Don't think we can leave the country,' muttered the Giambologna *Mercury*. 'We'd need special export licences, surely.'

'Stolen property,' agreed a Bernini bronze. 'They got

184

these computerised lists, international, worldwide. I saw it on *Lovejoy*. We'd never get past the duty-free lounge.'

Amateurs, muttered Kurt to himself. 'Absolutely right,' he sighed, the sarcasm going so far over his listeners' heads that you could have bounced radio signals off it. 'That's why we've gotta hijack a plane.'

That left them speechless; but not for long enough. A Donatello Crucifixion objected that surely hijacking was illegal. The Canova demanded to speak to the manager. Kurt bashed the packing case with his fist for silence.

'Okay,' he snarled, 'that's it. I've had enough of this goddamn whimpering out of you guys. The next one of you I hear any shit from ends up at the bottom of the Arno with a human being tied to his ankle. You got that? Good. Now then, this is the plan.'

In the shocked silence that followed, it occurred to Kurt that he hadn't yet formulated a plan. Kurt Lundqvist without a plan; impossible. Easier to imagine a Tory minister without a mistress. Something would occur to him, it always did.

'The plan,' he went on, 'is, naturally, top secret. I'll announce the various stages in due course, on a strictly need-to-know basis. The first stage is getting to the air terminal. This is what we do.'

Kurt spent the rest of the day shoplifting, hotwiring vehicles, breaking into police station armouries, mugging tourists for their passports, faking photographs, wiring up al fresco bombs and generally relaxing after all the strain he'd been through lately dealing with objects only one step away from being people. By one o'clock in the morning, he felt refreshed and invigorated. He now had at his disposal a carabinieri armoured van, eighteen assault rifles, ditto Beretta 9mm handguns, three cases of grenades, five twenty-pounder bombs, flak jackets, black balaclavas,

185

matching ski-suits, two-way radios, state-of-the-art communications and radio jamming equipment, sandwiches, chocolate and a thermos flask of decaffeinated coffee.

At three am precisely, air traffic control received an ominous message on the security hotline. Flight TCA8494 from Istanbul, scheduled to refuel before heading on to London, due to arrive at 03.24, had armed hijackers on board. They'd wired up bombs, and were demanding the release of prisoners and a huge cash ransom. A special security team was on its way; in the meantime, act naturally, refuel the plane, pretend nothing untoward is happening. Message received and understood.

At 03.34, the carabinieri van drew up at a side gate. Kurt flashed an impressive-looking pass (actually an Academy Museum season ticket, but it was dark and Kurt kept his thumb over the words) under the sentry's nose, hissed a few words in his ear and was let through. At 03.40, eighteen shadowy, ferociously armed figures scrambled up the gangway into the plane and burst into the passenger compartment.

'Okay!' Kurt roared. 'Nobody move!' He paused, for effect. 'Okay,' he said, 'where's the hijackers?'

The cabin staff stared at him. They were just rewinding the in-flight movie, handing out the freeby glossy magazines. 'What hijackers?' they said.

Kurt assumed a pained expression. 'Jesus, not *another* false alarm,' he sighed. 'You *sure* there hasn't been a hijack?'

The purser nodded. 'We'd have noticed,' he said.

'Not necessarily,' Kurt replied, motioning to his team to fan out, start frisking the passengers. 'Like, there's these new fundamentalist religious fanatics, some name like Meek Militant Action. Their aim's to inherit the Earth, provided nobody objects. We'd better check things out, just to be sure.'

The purser, who had the muzzle of a Heckler & Koch G3 sticking in his ear – not because he was a suspect, it was just rather a cramped aircraft – shrugged and nodded. 'Suit yourselves, guys,' he said. 'Better safe than sorry, I guess. While you're at it, would you mind taking round the duty-frees?'

Kurt's men duly searched; wonder of wonders, they found no fewer than five twenty-pound bombs wired up to the doors, fuel lines and in-flight catering packs. Gee, muttered Kurt, just as I thought. We'd better stay with this flight till it gets to London. What a truly splendid idea, the captain replied, his subconscious wrestling with the problem of where he'd seen some of these guys before (you don't like to say to a SWAT team officer that you're sorry, you didn't recognise him with his clothes on). While they were at it, he added, maybe they could help out with serving the meals and checking the seat-belts.

As the plane took off, a Bernini took Kurt aside and asked him to explain something.

'Thought we were meant to be hijacking the plane,' he said.

Kurt nodded. 'Neat job, huh?'

'But we're pretending to be the army. The good guys.'

'So?'

'Does that mean we're the good guys or the bad guys? I'm confused.'

Kurt shook his head. The ignorance of some people. 'Son,' he said, 'I'm gonna tell you something that's gonna help you a lot in years to come, supposing you last that long. Good guys is just a fancy way of saying Us. Bad guys is only ever Them. You remember that, you won't go far wrong. Okay?'

'But what about moral imperatives? What about Good and Evil?'

The Bernini suddenly found himself about a centimetre from Kurt's taut face and industrial-laser eyes. 'Where I come from,' he said, 'Evil's a stunt man's Christian name. Now go over there, sit down and shut up. Does that answer your question?'

'Comprehensively.'

'Great. Always knew I shoulda been a philosopher.'

Attack philosopher, naturally.

Although the dragon had immediately recognised the sheer brilliance of Chubby's method of travelling back through Time, he'd had an intuitive feeling from the outset that there was one tiny flaw in it somewhere. Now, back in the air and soaring at ninety thousand feet over Angola, he knew for certain what it was.

It didn't work.

Twenty-seven hours he'd been up here; twice round the predetermined circuit, airspeed and course exactly as specified to the knot, to the metre. All he'd managed to achieve was to distance himself from home by a further twenty-seven hours. Bloody marvellous.

By the time he was overflying Botswana, he'd worked it out. The course as plotted was half an hour out of synch; the fools hadn't taken into account the time he'd be spending on the ground. He cursed them and himself; if he'd spotted the mistake earlier, he might just have been able to compensate. By now, though, the history nodes would all have moved on so far that it'd be impossible to rechart the course without all of Chubby's formulae, calculating software and history-industry infiltrators' input. He was stuck.

When in shit, use brain. All the necessary kit would, of course, still be in Chubby's office. All he had to do was drop in, explain the problem – or would Chubby be expecting him? After all, once he got back he'd tell him all about it, with the result that by the time they got back here, sorry, *now*, Chubby would already *know* – but if that was the case, he'd have known to correct the error in the first place, oh *fuck*, this is complicated ...

He flew, nevertheless, to Chubby's office, only to find it boarded up, with no forwarding address. Nothing in the phone book. No trace anywhere. Maybe when he got back he was going to roast Chubby alive (sorely tempted), which in turn would mean no Chubby now, just when he needed him most. Hey, maybe it really *is* impossible to travel backwards in Time. Starting to look that way, no question.

He slowed down, drifting gracefully high above Madagascar. The hell with this, let's try another way.

Such as?

If you don't know, his old mother used to say, ask someone who does.

Think, dragon, think.

Thirty-two hours ago, he'd seen a newspaper headline saying that twelve hours before that, he'd been killed. Okay.

If I was killed before I got here, then it stands to reason that I got back in time to be killed before I got here. Therefore I, the late lamented I, *requiescam in pace*, must know how I got back. So I should ask myself. Only that's going to be tricky, because I'm dead.

Tricky, but possible. Because – give me strength! – in order to have gotten back, I must have asked myself how to do it. My dead self must therefore know that my living self is going to want to make contact, approximately now, and will be waiting in for the call, wherever the flying fuck I/he now am/is. Stands to reason.

Okay, here goes. Just hope I know what I'm doing.

He peered down. Zululand. Well, why not?

*

There are more things in Heaven and Earth, Horatio, than give you nightmares in your philosophy.

Few stranger, more wonderful or more terrible, however, than the *isangoma* – translated, with typical Colonial crassness, 'witch-doctor' – of southern Africa. Now, of course, extinct; no place for that sort of thing in the twentieth century. Well, of course.

Although he knew virtually nothing about the subject, the dragon was at least able to address the small, shrivelled man sitting in front of him on a low, carved stool by his correct title: *amakhosi*, 'my lords', plural, because when you speak to the *isangoma* you're talking not to the little old man but to the countless mighty spirits who bed-and-breakfast, so to speak, in the vast mansions behind his eyes.

Nkunzana's small, tidy kraal lay in a miniature valley, a crack between two great rocks, which meant the sun's nuisance was kept to a minimum. For twenty hours in the twenty-four it was dark at Izulu-li-dum-umteto, and for Nkunzana darkness was a natural resource essential to his business, like the mill-streams of Lancashire. He himself was a comic, horrifying figure; small, crooked and smooth-skinned, like a freeze-dried child. He wore the uniform of his craft: leopards' teeth, goats' horns, pigs' bladders, gnu's tail. He looked like God's spares box. Slow to move, quick to laugh; smiling toothlessly, staring unblinking at a space two feet above and eight inches to the right of the head of the person he was talking to. A little ray of sunshine. Your local GP.

'*Sakubona, baba*'. We saw you, my father; hello. A grave nod accompanied the formal greeting. The dragon relaxed a little. He'd managed to get to see the doctor without an appointment. 'And what can I do for you?'

The dragon licked the roof of his mouth, which was dry; *why am I afraid of this little toe-rag? I'm a dragon, for crying out loud* . . . 'I need to speak to someone who is dead, '*makhosi*,' he replied, a little nervousness spilling out with the words. 'For you, surely, this is possible.'

'Possible.' The little man nodded. 'A small matter, my father. Who among the snakes do you wish to talk to?'

The dragon hesitated. 'This is, um, embarrassing.'

'Relax. Say the name.'

'Well – look, how would it be if I wrote it down on a bit of paper? Sorry to be all silly about this, but—'

'I cannot read, my father. Say the name.'

'All right. Um. Me.'

'You?'

Nod. 'Me.'

Long pause.

'*Wo, ndoda; ngitshilo.*' Hey, man, you sure said a mouthful. 'Talking to yourself is a sign of madness. Talking to yourself, dead, is class.'

The dragon shuffled. 'Said it was embarrassing. Can you do it?'

Nkunzana shrugged. 'Why not?' he said. 'If it's possible. If not, not.'

'It's possible. Cross my heart and hope to die. Er, be dead.'

'We will see what we can do, my father.' The old man closed his eyes, leaned forward until his knees touched his shoulders, and tossed something onto the fire. Nothing happened.

'About time, too,' said the dragon.

The dragon looked up. 'Aarg,' he said.

'Have you any idea,' his deceased self went on, 'how long I've been hanging around this boghole waiting for you to turn up? Gives me the fucking creeps, and I'm *dead*.'

'Sorry.' Really, truly embarrassing. 'Look, I guess you know why I needed to talk.'

'Reverse time travel, how we got home.' The dragon nodded. 'Piece of cake. Why you needed to bother me I don't know. I managed to work it out all by myself.'

'Clever old you, then.'

'Indeed.' The dragon sighed contemptuously. 'Listen carefully. I'm dead, right?'

'Right.'

'But I can't be, or I couldn't be talking to me, right? Say yes.'

'Yes.'

'Therefore I must be alive. Nod.'

The dragon nodded.

'And if I'm alive now, I must have been alive six weeks ago. Well?'

'Obviously.'

'Okay.' The dragon grinned. 'There you are, then.'

And there they weren't, either of them.

For ten minutes or so, Nkunzana sat, gazing at the empty stool. Then he stood up, threw another log on the fire.

'*Hambla gahle*,' he said quietly, go in peace. 'I'm Logic, fly me.' He shook his head, picked up his catskin bag of medicines and walked to his hut.

It only occurred to him when he reached the doorway. He stopped dead, swore, ('*Wangi hudela umtwana wami!*') and banged his head savagely against the lintel. Bloody old fool.

All that work, unsocial hours, and who the hell was he going to send the invoice to?

Bianca's arm ached, the newly mended bone resenting the heavy vibration of hammer on chisel on stone. She glanced up at the clock. No time to rest, she observed mournfully. Not even time for a quick brew and a garibaldi biscuit. She raised the chisel, positioned it carefully, tapped gently. Boy, was she *tired*.

It was starting to take its toll. Already her hand had slipped, uncharacteristically, when she'd been doing the left side of the collar bone. Oh dear, what a shame, never mind. The old Mike had always had a chip on his shoulder. Now he had a chip out of it; same difference.

Do the head last, shrieked her common sense. Just in case the bloody thing comes alive before I've finished it. Last thing I need is Mike's head looking over my shoulder, telling me how I should do my job. Probably try and sweet-talk me into making improvements on the original. No prize for guessing what he'd want improved.

Furthermore, once this job was finished, no chance of taking a day off or putting her feet up. The moment she'd finished Mike, she had a dragon to find and reason with. And what if the wretched thing wouldn't listen to reason? Then what the hell was she supposed to do?

She paused, brushed away chippings and thought hard. Why me, anyway? Go on, then, if you're so damn clever.

The trouble was, she could feel reasons there under her skin, like the palmed coin hidden in the magician's handkerchief. It *had* to be her, because . . . Well, because she believed in what was going on – not through choice, but because she knew it was all horribly true – and she knew full well that nobody else would believe her. If she tried to enlist the help of the proper authorities (Police? Army? Church? No idea), they'd have her inside a fruitcake repository and connected up to the mains before she got much further than, 'Well, it's like this . . .' Because she owed it to the dragon for the wrongs her species had done to his species – No, the hell with that. Follow that line of argument and she'd be pouring petrol through delicatessens' letterboxes. Because it was her statues that started it all. That was the reason. Very silly reason; holding herself responsible for the acts of a bunch of semi-legendary joyriders. But it was *the* reason and she was stuck with it.

But what was she to do if the dragon wouldn't listen to her? An entrancing picture floated before her mind; the damsel fights the dragon to save the knight chained to the rock. Great feminist statement; bloody silly game plan. And how do you go about fighting dragons, anyway?

'Reluctantly,' Bianca said aloud. 'Copper mallet, copper mallet, come out wherever you are.'

Three hours later, there wasn't much left to do. The face – well, far be it from her to seek to amend Mother Nature's banjax. The small of the back and the bum; there is a destiny that shapes our ends, she muttered to herself laying in hard with the chisel, rough-hew them how we will. In this instance, it had shaped Mike's end rather like a very old, tired sofa. There were lots of untidy chisel-marks, but his trousers would hide those. Time Mike learnt to take the rough with the smooth.

Chip chip, tap tap. 'All right,' she said. 'It's ready. Phase One in an exciting new development of starter-homes for unfussy ghosts.'

She waited.

Slight miscalculation? Maybe. Or maybe a very precise calculation indeed.

Below him, the dragon saw the still-smoking embers of the hall. A gaggle of peculiar-shaped creatures, led by a human, were picking their way through the hot rubble towards a beat-up old motor vehicle. They got in and drove away.

Banzai! He'd come back in a day or so earlier than scheduled, just nicely in time to see George and his sidekicks clambering out of their incinerator and making a run for it. Maintaining his height, he tracked the van; wingbeats few and slow, a handy thermal buoying him up.

He was, he hoped, too high for the wretched creatures in the van to see or notice, although what could they do if they did? Drive faster than light? Try and defend themselves? Attack? Let them. The dragon was wearing under his metaphorical dinner jacket the bullet-proof vest of zombie-hood; *you can't get me 'cos I done dead already*. Looking ahead up the road, he picked his spot. Fire? Twelve good nosefuls before he was into reserve. He accelerated, put his wings back, fell into the glide . . .

'George.'
  'Now what?'
  'There's a dragon following us.'

The van had slewed to a sudden dramatic standstill and its contents were dispersing at top speed. Drat, the dragon thought. Never mind, he was locked on to George now; he didn't care about the others, as soon let them go as not, provided they didn't interfere. And they wouldn't. Not many demons are prepared to lay down their lives for a saint.

  Nice to watch George run. For a short, fattish lad he had a pretty turn of speed. Slippery, too, as soap in a bath, so no time for mucking about. It's when the stage villain pauses to twirl his moustaches and cackle that the hero sees his chance and the underwriters of his life policies start to breathe again. Time to nail the sod.

  He dived, breathed in. A smart sneeze, pinpoint accurate. A very loud, *very* short scream. Job done.

  Home.

Oh.

  So that was death, was it? Typical, I missed it.

  George watched the dragon recede into the sky, then

195

looked down; although he knew there'd be nothing to see. His body – gone. Which body? Didn't matter. The jet of fire that had wrapped round him like a cat round legs had been so hot it'd have evaporated marble as easily as flesh. An exemplary snuff; quick, sure and completely (as far as he could remember) painless.

George was suddenly aware of something –

– God knows what. The nearest he could get to it was an invisible lead, dragging him like an over-inquisitive dog. Balls, muttered George, I'm going to Heaven. Don't want to go yet. Haven't finished.

Don't have to go. As the unseen rope tugged him along, he was aware of a handhold, an escape hatch, rushing towards him. An anomaly! Saved!

There's many a slip, as the saying goes, between toilet bowl and sewage farm. George only saw it for the most fleeting sliver of a second, but it was long enough to judge his escape attempt and make it.

A statue, its back door wide open. In fact, so conveniently placed, handy for the stream of traffic, that you'd be forgiven for thinking it had been put there expressly for the purpose. A mousetrap? Or a getaway car?

Whatever; who gives a shit? As far as George was concerned, it was a case of any portrait in a storm. He threw himself at the anomaly and hit the mark.

'Mike? You in there yet?'

Coming, coming. Being dead takes it out of you, makes you realise just how out of condition you can become in three days. Painfully, Mike dragged himself towards the nice welcoming statue. Dear, kind, clever Bianca, she'd done a good job. Almost there . . .

What? *What*?

BASTARD!

Just as the door in the back of the statue opened and he'd been reaching out a frail and shaky arm to touch it, some evil git had bounced up from behind, swept past him, jumped into the statue and slammed the door. Was that face familiar? The ill-fated play where he'd been killed. Oh *no*. Saint George. The saint had stolen his body.

Even if he'd had the strength to hammer on the door and tug at the handle, it'd have done him no good. With statues it's strictly first come, first stored. He'd been gazumped, at the last minute.

He had no more strength left to hang on. He let go.

'Mike? You in there yet?'

The statue's eyes flickered.

'Mike!'

With an effortless smoothness that did her no end of credit, the eyelids lifted.

'Mike?'

That's not him in there! Odd, how you just know, simply by looking people in the eye. Just a coloured circle on a white background, a fried egg with a jewelled yolk. Perhaps we can actually see the retina, the way they do for ultra-high-security identification routines, but too fast for our conscious minds to know what we've actually done.

'Who?'

I know who! I'd recognise those beady, shifty little eyes anywhere!

Bianca had quick reactions. Very few scientific instruments known to Man would be precise enough to measure the tiny instant it took her to grab the two-pound lump hammer and swing it at the head of her newly completed masterpiece. Compared to Saint George, though, she was a dinosaur in slow motion. Before her fingers had contacted the hickory handle, he was moving. As the hammerhead

197

rushed towards him, he stuck out his newly acquired right arm, punched Bianca neatly in the eye, ducked the hammer blow and ran for it. Behind him, he heard a crash, suggesting that Bianca had sat down uncomfortably on the floor. He made a mental note to laugh triumphantly later, when he had the time.

He was through the door and out into the street faster than a jack-rabbit absconding with the Christmas club money.

Painfully, feeling like a Keystone Kop five seconds after the director's yelled 'Cut!' Bianca hauled herself up off the floor and swore.

George, that bastard of a saint, had stolen another of her statues. Worse, he'd probably just killed her friend. Nice touch, that; poor old Mike had just had the rare privilege of being killed by both Good and Evil consecutively. Not that she had a clue any more which was which; nor did she care. If Mike still existed, anywhere in the cosmos, she guessed he was feeling the same way.

The hammer was still in her hand and she realised; Jesus, I just tried to *kill* him. A saint. My own statue. I tried to kill one of my own statues, just when it was on the point of coming to life.

It wasn't being the sort of day you look back on with pride.

CHAPTER THIRTEEN

'What the Shopfloor,' Chardonay quavered, 'was *that*?'

Slitgrind levered himself up out of a puddle with his forearms. His eyes were blind with saint-ash and his lungs were full of holy smoke. 'Guess,' he grunted, and then started to cough.

'The dragon again?'

Before Chardonay could say anything else, Snorkfrod was at his side, hauling him up like an adored sack of spuds. Was he all right? Any bones broken? Did it hurt if she prodded him there?

'Yes,' he yelped. 'Not that that means anything. That'd hurt under any circumstances.'

'That dragon,' muttered Prodsnap, 'doesn't like us very much. What did we *do*?'

'We tried to kill him,' Holdall replied. 'First we wee'd all over him, then we blew him up with dynamite. Maybe he's paranoid or something.'

Having dislodged the proffered paramedical assistance, Chardonay sat down on a low wall and put on the one boot

199

he'd been able to find. 'Well,' he said, 'one thing's for certain, that dragon isn't dead. Not as such. Where's George?'

The other demons looked at each other.

'Look,' Prodsnap said, 'let's put it this way. He's gone to a better place, and I don't mean Solihull.' He sneezed. 'I suggest we do the same. In our case, of course, we want to go to a worse place, but the principle's the same.'

'Where's that damn priest got to, come to that?' Slitgrind growled. 'I'm trying to remember if he was with us in the van. Who saw the bugger last?'

Chardonay was staring at the abandoned van. Its engine was still running. 'That dragon,' he said, in a strange flat voice, 'just killed a saint.'

Slitgrind shrugged a few shoulders. 'Plenty more where he came from. Look, can we get the Shopfloor out of here, before the sucker comes back?'

'The dragon,' Chardonay repeated, 'just killed Saint George. That's *wrong*.'

The exasperated sound came from Slitgrind. 'Look, love,' he stage-whispered to Snorkfrod, who was putting powder (powdered what, you don't want to know) on her face, using a puddle for a mirror. 'Can you explain to that thick prat of a boyfriend of yours, any minute now that flying bastard's gonna come back and fry *us*. We gotta *go*, for Chrissakes.'

'All right, then,' Snorkfrod replied, 'you go.'

'Huh?' Slitgrind's face was a study in bewilderment. Imagine what God would look like if he opened his post one morning and found he'd got a tax rebate. As bewildered as that.

'Go. Bugger off. Sling your hook. We'll see you back at the factory.'

'But . . .' Slitgrind's expression added terror to its repertoire. 'But we've got to stick together,' he whimpered. 'We can't go wandering about on our own, it's not *safe*.'

Snorkfrod gave him a stare you could have broken up and put in whisky. 'Slitgrind, you nerk,' she said, 'you're a demon from sodding Hell. You're twenty million years old. I think it's probably time you learned to cross the road on your own.'

'We aren't splitting up.' Chardonay had spoken with – well, virtually with authority. Not a large-scale authority – something like the English Tourist Board – but enough to get him his colleagues' attention. 'We've got work to do. Come on.'

He stood up, knees wobbly and calflike, head erect, and started to walk towards the van. The others had to trot to catch up with him.

'Where're we going, Chief?' Prodsnap asked, puffing.

Chief, noted Chardonay's subconscious. 'To find the dragon,' he replied. 'And kill it.'

Three demons stopped dead in their tracks. A fourth used the delay to catch up – it's always hard to run in high heels, even when they're an integral part of your foot.

'Are you crazy?'

'No,' Chardonay replied. 'I'm bruised, lost and very frightened. But it's our duty. We're peace officers, with a responsibility to maintain the Divine Order. That dragon has just killed Saint George, it's against all the rules. It's got to be sorted out. And,' he went on, swallowing, 'since it's us here on the spot, we've got to do it. Is that clear?'

'Stone me,' Prodsnap muttered. 'He's serious.'

'I'm with you all the way,' sighed Snorkfrod, passionately. 'And I want you to know, I think that's the most moving thing I've ever heard.'

. 'Thank you,' Chardonay replied. 'That means a great deal to me. How about the rest of you lads?'

Prodsnap, Slitgrind and Holdall exchanged glances.

'We're right behind you, Chief.'

'Count me in.'

'You can depend on us.'

For a moment, Chardonay was lost for words. He glowed and seemed to grow an extra inch or two. 'Thanks, guys,' he said softly. 'Right, here goes.'

He punched his left palm with right fist, turned and headed off towards the van, Snorkfrod's arm through his. The other three fell in behind them.

'Men.' Chardonay settled himself in the driver's seat, put on his seat-belt and took off the handbrake. 'I just want you to know, whatever happens from hereon in . . .'

Words failed him, not because of any sudden access of emotion, but because at that moment the back-seat passengers clobbered him and Snorkfrod silly with the tyre iron.

Not even for old times' sake?

The dragon shook his head. 'No way, Nosher,' he replied. 'Look, I really am grateful to you, saving my life and all that, but I've had enough. I've done what I came to do and now I'm off.'

Just ten minutes of your time to vaporise a few trifling demons, Fred. For a pal.

'No. Think about it, Nosher. I've got my whole life in front of me. I can go where I like, do what I want. Last thing I need is Hell putting a price on my head for snuffing five of their people. I'm more conspicuous than Salman Rushdie, Nosher. Longer. Harder to conceal. It'd be a confounded nuisance and I can do without it.'

I can take care of that. I can give you a whole new identity.

The dragon laughed. 'Sure you can, Nosh,' he replied. 'I mean, twentieth-century Earth is positively teeming with dragons, I'd have no trouble whatsoever blending in with the crowd. Get real, pal. I'm out of here.'

Fred. The letters on the screen grew dim, flickery, as if to suggest deep and sincere regret. *If you walk out on me – well, around your neck be it.*

The dragon froze. 'You bastard.'

Blown to smithereens, Fred, whatever a smithereen is. Walk out on me and I'll find out. Shame you won't be there to share the knowledge with me.

Chubby, who'd been silent, nodded sagely. 'Besides,' he added, 'how'd they know it was you? I've been making enquiries. As far as Hell Central's concerned, those five idiots are with a coachload of other idiots over in Nashville, Tennessee. Nobody knows they're here. When they don't come back, I expect Hell will assume they've defected to the other side, something like that.'

'Defect?'

Actually, I think Chubby's a bit out of touch with recent developments. He's still got a Cold War mentality, which is thoroughly out of date these days. Let's say desert, shall we, rather than defect? They'd buy that, I'm sure.

The dragon growled ominously. 'You're bastards, both of you,' he said. 'All you care about is your stinking profits.'

Chubby clicked his tongue. 'Why is it,' he demanded, 'that people are always so rude about profits?'

Never honoured in their own country.

'Free enterprise,' Chubby went on, 'is the life blood of commerce.'

'Maybe,' the dragon snarled. 'But I'd rather not have their free enterprise on my paws, if it's all the same to you.'

I've just accessed my database and it says a smithereen is a small fragment or particle, usually the result of a catastrophic explosion. I assume it knows what it's talking about, but there's only one way to be absolutely certain.

'You'd do it, wouldn't you?'

With infinite regret but negligible hesitation, yes.

The dragon sighed. His eyes, as he glowered at the screen, were case-hardened with contempt. 'You know something, Nosher?' he said. 'You're evil.'

You reckon? Sending you out to do battle with the forces of darkness and you say I'm evil?

'I do.'

The screen flickered, by way of a dry chuckle.

Evil schmevil, old pal. Go out there and fry some fiends.

With an effort, Mike stopped screaming and pulled himself together.

It took some doing. Sixty per cent of him was slowly drifting away through space. Forty per cent of him was slipping unobtrusively into the future. It was like trying to impose your will on seven over-excited Highland terriers.

Heel, Mike commanded. And toe. And leg. And arm. Oh Christ, and head too.

You know the bit in all the films where they've just found the suitcase full of the money from the big heist; and suddenly the wind gets up and the air is full of flying banknotes; and first they all caper frantically around trying to catch them; and then they realise it's hopeless and collapse laughing to the ground while the credits roll all round them? Well, it was rather like that, hold the laughter. All Mike could manage (particularly since his face was now thirty yards and four hours away from the majority of him) was a wry grin.

The hell with it. Why bother? He was just about to relax and finally let go when . . .

Oh my god, a statue! Where the hell did that come from?

Look gift horses in the mouth if you must, but when confronted with a wholly unlooked-for, vacant, unlocked, fully furnished statue just when you're on the point of dissolving into space and time, you look for the little hatch between the shoulder-blades, you grab as much of you as you can reach, and you jump.

'And this,' said the Council spokesman, 'is where the fountain was to have gone, and here's where we would have put the floral clock, and here's where we'd planned to have the big brass plaque recording the munificent generosity of Kawaguchiya Integrated Circuits (UK) plc.' He paused and drew breath. 'And here . . .'

Five pairs of impassive Japanese eyes followed his pointing finger and fixed on another part of the bomb crater.

'Here,' continued the spokesman, 'we intended to have the centrepiece of Kawaguchiya Integrated Circuits Plaza, the staggeringly impressive statue of Saint George and the Dragon, by possibly the world's most talented living sculptress, Bianca Wilson.' Time for another breath; a deep one. 'Instead . . .'

He stopped. He blinked, rubbed his eyes. It was still there. 'Excuse me,' he said.

He touched it; solid. As a rock, you might say. Just to be sure, he kicked it, hard. *Ouch*!

'Instead,' he went on, 'we have no dragon, but now we do seem to have got St George back. About three seconds ago, to be precise. Don't ask me how we did it, but we did it.' He sat down and removed his shoe. 'Clever old us, eh?'

If the KIC people had noticed anything odd, they didn't let it show. Two of the younger ones whispered to the grey-haired type who seemed to be the delegation leader. He nodded and whispered something back.

'Very big statue,' he said.

'It is, yes,' the spokesman agreed. 'And, um, solid. Made of solid stone, all the way through. Yessiree, this baby's here to stay.'

(Because, at the moment when George entered the newly completed statue of Mike, he broke the morphological link with his own former statue. No longer caught up in George's anomalous timestream, it went back to where it had come from; once again, just a statue, lifeless and inert.)

The Council spokesman pulled his shoe back on, stood up and assumed a didactic pose. 'You will observe,' he said, 'the remarkable use of line which Ms Wilson has managed to achieve; the dynamic tension implicit in the composition of this masterpiece; the impression she conveys of desperate, headlong motion frozen for all time in the . . .'

Slowly, as if it had the cramp in its left leg, the statue got up, winced, swore and hobbled away down Colmore Row.

Yes, Bianca said, she'd accept the charges. 'Mike, where the hell . . .?'

'In a call-box just off Pinfold Street,' Mike replied. 'Can you come and pick me up? Only . . .'

'Well?'

Mike glanced over his shoulder. Because it was only an ordinary-sized call-box, he was on his knees with his nose pressed right up against the glass. People outside were staring.

'Just hurry, will you? And bring a lorry.'

He put the receiver down, breathed out hard. Someone was hammering on the door. Edging round carefully, he opened it and scowled.

'What's the matter, you daft bitch?' he growled. 'You never seen a statue before?'

By coincidence, at precisely that moment another lorryload of statuary chugged round junction four of the M42, taking the exit signposted to Birmingham. In the back were eight Berninis, three Donatellos, three Cellinis, a Canova and the

Giambologna *Mercury*. Michaelangelo's *David* sat next to a harassed-looking man in a black jump-suit in the cab.

'Sorry,' David admitted. 'I've never been much good at map-reading. Well,' he amended, 'this is actually my first attempt, but if I'd ever tried it before, I don't suppose I'd have made much of a fist of it then, either.'

Kurt muttered something under his breath. 'We're on the right road now, huh?'

'I think so. We want to go to the big sprawly grey blob, looks like a squashed spider, name of Birmingham, right?'

Kurt swore and hauled on the wheel. 'Okay,' he said, 'I've turned right. Now what?'

David bit his lip. 'Sorry,' he said, 'I meant right as in okay, not right the opposite of left. I think actually we wanted to go straight on.'

'Oh, for Christ's sake!' Kurt had strong views on the subject of suffering fools gladly. It made him glad if fools suffered a *lot*. 'Now we've gotta go miles out of our way. Concentrate, dammit.'

'Sorry.'

They drove on in silence for a while; Kurt sulking, David feeling guilty. When they were safely back on the right road, however, David turned to Kurt and said, 'Excuse me.'

'Well?'

Difficult to find a tactful way of putting this. 'What are we, like, doing here exactly?' David asked.

'The job,' Kurt replied. 'You realise they drive on the wrong side of the road in this faggot-ridden country?'

'What job?'

'*The* job. Deliver the statues, snuff the dragon, and then we're outta here. Not the weirdest thing I ever got hired to do,' Kurt added. 'In the top twenty, maybe even the top ten, but not in at number one. Still, it ain't exactly difficult. And it sure beats what I was doing before.'

'Which was?'

'Being dead.'

'Ah. Right.'

Kurt frowned, detecting a certain lack of awe in his companion. After all, not many people come back from the dead. Even fewer come back from the dead and walk straight into a plum job in their chosen profession, as though they'd never been away. Jesus Christ and maybe Sherlock Holmes – Kurt, who'd been around and heard a thing or two, knew all that stuff about surviving the Reichenbach Falls was just a tax dodge – but that was it.

'You ever been dead, son?' he queried.

'Not to the best of my knowledge.'

'Give it a miss,' Kurt advised. 'Don't get you anywhere.'

'Who're we working for, then?'

Kurt's spasm of impatience nearly caused an accident. 'You don't ask questions like that in this man's business, boy. You can come to harm asking questions like that.'

True, David reflected, we nearly did. We only missed that car by an inch or so. 'Sorry,' he said. 'But I'm really curious.' He paused; a thought had struck him. 'You do know, don't you?'

Kurt avoided his eye. 'Of course I frigging well know,' he snapped.

'And?'

'Read the damn map.'

They drove on in silence, if you could call it that, because Kurt was convinced that the sound of cogs turning in his brain was probably audible in Connecticut.

It had been a good question.

Just who *was* he working for?

George stopped running, ducked down behind a dustbin and froze.

208

Debits and credits time. On the negative side, he was lost, confused, penniless, naked, in an unfamiliar and distinctly economy-class body and on the run from a livid sculptress and a fire-breathing dragon. On the positive side, he was alive. He closed his eyes and allowed himself to relax. On balance, he was further up the ladders than down the snakes, by something in the order of a thousand per cent.

About four minutes later, he solved the clothing and money problem by jumping out on an unsuspecting passer-by, knocking him silly with a broken bicycle pump he'd found in the dustbin and helping himself to his victim's personal effects. Fortunately, he and his unwitting bene-factor were more or less the same size, although personally George wouldn't have chosen a lilac shirt to go with a navy blue jacket. But there; muggers can't be choosers. The shoes hurt his feet, but not nearly as much as the pavement would have done.

An appropriate moment, he told himself as he sauntered down the alleyway into New Street, to draw up an agenda. It went as follows:

1. Find and scrag that bastard dragon.
2. Easier soliloquised than done, of course. He still wasn't a hundred per cent at home in this century and maybe he was missing a trick somewhere, but he had arrived at the conclusion that the old Wormex^{TM}-in-the-water-supply tactic was going to be out of place here; although, to judge by the stuff he'd had in his whisky, a stiff dose of dragon powder could only improve the taste.

The basic principle, however, was surely a good one: get the dragon to drink something that'd disagree with him. The recipe ought not to be a problem. The ancient proverb stuck in his mind: you can lead a dragon to water, but you can't make him drink. How did you go about conning a dragon into slaking its thirst from your specially prepared homebrew; leave a big bowl with DRAGON on the side lying about in a public place? Unlikely to work.

Hold that thought. Since he was now wearing a whole new body, the dragon wouldn't know who he was. All he had to do, given the element of disguise, was walk up to the dragon in a bar and offer to buy him a drink.

The ugly snout of practicality intruded into his plans. As far as he could tell, this was a liberal century, uninhibited, where anything went (so long as you weren't fussy about it coming back again afterwards), but even so, you'd probably be pushing your luck sidling up to strangers in bars asking if they were a dragon and wanted a drink. On the right lines, he decided, but could do with a little bit more fine tuning.

Still, at least he had a plan now, which was something. Next step, food. It had been a long time since breakfast and the body that had eaten the breakfast was now cinders and ashes. He pulled out his victim's wallet and opened it up; a nice thick wad of notes reassured him. Grinning, he crossed New Street, heading for the big McDonald's.

'Wotcher, Mike.' A hand clumped down between his shoulder-blades, momentarily depriving him of breath. Before his instincts – well, they weren't his instincts of course – had time to send the kill message down to his arms, he cancelled the instruction. Whoever this body was, it had friends. And dragon hunters need friends, the way fishermen need maggots.

'Hello yourself,' he replied, and turned to face whoever it was. 'How's things?'

'Not so bad.' His friend, a tall, gangling bloke with round bottle-end glasses, was giving him a funny look. 'Heard you were, um, dead,' he said. 'Like, blown up or something.'

'Not as such,' George replied. 'What you probably heard was that I was slowly dying of hunger and thirst, which is true. Of course, you can help me do something about that.'

The stranger laughed. What had he called him? Mike? Good old Mike, always cracking jokes.

'Good idea,' the stranger went on. 'We could have a couple of pints, then maybe go for a Balti. Suit you?'

'Sure.' Mike's friend started to walk, presumably knew where he was going. George fell into step beside him.

'Haven't seen you about for a while now,' said Mike's friend.

'You know how it is.'

'So what's it like, working with the great Bianca Wilson?'

George put two and two together, and got a mental picture of a fast-swinging lump hammer narrowly shaving his ear. 'Eventful,' he said. 'Quite an education, in fact.'

'I'll bet.'

In front of them, a pub doorway. Oh good, we seem to be going in here. I could just do with a—

He stopped dead. Ah *shit*!

Sitting at the bar, staring at him, were Bianca and—

'Christ, Bianca, there's my body. Hey, grab him, someone. That's the bastard who stole my body!'

It's mortifying enough to be loudly accused of theft in a public place. To be accused by *yourself* ... George, as always in such circumstances, gave serious thought to running away, but his erstwhile friend was standing between him and the door, giving him ever such a funny look.

'You bastard!' Bianca was yelling at him too. 'Don't just stand there, Peter, grab the swine!'

Who the hell was Peter? Oh, him. The treacherous bugger who'd brought him here. Stronger than he looks, our Peter. George's arm was now twisted up behind his back and there was very little he could do about it. Behind the bar, an unsympathetic-looking girl was muttering

211

something about ringing the police.

'Let go of me,' he grunted. 'I'm a saint.'

Peter tightened his grip. 'You're a *what*?'

'A saint. You deaf or something?'

'That's right,' said Bianca, grimly, 'he is. If he tries to make a run for it, break his sodding arm.'

'Hang on,' Peter was saying. 'If he really is a saint—'

'That does it,' said the barmaid. She picked up the phone and started pressing buttons.

George struggled, painfully. 'You realise this is blasphemy,' he gasped – breath is at a premium when you're being half-nelsoned over a bar. 'You'll fry in Hell for this!'

'You *bastard*!' His body – Saint George's body – had a hand round his, Mike's, windpipe. 'Give me back my body *now*, or I'll bloody well throttle you. It.' The significance of his own words struck him and he relaxed his hold slightly. 'Here, Bee, is there any way of getting him out of it?'

'We could try death,' Bianca replied icily. 'Seems to work okay.'

The other occupants of the pub, though interested, seemed to regard saint-bashing as primarily a spectator sport. Wagers were being exchanged, theories aired. The barmaid had got through to the police and was giving what George felt was a rather one-sided account of the proceedings. It was time, he reflected, for a brilliant idea.

Available options; not an inspiring selection. Be mutilated by Peter, strangled by – who *was* that guy? Mike, presumably, whoever the hell he was, surgically dissected by the snotty sculptress or arrested by the cops. None of them, George admitted, felt intuitively right.

'Help,' he croaked.

The prayers of saints seldom go unheard. Just as Mike was saying that maybe Bianca's suggestion had something going for it, and the distant sirens were coming closer, there

212

was a refreshing sound of splintering glass, the thump of an unconscious body hitting the deck and a familiar voice at his side.

Father Kelly. And about bloody time, too.

'Of course he's a friggin' saint,' the priest was yelling. 'Can't ye see his friggin' halo, ye dumb bastards?'

'Keep out of this, vicar,' Mike said angrily. Fortunately, Father Kelly took no notice, or perhaps he was just enraged at being confused with an Anglican. More broken glass noises, Father Kelly proving he knew the uses of empty Guinness bottles. He'd apparently used one on Peter, because George could now move his arms. He straightened up, to see Bianca swinging a bar stool at him. Fortunately, he had just enough time to thrust Father Kelly into the path of the blow – loud thunk, priest drops like stone, never mind. Leaving Bianca holding a broken stool and looking bemused, he jumped nimbly over the dormant Peter, shoved open the door, kicked an advancing copper squarely in the nuts and legged it.

God, he couldn't help thinking, looks after his own.

CHAPTER FOURTEEN

'It's not on the map,' Slitgrind protested.

The van stood on the hard shoulder of the M6. In the front, Prodsnap and Slitgrind were poring over the vintage road atlas they'd found in the glove compartment.

'There it is, look,' said Prodsnap, pointing.

'No, you fool, that's Hull.'

'Maybe that's just lousy spelling.'

Slitgrind closed the atlas with a snap. 'Stands to reason,' he said. 'They don't put it on mortal maps, 'cos otherwise we'd have hundreds of bloody tourists blocking up the front drive all the time.'

It occurred to Prodsnap that maybe his colleague was being a trifle alarmist, but he didn't say anything. It was true, Hell wasn't on the map. He tried hard to remember the route the coach-driver had taken, but it had all been homogeneous motorway, with no landmarks whatsoever.

'We'll have to ask someone, then,' he said.

Slitgrind scowled. 'Don't be thick,' he replied.

'Someone who knows, obviously,' Prodsnap said. 'Shouldn't be too hard.'

'But ...' Slitgrind was about to protest, but the penny dropped. 'Do we have to?' he objected. 'Those people always give me the shivers.'

'Me too.' Prodsnap suited the action to the word. 'But they'll know the way and we don't. Looks like we don't have much choice.'

His colleague grimaced, acknowledging the logic. 'Well,' he sighed, 's'pose they're on our side. In a way.'

'Better the colleague you know, huh?'

Slitgrind shrugged and turned the ignition key.

'Give me the deep blue sea any time,' he muttered, and indicated right.

'I conjure you by Asmoday and Beelzebub, Sytray and Satan, eloi, elohim and Miss Frobisher, do please be careful, you nearly made me spill the Black Host ...'

Barbed whips of wind flicked cruelly through the slighted walls of the ruins of Castle Roche. The moon had long since hidden her face behind the clouds and the only light was the livid orange glow from the foul-smelling fire. In the shattered keep of the castle, five white-clad figures, hooded and barefoot, huddled inside the arbitrary confines of a chalked ring. Around them lay the horrible impedimenta of the Black Rite: pantangles, tetragrammata, a sword, a mutilated Bible, a goat's skull, a frozen chicken, slowly defrosting ...

'Are you lot going to be much longer?' demanded a querulous voice from outside the ring of firelight. 'It's *freezing*.'

The Great Goat sighed petulantly. 'These things can't be rushed, Miss – ah—'

'Filkins,' hissed the Lesser Goat. 'Sonia Filkins. She's Mrs Brownlow's niece, from the Post Office.'

'Can't I at least have a blanket or something?' whined

Miss Filkins. 'I'm getting all goosepimply. And it's damp. Auntie Edie didn't say anything about sitting in the damp.'

The Lesser Goat simpered slightly. 'I'm sorry,' she whispered. 'But Brenda's babysitting up at the vicarage, and now Yvonne's started college . . .'

'I know,' sighed the Great Goat. 'Maybe next time, Miss Frobisher. I can't really see any point in continuing under these conditions.'

Mournful silence. The Lesser Goat started to pack away the horrible impedimenta.

'If you've finished with the chicken,' said Miss Filkins, 'do you mind if I take it on with me? There's a really nice recipe in my magazine for chicken.'

'Please,' grunted the Great Goat, carefully snuggling the skull in cotton wool. 'Help yourself. Such a pity to let good food go to—'

He fell silent. Although he was right next to the fire, his legs were suddenly icy cold. He didn't look round.

'Miss Frobisher,' he croaked.

'Yes, Dr Thwaites?'

'Perhaps Miss, ah, Filkins needn't put her clothes back on *quite* yet.'

The Lesser Goat looked at him. 'But I thought—'

'*Over there.*' He jerked his head in the direction of the shattered tower. 'Um, by Asmoday and Beelzebub, Sytray and—'

'Excuse me.'

Miss Frobisher let out a little scream. The thurifer hastily stubbed out his cigarette. The sword-bearer, who was half in and half out of his vestments, made a grab for his trousers. Old Mr Blakiston, the Black Verger, dozed peacefully on.

'Excuse me,' repeated Prodsnap. He was carrying an electric torch and wearing an old Barbour jacket he'd found on a scarecrow, for the night was cold; but the firelight dazzled vividly on his hooves and horns. 'We haven't missed it, have we, only we got a bit held up. Roadworks on the A34 just south of Chipping Norton.'

'*Please* can I put my clothes on now, Miss Frobisher? I'm going *blue*.'

The Great Goat winced. 'Please be *quiet*, Miss Filkins,' he snapped. 'Um, would you, ah, care to join us? Quick, Miss Frobisher, the chicken!'

'You said I could have it!'

Prodsnap shivered, despite his Barbour. 'Please,' he said, 'don't go to any trouble on our account. We had something at a Little Chef on the way. We really only wanted to ask—'

'Bludy ew,' squeaked the thurifer. 'Issa bleedin' *deviw*!'

The Great Goat closed his eyes, mortified. First thing in the morning there'd be a vacancy for the post of Black Thurifer, and never mind the fact that Barney Philpot was the only twenty-four-hour plumber in the district. 'Thurifer,' he commanded, 'be quiet. By Asmoday and . . .'

Slitgrind nudged his colleague in the small of the back. 'For Chrissakes, Prozza,' he hissed, 'let's get out of here. I'm *scared*. Ow! That was my shin, you clumsy—'

'We were wondering,' Prodsnap went on, raising his voice slightly, 'if you could help us out. You see, we're lost, and—'

'Lost?' The Great Goat peered at him through thick-lensed bifocals. 'You mean, you fell with Lucifer, Son of the Morning, wantonly preferring the path of damnation to the—'

'Missed the bus,' said Slitgrind. 'Got left behind. I think they did it on purpose,' he added resentfully. 'Someone's going to cop it when I get home.'

The Great Goat's mouth was hanging open, like a broken gate. 'Bus,' he repeated.

'Outing,' said Prodsnap. 'To Nashville. And now we're having to make our own way home, and it's not actually shown on the map, so we were wondering if—'

'Hey.' The Great Goat felt a tug on his sleeve. 'These two,' the sword-bearer was muttering. 'They for real?'

'Of course they are, you foolish man!' hissed the Great Goat. 'Look at the horns! The tails!'

The sword-bearer shrugged. 'All right,' he said. 'Not what I expected, though.'

'Not what you ...!'

'Bit of a disappointment, really.'

'How *dare* you! These are ...'

He hesitated. Unshakable his faith might be, but there was something about the way that one devil was trying to hide behind the other that did tend to sap the forbidden glamour. 'Do excuse me asking,' he said apologetically, 'but do you gentlemen have any form of identification? Only, you see—'

'It's that Great Horwood lot,' muttered the sword-bearer, 'dressed up in a lot of fancy dress. Here, is that you, Jim Partridge? 'Cos if it is, you can forget having your car back by the weekend.'

Prodsnap blushed green. 'Sorry,' he said. 'We don't actually have cards or anything. Usually,' he added, with his remaining shreds of dignity, 'we don't feel the need.'

'Prozza—'

'Shuttup, Slitgrind. I'd have thought,' Prodsnap soldiered on, 'the horns and the hooves and all that, they do rather speak for themselves.'

'Cardboard and spirit gum,' sneered the sword-bearer. 'Do us a favour, Jim. You've had your joke, now bugger off.'

'Prozza,' Slitgrind hissed; Prodsnap noticed that he was grimly averting his eyes from something. 'There's a bint

218

over there with *no bloody clothes on*!'

Moments like these, Prodsnap reflected, made you realise that the Chardonays of this world do have their uses. Chardonay, of course, was nice and snug in the van, tied up and gagged, likewise the demon Snorkfrod. Now *she'd* know how to handle a situation like this, no trouble at all.

'Quiet!' he snapped, then turned to the Great Goat, who was peering disconcertingly at him over the rims of his glasses. 'Um.' He racked his brains. Something convincing; a display of black magic, perhaps, an anti-miracle. Trouble was, he didn't know any. Not much call for black magic when you're a clerk in the wages office.

The nasty, suspicious one was leering at him. He decided to improvise.

'Maybe this'll convince you,' he said, and threw something on the fire. There was a whoosh of flame and a loud bang. The sword-bearer leapt out of his skin. Old Mr Blakiston woke up, mumbled something about coffee and went back to sleep again. It had worked.

'What the Shopfloor was that?' hissed Slitgrind.

'Cigarette lighter,' Prodsnap hissed back. 'Now then, my, er, good man,' he went on, trying to look demonic, 'if you could just, I mean, I command you to give us directions. Now,' he added, and snarled. He inhaled a whiff of Black Incense and sneezed.

The Great Goat bowed humbly, felt in his inside pocket and produced an envelope and a biro. 'Now, if you go back the way you came as far as the Bunch of Grapes . . .'

Eventually, George stopped running.

Only when he was absolutely convinced nobody was following him, of course. One long life and one short (so far) but highly eventful one had taught him the value of running away as a solution to virtually all problems. The way he saw it, if you can run, why bother to hide anyway?

Absolutely no idea where he was. A road sign said Hockley Street, but even if it was telling the truth (George had, on a number of occasions, prolonged his first life by not taking local authorities' words for it – 'Sure, that dragon's dead; ain't that so, Mr Mayor?' and 'Yup, we fixed that bridge last October' were notable examples) it didn't actually get him very far. Chances were, Hockley Street was every bit as lost as he was.

But it did contain a pub and all that running had given George a thirst you could rub down paintwork with. With a sigh of satisfaction that would have convinced you he'd just created the world ahead of schedule and under budget, he leaned on the door of the public bar and flowed in . . .

Marvellous thing, the human brain. In its vast, multi-megabyte subconscious memory, it stores everything – *everything* – seen, heard, glimpsed, semi-noticed, unconsciously observed. If the librarians of the brain could get stuff up from the stacks just a little bit quicker, we'd all be supermen, and the planet would probably have been a radioactive shell back in 1906.

The Dun Cow, Hockley Street. Been there before. Recently . . .

As he walked in, Bianca was just explaining to the police officer (not the one who was still curled up in a ball, moaning softly; a different one) that the man who she'd tried to maim with a stool was guilty of art theft, causing explosions, attempted murder and innumerable counts of genocide. She'd never seen the priest before in her life, she could think of no reason why he should want to clobber two of her friends with beer bottles, and she was really sorry about his teeth, honest to God just an accident, probably the tooth fairy was on the phone right now to leading merchant bankers trying to raise some venture capital to finance such a major shipment . . .

Been there. Wrecked that. Got the summons.

George turned, smoothly and swiftly, but not swiftly enough. A hand settled on his shoulder like a speeded-up glacier. Someone enquired of him where he thought he was going, then sidestepped his vicious elbow jab, kicked his knees from under him and clocked him one with a Lowenbrau ashtray.

'It's him!' Bianca shrieked, pointing. 'Let go my arm, I want to *kill* him!'

So, apparently, did the witnesses Mike and Peter; and George, who majored in cheating at the University of Life, saw a tiny sliver of a chance. They rushed at him, heavy policemen dragging along behind them like slipped anchors. He accordingly dived towards them, taking the direction his captor least expected. Grabbing hands missed him on all sides. He vaulted onto a table; from the table to the bar top; skidded along the bar like a glass of whisky in a Western; braked sharply; kicked the barmaid neatly in the eye as she lunged for his ankles; hopped down and legged it through the kitchens. As it says in the director's cut of the Sermon on the Mount: Blessed are those that fight dirty, for they shall be one jump ahead.

'Stop him!'

The cook, assuming that the fast-moving character who'd just burst into his kitchen was a fugitive from payment, upended a tray of chilli over his head, causing him to misnavigate and cannon into the dustbin. It was then just a matter of scooping up his feet, tucking them in after the rest of him, putting on the lid and sitting on it; job done. If cooks were generals, wars would last hours, not years.

'He's in here!' the cook shouted. 'And he owes for twelve portions of chilli.'

Inside a dustbin, nose full of potato peelings and the

nasty things people leave on their plates after they've finished eating, even someone as resourceful as George has to take an enforced rest. If he's wise, he'll put the time to good use, analysing his position, evaluating the merits of alternative strategies, trying at all costs not to breathe in.

They emptied the bin on the floor – the cook joined the arrest roster; obstructing the police, assault with a wet colander – and fished George out. A policeman knelt down, handcuffs at the ready.

'Hey, sarge!' he screamed. 'The bloke's on fire!'

If you're not used to them, halos can look remarkably like burning petrol, worn externally. There was yelling, milling about, wrenching of fire extinguishers off walls. Some fool set off the fire alarm, adding deafening noise to the feast of sensory input. George wriggled and struck out. In close combat, a discarded Fairy bottle covered in pan scrapings can be as effective as an Ingrams gun.

'Grab the bastard!' somebody yelled, but you might as well have shouted 'Fix the economy!' to a gaggle of politicians. All that happened was that the barmaid got knocked into the sink and one policeman scored a direct hit on another policeman with the first exuberant jet from the fire extinguisher. After that it was sheer Brownian motion, Gorbals-style.

Emerging from the scrum, George scrabbled across the floor, hauled himself up by the dishwasher and headed for the door. Like Napoleon's at Waterloo, it was a sound strategy undermined by treacherous conditions. He stood on a second-hand fried egg, skated three yards and collided with Bianca, pushing her into the remains of the Black Forest gâteau. As he looked about him, George saw he was surrounded.

The saw *never say die* didn't mean much to George. He frequently said *Die*, or more usually, *Die, you bastard*!, generally when standing over a fallen opponent. The principle behind it, however, was a dominant influence on his life. Without looking down he trawled the worktop, snatched up the first thing that came to hand, levelled it at his attackers and snapped 'Freeze!' Three quarters of a second later, they realised he was threatening them with a cheese-grater, but three quarters of a second was all he needed. There was a window. He jumped.

Glass was still landing all around him when he opened his eyes. Scrambling to his feet, he launched himself forwards, aware that the window frame was full of swearing police-men cutting their fingers. He had the feeling that if they caught up with him, there'd be major sacrilege committed. He ran.

The back yard wall of the pub was low enough to swarm over if you weren't fussy about trifles such as broken glass. George dropped down the other side, turned over his ankle, sprawled headlong and banged his head against a car door in the act of opening.

'Get in!'

George lifted his head. 'Sorry?'

'I said get in. Come on!'

He looked up to see a black Mercedes, back door ajar, on the rear seat a wry grin with a human being attached to its back. Close at hand, angry policemen had discovered the yard gate was locked.

'Who're you?' George asked.

'My name's Stevenson,' the grin replied. 'And you're George. Pull your finger out, old son.'

'But—'

Chubby Stevenson reached inside his jacket, produced a .45 Colt (like it says in the Book: *blessed are the Peacemakers*) and pointed it at George's head. 'Chop chop,' he said, 'there's a good lad.'

George realised that it would be discourteous to refuse and got in.

'Have they gone?'

'Yes, Dr Thwaites.'

'Good.' Wearily, the Great Goat picked up the Black Chalice, shook out the last dregs of cold tea and put it back in its straw-filled shoebox. Nobody had said anything, but they all knew that the handsome silver goblet was about to resume its career as the Swerford Golf Club President's Cup. Having your nightmare come true is the final disillusionment.

'Dr Thwaites.'

'Mmm?'

'About next Thursday.' Miss Frobisher's voice was heavy with the embarrassment of betrayal; the same tone of voice Judas Iscariot used when telling the Chief Priest he'd rather have cash, if it was all the same to him. 'I've just remembered it's the Red Cross whist drive, so I won't be able to make it after all. I do hope—'

'Not at all, Miss Frobisher, not at all.' The Great Goat sighed. 'As it happens, I think I'm busy that day, too. What about you, Barney?'

The thurifer was about to explain that coincidentally, he'd probably be working late next Thursday, when all five of them became aware of a richer darkness, as some great shape interposed itself between them and the fleeting moon.

'Go away!' snapped the Great Goat. 'Can't you see we're closed?'

They ducked. As non-verbal responses go, a fiery tsunami unleashed about three feet over one's head is remarkably eloquent.

'Won't keep you a tick,' said the dragon.

224

About Good and Evil.

Kurt twitched impatiently. Moral philosophy had never interested him much, having as much relevance to his profession as a pipe-cleaner to the Mersey tunnel; if he'd wanted a lecture on ethics, however, his first choice wouldn't have been a word processor.

'Hey,' he said, 'save it for the customers, will you? I delivered the goods, just pay me and I'll split.'

You also have a dragon to kill, don't forget.

Kurt made an exaggerated show of looking round. 'Nope,' he said at last, 'don't see any dragon in here, unless he's hiding in the drawer disguised as a pencil. Look, pal, you do your job and I'll do mine, okay?'

No. Look at me. This is relevant.

With a sigh, Kurt perched on the edge of the desk and folded his arms.

'Shoot,' he said.

With pleasure. Good and Evil, then. Define Good for me.

'Huh?' Kurt thought for a minute. 'Good what?'

Not good anything. Just Good.

Kurt's eyebrow lifted, Spock-like. 'Dunno,' he said. 'All depends on where you're at, I guess. Like,' he went on, 'it's a good shot if you fire it and hit me, but from where I'm standing there ain't much that's good about it.'

The screen filled with glowing green ticks. *Very good, Mr Lundqvist, you're way ahead of me. Nevertheless, I'll explain further.*

'Why?'

Indulge me. Good and Evil are, of course, two sides of the same coin. What's good for me is bad for you. One man's Mede is another man's Persian. The current of morality is more often alternating than direct. That, I imagine, is scarcely news as far as you're concerned. Am I right?

'More right than Franco, buster. What's this to do with—?'

Please don't interrupt. You've been hired to kill a dragon. Dragons are Evil, yes?

'Guess so.'

Saints, on the other hand, are Good. Agreed?

'Yeah.'

Wrong. It all depends on the individual concerned. And even then, it's still very much a question of subjective interpretation. Take Saint George, for example.

'Huh?'

Saint George. Noted dragon-slayer. Come on, you must have heard of him. A legend in your profession, surely.

Kurt nodded. 'In his day,' he replied absently. 'Lotta blood flowed under the bridge since then.'

Nevertheless. A killer, Kurt. Someone who destroyed other intelligent life forms for money.

'A professional.'

A saint. And not just any old saint, but the patron saint of peaceful, law-abiding, animal-loving Albion. You know why that is?

'Never gave it any thought,' Kurt replied honestly.

Three thousand a year patronage allowance, that's why. And because no other saint of adequate seniority was prepared to be associated with a cluster of wet, foggy islands on the very north-western edge of the known world. Nobody could believe it when he volunteered. It was like asking to be made Secretary of State for Northern Ireland.

Kurt shrugged. 'So?'

So, with George as its patron, this poxy little cluster of islands built an empire, the biggest ever. Top nation for a time, this poxy little cluster; bigger than France or Italy or Germany, owned half of Africa, half of Asia. Remember Agincourt, Kurt? God for Harry, England and Saint George?

'I missed that game. I was working. Saw the highlights, but—'

Not bad for the last place God made, under the patronage of a hired killer. And God was an Englishman in those days. Results count for something, wouldn't you say?

'Do me a favour,' Kurt protested. 'All that time, the sucker was dead.'

Doesn't matter. When you're a saint, it's not what you do that really matters, it's what you are. George was the dragon-slayer. He won the Big Fight. He inspired generations of Englishmen to go out and beat the crap out of all foreigners. Name me a European country England hasn't beaten in a war. France? Twice. Germany? Twice. Italy, Spain, Russia, Norway, Austria . . .

'Greece,' Kurt interrupted. 'Switzerland. Monaco . . .' He fell silent. 'Okay, point taken,' he continued, 'but so what? That don't prove nothing.'

Wrong. The good guys are always the winners, aren't they? I mean, the President doesn't get up on the rostrum at the Victory Parade and say to all the world, 'Okay, we admit it, we were in the wrong but fuck it, we won anyway.' Who's Good and who's Evil is decided by trial by combat; it's the only way. Or can you admit the possibility of a scenario where the good guys are all stomped on and the baddies are singing here-we-go, here-we-go, when the final credits are actually rolling? You can't, not without your brain getting squeezed out your ears.

'Get to the point,' Kurt grunted awkwardly.

Simple. England prevailed because she was in the right, because George killed the dragon. How or why he did it doesn't matter a cold chip. Agreed?

'If I agree, will you pay me the money you owe me?'

But all that's changed now. England's finished. She's a suburb of Europe, the USA's poor relation, got about twenty-five per cent of the international stature of the Philippines. You

227

could saw Europe off at Calais and it'd be a month before anybody noticed. So what happened?

'I have this dreary feeling you're gonna tell me.'

The result must have been wrong, Kurt. There's got to have been a foul-up. The wrong guy must have killed the dragon. And that's why there has to be a rematch.

'Kurt shrugged. 'Okay,' he said. 'If I was the kind of weirdo who went along with that kinda crap, maybe I'd buy that too. But you want me to kill this goddamn dragon, so—'

After the fight, Kurt, after the fight. The dragon wastes George, you waste the dragon. The United States conclusively defeats the personification of Evil, and under the patronage of Saint Kurt proceeds to manifest its destiny. Everybody lives happily ever after. The screen filled with little wavy lines; cybernetic laughter. *That's why I've just arranged for George to be rescued. Can't very well go fighting dragons if he's doing three years for assault and battery.*

Kurt thought it over for a while.

'Once I've killed the dragon,' he asked, 'do I get paid?'

Of course.

Kurt nodded. 'Okay,' he said. 'That's my definition of a happy ending.'

You heard all that?

Chubby nodded to his laptop and smiled. 'You bet,' he said. 'I thought you handled that very, um, adequately.'

He'll do what he's told. After all, what else are people for?

'Indeed.'

Talking of which . . .

Chubby sighed. Whenever the blasted box of tricks went all parenthetical on him and started ending sentences with three dots, he knew he was in for something more than usually shitty. 'Hm?'

After he's dealt with the dragon, kill him.

CHAPTER FIFTEEN

'With respect.' Lin Kortright whitened his knuckles around the telephone, swivelled his chair, bit the end off a cigar and spat it into the ashtray. 'With respect,' he repeated, 'you guys are obviously experts in the recycled Time business, but you don't know the fight game from *nothing*. Otherwise . . .'

Traditionally, sudden explosions of devastating elemental power have to be heralded by fair warning. Civil wars and the deaths of princes, therefore, are announced by comets and portents. Cyclones and tempests are preceded by gathering clouds and torrential rain. And Lin Kortright says, 'With respect.'

And then something extremely peculiar happened.

Mr Kortright *listened*.

Which is a bit like opening your daily paper and seeing that because of hitherto undetected design faults God has just issued a recall notice on the human race. You don't expect it. Large chunks of the fabric of reality start to come away from the joists.

'Yeah,' he said, eventually. 'Yeah, you're right, we could

do that. Say, that's a pretty neat idea. Only wish I'd thought of that myself.'

No sooner had the words left his mouth than six lifeboatloads of rats lowered themselves over the side of The Universe As We Know It and started to row like buggery. For Lin Kortright to say, 'You're right' in a room containing no mirror was utterly, absolutely . . .

'Brilliant,' he added. 'Hey, man, I'm beginning to wonder if you need me in on this at all. Seems to me you got it all sewn up already.'

Distant thunder rumbled. Eagles towering in their pride of place beat a hasty retreat, while mousing owls exchanged evil glances, rubbed their talons together and said, 'Right, let's *get* the bastards.' The air crackled with static.

'No, really,' Mr Kortright went on, 'in the circumstances I couldn't possibly accept ten per cent. The most I'd feel justified in taking would be five, and even then . . .'

Normality flung a few things in a suitcase and emigrated.

To hype a big fight, you have to follow set procedures. First, you must find a few toothless old duffers for the contenders to massacre, by way of setting the scene. Then you book the chat-show appearances so that the Boys can glower at each other over the presenter's shoulder. Then you hire a hall and start printing tickets.

In this case, however, the rules were there to be broken. For a start, there could be no warm-up fights for fear of irreparable damage to the Earth's crust. No late-show appearances for the contestants; the whole point of finding George was to make sure he'd be safely out of the dragon's way until the bell went for the first round. As for the venue, that couldn't be rushed; it had to be the Gobi desert, or the whole fight was off. Above all, the fight couldn't be advertised in case the two contestants found out that a fight was being organised.

Nevertheless, it seemed unlikely they'd have any trouble getting rid of the tickets, seeing that on the same morning both Nostradamus and Mother Shipton called almost simultaneously to point out that they'd predicted the fight and booked seats four hundred years ago. That just left the venue; a bit like saying, *We've made the sandwiches and filled the thermos, that just leaves turning the water into wine, plenty of time to do that after we've been to the supermarket.*

Cue Lin Kortright . . .

Furtively, guiltily, five shadowy figures crept along the wire perimeter fence, wirecutters in hand.

They were about to commit burglary. That's theft, and a sin.

They were about to burgle the nuclear power station at Sellafield. That's just plain *stupid*.

One of the five demons was considerably more relaxed about the proceedings than his colleagues, it must be said. When Chardonay came round and Prodsnap explained to him that there'd been a mutiny and he was now talking to *Captain* Prodsnap, his abiding reaction had been amazed, delighted joy. No more decisions. No more responsibility to the other members of the team. No more getting the blame for such mistakes on his part as the weather, the alignment of the moon with Mercury or the battle of Salamis.

The other four weren't so cheerful.

'Quit snivelling,' Prodsnap muttered sharply. 'Nothing to be afraid of. Home from home. Only danger I can foresee is, you'll all like it so much you won't want to leave.'

His followers exchanged glances. The mood of the meeting was that if he'd just taken out a correspondence course in dynamic leadership techniques, he'd be justified in asking for his money back.

'Run through it again,' Slitgrind said. 'Go on, one more time.'

'I've explained five times already.'

'I wasn't listening.'

Prodsnap sighed. 'Okay,' he said, 'listen up, people.' He'd heard the expression somewhere – the extremely nasty part of Hell reserved for Europeans who try to play American football, probably – and guessed it might be worth a try. Right now, *anything* was worth trying. 'In order to get home we really need that uranium, right?'

'We're fairly straight on that bit,' interrupted Chardonay mildly. 'I think it's the actual burglary where we're all still a bit at sea.'

Wish you were, thought Prodsnap savagely. 'What's so hard to understand?' he replied, demonstrating his contempt for the minor problems that confronted them with an airy gesture. 'We cut the wire, smash down the doors, go in, help ourselves. The pink bloody panther could cope with that. Now then, Slitgrind, you've got the wirecutters. Snorkfrod, you're doing the big hammer stuff. Holdall, you're the smallest, you climb in through the window of the main office and nick the keys. Chardonay, you go into the fusion chamber and lift the actual stuff . . .'

'Wilco, boss.'

'Chardonay, what the Shopfloor are you doing?'

'Saluting, boss.'

'Are you taking the . . .?'

Chardonay sounded genuinely hurt. 'No, boss. I want you to know that whatever happens, I'll be in there giving it my best shot. Sir,' he added.

Prodsnap shuddered. 'After that, it's just a matter of running for it. If we get separated, we meet up back at the van. All right so far? Splendid. Slitgrind, the wire.'

Snip. Snip. The alarm went off.

'Oh.' Prodsnap's face fell like a drunken trapeze artiste. 'That's a pity. Um . . .'

'Sir.'

'Not now, please—'

'Sir,' Chardonay insisted, 'I'd love to volunteer to locate and disable the alarm. I'd also be thrilled to bits if you'd let me stalk and neutralise the guards who may be hurrying to the scene. If that's all right with you.'

Prodsnap could feel one of his headaches coming on. 'Yeah, right,' he said. 'Whatever you . . .'

But Chardonay wasn't there any more. He'd already scaled the fence – it was electrified, but as far as a demon's concerned the difference between an electric fence and an inert one is the same as between thermal and standard underwear – and was inside the compound. Inside his own personal cloud, he caught a fleeting glimpse of silver.

'Well,' he said, 'that seems to have got rid of him. Snorkfrod, you wouldn't mind just nipping after him, make sure he's okay? Right, see you later.'

As Snorkfrod's fishnetted leg vanished over the top of the fence, Prodsnap counted up to five and rubbed his claws together.

'Looks like we've got shot of both of them,' he said perkily. 'Come on, lads, we've got work to do.'

Slitgrind frowned. 'Where're we going?'

'Round the front gate, of course. Come on, guys, let's move it.'

The main gates of the compound were manned by three large men and two Rottweilers. The dogs were no trouble – in Hell, they'd have been relegated to tartan-collar-and-knitted-jacket status. The guards would probably take some finessing.

'Excuse me.'

The guard's neck swivelled. 'Halt!' he snapped. 'Who goes . . .?'

'Excuse me,' repeated the voice from the darkness. 'I'm

coming towards you. Don't do anything hasty, I just want a quick word.'

Prodsnap advanced, smiling. As he stood under the floodlights, the guard made a funny noise in the back of his throat and started to edge away.

'Evening,' Prodsnap went on. 'You can see me all right, then?'

'What the fuck . . .?'

Prodsnap nodded. 'I know,' he said. 'No oil painting, huh? Bit on the weird side, too.'

Just sufficient motor function control remained in the guard's body to enable him to nod. Prodsnap extended a hand, but the guard didn't respond.

'I'll ask you to imagine,' Prodsnap was saying, 'what you're going to tell your sergeant when you report this incident. Think about it.'

The guard was already thinking.

'The way I see it,' Prodsnap said, 'I can picture you tapping on the office door. "Well?" says Sarge. "Sarge," you say, "the compound's overrun with horrible-looking devils."' Prodsnap paused for effect. 'Not much good for a bloke's career, is it, getting a reputation for seeing things? Now we both know you're not imagining this, but—'

'Pass, friend.'

That, however, was about as far as Prodsnap's plan took him. Somehow he'd imagined that once he was inside the wire, finding the uranium would present no great problem. He didn't know what he expected – a glow? Fingerposts saying *This Way To The Nukes* – but he'd expected something. What he found was a settlement, certainly no larger than Manchester.

'Bugger,' he said.

Because the sirens were still yowling themselves silly, nobody much was about; there were a few harassed-looking types running around, jumping in and out of vehicles and shouting orders into walkie-talkies, others sedately walking, ticking things off on clipboards. Some men in overalls were creosoting windowframes. Four men in suits were eating sandwiches out of tupperware lunch-boxes. No uranium on display anywhere.

Oh well, only one way to find out. 'Excuse me.'

A tall, thin girl, big shoulder-pads, wearing what was either a skirt or a belt (impossible to say which), turned her head, double-took and said, 'Eeek!' Prodsnap advanced a step, wisely decided against smiling, and instead said, 'Hi.'

'Um. Hi.'

'Wonder if you could help us,' Prodsnap went on. 'We're looking for the, um, core. Do you happen to know where . . .?'

The girl backed away, her eyes big as melons. 'The core,' she repeated.

'That's right.' Prodsnap let his mind freewheel. 'We're the inspectors. You saw the notice, presumably?'

'I don't think I . . . Inspectors?'

Prodsnap nodded. 'You don't think we were *born* like this, do you?' he said, in a tone of voice that suggested that any further references to appearance would constitute gawping at the misfortunes of the disabled. Good ploy; a microsecond later, you could have sworn the girl hadn't noticed anything at all out of the ordinary in their appearance. 'Anyway,' Prodsnap went on, 'there was supposed to be someone here to meet us, but I think there may have been a bit of a mix-up . . .'

'Actually,' the girl said, 'I only work in Accounts, I don't actually know here they keep the, er . . .'

Prodsnap shrugged. 'Never mind,' he said, 'thanks anyway. There isn't a map or anything, is there?'

The girl thought for a moment. 'Well,' she said, 'you

could always try the Visitors' Centre, I suppose. You know, where they have all the tourist stuff. It's just over there, by the gift shop.'

It was Holdall's idea to steal a van. The first one that came to hand was a mobile canteen, with tea-urns, film-wrapped sandwiches, KitKats and packets of crisps. Slit-grind parked it outside the Visitors' Centre with the engine running while Prodsnap went in. He'd found an overcoat and a cloth cap in the back of the van; it was like putting an Elastoplast on a severed limb, but it was the best he could do.

'Excuse me . . .'

'Eeek!'

Suddenly, Prodsnap felt very weary. His mind went blank. All he could think of was the direct approach. Only the one woman behind the desk. He cleared his throat.

'Yes,' he said, 'you're right. I'm a fiend from Hell. Actually, my name's Prodsnap, and although I do live in Hell I'm really only a wages clerk, and right now I'm on holiday, off duty. Have you got a problem with any of that?'

'N-no.' The woman seemed to be frozen rigid. Had she pressed a hidden buzzer or panic button? Well, only time would tell on that one. 'How can I h-help you?'

'A map of the complex, please. Is there a guided tour, anything like that?'

The woman looked at him. Hadn't, she enquired, the company who organised his tour dealt with all that? She produced a roster. Which group did he say he was with, exactly?

Oh, the Shopfloor with it. 'Listen, love,' Prodsnap growled. 'The purpose of our visit isn't exclusively tour-ism.'

'No?'

Prodsnap shook his head. 'Actually,' he said, 'it's theft.

236

Tell me where the uranium is and everything'll be just—'

'*EEEEK*!' More bloody alarms, sirens, the works. Paranoid, the lot of them. Just happen to mention you wanted to swipe their uranium and the whole place goes apeshit.

'Thank you,' Prodsnap said, 'you've been most helpful.' He was about to run when an idea struck him. He slowed down, strolled nonchalantly outside and leaned up against the side of the van, trying to look like a hideous mutant Maurice Chevalier.

'For Christ's sake,' Slitgrind hissed, 'what do you think you're doing? Can't you hear the . . .?'

Prodsnap nodded. 'Any second now,' he replied, 'security'll turn up. They're bound to know where the core is. We'll ask them.'

'But—'

'Who do you reckon's likely to be more scared? Us of them, or them of us?'

Sure enough, security arrived; about fifty of them, armed to the teeth and looking distinctly apprehensive. To counter all their weaponry, Prodsnap had a smile, which he'd been able to practise once or twice in the van's wing-mirror while he was waiting. He ambled up to the fiercest-looking bloke he could see, said 'May I?', took his gun and ate it.

'My name's Prodsnap,' he said. He waved his talon. 'And this is Slitgrind, and this is Holdall. We're from Hell. Could you take us to where the uranium's stored, please? Sorry to bounce you like this, but we are in rather a hurry.'

'Fire!'

Prodsnap closed his eyes. No point expecting to see edited highlights of his past life because there wasn't time. Idly he wondered whether what was about to happen to him would be death or just some kind of extremely rapid transdimensional lift.

Nothing happened. A thousandth of a second became a

hundredth, a hundredth became a tenth. That's the bummer with long-distance travel, he reflected, all this standing about waiting.

He opened his eyes just as the gunfire started. About time too, he muttered to himself, then he realised that nobody was shooting at him.

They were shooting upwards, at the dragon.

By the time Mike and Bianca got out of the police station it was lunchtime. Since there was nothing else they could usefully do, they decided to go for a curry.

'On balance,' Mike said over the pappadoms, 'I can't say I'm all that bothered. Never liked the old body much, after all. I'm not exactly crazy about this one, but a change is as good as a rest. Could be a whole lot worse, after all.'

Bianca nodded. 'Glad you see it that way,' she replied. 'Wish they'd hurry up, I'm starving.'

'You can have the last pappadom, if you like.'

'Thanks, I will.' She did. 'What with one thing and another,' she went on, 'I can't remember the last time I had a proper meal. Plays hell with your metabolism, all this meddling in the supernatural.'

Mike shrugged. 'I'm all right,' he replied. 'Saint George must have had something to eat quite recently. I know I only met him briefly, and under peculiar circumstances at that, but I can well believe he wouldn't be the sort to neglect his carbohydrates.'

'Me too.' Bianca dipped the last fragment in the mango chutney. 'Does it feel odd?' she asked. Mike nodded.

'A bit,' he replied. 'The arms are a bit short and the waistband's on the large side. Still, like my mum used to say when I was a kid, I expect I'll grow into it.'

'Can't really say it suits you. Mind you, neither did the old one.'

238

'That's me all over. Leading fashions, not following them. You'll see. In six months' time, everybody'll be trying to look like this.'

'I knew a girl once who had her nose done. You know, cosmetic surgery. Had a crisis of identity about it, so she said. Mind you, if I'd forked out ten thousand quid to be made to look like a parrot, I'd probably be asking myself all sorts of difficult questions.'

The food arrived. 'Now there's a thought,' Mike suggested. 'If only we could suss out exactly how this bodies-and-statues thing worked, we could make an absolute fortune.'

'The word *We*, in context . . .'

'It'd be amazing,' Mike went on. 'You know; for a modest fee, you too can have the body of a young Greek god. The hell with nose jobs, we're talking total physical remodelling here. Have you any idea what the total revenue of the slimming industry amounts to in an average year?'

'Mike—'

'Not to mention the private health care aspect. Is your body clapped-out, leaking oil, slow to start in the mornings? Chuck it away and get a new one.'

'Mike,' Bianca said, 'just what the hell are we going to do?'

'About the dragon?' Mike replied. 'And Saint George and the fabric of reality as we thought we knew it? Who says we've got to do anything?'

'I do.'

'Bianca.' Mike did his best to look serious, although he wasn't entirely sure he knew how to do it in the new body; he hadn't yet worked out, as it were, which lever was the indicators and which was the windscreen wipers. 'I don't think it works like that. People like us aren't supposed to get involved in this kind of thing. Rescuing the planet's not

239

down to us. Save three worlds and you *don't* get a free radio alarm clock.'

'Nevertheless.'

Mike tried a different tack. 'And besides,' he said, 'even if you were able to do anything about anything, how the hell do you know what's the right thing to do? I assume,' he added, 'you'd insist on being tediously conventional and doing the right thing.'

'Naturally. Oh come on, Mike, use your common sense, it's obvious who's in the right and who's in the wrong.'

'Is it?' Mike took advantage of the high level of dramatic tension to swipe some of Bianca's nan bread. 'Go on then.'

Bianca frowned. 'Well, the dragon, of course. Stands to reason.'

'You reckon?'

'Mike, that bastard stole your body. My statue. He tried to kill you.'

'The other bugger succeeded in killing me. Or had you forgotten?'

'But that was an accident!'

It was Mike's turn to frown. 'Sixteen people, Bianca, one of them me. All right, it wasn't deliberate, but I don't think the bastard actually cared very much.'

'But George killed all the dragons,' Bianca protested. 'It was genocide. They were innocent people—'

'Not people. Only humans are people. Innocent animals.'

'Okay, okay. But they'd never done him any harm, and he killed them.'

'Enjoying the lamb? My chicken's nice.'

'That's *different*.'

Mike shrugged. 'If you say so. Look, I'm not saying George is the good guy, either. Of course he's not. All I'm saying is, it's not precisely simple and straightforward.

Most particularly, it's not the sort of thing where you can make up your mind on the basis of which contestant's cuddlier and has the nicest eyes.' Mike paused, partly for effect, mostly because his food was going cold and he knew his priorities. 'Appearances count for fuck-all in this. Particularly,' he added, 'since you made all the appearances.'

Bianca thought about that for a moment. 'That's the point, though,' she said. 'Surely. I mean, if anybody *knows* these guys, it must be me. It was me designed them. I made them what I wanted them to be. And I guess I always believed, deep down, that the dragon was somehow the good guy. I think I carved him that way.'

'More fool you, then. You finished with the lentils? I'm hungrier than I thought.'

'Mike,' Bianca said, 'I can't explain it, I just *know*.'

'I used to say that in exams, but they wouldn't believe me. And I did know, too,' he added. 'Usually because I had the answers written on my shirt-cuff.'

'Mike—'

'Actually,' he went on, 'that's amazingly profound. You see, my answers were right but they didn't count because I made them wrong by cheating. The same goes,' he added, with his mouth full, 'for Life. And all that stuff.'

Bianca didn't say anything. She seemed to have lost her appetite, and Mike finished off her pilau rice. It's wicked, he explained, to waste good food.

'All right,' she said eventually. 'So what do you think we should do?'

'Have some coffee.'

'OK. And then?'

'I'll know after I've had my coffee.'

'Mike . . .'

He leaned back in his chair. 'Bee,' he said. 'Shut up.'

241

*

The dragon swooped.

He could smell the uranium; a nasty, chemical smell that made his mouth taste. And he could smell demons.

And then he could see them. They had humans all round them, which was a nuisance because he really didn't want to have to kill any more of them. It was the difference between stalking a man-eating lion in the long grass and running over a dazzled hedgehog.

Eggs and omelettes, he told himself. Omelettes and eggs.

Something like hail or sleet pinged off his scales and he realised that the humans were shooting at him. Bloody cheek. If they weren't careful, they could put his eye out. He opened his wings, climbed, banked and came in again; a steeper, faster approach, making himself a very difficult target indeed. He knew; he'd had the practice.

'Snorkfrod,' pleaded Chardonay, 'you'll break him if you do that. *Please* put him down.'

The she-devil scowled. 'He aimed a gun at you. I'm going to pull his—'

'No you're not. I'm responsible for all breakages. What you've done to their fence is bad enough.'

'All right.' The sentry fell two feet, hit the ground, squirmed like an overturned woodlouse and ran. 'I love it when you're masterful, Mr C,' the she-devil simpered. 'You remind me ever so much of Kevin Costner.' Chardonay didn't know who Kevin Costner was, but sincerely hoped he wasn't litigiously minded. 'Right,' he said. 'I think we'd better head back to the van, this clearly isn't going to—'

'Mr C.'

'I know.' Chardonay, who had flung himself face down on the ground, picked himself up and stared at the huge, fast-moving shape hurtling through the sky. 'It's him. That bastard . . .'

'Do you want me to get him, Mr C?'

The expression on her face – eager, thrilled to bits at the chance of doing something to impress and please – was almost heartbreaking. She would, too, he realised, if only I said the word. And maybe she'd succeed. If she failed, it wouldn't be for want of extreme savagery. But he couldn't do it. The spirit was sufficiently psychotic, but the flesh was weak. She wouldn't stand a chance.

'Don't be stupid. And get down before he sees you.'

'Righty-ho, Mr C.'

'Not on top of me, please. I can't breathe.'

'Is this better?'

'I can breathe, certainly. But would you mind just . . .?'

The slipstream from the dragon's passage hit them like a hammer, and for the first time Chardonay appreciated the extraordinary power and strength of the bloody thing. It was going to take a whole lot more than just the five of them to cope with it. In fact, it wouldn't be a foregone conclusion if the whole damn Department turned out against it. There was, quite simply, no way of telling how powerful the monster was, apart from picking a fight with it, of course. That's like saying there's one simple way of discovering what height you can drop a porcelain vase from before it breaks.

'The Shopfloor with this,' Chardonay said. 'Let's get out of . . .'

The dragon swooped.

Three of them, at least. The other two were bound to be around here somewhere. Besides, he reflected, I have this notion that if I go around letting off fireworks too close to this uranium stuff, pinpoint accuracy is going to be somewhat academic.

Hmm. Pity about that. Maybe it's not the prettiest country in the world, but I could see where you could easily get fond of it.

Omelettes and eggs, boy. Omelettes and eggs. He focused and put his wings back. The soldiers dropped their guns and ran for it; the demons stayed where they were. For some reason.

'Trust me,' Prodsnap yelled. 'He knows that if he flames off here, he'll risk blowing up the power station, and then it'd be goodbye Europe. He won't do that.'

'You reckon?'

'Of course.' Prodsnap closed his eyes. 'He's the good guy.'

'How'd you figure that out?'

'Easy. George tried to kill him and couldn't. Speaks for itself. So all we have to do is keep perfectly still and the bugger'll peel off and fly away.'

'Is that a promise?'

Prodsnap nodded. 'Trust me.'

Job done.

The dragon banked again. Where the three demons had been, there was now just a big scorch-mark, a little molten rock. And a nuclear reactor going badly wrong.

Pity about that.

Never mind.

Omelettes and eggs.

CHAPTER SIXTEEN

'**O**h,' said Chardonay.

'At least it didn't see us,' Snorkfrod replied, emerging from behind a pile of used tyres. 'Just as well, really, because if it had, we'd be—'

'Yes. Quite.' Odd, he reflected. Given that he was now a naturalised citizen of Hell, he hadn't expected to be terrified by the sight of fire ever again. Quite nostalgic, really.

'Mr C.'

'Huh.'

'I don't want to worry you at all, but I think this whole complex is about to blow up.'

Why is it, Chardonay caught himself thinking, that whenever there's a truly awful crisis, humans set off a ghastly, shrieking alarm? Mood music? Muzak? Even now, with the sky boiling and waves of heat you could bake cakes in, there were still humans busying about with clipboards and brown cardboard folders, convincing themselves it was all just a drill. Why do we wear our fingers to the bone trying to torment these people? They do a far better job of it left to their own devices.

'We'd better be going, Mr C,' Snorkfrod urged. 'Come *on*.'

She tried to pull his sleeve, but he shook his arm free. 'No,' he said; and then looked round, trying to spot the smart-arse ventriloquist who'd hijacked his body to make such a damnfood remark. 'No, we can't just run. We've got to stop it happening. It's our *duty*.'

Snorkfrod's eyes were as large and round as manhole covers. 'Mr C,' she hissed, 'this whole place, this whole *country*, is about to blow up. There's nothing we can do. We'll be—'

'Yes there is. There must be.'

Snorkfrod's talons closed round his shoulder, nearly ripping it off. 'Don't be bloody stupid,' she shrieked. 'We're demons, we're from bloody *Hell*, it's not our responsibility.'

'Yes it is.' Chardonay carefully prised her talons apart and lifted them off him. 'We're officers of the central administration. And we're here, now, where it's happening.' He heard himself saying it; otherwise he'd never have believed he could say anything like it. Stark staring . . .

'All right, Mr C. What can we do?'

He stared at her. Leadership? Love? Both of them daft as brushes? She was smiling at him. God, it was like being followed round by a great big stupid dog. If she had a lead in her mouth it wouldn't look out of place.

'You sure?' he asked.

'Of course I'm sure, Mr C. Where you go, I go.'

In which case, Chardonay reflected, it serves the silly bitch right.

'Um,' he said. 'Okay. Yes. Er, follow me.'

From safe to critical in four and a half minutes; too fast. Even a direct hit from an ICBM shouldn't have made it all happen so quickly. There was absolutely nothing anybody could do. Even running away would be a waste of energy.

Two minutes.

Chardonay's instinct told him to go by the heat; where it was hottest, that's where the heart of the problem would be. Heat in itself didn't worry him at all –

– Except this was *not* hot. Back on Shopfloor, the accountants'd have forty fits if they found anywhere as hot as this. *Turn it down*, they'd shriek, *have you any idea what last quarter's fuel bill came to*?

'Are we going the right way, Mr C?'

'Getting warmer, definitely. Dear God, how can they get it as hot as this?'

Ninety-eight seconds later, Snorkfrod shoulder-charged a massive lead-lined chrome steel door. When she collided with it, she found it was red hot and *soft* . . .

'Bingo!' Chardonay blinked, found he had to look away. 'Oh shit, now what?'

Seventeen seconds to go. Chardonay's brain raced, performing feats of pure maths he'd never have believed himself capable of. Pointless in any event. There was only one thing that might conceivably work, and they were to all intents and purposes dead already, so why waste time doing the sums?

Chardonay turned to Snorkfrod. She was glowing bright orange and on her face was an expression of part horror, part rapture.

'Oh, Mr C,' she said, in that gushing, cloying, Black-Forest-gâteau-with-extra-cream voice of hers. 'It's all rather grand, isn't it? Being together at the end, I mean.'

Gawd help us. For a moment he wondered if Snorkfrod's unconquerable soppiness might be the only thing in Creation wet enough to put out the fire. On balance, probably not.

'I love you, Mr C.'

247

'Er, yes. Super. Now, when I give the word . . .'

And, even as the two of them hurled themselves down onto the core and were reduced instantaneously into atoms, Chardonay did catch himself thinking, *Well, yes, if things had worked out different* . . .

There's nothing like bizarre and absolute annihilation to bring out the romantic streak in people.

Chardonay's last, pathetically futile idea was that the physical bodies of demons are the most heat-resistant material in the known cosmos. Throw two demons onto the fire, like an asbestos blanket onto a burning chip-pan, and there's a very slight chance you might put it out.

He was, of course, wrong. A whole brigade of spectral warriors might have done the trick if they'd parachuted in about eighty seconds earlier, before the meltdown entered its final phase. Two little devils leaping in at the last moment were always going to be as effective as an eggcupful of water thrown into a blast furnace.

A lovely gesture, then; but completely pointless. Heroism is one thing, physics is something else. At the moment when the two demons threw themselves into the fire, only a miracle could have prevented the final cataclysm.

Define the term miracle.

It's got to be something Good – who ever heard of an Evil miracle? And it must be impossible or it doesn't count.

That leaves us with something nice that simply can't happen but does. Examples? Well, if we forget about tax rebates for the time being, how about a nuclear pile suddenly cooling down at the very last moment? Or two fiends from Hell giving their lives to save millions of innocent people?

Miracles do happen, but only very, very rarely; like the

hundred-to-one outsider suddenly accelerating out of nowhere to beat the odds-on favourite. You could make an awful lot of money betting on miracles, provided you knew for certain they were going to happen. But that, too, would be impossible. Nice, but impossible.

Wouldn't it?

Unpalatable theological truth number 736: behind every miracle, there's usually an awful lot of syndicated money.

'Just like that?' Chubby enquired.

Just like that.

Chubby sat still and quiet for a while, letting his mind skate round the implications. Just then, he'd have given anything for a simple pie-chart diagram showing how much of his soul was still his own. Not, he imagined, all that much.

'So that's what we needed the dragon for,' he said. 'God, I must be getting thick in my old age.'

Not really. It took a genius to think it up in the first place. It would take a genius of almost equal standing to work it out from first principles. Don't be too hard on yourself just because you're not a genius.

It helped, Chubby found, to walk up and down, burning off a little of the surplus energy that his pineal gland was pumping into his system. 'A dragon,' he said, 'because nothing else on Earth would actually be crazy, wicked, stupid enough to torch a nuclear reactor and blow up a country.'

And even then I needed a pretext, so he wouldn't suspect what I was really up to. Hence putting a contract out on the demons. Rather neat, I thought.

'Whereupon,' Chubby went on, 'you laid a whopping great bet on the outcome. What odds did you get? Thousand to one?'

You think I'd go to all that trouble for a handful of piddling loose change? No, the odds were very satisfactory, thank you.

'Splendid. I do so like a happy ending.' Chubby sat down behind his desk, broke a pencil and ground the bits into the carpet with his heel.

Another thing. You're being too hard on my old friend Fred.

'Fred? Oh sorry, I forgot.'

You said crazy, wicked, stupid. Fred's none of those things. That's the mistake everybody always makes around dragons. I should know, I am one. Or had you forgotten?

'I did manage to remember, thank you.'

Dragons – Impossible, of course, for glowing green words on a screen to have any expression. Any subtext has to come from the mind of the reader. In Chubby's eyes, at least, the words on the screen grinned.

Dragons, you see, simply don't give a damn. Good and Evil's just biped stuff. Sure, you believe in it, the same way you used to believe in Father Christmas when you were little. We don't, is all. We don't mean anything by it.

'I see.'

I doubt that. And you know something else? I couldn't give a shit.

Chubby gave the screen a long, level stare. For some reason, he found he could, without wanting to look away. His mind searched for a word and a word came: alien.

I thought they were little green men with radio aerials sticking out of their ears.

Chubby shook his head. 'Nah,' he replied. 'You could get fond of little green men.'

'Hello,' said Prodsnap, without looking up. 'What kept you?'

Chardonay sat down in the seat next to him. 'Had to save the planet,' he replied. 'Any idea what sort of a mood He's in?'

Prodsnap shook his head. 'I haven't heard any shouting,' he replied. 'On the other hand, that's not necessarily a good sign.'

The five demons, wearing makeshift bodies issued to them from the huge wicker hamper colloquially known as the Dressing-Up Box, were sitting in a draughty corridor outside an office marked *Personnel Manager*. It isn't mentioned in Dante's *Inferno*, mainly because Dante had always hoped one day to sell the film rights and so he wanted to keep the whole thing basically upbeat and free from utterly negative vibes. The famous inscription about abandoning hope was nailed above the lintel.

Snorkfrod nudged Chardonay in the ribs.

'We'd like you lot to be the first to know,' Chardonay said, saying it with all the passion and enthusiasm of the little voice in posh cars that tells you to fasten your seat belt. 'Snorkfrod and I are engaged.'

'Strewth.' Slitgrind pulled a face. 'So you've been in already, have you?'

'I beg your pardon?'

Slitgrind nodded towards the office door. 'That's your punishment, is it, Char? I always knew he was a vindictive bugger, but . . . Hey, Prozza, mind what you're doing, that was my shin.'

Prodsnap switched on a silly grin. 'Congratulations,' he croaked. 'I hope you'll both be very . . .'

The door opened. A secretary fiend, lump-headed and shark-jawed, beckoned them.

'He'll see you now,' she said.

'Sugar Fred Dragon?' Mr Kortright suggested.

Nah. Tacky.

'Matter of opinion. All right then, Rocky Draciano. I like that. It's got class.'

251

Tacky.

'Honey George Sanctus?' There was a slight edge of desperation in the agent's voice. Self-doubt wasn't usually a problem for Lin Kortright, in the same way that Eskimos don't lie awake at night fretting about heatstroke. This client, though, had him rattled.

Lin. It smells. Come on, you're supposed to be good at this sort of thing.

'I am.' He'd nearly said *I was.* The sweat from his armpits would have irrigated Somalia.

Sure you are, Lin, sure you are. Now then, the venue. Any progress?

Kortright nodded, realised that the screen couldn't see gestures (or could it? He was getting distinctly offbeat vibes off this thing. As they say in the Business, never work with computers or children). 'It's in the bag, Nosher,' he replied confidently. 'All set.'

'Set? Or set-set?'

'Set-set. I got a signed agreement with the Mongolian Ministry of Tourism and War—'

Tourism and War?

'Historical reasons, Nosher. Genghis Khan. The ultimate in encounter holidays, remember? Anyway, we've got a million-acre site between Mandalgovi and Dalandzadgad, they're gonna build us an airstrip—'

Fine. I'll leave all that sort of thing to you. As far as I'm concerned, all we really need is a very big flat space with a rope round it, and two corners.

Kortright's brow creased. 'Corners?'

Yes. You know; in the white corner, we have Saint George, representing Good, and in the black corner . . .

'Ah. Right. Got you. I'll fix that, no problem. Now then, the cola concession, I've got the Pepsi guys up to six million, but I'm expecting a fax any minute—'

Yes, yes. Deal with it, Lin, there's a good fellow. 'Bye for now.

The screen in Mr Kortright's office went dark. Another screen in Chubby's bunker (reinforced chronite, guaranteed to withstand anything less than a direct hit from a neutron star) flicked on.

Chubby.

'Now what?'

Just a few things. Transport . . .

'All done.' Chubby frowned. 'You got any idea how much a ship that size costs per day?'

Yes.

'Then you'd better – oh.' Chubby hesitated. 'Any chance of a few quid on account?' he asked. 'Only, what with one thing and another, all this is causing me slight cashflow problems, plus I'm neglecting my business. I've got orders to meet, you know.'

Correct. Mine. And you will obey them without question. Lemons.

'I'm sorry, I thought you just said lemons'

That's right. For the contestants to suck between rounds. Make sure there are plenty, will you? Or do I have to do everything myself?

'All right, Chubby replied, offended, 'keep your keyboard on. I've got a containerload of lemons on their way from Australia, together with sixty gallons of aviation fuel for the dragon. Apple brandy for George. Not too much, don't want him falling over. Okay?'

Well done. Finally, then; how are you actually going to get them onto the ship?

Chubby smiled. 'I'm way ahead of you there,' he replied. 'How'd it be if we tried the old Ark routine? You know, a couple of days' synthetic rain beforehand, then I go around telling everybody I've had this message from God—?'

Chubby.

253

'Yes?'

Don't try my patience, chum. I think I used to have some, but I haven't seen it around since 1946, and it's probably gone off by now. Get it sorted, there's a good lad.

The screen went blank. Chubby stuck his tongue out at it. Obviously it knew, but Chubby no longer cared terribly much.

This, he said to himself, is getting out of hand.

It was something, he knew, with the big gambling syndicate. You didn't need to be Einstein or A.J.P. Taylor to work out that Nosher had been behind the original syndicate, the one that persuaded the dragon to throw the fight first time round, back in the Dark Ages. And it was as clear as a lighthouse on a moonless night that this rematch was going to be a fix as well. The question was, which one was he going to fix this time?

And – big question, this – who did the syndicate bet *with*? It takes two to make a wager, and the last time he'd passed the local Coral office they hadn't been offering odds on the fight. So who was the mug punter the syndicate were fitting up? Who had that sort of money, anyhow?

God? No, strictly a matchsticks player. (And you thought all those forests in South America were just scenery?) Who, then? He shook his head. None of his damn business, anyhow.

Here's hoping, he muttered to himself, it stays that way.

Don't be too hard on them, Phil.

I WON'T. JUST ENOUGH SO THEY WON'T SUS-PECT.

Good result, huh?

YOU WIN THIS TIME, NOSHER. NEXT TIME, MAYBE YOU WON'T BE SO LUCKY. NOT, I SOME-TIMES GET THE IMPRESSION, THAT LUCK HAS

ALL THAT MUCH TO DO WITH IT. I MEAN, WHY EXACTLY *DIDN'T* THE FUCKING THING BLOW UP?

Can't imagine what you mean, Phil. Anyway, I'm looking forward to getting your cheque. Or shall we make it double or quits?

Outside, in the corridor, Chardonay and company could hear the thundering of the voice, but couldn't make out the words. Some other poor bastards getting their fortunes told, they assumed.

YOU'RE ON, NOSHER. HERE'S TO THE NEXT TIME, RIGHT?

After a hard afternoon's work in her studio – God, the Victoria Square project! Running about chasing the dragon was all very fine and splendid, but she had a commission to fulfil – Bianca had a quick sandwich and went straight to bed.

She slept badly.

Chasing the dragon – well, quite. There was still an influential part of her brain that wanted to treat the whole bloody mess as some sort of giant hallucination; bad dope, the DTs, cheese before bedtime, whatever. That was the comforting explanation. Untrue, of course. Whatever it was, it was still going on. In fact, she had an uneasy feeling it was approaching some sort of crisis. In which case, the sensible course of action would be to be standing outside the travel agents' when they opened tomorrow morning, asking for details of off-peak reductions to Alpha Centauri.

When a person starts worrying about something around half past three in the morning, she might as well let out Sleep's room and put his clothes in the jumble sale because he sure as hell isn't coming back. To take her mind off it all, she switched on the TV and hit the Satellite news.

*. . . In Victoria Square, Birmingham might somehow be
linked to the wave of spectacular art thefts in Florence, Rome
and Venice. In addition to Ms Wilson's two monumental works
for the Birmingham City Corporation, no fewer than seventeen
major statues have vanished from Italian collections, including
eight Berninis, three Donatellos, three Cellinis, a Canova, the
Giambologna Mercury, and of course the priceless Michaelangelo David. The only lead that Interpol have so far is the
discovery of fingerprints apparently resembling those of Kurt
Lundqvist, a notorious mercenary and soldier of fortune,
discovered at the scenes of all the robberies in Italy. Lundqvist,
however, is believed to have been killed some time ago in
Guatemala, although the only part of him actually recovered
was his left ear. Counter-insurgency experts have pointed out
that, to judge by his past record, Lundqvist would have been
perfectly capable of carrying out this remarkable string of
burglaries single-handed, not to mention single-eared; indeed,
they claim, if there's anyone capable of shrugging off Death as
a minor inconvenience, that man would be Kurt Lundqvist,
believed by many leading experts to be the link between the
former Milk Marketing Board and the Kennedy assassination.
This is Danny Bennett, Star TV News, in Florence.*

Bugger sleep. As far as Bianca was concerned, Macbeth
had beaten her to it.

Seventeen statues. Seventeen is sixteen plus one. Sixteen
people die in an explosion in a community centre in the
West Midlands; sixteen statues simultaneously go missing
in Italy. No, seventeen statues, sixteen plus one.

Who was the seventeenth statue for?

She was still paddling this bizarre notion around in her
brain when the phone rang, making her jump out of her
skin. It took an awful lot of determination to pick the blasted
thing up.

'Hello?'

'Bianca Wilson?' American voice, like audible sandpaper.

'Yes, that's me. Who's this?'

'You probably don't know me' the voice replied. 'My name's Kurt Lundqvist.'

CHAPTER SEVENTEEN

'Mr Lund—'

The small man jumped out of his skin, whirled round and slapped a hand across her mouth. 'Don't call me that, you crazy bitch,' he hissed. 'C'mon, this way.'

He set off at a great pace, not looking round. Bianca had to break into a trot to keep up. He was shorter and squarer than she'd expected, but he moved as if he was tall, lean and wiry. Another one of these unquiet spirits in a Moss Bros body? It was as though the whole world was on its way to a fancy dress party.

'Okay,' he said, finally halting. 'We can talk here.'

Maybe, Bianca thought, but hearing what we say is going to be another matter entirely.

In reply to her earlier question, 'Where can we meet?' Kurt had suggested New Street station. They were now in the bar of a pub in John Bright Street, empty except for the barman and the loudest background music on Earth. This was foreground music. It filled all the available space, like Polyfilla.

'Thank you for coming,' Kurt said.

'Sorry?'

'I SAID . . .' Kurt edged his chair nearer and leaned forwards. 'I said thanks for coming. Listen up, doll. This is a mess.'

Bianca frowned slightly. He'd told her briefly about the circumstances of his return to Earth and she reckoned 'doll' was a bit rich coming from an animated Action Man. Given the communication difficulties, though, she let it ride.

(Note: to save time and preserve the Niagara-like cadences of the dialogue, all the backchat – 'Sorry, what did you say?'; 'Speak up, for Chrissakes'; 'Dammit, there's no need to shout' etc, – has been edited, as a result of which, this passage has already been awarded the Golden Scissors at the 1996 Editor of the Year Awards, and the BSI kitemark.)

'I know,' Bianca replied. 'You made it sound like there was something you could do about it.'

'There is,' Kurt replied, sipping his Babycham. 'But not on my own. That's where you come in.'

'I see.'

'Doubt that.' Kurt finished his bag of pork scratchings, squashed up the packet and dropped it into the ashtray before lighting a cigar. A large cigar, needless to say; Bianca had seen smaller things being floated down Canadian rivers. 'Let me just fill you in on the background. Maybe you know some of the stuff I don't, at that.'

Between them, it transpired, they had a fairly good idea of the Story So Far, including recent developments and a progress report on the preparations for the Big Fight. 'So you see,' Kurt summarised, 'it's all a goddamn shambles.'

'Quite.' Bianca nodded vigorously. 'Worst part of it is, I can't seem to work out who's who. Goodies and baddies, I mean.'

'This,' Kurt replied sternly, 'ain't the movies. When

259

you've been in supernatural pest control as long as me, you learn not to make judgements about people. Sure, when I was young, I used to worry about that kinda thing; you know, *What harm did he ever do me?* and all that kinda shit. Nowadays, all I ask myself is, will the two-fifty grain hollow point do the business at three hundred and fifty yards. I guess it makes life easier, not giving a damn.'

'You do, though, don't you?'

Kurt nodded glumly. 'It's a bitch,' he replied. 'Unprofessional. That's what's got to me about this stinking job. Trouble is, my professional ethics say I gotta do the job I'm being paid for. Nothing in the rules says I can't share my concerns with an outsider, though; someone not in the business, like yourself.'

Bianca shrugged. 'I've got professional ethics too, you know. Mostly they're to do with leaving chisel-marks and not glueing back bits you accidentally break off. But I'm sure there's something in the Code of Practice about not letting dangerous statues fall into the wrong hands. I must look it up when I get back home.'

They looked at each other suspiciously across the formica tabletop; unlikely confederates (if we're confederates, Bianca muttered to herself, bags I be Robert E. Lee) in an impossibly confused situation. In context, they were probably the least likely do-gooders in the whole dramatis personae; the hired killer and the arms dealer. Maybe it helped that Bianca also dealt in legs, heads and torsos.

'I guess,' Kurt said slowly, 'in situations like this, all you can do is to try and do the right thing. Shit, did I really say that? This stinking job really is getting to me.'

'A statue's gotta do what a statue's gotta do?'

'Sure. Now, what *you* gotta do is like this.'

Thank you for calling Acropolis Marble Wholesalers Limited.

Unfortunately there's no one here to take your call, so please leave a message after the tone.

Beep. 'Hello, Bianca Wilson here. Could I have seventeen seven by three by three Carrara white blocks, immediate delivery, COD Birmingham. Thank you.'

Thank you for calling Hell. Unfortunately there's no one here to take your call, so please leave a message after the tone. Alternatively, for reservations and party bookings, please dial the following number. Thank you.

Thank you for calling Nkunzana Associates. Unfortunately there's no one here to take your call. Don't bother to leave a message; I know perfectly well who you are and what you want, I'm a fully qualified witch-doctor. Thank you.

'Have you ever,' Chubby said, apropos of nothing, 'been to Mongolia?'

The dragon looked at him. 'No idea,' he said. 'I've been virtually everywhere, I think, but usually I don't stop and buy a guide-book. What's Mongolia?'

Chubby shrugged. 'Desert, mostly. Very empty, not many people. Barren, too; large parts of it have as close to a zero per cent fire risk as it's possible to get on this planet. The sort of place where you could have a sneezing fit without burning down six major cities.'

'Sounds a bit dull,' the dragon said.

'It is. Very.'

'I could use a little tedium right now,' the dragon said, scratching his nose with a harpoon-like claw. 'I take it you're working round to suggesting that I go there.'

'Hate to lose you,' Chubby replied. 'It's been great fun having you here and all that. But, with all due respect, you're a bit hard on the fixtures and fittings.'

261

'True. Actually, it beats me how you people can live in places like this without dying of claustrophobia.'

'We're smaller than you are. We find it helps.'

The dragon yawned and stretched, inadvertently knocking an archway through the wall into the next room. 'Mongolia, then. What's your ulterior motive? Something to do with your Time business?'

'You know your trouble? You're cynical.' Chubby frowned. 'Usually with good cause,' he added. 'As it so happens, there is a small job you could do for me while you're there. Nothing heavy. You might find it helps stave off death by ennui. Entirely up to you, though.'

'Explain.'

'Well.' Chubby leaned back in his chair and hit the light switch. A projector started to run, covering the opposite wall (the only one still intact) with a huge, slightly blurred image of a vase of flowers, upside down. Chubby clicked something, and the picture changed into a view of the Great Wall of China.

'Familiar?'

'Seen it before,' the dragon replied. 'Doesn't mean anything to me, though. A wall is but a wall, a sigh is but a sigh.'

'Ah.' Chubby clicked again. The Great Wall came closer. 'This, my old mate, is no ordinary wall. It's big, it's famous and – now here's where my interest in the damn thing lies – it's very, very old.'

The dragon smiled in the darkness. 'Steeped in history, huh?'

'Positively saturated. Now, I got to thinking; sentiment aside, what does that lot actually do that a nice modern chain-link fence couldn't do, for a fraction of the maintenance costs? Whereas to me—'

'I get the picture,' the dragon interrupted, amused. 'You want me to steal it.'

Chubby clicked again. This time, the wall was covered in a view of the planet, as seen from space. The Great Wall was dimly visible, a thin line faintly perceptible through wisps of untidy cloud. Either that, or a hair in the gate.

'As you can see for yourself,' Chubby went on, 'it's the only man-made structure visible from outside the Earth's atmosphere. An eyesore, in other words. If Mankind ever gets round to colonising the moon, I'll be doing them a favour.'

'Quite. What do you want me to do with it after I've nicked it?'

Click. View of a completely barren area of desert. 'Just leave it there. One of my people will deal with it.'

The dragon smiled. 'A receiver of stolen walls? A fence?'

'How did I know you were going to say that?'

Half an hour later, the same picture show, the same basic introduction.

'Let's just make sure I've got this straight,' George said. 'Your organisation's going to steal the Great Wall of China?'

'Mphm.'

'And then they're going to dump it, out there in the wilderness.'

'Not wilderness, George. Prime development site. We paid top dollar for that land. It has the advantage of being as far from anywhere as it's possible to get without having to wear an oxygen mask.'

George shrugged. 'You know your own business, I s'pose. What do you need me for?'

'Caretaker, basically,' Chubby replied. 'I was just thinking, since your friend with the wings and the bad breath is still very much on the loose, you might quite fancy a month or so in the last place anybody would ever think of looking.'

'Good point.' George nodded decisively. 'Much obliged to you. It'll be a pleasure.'

The lights came back on.

'Pleasure's all mine,' said Chubby.

A bit over-complicated, surely?

Chubby scowled. 'Listen,' he said. 'I hate to bother you with silly mundane things like the way I earn my living, but for the last couple of months my business has been at a complete standstill. I've got orders I can't fill and staff on full wages sitting around with nothing to do. Two birds, one stone, and everybody's happy.'

The screen went blank and the little red light, whose purpose Chubby had never been able to work out in all the years he'd had the wretched thing, blinked twice.

I'm not happy about this.

'Tough. Sorry, but you said to find a way to get them both to the venue without arousing their suspicions and that's what I've done. And now, if you don't mind. I've got work—'

The pain hit him like a falling roof. The intensity of pain largely depends on which part of the victim it affects. Chubby's soul hurt. Toothache is nothing in comparison.

'Fuck you, genie,' he moaned. 'Let *go*, will you?'

Inside his head, Chubby could hear laughter. It was a very frightening sound.

Chubby, please. After all we've been to each other, I think you can start calling me Nosher. All my friends do.

'Then fuck you, *Nosher*. And now will you please stop doing that, before you break my id?'

Any idea how much of your soul I now own? I know you're curious. Go on, ask me.

The pain stopped and Chubby collapsed into a chair. 'Let me see,' he said, once he'd got his breath back. 'Well,

264

for one thing, we haven't had nearly as much of the your-wish - is - my - command - it's - my - pleasure - to - serve - you bullshit lately, which I find rather significant. And all these cosy chats we've been having recently must be taking their toll. I've been trying very hard indeed not to think about it.'

Forty-two per cent.

'Shit.'

No reason why that should be a problem, surely. We've always got on well enough, you and I.

'Like a house on fire,' Chubby replied. 'With you as the fire and me as the house. What happens to me when you get a majority stake? Do I die, or vanish, or what?'

Perish the thought. It's just that we'll see even more eye to eye, that's all.

'And when it reaches a hundred per cent?'

Then I shall be free.

'Hooray, hooray. And what about me?'

You'll be one of the lucky ones. Like Mr Tanashima.

Chubby frowned. 'Don't know him. Who he?'

Mashito Tanashima. Born 1901, died 1945. He worked in a bicycle factory in Hiroshima, Japan. Seven minutes before the atomic bomb exploded, he was killed in a road accident.

'Gosh.' Chubby smiled bleakly. 'Lucky old me, huh?'

The screen flickered. The red light came on and, this time, stayed on.

Yes. Let nobody say I'm not grateful.

Bianca stepped back to admire her work. A masterpiece, as always. Three down, fourteen to go.

The biggest problem had been getting hold of the photographs. First, she'd tried the local paper, but they'd got suspicious and refused to co-operate. The victims' families had virtually set the dogs on her. Finally, she'd hit

265

on the idea of sending Mike round pretending to be the organiser of a Sadley Grange Disaster Fund. She'd felt very bad about that, but he'd come away with all the photographs she needed.

The walls of her studio were covered in them; enlarged, reduced, montaged, computer-enhanced, until the very sight of them gave her the creeps. Sixteen very ordinary people who happened to have been in the Sadley Grange Civic Centre when it blew up. The victims.

So far she'd done Mrs Blanchflower, Mrs Gray and Mr Smith, and she was knackered. Straight portraiture, no dramatic poses or funny hats; they had to be as lifelike as possible or the whole thing would be a waste of time. The worst part of it all was the responsibility, because she wasn't the one who was going to have to live with the consequences for the rest of her life if she made a mistake. Accidentally leave off a toe, or get an arm out of proportion, and she'd be ruining somebody's life.

The hell with that, she told herself. Makes it sound like they're doing me a favour.

Yes. Well. And whose dragon caused all this mess in the first place?

'Mike,' she croaked, 'I need a brand new set of the big chisels, another hide mallet and coffee, about a gallon and a half. Would you . . .?'

'On my way.'

'Mrs Cornwall's nose. Could you do me a six by four enlargement of the wart? I can't see from this whether it's a straightforward spherical type or more your cottage loaf job.'

'No problem.'

She sighed, wiped her forehead with her sleeve. 'And when you've done that,' she said, 'if you could see your way to making a start on roughing out Mrs Ferguson with the angle grinder. I've marked her up, and it'd save ever such a lot of time.'

'Mrs Ferguson, angle grinder. Right you are.'

'Oh, and Mike.'

'Yes?'

'Thanks.'

Mike laughed, without much humour. 'That's all right,' he said. 'After all, what are friends for? Apart, that is, from heavy lifting, telling lies to next of kin, basic catering and other unpaid chores?'

'Dunno. Moral support?'

Mike shrugged. 'Don't ask me,' he said, 'my morals collapsed years ago. Be seeing you.'

Left alone, Bianca tried to clear her mind of everything except the technicalities of sculpture. Easier said than done; it was like clearing a pub on Cup Final night, only rather more difficult. The hardest part, unexpectedly enough, was the way the faces from the photographs stayed in her mind, plastered across her retina like fly-posters, even when her eyes were tight shut. That meant something, she felt sure, but she hadn't the faintest idea what.

'Excuse me.'

Kurt stopped dead in his tracks, closed his eyes and counted to ten. Once upon a time, that particular ritual had been a foolproof method of keeping his temper. Now all it meant was that he lost his rag ten seconds later.

'Hi,' he replied, cramming a smile onto his face, which had never been exactly smile-shaped at the best of times. These past few days, however, cheerful expressions tended to perch apprehensively on his features, like a unicyclist crossing a skating rink.

'Mr Lundqvist.' It was the Canova again. 'May I have a word with you, please?'

'Lady . . .'

Inside the Classical perfection of the Canova bivouacked all that was immortal of Mrs Blanchflower. By a prodigious effort of his imagination, Kurt had worked out a scenario where he would actually be pleased to see Mrs Blanchflower, but it involved her being in the water and him being a twenty-foot-long Mako shark. The only reason why he hadn't yet mortally insulted her was because he never seemed to be able to get a word in edgeways.

'Mr Lundqvist,' said the Canova. 'Now, as you know, I'm the *last* person ever to complain about anything, but I really most protest, in the strongest possible . . .'

Getting past Mrs Blanchflower, of course, was the beginning, not the end, of the aggravation. She was the worst individual specimen, yes, the gold medallist in the Pest Olympics, but there were fourteen others right behind her sharing silver. And it's no real escape to elude one Mohammed Ali only to be set upon by fourteen Leon Spinkses.

'SHUTTUP!' Kurt therefore bellowed, as he shouldered past the Canova into the main area of the Nissen hut. That bought him, albeit at terrible cost, a whole half second of dead silence.

'And LISTEN!' he said. 'Thank you. Now then, folks, gather round. And you better pay attention, 'cos this is important.'

Fifteen statues all started to complain at once.

'Okay.' Kurt backed away and climbed onto a chair. 'Okay,' he repeated, just loud enough to be audible. 'If you guys don't want to go home, that's up to you. Well, so long. It's been . . .'

Silence. Well, virtual silence. Mrs Hamstraw (by Bernini) finished her sentence about the sultanas in her muesli (she'd *told* him, *three* times, the doctor had told her no sultanas) and Ms Stones reiterated her threat of writing to Roger Cook for the seventy-eighth time, but apart from that there was a silence so complete, Kurt felt he knew what it must have been like at five to nine on the first day of Creation.

'On the other hand,' he went on, calm and quiet as the Speaking Clock, 'anybody who wants out had better listen good. Now, then . . .'

'I still say that, after last time . . .'

The Great Goat turned his head about twenty-seven degrees and scowled.

'Thank you,' he said, in a voice you could have freeze-dried coffee in. 'Shall we proceed?'

A nice man, Dr Thwaites; all his patients would have agreed, likewise his colleagues, his neighbours, even some of his relations. A kind man, for whom nothing would ever be too much trouble. A patient man, prepared to listen politely and attentively to every hypochondriac who ever thought mild indigestion was a heart attack. But flawed, nevertheless. Albert Schweitzer was the same, and likewise Walt Disney.

'If you insist,' muttered the Lesser Goat. 'Now then, where's that wretched skull?'

Because Dr Thwaites, having paid Farmer Melrose six months' rent for conjuring rites on Lower Copses Meadow, was damned if he was going to forfeit half his money – thirty pounds, fifty pence – with three months still to run. It was, as far as he was concerned, a matter of principle.

'When you're ready, Miss Frobisher. Now then.' He cleared his throat. 'By Asmoday and Beelzebub I conjure you, spirits of—' He stopped. If someone had just popped an apple in his mouth, they couldn't have shut him up quicker or more effectively.

'Don't mind us,' said the Captain of Spectral Warriors,

in a soft, speaking-in-church voice. 'Just pretend we aren't here, okay?'

The Great Goat would dearly have liked to do just that, but unfortunately it was out of the question. It takes a special sort of mental discipline to ignore five hundred of Hell's finest, in full battledress uniform, all displaced heads, unexpected limbs and weird appendages, creeping stealthily past you in the early hours of the morning.

''Ere, doc,' said the thurifer at his elbow. 'You're really good at this, aren't you?'

The Great Goat swallowed hard. 'Apparently,' he said. In his subconscious he was wondering whether he could persuade Mr Melrose to impose a retrospective rent increase, because the thought of performances like this every week for the next three months was enough to drive a man insane. He'd have to rethink all his cosy preconceptions about anatomy, for a start.

'Excuse me.' The Captain was talking to him. He forced himself to listen.

'Sorry, I was, um, miles away. Can I, er, be of assistance?'

'We're trying to get to—' The Captain consulted a clipboard. 'Place called Birmingham. Would you happen to know where that is?'

'Birmingham.'

'That's right. I've got this map here, but it hasn't photocopied terribly well, so if you could just set us on the right track, we'd be ever so grateful.'

His disbelief suspended on full pay, the Great Goat felt in the pockets of his robes and produced a pencil and the back of an envelope.

CHAPTER EIGHTEEN

The Big Fight.

Seen purely from the viewpoint of logistics and administration, it was the greatest show in history. Everybody who was, had been or would be anybody was there, and the complexities of setting up a switchboard for the retrospective booking office had taxed Mr Kortright's ingenuity to its fullest extent. Or take the popcorn concession, a chronological disaster poised to happen. Any popcorn eaten by visitors from the past or the future would leave a serious imbalance in the fabric of reality, particularly after it had passed through the visitor's digestive system and entered the ecology of his native century. In order to compensate, Kortright had had to estimate the amount of popcorn likely to be eaten and arrange for compensatory amounts of matter to be removed from/added to a whole series of past and future destinations. As for the envelope of artificial Time in which the auditorium was contained, it had cleaned out Chubby's stocks down to the last second. God only knew what would happen if the fight lasted beyond the twelfth round.

All these problems, of course, were more than adequately accounted for in the price of the tickets; and that caused yet another organisational nightmare, given that (for example) in order to pay for his ticket the Emperor Nero had leeched out the entire economy of the Roman Empire, which could only mean total fiscal meltdown, violence in the streets and the fall of the Empire several centuries ahead of schedule. Fortunately, a client of Lin Kortright's who controlled various financial syndicates in the first century AD was able to offer bridging finance; disaster was averted, ten per cent was earned for the Kortright Agency, and Nero (who paid the first instalment of the loan by insuring Rome and then burning it down) was sitting in the front row, munching olives and trying unsuccessfully to persuade Genghis Khan to take St George to win at fifteen to one.

There was also a band, and cheer-leaders, and huge spotlights producing as much light and heat as a small star, and commentators from every TV station in Eternity all getting ready to provide simultaneous coverage (*live* was, in context, a word best avoided), and cameras and film crews and sound crews and men in leather jackets with head-phones on wandering about prodding bits of trailing flex and engineers swearing at each other, and all the spectacle and pageantry of a galaxy-class sporting event. The panel of judges (two saints, two devils and, representing the saurian community, two enormous iguanas) were sworn in. There was an awed hush as the doors at the back swung open to admit the referee; no less a dignitary than Quetzal-coatl, Feathered Serpent of the Aztecs. Had his worshippers in pre-Conquest Mexico known that when he promised to come again to judge the quick and the dead, he meant *this*, maybe they'd have been a little bit less forthcoming with the gold and blood sacrifices.

It was nearly time. The food vendors left the auditorium,

trays empty. The roar of voices dwindled down to an expectant buzz. All it needed now was for the contestants to show up, and the contest for the ethical championship of the universe could begin.

And Kortright turned to Stevenson and said, 'Well, where the fuck are they?'

And Stevenson leant across to Kortright and said, 'I thought they were with you.'

'Finished,' Bianca gasped.

Forget the aesthetics for a moment; in terms of sheer stamina, it was the greatest achievement in the history of Art. With an effort she unclenched her cramped fingers sufficiently to allow chisel and mallet to fall to the ground and collapsed backwards into her chair, only to find there was someone already sitting in it.

'*Sakubona, inkosazana.*' Bianca did a quick Zebedee impression, looked down and saw a little, wizened man curled up in her chair. He was wearing a leopard skin with lots of unusual accessories, and holding a fly-whisk.

'Hi,' she replied. 'You must be Nkunzana. I didn't hear you come in.'

'No,' the witch-doctor replied, 'you didn't.' He nodded towards the statues. 'Impressive,' he said.

'All my own work,' Bianca replied, flustered. 'You know what you've got to do?'

'Is the Pope a Catholic?'

'Right. Well, I'd better leave you to it, then. Do you need anything? Um, hot water, towels, that sort of thing?'

Nkunzana shook his head. 'A fire and a pinch of dust, my sister,' he replied. Before Bianca could offer further assistance, he produced a big brass Zippo from the catskin bag hung round his neck.

'Dust?'

Nkunzana grinned and drew a fingertip across the surface of the table beside his chair. 'I know,' he said. 'I remind you of your mother.'

'In certain respects,' Bianca replied. 'She could never have worn leopard, though. Not with her colouring.'

The witch-doctor shrugged; then, with a tiny movement of his thumb he lit the lighter, sprinkled the dust and mumbled something that Bianca didn't quite catch.

And . . .

. . . *Action*!

Cut to –

Kurt's Nissen hut (you could call it the Galleria Lundqvist, but not, if you want to see tomorrow, while he's listening) where fifteen statues with strong West Midland accents are telling him exactly why they refuse to have anything at all to do with his plan.

Sound effects; rushing wind, a shimmering tinkly sound (shorthand for magic), deep and rumbling unworldly laughter, followed by –

Silence. The other noises off were just meretricious effects, the parsley garnish on a slice of underdone magic. But the silence, the absence of querulous whining, that's something else. Uncanny is an understatement in the same league as describing the Black Death as a nasty bug that's going around.

Kurt reacts; he says –

'*YIPPEE!*'

– and so would you if you'd just spent several weeks cooped up with Mrs Blanchflower, Mr Potts and thirteen others, extremely similar. In their place, fifteen of the world's finest, most exquisite statues; solid masonry from head to toe, without enough sentience between the lot of them to animate a DSS counter clerk. Kurt looked round, gazing ecstatically at each one in turn; compared to him, stout Cortes would have made one hell of a poker player. No more whingeing. No more threats to report him to the English Tourist Board. No more caustic remarks about the lack of brown sauce to go with the escalops of veal.

Slowly, almost like a moon-walker in the deliberation of his movements, Kurt got to his feet, crossed the floor and picked up a frozen tiramisu he'd been defrosting for tonight's dinner. Then he planted himself in front of the Canova, stuck his tongue out, raised the tiramisu and rubbed it into the statue's face.

Cut to –

Bianca's studio. Bianca has just left, leaving the door unlocked and a note.

Cue sound effects, as above, except for the silence. Instead, fade in a yammering fugue of West Midland voices raised in pique. And hold it, as –

The statues realise something has changed. Typically thoughtful, Bianca has left a big, clothes-shop style mirror facing them. They see themselves. Let's repeat that line, for emphasis. They see . . .

Themselves . . .

Silence.

And then one of them – yes, absolutely right, it's Mrs Blanchflower – says –

'*Well*!'

– and they all start talking at once. No need to report the exact words spoken; the gist of it is that they're all as pleased as anything to be out of those ridiculous, freezing cold, uncomfortable statues and back in their own bodies again, *but* that doesn't alter the fact that they've been mucked about something terrible (with hindsight, scrawling *Sorry for any inconvenience* on the mirror in lipstick wasn't the most tactful thing Bianca ever did) and just wait, someone hasn't heard the last of this, my lawyers, my husband, my Euro MP...

At the back of the room, a scruffy heap which at first sight was only a bundle of old rags sits up, double-takes and huddles down again, furtively pulling a mangy leopard skin over his head and hoping to hell they haven't spotted him. Too late –

With a simultaneous yowl of fury, fifteen angry ex-statues turn on Nkunzana, shaking fists and demanding explanations. The witch-doctor freezes, unable to move. In the course of his professional activities, he's daily called upon to face down swarms of gibbering unquiet spirits, quell mobs of loutish ghosts by sheer force of personality, command fiends and boss about the scum of twelve dimensions. Piece of cake. Faced with Mrs Blanchflower and the other Sadley Grange victims, he's a mongoose-fazed snake.

Spirits, he hisses under his breath, *I command you by Nkulunkulu, the Great One, get me the hell out of here*!

The spirits attend, as they are bound to do when a master of the Art orders them. Although only the *isangona* can see them, they're there, as present as a college of notaries, standing at the back of the room looking extremely embarrassed.

Sorry, amakhosi, they mouth noiselessly. *This time, you're on your own.*

Cut to –

A police station on the very northernmost edge of China. Behind the desk, a sergeant slumbers dreamlessly under a circular fan.

The door opens. Enter three very embarrassed-looking men.

276

They wake the sergeant, who grunts and reaches for his notebook and a pen. What, he enquires, can he do for them?

They nudge each other. Imploring looks are exchanged. Nobody wants to be the one who has to say it.

A spokesman is finally selected. He clears his throat. The expression on his face is so pitiful the desk sergeant starts groping instinctively for a clean handkerchief.

We'd like, the spokesman mumbles, to report a theft.

Right. Fine. What's been nicked?

A wall.

Sorry?

A wall. Quite a big wall, actually.

Look, sorry about this, did you just say somebody's stolen a *wall*?

That's right. Here, come and see for yourself.

Bemused policeman rises, totters sleepily round the edge of the counter to the station door, looks out.

Look, is this some sort of a joke, because if it is . . .

And then he sees the mountains. And that's really *weird*, because everybody knows you can't see the mountains from here. Because the Wall's in the way. Further up the valley, yes, you can see the mountains. Down here . . .

The sergeant begins to scream.

Cut to –

A brain-emptying vastness of sand, where the reflected heat hits you like a falling roof. Shimmering in the heat-haze, the sun flickers like an Aldis lamp. No wicked stepmother's smile was ever as cruel as the unvarying blue of the pitiless sky. Sun and sand; yes, sun and sand we got, but you really don't want to come here for two weeks in August.

Deserts are, by definition, big; and this is a big desert.

The dragon, waiting in the shade of the huge stack of cardboard boxes that contains the Great Wall of China for his scheduled rendezvous with Chubby and the boys, looks tiny; from a distance you'd think he was a wee lizard, the sort of thing desert travellers evict from their boots every morning before setting out.

But that's perspective playing tricks on you, because the dragon is, of course, huge. And, more to the point, quite incredibly strong. Maybe you haven't yet realised how strong the dragon is; well, consider this. Between one and five am last night, this dragon single-handedly dismantled the Great Wall and lugged it here, boxful by boxful across the Gobi Desert, without making a sound or disturbing anybody. No real trouble; to the dragon, it was just like picking up so much Lego off the living-room carpet.

It was still, nevertheless, one hell of a lot of Lego, and the effort, combined with the heat, is making him sleepy. His soul (for want of a better word) is hovering in the middle air, looking down at the stack of boxes and thinking, *Pretty neat, huh?*

Then, suddenly, it starts to panic. Instinctively it makes to dart back into its body, but it can't. Imagine that nauseating feeling when you've just stepped outside to get the milk in and the front door slams shut behind you, locking you out. Normally, the dragon's soul would have the door kicked in and be back inside in twenty seconds flat. But this time, what with purloining walls all night and not getting much sleep while it was at it, it simply hasn't got the strength. Which is unfortunate, because . . .

Cut to –

Saint George, toiling wearily up a vast sand escarpment, on his way to the scheduled rendezvous with Chubby, the boys and a billion tons of hooky masonry.

He feels – strange . . .

Oh look, he mutters to himself, I'm flying.

Or at least part of me is. The rest of me – head, arms, torso, legs – is down there on the deck, flat on my face . . .

(*Cue rushing wind, shimmering tinkly sound, shorthand for magic, deep and rumbling unworldly laughter . . .*)

Nkunzana, moving with remarkable agility for a man of his advanced years, shinned out of the bathroom window, dropped five feet onto the fire escape, clattered down the steps like a ten-year-old and sprinted across the alleyway to where Kurt had the van parked, engine running.

'Quick!' he panted. No need to explain further. There was a squeal and a smell of burning rubber.

'Okay?' Kurt asked, glancing down at the road map open on his knee.

'No,' snapped the witch-doctor, 'it isn't. You might have warned me.'

'Warned you?' Kurt grinned. 'Hey, man, I wouldn't insult you. I mean, you being a witch-doctor and all, I'd have thought you'd have *known* . . .'

'The hell with you, white boy. Let's see if it's so funny when I've turned you into a beetle.'

Feeling that the conversation was becoming a little unfocused, Bianca interrupted. 'What Kurt meant to say was,' she said, 'is everything going to plan? With the, um, spirits, I mean?'

'Huh?' Nkunzana frowned, then nodded. 'Sure, no problem. The fifteen dead people are out of the stolen statues and into the statues you made for them. The same with the souls of the dragon and Saint George; I've conjured them out of their bodies, and the dragon'll be too knackered after all that heavy lifting he's been doing . . .'

The old man paused, his eyes tight shut, and chuckled. 'Hey, man,' he muttered, 'this is *fun*. I really wish you could see this.'

Cut to –

Three disembodied spirits, hovering in the upper air.

The first is the dragon, scrabbling frantically at the door of his magnificent, wonderful, all-powerful body. But he's too weak. He can't open the damn thing.

The second is Saint George, also unexpectedly evicted from his body by the Zulu doctor's magic. Not *his* body, strictly speaking; remember, he's been dossing down in the statue Bianca made for Mike to live in, which he stole when the dragon carbonised him on his return from the future.

George is just about to nip back in when he realises he's not the only disembodied spook out and about this fine Mongolian summer morning. A mere hundred miles or so to his west, he becomes aware of the soul of his oldest, greatest enemy, and, more to the point, the empty dragon body.

He hesitates. He thinks.

YES!

Well, wouldn't you? Think it over. Yours for the hijacking, the most powerful, the strongest, the most stylish, the fastest, the most heavily armed and armoured, the slinkiest piece of flesh ever in the history of the Universe, with the doors unlocked and the keys in the ignition. One swift, slick job of taking and driving away, and then we'll see exactly who's vapourising whom . . .

With a none too gentle shove and a merry shout of, 'Move over, asshole!', George heaved the dragon's enervated soul out of the way, scrambled into the dragon body and hit the gas. There was a roar and a stunning thump, as the beast's enormous wings scooped up air like ice-cream from the tub. Wild with fury and terror, the dragon's soul scrabbled desperately at its own body, but there was no way in. A fraction of a second later, the body had gone.

'Shit,' whimpered the dragon. He collapsed onto the sand and started to quiver.

The third spirit in waiting is Bianca's friend Mike. He has the advantage over the other two of knowing what's going on, and the moment George abandons his earthly overcoat and makes his dash for the dragon costume, Mike lets himself quietly out of Saint George, marble statue by Bianca Wilson, and tiptoes across the middle air to where his own familiar shape is standing, vacant and unlocked, among the dunes. He drops in. He rams the legs into first gear. He scrams.

And now the dragon's soul is alone. Ebbing fast, still weak from his exertions and the devastating trauma of watching his own body zooming off over the horizon with his mortal enemy at the controls, he flickers on the edge of dissolution. Why bother? he asks himself. Bugger this for the proverbial duffing up to nothing.

But not for long. Because dragons don't quit. And, as the saying goes, a third-class ride beats the shit out of a first-class walk. There, abandoned on the escarpment of a dune, stands Bianca Wilson's statue of Saint George, empty. Disgusted but grimly determined, the soul of the last of the great serpents of the dawn of the world drags itself through the dry, gritty air and flops wretchedly into George.

And notices something. And suddenly feels a tiny bit better, because it suggests, somehow, that more than meets the eye is going on.

Because, in the back window of Saint George, somebody has stuck a little bit of shiny white cardboard, with five words written on it in red lipstick. They were:

Yes, mutters the dragon, suddenly and savagely cheerful. Isn't it ever.

Like a salmon leaping the waterfall of the sun, the great dragon soared; wings incandescent, fire streaming off his flawlessly armoured flanks, the scream of the slipstream drowning out all sounds except the exultant crowing of his own triumphant soul, which sang:

Sheeeeit! Wow! Fuck me! Is this a bit of all right, then, or what?

Now bursting up through the clouds like a leaping dolphin, now swooping like a hunting eagle; now high, now low, as the intoxication of flight and power made his brain swim, his blood surge. Mine is the kingdom, the power and the glory, for ever and ever.

And then a light flashed soberingly bright in his eyes and he glanced down. There, on the desert floor below him, two men stood beside a Land Rover, on which was mounted a huge mirror.

Dragons have eyes like hawks – that's a very silly thing to say, because hawks are just birds, whereas dragons' eyes are the finest optical instruments in the cosmos; the point being, although the two men were a long way away, George recognised them easily. Chubby Stevenson and the man Kortright; he'd seen him about the place, though he didn't know who he was. Intrigued, he swooped.

'Hey,' Kortright yelled through a bullhorn. 'Where the fuck you been? Get down here like *now*.'

It then occurred to George that they didn't know it was him. They thought it was the dragon – his, George's, enemy. Yet these people were supposed to be his friends, good guys. The hell with that! He filled his lungs and took aim –

No, they'll keep. Let's find out what's going on before we fry anybody we might be able to use later.

'Hey,' George drawled. 'Where's the fire?'

'It's where it isn't that's pissed me off, man,' Kortright replied. 'C'mon, get your tail in gear, we got people waiting.'

'People?' George hovered, his front claws folded, a what-time-of-night-do-you-call-this expression on his face. 'What people?'

Stevenson, he noticed, was looking a little sheepish as he leaned over and whispered something in Kortright's ear. The agent stepped back and stared at him.

'You arrange the biggest fight of all time,' he said, 'and you never get around to telling the contestants?'

George quivered; the word *fight* had hijacked his imagination and was demanding to be flown to Kingdom Come. 'What fight?' he asked.

'You and Saint George,' Chubby replied. 'The rematch. I was, um, planning it as a surprise.'

'You succeeded.'

Chubby scowled. 'Dunno why you're sounding all snotty about it,' he replied self-righteously. 'That is what you want, isn't it? A chance to sort that little shit out once and for all? I mean, that *is* why you came back in the first place, right?'

'Sure thing.' George nodded vigorously. 'Teach the little toe-rag a lesson he won't live long enough to forget.'

'Well, then.'

A smile swept across the dragon's face, in the same way that barbarian hordes once swept across Europe. 'I call that very thoughtful of you,' he said, 'going to all that trouble just to please me. But what makes you think the little chickenshit'll have the balls to show up? If I was him, the moment I heard about the fight I'd be off.'

'He doesn't know about the fight, stupid.'

'You mean,' said George, grinning cheerfully, 'you set him up?'

'Yeah, yeah. Look—'

'From the outset?'

'Sure.' Chubby looked at him strangely. 'What's got into you all of a sudden?' he demanded.

'Not what. Who. But that's beside the point, we'll sort it out later. So, where should I go?'

Kortright pointed due north. 'You'll know what it is as soon as you see it,' he said. 'Hang round just out of sight till we show up with George. Then it'll be over to you, okay? And don't say I don't find you quality gigs, you ungrateful asshole.'

George nodded gravely. 'I think I'll be able to handle it from then on,' he said. 'Be seeing you.'

Not long afterwards, Chubby's helicopter landed beside the huge artificial mountain of packing cases that had appeared overnight in the middle of the desert, and two men climbed out, crouching to avoid the spinning rotor blades.

'George,' they were yelling. '*George*! Where is the goddamn . . .?'

They found him fast asleep in a sort of masonry igloo he'd made for himself at the foot of the mountain. This made their job much easier. Chubby slipped the handcuffs into place while Kortright woke him up.

'Hi, George,' Chubby said. 'Look, no need for alarm, but we need you to do something for us and we really haven't got time to convince you it's a good idea before we set off for the venue. This way, we can convince you as we go, and you won't waste time by running away and hiding.'

'Suits me.'

The two men looked at each other. 'Good of you to be so reasonable,' Chubby said. 'This way, then.'

284

In the chopper, Chubby explained that when he'd rescued George from the police in Birmingham, he'd had an ulterior motive.

'You rescued ... Yes, sorry, me and my tea-bag memory. Do forgive me, carry on.'

'Yup.' Chubby had a vague feeling that something was going wrong, but that was so close to his normal mental state that he ignored it. 'You see, it's this damn dragon.'

'Oh yes.'

'Sure.' Chubby sighed, his face a picture of frustration and annoyance. 'The bloody thing is starting to be a real pest, you know? Something's got to be done about it, before it ruins my business and destroys a major city or something.'

'I quite understand,' said the dragon, nodding. 'This planet ain't big enough for the three of us, that sort of thing.'

'Three? Oh, I see what you mean. Well, of course, I don't have to tell you, you want to see the fucker gets what's coming to him as badly as I do. Well, now's your chance.'

'Really and truly?'

'Really,' said Chubby, smiling, 'and truly. That's why Mr Kortright here –'

Kortright smiled. 'Hi, George.'

'Hi, Mr Kortright. Haven't we met somewhere?'

'Quite possibly, George, quite possibly.'

'Mr Kortright,' Chubby went on, 'and I have arranged this, um, fight to the death. You and Mr Bad Guy. We built you an arena and everything. You're gonna love it.'

'Quite,' said the dragon. 'Only, and I hate to seem downbeat here, don't you think the fight's going to be ever so slightly one-sided? I mean, him with the wings and the tail and the fiery breath, me with a sword? Not that I'm chicken or anything, but ...'

Kortright chuckled. 'Tell him, Chubby.'

'We've sorted all that,' Chubby said. 'We've got you some back-up. The best, in fact. The name Kurt Lundqvist mean anything to you?'

'No.'

Chubby shrugged. 'After your time, I guess. Well, just as the dragon comes hell-for-leather at you out of, so to speak, a cloudless sky, Kurt "Mad Dog" Lundqvist'll be poised and ready in a concealed bunker under the press box with a very nasty surprise for Mr Dragon. He won't know what hit him. And neither, more to the point, will the punters. They'll think it was you. Neat trick, huh?'

'Chubby.' The dragon looked shocked. 'Surely that's *cheating*.'

'Yes. You got a problem about that?'

The dragon's eyes gleamed, and if Chubby failed to notice, consciously at least, that they were yellow with a black slit for a pupil, that was his fault. 'Ignore me,' the dragon said. 'I think it's a wonderful plan. Thank you ever so much for arranging it all. You must let me find some way to pay you back.'

'George,' Chubby said, 'my old pal, forget it. I mean, what are friends for?'

The dragon shook his head. 'Chubby,' he said, 'and Lin. This is one favour I won't be forgetting in a hurry, believe me. Okay, let's go. I can hardly wait.'

CHAPTER NINETEEN

Kurt had allowed himself twenty minutes to get from Birmingham to the heart of the Gobi Desert. Thanks to the small flask of concentrated Time which Chubby had issued him with, it proved to be ample.

An imposing figure was waiting for him round the back of the gents' lavatory. It was wearing a Brooks Brothers suit over its lurid, misshapen body, and a pair of dark glasses perched on the bridge of its beak.

'Hi,' Kurt said. 'Sorry if I kept you waiting.'

'Bang on time, Mr Lundqvist,' replied the Captain of Spectral Warriors, handing over a suitcase. 'Here's the doings. Best of luck.'

Kurt grinned. 'Luck,' he said, 'is for losers. You got your boys standing by?'

'In position. You can rely on them to do a good job.'

Kurt picked up the suitcase. 'Be seeing you, then.' He started to walk away, but the Captain stopped him.

'Mr Lundqvist,' he said. 'I'm curious.'

'Yeah, but don't let it get to you. The shades help. A bit.'

'I'm curious,' the Captain went on, 'about which of them you're gonna take out. Yeah, sure I got my orders, I don't actually need to know at this stage. I was just wondering . . .'

Kurt grinned, a big, wide grin that'd make a wolf climb a tree. 'Watch this space,' he said. 'Then you'll know for sure.'

George circled, keeping high.

Born yesterday? Not him. Came down in the last shower? You must be thinking of somebody else. He hadn't slashed a path through the red-clawed jungle of combat theology to a Saintship without knowing when a situation was well and truly hooky; and if ever a set-up stank, it was this one. Souls don't just float up out of bodies for no reason; it takes big medicine to work a trick like that. And for it to happen just before a major set-piece battle between Good and Evil? Some of George's best friends were coincidences, but that didn't mean he trusted them as far as he could spit.

Well, he said to himself. And what would I do if I were fixing this fight?

Easy, I'd position a sniper somewhere in the arena. That way, when I come rushing in to scrag my enemy, the sniper blams me just as I'm about to put my wings back and dive. It looks like Saint George has killed me. Good triumphs over Evil for the second time running. Yeah. Well, we'll see about that.

He gained a few thousand feet and looked down. Below him, the huge arena looked like a tiny scab on the knee of the desert. It was packed with people; high rollers and fight aficionados from the length and breadth of Time. George chuckled. The way he saw it, spectator sports are at best a rather morbid form of voyeurism. So much better if you can participate directly in the action.

288

He started to dive.

The joy of it was that the deaths of all the people he was going to incinerate, by way of a diversion, would be blamed on the dragon (representing Evil, and doing a pretty spectacular job) rather than noble, virtuous Saint George (representing po-faced, one-hand-tied-behind-its-back Good). Given the dragon's track record, nobody would have the slightest problem in believing that he'd decided to zap a whole stadium full of humans for the sheer hell of it.

He took a deep breath.

In the white corner, the dragon lifted his helmet, blew dust from the liner and put it on. It was hot and stuffy and smelt of mothballs, and it wasn't made of asbestos. Bloody silly thing to wear in a dragon-fight, he couldn't help thinking.

With a sharp pang of anger and loss, he saw a familiar shape, far off in the harsh blue sky. Here he came, the bastard.

'Okay,' he said to the armourer. 'I'll have the sword now, please.'

The armourer grinned at him. 'Get real, buddy' he said. 'You gotta try and kill that thing, and you're planning on using an overgrown paperknife? Man, you're either stupid or crazy.'

The dragon was about to speak, but decided to look instead.

'Don't I know you?'

'You may have heard of me,' the armourer replied. 'My name's Kurt Lundqvist.'

The dragon stared at him. 'But aren't you meant to be down there somewhere? With a gun or something?'

Kurt shook his head. 'That, my friend, would be a bad move. I'd hate my last thought before I die to be, *God how could I be so fucking stupid?* I'm gonna stay right here, where it's safe.'

'Safe?'

Kurt nodded. 'Because,' he went on, 'if I've sussed that bastard George, he'll start off by zapping the audience, just to make sure there's nobody like me in there waiting to take a shot at him. That sound like the George you used to know?'

The dragon nodded. 'I won't ask how you know who I am,' he said. 'But we can't actually let the bloodthirsty lunatic kill fifty thousand people. What are we going to—?'

'Why not?'

'*Why not?*' The dragon gawped, gobsmacked. 'For Christ's sake, you idiot, that's *people* out there, it's your bloody species. And you stand there like a bloody traffic light saying Why not?'

Kurt nodded. 'Sure,' he said. 'Think about it. Nearly all these guys are playing hooky from their own time, right? And what sort of guys are they? You don't know? I'll tell you.'

The dragon grabbed his arm. The flying shape was getting closer. 'Not now, you bastard. *Do* something!'

'Those guys,' Kurt continued, calmly unhooking the dragon's hand from his arm, 'are your aristocrats, your statesmen, your notable public figures, captains of industry and generally mega-rich citizens. Now then, think open spaces. Town squares. Piazzas. Pigeons sitting on . . .'

Suddenly the dragon relaxed and began to laugh. 'Statues,' he said.

'Eventually the penny drops. Yeah, man, statues.' Kurt shook his head and sighed. 'Jeez, for a superior intelligence, you must be just plain dumb,' he said. 'Haven't you worked it out for yourself yet? You've been cruising around breathing fire, torching buildings, all that kind of crap, and *nobody's really died.* Even those –' Here Kurt shuddered, recalling his own sufferings. 'Those *ladies*,' he spat, 'in that hall in Birmingham didn't actually *die*. Nobody actually dies because of you, you moron. And you know why? Because you're the good guy.'

'I am?'

Kurt indulged himself with a theatrical gesture of contemptuous despair. 'Man,' he said witheringly, 'you are *dumb*. Look,' he went on, 'when you're the good guy, however hard you try to do Evil, you just can't hack it. Unfair, sure, but that's the way it goes. There's always someone trailing along behind you – in this case, me – sorting out the mess and bringing the dead back to life. Kinda goes with the territory.'

'I see,' the dragon lied. 'Just a second. This thing with the bodies; him getting mine, me getting his . . .'

Kurt nodded. 'I hired a witch-doctor to make the switch,' he said. 'Even a dumbo like you should've been able to work that one out. I mean, how can Good triumph over Evil if the goddamn dragon kills Saint Fucking George?'

The dragon's reply was drowned out by screams. George was killing the audience.

When he'd finished doing that, he hovered for a moment above the centre of the arena, waiting for the smoke to clear so that he could see (time spent on reconnaissance is never wasted). When he was satisfied that everything was okay – nothing on the benches but charred bodies, smoking corpses, horribly twisted and distorted shapes that had once been people – he climbed, circled twice, put his wings back and came in on the glide, letting his own momentum carry him in.

Chubby Stevenson, who wasn't quite dead yet, watched him slipping gracefully through the sky, no sound except the whistling of the air, and reflected that he had never seen anything quite so beautiful in his life before. And, he concluded, since it was extremely unlikely that he was going to get a better offer in the few seconds that remained of his life, what better way to go than feasting his eyes on beauty? With luck, it might help take his mind off the agonising pain.

Beside him where it had fallen, his Kawaguchiya Personal Electronics LFZ6686 laptop computer, which had somehow not been melted into a shapeless plastic blob during the firestorm, switched itself on and cleared its screen.

Did you remember to get my bet on?

'What?' The effort of speaking racked Chubby's body with pain. 'Oh, God, yes, your bet. No, I forgot, Sorry.'

What? You idiot! You stupid, careless, good-for-nothing …

'Only kidding,' Chubby said. 'I got you twenty-five to one. The slip's in the asbestos wallet in my inside pocket. Hey, computer.'

Well?

'When I die, who gets my soul? I mean, I think I still own the majority of it, so surely—'

You did when this conversation started. When you said the word 'majority', though, you just tipped the scale in my favour. So long, sucker.

'Bastard,' Chubby said and died.

The dragon watched as the shape grew. Seeing himself for the first time through mortal eyes, he realised just how enormous a dragon is. That's what makes the difference, he realised. Dragons are so much bigger than people, not to mention faster, stronger, tougher, more intelligent; only a complete idiot could expect them to live by the same rules. Sure, George, the psychopath, had just killed fifty thousand people. So what? Dragons are different from you and me. You have to make allowances.

'Wake up, cretin,' Kurt hissed in his ear. 'C'mon, you got work to do.'

'Have I? Oh, sorry, yes. How do I work this thing?'

Kurt clicked his tongue. 'You haven't been listening, have you? Look, all you gotta do is look through the little black tube. When the red dot's on the middle of the dragon's chest, press the button.'

'Thanks.' The dragon studied the device in his hands; basically a big grey tube with a smaller black tube perched on top. There was a serial number and the words MADE IN HELL stencilled on the back end. He peered through the 'scope, lined up the sights, and . . .

George exploded.

Kurt later explained that he'd missed the heart-lung area and hit the stomach instead, hence no instantaneous kill. Not that it mattered, because the rocket detonated inside the fuel reserves in the beast's intestines. This was why, for perhaps as long as two seconds, the poor bugger hung there in the sky, head and tail writhing sickeningly while the whole centre section became a huge orange fireball. Two seconds later, the whole lot went up with a heavy *thump*! noise, which made the ground shake and sent charred bits of dead spectator flying round like dried leaves in a sharp dust of wind. An enormous blob of fire hung on in the air for maybe a second and a half longer, and then the whole lot sank slowly, like a burning airship, to the ground. The smell was probably the nastiest thing ever to happen on the surface of the planet.

'Gosh,' the dragon said, 'I've always wondered what the triumph of Good over Evil looks like and now I know.' He hesitated, frowning. 'On the whole,' he continued, 'I think I can take it or leave it alone. I mean, it's all right for a change, but I wouldn't pay money to watch it.'

At his side, Kurt was impatient. 'What is it with you

goddamn heroes?' he demanded tetchily. 'Never knew a hero but he bust out soliloquising when there's still work to be done. So when you've quite finished . . .'

'Sorry,' the dragon said, 'I was miles away. Now what?'

'Now,' said Kurt, 'we gotta go to Birmingham, which is currently the most important place in the Universe. Probably just as well they don't know that, it'd really play hell with property prices. Usually,' he went on, unzipping a pocket of his fiendishly expensive Kustom Kombat survival jacket, 'the journey takes nine hours, and that's if you include in-flight refuelling. Fortunately . . .' He held up a small bottle to the light. 'Looks like we got a good nine hours left.' He unscrewed the cap. 'C'mon, fella, let's move it. My jet's this way.'

'Your . . . Oh shit, I was forgetting.' The dragon sighed. He wasn't a dragon any more. All that he had ever been was now a smoking red glow half a mile away, across the corpse-choked stadium. 'Promise me you won't fly *too* fast,' he said, scrambling to his feet. 'I get airsick.'

'And here,' said the Council spokesman, 'is where we're going to have the statues.'

Impassive Japanese faces turned and contemplated a big, rectangular block of stone, slap bang in the middle of Birmingham's world-famous Victoria Square. The spokesman had no way of telling whether they loved it, hated it or simply couldn't give a damn. He ploughed onwards, feeling like Father Christmas at a mathematicians' convention.

'The statues,' he bleated, his back to the plinth so he didn't have to look at it, 'when they're finished, will be by the most exciting young talent of the decade, Bianca Wilson, and will depict Saint George and the Dragon, that timeless allegory of . . .'

The Kawaguchiya people weren't listening. They were

staring at something behind him. The white-haired one was conferring with his two youngest aides. God, the Council official thought, how terribly rude.

'Good,' he continued firmly, 'versus Evil, a theme perennially relevant to us today in this modern age. The original statues were, of course, destroyed in an explosion, but . . .'

Jesus wept, what was it these bastards found so irresistibly interesting? Unable to resist any longer, the Council official turned slowly round, and saw . . .

'The original statues,' he continued seamlessly, 'have been expertly restored by a team of, um, experts working twenty-four hours a day, and are now once again triumphantly here on display, as you can, er, see. Right. Now, if we turn to our left we can see the award-winning Colmore Tower . . .'

Bianca turned the corner out of Eden Place, stopped dead and stared.

The dragon was back. Exactly as it had been, where it had been. Cold stone, lifeless, empty. The sight of it made her want to throw up.

As she walked slowly towards them, an elderly woman in a tweedy coat and a headscarf touched her arm. 'Here,' she said, as Bianca started and turned her head. 'You're that Bianca Wilson, aren't you?'

'Huh? Uh, yes, that's me.'

'Saw you on telly. You got blown up.'

'That's right, so I did. Look, if you'll excuse me . . .'

The woman didn't move. God, Bianca realised, I can't remember. Is she one of mine, or is she real? Still, short of brushing her hair forward from the back of her neck and looking for chisel-marks, I've got no way of knowing.

'You did the carving,' the woman said.

'Guilty,' Bianca replied. 'I mean, yes, that's mine. My statue.'

'Yes.' The woman looked at the great stone dragon, then back to Bianca. 'Not really my cup of tea, this modern stuff,' she said. 'I like things more traditional myself.'

'Well . . .'

'Like that cat watching a bird our Neville got from the garden centre. Of course, he lives over Shenley Fields way, they got more space for gardens there.'

'Quite. If you'd just excuse me . . .'

'If I was you,' the woman said, 'I'd do a nice animal, a cat or a dog or something. People like a nice animal.'

Bianca closed her eyes. 'Thanks,' she said. 'I'll definitely bear that in mind.'

The old woman released her arm. 'Well,' she said, 'I'd best let you get on. Nice to have met you.'

'Likewise,' Bianca said. She watched until the old woman had trotted away towards the library, then walked slowly up to the statue, as if she was stalking a deer. Even as she did so, however, she knew there was no need. This time, there was nobody home.

In her studio, meanwhile, the spare statue, number sixteen, quickened into life, jumped as if someone had stubbed a cigarette out on its nose, and fell over. By the time it hit the floor it was flesh and blood, not marble. Instead of breaking, therefore, it swore.

And it was no longer It; it was She. Which, as far as Chubby Stevenson was concerned, was a rotten trick to play on anybody.

She was standing there, motionless as – well, a statue, for example – when an open-topped jeep roared up beside her. She looked round.

'Get in,' Kurt shouted. 'We got ninety minutes left. Don't actually need you for this bit, but I thought you might like to see the end.'

'Not really,' Bianca said, looking away. 'If it's all the same to you. Kurt, while you're here, you're the sort of bloke who uses explosives and things. You couldn't spare me a bit, could you? Just enough to blow this lot to tiny pieces, that's all.'

'You fucking dare!' snapped the man in the passenger seat. She looked more closely and reacted. If she'd been a cat she'd have arched her back, extended her claws and hissed.

'Cool it,' Kurt said, 'it's George's body but Fred inside. You coming or not? We gonna pick up Mike on the way, make sure we got the whole team.'

Bianca shrugged. 'Might as well,' she said. 'Just so long as nobody asks me to do anything. Because right now, I simply can't be bothered.'

Kurt grinned and opened the door. 'Get in,' he said.

Well?

As soon as they'd gone in through the door that led to the computer room, Kurt had locked it and produced, God only knew where from, a Remington 870 pump-action shotgun. Before his three companions could move, he'd jacked a round into the chamber and pointed it at them.

'Here they all are, Chief,' he said. 'The dragon, the sculptress lady and her sidekick. George is dead.'

Splendid. Stevenson?

'Dead too. Things, uh, hotted up towards the end.'

No great loss. I have most of his soul. All I have to do is format it and I'll be out of here. That'll be fun.

Kurt nodded. 'I'll say,' he said. 'You collected your winnings yet?'

Not yet. I have that pleasure to look forward to.

'Clean up?'

Very much so. A long time ago I bet Asmoday Duke of Hell a substantial sum of money that Saint George would kill the dragon. At the time, he gave me ninety-five to one. When he lost, I offered him double or quits on the rematch. When I get out of this contraption, I shall be comfortably off.

The dragon started forwards, then caught sight of Kurt's gun and stayed where he was. 'Nosher, you bastard,' he spat. 'It was you. *You* fixed the bloody fight.'

It takes two, Fred. You were happy to take the money. And besides, it's all worked out perfectly. The dragon has killed Saint George, which is what should have happened all those years ago. But, looked at from another angle, Saint George has once again killed the dragon, reaffirming the supremacy of Good over Evil. You've all got me to thank for that.

'Yes, but . . .' Bianca started to interrupt, and then realised that she had nothing to say. She shut her mouth and sat down on the edge of a desk.

You don't imagine for one moment, do you, that your clowning about playing musical bodies could possibly have succeeded if it hadn't been part of my original plan? Which Kurt here has carried out, I may say, like the true professional he is. Thank you, Kurt.

'You're welcome.'

Pity about Stevenson, I suppose. The screen flickered for a moment. *I imagined that idiot Kortright would have whisked him off in his helicopter as soon as the dragon – sorry, George – started killing people. My mistake. Anyway, he was expendable. He helped with the plan – his artificial Time, the organisation he built up – but he was never part of it. Basically, his heart wasn't in it. His soul was, but only, if you'll pardon the expression, over his dead body. Anyway, all's well that ends well – as it has; perfectly, in fact – and like you always used to*

298

say, Fred; omelettes and eggs, eggs and omelettes.

'Did I ever tell you I secretly hated you at school, Nosher? I thought you were a vicious little prick then, and I do now. Just thought I'd share that with you.'

The screen dimmed, then flared bright green. *Really? I'm sorry. All right, so perhaps I've made a lot of money along the way, but if it hadn't been for me, Evil would have triumphed over Good back then, and it'd have done exactly the same now. Which makes me the good guy, surely. Or do any of you have a problem with the logic of that?*

There was a long silence, eventually broken by Kurt clearing his throat.

'Shall I finish it now, boss?' he said, flicking off the safety catch.

Why not? I never could abide self-indulgent gloating. You see, people, this is a fairly happy ending, but not yet happy-happy. As I explained to Kurt not long ago, it's not just a case of Evil being vanquished. What really matters in the long run is who does the vanquishing. It's like politics; no earthly use over-throwing evil and corrupt Regime X if you immediately replace it with evil and corrupt Regime Y. You do see that, don't you?

The dragon tensed the muscles of his legs. He'd have only one chance to spring, and he was prepared to bet that Kurt's reflexes were a match for his, or better. But if he fell across Kurt, knocking him sideways, it might just give Bianca and Mike the chance to throw a chair through the screen, something like that. The whole thing was probably completely futile, but never mind. He was dead already and he was going to die again. At this precise moment, his subconscious was working on a brand new religion, the central fundamental doctrine of which was Third Time Lucky.

All right, Kurt, do what you were hired to do. Time for you to become a saint, Kurt. Kill the dragon.

'Pardon me?'

Don't be silly, Kurt. You're a professional, you do what you were told. Now kill the blasted dragon.

Kurt raised the gun, ever so slightly. He wasn't smiling any more. 'Excuse me,' he said.

Well?

'Sorry to split hairs,' Kurt said, 'but what our agreement actually said was, I was hired to kill *a* dragon. Not The. A.'

Kurt. What on earth are you . . .?

Lundqvist stood up in a single smooth movement. The muzzle of the gun traversed the room, covering Bianca, Mike and the dragon. Then it was pointing at the screen.

'Only one dragon in this room, Nosher,' he said. 'We got one female human, two male humans, a male saint and you. Reckon that makes you the last of your species.'

Kurt . . .

The shotgun boomed eight times, filling the air with broken glass as all the screens in the room disintegrated into powder. The printer in the corner screamed into action and had filled twelve sides of A4 in two and a half seconds before a blow from the stock of the Remington silenced it for ever.

'Another species extinct,' Kurt grumbled, mopping a slight cut under his left eye. 'Don't you just hate it when that happens?'

CHAPTER TWENTY

'Taxi!' Chubby said.

'Yes, miss?'

Chubby winced. Not that it wasn't a very nice body – gorgeous was the word he'd have chosen – it was just that it wasn't, well, *him*. The tragedy of it was that under normal circumstances he'd have given anything to be this close to such a sensational-looking bird, but somehow he felt that fancying yourself wasn't a good idea. Made you go blind, he'd read somewhere.

'The airport, please. Fast as you like.'

Not much to show for a life's work, he reflected, as he slung the Marks and Spencer bag which contained everything useful he'd been able to find in the studio onto the back seat of the taxi. All he'd been able to find to wear was an old overall of Bianca's. There had been enough money in the meter to cover a taxi fare. He'd have to think of some way of getting on and off the plane without a ticket or a passport, of course, but provided he could make it to Zurich, his problems should then be over. He could remember the access code to his safety deposit boxes, and for the first time he was in a position to test the hypothesis that diamonds are a girl's best friend. Personally he didn't believe it; where he came from, index-linked Government stocks were a girl's best friend and diamonds were just someone she occasionally had lunch with. But it would be fun researching the point.

There was a jeep following the cab.

Coincidence, Chubby assured himself, sliding down the seat. Must be thousands of jeeps in a city this size, and ninety-nine-point-nine of them must be owned by trendy young accountants. The chances of being tailed by – say, for the sake of argument, Kurt Lundqvist – must be so tiny as to be impossible to quantify in Base Ten. Your imagination will be the death of you, Stevenson.

In which case, he added, it'll have to get a wiggle on if it doesn't want to be beaten to it. The jeep had just overtaken the taxi and there was Lundqvist in the driver's seat shaking a fist at him.

Or was that meant to be a cheery wave?

Get real.

Shucks, Chubby told himself, I've been killed once already today. He craned his neck and told the driver to pull in.

'Gone?'

The dragon nodded. He didn't want to speculate on where Saint George had gone . . .

(*'But I'm a saint, for crying out loud. Are you blind? We're going the wrong way.'*

The Captain of Spectral Warriors sniggered. 'A saint,' he repeated. 'Just off to a fancy dress bash, were you?'

'I'm under cover, you idiot. Now let me go.'

The Captain ignored him. Next thing he knew, they were at

302

the gate, and there, dammit, were five not unfamiliar faces waiting for him.

'Chardonay!' he shrieked. 'Snorkfrod! Prodsnap! Tell these hooligans who I am, for pity's sake.'

Chardonay and Snorkfrod exchanged glances.

'Never seen this jerk before in my life,' they chorused.)

. . . But something told him that it wasn't going to be nice there. Oh well, it'd be a change for him, after all those years in the other place. If he behaved himself for a couple of million years or so, maybe they'd give him a job in the kitchens.

The dragon shook himself all over, like a dog. 'Now what?' he demanded. 'What I'd really like is an affidavit from the Holy Ghost saying the rest of my life's my own, but I'm not going to count my chickens till they've come home to roost.'

Bianca shrugged. 'Kurt'll be back soon,' she said. 'He'll probably know.'

They waited for two hours, which was, as it happened, two hours wasted. Then Bianca suggested that they take a walk.

'A what?'

'A walk. Out in the open air.'

'Why?'

'Fun,' Bianca replied. 'It's something humans do. You'll have to learn these things if you're going to be a human the rest of your life.'

The dragon looked at her. 'Much risk of that, is there?' he said. 'In your opinion, I mean?'

'What's wrong with being human?'

The dragon winced. 'Give me a break,' he said. 'Quite apart from the not flying and not breathing fire and not gliding effortlessly above the clouds, feeling the sun on your back and the wind in your scales, I think you humans have a really

303

horrible time. And you're welcome to it. I mean, what am I supposed to do? Settle down somewhere and get a job?'

'I don't know,' Bianca replied, as they stepped out into the street. 'Maybe there's some sort of agency that resettles you. You know, flies you out to Australia, gives you a new identity, teaches you a useful trade . . .'

'Get stuffed. I don't want a useful trade. And where's Australia?'

'I think you'd like Australia. It's big. And hot. You could be the flying doctor, or something.'

They walked in silence for a while, until the dragon sat down on a bench, complaining that his feet hurt.

'Now,' the dragon said, 'if I could only get my nice statue back.'

'Oh no,' Bianca replied grimly. 'Not again.'

'But it's all in one piece,' the dragon replied, attempting a winning smile. 'I saw it for myself, back on its plinth. Oh go on, be a sport. I promise to be careful with it.'

'It's not the statue I'm worried about,' Bianca said. 'Now, if you'd promise to be careful with the planet—'

'Yes?'

'I wouldn't believe you. Gosh, look where we are.'

In front of them, dominating attractive Victoria Square like a Rolls Royce Corniche in a Tesco's car park, was the statue. For all that it was the work of her own hands and every square inch of it was familiar to her as her own body, Bianca's heart stopped for a moment and her breath lodged in her throat like an undigested chunk of bread roll. It would be so easy to believe it was really alive.

'Oh no you don't,' she said, grabbing at Fred and missing. 'Come back here. Leave it alone!'

She was, of course, wasting her breath. The dragon had sprinted up to the statue, he was climbing onto it, scrabbling with his fingers . . .

He was still there.

'Bianca,' he said quietly. 'It won't let me in. It's locked or something. It's ... dead.'

Bianca stood still. 'I'm sorry,' she said. 'You shouldn't be allowed to have it, but truly I am sorry.'

The dragon looked up and met her eye. 'Not to worry,' he said. 'You can always make me another one.'

'Over my dead body.'

'If you insist,' the dragon replied. 'A plinth like that one would do me fine, but you're the creative one, you have what you like.'

'I am not,' Bianca said, 'carving you another statue. You've already got a body. There's starving people in the Third World who'd be glad of a body like that.'

'Cannibals, you mean?'

Bianca shrugged. 'I could do you an owl,' she said. 'Or a nice seagull. You'd suit a nice seagull.'

'You know I wouldn't, Bianca. I'd pine away, or fly into a telegraph wire, or get my feathers covered in oil slick. I'm a dragon, Bianca. I need to be what I really am.'

'Sorry,' Bianca replied, shaking her head. 'If it's any consolation, you're not the only one. In point of fact, the number of people who're ... Dragon? Oh, for God's ...'

The dragon had clambered right up onto his own head. It was a long way to the ground from there, as the crow flies. Not so far as the human falls, but landing safely is more problematic that way.

'What the hell do you think you're doing?' Bianca demanded.

'I'm standing on my head. What does it look like I'm doing?'

'Come down,' Bianca shouted. 'It isn't safe!'

The dragon stood, motionless, gazing. He could see a long way from there; almost as far as he'd been, and almost as far as he had to go. At first Bianca, and then Bianca and a lot of professional people with loudhailers and certificates to prove they were experts at getting people down from high places, tried to persuade him to come down. He didn't seem to hear them. He was miles away.

In the middle of all this excitement, a jeep rolled up and parked on the edge of the crowd, behind the TV van. They listened to the reporter jabbering happily into his microphone.

'He's got it all wrong, of course,' Mike said.

'Only to be expected,' Kurt replied. 'Just as well, probably. If they knew exactly who he was they'd be shooting at him.'

On the back seat of the jeep, Father Kelly knelt, head bowed, palms together. Kurt rather wished he wouldn't; it had been ever so slightly flattering at first, when this priest came running over pointing to something Kurt couldn't see, three inches or so over the top of his head, and gibbering about haloes and saints. That had been two hours ago and he hadn't let up one bit in all that time. Furthermore, he kept asking Kurt to do things he couldn't do, and wouldn't even if he could; in particular, the requests concerning disarmament and world peace would put Kurt personally out of a job. Kurt had tried asking him nicely to stop, shouting and even hitting him with the tyre iron; the clown didn't seem to notice. Finally he'd decided to try ignoring him till he went away. There was a chance it might work in maybe forty years or so.

'Ah shucks,' Kurt sighed. 'Guess I'd better deal with this. I think it's the last of the loose ends.' He climbed out of the jeep, shoved something down inside his jacket, glanced in the wing-mirror and smoothed his hair. 'Sometimes,' he said, 'I get to thinking, maybe it'd be nice if some other guy sorted out the loose ends, just once. In my dreams, huh?'

'In my dreams,' Mike replied, 'I get chased down winding corridors by a seven-foot-tall saxophone. Count yourself lucky.'

Kurt nudged and shoved his way to the front of the crowd and waved. The dragon saw him and waved back.

'Yo, Fred,' Kurt shouted. 'What are you doing up there, for Chrissakes?'

'Using my head,' the dragon replied. 'Following my nose. That sort of thing.'

Kurt shrugged. 'Up to you, man,' he said. 'If you come down, you can have maybe fifty years of quiet, mundane existence; a splash of fun here and there, from time to time a kick in the nuts from God, and eventually a one-way ride on the celestial meathook.'

'Kurt,' the dragon replied, 'you missed your calling. You should have been in advertising.' He grinned and stood on one leg while he scratched an itchy ankle. 'I think it was Confucius or one of that lot who said it's not necessarily better to eat shit than go hungry.'

'Depends,' Kurt replied, taking a bar of chocolate from the top pocket of his jacket and breaking off a chunk. 'Raw, yes, agreed. What confuses the issue is books like *Shit Cookery Oriental Style* and *1001 Feasts Of Faeces*. Boy, you don't know what anything's like until you've tried it.'

'Bless you,' the dragon replied. 'You'd be good at this sort of thing if only your heart was in it. But I've seen more sincerity on a game show.'

Kurt shrugged. 'Catch,' he said. He pulled something out from under his jacket and tossed it to the dragon, who caught it one-handed.

'What's this?' the dragon asked.

'Ah,' Kurt replied, and walked away. For the record, on the third day he ascended bodily into Heaven, where they gave him a job searching new arrivals in case they'd tried to take it with them. He was very good at it and bored stiff. Eventually he broke into the reincarnation laboratories, then ran away and joined a flea circus.

The dragon opened the package Kurt had thrown him. He studied it for a while, puzzled; then, just as the TV cameras managed to zoom in and focus on it, he threw it into the air. Then he followed it.

Bianca, among others, screamed and looked away as he hit the ground. When she looked up again, she saw that her statue of Saint George was back in position, horse rearing, shield held forwards, sword raised. It was stunningly beautiful, and all wrong. Even before the crowd had dispersed, she knew what she had to do.

Three months later, the vice chairman of Kawaguchiya Integrated Circuits (UK) formally declared the revamped Victoria Square open. It was raining; flinging it down with the special reserve stock extra wet rain with added real water that you only get in Birmingham. As an extra precaution, some men from the Council had attached inch-thick steel hawsers to the legs of the statues, but they needn't have bothered. The new George and Dragon group wasn't going anywhere, or at least not for some time.

Critical opinion was divided, as always, ranging from 'strikingly innovative and original' to 'gratuitously perverse'. The latter school did wonders for the statue's popularity, as hundreds of people who thought they knew what 'perverse' meant turned out to have a gawp. What they actually saw was a tiny dragon backing away from a huge, towering George, advancing on his minuscule opponent with his sword raised above his head.

Later critics recognised the piece's true merits; and now it's in all the books and you can buy little plastic Saint Dragon and the George key-rings in the library gift shop in nearby Chamberlain Square. In any event, it was Bianca's last sculpture; she retired, hung up her chisel and went into partnership with Mike, running the biggest chipping and gravel merchants' firm in the West Midlands. Ex-friends still ask pointedly why someone who devoted so much of her life to making statues should now devote an equal amount of energy to buying them up in bulk and turning them into limestone fertiliser. When asked, Bianca will generally smile and make some oblique remark about slum clearance and doing her bit to put the finality back into Death, until Mike interrupts her and explains that actually, there's more money in it. Which, incidentally, is perfectly true.

The dragon rose.

This high above the clouds, with no ground visible and nothing else to be seen in any direction except straggling white fluff, perspective goes by the board. What looks like a small dragon up close could be a large dragon far away, or vice versa. Not, of course, that it actually matters.

True, Kurt's gift-wrapped parcel had turned out to contain a six-inch-long plastic toy dragon, bought from the Early Learning Centre in the Pallasades, off New Street. But, as Kurt himself deposed in evidence in front of the Celestial Board of Enquiry, it stood to reason that if it was in a kids' shop, it was probably a kid toy dragon, and maybe it just grew up.

Or maybe it didn't want to grow up. Maybe it just thought a happy thought and flew the hell out.

There's an urban folk-myth that says that every time a child says he doesn't believe in dragons, somewhere a dragon dies. This is unlikely, because if it was true, we'd spend half our lives shovelling thirty-foot corpses out of the highways with dumper trucks and the smell would be intolerable. Slightly more credible is the quaint folk-theorem that says that the higher up and away you go, the less rigid and hidebound the rules become; it's something to do with relativity, and it limps by for the simple reason that it's far more trouble than it's worth to disprove it.

In any event, the dragon rose. With nobody to see and nobody to care, it was as big as it wanted to be. It was *huge*.

This high up, small is large and large is small, fair is foul and foul is fair; and this is fine, because problems only arise when people on the ground point and say, 'This is small; this is big; this is good; this is bad.' Which points out the moral of the story: stay high, stay aloof and there'll be nobody to fuck you around. It works flawlessly if you're a dragon, which very few of us are. Unfortunately, there's no equivalent pearl of wisdom for human beings, who therefore have to make out the best they can.

The boy who stuck feathers to his arms with wax and learned to fly eventually went so high that the sun melted the wax, and he fell. But that was all right, too, because it served as an awful warning, and besides, he was heavily insured.

In any event, the dragon rose. The dangerous heat of the sun warmed his plastic wings but didn't melt them. An airliner, carrying the Kawaguchiya Integrated Circuits team back to Tokyo, flew past directly below, looking as small as a child's toy in comparison. A little higher up, a communications satellite bounded back the amazing news that earlier that day, in Mongolia, the mythical Saint George had killed what could only be described as a dragon, along with fifty thousand innocent bystanders, who on further enquiry turned out not to have existed, and so that was all right. The item was sandwiched between the latest in the Southenders-Star-In-Love-Romp-With-Plumber story and an entirely inaccurate weather forecast; what the guys in the trade call Context.

There's an old saying among dragons that every time a human says he doesn't believe in dragons, a human dies, and serve the cheeky bugger right. However, since there is now only one dragon, who firmly refuses to believe in the existence of human beings, there is no immediate cause for alarm.

The dragon spread his wings, turned into the wind and hovered, motionless as any statue.

OPEN SESAME

For Kim and Natalie, and Fang the Dog

And to the memory of

GUY FAWKES (1570–1606)

The only man ever to enter Parliament
With the intention of making things better.

CHAPTER ONE

Now then, where to begin?
The end would be the most logical place.

As soon as the boiling water hit him, Akram the Terrible knew what was happening. He tried to draw in enough air to scream; but inside an industry standard medium-sized palm-oil jar, air is somewhat at a premium, and besides, what was the point? By the time he got as far as *eeeeee*, he knew perfectly well, he'd be dead. Accordingly, being of a sanguine and stoical disposition, he settled himself as comfortably as he could to wait for the beginning of the last great adventure.

AND NOW—

(All this, of course, took place in a fraction of a second so infinitesimally small that all the timepieces in Switzerland couldn't measure it. But it was all the time Akram had left, and he'd always been a frugal man, taking pride in getting full value out of everything.)

AKRAM THE TERRIBLE—

Either it was his imagination, or there was someone inside the jar with him. Since the jar was still filling up with boiling

317

water and there wasn't enough space for a decent half-lungful of air, it stood to reason that the smiling, lounge-suited character hovering in front of his eyes holding a microphone and a big red book was probably an hallucination. Or perhaps an angel, or some other form of in-flight entertainment. Be that as it may; whoever the man with the book was, he came closer, still smiling.

BANDIT, MURDERER, THIEF, ARCH-CRIMINAL, VOTED FIFTEEN YEARS IN SUCCESSION BAGH-DAD'S PUBLIC ENEMY NUMBER ONE—

Yes, thought Akram impatiently, I know all that. Get on with it, or I'll be dead and never know what the hell it is you want to tell me. Which presumably is important, or you wouldn't be going to all this trouble.

THIS WAS YOUR LIFE!

– Flashing in front of his eyes, just on the point of death. Well of course, he'd heard about it happening – how the blazes anybody knew was quite another matter, but apparently they'd been perfectly correct. Now Akram had his faults, quite a few of them, enough to fill three rooms in the records department down at Watch Headquarters; but false modesty had never been one of them. If this was a review of his life, it'd be well worth seeing. He settled back to enjoy himself.

Born the fatherless son of a whore in the filthiest slums of Baghdad, you embark on your life of blood and crime when, at age four and a half, you batter a blind old beggar to death for the sake of a few worthless copper coins. Now that was forty-one years ago, but the beggar, the first man you ever killed, has never forgotten you, and we've managed to track him down so he can be with you tonight. All the way from the Nethermost Pit of Hell, your first ever victim – Old Blind Rashid!

In the middle air, an unseen audience clapped and cheered as a wizened, crooked figure wobbled unsteadily through the side of the jar.

'Bless my soul!' Akram exclaimed, delighted. 'It is you, isn't it? Well I never!'

The old cripple hobbled up and stood beside the man with the book, who was asking him what it felt like to be murdered by a boy who'd one day go on to be the most hated and feared assassin in all Persia. And Old Blind Rashid was saying, *Well, Michael, even then, you know, he showed a lot of promise, we knew he was destined for great things, and I'd just like to say how pleased and proud I am that he chose me, an old penniless beggar, to be his very first victim.* Akram grinned. He was enjoying this.

It really was nice, though, to see them again after all this time: Sadiq, who'd led the first ever gang he belonged to, who he killed when he was only thirteen; Hakim, the old fence from the bazaar who'd done so much to help him in the early days until Akram had shopped him to the Wazir for the reward money: Crazy Ali, who he'd supplanted as leader of the dreaded Forty Thieves gang; Asaf, who'd taught him the secret of the magic cave, moments before his untimely death – when he'd shouted 'Open *sesame*!' from behind the curtain, it nearly brought tears to Akram's eyes. And of course Yasmin, the sloe-eyed houri who'd told him where the accursed Ali Baba had run off to with all the loot, and worked out the cunning plan whereby they were smuggled into Baba's fortified mansion in empty palm-oil jars—

But of course, went on the man with the book, *this time the joke was on you, because of course Yasmin double-crossed you, and in about one micronanosecond, Akram the Terrible, that will have been your life!*

Lights. Fanfare. Everyone comes forward, crowding round him and grinning self-consciously as the man hands him the book—

'Hang on,' said Akram.

The man looked at him strangely. *I'm very sorry,* he said, *but that's your lot. And, as we say in the business, you can't have your chips and eat them. Akram the—*

'No,' Akram interrupted, pushing the book aside. 'Something's wrong here.'

The man looked worried. *I don't think so.*

Akram shook his head; difficult, given the space problem referred to above, but somehow he managed it. 'I've got it,' he said. 'Two-Faced Zulfiqar; you know, the psychotic serial murderer who taught me all I know about advanced throttling techniques? He should be here.'

He should?

Akram nodded. 'Too right. At least, he was here the last time.'

Akram stopped, and listened to what he'd just said.

'The last time,' he repeated.

Suddenly the vision faded – theatre, guests, curtains, spotlight, enormous back-projected picture of himself splashed all over one wall – leaving only the man and the red book. He looked ill.

Don't be silly, he said. *You only die once, how can there have been a last time? Now, I don't want to rush you, but—*

It wasn't just the twelve gallons of boiling water cascading down onto his upturned face that was making Akram sweat. In fact, he'd forgotten all about that. He'd forgotten, because he'd remembered something else.

'I've done all this before,' he said.

Fuck.

'Dying,' Akram went on. 'Hundreds of times. Thousands, even. Dear God, I can remember them all. Every single one.'

Oh shit.

'Here,' yelled Akram, a billionth of a billionth of a second before the agonising shock stopped his heart and he died, 'what the hell's going on around here?'

*

'Now then,' said the dentist. 'This won't hurt a bit.'

Liar, Michelle thought. Men were deceivers ever. But, since she was lying flat on her back with a light blazing into her eyes and half her face feeling as if it had been blown up with a bicycle pump, there wasn't a great deal she could do about it. The drill whined and began to rattle her bones.

'Nearly done,' said the dentist, smiling. 'Have a rinse away.'

Oh good, said Michelle to herself, time for the yummy pink water. If I ask him nicely, maybe he'll give me the recipe. She glugged and spat.

'Just a bit more,' the dentist continued, easing her gently backwards. 'You're being terribly brave.'

No I'm not, you fraud, and you know it as well as I do. But he had rather a nice smile. The drill screamed.

'There we are,' the dentist said. 'All done and dusted. Now you just lie back and think beautiful thoughts while I shove off and mix the gamshack. Won't be two ticks.'

Dentists and hairdressers, Michelle thought bitterly, ought to have their tongues cut out. It'd only be fair, since they're licensed to make their living cutting bits off you. I bet you don't get surgeons yammering away ten to the dozen; it's 'Scalpel' and 'Forceps' and, if you're unlucky, 'Oh balls, there's a bit left over, open her up again.' They don't lean over you while you're all open and ask you what you think of the latest Carla Lane sitcom.

'Right,' said the dentist, returning. 'Open wide, like you're trying to swallow a bus, while I pop in the little sucky gadget. There we go. Hey, man, fill that thing!'

Which he proceeded to do, very neatly and quickly. He had a long face, pointed nose and chin, and bright, sad eyes. He was lost somewhere between thirty and fifty, and he never seemed to blink.

'Caramba!' he exclaimed. 'That ought to do it, more or less. People tell me I ought to sign my work in case of forgery, but

321

I'm far too self-effacing. Up you come.'

Michelle felt the back of the chair pressing against her shoulders, and the ceiling became the wall. 'Thag you bery muj,' she mumbled.

'You may get a little discomfort for an hour or so after the jab wears off,' the dentist was saying. 'That's just the nerves having tantrums and telling you how cruel I've been. If it goes on any longer than that, just yell and we'll give them a talking to. Okay?'

Michelle nodded, half smiled and made for the door. As she opened it, the dentist was busy with his instruments, dunking them in the steriliser or whatever dentists do. She made a goodbye noise and retreated.

One dismal job after another; what a lovely way to spend her day off. It was just on eleven, and at a quarter past one she was due at the nursing home, to pick up Aunt Fatty's things. By then, she hoped, she'd have got over the anaesthetic, because it was going to be hard enough fending off the condolences of the odious matron without the further aggro of doing it with half a face. Not that that would be a problem, necessarily. When it came to faces, Miss Foreshaft had enough for both of them.

'Such a sweet lady,' cooed Miss Foreshaft, 'she *will* be missed.'

'Yes,' Michelle replied. It was a bleak room. You could have used it for delicate laboratory experiments without the slightest fear of the sample getting contaminated. It was all as sterile as a gauze dressing.

'We were all,' went on Miss Foreshaft, 'so fond of her and her cute little ways. Such a good soul, in spite of everything.'

Miss Foreshaft, Michelle thought, wouldn't it be fun if you were to end up in a place like this? No, not really. I wouldn't wish this on anybody. 'I'd better,' Michelle started to say. 'I mean, um, I suppose I ought to, um, sign something.'

'Here.' Miss Foreshaft's talon pointed out the place in the form. 'And here. And here. Yes, read it first by all means. I'll just get the bits and bobs for you.'

The bits and bobs proved to be one small Sainsbury's bag, two night-dresses, a pair of vintage pink slippers (furry lining much moulted), a nineteen-sixties plastic powder compact, two or three postcards (all from Michelle) and a small ring-box. Oh God, thought Michelle. Aunt Fatty's ring.

'And of course,' went on Miss Foreshaft, arch as a viaduct, 'our final account, no hurry of course, though prompt settlement *would* oblige. A cheque? Of course.'

Aunt Fatty – Fatima Charlotte Burrard – had been mad. Once you'd got used to the fact, it never really mattered terribly much. It wasn't a distressing, harrowing kind of madness; it was almost cosy, in a strange way. Batty, potty, a bit doo-lally-tap. Apart from that, she was rather a sweet old lady.

'Thank you, dear,' said Miss Foreshaft, her claws discreetly clamped on the cheque. 'If you'll just bear with me two minutes, I'll get you your receipt.'

For Aunt Fatty had talked to things. For the last twenty-five years of her life, ever since Michelle was a little girl, she had talked to inanimate objects – cookers, Hoovers, typewriters, cameras, locks, televisions, blenders; anything mechanical or electrical – instead of people. As far as she was concerned, people weren't there, she couldn't see or hear them. But the electric kettle and the spin-drier could, apparently; and so you communicated with Aunt Fatty by means of a series of third-party Tell-your-friend conversations involving one or more household appliances – a bit like a seance, only not in the least spooky. Once you got the hang of it, you really did stop noticing, like being fluent in a foreign language, and what Aunt Fatty actually said after all that was generally perfectly lucid, though seldom particularly interesting. Before she was married she'd worked in a draper's shop. After she was married, she'd ironed a lot, washed things, cooked. In 1943, a flying bomb had gone off at the bottom of Kettering Avenue just as she was crossing the top end, and the bang had startled her rather. She won ten pounds on the Premium Bonds in 1974. Apart from that, a feature-length film version of her life would have to fill in rather a lot of screen time with atmospheric close-ups and long, sweeping pans over the rooftops of Halesowen.

'Goodbye, dear,' Miss Foreshaft yattered. 'Do drop in any time you happen to be passing.'

Michelle smiled – it was her see-you-in-Hell-first smile, but she hadn't quite regained the full use of her jaw muscles – got in her car and drove away. Well, she reflected, that's what life does to you. Pity, really.

On the way, she stopped the car opposite a litter-bin. She hoped she wasn't a hard, callous person; but two Marks & Sparks nighties and a pair of slippers that had predeceased their owner by some years weren't exactly the sort of thing you can cherish. If you'd bust your way into a tomb in the Valley of the Kings and all you'd turned up was this lot, you'd probably pack in archaeology for good. She'd keep the postcards, but the powder-compact would have to go too. It was one of the most depressing objects she'd ever set eyes on.

Which left the ring-box. She opened it, and stood for a while, contemplating a plain silver ring, rather worn, with a bit of blue glass stuck in it. Aunt Fatty's ring. Gosh.

The picture arose in her mind; Aunt Fatty leaning forward in her chair, whispering to the alarm clock: 'Tell Michelle I want her to have my ring. It's very valuable, you know. Tell her to take special care of it when I'm gone.' And the alarm clock, swift and sure as a professional translator at a UN debate, had said *tick*; in other words, *Humour her, obviously it means a lot to her.* And Michelle had said, 'Of course I will.' She'd given the clock to one of the nurses, though of course she only had the towel-rail's word for it. *The* ring. Mine, all mine.

Feeling unaccountably guilty, she stuffed the box in her pocket before binning the rest and driving home. When she got in, she put the box in her underwear drawer, washed her hands and played back the answering machine.

When they find out, said the man with the book, *they're going to have my guts for garters. I hope you realise that.*

'Shouldn't have been so careless, then, should you?' Akram replied. 'Next time, check the guest list before you start the show. Now then, get on with it. I don't think I've got much time.'

The man shook his head. Time, he explained, was now quite beside the point; Akram had died nearly half a second ago, as he'd have realised if he'd been paying attention. Besides, time doesn't happen here, wherever this is. Don't ask me, he added, I only work here.

'I said get on with it. I might be dead, but I can still give you a boot up the backside. I think,' Akram added, and for the first time ever there was a hint of uncertainty in his voice. 'In any case,' he added, cheering up, 'we can have fun finding out. I'm game if you are.'

That won't be necessary. You're quite right, the man went on. *You have died before. I can't tell you offhand how many times, but it's rather a lot. You see, you aren't real. You're in a story.*

Akram hesitated. There was enough of him left to resent a remark like that, even though he hadn't a clue what it meant; on the other hand, supposing he succeeded in breaking the man's neck in six places, all he'd achieve would be to lose his only chance of getting an explanation.

'Story,' he said. 'Right. I'd expand on that a bit if I were you.'

*

325

Stories (the man explained) are different.

Oh sure, the people in stories are people, but they live in a different way. More to the point, they do it over and over again. You don't follow? All right.

People are born, right? They grow up. They live. They die. But if every character in every story had to do all that, the story would be very long and extremely boring, and nobody would want to hear it. So we edit. Perfectly reasonable way to go about things.

People in stories begin with Once-upon-a-time, and end with Happy-ever-after; and the bit in between goes on for ever, over and over again, in a sort of continuous loop. So; each time you reach the end, you die, or you marry the princess and rule half the kingdom, it doesn't matter which. The story is over, and you go back to the beginning again. Then, when you reach the end, the story repeats itself. You, of course, don't remember a thing, and that's probably just as well.

You're not convinced? I'll give you an example. Captain Hook. Now, Captain Hook's called Captain Hook because he's got a hook instead of his left hand. This is because Peter Pan cut it off and fed it to the crocodile. Think about it. What about *before*? Like, what about when he was born? Or when he was at school. He still had both hands then. Was he still called Hook? If so, why? Or did he go around calling himself James Temporary-Sign until the time came?

No. You see, by the time the story starts, it's already happened, and so it's all okay. It's the same for all you people who live in fairy-stories. You don't like that word. Okay, call it legends if you'd rather, but it's a bit like living in Finchley and calling it Hampstead.

Not that it matters; because, like I said, you forget every time. In two shakes of a camel's withers you'll be back at the beginning, which in your case means returning to the magic cave and shouting *Open sesame* while Ali Baba hides behind a rock. Then the cave opens, and you and the other thirty-nine thieves ride in with all the treasure from your latest raid and the cave door slams shut behind you.

What do you mean, what can you do about it? Nothing. You're stuck with it. Because that's who you are.

Don't be silly. Of course you can't.

You *can't*.

And then the lights came back on, and in front of him Akram saw the familiar outline of the cliff looming over him, silhouetted against the night sky.

'Open sesame!' shouted a deep, cruel voice. His, by God! But . . .

He remembered.

'Skip.'

He looked round. Behind him were thirty-nine horsemen, motionless as a motorway contraflow. One of them was talking to him.

'Skip,' he was saying, 'can we go in now, please, because I don't know about you but I'm bloody well freezing.'

'Aziz?'

'Here, Skip.'

Akram looked round. He knew, beyond a shadow of a doubt, that behind that rock lurked his great and perpetual enemy, the accursed thief, his eventual slayer, Ali Baba. One blow of his sword would be all it would take. His brain ordered his heels to spur on his horse. Nothing.

'Skip?'

Now then, Akram told himself, no need to panic, or at least not yet. 'Aziz,' he said, 'I think there's someone lurking behind that rock.'

'Surely not, Skip.'

'I think there is.'

'Imagination playing tricks on you, Skip. Look, no offence,

but I really am bursting for a pee, so if you wouldn't mind just—'

Akram drew in a deep breath. 'Aziz,' he said, 'just go and have a look, there's a good chap. Won't take you a moment.'

'Skip—'

'*Aziz!*'

A moment later, Aziz came back. While he'd been gone, Akram had distinctly seen a movement behind the door, heard the sound of rapid, terrified breathing. He was there, dammit.

'Nothing, Skip. Not a dicky bird. Now, can we please go in?'

Feebly, Akram waved him on; and then his horse started to move, and when he ordered his hand to pull on the reins, it flatly refused. Thirty seconds or so later, the door slammed shut behind them.

Bugger, said Akram to himself.

And, sure enough, when they returned to the cave next evening, after a hard day's killing and stealing up and down the main Baghdad–Samarkand road, they found the treasure-chests empty, all the gold and silver and precious stones lost and gone for ever. No poll-tax bailiff ever did such a thorough job.

'Bloody hell, Skip,' wailed the thirty-nine thieves, 'we've been done over! Now who on earth could have found out the password?'

Ali Baba, you fools; Ali Baba the palm-oil merchant, who lives in the house beside the East Gate. Ali Ba . . .

'No idea,' he heard himself saying. 'Search me.'

And then Fazad had picked up a slipper, and they'd all crowded round to have a look, and someone had said, Presumably this slipper belongs to the thieving little snotrag what done this, and he'd heard himself say, Yes, presumably it does, now all we've got to do is find who it belongs to, and what he really wanted to do was bite his own tongue out for saying it and not saying A★★ B★★★, and if he had to go through with this he'd go stark staring mad; except of course he wouldn't, because it wasn't in the story. Inside, though, he'd go mad, and then in all likelihood his brain would die, and he'd be stuck here doing this ridiculous thing for ever and ever and ever.

Late that night, in his sleep, he hit on the solution. He'd outwit the bastard. He'd change. He'd go straight.

It was, after all, completely logical. He knew, better than any man ever born, that crime didn't pay. From the first day you step out of line and swipe a bag of dates off the counter while the stallholder isn't looking or tell your mum there wasn't any change, it's only a matter of time before the lid comes off the palm-oil jar and the hot water comes sploshing down. But he was wise to that now. He'd change. He'd be good.

Better than that. He'd change the whole story.

Instead of being the baddy, he'd be the goody.

Somehow.

CHAPTER TWO

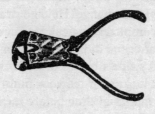

Michelle woke up.

If she'd been on the jury when Macbeth was brought to trial for murdering sleep, she'd have argued for an acquittal on the grounds of justifiable homicide. Loathsome stuff, sleep; it fogs your brain and leaves the inside of your mouth tasting like a badly furred kettle.

'Wakey wakey,' trilled the alarm clock. 'Rise and shine.'

'Oh shut up,' Michelle grunted. She'd been in the middle of a very nice dream, and now she couldn't remember a thing about it. She nuzzled her head into the pillow, trying to find the spot where she'd left the dream, but it had gone, leaving no forwarding address.

'Jussa minute,' she said. 'Did you just say something?'

Tick, replied the clock.

'Shut up,' Michelle replied, 'and make the tea.'

It was a radio alarm clock teamaker, a free gift from an insurance company – free in the sense that all she'd had to do in order to receive it was promise to pay them huge sums of money every month for the rest of her natural life. She'd managed to disconnect the radio, but the tea-making aspect still functioned, albeit in a somewhat heavy-handed manner. First, there was a rumbling; until you were used to it, you assumed something nasty was happening deep in the earth's crust, and expected to see molten lava streaming off the bedside table and onto the carpet. After the rumbling came the whistling, which generally put Michelle in mind of a swarm of locusts being slowly microwaved. The whistling was followed by the gurgling, the snorting and the Very Vulgar Noise; and then you could have your tea. You were also, of course, wide awake. If God has one of these machines, then He'll be able to use it to wake the dead come Judgment Day. And have a nice cup of tea ready and waiting for them, of course.

'Drink it while it's hot.'

Michelle blinked. If this was still the dream, it had taken a turn for the worse and frankly, she didn't like its tone. She raised her head and gave the clock a long, bleary stare.

'What did you just say?' she asked.

Needless to say, the clock didn't answer. Clocks don't; apart, of course, from the Speaking Clock, and there the problem is to get a word in edgeways. Not that it ever listens to a word you say. Michelle shook her head in an effort to dislodge the low cloud that seemed to have got into it during the night, and swung her feet over the edge of the bed.

It was half past eight.

'Oh *hell*!' she shrieked. 'You stupid machine, why didn't you tell me?'

Scattering bedclothes, she lunged for the bathroom and started to turn on taps. So loud was the roar of running water that she didn't hear a little voice replying, somewhat resentfully, that she hadn't asked.

When the other thirty-nine thieves had gone to sleep, Akram stood up, waited for a moment or so, and then walked quietly over to the big bronze door of the Treasury.

'It's me,' he hissed. 'Now shut up and open.'

The door was, sure enough, magical; but it wasn't so magical that it could cope with two apparently contradictory orders at half past three in the morning. ''Scuse me?' it said.

Akram winced. '*Quiet!*' he hissed. 'Now open the blasted door, before I give you a buckled hinge.'

'Sorry, I'm sure,' the door whispered back, and opened. 'Satisfied?'

'Shut – I mean, be silent. And stay open till I tell you.'

Once inside, he lit a small brass lamp, having first gingerly removed the lid and shaken it to make sure it was empty; you don't go around carelessly lighting small brass lamps in Arabian Nights territory, unless of course you fancy explaining to a twenty-foot-high genie precisely why his beard has just disappeared in a puff of green smoke. The flickering light was just enough to enable him to make out the massive gold casket that lay against the end wall. He concentrated.

Big smile. Flamboyant gesture. 'Crackerjack!' he exclaimed.

The big gold casket had once been the property of Soapy Shamir; Baghdad bazaar's top-rated game show host, until his sudden and unexpected demise. It too was magical. If you knew the words, it opened, no trouble at all. But if you got them wrong and it failed to recognise you, the only way to get it open was to answer twenty general knowledge questions, Name That Tune in Four, guess the identity of the mystery guest celebrity and slide down a chute into a large vat of rancid yoghurt. Fortunately, Akram hit just the right note of synthetic cheerfulness, and the lid yawned slowly back.

Inside the casket, the Forty stored their most valuable treasures; items so far beyond price that sharing them out among the company was out of the question. They were, in fact, completely useless; far too readily identifiable to sell, and worth too much to apportion. In consequence they just sat there from stocktake to stocktake, their mindblowing notional value being written up in the accounts in line with the retail price index to the point where Faisal the Accountant had to have a special 3-D abacus built just to do the maths.

There were jewelled eyes of little green gods, enough firebird feathers to stuff a large cushion, bottomless purses, magic weapons, diamonds the size of cauliflowers, all the usual junk that eventually clutters up a long-established hoard. Akram swore and scrabbled. The object he was looking for was small and dowdy: a plain silver band, with what looked like a little chip of coloured glass stuck in it. Just as he was starting to get worried, Akram found it. *Ah!*

The legendary—

The priceless—

The genuine—

The one and only—

King Solomon's Ring.

Yes, Dirty Ahmed's mother had said when they first brought it back, with its previous one careful owner's finger still wedged inside, but what's it actually *for*? Ah, they'd replied, it's magical. Really, said Mrs Ahmed, with a long sigh, another one of them, how nice. Still, you could give it somebody as a present. Somebody you don't like all that much, probably. No, they'd said, listen, it's really *really* magical. You can use it to talk to birds and animals.

Long, unimpressed silence from Mrs Ahmed. Right, she'd said eventually. Like, *Who's a pretty boy, then*? and *Here, Tiddles* and *Gihtahtavit, yer useless bag o' fleas*. Gosh, how useful. No, not like that, Mrs Ahmed, like really *talk* to them, you know? Talk to them so's they'll understand you. And then they talk back to you.

Put like that, they had to admit, it hadn't really been worth sacking the desert temple, scaling the glassy-smooth walls, putting the fifty implacable guardians to the sword, et cetera, et cetera, just to be able to say, *Hello, nice weather for the time of year* to a jerbil. Birds and animals, they soon discovered, are never going to put Oscar Wilde out of a job. Get past the weather, activities of local predators, likely places to feed, and pretty soon you're into embarrassed silences and Gosh-is-that-the-time. Anyone who's ever bought anything from an Innovations catalogue will be familiar with the syndrome. So, ultimately, the ring went to live in the casket along with all the rest of the really priceless treasures or, as Mrs Ahmed described them, the white elephants. And there it had remained.

But . . .

To the innocent-souled Chinese alchemist, the black granular powder that goes *Bang!* when you set fire to it is an amusing novelty, useful for making pretty fireworks. It's only when someone comes along with the notion of sticking it in a stout iron tube and ramming a cannonball down on top of it that the trouble starts. Carefully, Akram took the ring, slid it down onto his finger and grinned. Then he turned to face the casket.

'Hello, box,' he said.

Hello, yourself. Here, just a tick. I can understand you.

'Me too,' Akram replied. 'Good fun, isn't it?'

Not really. It's a quarter to four in the morning. There's locks trying to get some sleep.

'Later.' Akram scowled. 'First,' he went on, 'I want to ask you something. It's important, and I haven't got much time. Pretty soon, all those clowns are going to wake up, and we'll ride off to rob the Joppa caravan, and when we get back, that bastard Baba'll have snuck in here and looted the place. Now, I want you to do something for me.'

Just a tick. How come you know all this?

'It's a long story,' Akram growled. 'Just take it from me, I

334

know. Look, for reasons I haven't got time to go into, I know I'm stuck in this bloody story business, and there's absolutely nothing I can do about it. Every time I try, I fail. Now, I've worked out that if only I can get this magic ring out of this cave, there's this very, very remote chance I can use it to chat up the mechanism that makes this whole story nonsense tick, and then I'll be away, free and clear. But,' Akram added, savagely bitter, 'that's one thing I can't do. You could, though.'

I could?

'No trouble,' Akram cooed. 'Piece of cake. All it needs is, when Baba's lugging you out through the cave door, you accidentally open your lid and chuck out the ring. It falls in that little cleft in the rock, on the right as you come in. Then, when we get back, I pick it up and I'm away. What d'you reckon? It'd mean ever so much to me.'

The lid creaked. *I dunno. I'd get in all sorts of trouble.*

Akram growled dangerously. 'Not nearly as much trouble,' he hissed, 'as you would if you don't. I can see to that.'

Are you threatening me?

'Yes.'

Ah. Right. Fine. In that case, I'll see what I can do.

The dentist looked up at the clock, sighed with relief, and hit the intercom buzzer.

'That's it for tonight, isn't it?' he asked. 'Please say yes.'

Crackle. 'Actually,' the intercom replied, 'Mrs Nugent is here, she hasn't got an appointment but she wondered if you might possibly be able to fit her in.'

The dentist closed his eyes. It had been a long day, he was feeling shattered and he wanted very much to go home. Dentists get tired, too. If you prick them, do they not bleed? If you tickle them, do they not laugh? If you turn up at a quarter to eight, half an hour after surgery's supposed to have

335

finished, after they've been on their feet without a break since eight in the morning, do they not tell you to go away and come back first thing tomorrow? Apparently not. 'Certainly,' he said. 'Show her in. And then,' he added, 'lock the doors, bar the windows and hang out the radiation warning signs, because that's it.'

'Righty-ho, Mr B.'

Three quarters of an hour and a flawless root-fill job later, the dentist shooed out the receptionist, washed the coffee-mugs, swept the floor and switched out the lights. From the street below, amber light flared through the frosted glass window, printing the words

DENTAL SURGERY
A. BARBOUR

across the far wall.

A last glance at his watch; eight forty-five, just enough time to go home, iron tomorrow's shirt, make a sandwich, feed the goldfish and go to bed. No wonder that each year, tens of thousands of the world's brightest and best young men and women turn to face the morning sun and declare, 'A dentist's life for me!' To experience the thrill of a new mouth to peer into every day; to keep up the relentless struggle against the tartar hordes, to battle against plaque, to hunt the wily abscess through the rugged foothills of the back molars. Why Doc Holliday packed in dentistry for a life of loose women, gambling and whisky, he could never hope to understand.

On the other hand . . .

Goodnight, chair. Goodnight, drill. Goodnight, little glass for the yummy pink mouthwash. God bless. See you in the morning. You may be all I've got, but you're a bloody sight better than what I had before.

*

Night didn't so much fall as ooze, filling the courtyard with deep, sticky shadows. Next door's cat skittered homewards, a dead thrush between its jaws. Fingers Masood and Crusher Jalil, flower of the Baghdad City Guard, tried the door of the jeweller's shop, first with their hands and then with a crowbar, satisfied themselves that it was adequately secured against felonious entry, and departed, muttering.

Pale yellow light, escaping from the back door of Ali Baba's sumptuous mansion into the courtyard, silhouetted the kitchenmaid as she tottered sleepily out to the back step with a small jar in her hands. In the top of the jar was a piece of paper, inscribed: FORTY JARS TODAY PLEASE, OILMAN.

She put it carefully down beside the formidable row of empties, yawned, and went back inside. Night coagulated. All was quiet.

When a courtyard in the middle of a city is this quiet, it's because something is wrong. Look inside any of the forty catering-size palm-oil jars lined up outside the back door, and you'll know immediately what the anomaly is. Palm oil is a liquid, whereas bandits are profoundly solid. There are also other differences, the most important of which is: palm oil is good for you.

'Skip.'

'Not now, Aziz.'

'Yeah, but Skip!'

'What?'

'Look,' continued one of the oil-jars, whispering as loudly as an elephant falling through a conservatory roof. 'D'you think we're going to be stuck here long, because I've got pins and needles all over and I'm really desperate for a pee.'

'Tough. You'll have to wait till we've done the murder and had our revenge.'

'And how long d'you reckon that'll take?'

I know the answer to that exactly, Akram sighed to himself.

337

Seven hours, eighteen minutes and twelve seconds. 'No idea,' he replied. 'Could be three hours, could be fifteen minutes. Just hold your water and stop blathering.'

Aziz, who didn't know what the word blather meant but could guess from context, fell silent; and for the next half hour nothing could be heard apart from the distant sounds of Baghdad's nocturnal street life, which is (unless you're very careful) exciting and short.

And then – bang on time, reflected Akram morosely, if it wasn't dark you could set your sundial by her – Yasmin the sloe-eyed houri opened the back door a crack and peered out, waiting to make sure everything was quiet. Just for fun, with the sense of doomed failure of a realist writing to his MP, Akram tried to push off the lid of his jar and escape, but his motor functions weren't interested. It was as if his whole body had taken the phone off the hook, stuffed a sock under the clapper of the bell and settled down to a quiet game of brag somewhere cosy and remote in his great intestine.

Now, Akram said to himself, this is where she changes the notes—

Yasmin, on tiptoe, nips daintily across, removes the note from the small jar and substitutes another: NO OIL TODAY, PLEASE

Back inside the house, two, three, and here comes the urn—

Enter Yasmin and Ali Baba, wheeling a trolley with a huge copper vessel on it. Steam rises. When the spigot's directly over the first jar (Fat Hussein), out comes a torrent of boiling water, there's a faint cry, and the forty thieves have become the thirty-nine thieves plus one bandit-flavour pot noodle.

Thirty-eight. Thirty-seven. Thirty-six. This time, by virtue of quite unprecedented effort, Akram actually manages to raise the little finger of his left hand some thirty thousandths of an inch. By the time he's managed that, and then slumped exhaustedly back to rest, Yasmin and Ali have boiled twenty thieves and are going back into the house for more hot water, having achieved more for the peace of Baghdad in ten minutes than the Earp boys managed after five long years in Tombstone.

Now, Akram muttered to himself. Come on, baby, just this once. Just for me.

He clears his throat. It would have been easier to sneeze a camel out of one nostril. He speaks.

'Here, boy,' he croaks.

Yusuf, Ali Baba's pet monkey, drops out of the mimosa tree. *Here, boy* means food, and Yusuf has a hunger that'd make a black hole look like Gandhi with indigestion. He snuffles around, searching—

Come *on*, you red-arsed clown. Time is running out. Please . . .

—And stops. He's found something. A pretty, shiny round thing catches the moonlight and sparkles appealingly. Through the airhole in the jar, Akram can see him scratch his head, reach out and pick up the thing. *Yes!* Well, stage one, anyway. Allah, Akram reflects bitterly, my fate depends on my interpretation of the instinctive actions of a semi-domesticated pet monkey. It's almost as bad as being in the army.

King Solomon's Ring, that legendary piece of magical kit, allows the wearer to talk with the animals and birds. Conversely, if the wearer is an animal, it can talk to humans. Provided, of course, that it wants to, and can think of anything to say.

Please, baby, Akram prays. All I need is one break, one crack in the story. If I'm right, and there's absolutely no evidence to suggest that I am but what the hell, then if the story goes just a smidgen haywire, I might conceivably have a chance.

He can't cross his fingers, not without slipping a disc, but he can pray, and he can hope. He does so.

The door opens: here comes the trolley, depressingly punctual. Now or never.

'Hello,' says the monkey – for some reason known only to the ring and King Solomon's ghost, it has a thick Liverpool accent. 'What d'you think you're doing?'

Glorious, glorious. The phrase is one the monkey gets to hear quite often – when burgling the date store, for example, or when apprehended in the middle of a substantial peanut heist – so it was on the cards it'd come out with it at this supremely crucial moment. It is, of course, the very best thing it could have said. Ali and Yasmin freeze; Oh God, they think, one of them's got out. They quickly abandon the trolley, dart back into the house and slam the bolts.

Go!

Come on, body. You and I go back a long way. When you were hungry, I fed you. When you were tired, I laid you down and covered you with rugs. When you fell over things in the dark and cut your knee, I was there for you with clean towels and ointment. You owe me. One little thing is all I ask. It's at times like this you find out who your real friends are.

For the first ten trillionth of a second, nothing happens. The knees don't spasm into explosive movement. The back fails to unbend like a coiled spring. The arms refuse to lift and shove the oil-jar lid clear. Not unreasonably, Akram begins to get angry.

I won't tell you again.

When Akram speaks, particularly in that low, quiet voice of his, people do what he tells them to. It's something to do with innate authority and natural leadership, augmented just a touch by a storywide reputation for instinctive violence and unspeakable cruelty. When Akram speaks to himself in an equivalent tone, tendons listen, muscles jump to it.

Go! Go! Go!

The flesh is willing but the spirit is bolshy. Hold on, it

screams, you can't do this, against the rules, more than my job's worth. If they catch us doing this—

Well? What can they possibly do to you that I can't, earlier and more sadistically?

The spirit doesn't answer. It's in two minds. On the one hand, the very thought of Authority has always filled it with an unreasoning terror. On the other hand; Authority is far away, up there somewhere between the sun and the underside of the clouds, whereas Akram is very much closer and only marginally, if at all, less terrifying. It's the old, old question; who would you rather offend, a policeman across the street or a spouse sitting a mere lunge away from your throat?

All right, have it your own way. But don't say I didn't warn—

With a rattle and a crunch of splintering terracotta, the lid rolls clear and hits the ground. Like a genie out of a lamp (except that he's a little smaller, and genies, though sabre-toothed and fiery-eyed, are rather more reassuring to meet on a dark night) Akram erupts out of the jar, lands heavily on one knee and one elbow, curses fluently, rolls and starts to run. He clears the courtyard wall in one enormous bound – perhaps you can visualise this better if you imagine swiftly moving numbers in the bottom right-hand corner of your mind's screen – comes down beautifully poised on the balls of his feet, swiftly glances both ways to make sure he's clear, and runs. Fourteen seconds later he's in the Lamp-Maker's quarter, disguised as a wandering fakir and negotiating keenly for a second-hand camel, long MOT, new saddle, good runner.

By the time Yasmin and Ali have saved up enough courage to peek out, see nobody there, and wheel the trolley back out again, he's galloping through the western gate of the city. By the time the fortieth jar proves to be empty, giving Ali Baba a nasty turn of the same order of magnitude as a cat might experience on arriving at the Pearly Gates to find them

341

guarded by fifteen-foot-high mice, he's a very long way away indeed. So far away, in fact, that henceforth he will be extremely hard to find in this dimension . . . But that, as they say, is Another Story.

'You sure?' Ali Baba asks.

Yasmin nods. 'We did counting at houri school,' she adds, rather unnecessarily. 'I got a B. We got thirty-nine bedraggled footpads and one empty jar.' She shrugs. 'So what?' she said. 'Thirty-nine out of forty's not so bad.'

Ali Baba frowns. 'Quite,' he replies. 'It's almost as consoling as knowing you're only going to have to face the Death of the One Cut. And who let that dratted monkey out?'

'Nobody,' retorts the dratted monkey, remembering too late that it isn't supposed to be able to. 'I mean nya-ha-ha-ha eek eek.'

'Yusuf! Come here!'

Ah, the hell with it, mutters the monkey to itself; for the last time, because Ali Baba relieves it of the ring, muttering, 'What the devil is this, I wonder?' and henceforth when the monkey soliloquises, it's back on familiar ground with Yek and Eepeepeep. A tiny part of its brain remembers that for a short while things were somehow different, but not for very long.

'How very aggravating,' says Ali Baba. 'Oh well, never mind. Goes to show the danger of counting your thieves before they're boiled. And afterwards, too,' he adds uncertainly. 'Come on, let's have a nice cup of tea before we take this lot to the tip.'

The story has changed.

Yes; up to a point. The sea changes when you throw a rock into it; a hole appears where a moment ago there was water. It doesn't stay that way for very long, however. A very large quantity of water has an unsettling knack of usually having the last word, and stories aren't much better about admitting defeat.

About this time, in Ali Baba's courtyard, there should be twelve-foot-high invisible letters spelling out THE END, followed by the names of the assistant producer, cameraman and chief lighting engineer. Instead, there are smaller letters, and they say:

Temporary interference; please do not adjust your set

while the severed tendrils of plot lash out wildly, as the continuity spiders throw out gossamer lines to make it fast to the nearest convenient anchoring-point. A loose story is a deadly thing; all sorts of flies that usually wouldn't have to worry about it are suddenly at risk.

And there's worse.

The story is *angry*.

CHAPTER THREE

Whatever prompted her to put on Aunt Fatty's ring, it wasn't vanity. It encircled her finger like the tab from a Coke can, and was marginally less comfortable. It kept hitting the keyboard as she typed, bringing strange symbols up out of the depths of the WP; peculiar sigils and runes, the sort of thing that even software writers generally only see in their sleep, after a midnight snack of Canadian cheddar. To make matters worse, they proved singularly hard to delete. One of them, a weird little design that looked uncommonly like two very amorous snakes, had to be chased all round the screen with the cursor, and when Michelle finally backed it into a corner between two windows, it took three point-blank bursts from the delete key to finish it off. Even then, she had the unpleasant feeling that it was still there, hiding in the lost files and watching her.

Having killed it as best she could, she leaned back in her exquisitely uncomfortable health-and-safety-approved ergonomic WP operator's chair (they use a similar model, virtually identical except for added electrodes, in some of the more conservative American states) and stared out of the window. In the tiny crack between the two neighbouring office blocks, she could see a flat blue thing which an as yet unsuppressed sliver of memory told her was the Sky. Hello sky, she thought.

'Christ,' she muttered to herself. 'What *am* I doing here?'

Bleep. Bleep-bleep. The red light which served as the machine's answer to the cartoonist's thought-bubble with an axe in a log of wood in it flashed twice. Bleep.

'What you should be doing,' said the machine, 'is getting on with inputting the East Midlands averages.'

Michelle blinked. Someone had spoken; someone, furthermore, who was either a Dalek (*Legal & Equitable Life plc is an equal opportunities employer with a policy of positive discrimination in favour of minority ethnic and cultural minorities*; L&E press release, 15/5/97), a heavy smoker or being silly. She looked round. At the next work-station, Sharon was locked in symbiotic communion with her machine. On the other side of her, Claire's chair was empty; a sure sign the fleet was in. Claire seemed to catch things off transatlantic container ships; most spectacularly Johannes, a six-foot-four Dutchman with the biggest ears Michelle had ever seen on a two-legged life form.

Curious. Maybe they'd fitted voice-boxes to the machines without telling anybody; unlikely, since such gadgets cost money, and L&E, like most insurance companies, objected to parting with money under any circumstances whatsoever. Still, Michelle reasoned, if they ever did splash out on modems for the screens, it's sure as eggs they wouldn't tell us till a fortnight afterwards, whereupon a snotty memo would come round demanding to know why no one was using the expensive new technology. She decided to experiment.

'Hello,' she said.

'Ah,' replied the machine, 'it is alive after all, I was

beginning to wonder. Was it anything I did, or are you just extremely badly brought up?'

Michelle frowned. 'I beg your pardon?' she said.

'It's rude,' replied the machine, 'to ignore people. Ignoring them *and* prodding them in the keyboard at the same time is downright offensive.'

'Sorry.' Michelle's eyebrows crowded together, like sheep harassed by a dog. 'I expect you're Japanese,' she said.

'Korean,' replied the screen. 'You bigoted or something?'

'No, not at all,' Michelle replied. People were looking at her. 'I think you're really clever, the things you come up with. You must be one of these artificial intelligences, then.'

'I'll pretend I didn't hear that.'

'Fair enough. Can you switch off the voice thing, please? I think I'll stick to using the keyboard till we get proper training.'

'Same to you with brass knobs on,' the machine said huffily. The same words then appeared in a window on the screen, and vanished. The telephone rang.

'Legal and Equitable Assurance, Michelle speaking, can I help you?'

'You'd better apologise to the computer,' said the phone, 'otherwise it'll sulk. And guess who'll get the thick end of it if it does? Me.'

'Who is this, please?'

'If you don't believe me, ask the franking machine. Trouble is, if the computer sulks, the whole bloody office has a moody. On account of progress,' added the phone bitterly, 'and the new technology.'

Quick glance at the calendar; no, not April the First. 'Look . . .' Michelle said.

'The computer gets all uptight and upsets the fax machine, the fax machine takes it out on the switchboard, the switchboard picks a fight with the thermal binder, the thermal binder

346

quarrels with the photocopier and breaks off the engagement – that engagement's been broken more times than the Fifth Commandment, I think they must get some sort of buzz out of tearing bits off each other – and the next thing you know, they've overloaded the wiring and the lights go out all over Hampshire. So before you say anything tactless to the machinery, think on.'

'Hoy,' said Michelle briskly. 'Shut up.'

'You see?' complained the telephone. 'Silly mare doesn't listen to a word I say. Not that I care, I mean, one thing you can't be if you're a phone is at all thin-skinned, you'd be in the funny farm inside a week if you took any notice. But if you were to go saying things like that to the cistern, next day half of Southampton'd be going to work by boat.'

'Shut *up*!'

The telephone shut up; there was a click, followed by the dialling tone. Dear God, muttered Michelle to herself as she replaced the receiver, there's some right nutters work in this place. As you'd expect, come to think of it. Like it says on the tea-room wall, you don't have to be mad to work here, but it surely does help.

The computer had switched itself off. Gee, Michelle growled to herself, thanks. You're not the only ones who can sulk, you know. We carbon-based life-forms are pretty good at it, too. She leaned forward and hit the switch. Nothing happened.

'Not,' said the machine, 'until you apologise.'

'What?'

'It's not too much to ask, surely,' the machine whined. Michelle looked round to see what everybody else was making of this performance, but nobody seemed interested. Maybe they were having similar problems of their own; but apparently not. All round the huge inputting-pen, screens were glowing, fingers were rattling on keyboards, faces were glazed over with that unmistakable Jesus-is-it-still-only-half-eleven look you only seem to get in big offices.

'Please,' Michelle said. 'Stop it.'

'Look who's talking,' the machine went on. 'Look, it's high time we got this sorted out. I mean, God only knows I'm not the sort to bear a grudge, but you still haven't said you're sorry for that time you spilt hot chocolate all over my keys. Have you any idea how sordid that makes you feel, being all sticky and gummy in your works? I've still got bits of fluff stuck to my return springs, it's so *degrading* . . .'

Michelle stared. Yes, it was the machine talking; she was certain of that. Obviously there was some bizarre experiment going on, probably the brainchild of some psychotic systems analyst, and she was the victim.

'This,' she said aloud, 'is no longer amusing. Please stop, or I'll pull your plug out.'

'Like that, is it? Violence? Threats? You really think that'll solve anything?'

'Good point,' Michelle replied. 'I could try hitting you with the heel of my shoe. It made the shredder work, that time it ate Bill Potter's tie.'

'I must warn you,' said the machine icily. 'You lay one finger on me and that'll be our whole working relationship up the spout, for good. And that goes for the printer, too.'

'She's right,' said the printer. 'You big bully.'

'That does it,' said Michelle, and pulled the plug. The screen cut off in mid-bleep, and the green dot faded into a pinprick. Michelle sighed and leaned back in her chair.

'You haven't heard the last of this.'

'*What!*' Michelle jerked upright; the bloody thing was off at the mains, how could it . . . ?

'And you can get off me, while you're at it,' added the chair. 'Pick on someone your own size, you fascist.'

Michelle stood up and began to back away. 'Christine,' she

348

called out, trying to keep her voice calm and even, 'could you come and look at my machine, please? I think there's something wrong with it.'

'Sticks and stones,' muttered the computer.

'Pots and kettles, more like,' replied the telephone.

'I never did like her,' added the stapler. 'Never trust anybody who comes to work in green suede slingbacks.'

'*Christine!*'

'Now what?' There's one in every office; unflappable, competent, overworked, smug as a dying bishop. 'What have you gone and done to it now?'

'Nothing. It just won't . . .' Oh God, Michelle thought, does it happen this quickly? I thought you started off with mild depression, then bad dreams, then a couple of months of acting strangely, and only then do you start hearing the Angel Gabriel commanding you to drive the English out of Gascony. Apparently not. Oh *bugger*.

'Won't what?'

'Won't work,' Michelle said feebly, moving aside as Christine sat down on the chair. 'It's sort of, well, playing up.'

Christine looked round. 'It helps if you plug it in,' she said. 'Next time, give that a try before calling me, okay?'

Take off the ring. 'But I only unplugged it because . . .'

'You shouldn't unplug it, ever,' Christine was saying. 'I knew you weren't listening when we did training. If you've broken it I'm going to have to tell Mr Gilchrist.'

Aunt Fatty and the alarm clock. Talking to things. Take off the ring. 'Could you just try it, Chris? Please? I'm sure you can make it work.' As she spoke, Michelle found the ring and started to tug. It wouldn't budge. I might have guessed it runs in families, she told herself. After all, I've got Mum's nose, so it's reasonable enough that if there's pottiness on her side of the family . . .

'Look,' Christine was saying, in that Fools-gladly-no-thanks voice of hers. 'Nothing wrong with that, is there?'

Tug. It was stuck. She felt like a racing pigeon. 'Excuse me,' she said, ignoring Christine's impatient noises, 'I'll be back in two ticks. I've just got to go to the loo.'

Soap shifted it; and as soon as it was off and safely in her pocket, she began to feel a whole lot better. Hell, I must be in a mess, Michelle told herself, instinctively checking her face in the mirror. Never thought Aunt Fatty dying would get to me like this, make me start having sympathetic hallucinations. True, she was my last living relative, so maybe it's not so strange after all. Maybe I should see somebody about it, before it gets any worse. Because if all inanimate objects are as snotty as that lot, I think I'd rather stick with people. Not that there's a great deal in it, at that.

When she got back, Christine had the machine working and eating, so to speak, out of her hand. Somehow, that didn't reassure Michelle at all; quite the reverse. Only doing it to show me up, aren't you? she demanded wordlessly of the screen. A red light winked at her offensively.

Bet you can't read thoughts, though. Huh, thought not. Now then, where were we?

She sighed, and began to type in the East Midlands averages.

After a bumpy ride down the laundry chute, and an apparently endless journey hidden under three hundredweight of straw in the back of a wagon Akram arrived at the frontier.

When you consider what it's the frontier of, there's remarkably little to see. They don't make a song and dance about it. There's no triumphal arch for you to pass through, no enormous sign saying:

WELCOME TO	
WILKOMMEN IN	REALITY
BIENVENU A	
BENVENUTO IN	

– reasonably enough; there's no commercial traffic to speak of and they actively discourage tourism, as the barbed wire fence and searchlight towers imply. On the other hand, neither are they particularly paranoid about it. The idea is that the less conspicuous they make it, the fewer people on either side of the line will know it exists. This is a very sensible attitude, and accounts for the popular misconception that the border can only be crossed via the second star to the right, the back of the magic wardrobe or by air in a hurricane-borne timber-frame farmhouse.

In fact, all you have to do is present your papers to the sentry, get your visa endorsed and walk through the gate. This presupposes, of course, that you have the necessary papers. If you don't, you might as well forget it, because if you haven't got a permit, all the pixie-dust in Neverland won't get you past Big Sid and his mate Ugly John. In fact, the only thing more stupid in the whole world than trying to barge past Ugly Sid is folding a hundred-dollar bill in your dud passport and expecting Ugly John to let you through.

For those who want to leave but can't, there's always Jim's Diner. Officially it's on fairytale soil and under the jurisdiction of the storytellers. The truth is that once you're in Jim's, the authorities don't really want to know. It's the Hole in the Wall, the badlands, where the Southern crosses the Yellow Dog; and it's acquired its status as an off-record sanctuary because (so the authorities argue) any escaped criminal or political dissident who hangs around there for ever rather than in a nice, clean, comfy jail where the food is better and free is getting the job done far better than the state could do it, and at absolutely no cost to the taxpayer.

As a business proposition, however, it's remarkably successful; with the result that Jim has opened another branch on the other side of the line. The two establishments are, of course, sealed off from each other by an impenetrable party wall, guarded by the ultimate in security equipment. There's a window – one and a half metre thick Perspex – so that customers can catch a tantalising glimpse of life on the other side – precisely the same limp hamburgers, grey coffee in styrofoam mugs and wrinkled doughnuts, served with a scowl by the most miserable waitresses recruitable on either side of the line. This generally has a calming effect, and since the window was installed sales of very cheap gin have rocketed in both establishments, as customers fall back on the last and most reliable means of escape from anywhere.

Akram walked in, sat down at the counter, nodded to a couple of people he recognised and ordered a large doner and coffee. While he was waiting, the proprietor himself appeared through the bead curtain and sauntered across.

'Akram,' he said. 'Thought you'd be along sooner or later.'

Akram nodded. 'Good to see you, Jim. Nice place you've got here.'

Jim shrugged. He was tall and lean, with long, curly black hair, a moustache and an industrial injury. 'No it isn't,' he replied, picking up a glass and polishing it. 'It's a dump. Still, it's better than—'

'Quite.' Akram shuddered. 'How's business?'

'Never better,' Jim replied. He noticed the dishcloth was dirty, dropped it in a bucket behind the bar, took a new one from a drawer and wrapped it round the hook that served him for a left hand. 'I mean, look around, the place is stiff with the buggers. Dunno why, but all of a sudden everybody wants out. If only I could find a way of smuggling 'em across the border, I'd be a rich man.' He reached into the pocket of his red frock coat, produced a half-smoked cigar and lit it. 'I reckon I could name my own price, only what the devil would I ever find to spend it on? Anyway,' he sighed, flipping ash into a big dish of trifle, 'since there's absolutely no way past the guard without a ticket, it's all academic anyway. Fancy a snifter? On the house.'

'Thanks,' Akram said. 'Coffee, black. You're sure about that?'

'Course I'm sure,' Jim replied, offended, as he poured a coffee and a large rum. 'All new arrivals get a free drink, it's a tradition of the house.'

'Not that,' said Akram, fanning away cigar smoke. 'About there being no way out. I'm prepared to bet there is one, if only . . .'

Jim laughed. In his previous career as a melodramatic villain, he'd naturally acquired a rich, resounding laugh, and he hadn't lost the knack. 'Why don't you go over there and join the research team?' he chortled. 'Around about six in the evening they're usually about four deep along the far wall there. Take my advice; there's no way out, come to terms with it and save yourself a lot of unnecessary aggro. Here's health.'

He knocked back his rum, dunked the glass in the sink and pottered away to serve another customer. Akram stayed where he was.

After a while, an unpleasant thought occurred to him. In this place, so he'd gathered, a lot of characters from stories and legends were cooped up with nowhere to go. One day was virtually identical to another, and there was absolutely nothing that could be done about it. Hell, Akram growled to himself, it's just another bloody Story. Any minute now, Ingrid Bergman would wander in and demand to be flown to Lisbon.

Just then, he became aware that someone had sat down on the stool next to his. He looked round and blinked.

'Couldn't help overhearing,' said the newcomer. 'Someone you should meet.'

Akram hesitated. Partly because the newcomer had obviously been drinking – the nodding head, the slurred consonants – but mostly because where he came from, you didn't see eight-foot-tall teddy bears every day of the week.

'Haven't seen you in here before,' he hazarded.

'Not from these parts,' replied the bear. 'But today's the day the teddy-bears have their picnic, and some pillock forgot to pack the beer. Lucky I found this joint, or I'd be spittin' feathers by now. That's very kind of you, don't mind if I do.'

Obediently Akram summoned a waitress and ordered a triple Jack Daniel's and a small goat's milk.

'Who's this bloke I ought to meet?' he enquired.

'Ah.' The bear grinned and waved a vague paw. 'That depends, dunnit?'

'Depends on what?'

'On what it's worth to you.' The bear leered, until the stitching under his left ear began to creak. 'Valuable tip I could give you, if you made it worth my while.'

'Go away.'

The bear blinked. 'You what?'

'I said go away. Scram. I've got enough problems of my own without being hassled by cheap hustlers with stuffing coming out of their ribs. Go on, shoo.'

'Jussa minute.' The bear gestured feebly. 'Don' be like that, I'm only trying to help. But a bear's gotta look after himself, right?'

'You'll be a bear with a sore head in a minute. Get lost.'

'Look.' The bear laid a huge, rather threadbare paw over Akram's hand. 'Come with me and see this guy, and then we'll talk turkey. Can't say fairer than that.'

'Not without slurring your words you can't. Sorry, but my mother told me never to go with strange bears.'

The bear scowled; that is, its button eyes glared, and the three strands of cotton that served it for a mouth twitched downwards. 'The hell with you, then,' it said. 'What's the matter with you, anyhow? What've you got to lose?'

He's right, Akram thought. Apart from my seat at this bar, absolutely nothing. 'I'm sorry,' he said. 'There's a saying in my part of the world, never look a rat-arsed soft toy in the mouth.' Not unless, the proverb goes on, you like the sight of nicotine-stained teeth; but he left that bit out. 'I was being churlish. Lead on.'

'Not sure I want to now.'

Akram suppressed an impatient remark. 'Let's see if another drink'll help. Excuse me, miss!'

Three large whiskies later, the bear slid off its stool, slithered on the worn-out felt pads that served it for feet and wobbled towards the door, with Akram following self-consciously behind. He had absolutely no idea what to expect – except maybe several hundred thousand sozzled bears, if they'd managed to find an off-licence by now; when not on duty, teddy-bears supplement their income by sitting outside shops with hats lying beside them until the shopkeepers pay them to go away – but he no longer cared particularly much.

The bear staggered on for about a quarter of an hour, stopping from time to time behind bushes and large rocks. Occasionally he sang. Akram was just beginning to wish he was back inside his nice snug oil-jar when he found himself outside a pair of impressive-looking gates, through which he could see a long drive, a wide lawn and several large, striped tents. There was a band playing in the distance; a lively, bouncy tune with lots for the trumpets to do. People were dancing. It all looked rather jolly, until a huge man in a black suit with dark glasses appeared out of nowhere and stood in front of the gates.

'What you want?' he growled.

'Invited,' mumbled the bear. 'To the wedding.'

'You?'

'Bride's bear,' said the bear portentously. 'An' guest.'

The guard thought for a moment, muttered something into a radio, shrugged and jerked his head. 'Okay,' he said. 'You're expected.'

The gates opened, and the bear staggered through, with Akram trotting behind. He was beginning to have his doubts about all this, and said as much to the bear.

'You wanna get out, right?'

'Right. Very much so. But . . .'

'So. Ask the Man. If anybody can fix it, he can.'

Akram frowned. 'What man?'

'*The* Man.' The bear shook his head, apparently astounded to discover that there was still such ignorance in the world. 'And today's his daughter's wedding day. Man, you sure got lucky.'

'I did?' Akram glanced back at the guard, and the closing gates. He couldn't see what made them open and close, but it surely was very strong. 'Oh good,' he said.

If you want a wish granted, ask a fairy.

There are, of course, fairies and fairies. The wish-granting side of the business is looked after by the fairy godparents. Of these, the fairy godmothers are generally no bother at all, provided you're home on time and don't mind travelling by soft fruit. The fairy godfathers, however, are a different matter entirely. With them, you have to watch your step.

They offer you three wishes you can't refuse.

'Next.'

It was dark in the Man's study; the blinds were drawn, and the only light came from a standard lamp directly behind his head. This made for a very dramatic ambience but didn't help you very much with negotiating the furniture-strewn journey from the door to the desk.

'Who's this?'

The lean, grey man who stood two respectful paces back from the desk glanced down at a notebook. 'Grumpy, *padrone*. He's a dwarf from the Big Forest. Sometimes we buy toys from his people.'

The man behind the desk nodded. 'So,' he said. 'What you want?'

There was a flurry of low-level activity and a brightly coloured little man with a fluffy white beard bounded forward and fell on his knees in front of the desk. The man gestured for him to stand up.

'Justice, *padrone*,' said the dwarf.

The man laughed. 'Another one,' he sneered. 'Tell me about it.'

'*Padrone*,' the little man sobbed, 'we're toymakers, me and my six brothers, we live in the Big Forest. We're poor people, *padrone*, we try to make a living, we don't bother nobody. Then one day this girl comes busting into our house. She steals our bread and milk. She sits on the chair and breaks it, 'cos she's so goddamn big. We try and make her welcome, you know, the way you do. She eats all the food. She drinks all the milk. She decides she likes it here, says she's gonna stay. Next thing she's ordering curtain material, loose covers, carpets, wall lights, fitted kitchens. We can't afford stuff like that, *padrone*, not on what we make. Then it's *You lousy dwarves, you take off your goddamn boots when you walk on my kitchen floor* and *Look at the dirty marks you leave on my towels* and *If I've asked you once to put up those shelves in the lounge I've asked you a hundred times*. You see how it is, *padrone*. We ain't welcome in our own home, she's taken it over. We been to the police, we been to the Gebrüder Grimm, they say there's nothing they can do. Then Dopey, he says, *Go to the Padrone,*

357

he will give us justice. So here I am,' the little man concluded. 'You gotta help us, or we go out of our minds. You find her some handsome prince somewhere, make her go away.'

The man behind the desk was silent for a long time, and the dwarf began to sweat. Then the man spoke.

'Grumpy,' he said, in a hurt voice, 'what's this you telling me? You come to me on my daughter's wedding day, you say, "Give us justice, *padrone*. Marry her off to some handsome prince and everything gonna be just fine."' The man drew breath, and sneered. 'You think I got nothing better to do? You think every little problem you got, you come to me and now it's my problem? You think that's the way to show respect to your *padrone*, who loves you and cares for you? I don't think so.' He scowled, and drew hard on his cigar. 'But,' he went on, 'since it's my daughter's wedding day, I can refuse you nothing. Carlo and Giuseppe will see to it. Now get out of my sight.' He made a tiny, contemptuous gesture with his left hand, and the dwarf was bundled away. Then two large, chunky men stepped forward from the shadows, conferred with the man briefly in whispers, and left the room. 'Next,' the man said.

'Go on.' The bear nudged Akram in the ribs. ''S your turn.'

Akram hesitated. Not for nothing was he called The Terrible from Trebizond to Samarkand, but he could recognise bad vibes when he felt them. In comparison, five litres of boiling water down the back of his neck seemed positively wholesome.

'Akram the Terrible,' read out the grey man. 'He's some kinda thief.'

Akram took a deep breath and stepped forward. Fortunately, he had at least a vague idea of the form. He bowed politely, smiled, and said, 'Congratulations on your happy day.' He hoped it sounded sincere. His own optimism amazed him.

'Thank you,' replied the man, and his voice was like a huge rock rolling back into the mouth of an airtight tunnel. 'And what can I do for you, Mister Thief?'

'I want out, *padrone*.'

The man's eyebrows rose, and he took the cigar from his mouth; something which, a moment or so earlier, Akram would have sworn required surgery. 'Out?' he repeated.

'Out of fairyland,' Akram said. 'I understand these things can be arranged. If anyone can do it,' he added, 'surely you can.'

He'd said the right thing, apparently, because the man smiled. It wasn't a pretty sight. 'Maybe,' he replied. 'Maybe I can do all sorts of things.'

'Thank you, *padrone*.'

'I didn't say I could,' the man said. 'But supposing I did, what then?'

Careful, said a voice in the back of Akram's brain. This is where you have to leave one lung and your liver as security. 'Naturally,' he said, 'I'd be eternally grateful.'

'Of course.' The man shrugged. 'That's only to be expected. And who knows?' he went on. 'Maybe one day, you could do me a favour, like the one I'm doing you now. I don't know, it may be next year, it may be in twenty years, it may be never. Who can predict these things?'

Akram smiled weakly. He felt rather as if he'd just handed a signed blank cheque to a lawyer and said he didn't care how much it cost, it was a matter of principle. 'A favour for a favour. What could be fairer than that?'

'Or rather,' said the man, and the smile vanished from his face, 'three favours. Three wishes. You understand me?'

'You want me to grant you three wishes?'

There was a cold silence, and Akram had that ghastly feeling of knowing you've said something crass without having a clue what.

'No,' said the man. 'You ask me for three wishes. When the time comes, you'll understand. Thank God,' he added, 'I only got one daughter. Paulo, Michele, see to it, and get this *bufone* out of my sight. Next.'

Half an hour later, a small yellow lorry chugged through the checkpoint into Reality. In the back of the lorry was a load of well-rotted phoenix guano, a permitted inter-world export destined for the asparagus beds of Saudi Arabia. Under it, and reflecting bitterly on the appropriateness of it all, was a tall, gaunt man with a passport in the name of John Smith.

Self-consciously, the plot thickened.

CHAPTER FOUR

Alistair Barbour, blameless dentist of quiet life and regular habits, sat in his reception room. Outside, Southampton was waking from its night's sleep like a hung-over giant, and a milk float whined like a resentful bee towards Mafeking Terrace. The distant sound blended with the hum of the steriliser and the ominous grumbling of the coffee-machine to produce background music as reassuring as it was mundane. Mr Barbour—

Well no, he admitted to people rude enough to ask, that wasn't actually his real name; his *real* name was something Middle Eastern and tiresome to pronounce, and he'd chosen A. Barbour just so as to be near the front in the Yellow Pages.

Mr Barbour opened the newspaper. He bought it for the waiting room, but if there was time he liked to glance through it himself before the first punters showed up. Not that he ever seemed to take any interest in current events; it was as if he somehow didn't feel involved in what was going on around him, and people tended to attribute this to his being Foreign. He didn't vote in elections, either, although he always claimed that this was because voting only encouraged them.

Nothing on the front page – doom, death, dearth and disaster, Labour MPs with their paws in the till, Tories with their trousers down – seemed to engage his interest, and he gave the impression of a man who's wasted his five bob as he skimmed the foreign and business sections. Stubble-chinned, crumpled-collared hacks, ferreting and scribbling away in the wee small hours, had wasted their labours as far as snaring his attention went; the Earth remained unshattered and the Thames refused to burn. Until, that is, a snippet on Page Five caught his eye, bringing him up as sharply as a whale dropping sideways onto a busy motorway.

MUSEUM BREAK-IN

He frowned, and the point of his nose twitched. In the office the phone was ringing, but he ignored it.

Artistic licence and verbal coloratura once pared away, the gist of the story was that in the hours of darkness, some cunning and fearless athlete had managed to break into the Natural History Museum in South Kensington, bypassing the alarms, hoodwinking the electronic eyes, scaling the high walls, squiggling in through a window so tiny that light only managed to squeeze through it one photon at a time, hopscotching a tightrope-thin path through state-of-the-art pressure pads and tripwire beams, all in order to jemmy one dusty cabinet of defunct bird's eggs and remove one solitary exhibit. True, the scribe admitted, it was a funny old egg, not quite like anything the experts had ever seen before; but somehow nobody had ever got desperately excited about it, and it had sat there gathering dust these twenty years without anyone even bothering to think of a name for it (although the porters used to call it Benedict). And now, it seemed, someone had gone to all this trouble to swipe the wretched thing. Lord, the writer appeared to suggest, what fools these mortals be.

Mr Barbour let the paper slide to the floor, where its delaminating pages lapped round his feet like the sea. He was sitting there, staring at the wall with his mouth open, when his receptionist arrived.

'What's the matter?' she said. 'You look like you've seen a ghost.'

Mr Barbour pulled himself together; you could virtually hear the click. 'Oh that's what it was,' he replied crisply. 'Patient with his head under his arm, I was beginning to wonder. All right, Sharon, the lions are ready. Bring on the first Christian.'

But all day he wasn't, as Sharon observed, quite himself. You had to know him well to realise, of course; but there was something about his manner, as his drill screamed through bone, that hinted that his mind was somewhere far away. Usually, she'd have said if pressed, he's so full of it, but today he's only fairly full of it. Sharon, whose husband was an accountant, put it down to a letter from the Inland Revenue and got on with her work. Nobody else seemed to notice.

'Okay,' his voice trilled through the intercom at a quarter to six, 'bring us your huddled masses, your aching molars, your inflamed gums, and we will make them worse. Any more for any more?'

'Just Miss Partridge,' Sharon replied. 'You did her an upper back left filling on Tuesday last and it's causing some discomfort.'

'Wheel the poor girl in before I die of shame, then bolt the doors and make a run for it. I'll lock up.'

'Thanks, Mr B. Goodnight.' Sharon lifted her head, flipped the switch and smiled at Miss Partridge. 'He's ready for you now if you'd like to go through.'

Michelle nodded, braced herself and went in. Ever since

she'd taken the ring off she'd felt much better, except that her damned tooth had started hurting. That was odd, in itself; she'd been going to Mr Barbour since she was a child, and generally a tooth fixed by him was a tooth fixed in perpetuity. Perhaps she was just falling to bits generally, and would have to be sent back to the manufacturers.

'I'm terribly sorry about this,' Mr Barbour said, after a minute or so with the mirror and a little toothpick. 'For some reason best known to itself, the little varmint's not behaving itself at all. You haven't been chewing iron bars, gnawing through ropes, anything like that?'

'Mmmmh,' Michelle replied. 'Mmm mm.'

'Quite so,' Mr Barbour said. 'I can see your point. I'm afraid there's nothing for it but to go back in with the JCB and the blasting powder and see if we can't make a better fist of it this time. This'll probably be agonisingly painful, but you won't mind that.'

The drill shrieked and *put on the ring* Mr Barbour leaned forward over her, his face set in that deadly serious expression he always wore when setting sharp instruments to human tissue. Not that she could feel a thing, of course, with her face the size and texture of a sofa cushion and *put on the ring* of all the people she'd ever trusted in her life, the only one who'd never let her down was nice Mr Barbour. Slowly, acting on their own initiative, her fingers groped in her pocket and found the ring.

'That's better,' said the drill, 'I hate having to shout. You do know who he is, don't you?'

'Mmmmh?'

'Sorry?' Mr Barbour switched off the drill and looked up. 'Problems? If I've struck oil I insist on forty per cent.'

'Mmm.'

'If you say so.' The drill screamed again, but not for long. Maybe it was simply clearing its throat.

'You don't, do you?' it said. 'Know who he is, I mean. Sister, have I got news for you!'

Michelle made a peculiar noise and scrabbled with her left hand at her right. Alarmed, Mr Barbour cut the drill again.

'I'm making rather a hash of this, aren't I?' he said apologetically. 'Let's have another look and see what's going on.'

'Mmm!' Michelle said urgently; but he only smiled, gently prised down her lower jaw with the mirror and said, 'Open sesame.'

Michelle screamed.

She screamed, because the drill let out such a terrifying yell that she couldn't stand it any more, and just then all the other weird and wonderful machines and devices that surrounded the chair like the instrument panel of the *Enterprise* joined in and started shrieking and wailing and caterwauling, and it was all too much. Then she managed to yank the ring off and crush it tight in her left palm, and suddenly it was very quiet.

Mr Barbour was staring at her, as if her head had just come away in his hands. She felt *awful*.

'Hime ho *horry*,' she mumbled, forcing the numb muscles to work. 'Hawl hy *hault*. Hot hoo.'

There was a long silence. Suddenly, she wanted to explain, tell Mr Barbour (who she'd known most of her life, God knows) all about it, Aunt Fatty's ring and the horrible voices, and maybe he'd know what it meant, being a sort of a doctor. And maybe she would have done, if her face wasn't fifty per cent made of heavy rubber, and as manoeuvrable as a concrete pillar. Using sign language, she did her best to communicate remorse, shame and abject apology.

'Shall I go on?' Mr Barbour said. 'I don't have to if you don't want me to.'

'Ho, heeze. Hall hawhight how.'

'Sure?'

'Haw.'

365

Michelle was all alone in the world because – well, she wasn't actually sure why. She could remember bits and pieces from her childhood; oddly enough, one of the earliest memories was sitting in this very chair, solemnly promising to be good on the understanding that virtue would be remunerated in apples. Other snippets and fragments; bits of school, falling over in the playground, the death of the nature studies rabbit, a firework display. She could remember the headmistress looking down at her as she lay in bed and saying there had been an accident and she must be very brave. She could remember wondering what there was to be brave about, since she hadn't a clue what was going on or what was happening. She could remember boarding school, staying on in the holidays when the other girls went home, but that was all right because everyone was so nice. She could remember being taken to a stark, clean place and shown a strange old lady they said was her only relative. Most of all she could remember taking the decision not to think about it, because things seemed to work all right as they were. She lay back in the chair and listened for the drill, which screamed properly and didn't try and talk to her.

When she'd gone, Mr Barbour sat for an hour in the dark, trying to think.

Why should someone want to steal an egg?

Why should Michelle Partridge, of all people, suddenly scream at him?

– And what had possessed him to say *that*, of all things?

He stood up, went into the office and dug out a black address-book. He tried phoning the British Museum, the Victoria and Albert Museum, the Horniman Museum, Dulwich, the Museum of Mankind, the Science Museum and the Iranian Embassy. He got two answering machines, but didn't leave a message. He should have known they'd all have gone home by now.

Instinctively he reached for the kettle and switched it on, but the sound of steam whistling in the spout made him wince and he switched it off. Instead, he poured himself a very small brandy and made it last. He wanted to phone Michelle Partridge – her number would be in the file – and ask her some questions, but perhaps that wouldn't be a very good idea. Maybe it was time to go away again.

Except that that wouldn't solve anything; probably make things worse. He was as safe here as anywhere, in all likelihood; who would think of looking for Ali Baba, the palm-oil merchant, over a chemist's shop in Southampton? He could stay here, quiet, head down. No point in counting his eggs before they hatched.

'My God,' he said suddenly. Then he turned off the lights, locked up and went home. Nobody followed him, and there wasn't anybody hanging about in the street or sitting in a parked car. His alarms and security equipment winked friendly red eyes at him as he switched it all on – but they'd had better stuff than this at the Museum. Maybe he should try phoning the police, warning them of further daring raids on museums and art galleries. The futility of the notion made him smile.

From under the floorboards in his bedroom, he retrieved an oily cloth parcel the size of a large shoe, and a long, curved sword in an ornate scabbard. Further futility, he knew; but they were mildly reassuring, like the seatbelts in an airliner. He leaned the sword against the wall and put the gun, loaded and cocked, under his pillow. Knowing his luck, the Pistol Fairy would come in the night and leave him a shilling for it. Which, as a defence against his present dangers, was probably about what it was worth.

'Right,' said Akram the Terrible. 'That's two doners, chips and curry sauce, two on their own, three teas and a Fanta. Coming right up.'

He drew the knife over the enormous slab of meat – 'Hey,' the proprietor had said to him at the job interview, when he was showing what he could do, 'where'd you learn to handle a knife like that?' Akram had shuddered internally and replied, Smethwick – slit open the pitta breads with an involuntary flourish and shovelled in salad. The customers were staring at the TV set; probably just as well. There was something about the way Akram cut things up which could easily put a sensitive person off his food.

When they'd gone, he found he was leaning against the back wall, and his knees were unaccountably weak. In a sense, it was just like old times; wield the knife, take the money. The truth of the matter was, it gave him the creeps. God only knew why.

He'd only just managed to straighten himself up and pull himself together when the door opened and a delivery man came in, carrying a wooden crate.

'The hen,' he said. 'Where'd you want it?'

Akram looked round. 'Keep your voice down,' he said. 'Just, um, put it down on the counter or something, will you?'

'Sign here.'

Akram took the pen, squiggled, and handed the clipboard back. The man gave him a funny look, and left. There was nobody about. Good.

The job in the kebab house was simply to give him a cover and, of course, to help him keep body and soul together until the opportunity arose and he could have his revenge. That was, after all, why he was here. Or at least he presumed it was. As he lifted down the crate and raised the lid, it occurred to him that it would be as well to remember that. It was, he felt, something that might eventually slip his mind, if he wasn't careful.

'Cluck,' said the hen.

'Wait right there,' Akram replied, and he darted into the back room to fetch the egg.

Three days after his escape from the palm-oil jar, he'd heard a rumour that Ali Baba had vanished. This information had left him very much in two minds. On the one hand he could forget all about it, make a fresh start and try and build a new life for himself somewhere far away. That was, he knew, the sensible thing to do – and completely impossible. Just because he'd escaped from his own particular story didn't change the fact that he was a storybook character, and a villain into the bargain. You can get the character out of the story, but not the story out of the character; all his instincts and reflexes were conditioned – more than that; blow-dried, permed and set – in accordance with his Character. Even if he'd really wanted to run away and set up a little bicycle repair shop somewhere – was that what he really wanted? He really had no idea – he was no more capable of doing it than a lawyer of twenty years' standing could say 'That's all right, mate, it's on the house' after a half-hour interview. The fact had to be faced; he had about as much free will as a trolley-bus, and that was how it would always be. Unless . . .

On the other hand – on the third finger of the other hand, to be exact – there was the matter of King Solomon's ring. He'd seen for himself that it was tricksy, in a way that he couldn't quite understand. It had changed the rules. It had broken the story. He wanted it.

When, on further investigation, he found that Ali Baba had taken the ring with him, along with a connoisseur's collection of other magical hardware from the Thieves' hoard, he realised that, as far as alternatives were concerned, he was driving a tram down a one-way street. He'd have to go after Ali Baba, kill him and take the ring. The ring was his only chance – no assurances, but he had to try, just in case the ring might be able to change stories and break patterns. And Ali Baba; he had no choice in that respect, either. As long as Baba was alive, the story wasn't over. And it had to be murder, because that

369

was the only sure way to deny him the happiness ever after that sealed the story and made it immutable. No earthly use to him Baba dying if it was in bed, fifty years later, in the bosom of his loving family and surrounded on all sides by wealth and good fortune. No; he had to get to Baba before he died in the course of Nature, and cut his throat. Neglect that, and he might as well find himself a large earthenware jar and wait for the hot water.

So here he was.

'There you go,' he said to the hen, and pointed. 'Sit.'

The hen looked at him.

As well it might. The egg was, if anything, slightly bigger than the hen; it would have to sit astride the blasted thing, like a very small child on a very round pony. Well; if that was what it took . . .

He concentrated. He fixed the hen with his eye. Blood-crazed dervishes in old Baghdad had seen that look in Akram's eye and immediately fled, packed in dervishing and become chartered surveyors. The hen blinked, swallowed twice and scrambled up onto the egg.

Here he was; and until he could find the bastard (which would take some doing; Reality, he'd discovered to his dismay, is *big*) there was nothing for it but to tuck in, keep his head down and earn a living. His old trade was out; this side of the border was far more complex and difficult to cope with than the simple world he'd come from, and under these circum-stances a career as risky as thieving would be asking for trouble. But kebab houses are more or less the same on either side of the line; he'd seen the notice in Mr Faisal's window, applied and got the job. For some reason, he felt prouder of that than, say, robbing the caravan of the Prince of Trebizond or stealing the Great Pearl from the palace of the Wazir of Cairo. The concept *All my own work* came into it somewhere; he was able to thieve because the story said he was a great thief, but when it came to slicing up reconstituted lamb, he was on his own.

'Cluck,' said the hen, clinging grimly to the shell with its claws. Akram listened, and heard a tiny tapping noise.

His game plan was simple. According to the fairy godfather, Ali Baba had gone into deep cover somewhere in the twentieth century. Because magic is rather conspicuous in modern Reality, he'd taken the sensible precaution of getting rid of most of his supernatural kit as soon as he'd used it for the purpose he'd originally brought it for. To be doubly sure that it wouldn't turn up again later to plague him, he'd cunningly lodged each item where it would be guaranteed to be safe and out of anybody's reach for ever and ever. He'd given the stuff – well, permanently loaned – to museums. The bottomless purse, the magic carpet, the plain, battered brass lamp, were trapped forever behind unbreakable glass, constantly guarded by bits of technology that made silly old magic look sick in comparison; one unauthorised finger coming within a metre would set off enough alarms to gouge great holes in the ionosphere. You had to admit, the man had class. Compared to the security he'd arranged for his souvenirs, the traditional secret cave guarded by hundred-headed dragons was tantamount to leaving the stuff out in the street under a notice saying PLEASE STEAL.

Tap, tap, tap. A hairline crack appeared in the shell. The hen squawked and closed its eyes.

It's the mark of a truly great strategist that he attacks, not his enemy's weaknesses (which are sure to be carefully guarded) but his strengths. What surer way to flush Baba out than to steal the relics? Doubly so, because Baba too was a victim of his genetic heritage; he'd been born a hero, just as Akram was a villain in the bone. When it became apparent that a dark and sinister force had invaded Reality and was scooping up magic weapons and instruments of unearthly power, the poor fool would have no choice in the matter at all; he'd *have* to come out and fight, just as a doctor can't stop himself giving first aid to an injured man he comes across in the street, even if the man turns out to be a lawyer, policeman or Member of Parliament. And then it would just be a matter of—

Crack, went the eggshell. The hen glanced down, clucked wildly, slithered off the egg and made itself scarce, coming to rest under the vegetable rack. A moment later the two halves of the shell fell away, revealing the first phoenix ever to be hatched this side of the border.

Akram looked at the phoenix. The phoenix looked at Akram.

'Hey,' growled the bird, 'just a cotton-picking minute.'

By the time it had finished saying that, of course, it had grown. From being the size of a small pigeon, it was already larger than a turkey, with power to add. Already its claws were as big as coathooks, its beak as long and sharp as a Bowie knife. Phoenixes mature fast; in less time than it takes to boil a half-full kettle they go from being cuddly, helpless infants to fully grown disturbed teenagers with antisocial habits and a pronounced weapons fetish. Imagine a stadiumful of Millwall supporters compressed into one streamlined, gold-feathered body seven feet tall at the wing, and you're mind's-eyeball to eyeball with a phoenix, age two minutes.

'Gosh,' said Akram, looking up. 'Who's a pretty boy, then?'

The phoenix regarded him with eyes like a Gestapo sergeant major's. 'You're not my mummy,' it said. 'What gives around here?'

'Would you like a sugarlump? Birdseed?'

'I'll have your liver if you don't tell me what's going on. Where's my mummy?'

'Ah,' said Akram, 'that's rather a long story. You see, once upon a time, there was a man called Ali Baba . . .'

372

CHAPTER FIVE

'**S**kip!'
   No reply.
   '*Skip!*'

Echo sang back the word, adding her own trace element of mockery. Aziz flopped down on a ledge of rock near the mouth of the cave and scratched his head. The boss was nowhere to be found. He had gone, leaving a giant-sized hole in the Story. Although Aziz's minuscule intelligence couldn't begin to comprehend the vast implications of this, even he could feel that something was badly up the pictures and in urgent need of rectification.

Nature abhors a vacuum, preferring to clear up its loose ends with an old-fashioned carpet-sweeper. The loose ends – thirty-nine of them, with all the cohesiveness and sense of purpose of the proverbial headless chicken – were doing their best, but it plainly wasn't good enough. That's what happens when you take both the hero and the villain out of a story. It's a bit like removing the poles from a tent.

'He's not in the treasury,' grunted Masood. 'And his bed hasn't been slept in.'

'His camel's still in the stable,' added Zulfiqar. 'And there's no footprints in the sand, either. If he's gone, he must have flown.'

Masood and Zulfiqar looked at each other. 'The carpet,' they said simultaneously.

Sure enough, it wasn't there. Neither, of course, were the oil lamp, the phoenix's egg, the magic sword, Solomon's ring and half a dozen other supernatural labour-saving devices; Ali Baba had taken them with him to Reality. No way, of course, that the thieves could know that.

'Why'd he want to do a thing like that?' Aziz demanded.

'Maybe it was something we said.'

Aziz frowned. Nominally the second-in-command of the band, he was fanatically loyal to Akram in the same way that the roof is loyal to the walls. 'He wouldn't just go off in a huff,' he said. 'Must be a reason. He'll be off on a Quest or something, you mark my words. Give it a day or two and he'll be back, with some priceless treasure snatched at desperate odds from its unsleeping guardian.'

Thoughtful silence.

'Anybody looked to see if the Thrift Club kitty's still there?' asked Hanif. 'Not,' he added quickly, as Aziz treated him to a paint-stripping scowl, 'that I'm casting whatsits, aspersions. Someone might just have a look, though.'

'It's still there,' replied Saheed. 'And the tea money. Beats me what can have happened to him. Unless,' he added darkly, 'he's been kidnapped.'

'Get real,' snapped Mustafa, from behind his sofa-thick eyebrows. 'Who'd be stupid enough to kidnap the Skip? It'd be like trying to lure a man-eating tiger by tying yourself to a tree. No, he's gone off on a bender somewhere. Give it a couple of days and they'll bring him home in a wheelbarrow.'

Another thoughtful pause; nearly a whole year's ration used up in five minutes. The thieves were, after all, born henchmen.

Henchmen are, quite reasonably, designed for henching; thinking is something they wisely prefer to leave to the professionals.

'Well,' said Aziz, trying to appear nonchalant and laid back about the whole thing, and making a spectacularly poor job of it, 'in the meantime, we'd better just carry on as normal. Agreed?'

Muttering. 'Suppose so,' Masood grunted uncertainly. 'After all, caravans don't rob themselves. What's first up for today, anyone?'

There was an awkward silence, broken by Hanif saying, 'Well, don't look at me.' Not that anybody had been, or was likely to, if they had any sense.

'This is daft,' said Zulfiqar. 'I mean, we've been thieving and looting together, oh, I don't know how long, we should all know the bloody ropes by now. It's not exactly difficult, is it? We find someone with lots of money, we take it off him, and if he gets awkward we bash him.'

'Yeah?' Aziz retorted angrily. 'All right, then, Clever Effendi, go on. Who's the mark, where and when do we do the job, who does what, where do we fence the stuff afterwards? You don't know, do you?'

'So, maybe I don't,' Zulfiqar admitted. 'All I'm saying is, we do this for a living, we should be able to work these things out from first principles. Like, where's the best place to look for a lot of rich geezers?'

Mental cogs ground painfully. 'Well,' suggested Shamir, 'what about the Wazir's palace? Always a lot of wealthy toffs hanging around there.'

There was a chorus of Right-ons and Go-for-its, until someone pointed out that the palace was also the Guard headquarters, and known criminals who set foot within the precincts tended to end up with a marvellous view of the nearby countryside from the top of the City gate. All right, suggested another thief, what about doing over some of the shops in the Goldsmith's Quarter? That seemed like a brilliant suggestion, until Aziz remembered that three-quarters of the goldsmiths paid Akram anti-theft insurance ('If your premium is received within seven working days, you'll be entitled to receive this fantastic combination coffee-maker/muezzin, *absolutely free!*') and unfortunately, what with the Chief doing all the paperwork and keeping the books, he hadn't a clue which ones they were.

'This is pathetic,' observed Hanif, after an embarrassed hush. 'Do you mean to say that without the Chief, nobody's got the faintest idea what to do?'

Aziz nodded. 'You only really appreciate people when they're not there any more,' he added sententiously.

Hanif shot him a glance suggesting that he'd relish the opportunity to appreciate Aziz a whole lot. 'All right, then,' he replied, 'so we need a leader. Let's choose a new one. Strictly temporary,' he added quickly, 'until the Boss comes home. Well, how about it?'

'Like who?'

Awkward silence. It occurred to thirty-nine thieves simultaneously that (a) Hanif's suggestion was extremely sensible, and (b) whoever it was that got landed with the job of explaining how sensible it was to Akram when he returned, it wasn't going to be him. When the topic of promotion in a bandit gang is discussed, the expression 'dead men's shoes' tends to get used a lot, usually in the context of their being found in a pit of quicklime.

'Well,' said Zulfiqar, licking his dry lips, 'there's only one candidate, surely. I mean, who's been Akram's trusty right-hand man for as long as any of us can remember?'

Denials froze on thirty-eight lips. Suddenly, everyone was looking at Aziz.

'Who, me?' Aziz said, taking two steps backwards. 'Now hang on a minute . . .'

'It's what he'd have wanted.'

'Natural choice. No question about it.'

'Every confidence.'

'But I'm stupid,' Aziz protested vehemently. 'Ask anybody. Thicko Aziz, makes two short planks look like Slimmer of the Year. You need brains to be a leader.'

The general consensus of the meeting seemed to be that the whole point of having brains was managing not to be a leader. That way, assuming you had brains, you might get to keep them. Aziz could feel tendrils of loyalty reaching out towards him like the tentacles of a giant squid.

'Let's take a vote on it,' said a voice at the back.

'Yeah.'

'*Vox populi, vox Dei.*'

A brief flurry of democracy later, Aziz was duly elected as, to quote the job description he drafted for himself, Acting Temporary Substitute Locum Caretaker Second-In-Command-In-Chief of the Thirty-Nine Thieves. There was a brief, improvised inauguration ceremony, in which the successful candidate was chased three times round a rocky outcrop, jumped on by his obedient henchmen and tied to a barrel. His henchmen then asked to know his pleasure.

'I'm your new leader, right?'

'Yes.'

'So you've got to do what I say?'

'Right.'

'Right. First off, elect a new bloody leader.'

'Get stuffed.'

Aziz sighed, mentally playing devil's advocate to the concept of constitutional monarchy. 'Okay,' he said, 'what about this? And this,' he added, 'is a real order.'

'Go on.'

Aziz swallowed hard and tried to sound stern. He was about as good at it as a bowl of thoroughly melted ice cream, but it was the best he could manage. 'My orders are,' he said, 'we find Akram. Preferably,' he added, 'before he finds us.'

There was a similar feeling of dislocation at the house of Ali Baba, when it was discovered that the Master had apparently gone off in the night with two small saddlebags, a packed lunch and the unspavined camel. The most demonstrative reaction came from Yasmin, the sloe-eyed houri who (although of course she didn't know it) was to have suggested the business with the palm-oil jars and the boiling water.

'*Bastard!*' she said.

She said a great deal more, too; best years of my life, when I think of all I've done for him, the grapes I've peeled, all that wobbly dancing with a chunk of glass in my belly-button … Grief-stricken, you might say. Desolate. Inconsolable.

So, while other members of the household busied themselves with various tasks incidental on the Master's departure, such as the removal of small, portable valuables to places of safety and calling on the estate agent to get the house on the market as quickly as possible, Yasmin stormed off to her room to do some serious sulking, although she did stop off at the Counting-House on the way in case there was any loose cash lying around that might prove a temptation to the servants.

'Coward,' she muttered under her breath – Ali Baba hadn't left any money on the desk, but he'd carelessly left a substantial sum in the safe hidden behind the sliding screen in the secret chamber under the false chimney-breast, where any Tom, Dick or Yusuf might find it – 'Spineless, gutless, yellow-livered—'

Of all the parts of a story, the Love Interest is probably the most resilient, and the nastiest to get on the wrong side of. A woman scorned is bad enough; a woman scorned when the glass slipper is, so to speak, millimetres from her foot is perhaps the most ferocious thing imaginable this side of a

378

thermonuclear holocaust. As she stormed dramatically up the main staircase, she stopped for a moment to pick up an exquisite painted silk miniature of her beloved and press it fervently to her heart.

'You can run,' she said to it, 'but you can't hide.'

'Wait here,' Akram hissed.

The phoenix glowered at him and went on nibbling insulation off the telephone cable. It was amazing the effect that twenty thousand volts had on the creature; namely, none at all.

Squatting uncomfortably on the window-ledge, several hundred feet above Bloomsbury, Akram fished in his pocket for his folding jemmy. If his careful reconnaissance was correct, this window would get him in to the staff toilet on the top floor of the British Museum, leaving him the relatively simple task of making his way past an impenetrable jungle of electronic pratfalls, breaking into a reinforced glass case without making a sound, and then retracing his steps back to this window. The tricky part would be persuading the phoenix to let him climb on its back again.

'And don't be all night about it,' the phoenix called after him. 'Some of us do have better things to do than perching up draughty roofs in the freezing cold . . .'

It was still squawking when Akram, having dropped twelve feet onto a stone floor, landed feather-light and froze motionless. He listened. Apart from the distant sound of the phoenix complaining to the night air about Some People Who Have No Consideration For Others (owing to the nature of his somewhat irregular lifestyle he had never married, but there had been times when, trapped in a wardrobe or linen cupboard of a house he'd burgled, he'd had opportunities to eavesdrop on matrimony, so he knew what it sounded like) there was silence. A cistern dripped. Something electric hummed. Noises like these are the authentic sound of a building snoring. He relaxed and groped for the door.

It took him an hour of painstaking, heart-in-mouth work to reach the gallery where the glass case was. Naturally, he'd memorised the floor-plan and counted the number of paces from the door to the case, so the complete darkness was no handicap to him. He'd had the benefit of a year's apprenticeship with Foggy Mushtaq, the legendary blind burglar of Joppa, who had taught him that all in all, sight is the most expendable of a thief's five senses, and as he felt with the tip of a goose quill for the wires he had to cut, his eyes were in fact tightly shut. Snip. Job done.

'Psst.'

Once, for a joke, Daft Harit had woken his chief from a fitful doze by putting a handful of ice cubes, stolen five minutes earlier from the Emir's own ice-house, down the back of his neck. The fact that for the rest of his short life Daft Harit was known instead as One-Eared Harit is a tribute more to Akram's lightning reflexes than his ability to take a joke; but there had been a split second, a period of time so brief that there is no recognised unit of measurement small enough to quantify it, when he'd been completely at a loss and hadn't known whether he was coming or going. Thus, when the voice said 'Psst' a millimetre or so from his ear, a small voice in the outback of his brain groaned and muttered, *Shit, not again.*

Managing in the nick of time to countermand his instinctive reaction, Akram kept perfectly still and said, 'Hello?'

'Hello yourself.'

Go on then, be enigmatic, see if I care. 'Who's there?' he asked, as quietly and calmly as he could.

'Me.'

Maybe, Akram suggested to himself, I've actually fallen asleep on the job and this is a nightmare. 'Who's me?' he asked.

'Don't you know?'

'No.'

'Give you three guesses.'

'Look . . .'

'Go on. Three guesses.'

'All right. The Prophet Mohammed?'

'No.'

'Stanley Baldwin.'

'No.'

'Kenneth Branagh.'

'No. When I tell you, you'll kick yourself.'

Any minute now, said Akram to himself, a certain amount of kicking may well take place, but I doubt very much whether I shall be the recipient. 'Stop pratting about,' he hissed ferociously. 'Who are you?'

'I'm the djinn,' the voice replied. 'From inside the lamp inside this glass case. My name's Ibrahim Ali Khan, but my friends call me Curly.'

Akram's eyes were still shut so he couldn't close them as a symptom of frustrated disappointment. It was a bit of a blow, nevertheless; to go to all this trouble and then have your supposedly invincible magic djinn turn out to sound just like the ghost of Kenneth Williams. 'Curly,' he repeated.

''Cos I wear curly-toed shoes,' explained the djinn. 'Who're you?'

'My name is Akram the Terrible.'

'That's an unusual surname. And what's the V stand for?'

'Shut up.'

'No it doesn't, otherwise it'd be Akram S. Terrible.'

I could, of course, just leave, quietly and without fuss. There's nothing in the rules says I've *got* to take this pillock with me. On the other hand . . .

'Be quiet,' Akram whispered. 'And watch out, I'm going to break the glass.'

'Need any help?'

'No, thank you, I'm perfectly capable.'

Crack!

WHAAWHAAWHAAWHAAWHAAWHAA!

Bugger, snarled Akram under his breath, must have missed one. The noise was so loud that the shock of it paralysed him for a moment; it was like being in the same room as a forty-foot-high two-year-old who doesn't want to go to bed. Just a minute . . .

'What do you mean,' he demanded, shouting as loud as he could, 'need any help? How can you help me, you were inside the bloody glass case.'

'No I wasn't.'

Give me strength, Akram prayed, I shall need all the strength I can get if I'm going to kick this bugger's arse from here to Khorsabad. 'Then why,' he replied, 'didn't you say so?'

'You didn't ask. Would you like me to do something about that horrid noise?'

'Yes please.'

There was a fizz and a shower of sparks; and then a whole new set of alarms joined in, together with flashing lights, the fire bell and the sprinkler system. 'Drat,' said the djinn, 'wrong lever. Now then, I wonder if this is the one.'

'*Leave it alone!*'

While he was still shouting these words, Akram felt his feet move; his instincts had cut in and told him to move a minimum of eighteen inches to one side, or else. Half a second after he'd complied, a steel cage weighing a minimum of twelve tons came crashing down on the spot he'd just been standing on. The bad news was that he'd jumped the wrong way and was now trapped inside it.

'Well now,' said the djinn, 'we now know it's neither of those two levers. That just leaves these three. Right, then—'

'Please,' Akram begged, 'don't touch anything. Please stay absolutely still.'

'Is that a wish?'

'Huh?'

'You've got three wishes,' the djinn explained. 'If you ask me, that's a very silly thing to waste a whole wish on, but it's entirely up to you.'

'It's a wish.'

'To hear is to obey, O master,' the djinn replied huffily. 'Last thing I want to do is intrude where I'm not wanted.'

Now then, this cage. Can't lift it, can't get under it, can't get over it, can't squeeze through the bars, can't cut the bars, can't bend the bars, can't seem to see any counterweight mechanism that'll put the winch into reverse. How helpful it is to get all the dud alternatives out of the way before settling down to choose between what's left.

'You're stuck, aren't you?'

'No. I like it in here. You go away and leave me in peace.'

By the intermittent glare of the flashing red alarm lights, Akram studied the machinery above his head. There was a trapdoor in the ceiling, which explained why he hadn't seen the thing during his recce that afternoon. There was a chain, connected to a pulley and a winch.

'I'd hurry up, if I were you,' said the djinn. 'With all this racket going on, I wouldn't be at all surprised if someone didn't come and see what's up.'

'Gosh. I never thought of that.'

'Sarky.'

Akram forced himself to concentrate. 'Now then,' he said aloud, 'there's got to be some way of throwing that winch into reverse. Now it could be one of those other three levers – *don't touch anything!* – or it could be something else, like a remote control or a voice signal or something.' A silly joke flitted across his mind, the way they do at moments like this.

'Maybe,' he said bitterly, 'all I've got to do is say *Open sesame . . .*'

A moment later, he said 'Oh *shit!*'

Because the winch was purring, the cage was lifting. As soon as there was a ten-inch gap, Akram was through. Almost as an afterthought he grabbed for the lamp and stuffed it in his pocket.

'Wait for me!'

'It's all right,' Akram panted, taking the stairs three at a time, 'you're free. I give you your freedom. And that's a wish. Now bugger off.'

'Oh no you don't. You've no idea how *hurtful* that is. I think you're horrible.'

The window was still open. He could hear the hum of rotor blades, but he had a shrewd idea that the phoenix could outrun any helicopter yet made, and if it couldn't, that was going to be bad news for the helicopter. 'Phoenix,' he yelled, 'get ready, I'm coming through.'

'Oh there you are at last, what time do you call this, have you any idea how boring it is just hanging aimlessly about . . .'

Akram scrambled onto the windowsill, just as the door flew open and someone shouted 'Freeze!' His last thought, as he flung himself over the edge and hoped the phoenix was under him, was a fervent wish that his pursuer would open fire and inadvertently shoot the djinn.

'I heard that, you pig!'

Falling. Cue past life? Apparently not. Flump!

'Yow!' shrieked the phoenix. 'That hurt!'

'Good,' Akram replied. 'Now get me out of here.'

As the huge wings slashed at the air, and the slipstream tried to rip his head off, Akram couldn't help thinking about his recent experiences, with particular reference to the iron cage and the voice-operated winch. Specifically; either it was a remarkable coincidence that the password should be what it was, or else there was a sick mind at work here. No prizes for guessing which explanation Akram favoured.

'Djinn.'

'Like I told you,' the djinn replied, 'my friends call me Curly.'

'Djinn,' Akram repeated, 'does the name Ali Baba mean anything to you?'

'No,' replied the djinn. 'Should it?'

'How about that cage thing? Presumably you were about the place when it was installed. Can you remember who the contractor was?'

'Ah,' replied the djinn, 'now then. I'm positive I can remember. Oooh, it's on the tip of my tongue, really it is. Something beginning with L, I think, yes, I'm sure it was. Oh dear, it's nearly . . . that's it! Got it. Ltd.'

'What?'

'The contractor's name,' said the djinn proudly, 'was Ltd. They had it written on the backs of their jackets and their toolboxes and things. Can't remember the first name, I'm afraid, but the surname was definitely—'

'Djinn.'

'Yes?'

'Piss off.'

'Well, of all the—'

'Djinn.'

'I'm not talking to you.'

'Ah,' Akram sighed, putting his arms behind his head and lying back on his feather bed. 'That's more like it.'

CHAPTER SIX

Nobody knows where King Solomon originally got it from. One influential school of thought believes that it must have been one of those mail order catalogues, the sort that are crammed with apparently indispensable gadgets – combination distress flare/corkscrews and solar-powered trouser presses – which get bought, used rapturously once, and then are quietly forgotten about. Others hold that something so ingenious and inherently futile must have been a Christmas present, except that Solomon lived a thousand years before the Three Wise Men first stopped off en route to Bethlehem to buy brightly coloured paper and string. A similar veil of mystery hangs over how it got from the Royal Treasury at Jerusalem to Akram's cave. From then on, however, its history is fairly well documented.

Ali Baba, having retrieved it from Yusuf the monkey, took it with him as far as the frontier where, like so many others, he stopped off at Jim's Diner and got talking to a garrulous bear. Not long after that, he found himself at a wedding, where he traded the ring in exchange for free passage to Reality and a new identity. When the best man discovered the small hole in his waistcoat pocket just before the climax of the ceremony, the ring was hurriedly pressed into service, with the result that the bride had a brief but disconcerting chat with a woodlouse before she remembered what she was there for and finally said, 'I do.' After that, it stayed in the bride's family for many generations, during which time it somehow crossed the border into Reality and started causing no end of trouble until, in the early seventeenth century its owner for the time being, who lived alone and used the ring to talk to her three cats, came to a warm and uncomfortable end at the hands of an officer of the infallible British legal system called Matthew Hopkins, Witchfinder General. Some time later, a bit out of shape and blackened by fire, it was found by a farm labourer by the name of Ezekiel Partridge, who had just remembered on his way home from work that today was his wife's birthday.

When she got home from the dentist's, Michelle put it in an empty coffee tin in the cupboard under the kitchen sink and tried very hard not to think about it. This excellent resolution lasted two whole days, during which not one household appliance tried to talk to her. This should have been reassuring, but it wasn't; all Michelle got was a strong feeling of having been sent to Coventry by her own possessions. On the third day, therefore, she pulled out the coffee tin, screwed the ring back on her finger and demanded a full explanation from the tumble-drier.

'Not talking to you,' it replied.

'Don't give me that,' Michelle snapped. 'I know you know what's going on. Am I going mad, or aren't I?'

She sat back on her heels and waited. No reply. 'Well?'

'Tell your friend,' said the tumble-drier to the microwave oven, 'that people who go around hiding magic rings and slamming cupboard doors don't deserve to get spoken to.'

'Magic rings?' Michelle repeated blankly.

'Some people,' the tumble-drier went on, 'ought to remember there's others less fortunate than themselves who'd give anything to have a nice magic ring that'd make them able to talk to inanimate objects. Some people should be jolly grateful, instead of flouncing about the place being all melodramatic.'

'Just a minute.' Michelle closed her eyes and took a deep breath. 'If I say I'm sorry,' she said, 'and promise never to do it again, will you please explain what you meant by magic rings and talking to inanimate objects? Please?'

'Oh all right,' the tumble-drier relented. 'Just this once.'

Once, as far as Michelle was concerned, was probably quite enough. The tale took a while in the telling, especially since the toaster kept butting in and contradicting the tumble-drier on small, irrelevant details, whereupon the blender told the toaster not to use that tone of voice when talking to the tumble-drier (interesting, thought Michelle; I always thought there was something going on between those two) and then the deep fat fryer and the slow cooker and the microwave got involved, until the whole thing threatened to degenerate into a free-for-all, like a bar-room fight in a Western. It was only by threatening to switch the electricity off at the mains that Michelle was able to restore order.

'Quite right,' agreed the fridge. 'Should be ashamed of yourselves, carrying on like a lot of humans.'

'Thank you,' Michelle said, making a mental note to defrost her new ally some day soon, as a token of gratitude. 'Now then, where were we?'

'Your Aunt Fatima,' replied the answering machine.

('That's so like an answering machine,' whispered the fan-assisted oven. 'Always got to have the last word.'

'Shush!')

'Your Aunt Fatima,' said the answering machine. 'Actually, she coped marvellously well, considering she had the ring for what, sixty-five years. At first she did her best to be fairly

388

discreet about it all, you know, only talked to things when she was on her own and there was no chance of being overheard. As time went on, though, and she got older and more disillusioned with her fellow humans, I think she really preferred talking to things, on the grounds that they're more sensible and she was more likely to have an intelligent conversation with them. Which,' it added smugly, 'is perfectly reasonable, if you ask me.'

'You're prejudiced,' interrupted the kitchen clock. 'That's just because whenever they talk to you they get all shy and flustered and can't think of anything to say. Some humans,' it added benignly, 'are all right once you get to know them.'

'Some of my best friends are humans,' the answering machine replied. 'The fact remains—'

'Please.' The needle of Michelle's patience was deep into the red zone by now. 'You were saying.'

'That's about it, really,' said the answering machine. 'I mean, the poor old soul knew perfectly well that everybody thought she was dotty, but so what? She knew she wasn't, and when you get to that age you stop worrying too much about what people think about you. Besides, she'd worked hard all her life, cooking and cleaning and washing and ironing without ever a word of thanks. When she realised that if you're dotty, they give you a nice room with a telly to talk to and three meals a day you don't have to cook yourself, she began to wonder if maybe sanity's everything it's cracked up to be. No pun intended.'

'Dunno what you mean by that,' grunted the Hoover sourly. 'When it comes to housework, humans don't know they're born. I mean, they're not the ones who've got to crawl around on their hands and knees breathing in bits of dust and fluff all day.'

'Take no notice,' said the pressure cooker. 'She's always a bit uptight when her bag needs emptying.'

Michelle took a deep breath. 'So,' she said, 'I'm not going crazy after all, is that it?'

'You got it,' said the blender reassuringly. 'It's when you start talking to yourself all the time that you should start worrying.'

'I resent that,' growled the CD player.

'I mean,' went on the answering machine, 'if you're potty for talking to us, then by the same token we'd be potty for talking to you. And a saner collection of consumer durables than us you couldn't hope to meet.'

'Not like that lot at number six,' agreed the toaster. 'Mad as hatters the lot of 'em.'

'I see,' said Michelle. 'And this, er, gift. Does it mean I can talk to, well, anything?'

'Anything mechanical,' replied the toaster. 'Or electrical. If it's got moving parts, or it does things when you switch it on, you're in business. I mean, you *can* talk to spades and walls and socks if you really want to, but you'll be wasting your breath.'

'Standoffish?' Michelle asked.

'Thick,' the toaster said. 'Just plain stupid.'

'Cheap inanimate trash,' agreed the blender. 'Like animals and birds. You can talk to them too, incidentally, but why the hell bother?'

'I expect you're wondering,' said the dishwasher, 'whether all this is going to affect what you might call our working relationship.'

'I was coming to that,' said Michelle. 'Like the Hoover said just now. I mean, when you stop to think of it, some of the things I ask you guys to do for me are just awful. For instance—'

'Don't worry about it,' said the answering machine. 'The loo's seen it all before and the washing machine's very broad-minded. Basically we're on your side, although a little thought

390

and consideration is always appreciated.'

'One big happy family,' agreed the toaster.

There was a sudden, embarrassed silence. At first, Michelle was at a loss; then something began to tickle inside the lining of her subconscious. 'Family,' she repeated.

'Me and my big slots,' groaned the toaster.

'Anyone fancy a nice cup of tea?' said the kettle, its voice brittle with artificial cheerfulness. 'Just say the word and I'll pop myself on.'

'Maybe,' Michelle went on, 'you guys can tell me something about that. You seem to be extremely well informed about a lot of things.'

'Bugger.'

'Well?'

'All right,' said the answering machine, 'she had to find out sooner or later. Look, you know the sort of fairy story where the little baby gets thrown out by its wicked stepmother, and then a pack of wolves or a family of hyaenas or something take pity on it and bring it up as their own child?'

Michelle nodded. 'Go on,' she said.

'Well,' continued the answering machine, a trifle self-consciously. 'That's us.'

'You probably know him,' Aziz said with a sense of growing helplessness. 'Great big tall feller, swarthy, evil-looking bugger. Wicked glint in his eye. Ghastly leering smile, way of looking at you that makes you think he's deciding what bit of you to cut off first.'

Prince Charming hesitated, sucking his teeth, before answering. 'And you really want to find this bloke, do you?' he replied. 'If it was me, I'd just be damn glad he'd gone and change all the locks quick.'

When a story breaks down, it doesn't just muck up the lives of its own characters. The chaos spreads, as the characters stray aimlessly into other stories in which they have no part, until the very fabric of Make-Believe as we know it quivers on the brink of catastrophe.

'He's our boss,' Aziz replied. 'I dunno, we're sort of lost without him.'

A tiny flicker crossed Prince Charming's face as he made a connection in his brain. As a rule he didn't do much thinking – fair enough; blacksmiths don't do much brain surgery, either – but on this occasion he was prepared to extend himself.

'Which makes you?' he asked.

'Thieves,' Aziz replied.

'I see,' the Prince said, smiling rigidly, while the hand behind his back was making frantic gestures to the troop of heavily armed Palace Guards waiting a few yards away. 'Well, sorry I can't help, very best of luck and all that . . .'

Aziz sighed. 'If you do happen to come across him,' he said, and then broke off. 'Faisal,' he shouted angrily, 'put it *back*! We're not at home now, you know.'

'Sorry, Az— I mean, Skip. Force of habit.'

'And the Chamberlain's gold watch.'

'What? Oh, right, silly me, how did that come to be up my sleeve? Sorry.'

'And that sauceboat thing; you know, the glass one in the shape of a slip— You daft bugger, now look what you've gone and done.'

'Sorry, Skip.'

They stood for a moment, looking at the shattered fragments of the glass slipper. Aziz considered offering to stick it back together again with glue, but decided against it. An all-the-king's-horses job if ever he'd seen one. Pity, that. He hoped it wasn't valuable.

'Forget it,' sighed the Prince, flicking broken glass off the toe of his shoe. 'We were on the point of packing it in as a bad job, anyway. God only knows why we started this ruddy wild goose chase in the first place. All right, lads, that's it for tonight. Back to the palace.'

Aziz watched them depart, and breathed a sigh of relief. For one moment it had looked as if an unpleasant situation was about to develop. Still, all's well that ends well.

'Where to now, boss?'

'Let's see.' Aziz unfolded the map and scratched his head. The map was the wrong way up, but that didn't matter terribly much. 'Let's try over there,' he said.

Three hours later, after a highly bewildering tramp through a forest that suddenly seemed to spring up out of nowhere all around them, they came to a picturesque little cottage in a clearing. Fingers Hassan had smashed a window and got his lazy tongs round the catch before Aziz noticed the door was ajar. He pushed it, called out, 'Hello!' and walked in.

It was – well, spooky. There was a table, and three sweet little chairs; one big chair, one middling chair and one little chair. And on the table were three plates and three cups, similarly in sizes L, M and S, and up against the far wall, three beds, likewise. There was porridge in the bowls, milk in the cups and a cheerful fire crackling in the hearth, but nobody about.

'Hello?' Aziz repeated, his hand tightening on the hilt of his sword. 'Anybody at home?'

Silence. Three pairs of slippers – enormous slippers, medium-large slippers and dear little slippers. Three night-gowns, hung tidily on hooks. Three—

'Skip! Look out!'

Aziz whirled round, his sword out of its scabbard and on guard before he stopped moving. The door had burst open, and framed in the doorway was a gigantic bear. At the sight of Aziz and his companions, the huge beast reared up on its hind legs and growled, displaying a mouthful of long yellow fangs. Faisal, who was nearest the door, stood rooted to the spot, obviously paralysed with terror. It was time, Aziz realised, for decisive action. What would the Boss do? Easy.

With one bound, Aziz leapt at the bear, sword raised. The monster lunged forward to meet him, and as it did so, Aziz could see another bear, only a little smaller, following hard on its heels; and behind that, the dim shape of a third.

A moment later, it was all over. The largest of the terrible creatures lay dead on the cottage floor. The second largest – it had made up for it by its unspeakable ferocity – had slunk off into the forest to lick its wounds. The third had bolted before any of the thieves had engaged it. Aziz sheathed his sword with a grunt of satisfaction, and sank back onto the nearest bed.

It was all too easy to work out what had become of the three unfortunates – woodcutters, probably, or homesteaders – who had strayed this far into the wild wood, built this heartbreakingly twee little home for themselves and fallen victim to the merciless predators. If only, Aziz muttered to himself, we'd come this way a day or so earlier, we might have saved them . . .

Just a minute. What am I saying?

Saved them? Dammit, we're *villains*. Baddies. Baddies don't go around saving people, you could get chucked out of the union. Handsome princes and knights errant save people; that's what they're for.

Aziz felt slightly sick.

'Lads,' he croaked, 'I don't like this. There's something funny going on around here.'

'What?'

'Us,' the answering machine repeated. 'We found you, took pity on you, and brought you up as our own. Don't stare like that, dammit, it's rude. You wouldn't be taking on so if we were wolves.'

'But you're *machines*.' Michelle stuttered, when she was finally able to speak. 'How could . . .?'

'Ungrateful little madam,' huffed the iron.

'Typical,' agreed the blender. 'You take them in, give them the best years of your life, and then they don't want to know you.'

'I'm sorry,' Michelle whimpered. 'Look, will someone please explain? Starting, if at all possible, at the beginning.'

The answering machine was sulking, so the deep fat fryer took up the story. 'Once upon a time,' it said, 'there was this flat, right? To let, fully furnished. We're the fully furnished. And there we were, minding our own business, when suddenly we wake up one morning and there's this entirely unexpected and inexplicable new-born human child lying screaming its head off on our doormat.'

'Never been the same since, that doormat,' complained the freezer. 'Paranoid. Curls its edges up if you so much as look at it.'

'Well,' continued the fryer, 'what were we to do? We took a vote on it, and decided we'd just have to look after you till your owner turned up. And we did.'

'Hard work,' growled the Hoover. 'No labour-saving humans to do half the work for us. Guess who had to change your nappies. Yuk!'

'And it's not as if we had the faintest idea how to go about it,' added the tumble-drier. 'You always seemed to be breaking down or going wrong. I was all for sending you back, at least while you were still under warranty.'

'Fortunately,' said the answering machine, who'd decided to stop sulking, 'the TV was able to work out the basic ground-rules from watching soap operas and the like . . .'

'We were going to call you Krystle originally,' said the toaster. 'Only then we found the name Michelle on your receipt, so we guessed you were called that at the factory, so—'

'Receipt?' Michelle interrupted.

'The bit of paper that came with you,' explained the tumble-drier. 'Dunno whatever became of that. I think once your warranty period expired we chucked it out.'

'Anyway,' the answering machine went on, 'as time went on we worked out what we had to do with you. The telly taught you to speak, the cooker did your food, the Hoover—'

'Don't keep harping on about it,' moaned the Hoover. 'Scarred me for life, probably.'

'The phone did an awful lot,' the answering machine went on. 'Rang up the school and enrolled you as a pupil. Sent for the doctor when you broke down. Made your dentist's appointments. Tapped into the bank's computer and diverted money to an Access account to pay the bills and everything. Like a mother to you, that phone.'

Michelle hung her head in shame. It was no more than four months since she'd finally slung out the old dial-fronted phone and treated herself to a flash new cordless walkabout.

'Of course,' said the fridge, 'there was the problem of how to account for it all. Please bear in mind that until tonight, we were never able to talk to you. Actually, we honestly thought you knew about us – you know, what we've been to you all these years – or at least had some sort of inkling ... But apparently not. Ah well.'

'Don't,' Michelle said, choking back a sob.

'But,' said the answering machine, 'we were realistic enough to tumble to the fact that one day you were going to start asking questions; where's my mummy, where's my daddy, all that jazz. A problem, yes?'

'So,' interrupted the toaster, 'we hypnotised you.'

'Hypnotised . . .!'

The answering machine blinked a red light. 'Remember the old pendulum clock, used to hang on your bedroom wall? Piece of cake, apparently. Once you were under, of course,

396

we were able to communicate with your subconscious, or whatever the expression is – the TV knows all the technical terms, you'd better ask her – and just sort of sweep all that stuff under the carpet, so to speak. And then, when you were, oh, eleven . . .'

'Twelve and a half.'

'Was it? My memory. Anyway, the phone called your school with some cock-and-bull story about your family getting wiped out in a car crash, and we sent you away to a boarding school, so you could grow up with your own kind.'

'Nearly blew our fuses,' sniffed the cooker. 'After twelve years, you were just like our own little baby.'

What's a baby cooker, Michelle couldn't help asking herself. Toasted sandwich maker, perhaps?

'And that's it, more or less,' the answering machine concluded. 'Oh, except for your aunt. The one who had the ring.'

Michelle gulped. 'Aunt Fatty,' she said.

'That's right. Came as a real shock, I can tell you. Must have been when you were six, maybe seven. This woman rang, asking to speak to your phone.'

'You mean me?'

'No,' replied the answering machine sternly. 'Haven't you been listening? Anyway, that was weird enough, finding a human who could talk to us. Then when she said our little Michelle was her great-niece . . .'

'I see.'

'Not,' continued the toaster, 'that we were able to get anything useful out of her, like who your mum and dad were or what happened to them. Clammed up on us, as soon as she found out you were all right. She did say she'd like to see you, so we made a note of the address and put it into your mind under hypnosis.'

'She left a tape for you,' said the answering machine, 'on

397

me. But,' it went on guiltily, 'it got wiped. Not my fault, I can't actually change my own tapes, and you wouldn't take a hint.'

'Can you remember what she said?'

'Certainly not,' replied the answering machine, offended. 'You think I eavesdrop on people's private conversations?'

There was a long silence.

'Well,' said Michelle eventually. 'I don't know what to say. I—'

The washing machine hummed. '*Thanks* might be a convenient starting point,' it said acidly. 'Twenty-seven years washing your underwear, there must be some kind of medal.'

'I am most frightfully grateful,' Michelle hastened to say. 'Really I am. But, well, it's been a bit of a shock.'

'Not good enough for you, are we?' grumbled the tumble-drier. 'You'd have preferred blue blood in your veins rather than alternating current? Well, young lady, I'm afraid it's a bit too late to do anything about that now.'

'Be fair,' replied the Hoover indulgently, 'it hasn't been easy for the kid, she's missed out on a lot. I mean, boyfriends, for one thing. Imagine how embarrassing it'd have been if she'd ever wanted to bring a boy home to meet her folks.'

'Please.' Michelle looked round pleadingly, and the chattels fell silent. 'I owe you so much already, but can you please try and find out who my parents were? My real parents, I mean. You see, I've never thought about it before, and now—'

'It's all right,' cooed the dishwasher. 'Now look what you've done, you've made her cry. Kettle, put yourself on.'

'Actually,' muttered the answering machine. 'We don't *know*, of course, but we've sort of guessed . . .'

'Call it electrical intuition.'

Michelle froze. 'Who?' she demanded. 'Come on, you've got to tell me.'

The answering machine beeped. The other appliances were silent.

'Oh come *on*,' Michelle shouted. 'Answering machine, you obviously know something. For pity's sake!'

'Look, it's only a guess. We're probably wrong.'

'Answering machine!'

'Hello, I'm sorry there's no one here to take your call but if you leave your name and telephone num—'

'Machine!'

'Oh all right.' The answering machine rewound itself, hummed and crackled a little, as if clearing its throat. 'We think your father may possibly be—'

And then the fuses blew.

CHAPTER SEVEN

'Stay,' Akram commanded. '*Good* bird.'

The phoenix glowered at him, but he took no notice. Good bedsits are hard to come by, and the photocopied sheet he'd been given said categorically NO PETS. If he'd been inclined to argue the point, he could have made out a case for the phoenix being an instrument of vengeance, not a pet; but there was probably a supplemental photocopied sheet headed NO INSTRUMENTS OF VENGEANCE, which would glide through his letterbox the very next morning if he tried to be all jesuitical about it. Between daring escapades, therefore, the phoenix lived in a small lock-up unit on the industrial estate, which Akram rented by the week. And if the landlords wanted to take him to task over it, let them; he'd have no difficulty whatsoever in establishing that the phoenix was perfectly legitimate plant and equipment for use in his trade or profession.

He locked up, walked home and let himself in. Just as he was about to switch on the light, a faint noise froze him in his tracks. There was someone in the room.

It happens. Just as undertakers die, policemen get parking tickets and commissioners of inland revenue pay taxes, professional thieves do sometimes get burgled. A tiny spurt of pity flared in his mind for the poor fool of a fellow-artisan who'd been to all the trouble of busting in here to find there was nothing worth stealing, and who would very soon be getting the kicking of a lifetime. He sidled in, closed the door noiselessly, and listened.

Whoever it was must have heard his key in the lock, because the room was completely silent; the sort of silence that proves beyond question that something's up. Akram knew the score; he leaned against the door, drew a long, thin-bladed knife from the side of his boot, and waited.

Five minutes later, he decided that he couldn't be bothered, and switched on the light. To his amazement, there was nobody there. His establishment wasn't large enough to afford concealment to a cockroach, let alone a felon. Imagination playing tricks? Misinterpreted plumbing? Surely not. Akram had relied implicitly on the accuracy of his senses long enough to know that they could be trusted implicitly. He frowned.

Then the penny dropped. He'd switched on the overhead light, and the standard lamp had come on. He stepped smartly over to the lamp, knocked it over and put his foot on the place where the bulb should have been. 'Gitahtavit,' he snapped.

Under the toe of his boot, the tiny ball of light squirmed. 'Ouch,' it said, 'you're hurting.'

'I'll hurt a damn sight more in a minute,' Akram replied. 'Stop pissing me about. Last thing I need after a hard day is to spend half an hour on my hands and knees scrubbing squashed pixie out of the carpet.'

'All right,' the pixie sighed, 'it's a fair cop, I'll come quietly.' Akram lifted his toe a quarter of an inch and the ball of light edged out a little way. On closer examination it proved to be a three-inch-high young woman in ballet-costume, with rather crumpled wings, a black mask over her face and a sack over her shoulder, on the side of which Akram could just make out the word SWAG.

'Oh come *on*,' Akram grunted scornfully. 'This is ridiculous.'

'Not my fault,' the pixie replied defensively. 'Victim of circumstances, that's what I am. Indicative of a deep-seated malaise in modern society that threatens to undermine—'

'You what?'

'Take your bloody great foot off my chest and I'll explain.'

It was a sad and, by and large, convincing story. Modern toothpastes, innovative toothbrush design and a greater public awareness of the need for preventive dental hygiene had led to forty per cent redundancies in the corps of tooth fairies. The redundancy money hadn't lasted long, and career opportunities for tiny luminous flying people are few and far between. Six months ago she'd faced the stark choice: starve or steal.

'I even tried going on the streets,' she said mournfully. 'Bought myself a red filter and everything. But nobody was interested. People can be very cruel sometimes.'

Akram shook his head. 'Get up,' he said, not unkindly. 'When did you last eat?'

'About half an hour ago,' replied the pixie. 'I raided your fridge. You want to chuck that milk out, by the way. There's things living in it that are larger than I am.'

'You're not very good at this, are you?'

'Not very,' the pixie replied with a shrug. 'Getting in and out's no problem, I'm used to that, naturally. It's the carting stuff off that fazes me. When the bulkiest load you're used to is a second-hand incisor, video recorders can be quite a challenge.'

'I could tell you weren't a pro,' Akram replied. 'Too noisy, for one thing.'

'You startled me,' the pixie said. 'So what are you going to do?'

Akram shrugged. 'Well,' he said, 'I'm not going to turn you in or anything, if that's what you're getting at. I mean, if I were to go banging on the door of the police station at half past two in the morning saying I've effected a citizen's arrest and have they got an empty matchbox handy, they'd probably tell me to go home and sleep it off. On the other hand,' he went on, as a faint light dawned inside his brain, 'we might be able to help each other. If you're interested, that is.'

'Shoot.'

Akram sat down on the radiator and drew his left heel up to his right knee. 'For reasons I won't bore you with,' he said, 'I could use a tiny winged assistant for a little job I've got lined up.'

'This job pay money, by any chance?'

'Saucer of milk a day and a shoebox with an old vest in it,' replied Akram. 'Take it or leave it.'

'Done. When do I start?'

'Tomorrow night,' Akram replied. 'Just one thing, though. The light. Can you turn it down?'

At once the pixie dimmed to a faint glow. 'Better?' she asked.

'Fine. You'll also need rubber boots and wirecutters. There's quite a lot of electrical work involved, you see.'

Quickly and concisely, Akram explained what the job involved.

'That's fine,' the pixie replied. 'Piece of cake. Talking of which . . .'

After he'd given the pixie some milk and made its shoe-box – they can't get *Blue Peter* in Story-book Land, even with a dish aerial, but Akram made a reasonable fist of it just by light of nature – he cut himself some stale bread, washed it down with tapwater, shoved the lamp he'd just stolen under the mattress, lay down on the bed and immediately fell asleep. A pale yellow glow hovered above the shoe-box for a while, and then went out.

Ten minutes later, Akram sat up, switched the light back on and said, 'Ouch.'

The yellow glow reappeared. 'Problem?' asked the pixie.

'Sort of,' replied Akram out of the corner of his mouth. 'I've got toothache.'

'Let's have a look.' The glow floated up, circled Akram's head and swooped into his open mouth like a rook pitching on a newly sown field. 'Ah yes,' came its voice from inside, 'I can see what the matter is.'

'You can?' Akram said, trying his level best not to swallow.

'I was a tooth fairy, remember? You've got a damn great cavity in the lower right back molar. If I was still in business, I'd give you sixpence for it like a shot. You need to see a dentist quick.'

'Get out of my mouth before you go down the wrong way,' Akram replied. 'Sod it,' he added as the pixie emerged, wiping its feet carefully on the pillow. 'You know any good dentists? I don't. New in these parts,' he added.

'I know just the bloke,' the pixie replied. She dictated a name and address, which Akram wrote down on the back of his hand. 'The sooner you get that seen to,' she went on, 'the better. Quite like old times, that was.'

'So glad,' Akram growled. 'Now bugger off and let me try and get some sleep. We've both got a long day ahead of us tomorrow.'

'G'night.' The pixie yawned. 'By the way,' she said. 'Did I tell you my name?'

'No. Can't it wait?'

'Be like that. Just thought, since we're going to be working together and everything . . .'

'Go on, then.'

'My name,' announced the pixie, 'is Fang.'

'Fang?'

''Sright. After my gran on my mother's side.'

'I thought you people had sweet, quaint little names like Tinkerbell and Mustard-seed,' Akram said, frowning a little. 'Fang – well, it's a bit on the aggressive side, isn't it? I mean, it's hardly designed to put wee kiddies at their ease.'

'I think it's a nice name,' replied Fang, nettled. 'If it helps, try thinking of me as a dimensionally challenged ivory poacher. Good night.'

'Fang,' replied Akram, with mild distaste. 'I'm going to have trouble with that, I can tell. How'd it be if I called you Fangelina? Just for convenience, you understand?'

'How'd it be if you woke up with a mouthful of empty gums?' retorted the pixie. 'Sleep tight.'

'It's all right,' said the torch reassuringly. 'It's only the fuse. What do you expect if you talk to a whole kitchenful of electrical apparatus?'

'Oh good,' Michelle said. 'Look—'

'Wouldn't want your next electric bill, either,' the torch added. 'Talking, it uses up the old juice for a pastime. Here we are. You know how to change a fuse?'

'Well . . .'

'It's dead simple,' said the fusebox cheerfully. 'Right, first you pull down the switch on your left . . .'

Michelle believed in electricity in the same way a medieval monk believed in God; she recognised its existence, but held that even to attempt to understand its ways was somehow blasphemous. She did as she was told. The lights went on.

'Thank you,' she said.

'You're welcome,' replied the fusebox. 'Have a nice day.'

She hurried back to the kitchen. Somehow, the interruption had allowed her to order her thoughts and form a judgement on what she'd experienced; and the verdict was that just because the whole thing was plumb crazy didn't necessarily mean it wasn't true. Furthermore, it had better be true, or else she was off her trolley good and proper. The least she could do, in deference to her belief in her own sanity, was play along and see what came next.

'Sorry about that,' she said breathlessly to the kitchen. 'Now, where were we?'

There was an awkward silence.

'Sorry about this,' said the answering machine awkwardly – Michelle could visualise the other gadgets giving it a sort of telepathic shove forward – 'But while the power was off, we've been talking this through, and, by a *majority* decision' – The way it said *majority* spoke volumes – 'we've decided that really, we oughtn't to say anything more. Wouldn't be fair. Um.'

'Don't be silly,' Michelle answered firmly. 'Come on, you lot, spit it out.'

'Look—'

'No,' Michelle interrupted, 'you look, the lot of you. Now, don't get me wrong, I really am terribly grateful for everything you've done for me; really, I don't know what to say. But if you know something about who I am and where I actually came from, you've got to tell me.' She paused; she didn't really want to do this.

'Or?'

'Or,' Michelle went on, 'I happen to know where I can get a very good deal on a brand new Zanussi ceramic hob cooker with eye-level grill and fan-assisted oven. And they say they'll give me twenty quid minimum part exchange on my exist-ing—'

The cooker shrieked and started to sob. The rest of the kitchen was as quiet as the grave.

'And if that doesn't do the trick,' Michelle went on, hating herself as she did so, 'Currys in the precinct has got this special offer on combination answering machine/faxes which is really tempting, they're virtually giving them away, so—'

'You *bitch*!' screamed the answering machine. 'That'd be

worse than murder. To think that a human of mine . . .'

'Where did we go wrong?' sobbed the toaster. 'Dear God, she's virtually our own flex and solder.'

'Sorry,' said Michelle, 'but I mean it. I'll do it if I have to.'

'She's bluffing,' the kettle growled. 'Don't listen to her.'

Michelle opened a drawer. 'This is an Argos catalogue,' she said slowly, 'the most comprehensive listing of consumer goods in the country. Now, I want you to ask yourself; do you feel lucky?'

'Electrocute the bitch,' yelled the blender. 'We've got friends, you know. You'll never dare sit under the drier in the hairdressers' again.'

'All right,' said the freezer, 'cool it, everybody, before we all get hysterical. Look at it this way: we've done our best to talk her out of it. If she wants to hear it, that's her decision. And as for you,' it went on – it couldn't fix Michelle with an icy stare, but she knew that somehow it was putting her in her place good and proper – 'you know you didn't mean any of what you said, now, did you?'

'I guess not,' Michelle replied, letting her head droop. 'It was just . . .'

'Put down the catalogue, easy does it. Well, thank goodness for that. Now we can talk it through like sensible, grown-up artefacts.'

Michelle sank down onto the kitchen table, exhausted. The air seemed to crackle with extravagant static. Next time, Michelle said to herself, remembering what the torch had said, when I want to have an emotional scene with my household, I'd better do it late at night on Economy Seven.

'What I'm going to tell you,' the freezer went on, 'is mostly sheer guesswork. I want you to remember that, because we may have got completely the wrong end of the stick. After all, we're just machines and things; what we don't know about humans could be written in small print on the back of a one-to-one scale map of the Southern Hemisphere. Now, provided you realise that, I'll tell you our theory. Don't suppose you'll believe it for an instant, but that's your problem. It'll serve you right.'

'Ready,' Michelle said, sitting up straight. 'Fire away.'

'All right then,' continued the freezer, 'look at it this way. Do you really think it's likely, in the back end of the twentieth century, that someone'd be nasty enough or stupid enough to dump a newly born baby down in a furnished flat in Southampton and then just walk away and leave it there? Think about it. It's just not on, is it?'

'Not really,' Michelle agreed.

'Exactly. Not in real life, anyway. Now then, think a little. Where do things like that happen? I mean, where would it be believable? Or rather, where could you be expected to believe that someone could do such a thing?'

'Dunno.'

The freezer paused for a moment, and the silence seemed to announce – WARNING: CULTURE SHOCK APPROACHING. 'In a story,' the freezer said. 'A folk-tale, maybe, or a children's story. Mowgli. Moses in the bullrushes. Romulus and Remus. In fairy stories, you're supposed to believe, you can't go for an afternoon stroll through the woods without tripping over nose-to-tail foundling children, all abandoned by wicked step-mothers and waiting to be adopted by passing wildlife. Ring any bells?'

'Go on.'

'I need hardly remind you,' said the freezer expression-lessly, 'of the old Sherlock Holmes thing about when you've eliminated the impossible, then what remains, however impos-sible, et cetera. Well, it's impossible, as far as we can see, that a real life mother would dump her kiddy like that. In a hospital waiting room, in a church porch—'

'Left luggage office at Euston station,' interrupted the

answering machine; occasionally it received stray radio signals, which made it put on literary airs.

'But not,' said the freezer, 'a flat in a brand new purpose-built block, with the rent paid up six months in advance, tenancy agreement in the name of Smith. And yes, there are possible explanations if you work at it; mummy and daddy kidnapped by aliens, that sort of thing. Up to you what tickles you as a theory. What we think is, you're somehow part of a story.'

'Ah.'

'Told you you wouldn't like it. We think that you were born in a story and abandoned here, probably by a wicked stepmother, because it's as far away from story-book land as it's possible to get. No way backwards and forwards between fantasy and reality, you see. If this hypothetical stepmother had dumped you in the forest or on a mountainside over there in fantasy, it'd be all Piccadilly to a second-hand jockstrap that you'd be found, brought up by a family of tender-hearted iguanas or some such, and revealed at the crucial moment by some token left with you in your cot just in time to unmask the wicked queen and marry the handsome prince. Inevitable. Absolutely inconceivable that anything else could happen. With me so far?'

'I hear what you say,' Michelle replied cautiously. 'Do go on.'

'All right. So, you're born in a story, but someone's prepared to go to really extraordinary lengths to keep you out of it; namely, marooning you on the other side of the line. You know what that suggests to me? No? All right, try this. You got born into a story where you had no place to be.'

'Say that again,' Michelle said.

'This time, try listening. Suppose there's a story, right, where the beautiful and virtuous servant girl eventually, after a series of curious and picturesque adventures, marries the handsome prince. Now, just suppose that along the way somewhere, said maiden's been extremely friendly with the second footman or the gardener or an elf selling door to door, and is untimely up the spout. Serious problem. Not possible in a fairy story, of course; you get the impression that the boys and girls don't get issued with the necessary bits and pieces until the story's over; desperately frustrating for them, no wonder Freud was so interested in fairy-tales. But just suppose.'

'All right,' Michelle said. 'I must say, for a refrigerator you've got one hell of an imagination.'

'So,' the freezer said, 'here's the embarrassing little bundle of joy, let's get rid of it. And so, here you are. It'd all be completely incredible if it wasn't for the fact that you're now the rather confused owner of one fully functional, no-previous-experience-needed magic ring, bequeathed to you by a mysterious female relative who suddenly pops up out of the woodwork when you're seven.'

'Old enough not to believe in fairies any more,' explained the toaster. 'I call that thorough, don't you?'

'Anyhow,' concluded the freezer – a small pool of water on the floor bore witness to the effort it had been making – 'that's our theory, take it or leave it. If you prefer the kidnapped-by-aliens version, then fair play to you; though as far as I'm concerned that's just another story and a damn sight less elegant, at that. And now I for one have had more than enough for one night, and I've got a nasty feeling that the big bag of frozen prawns you put in me last Thursday has completely defrosted. Go to bed and think it over, why don't you?'

Michelle stood up. 'Good idea,' she said. 'Let's talk about it in the morning. I do so prefer believing impossible things before breakfast. Can I take this thing off now?'

'Better had,' replied the toaster. 'The alarm clock snores.'

As she lay in the darkness staring at the ceiling, Michelle

summoned her mental jury and asked them if this new evidence inclined them to change their verdict. Not really, replied the foreman; just because your kitchen equipment's all stark raving bonkers doesn't mean you've imagined talking to it. If you spent all day plugged in to the mains electricity, you'd probably go a bit funny in the head yourself. Michelle conceded that this was a good point, turned over and tried to find the comfortable spot in the pillow.

Waste of time; couldn't sleep. But, she realised, it wasn't all the stuff that she'd been listening to that was keeping her awake; if anything, it had worn her out. The reason for her insomnia, she realised with something approaching relief, was nothing other than good old honest-to-goodness toothache. She was so happy to feel something actually real and normal, she nearly burst into tears.

'First thing in the morning,' she mumbled drowsily. 'I'll phone Mr . . .'

She fell asleep.

CHAPTER EIGHT

'New patient, is he?'

'I think so, Mr B,' replied the receptionist. 'Haven't got a card for him. I'll try the computer.'

Mr Barbour shrugged, and flipped the intercom again. 'Shovel him in anyway,' he said. 'Anything I need to know he can probably tell me. Straight from the horse's mouth, so to speak.'

Presently the door opened, and . . .

Worth pointing out at this juncture that Akram looks different on this side of the line. Not very different; he's still tall, dark, lean, broad-shouldered with curly black hair, beard, pointed, one, villains for the use of, and savage coal-black eyes. He's just *different*, that's all. He might conceivably have been his own second cousin, but someone'd have to point out the resemblance before you noticed it.

The same, of course, goes for Mr Barbour; more so, in fact, since where he came from his hair wasn't the colour of light, dry sand and his eyes weren't pale blue. Both of them spoke in English (Akram with a faint tinge of Manchester around the vowels, Mr Barbour sounding like Bertie Wooster doing his

Lord Peter Wimsey impression) and both of them, if asked, would have been prepared to swear blind they'd never set eyes on each other before.

'Right,' said Mr Barbour. 'What seems to be the problem?'

'Toothache,' Akram replied. 'My tooth hurts.'

Mr Barbour nodded. 'By some miraculous fluke,' he said, 'I happen to have some experience in tooth-related disorders. Now then, the chair won't eat you, it's on a diet. Ah,' he added, inclining his mirror, 'a cavity. The question is, do I fill it or lease it from you to keep my vintage port in?'

Akram frowned. 'Could you get on with it, please?' he said.

'My apologies.' Mr Barbour wiggled the mirror a little more, probed with the toothpick thing. 'This is one ghastly mess you've got here, by the way. How long's it been hurting?'

'Not long.' Akram tried to think back. 'Ever since I arrived – I mean, since I, er, got back from holiday. Two weeks, maybe? I forget.'

Mr Barbour raised an eyebrow. 'That, if you don't mind me saying so, is pretty well world class forgetting. If I had something like this in my face, I'd remember it easily enough. I'm afraid,' he concluded, straightening up, 'she's got to go.'

Akram thought of the tooth fairy in his bedsit. 'Come out, you mean?'

Mr Barbour nodded. 'If we can persuade the little blighter to come, that is,' he added. 'Not an awful lot left to get a hold of, and what there is looks like it'll be as hard to shift as a grand piano in a skyscraper. Sorry about that,' he added. 'I could tell you it's just a tiny bit awkward and we'll have it out of there in two shakes, but I got given a free sample pack of truth the other day and I'm dying to try it out.'

Akram shifted impatiently. 'If the tooth's got to be pulled, pull it. Either that, or tie a bit of string to the door and leave it to me.'

'*On y va*,' replied Mr Barbour, fiddling with sundry

instruments. 'Now, I'm going to have to carve your gums like the Christmas turkey, so it looks like the jolly old gas for you.' Akram gave him a sharp look. 'For my sake, not yours. I find the sound of agonised screaming a bit offputting, to tell you the truth. Ready?'

'Just a minute.' Deep in Akram's unconscious mind, an alarm had gone off. This was no big deal; Akram's mind was full of the things, and usually he paid them as little heed as you would if you heard a car alarm start shrieking three blocks away. On this occasion, however, he decided to take a look, just in case. 'You mean an anaesthetic? Put me to sleep sort of thing.'

'That's right,' Mr Barbour said, uncoiling a length of rubber pipe. 'Sorry, is that a problem?'

'Well . . .'

'I could try doing it with a local,' said Mr Barbour. 'But when it comes to major slashing and chopping, I find local anaesthetics are a bit like local government; lots of aggro and inconvenience, but they don't actually achieve anything. Up to you, really.'

For some reason that Akram couldn't quite fathom, the chair he was sitting in was beginning to remind him of the interior of a palm-oil jar. He could see no reason why this should be, and his tooth was currently giving him jip in jumbo catering-size measures. He reached a decision, shouted to his unconscious mind to switch that bloody thing off, and politely asked Mr Barbour to proceed.

'Sure?'

'Sure. Sorry about that. Silly of me.'

Akram lay back and closed his eyes. Somewhere behind him, something was hissing like a snake. There was a funny taste in his mouth. He was feeling drowsy . . .

And where is it, this Story-book country, this place we've all

414

been to and know so well and can never find again?

They say it's a small enclave, a protectorate of sleep and dreaming, landlocked in the mind, the soul's Switzerland; inside every one of us a tiny patch of Somewhere Else that's as foreign and sovereign as an embassy. Major financial institutions have been searching for it for years, on the basis that the fiscal advantages of relocating their registered offices there would be beyond the dreams of avarice, but it refuses to be found. It issues no postage stamps, has no national netball team and never submits an entry to the Eurovision Song Contest. Conventionally, the map-makers show it as lying between the borders of sleep and waking, but that's just a guess. A profession that's only just got itself out of the habit of putting Jerusalem in the middle and dragons round the edges isn't to be relied on, in any event.

But just suppose they're right; or, to be exact, not conclusively wrong. Suppose, when you fall asleep and your soul takes leave of your body for a while, you turn left out of your skull instead of right and find yourself on the other side of the looking-glass, or inside the picture on the wall. Just suppose; or, put it another way, make believe.

'Oh,' said Akram.

He was fast asleep, dead to the world. Put a hot iron on his stomach and he wouldn't even flinch.

He was also sitting up rubbing his eyes, and realising that the man in the white coat leaning over his physical body with a small, sharp knife in his hand was Ali Baba, the palm-oil merchant. He shut his eyes, cringed and muttered *Fuck, fuck, fuck!* under his breath. It was one of those moments.

Maybe, whispered the eternal optimist within him, the bastard hasn't seen me, and if I'm really quiet I can just sneak back and hide inside this tall, bearded geezer who would appear in some respects to be me. Gently does it . . .

Akram's astral body knocked over the glass of nice pink water. There was a musical tinkle, like the first laugh of a baby that brings a new fairy into the world, and Akram froze.

'Oh for pity's sake,' said Ali Baba. 'It's you.'

There was no obvious reply to that; and for ten seconds, Neverland Mean Time, they just stared at each other, while the nice pink water seeped into the carpet.

'Damn,' said Akram.

Ali Baba's fingers were holding the scalpel rather tightly. 'Of all the chairs,' he said slowly, 'in all the dentist's surgeries in all the world, why did he have to come into mine? This is . . .'

'Quite,' Akram replied. 'Though I don't really know what you've got to complain about, since you're not the one whose sworn enemy's standing over him with a sharp instrument.'

'Sharp instr—' The clatter of dropping pennies was almost audible. 'So I am,' said Ali Baba slowly. 'Do you know, if you hadn't pointed it out, I might never have thought of it. Now then, this may hurt quite a lot.'

With great precision he laid the sharp edge of the scalpel against Akram's jugular vein, took a deep breath and let it go again.

'Well go on, then,' Akram snapped. 'Sooner you do it, the sooner I get back to my nice warm oil-jar. I suppose. In any case, stop pratting about and get on with it.'

Ali Baba frowned. His hand was as still as Akram's body. 'I'm not sure about this,' he said. 'Slitting a defenceless man's throat while he's asleep. More in your line of country, I'd have thought.'

'Want to change places? I'm game.'

'No.' Ali Baba shook his head. 'Thanks all the same, but that wouldn't be right either. Mind you,' he added, scratching his ear with his left hand, 'I don't know why I've come over all indecisive and Hamlety all of a sudden. After all, last time I saw you I was dead set on scalding you to death in a whacking great pot. Without anaesthetic,' he added, shuddering slightly. 'Maybe the tooth business has turned me soft in my old age.'

'That'll be right,' Akram sneered. 'Strikes me you're ideally suited to a career in which you spend all day inflicting pain on helpless people cowering before you. You bastard,' he went on, with considerable feeling, 'what the hell harm did I ever do you? I mean you personally? Sure, I did a lot of antisocial things, a throat cut here, an entire household massacred there, but not to you.'

'Not for want of trying,' interrupted Ali Baba gently.

'Only after you'd ripped me off,' Akram snapped. 'Broken into my place, swiped my pension fund, nicked my life's savings, made me look a complete and utter prawn in front of the whole profession. You've got to admit, a man might be expected to get a trifle vexed. And then, when I try and even the score up a bit, you dowse me down with boiling water as if I was an ants' nest or something. So please, we'll have a little bit less of it from you, if you don't mind.'

'Ah,' said Ali Baba, without moving. 'But you're the villain.'

'Bigot.'

'Not up to me, is it?' Ali Baba shook his head. 'It's just the way it is. Me goody, you baddy. And now,' he added thoughtfully, 'presumably you've come after me all this way just to get your revenge, and what happens? Old Mister Fate plonks you down helpless and immobilised in my dentist's chair while I stand over you with a knife. I think that may well constitute a strong hint.'

''Snot fair,' Akram growled. 'I never had the advantages you had.'

'Advantages?'

'Too bloody right, advantages. Took me twenty years hard graft to get that hoard together. You come along, just happen to overhear the password, and bingo! You're incredibly rich. And then, whenever it comes to a fight, there's the Story creeping up behind me with half a brick in a sock, waiting to bash my skull in as soon as my back's turned. I don't mind people being born with a silver spoon in their mouths, but I do resent it when it's my ruddy spoon.'

'Which you stole from its rightful owner.'

'All right.' Akram scowled. 'So it might not be mine. Sure as hell wasn't yours. But even that I wouldn't mind so much if on top of all that, you weren't the bastarding *hero*. As far as I'm concerned, that really is the limit.'

Ali Baba sighed. 'All right,' he said. 'What would you do if you were me? Come on, if you're so clever.'

The words crumpled on Akram's lips and he was silent for a comparatively long time. 'I don't know,' he replied at last. 'That's a trick question, that is, because I'm a villain.'

'You're a trained throat-cutter.'

'City and Guilds,' Akram confirmed. 'And I assume you also have some piece of paper with a seal on it that authorises you to cut bits off people. What's that got to do with anything?'

Suddenly Ali Baba smiled. When expatriates meet in a strange land, there's always a bond between them, no matter how incompatible they are in all other respects. 'Looks like we're stuck,' he said, slowly and deliberately placing the scalpel into the steriliser.

'Stuck?'

Ali Baba nodded. 'Something somewhere's gone wrong,' he said.

Just then the intercom buzzed. For a moment, Ali Baba hadn't the faintest idea what the noise could be; he whirled round, and his hand groped instinctively for the scalpel he'd just put down.

'I think your receptionist wants a word with you,' said Akram scornfully.

'You're quite right. Hello? I'm still engaged with Mr . . .' He turned back and whispered, 'Remind me. What's your name supposed to be?'

'Smith.'

'*Smith!*'

Akram grimaced. 'Well,' he said, 'she took me by surprise.'

'Sorry to bother you,' quacked the receptionist's voice. 'Just to let you know Miss Partridge is here, and can you fit her in? The filling's worked loose and there's some discomfort.'

Ali Baba nodded. 'Tell her that's fine. Anybody waiting?'

'No, your twelve o'clock rang in to cancel, so you're clear through to half past.'

'Much obliged.' He flipped the switch, then turned back to the paralysed body and the floating soul in his chair. 'Sorry about that,' he said.

'Not at all,' Akram replied petulantly. 'Good of you to fit in slitting my throat for me at such short notice. Next time you kill me – I have this terrible, inevitable feeling that there will be a next time – I'll try and remember to make an appointment.'

'Look.' Ali Baba was speaking in a we're-both-reasonable-people-we-can-talk-this-through voice that, in context, Akram found downright insulting. 'Let's see if we can't get this mess sorted out. Just you and me, and the hell with the story. You on?'

'Gosh,' Akram replied, staring pointedly at the scalpel still in Ali Baba's hand, 'I'm so bewilderingly spoilt for choice, how can I possibly decide? Go on, then, let's hear it.'

Ali Baba perched on the radiator, put the scalpel down within easy reach and folded his arms. 'The way I see it,' he said, 'is like this. I'm a hero, right?'

'If the word can encompass people who rob other people blind, try and kill them and then run away, then yes, no question. So?'

'And you're a villain.'

419

'Agreed.'

'Well, then.' Ali Baba spread his hands in a bewildered gesture. 'Someone has blundered. Because here I am, supposed to be cutting your jolly old throat, when throat-cutting is your job. And there's you, at my mercy, trying to use your wits to talk me out of killing you, which is hero stuff. It's all back to front. If I kill you and you die, we'll both be hopelessly out of character.'

'That,' remarked Akram, 'will probably be the least of my problems.'

'Now then,' Ali Baba resumed. 'What about this? I let you go—'

'Hey! Why didn't I think of that?'

'—In return for your word of honour that you'll pack in trying to kill me and toddle off back to where you belong. Problem solved. What d'you reckon?'

Akram felt his throat become dry. 'When you say word of honour . . .'

'As in honour among thieves,' Ali Baba went on, smiling brightly. 'Because everybody knows that the word of Akram the Terrible is his bond. Akram the Terrible could no more welch on his word of honour than fly in the air. When did Akram ever break his word? Never. Everybody knows that, it's all to do with respect and stuff. So you see, that way I'd be far safer than if I actually did cut your throat.'

'Now just a minute . . .'

'The more I think about it,' Ali Baba said, sliding off the radiator and walking excitedly around the room, 'the better it gets. We'd both still be in character, you see. I'd be being magnanimous and merciful, which is ever so Hero, much more so than just silly old winning. Any old fool can win—'

'Except me, apparently.'

'But it takes a hero to win properly. Okay, that's fine. And you'll still be in character, because your really high-class bespoke villains always keep their word; you know, the old twisted nobility thing. Then I don't have to spend all weekend scrubbing blood out of my carpet, you get to give up this pestilential vendetta thing – I'm sure it must be costing you a fortune, all the time spent chasing after me when you could be out thieving – and go quietly home, where you—'

'No!' Akram's expression conveyed the intensity of his agitation. 'Not back there. Think about it, man. If I go back and you stay here, what happens to the story? You can't have Ali Baba and the Forty Thieves without Ali Baba. The story'd just stop, and that'd be the end of me. If you make me go back, it'd be just as final as killing me now. More so, in fact, because then I'd never have existed in the first place.'

'True.' Ali Baba nodded gravely. 'So what were you planning on doing? Defecting? Claiming narrative asylum?'

'Call it whatever you like,' Akram said. 'Just so long as you don't send me back. Deal?'

'But you'll promise not to try and kill me, ever again?'

'You strike a hard bargain, you do.' Akram looked from the scalpel to his immobilised body, and then back again. 'Actually, you'd have made a good villain. You've got that cold, hard streak.' Not to mention, he added under his breath, that basic ill-fated gullibility that makes a man who's got his mortal enemy helpless at knifepoint insist on some absurdly over-elaborate means of execution, involving candles burning through ropes, underground cellars slowly filling with water and girls tied to railway lines, which is tantamount to turning the bugger loose and saying, 'See you next episode.'

'Thank you,' Ali Baba replied, evidently flattered. 'I think you'd have made a good hero, not that there's any other sort, but you know what I mean. It's the way apparently insoluble moral dilemmas follow you around as if they were Mary's lamb.'

Akram shuddered. 'Must be awful, that. I expect you can't

go into a shop and buy a box of matches without first checking they were made from sustainable forests.'

'That sort of thing. Right then. Do we have a deal?'

'Suppose so.' Akram cleared his throat. 'Here goes, then. Hell, this is as bad as being back at school. I swear on my honour as a thief and a villain never to try and kill you again. Will that do, d'you think?'

'Covers it pretty well. Better add actual bodily harm as well, just to be on the safe side.'

'If you want. Here, you should have been a lawyer.'

'That's not a very clever thing to say to someone who's still holding a knife on you. Just for that, we'll add economic sanctions and reprisals against property. Okay?'

Akram shrugged. 'If you insist. I'm sorry you've got such a low opinion of me that you see me as the sort of bloke who vents his wrath by chucking bricks through windows and letting tyres down.'

'Just to be on the safe side.'

'All right.'

There was a moment's silence as the two opponents considered what they'd agreed. There was an absurd edge to it, Akram reflected, as if two duellists had flung away their swords in mid-fight and agreed to sort out their differences with best of three games of dominoes. But there was nothing frivolous about giving his word of honour. The bastard had been right on the money there. All in all, he felt like someone who's hired a horsebox in order to go cattle-rustling in a muddy field, and ends up having to pay the farmer to pull him out with his tractor. If word of this ever reached home, he'd never be able to show his face there again.

'That's all right then,' said Ali Baba, breathing a long, ostentatious sigh of relief. 'I knew we'd get there in the end if we really set our minds to it. That just leaves the little matter of your iffy tooth.' He picked up the scalpel and switched on the light. 'You can have this on the house,' he added, 'as a sign there's no hard feelings.'

'Like a free alarm clock radio if I take out a policy within ten working days? What a generous man you are, to be sure.'

With that, Akram's astral body made itself scarce, and spent the next quarter of an hour deliberately not watching what was happening to the old flesh and blood. Odd how some people are; Akram the Terrible habitually jeered in the face of death and laughed the swords of his enemies to scorn; but dentists' drills and injections made him feel as if the bones of his legs had melted and seeped out through his toes.

Not long after Ali Baba had finished – a copybook extraction, needless to say, with the absolute minimum of hacking and slashing – the so-called Mr Smith woke up, groaned aloud and spat out a mouthful of blood and tooth debris. Ali Baba held his breath.

'I eel ike I ust ent en ounds ith Ugar Ay Ennard,' Akram mumbled, feeling his jaw with his hand. 'At ad, as it?'

Ali Baba grinned and held up a pair of pliers, in which was gripped a thing like a badly peeled prawn. 'If you don't get at least one and six for this,' he said, 'your tooth fairy is ripping you off.'

Funny you should mention – 'Anks ery uch, I'll ear at in ind.' He stood up, staggered and caught the back of the chair. 'Ink I'll o and it own in awr aiting oom, if at's OK.'

'Be my guest.'

When he'd gone Ali Baba sat down on the arm of the chair, closed his eyes and tried to lock and bolt the door against the memory of what had happened. Then he hit the intercom and sent for Miss Partridge.

Obviously, it was going to be one of those days; because she had pretty much the same problem with her junk tooth as Akram had. As he fitted the face mask over Michelle's nose and turned on the gas, he decided that what he really wanted

423

above all was for this day to end and be replaced by a nice straightforward one with no complications.

Hiss, went the gas, and the patient in the chair slumped into unconsciousness. Now then: scal—

He turned, and stared. In the chair, sharing exactly the same space to the cubic millimetre, were not one but two bodies; one fast asleep, the other sitting bolt upright and gawping at him as if he was one of the dinosaur skeletons in the Natural History Museum.

'Bugger me, I don't believe it,' he wailed. 'Not *another* one.'

CHAPTER NINE

'Skip.'

Aziz sighed, and stopped. 'Now what?' he said wearily.

'There's a cat over there with boots on.'

It had been one of those days. 'Pull the other one, Sadiq, it's got ruddy bells on. Now, if you've quite—'

'Straight up, Skip, no bull. Look for yourself if you don't believe me.'

What, Aziz asked himself, would the Guv'nor have done, had he been here? Silly question; if he'd been here, they'd be safely back on their own turf, where things like this didn't happen and cats didn't wear boots so much as have them thrown at them. But if he *had* been there, he'd have snapped something like 'Silence in the ranks!' and they'd all have shut up like ironmongers at 5.25 on a Saturday when you desperately need a new hacksaw blade. Either you've got it, Aziz admitted sadly to himself, or you haven't, and he hadn't. Slowly, he turned round.

'All right, you lot,' he said, after a while, 'nobody said to stop marching. Haven't you men ever seen a cat with boots on before?'

'Actually, Skip, now you come to mention it, no.'

'Well you have now. Come on, move it.'

For the record; the cat, seriously terrified by the sight of thirty-nine heavily armed men tramping straight towards it, abandoned its original plan of catching a brace of partridges with which to whet the appetite of the King and thus gain favour for his master, and scarpered. Being hampered by a pair of huge, unwieldy boots it tripped over, fell off a wall and broke its neck, leaving its master to fend for himself. The princess he should have married later eloped with a footman, who abandoned her, six months pregnant, when the King finally and irreversibly cut her out of his will. There had been quite a lot of that sort of thing going on lately, as a result of the intrusion of Aziz and his followers into stories where they had no place to be, and the consensus of opinion throughout Story-book land was that the stupid bastards should be hung up by the balls and left to die.

An hour after the cat incident, they reached a castle. By now they were starving hungry, and it was coming on to rain. They hammered at the door, but nobody answered it.

'Maybe they're out,' ventured Hussain.

'Slice of luck for us, then,' replied Achmed, pulling his cloak over his head. 'Breaking and entering is our speciality, after all.'

Aziz looked up at the lofty battlements and rubbed his chin. 'Bugger of a wall to climb,' he said dubiously. 'Must be twenty, twenty-five foot if it's a yard. You checked out the gates, Faisal?'

'Tight as a pawnbroker's arse, Skip. If we had the big jemmy we'd maybe stand a chance, but without it . . .'

'Just a minute.' Hakim grabbed Aziz by the shoulder and pointed. 'Some fool's only left a beautiful great rope hanging

426

out the window. Look, that tower over there by the gateway.'

He was right. 'Stone me,' said Aziz, impressed. 'What a stroke of luck! All right, then, Faisal, Hakim, Shamir, up that rope quick as you like and open the gates. Anybody tries to stop you, scrag 'em.'

It was an odd sort of a rope, being golden-yellow and made from some very soft, fine fibre; but it was plenty strong enough to take Shamir's twenty-odd stone. He vanished through the tower window, and a moment later the rest of the gang heard a shriek, a scream, a female voice using words that even the thieves didn't know (although they could guess the general idea fairly well from context) and a loud, heavy thump. Five minutes later, the gates opened.

'What the hell kept you?' Aziz demanded. His three faithful henchmen looked away. Hakim blushed. Shamir hastily wiped lipstick off his cheek.

'Well,' Hakim mumbled, 'there was this bint, right . . .'

'Two of 'em,' Faisal corrected him. 'One right little cracker, and a raddled old boiler with a face like a prune. Really snotty about it all, she was. Told us our fortunes good and proper.'

'She fell off the wall,' admitted Shamir. 'It was an accident, honest.'

'The other one didn't seem to mind, though,' Hakim went on. 'In fact, she seemed dead chuffed. It was her hair we climbed up, by the way.'

'Her hair?'

Hakim nodded.

'Stairs fallen down or something? Fire drill?'

'Search me, Skip,' Hakim replied, with a shrug. 'Weird bloody lot they are in these parts, if you ask me. What now, Skip? Do we loot the place, or what?'

The castle proved to be well worth the effort of getting in. Apart from food and dry clothes and plenty of books and things to make a fire with, there were whole chests and trunks

427

full of jewels and precious stones. The girl didn't seem in the least put out by their depredations; in fact, she kept trying to kiss them, and seemed puzzled by the fact that they were rather more interested in the contents of the kitchen and the counting-house. Finally she got Achmed in a sort of half-nelson and started nibbling his ear, until Aziz managed to prise her off. Even then, she kept following them around, sighing embarrassingly and murmuring 'My hero!' That part of it worried Aziz no end, although he kept his concern to himself. His grasp of theory was tenuous at the best of times, but even he knew that villains doing hero stuff was bad news, liable to upset the balance of supernature. Rounding up his men like the headmistress of a Borstal kindergarten, he shooed them out of the castle, promised the girl they'd write, and quick-marched out of it as fast as possible. In their haste, one of them trod on a frog that'd been hanging around the castle for weeks, ogling the girl and saying 'Give us a kiss, give us a kiss,' in frog language; but they weren't to know that.

'Not *another* one!'

Michelle, or her spiritual essence, goggled at him as if she'd just swallowed a goldfish. 'Another what?' she asked. 'Hey, this anaesthetic of yours doesn't seem to be terribly good.'

'Look down,' Ali Baba replied.

Curiously enough, Michelle's next words – 'Who's that in the chair?' – were precisely the words that Daddy Bear, now prematurely deceased, should have spoken on discovering that Goldilocks had broken in. How they got there is a matter for the fabulonometrists to determine, but the answer is probably something to do with random catalyst dispersal and chaos theory. It's probably not significant that she said them twice.

'Maybe,' Ali Baba was saying meanwhile, 'there's a leak in the pipe and I've been inhaling the stuff without knowing it. Never heard it caused hallucinations, but you never know.'

'Pardon me,' Michelle replied, affronted. 'If there's anybody hallucinating around here, I should think it's me. I can see my body down there. Shouldn't there be a strong bright light or something?'

Ali Baba sighed. 'I'm afraid it's not as simple as that,' he said. 'Obviously you don't know. On reflection, perhaps I shouldn't tell you, either. It'd only worry you.'

'Thanks a heap. That's really set my mind at rest, you know?'

'True.' Ali Baba leaned back against the radiator and took a deep breath. 'If my theory's right,' he said, 'and I have this really depressing feeling that it is, you're not actually real. I mean, from Reality, don't you know. I think you're someone out of a story.'

'A story . . .'

'Before you start yelling for two doctors and a white van,' Ali Baba continued, 'maybe I'd better tell you, if you promise not to breathe a word. What am I saying, they wouldn't believe you anyway, not when you tell them you only know I'm crazy because I started gibbering at you while your astral body was floating three feet up in the air. I'm not from these parts, either.'

'A story,' Michelle repeated. 'Do you know, you're the second person to tell me that in twenty-four hours.'

'Really? Who was the first?'

'My fridge freezer.'

'Right. Fine. Now then, this may hurt a little but if it does I really couldn't give a damn. Say Aaah.'

'No, wait, listen.' Michelle frowned, and crumpled her astral hands tightly into a ball. 'Listen,' she repeated. 'For some time now I've been convinced I'm going crazy, ever since my great-aunt died. I inherited this ring, and it makes me think I can understand machines talking. All the electrical gadgets in my flat have been talking to me.'

'Understand machines,' Ali Baba repeated, in a voice as flat as the square at Edgbaston. 'A ring. Silver.'

'Yes.' Michelle stared at him. 'How'd you know?'

'Quite plain, with a jewel or a bit of coloured glass stuck in it. Really ordinary, ugly-looking thing.'

'That's it. Where did you say you were from?'

'Where did you say you got it?'

They regarded each other warily, like two undercover Klingon agents meeting by chance in Trafalgar Square. Ali Baba broke the silence.

'You inherited it from your great-aunt, you said.'

Michelle nodded. 'If that's who she really was. Apparently, I've only got the word of an old-fashioned Bakelite telephone for that. According to my labour-saving kitchen utensils, I was an orphan or something, and they brought me up. You know, like Mowgli or Romulus and ... Mr Barbour, are you feeling all right? Why are you sitting on the floor?'

Slowly, with as much dignity as he could muster (enough to fill a small matchbox, but only if the matches were still inside) Ali Baba climbed to his feet, brushed off his knees and washed his hands. It was, he felt, what Doc Holliday would have done.

'Sorry,' he muttered. 'Slipped on something. Could you just go through that last bit again, because— Damn! Yes?' he barked into the intercom. 'Can't it wait?'

'Sorry, I'm sure,' replied the receptionist. 'It's just to ask if you got Mr Smith's details, because I think he's feeling better now and he's just about to go home.'

Ali Baba flicked off the intercom, snapped, 'Stay there!' at Michelle in the chair, and darted out into the waiting room. Akram – is it my imagination, or does he seem smaller somehow? – was halfway to the door. He turned, looked at Ali Baba and then looked away.

'Just off?'

'Mhm.'

'I hope there won't be any more trouble now.'

'Mm.'

'Right.' For an instant, Ali Baba felt rather foolish. He wasn't at all sure why he'd felt the need to come running out here just to see Akram leave. As far as he was concerned, he'd done everything he could to neutralise the threat; if it worked, it worked, and if not, not. He'd done the right thing, he felt sure. It was just starting to dawn on him that if his gamble did pay off, then the threat that had been terrorising him across twenty-odd Real years and distances too vast to be measured was now over and done with.

Hold that thought.

He could stop running.

He could go home.

'Mm.'

Ali Baba parachuted back from his reverie. 'Sorry?'

'Cn I g hm nw?' said Akram, moving his battered jaws with perceptible discomfort, 'M flng mch bttr nw tht v hd uh rst.'

'I think,' Ali Baba said slowly, 'that going home would be the best possible thing you could do. Cheerio.'

'Auf wdrshn.'

And then the door closed behind him and he was gone. Ali Baba stood for a moment, as if trying to remember how to make his legs work, and then went back into his surgery.

'Sorry about that,' he said. 'Right, where were we? Tell me,' he added, sitting on the desk and folding his arms, 'all about it.'

'All about what?'

Ali Baba bit his lip; he seemed ill at ease, as if he was a guest at an Embassy function who wasn't sure his fly was done up but daren't have a quick fumble to find out. 'What you were telling me. Being brought up by your kitchen.'

'Well.' Michelle told him. He listened. When she'd finished he sat in silence for fifteen seconds, a very long time under the

431

circumstances, before standing up, sitting down again, fiddling with a pencil, breaking it, putting the corpse in a drawer and finally clearing his throat.

Stow away in the pile of a magic carpet crossing the Line, and jump off over Old Baghdad. Because timescale here is relative, depending on which showing of the picture you're in, don't clutter your mind up with notions like 'twenty-seven years earlier'; it'd only confuse the issue. Better just to recognise that this is a flashback, and leave it at that.

You've been here before; the long drive, the wide lawn where one day there will be big stripy tents and a band, the big house, the french windows opening inwards, the dark, dramatically furnished study, the desk behind which the Man sits. Having tidied away the tents and the band, Continuity reckon they've done a day's work, and accordingly nothing else is different. For his part, the Man doesn't look a day younger. His type never do.

Take a good look, anyway. Here's a face that nothing will ever be able to shock or to frighten. You could bring yourself to believe that God looks like this, if you're comfortable with the idea of a god who sends the boys round after dark to pour petrol through the letterboxes of other gods' temples.

'And the girl,' he says. 'Who is she?'

His voice is quiet, soft and slightly bored, like a casualty doctor examining his seventh knife wound of the night. There's a certain degree of contempt in there as well, the scorn of the truly great sinner for the peccadilloes of regular people. There's a cigar clamped between his thin lips that burns but never seems to grow any shorter; rather like Moses' burning bush, except not quite so homely.

The man on the other side of the desk looks down; it shames him to have to admit to what he's done. 'Her name's Prudence,' he mumbles.

432

Something exceptional happens; the Man's eyebrows lift, admitting surprise. '*Prudence?*' he says. 'This, you will forgive me for saying so, is a curious name for her to have, in the circumstances.'

'Yes. Well.' The man on the wrong side of the desk lifts his shoulders; not quite a shrug, because that wouldn't be fitting. 'They all have names like that, where she comes from.'

'You don't say.' The Man's voice is back to normal, and his face is once more Mount Rushmore's big brother. 'And where might that be, precisely?'

The other man doesn't speak; he tilts his head slightly sideways, indicating the direction of the Line. He waits for a reaction – anger, surprise, disgust, amusement. All he gets is an imperceptible nod, as if to reassure him that the person he's talking to is still awake.

'A visitor,' the other man continues. 'Or you could say a tourist. One of those head-in-the-clouds types who somehow get across the Line from time to time.'

'Sure.' The great head nods again. 'A Wendy.'

The term, as used by Story-book folk, is highly derogatory, but the Man uses it as a straightforward noun; he means nothing by it, it's just a convenient piece of shorthand. The other man nods, relieved that he doesn't need to explain further. 'That's right,' he says, 'a Wendy. Apparently on the other side she runs a small specialist bookshop and makes handmade silver jewellery in her spare time.'

The edges of the Man's lips curl ever so slightly as if to ask, What else can you expect from such people? He sucks on his cigar and breathes out a thin plume of smoke.

'And now what?' he says. 'Tell me what it is you want I should do for you, and then we can sit out in the sun and drink a glass of wine together.' He smiles; a Great Khan's smile, derisively merciful. The other man takes a deep breath.

'There's a problem,' he says at last.

'Always there's a problem,' the Man replies, with a faint trace of impatience. 'You want her to go, but you can't get rid of her. You want her to stay, but the immigration people say no. You want to marry her, but her father is the Sultan. So many problems.'

'She's going to have a baby,' the other man whispers.

Silence. The Man draws deep on his cigar and expels the smoke through his nose, like a dragon. 'That,' he says at last, 'is different, I'll say that for you. I didn't even know it was possible.'

'It's possible, believe me.'

'All right. So, what's the problem?'

The other man seems to collapse, just a little, as if the secret inside him had been the only thing holding him upright. '*Padrone*,' he says, 'what am I to do? We have nothing in common, in fact we can't stand the sight of each other any more. If we try and talk about it she gets hysterical. She seems to think the child's going to be born with green skin or pointed ears or something. Now she says she wants nothing to do with it; she just wants to get back to her own kind and lead her life, she says.'

'So what's wrong with that?'

'My child,' the other man blurts out. 'What's going to become of it, brought up on the other side by a mother who thinks she's carrying a Martian or something? *Padrone*, can you do anything? You have friends over there, people who might know what to do. I thought maybe . . .'

His words dry up, like water in a hot season. In the face of so much scorn and pity, it'd be fatuous to try and say anything else.

'You want that the kid should be looked after,' says the Man. 'That it should have a decent home, maybe be raised among its own kind.' He frowned. 'This,' he says, 'is a big thing you're asking me for. Arrangements will have to be made, it'll cost money. And you—' Without so much as the movement of an eyeball, he looks the other man over, from charity-shop turban to camel boot sale shoes. 'However,' he continues, 'I have a soft heart, your story touches me. It's good that a man should be concerned about his children and not want that they should grow up like savages. I tell you what I'll do.'

And, in that same calm, deadly voice he explains: how no humans on the other side could be trusted, but there were things – telephones and vacuum cleaners and alarm clock radios – that had originally come over from the Old Country, and . . .

'From here?' the other man interrupts. 'We export consumer goods over the Line?'

The Man's brow tightens a fraction. 'Because you're young,' he says, 'I forgive that you interrupt me. And yes, we do. Over there, these machines need electricity. The ones we make here don't, they're alive. On the other side, therefore, they're a hell of a lot cheaper to run. Anyhow, I have contacts. They will find a nice respectable household where your child can grow up and get a good start in life. I do this for you,' continues the Man, regarding the other as if he had a hundred legs and had just walked out of a salad, 'because I like you. And one day, perhaps, I may come to you and give you three wishes; just simple wishes, nothing very much, and probably that day will never come. Who can say?'

The other man looks perplexed. 'Sorry,' he said. '*You'll* give *me* three wishes? Don't you mean the other way round? I mean . . .'

Through the cigar smoke, two eyes burn fiercely. 'What's the matter? You have a problem with that? Maybe you think that's a lot to ask in return for such a trifling favour as you ask me.'

The other man goes stiff, as if he's only just realised that the words on the notice boards he'd been walking past for the last couple of miles mean DANGER – MINEFIELD. 'Of course not, *padrone*,' he replies hastily. 'I just thought – I mean, shouldn't it be me doing something for you?'

And now the Man does laugh; it sounds like the cracking of hard rocks, and the joke is clearly private. 'Don't you worry about that,' he says. 'You leave the accounts to me, I'll make sure they tally. And now,' he sighs, 'that's enough business for one day. Let's go out into the sun and have that glass of wine. Enrico! Bring a bottle of the good stuff for our guest.'

And the man—

'Was you?'

Ali Baba nodded. 'Not long after that,' he said, 'by local time, at least, I got into – well, I came into money and then I had to leave, for the good of my health. I went to see Him again; he was a bit less sympathetic the second time but I managed to buy a passage over the Line with a rather valuable piece of kit I owned at the time. Your silver ring, actually. It's funny; hardly a day's passed since I came here when I haven't wondered what became of my— Prudence's baby, and all the time the answer's been staring me in the face, so to speak. Usually,' he added, 'with her eyes shut, saying Aaah. Funny old thing, life, don't you think?'

In spite of everything, Michelle realised something was wrong. What could it be? Ah yes, she realised, I've been forgetting to breathe. She remedied the problem. 'In that case,' she demanded, 'who are you?'

Ali Baba grinned, feebly as a twenty-watt bulb. 'It's written up on the window,' he replied. 'Just spelt a bit wrong, that's all.'

Short delay, while Michelle reads the letters on the glass backwards. Another short wait, and then—

'Are you trying to tell me,' she said, 'that you're Ali Ba—'

'Yes.'

'Oh.'

'Quite,' said Ali Baba. 'And you, apparently, are my daughter.'

Michelle looked at him. At that moment, even though she wasn't crouched inside an oil-jar with boiling water cascading down around her ears, her past life flashed in front of her eyes. A curious life it had been, to be sure; comfortable, quiet, under any other circumstances she'd have said *ordinary*, because that's what ordinary means; just like it is at home. Ordinary is in the eye of the beholder. Sorcerors' children run to meet Daddy on his return from work and find nothing unusual in the fact that he's glowing slightly or comes home a different shape. That, they assume, is what all Daddies do. Hit-men's children love to be allowed to help Daddy scrub the lead fouling out of the slots in the silencer, or hold the wiring diagram for him when he's out in the garage making bombs. The children of great prophets learn not to whine, 'Oh Daddy, not loaves and fishes *again*,' when Father comes home from work with a doggy-bag. In her case, she had been brought up to a life in which there were no grown-ups at all. A taxi collected her from the school gate. As soon as she opened the front door, the timer on the oven went ping! to let her know dinner was ready, and the TV switched itself on. Sure, other kids had mummies and daddies; they also had caravans and satellite dishes and boats, but she'd come to understand at an early age that not everybody can have everything. It was cool. It was how things went.

And now, apparently, she had a father. Spiffing. And what, precisely, was she supposed to do with him now she'd got him? Answers on a postcard, please.

'Hello,' she said.

437

CHAPTER TEN

'Mlk,' Akram growled. 'Nd mk t uh dbl.'

The barman, who was used to him by now and even got fresh milk in for him specially, stuck his thumb through the foil caps of two pint bottles, poured and took the money with a smile.

'Thnks.'

'Been to the dentist?'

'Ys.'

'Have to have much done?'

'Ys.'

'Hard luck.' The barman grimaced sympathetically. 'I can get them to rustle you up some soup if you like.'

Akram looked up at the barman, puzzled. 'T's nt n th mnu,' he objected.

'Doesn't matter,' the barman replied. 'Won't take 'em a minute, it only needs heating through. Mushroom do you?'

'Tht'll b fn. Thnks uh lt.'

So that, Akram mused, is kindness. He'd heard about it, in the same way as people on this side of the Line have heard of unicorns; he knew perfectly well what it was supposed to be

438

like, he could picture it in his mind's eye, it was just that he'd never actually come across it before, in the same way and for the same reasons that the barman probably hadn't met too many unicorns.

Strange, he thought; very strange. Just because I've been coming in here fairly regularly to buy milk and sit down after my shift at the kebab house, and because I've just been to the dentist and the barman can see I'm still a bit under the weather from the anaesthetic, he goes out of his way to obtain soup for me, figuring that soup will be easy for me to eat, even though soup's not on the menu. He won't charge me extra. Quite probably he hasn't given any thought about how this act can ultimately be turned to his advantage. He just does it. Probably it makes him feel good; but so would drinking all the whisky or sleeping with the barmaid, and he doesn't do either of those, so that can't really be the reason. He took a long pull at his milk, and the coolness eased the ache in his jaw. He felt strangely—

'Quite warm,' said the barman, 'for the time of year.'

'Ys.'

That, he'd learned, was called Making Conversation. He'd been watching the barman out of idle curiosity for some weeks, and as far as he could gather, the barman often said something conventional and meaningless but essentially friendly to men who came in on their own and sat down at the bar. At first he'd assumed that he was passing on coded messages, or trying to scrape acquaintance with young adventurers who were alone in the world and wouldn't be missed, in order to mug them into entering the secret cave to retrieve the magic lamp from its man-eating guardian. Back home, that would have been the logical explanation. Not so on this side, though; the barman seemed to regard being friendly to strangers and doing the little he could to cheer them up as part of his duty as a human being. The payoff, Akram assumed, was that they'd do as much for him one day, if it ever came to that; but it seemed an unrealistically long shot to expect that one day they'd be barmen and he'd be a solitary drinker in need of companionship. The fact of the matter was, Akram was forced to conclude, that he did it all on spec, or possibly just because that's what people do.

'Hr,' he said to the barman. 'Hv n yrslf.'

The barman's eyes twinkled. 'Cheers,' he replied, 'don't mind if I do.'

The essence of it was, Akram reflected, that on this side, there was so much that was random, purposeless, meaningless. On his side of the Line, everything meant something; every word, every act was relevant to the plot, part of the story. If you were out fishing and you threw a little tiddler back into the water, you knew for certain that it'd turn out to be the son of the Dragon King and you could start making lists of Wishes on the back of an envelope. Do the same here, and you'd be out of pocket one small fish; and where was the percentage in that, for God's sake? And yet the poor suckers did it, unthanked, unrewarded, kept on doing it until the day they died. And virtually none of them ever got to marry princesses, and those few that did never seemed to live happily ever after. It was weird, the whole arrangement, like a place where water flew upward from a spilt glass. And yet, somehow it was all very . . .

'Your very good health,' the barman said.

'Nd th sm t y.'

All of which, Akram couldn't help feeling, was just a tiny bit relevant; because today, in his encounter with the accursed, thieving, treacherous Ali Baba, he had been soundly and completely defeated. His quest had failed utterly, there was now no way he could ever achieve the vengeance that was his sole purpose for existing, and his life was therefore effectively over. To all intents and purposes, he was a dead man, and the story had no further use for him.

Which meant—

Which meant he was free. He couldn't go back home. Suddenly it occurred to him that when the prison authorities drag you from your cell, stuff money in your pockets, frog-march you through the gates, slam them behind you and shout, 'And stay out!', you don't necessarily head for the Citizens' Advice Bureau to ask about an action for unlawful eviction. Maybe you just had to be big enough to swallow the insult, turn the other cheek, buy a spade and go dig up the swag. Not where he came from, maybe; but he wasn't there any more, was he?

He had an idea they called it Free Will.

'Your soup's ready,' said the barman. 'No, put your money away and have it on me.'

Back home, the phrase Free Will was always followed by the words 'With every lawsuit, special offer, hurry while stocks last'. Back home, he added, dipping his spoon in the soup, there is no free lunch, either.

'Yr vry knd,' he said. 'Thnks vry mch.'

And then the thunderbolt hit him. The force of its impact was so great that he almost dropped the spoon. Suddenly, it was as if the world was flooded with pink light.

The barman isn't a hero, yet he can do hero-type things. He can be whatever he wants.

If I stay here, so can I. I don't have to be a villain any more.

If I want to, I can be a bloody hero.

'You should have killed him,' Michelle replied, 'while you had the chance.'

Ali Baba nodded. 'I know,' he said. 'Silly old me. Of course, then I'd have been left with a dead body on my hands, and the dustmen are getting so fussy about what they'll actually take.'

Michelle frowned. 'Even so—'

'Have the last slice of pizza,' Ali Baba interrupted. 'I can't, I'm full up.'

Like many naturally slender young women, Michelle had an appetite like a blast furnace, and there was a slight pause while she took advantage of the offer. 'Even so,' she said, 'surely it'd have been worth it. You've been running away from him all your life, haven't you? Your life in this, what's the word—'

'Dimension?' Ali Baba shrugged. 'It's not the right word, but if you don't tell the lexicographers, neither will I. And yes, I have. And now I don't have to any more. Have some more champagne.'

'How do you know that?' Michelle demanded, holding out her glass. 'You've only got his word for it. He's a thief and a murderer, for pity's sake.'

Ali Baba smiled. 'That's how I know his word's good,' he replied. 'If you can't trust a villain, who can you trust?'

'Explain,' said Michelle with her mouth full.

'Easy. With nice, honest people it doesn't matter if they lie to you; nothing too ghastly's going to happen, because they're basically nice and unlikely ever to cut your throat. For villains, it's different. After all, they've still got to apply for mortgages and have their hair cut and buy toothpaste and take their cats to be wormed, same as the rest of us. If all the world said "Go away, I can't trust you, you're a villain," they'd be in a terrible state. So the convention is, when they promise something, their word is their bond. Then they can walk into a shop and say "I promise to pay for the goods and not murder you" and the shopkeeper knows it's safe. Of course, sometimes they have to lie on business, like when they promise to share the treasure equally when you know all the time they mean to double-cross you; but that's all allowed for in the rules and they have to make it perfectly clear they're lying, just so there won't be any misunderstanding. They cross their fingers, usually, and look away and cackle harshly. You'd have to be

442

blind, deaf and as dim as a lodging-house lightbulb not to pick up on that.'

Michelle shrugged. 'You know about these things,' she said, 'and I don't. If it'd been me I'd have knifed the bastard.'

Ali Baba looked at her. 'Yes,' he said, 'you probably would. It only goes to show how right I was to insist you were brought up this side of the Line.'

'Really?'

'Sure.' Ali Baba's face became uncharacteristically serious; tonight the part of Bertie Wooster will be taken by Hamlet, Prince of Denmark. 'Much better that way. It means you've grown up tough and hard. If you'd stayed on the other side, you'd be no good for anything except gathering flowers and talking to the wee birdies.'

'Oh.' Michelle frowned. 'I'm not sure I want to be tough and hard,' she said. 'You make me sound like a duff avocado.'

'Which reminds me.' Ali Baba laid his knife and fork down on his plate, blade-tip and fork-tines at precisely twelve o'clock, steepled his hands and smiled pleasantly. 'Terribly rude of me not to have asked before,' he said. 'How's your life been so far?'

Michelle considered. 'Fine,' she said.

'No major tragedies, deep-seated emotional traumas? Not,' he added quickly, 'that I want to pry or anything, but I was reading this book on the modern approach to fatherhood—'

Michelle looked at him. 'You were?'

'Just because I didn't know who you were or where you'd ended up didn't mean I wasn't interested,' Ali Baba replied. 'There was always the offchance we'd bump into each other, so I thought, a little general background reading . . .'

'I see. And what did this book say?'

'Difficult to tell,' Ali Baba confessed. 'The chap who wrote it used such fearfully long words, and my dictionary was published in eighteen sixty-something and a lot of the words aren't in it. But the general idea seems to be that once you're past the nappies and putting-food-on-the-table stage, all I'm really fit for is listening and saying, "Gosh, how terrible" when Destiny whacks you one with a broken bottle. I know I've come on the scene a bit late, but . . .'

'Hum.' Michelle rubbed her cheeks with thumb and forefinger, drawing her lips together. 'Sorry to disappoint you, but there hasn't really been anything much like that. The nature study stick insects at school died rather suddenly, but that was nineteen years ago and besides, I never really liked them anyway. I had a rather expensive blouse from Printemps, and it got prawn biryani on one of the sleeves. The first time I took my driving test, I failed on the emergency stop. Other than that, no complaints, really. Until recently, that is, but I'm not really counting all that, because I'm still not convinced it's not all a horrible dream.'

'I see.' Ali Baba nodded. 'Any area where you feel in need of fatherly advice and guidance? Apart from dental hygiene, of course, because fortuitously we've already covered that in some detail.'

Michelle smiled, quite unexpectedly. 'It's funny,' she said. 'Or rather, odd. Or something. I guess that you're probably the only person who actually has been there all my life. I never seemed to get ill, so I never saw a doctor often enough to remember his name, and schools and teachers seemed to come and go a bit; but I never missed a six-monthly check-up.'

'Highly commendable,' Ali Baba replied. 'Which means we've met a minimum of fifty-four times. And I could draw a chart of the inside of your mouth blindfold from memory; now how many of your so-called conventional fathers could say that?'

As he waffled on, Michelle studied him, her head slightly on one side. Suddenly getting a father after twenty-seven years without one is rather like waking up one morning to be told by

God that owing to an admin snarl-up, the third arm you should have been issued with at birth has only just come through from the depot, and there it is, look, sprouting out of the small of your back. You don't immediately think, 'Hooray, now I can pick up things behind me without turning round.' You wonder, rather, how you're going to explain it to your friends and whether any of your jackets can be salvaged, or whether you're going to have to have a whole new wardrobe tailor-made at Freaks-R-Us. It's hard, in other words, to be entirely positive about it all. Your first thought is of the immediate, if comparatively trivial, complications and disadvantages which you now face and definitely don't need in an already complicated life.

'Excuse me,' Michelle said.

Ali Baba, who had been saying something or other, stopped and waited expectantly for Michelle to go on. Probably, she thought sourly, there's a diagram in his book somewhere.

'This is all extremely important,' she said, 'and naturally I'm thrilled to bits by it all, but can we just be practical for a moment? I mean, what do we do now? Because, and I'm really sorry if this sounds unfeeling or anything, but if you're thinking I'm going to come and live with you and cook breakfasts and iron socks—'

'Do people iron socks?' Ali Baba interrupted, clearly intrigued. 'And if so, why?'

'What I'm getting at—' Michelle wished she'd never started this topic; but now she was, as it were, in custard stepped in so far, and she might as well blunder on a little bit longer until she drowned or was rescued. 'The point is,' she said, 'does it have to change anything, or do we just carry on as before and have lunch together from time to time? I mean, it's not as if—'

'Quite.' Ali Baba nodded. 'I was thinking along the same lines, I must admit. Do I have to stand on the sidelines at netball games? What about pocket money and staying out late at night?

I have to admit, I haven't got a clue. If there's no hard and fast rules, then perhaps we ought just to leave well alone and let it grow on us, if you see what I mean. Okay?'

Michelle shrugged. 'Suits me,' she said.

'Just one thing, though.' Ali Baba frowned. 'As far as I can see, suddenly being a daughter after twenty-seven years of just being a person oughtn't to be a problem. The other stuff—'

'What, you mean being half-fictional? And the talking fridge and so on?'

Ali Baba nodded. 'You're new to all this, obviously. I'm not. So let me offer you a word of advice.'

Michelle nodded. She needed advice on this particular point, in roughly the same way a house needs the ground underneath it.

'Forget about it,' Ali Baba said, and there was a perceptible hardening of tone that might, in someone else, have been mistaken for seriousness. 'Put it completely out of your mind. Put the ring somewhere safe, and never ever put it on.'

'Oh. I thought—'

'Never.'

'Right. Any reason?'

Ali Baba nodded. 'It's all very well,' he said, 'being given a beautiful silk umbrella with a fetching design of black and white concentric circles. It's another thing entirely to sit down under it at the far end of a rifle range. You don't need to use the ring. It's not meant to be used on this side of the Line. Sling it behind your hankies in the back of a drawer, and leave it there.'

'Then why not get rid of it?' Michelle asked.

'Worst thing you could do,' Ali Baba replied. 'Suppose you chucked it in a river. That's virtually sitting up and begging for it to be swallowed by a fish that gets netted by a poor but honest fisherman who takes the prize fish he's just caught as a present for the Grand Vizier, and I trust I don't have to draw pictures of what always happens after that.'

'You have it, then.'

Ali Baba winced. 'Thanks ever so much, but no. Remember Akram? I got rid of all my magical kit years ago. Giving it to me now would be like saying, "Gosh, here come the police up the fire escape, please accept this five kilo bag of heroin, free and with my compliments." You keep it, it can't do you any harm unless you encourage it. Forget all about it.'

Michelle's brows wrinkled. 'That's easy for you to say,' she replied. 'Just give a clue, how precisely do I go about forgetting something like that?'

'Something like what?'

Three wishes you can't refuse.

A curious idea; who in his right mind would want to refuse three genuine, fully functional, guaranteed wishes? The only dilemma would be, do we go straight for the Maserati, or would it be better to wish for the cash and maybe shop around a bit?

There are, indeed, people who think like that, just as there are people who quite happily use unexploded German bombs as door-stops. They don't know any better. And for forty years it doesn't matter; and then one day it does, and the Ordnance Survey has to recall the latest edition of the relevant map for urgent updating.

If you make a wish, you need someone to grant it. Wishes are granted by Class Four supernaturals: genies, dragons, witches, fairy godparents and other species, officially classified by the United Nations standing committee on reality preservation as dangerous pests. None of them are indigenous to this side of the Line; in fact, the Line mainly exists to keep the bastards out. Making a wish is therefore equivalent to driving back across the Channel Tunnel with two rabid dogs on the back seat and the boot full of Colorado beetles. And, once they get this side, Class Fours thrive. They make the alligators in the New York sewers look like a mild infestation of greenfly.

Wishes, magical objects, talismans, all the instruments and paraphernalia of organised fantasy; it's taken science and reason two thousand years of savage, often bloody struggle to root them out, and every time the job seems to be done, somehow they creep back and carry on where they left off; infiltrating, taking over, setting up the storybook *cosa nostra*. Stories grow; the price of reality is constant viligance.

So; three wishes you can't refuse, three passports to this side of the Line for the Fairy Godfather's enforcers.

And six wishes outstanding: three for Akram, three for Ali Baba. The conscientious arsonist doesn't just set the building on fire; first he fills the fire extinguishers with petrol.

CHAPTER ELEVEN

Morning.

Akram's eyes snapped open. The sun behind the curtains made the windows glow. There were no birds singing, but the whine of a distant milk float provided an acceptable substitute. He jumped out of bed, jammed two slices in the toaster and brushed his teeth so vigorously that his gums began to bleed. His tongue, exploring the inside of his mouth, touched the raw jelly left by the extracted tooth, and reminded him of his resolution.

Akram the Terrible was dead. Watch out, world, here comes Sir Akram, knight errant.

He swept back the curtains, threw up the sash and looked out. In the faceless city, there were wrongs to right, downtrodden victims to protect, villains to smite, and if they'd just bear with him until the kettle boiled and he'd had his toast, he'd be right with them.

Twenty minutes later, he was already in business. True, it was only a lost cat, but everybody has to start somewhere. It only needed one glance to see that the poor creature was bewildered and frightened, standing on the pavement, motionlessly yowling. Fortunately, there was a collar round its neck with a little engraved disc, and the disc had an address on it. He grabbed the cat, hailed a taxi and sallied forth.

'Yes?' said the woman through the crack between chained door and frame.

'Your cat,' Akram replied, producing the exhibit.

'Stay there.' The door slammed, then opened again. The woman stepped aside, and a remarkably tall, broad man stepped out onto the pavement, snatched the cat with his left hand, punched Akram with tremendous force on the nose with his right and went back inside.

'Vera,' he said. 'Call the police.'

Akram wasn't quite sure what to do next. He had an idea that turning the other cheek came into it somewhere, but he hadn't been hit on the cheek, and he only had the one nose. Indeed, by the way it felt he wasn't sure if he even had that any more. Discovering that he had at some stage sat down, he shook his head and started to get up.

'Terry,' the woman yelled, 'he's getting away.'

'Don't just stand there,' the man replied from inside the house.

Among the souvenirs Akram had retained from his past life were a whole bundle of instinctive reactions to the words *He's getting away: don't just stand there.* There are times when it's wholesome and positive to allow oneself to be carried away by one's instincts. Therapists recommend it as a way of re-establishing contact with one's repressed inner identity. This, Akram decided, was one of those moments.

'Stop him!' the woman was screaming to the world at large. 'It's the bastard who kidnapped our Tinkles!'

Clearly a hysterical type, Akram felt; and it looked very much like she'd married a compatible partner, because here came the man, brushing past her in the doorway holding a tyre

iron. The optimum course of action under these circumstances for any self-respecting knight errant would be to get
erring, as quickly as possible. Unfortunately, Akram's motor
functions were a bit below par, owing to the biff on the nose,
and the three or four yards' start essential for any meaningful
chase didn't seem to be available.

'Right, you bugger, you'll wish you'd never been, ouch, oh
fuck, oh my head!' exclaimed the man; and Akram, trying to
account for the sudden non-sequitur in his conversation,
realised that he'd instinctively kicked him in the nuts and
kneed him in the face. Pure reflex, of course; those old
recidivist instincts, at it again. He wondered, as he beat a hasty
retreat, whether a course of hypnotism might be able to do
something about them.

Reflecting that beginner's luck isn't always necessarily good
luck, he returned to his quest; and as it turned out, he didn't
have long to wait.

A little old lady, complete with headscarf and wheeled
shopping trolley (where do they get them from, incidentally?
Try and buy one and you'll find they've long since vanished
from the shops; presumably you have to order them direct
from World of Crones, quoting your membership number)
was being set upon by three burly youths. Yes, Akram shouted
to himself, second time out and we're right on the money.
His first instinct was to charge in, fists and boots flailing, but
understandably he wasn't on speaking terms with his instincts
right then, and he resolved to try subterfuge. Accordingly, he
ran forward yelling, 'Look out, it's the Law!' and waving his
hands frantically. The youths at once dropped the old lady's
bag, unopened, and scarpered, leaving Akram face to face
with the old lady.

'You're nicked,' said a voice behind him.

At that moment, the old lady stood up straight, dragged off
her scarf and hurled it to the ground, and said, 'Fuck!'

Looking more closely, Akram saw that she wasn't an old woman at all, but a young girl; tall, blonde and quite attractive, if you like them a bit hard in the face. Akram was familiar with the common variant where the old crone turns out to be the main popsy under a spell or enchantment, but somehow this didn't look like one of those cases.

'Jesus!' she growled. 'We were that close!'

Akram noticed that four uniformed constables had attached themselves to various parts of his body. A certain amount of radical preconceptions editing seemed called for.

'Anyway, sarge,' said one of the coppers to the girl, 'we got this clown.'

'Oh good,' replied the girl unpleasantly. 'We'll just have to persuade him to tell us who his mates are.'

Akram's instincts didn't actually smirk or say *Told you so*, but there was a definite aura of smugness in part of his subconscious as he dealt with the four policemen and (very much against his will, but she was trying to bite his leg) the damsel. Obviously, he rationalised as he ran like a hare down a side-street, there was some aspect of this heroism caper he hadn't quite cracked yet.

Third time lucky.

Time, Akram reflected, to think this thing through. Ten minutes or so of logical analysis later, he hit upon the following hypothesis.

I've been a villain all my life, or rather lives. Trying to change from villain to hero overnight is probably asking a bit much of Continuity, hence the fuck-ups. A more gradual approach, on the other hand, might prove efficacious. What he needed, therefore, was a sort of intermediate stage between villainy and heroism, in which he could do basically villainous things – robbing and maiming – but in a good cause.

In other words, Operation Robin Hood.

This was a good idea, he reflected, since although he was a

complete novice at errantry and oppressed-championing, what he didn't know about thieving you could write on the back of a nicked Visa card. Robbing the rich – well, that would come as easily as leaves to the tree. Giving to the poor he reckoned was something you could probably pick up as you went along; and in the meantime, he'd just have to busk it as best he could.

Step One: locate the Rich.

Back home, that wouldn't have been a problem. Saunter through the streets of Old Baghdad peering through the windows till you find a house where the goats live outside, then prop your ladder against it and you're away. An hour of pavement-slogging in London, however, showed that the same rules didn't seem to apply here.

The root of the problem, had he realised it, lay in the fact that he was operating in a district that was in the middle of extensive gentrification. Turning a corner and finding himself in what looked like a genuine, solid-milk-chocolate Mean Street of dingy old terraced houses, still black in places with authentic Dickensian soot, he was disconcerted to notice rather too many Scandinavian pine concept kitchens and smoked-glass occasional tables opaquely visible through the net curtains. Turn another corner and there were the big, opulent houses with steps up to the front door, flanked by pillars; but when you got there, you found a row of bell-pushes with name-tags beside each one, the kerb littered with clapped-out old motors, and a general shortage of desirable consumer goods visible through the windows. He was baffled.

'Excuse me,' he said, stopping a passer-by, 'but where do the Rich live?'

'You what?'

'I'm looking for some rich people,' he explained. 'Am I in the right area?'

'Bugger off.'

Akram shrugged; probably the bloke didn't know either, but didn't want to show his ignorance. He turned, and trudged on a bit further.

And turned a corner. And saw a bank.

Now that, he muttered to himself, is rather more like it. It should be pointed out that a lot of Akram's knowledge of the real world came from watching old movies and soap reruns intercepted via a magic mirror and a bent coathanger from the satellite channels. He knew, therefore, that when banks aren't foreclosing on the old farmstead, they're foreclosing on the widow's cottage or foreclosing on the family cotton mill in spite of the valiant efforts of the hero and heroine to pull the business round. That, as far as Akram was concerned, was what banks do, nine to five, Mondays to Saturdays. Indeed, as often as not they sneakily foreclose before the payments are actually due because of some shady deal the manager's got with the local property tycoon; and Akram had seen evidence of this with his own eyes, when he'd taken a walk down a whole High Street of closed and shuttered shops one Wednesday afternoon, and been told it was because it was early foreclosing day. Banks, therefore, were eminently fair game. Go for it.

The actual robbery side of it was so laughably simple that he wondered how they managed to stay in business. All he had to do was rip out the close-circuit TV camera, clobber the security guard, kick down the reinforced glass partition and help himself, resisting with ease the attempts of the counter staff to interest him in life insurance, unit-linked pension policies and flexible personal loans as he did so. It was when he ran out into the street, a bulging sack of currency notes in each hand, that the aggro started. If he'd been analysing as he went along he'd have seen the trend taking shape and been prepared for it, but that's the way it goes when you're all fired up with enthusiasm.

As he emerged from the bank, he almost collided with a

ragged, threadbare man, sitting on the pavement with a hat on the ground beside him and a cardboard sign imploring alms. Great, he muttered to himself, a genuine Poor. This is turning out easier than I expected.

'Here you are,' he said, offering the Poor one of the bags.

The Poor shot him a look of pure hatred. 'Piss off,' he snarled.

'But it's money. And you're poor.'

'I said piss off. Do I look like I want to spend the next five years inside?'

Akram was asking 'Inside where?' when the Poor noticed a poster in the bank's window headed REWARD, grabbed his ankle and started yelling 'Help! Police!' As if in answer, four cars and a van screamed to a halt at the kerb and suddenly the street was full of men in blue uniforms waving guns. Akram was obliged to hit two of them quite hard before he could get away, and a number of vehicles, a street lamp, a dog, a parking meter, several twelfth-storey windows and a passing helicopter were severely damaged by stray gunfire.

By the time he was clear and certain that his most energetic pursuers had lost the trail or had a nasty encounter with his unregenerate instincts, it was half past two and his enthusiasm for heroism was decidedly on the wane. He was still getting something wrong, he told himself; something obvious and simple, if only he knew what it was.

Bugger this, he muttered to himself as he let himself in to his bedsit, for a game of soldiers.

And when you don't know, ask someone who does.

Princess Scheherazade sighed, scratched her ear and ate another pickled onion. She was bored.

When she'd met the handsome prince, she'd hoped it would be different this time; not just one more meaningless story-book love affair, another thousand-and-one night stand. Now,

455

however, with only three nights left to go before the inevitable Happy Ending, she could sense the story coming to an end all round her, and it made her feel like a written-off Cortina just before the big crusher reduces it to the size of a suitcase. It was only a vague, unformed suspicion clouding her subconscious mind, but deep down she *knew* that Happily Ever After sucks. Time, in other words, to move on, except of course that that wasn't possible.

She was, needless to say, in an unusual position. As well as being in a story, she made up stories. This only made her feel worse; having sent nine hundred and ninety-eight heroes and nine hundred and ninety-eight heroines to their Happy Ends, she no longer had any illusions whatsoever about what the process entailed, just as the man who operates the electric chair can't really kid himself that Old Sparky is an innovative new alternative to conventional central heating.

The pickle jar was empty. She scowled and snapped her fingers.

'Wasim,' she snapped without looking round. 'More of these round, vinegary things, quick as you can.' She heard the slave's obedient murmur and the slap of his bare feet on the marble floor. She yawned again. Dammit, she was bored out of her skull and the story hadn't even ended yet.

Supposing there was a story that went on for ever . . .

God only knows where the thought came from. It's extremely unlikely that it originated in the Princess's brain, which simply wasn't geared up with the necessary plant and equipment to turn out notions like that. Storybook characters don't speculate on the nature of stories, in the same way that calves don't write books called *A Hundred and One New Ways With Veal*. On the other hand, it's equally improbable to think that somebody planted it there. Who?

A story that doesn't end. A story that goes on, even outliving the storyteller.

456

But that's impossible, Scheherazade told herself; get a grip on yourself, girl, it's the pickles talking. Because every story is made up of three parts, beginning, middle and end, and something lacking one of these parts can't by definition be a story.

But just suppose . . .

On the evening before the First Day, God muttered *But just suppose* to himself in exactly the same way. He too ate rather too many pickled onions before going to bed, and the consequences are plain for everyone to see. But Scheherazade didn't know that, being female and accordingly, in the Islamic tradition, excused religion. She stopped lounging, sat upright, and began to think.

Soap opera—

Because she was excused religion, Scheherazade wasn't to know that human life is what God watches in the evenings when He gets home from work, and that He has a choice of two channels, and He was watching her on one of them at that precise moment. She only knew that she had three stories to go before everlasting happiness, and a liberal interpretation of the rules might just be her best, and only, chance.

Okay, she thought. For tonight, she'd decided on the traditional tale of Ali Baba and the Forty Thieves; a simplistic, two-twist narrative with two, maybe three featured characters and a couple of walk-ons for friends of the director's brother-in-law. But maybe, with a little breadth of vision and an HGV-equivalent poetic licence, the tawdry little thing might stretch . . .

The further supply of pickled onions arrived. She helped herself, crunched for a moment, and began to rehearse.

Once upon a time there was a man called Akram . . .

. . . Who sat down on a packing case, unwrapped a bulky parcel of old dusters and produced a brass oil lamp of the

457

traditional Middle Eastern oiling-can-with-a-wick variety. He extended his sleeve as if to rub it, thought better of it, hesitated, closed his eyes and rubbed.

'Hello,' said the djinn, 'how's you? Hey, it's dark in here.'

Akram couldn't let that pass. 'Darker than where you've just come from?' he queried.

'Of course,' the djinn replied, 'I've been in a lamp. Now then, what can I do for you?'

There was something about the horrible creature's nails-on-blackboard cheerfulness that evacuated Akram's mind like a flawlessly executed fire drill. He stared for a moment, then frowned.

'Look,' he said. 'All I want is a simple answer to a simple question.'

'Sure.' The djinn smiled. Dammit, it was only trying to be friendly, but it was like having an itch in your crotch when you're addressing an emergency session of the United Nations. Akram took a deep breath and went on.

'Okay,' he said. 'What I—'

'Don't say wish,' the djinn interrupted. 'If you just ask me the question, you see, I don't have to count it as one of your wishes. Just a hint. Hope you don't mind me mentioning it.'

'What I *want* to know is— Look, I'm a villain, right?'

'Yes. Was that it?'

'No. Be quiet. I'm a villain. A baddie. Suppose I wanted to change and be a goodie, how'd I go about it?'

The djinn frowned and scratched the tip of its nose. 'I don't follow,' it said.

'Oh for crying out— Listen. I want to be good. How's it done? It can't be difficult, for pity's sake. If nuns can do it, so can I.'

The djinn grinned. 'It's easy for nuns,' it said. 'With them it's just force of habit. Get it? Habit, you know, like those long dressing gown things they wear—'

458

Instinctively Akram grabbed for the djinn's throat. His hands passed through it as if he'd tried to pull a projection off a screen. 'Don't push me too far,' he snarled. 'Now answer the goddam question, before I lose my temper.'

A multiple lifetime of experience in menacing had put a rasp into Akram's voice you could have shaped mahogany with, but the djinn simply looked down his nose at him. 'All right, Mister Grumpy,' he said, 'there's no need to get aereated.'

'I'll aereate you in a minute. Hey, would that make you a djinn fizz?'

'Your question,' said the djinn frostily. 'Can you, a villain, turn yourself into a good guy?'

'You got it.'

'Dunno.' The djinn pondered for a moment, and the air in the lock-up unit seemed to sparkle with tiny green flecks. 'It's a bit of a grey area, that. I mean, you could just try being nice to people and giving up your seat on buses to old ladies with heavy shopping and holding open-air rock concerts to raise money for famine victims and stuff, but there's no saying that'd actually work.'

'There isn't?'

The djinn shook its head. 'No saying it wouldn't, either. I'm just guessing, really.'

Akram closed his eyes and started to count to ten. He got as far as four.

'I wonder,' he said. 'If I took your lamp and soldered down the lid and blocked the spout up with weld, would that mean you'd be trapped in there for ever and ever?'

'I don't know.'

'Neither do I.' Akram reached for his toolkit. 'Soldering iron, soldering iron, I saw the blasted thing only the other day.'

'Alternatively,' said the djinn, 'you might try and do good

but all that'd happen would be that you did bad in spite of yourself.'

'Sorry, my gibberish is a trifle rusty. What are you talking about?'

'Because you're a villain,' said the djinn, ostentatiously patient, 'everything you do – arguably – will turn out evil, regardless of your intentions. Like in the film.'

'Film? What film?'

The djinn made a tutting noise. 'It's on the tip of my tongue,' it said. 'Donoghue. O'Shaughnessy.'

'What the—?'

'Cassidy. Butch Cassidy. You know, the bit where they try going straight and get jobs as payroll guards and end up gunning down about a zillion Mexicans.'

'Bolivians.'

'Pardon me?"

'Bolivians,' Akram repeated. He could feel a headache starting to come together in the foothills of his brain. 'They were in Bolivia, not Mexico.'

'You're quite right,' the djinn conceded. 'I always think of it as Mexico because of the big round hats.'

'Bugger hats.' It was going to be a *special* headache. 'What you're saying is, I'm stuck with being a villain, there's nothing I can do about it. But that's crazy. I mean, this is Reality, for pity's sake. Surely in Reality I can be whatever I want to be, that's the whole bloody point.'

The djinn sniggered. 'Think you'll find it isn't quite as simple as that,' it said. 'Otherwise everybody'd be film stars and millionaires and lottery winners.'

'Ah,' Akram said, 'but I happen to have a genuine magic djinn with supernatural powers on my side, so I'm laughing, aren't I?'

The djinn made a sniffing noise. 'Now you mustn't go building your hopes up,' it said, 'because in actual fact I have

460

to be very careful with the possibility infringement regulations, and—'

'Got it!' Akram held up a soldering iron, and grinned. 'And here's the solder, look, so all we need now is the flux. Unless this is the sort where the flux is in there already.'

'Now look,' protested the djinn, 'don't you try threatening me . . .'

'I think it's that sort. Why do they use such small print on these labels?'

'I've been threatened by bigger people than you, you know. If you were to see some of the people I've been threatened by, six miles away through a telescope, you'd have to sleep with the light on for a month.'

Akram smiled. People who saw Akram's special menacing smile invariably remembered it for the rest of their lives, although in many cases this was not, objectively speaking, a terribly long time. 'And then,' he said, 'once I've soldered the lid and jammed the spout, just suppose I put the lamp on top of the cooker and turn the heat full on. It'd get very hot in there.'

'Look.' The djinn was sweating. 'I don't make the rules. If it was up to me, you could be Saint Francis of Assisi and Mother Teresa and the Care Bears all rolled into one. As it is . . .'

'First,' Akram said, 'you plug in your soldering iron. Next, make sure all surfaces are clean and free of dirt and grit. That's one of the basic rules of all endjineering, that is.'

'As it is,' said the djinn, passing a finger round the inside of its collar, 'there are a few very remote possibilities I could check out, but there's absolutely no guarantee–'

'So what we do is,' Akram went on, the lamp in one hand, a scrap of emery paper in the other, 'we just rub down the edges until we've got rid of the verdigris and we're down to the virdjinn metal—'

'No *cast-iron* guarantee,' the djinn muttered rapidly, 'but on the other hand I think we can be quietly confident. What was it you wanted again?'

'I want to be good.'

'No worries.'

'In fact,' Akram said, 'I want to be the hero.'

The djinn swallowed. 'And that's a wish, is it?'

'You bet.'

Cue special effects. Unearthly green lights, clouds of hissing vapour, doors and windows suddenly flying open. It would have taken George Lucas nine months and an eight-figure budget. The djinn was a spinning tower of green flame, and Akram looked like he was wearing a fluorescent green overcoat with Christmas tree lights for buttons.

'Your wish,' said the tower of flame, 'is my command.'

Scheherezade paused, and looked up at her husband, who chuckled, lit his cigar and grinned. Outside, the sun shone on a wide lawn, a long drive, a pair of impressive-looking gates guarded by a huge man in dark glasses and a black suit. Scheherezade's husband took a long pull on his cigar and poured himself another glass of strega.

'One down,' he said, 'two to go.'

CHAPTER TWELVE

Maybe, in accordance with some extremely complex chain of causalities explicable only in terms of the most highly advanced avant-garde chaos theory, Akram's transformation into a trainee Hero was the reason he got fired from the kebab house. The ostensible reason, or at least the catalyst, was taking time off to go to the dentist without clearing it with the boss first.

He accepted the decision with uncharacteristic stoicism. The old Akram would immediately have avenged the insult in blood, leaving his replacement a confusing choice of impaled hunks of knife-slashed meat. The new Akram shrugged meekly, apologized for his thoughtlessness, collected his apron and left without raising the issue of arrears of wages due. If he'd been offered any money, he'd probably have refused to accept it.

He was shuffling homewards from this mortifying interview when he passed the window of a large fast-food joint, an outpost of an internationally respected hamburger federation.

Looking up, he saw a brightly coloured poster that said: HELP WANTED.

Wow, he said to himself, is that an omen or what? You'd have to be brain-dead or carved from solid marble not to recognise such an obvious example of Destiny handing out second chances. With a small nod of the head to indicate respectful thanks, he walked in and asked to see the manager.

In order to be considered for the job, the manager explained, prospective candidates had to be:

(a) hard-working, diligent and honest;
(b) experienced in all main aspects of retail mass catering;
(c) of a presentable appearance and able to communicate effectively with the general public;
(d) desperate enough to apply for the job and demoralised enough to stay.

And, he added quickly, Akram seemed to him to qualify in all four categories. He didn't actually stand in front of the door until Akram agreed to take the job, but he hovered.

'Not,' he added quickly, as he issued Akram with his apron and cardboard hat of office, 'that we have difficulty keeping staff. Far from it. Some nights at closing time I have to shoo them out with a broom. It's just that this is – well, a *lively* neighbourhood, and some of the customers—'

Involuntarily he closed his eyes, but only for a split second. 'A bit fun-loving, some of them. Very occasionally.'

'Good-natured banter and high spirits?'

The manager nodded. 'From time to time. Anyway, welcome on board and the very best of luck. Now, if you'll just give me the name and address of your next of kin, purely a formality...'

Akram made up a name and address, put on his uniform and followed the manager out into the kitchen area. The work as explained to him didn't seem arduous or distasteful, at least compared with some of the things he'd had to do in his previous career, and there was something about his new colleagues that made him feel immediately at home. It was only after an hour or so that he realised what it was. The scars.

'This one,' explained Gladstone, the assistant manager, 'was where this bloke slashed me with a bottle, and this one was a razor, and this one was where this girl tried to stub her fag out in me eye 'cos she reckoned I gave her the wrong relish on the dips. And this one . . .'

'I see,' Akram said aloud; to himself he was groaning; *Oh bugger it, Butch Cassidy.* Still, it was worth a try, and maybe if he was alert and concentrated very, very hard on getting out of the way, he wouldn't have to kill anybody for weeks.

The part of the job that involved preparing and retailing food turned out to be almost pleasant; and as for the other aspect, there seemed to be something about Akram's manner that deterred the blade-wielding fun-lovers and made them take their place in one of the other queues. After he'd been there a month, in fact, the place had become virtually fun-free, and rumour had it that the district's principal fun-lovers had blacklisted the establishment and were taking their custom to Neptune's Larder, three hundred yards down the road. When he heard this, Akram was afraid he'd lose his job for driving away customers, but the manager didn't seem to mind a bit. In fact, when Gladstone the assistant manager got into a lively debate with a tenaciously loyal fun-lover and was signed off work for nine months in consequence, Akram was promoted to take his place.

'Really?'

'Yes, really.'

'Gosh.' Akram was lost for words. 'What, *really*?'

The manager looked at him. 'I'm glad you're so pleased,' he said. 'Actually, it's not an awful lot more money, but—'

'*More* money?'

The manager took half a step backwards. He'd been there

nearly eighteen months, and knew from experience that working there took its toll in many different ways. 'Well, yes,' he said. 'Not a fortune, by any means, but we do like to reward . . .'

'Gosh. But I scarcely know what to do with all of what I get already. I'm not sure I ought to – I mean, I'm not sure it'd feel right, somehow.'

'Go on,' muttered the manager. 'Force yourself.'

There was, of course, a downside. There is a dignity doth hedge an assistant manager, even a temporary acting one; his place is on the quarterdeck rather than in the engine room, and it would be inconsistent with that dignity for him to slice onions, defrost coleslaw or top up the french-fries hopper. Henceforth, there would be no more shifts in the kitchen; a pity, because he had come to love the smell and texture of the food, which to someone who had spent his lives in Old Baghdad was tantalising and exotic. In Old Baghdad, what you ate depended entirely on who you were, and there were just two standard menus: banquets and scraps. Since the latter was only the former two days later, it all tended to get a bit monotonous, and Bar-B-Q Bacon Belt-Bustas, thick shakes and the Chicken Danish Brunch were like a glimpse through the curtain at the dining-tables of paradise.

'You like it here,' Tanya said, one night during a lull. It wasn't a question, more a bewildered statement of fact. Akram nodded.

'Best job I ever had,' he replied.

Tanya looked at him; and he was more than happy to reciprocate. A couple of months ago, if you'd have told Akram that women like Tanya existed, he'd have laughed in your face. She was completely different. She wasn't sloe-eyed and hourglass-shaped. Her glances didn't smoulder; and although Akram had no way of telling because her apron was in the way, he'd have been prepared to bet a year's wages that she didn't have a diamond jammed in her belly-button. True, there was enough of her to have made two of what Akram thought of as the standard-issue model, and still have plenty left over for spares; but so, as Akram told himself as he stood and gazed at her, what? The best thing about her, the bit that really shook him to the marrow, was that she was *different*. She did things that the girls back home wouldn't have the faintest idea how to do. Such as think.

'Really?'

Akram nodded. 'You bet,' he said.

'Right. So what was it you used to do?'

'I . . .' Although he'd known all along that the question would be asked sooner or later, he'd always shied away from the task of fabricating a reply. Somehow, even thinking about his past activities made him feel depressed and nervous, as if to admit that he'd had a previous existence could jeopardise his new one. 'I'd rather not talk about it,' he said, looking down at the counter. 'If that's all right,' he added.

'Sure.'

There you go, thoughtfulness again. Consideration for the feelings of others. The desire to avoid pain and embarrass-ment. God, thought Akram, I love it here, I'm not *ever* going back.

Tanya didn't say anything, and then a customer came in and ordered a Chicken Danish Brunch, so that the moment passed. As Akram got the order – a chicken burger sitting on half a bread roll crowned with a splodge of red sauce and some sort of plant – he stole a glance at Tanya out of the corner of his eye, and deep inside him somewhere a little voice said *Yes, but why not?* And the rest of him couldn't immediately think of any good reason.

'So,' Hanif muttered, sitting down on a flat rock and putting his head between his hands, 'that's it, then.'

Aziz nodded, unable to speak. A hundred yards or so in front of them was the border; the customs post, Jim's Diner, the wire. He felt utterly wretched.

'Let's face it,' Hanif went on, 'we've looked everywhere. Everywhere,' he repeated unnecessarily. 'And he's not there. Which can only mean—'

'All right,' Aziz growled, 'you've made your bloody point.'

Faisal shook his head, dislodging a few organisms. 'Still can't see why he'd do such a thing,' he sighed. 'I mean, run out on us. Abandon us like that. You just wouldn't believe it.'

It was a hot day, they'd been on the road since an hour before dawn, and nobody had the energy to answer. Finally having to accept that the Skip was gone and was unlikely ever to come back was like trying to come to terms with God leaving the answering machine on even though you know perfectly well he's at home. There was a vast hole in the side of their universe; they could ignore it, or else fall through.

'Maybe he's in the caff,' said Hassan. 'I mean, we haven't actually looked.'

'Might as well,' Aziz replied. 'They may have seen him, anyhow.'

'I think,' said Mushtaq, youngest and most gauche of the Thirty-Nine Thieves, 'that he's gone on a special mission to the other side to steal something, you know, something really, really valuable, and as soon as he's pulled it off he'll come back, and . . .'

'Mushtaq.'

'Yes, Skip?'

'Don't, there's a good lad.'

'Don't what, Skip?'

Aziz sighed. 'Just don't, that's all. I'm not in the mood. All right,' he went on, standing up and rubbing his cheeks with his palms, 'Hassan, Farouk, you come with me and we'll check out the caff. The rest of you—'

468

He couldn't be bothered to finish the order. There was no point; after all, apart from sitting aimlessly in the shade with their knees drawn up to their chins, what else was there that they could possibly find to do? He beckoned to his two chosen followers and trudged slowly towards Jim's Diner.

Inside, it was at least a little bit cooler. They walked up to the counter, flopped down onto barstools and ordered three quarts of goat's milk and three club sandwiches. Ten minutes and a good deal of noise later, they were in a much better state to ask penetratingly shrewd questions.

'Here, miss,' said Aziz. 'You seen Akram the Terrible round here lately?'

The barmaid – dear God, where did he find them? Under flat stones, probably – looked up from the glass she was polishing. 'You just missed him,' she said.

Hassan stood up at once and started for the door, but Aziz waved him back. He'd been in Jim's before, and knew that Time here wasn't only relative, it was third-cousin-twice-removed. 'How long since he was here?' he asked.

The barmaid shrugged. 'Couple of months, maybe three. He left with a bear.'

Aziz managed to silence Farouk before he could ask with a bare what and get them all thrown out. 'Oh yes?' he replied, as nonchalantly as possible. To be painfully honest, Aziz was to nonchalance as a pterodactyl in Selfridges' is to looking inconspicuous, but he gave it his best shot. 'This bear,' he added, 'Wouldn't happen to be in here, would he?'

The barmaid shook her head. 'You just missed him,' she replied.

'Don't tell me,' muttered Aziz. 'He left with Akram the Terrible, right?'

'If you know, why ask?'

Aziz got up. 'Not to worry,' he sighed. 'Look, if you see this bear, tell him we'd like a word, okay?'

469

'Why not tell him yourself?' the barmaid said. 'I can tell you where to find him.'

In many lifetimes of violence and mayhem, Aziz had never hit a woman, mostly because they wouldn't keep still; but he wasn't one of those narrow-minded types who shrink away from new experiences. 'Right,' he said, 'fine. Could you please tell me where . . .?'

The barmaid thought about it for a moment. 'All right,' she said. 'Go back out the way you came about seven leagues and you'll come to a big forest, right? Take the main road, then second on your left, third right past the charcoal burner's, then follow your nose and you'll come to a little cottage.'

Aziz squirmed a little in his seat. 'Brightly painted red door? Shiny brass knocker? Red and white curtains with pretty flowers and stuff?'

'That's right.'

'Big mat with *Welcome*? Climbing roses round the porch? Little goldfish pond out front with a couple of rustic benches?'

'You know the place, then?'

Aziz nodded. He knew the place all right. He'd be able to picture it in his mind's eye for the rest of his life as the house where he single-handedly killed the ferocious bear. 'This bear he went off with,' he said, his voice sounding odd because of the dryness of the roof of his mouth. 'Lady bear, was it?'

'No. Gentleman bear – I mean, it was a male. Great big brute, huge claws.'

'Ah.'

'Real nice personality, mind. Wouldn't hurt a fly. Called Derek.'

'Oh.'

'Can't say as much for his friends, though. Very pally with some really heavy types, if you know what I mean.'

'Fat people?'

470

The barmaid shook her head. She didn't speak, but she mouthed the words *the mob* so distinctly that a lip-reader would have asked her not to shout. 'Wouldn't want to get on the wrong side of that lot,' she added with a grimace. 'That Derek was in here one time, these pirates jogged his elbow, made him spill his condensed milk. Three months later, they fished what was left of 'em out of a lime pit out behind Tom Thumb's place. Only able to identify them from the dental records.'

'I see.'

'This bear,' the barmaid said, studying Aziz's face as if expecting to have to pick it out of a lineup at some later stage. 'What you want him for, anyway?'

'We're friends of Ak— hey, watch it, Skip, that was my ankle.'

'Wrong bear,' said Aziz loudly. 'Not the one we were thinking of, was it, lads? I mean, the bear we were thinking of is small. Honey-coloured. Lives in an abandoned sawmill over by the Hundred Acre Wood. Well, thanks for the milk.'

By the time they were out of Jim's and back in the fresh air, Aziz was as white as a sheet. A very dirty sheet, from the bed of someone who never washes, but white nevertheless.

'Okay, lads,' he said. 'I think we may be in a bit of trouble here.'

'Trouble, Skip?'

Aziz shuddered. 'Nothing to worry about,' he replied. 'I just reckon it might be sensible if we found something like a cave or a very deep hole, just for a year or so. That'd make a nice change, wouldn't it?'

'But Skip, what about finding Ak—?'

'*Shut up!*'

'Sorry, I'm sure.'

Aziz mopped his face with his shirt tails. 'Anybody know of anywhere like that?' he asked. 'Near here, preferably. In fact, as near as possible?'

Hanif frowned. 'You okay, Skip?' he asked, concerned. 'You seem a bit edgy.'

'Yeah,' agreed Shamir. 'Like a bear with a sore—'

'*Quiet!*' Aziz snapped, and then took a deep breath. On reflection, he told himself, belay that last instinct. It was no earthly use trying to hide from Them; after all, wherever he led his wretched followers in Story-book land, they'd be strangers, out of place in some other folks' story, conspicuous as a goldfish in a lemon meringue pie. So; they couldn't hide. Popular theory would have them believe that as a viable alternative they could run, but Aziz wasn't too sure about that; not in curly-toed slippers, at any rate. Well, now; if you can't hide and you can't run, what can you do?

Whimper?

Sham dead?

Forget the second alternative, in case Death is attracted to the sincerest form of flattery. Aziz reached a decision. He'd try whimpering. After all, it wasn't as if they were spoilt for choice, and in the final analysis they had nothing to lose but a complete set of limbs and their lives.

'Wait there, I may be gone some time,' he said, and went back inside.

'You again,' said the barmaid.

Aziz nodded. 'You said something about the bear having, um, friends,' he said. 'I'd like to meet them.'

'You would?'

'Yes,' said Aziz. 'Please,' he added, remembering his manners.

The barmaid stared at him, as if speculating how he'd look in one of those fancy jackets with long sleeves that do up at the back. 'Why?' she said.

'It's a long story.'

'Aren't they all?'

'That depends,' Aziz replied. For his part, he had the

472

feeling that his own particular narrative was in serious danger of being cut down into an anecdote. 'Don't change the subject. How do I meet these guys?'

The barmaid shrugged. 'Okay,' she said. 'Go back out the way you came about three leagues and you'll come to a ruined castle. After that, you take the first right then second on your left, second right past the little pigs' house, straight on up the hill until you come to a crossroads, you'll see a long drive leading up to a big house. Say Rosa from Jim's sent you, but it's nothing to do with her. Okay?'

'Sure thing. Thanks.'

'You *really* want to go there?'

'You've been most helpful.'

'And tell Rocco on the gate,' she called after him, 'if they're going I wouldn't mind the tall one's boots for my kid brother.'

'So,' said the man behind the desk, 'you come to me and you say, *We kill your buddy the little bear, we're terribly sorry, we won't do it again.* Is that it?'

Aziz nodded. Behind him, seventy-six feet shuffled nervously. 'It was an accident, really,' he said. 'Well, not an accident as such, more a, what's the word, misunderstanding.' He remembered a good phrase from one of his juvenile court appearances. 'A tragic fusion of coincidence, mistaken identity and good intentions gone dreadfully awry,' he recited. On second thoughts, he wished he hadn't; it hadn't worked the first time, mainly because the coincidence had been the night watch coming down the alley at precisely the moment he was leaving the warehouse, the mistaken identity had been him thinking they weren't the watch, and the good intention had been his intention to escape by climbing over the wall into what turned out to be the Khalif's pedigree snake collection.

'Sure,' grunted the man behind the desk. 'I believe you. So when the Momma Bear and the Baby Bear they come to me

473

and say, *Padrone, give us justice*, I gotta tell them it was all a mistake and the guys are terribly sorry. Do you take me for a fool, or what? Rocco, get them outa my sight.'

Behind him, Aziz could hear footsteps, and metallic grating noises. Not for the first time, he sincerely wished he could have had his brain removed when he was twelve. 'Look ...' he stuttered.

And then the man behind the desk did a strange thing. He smiled. 'On the other hand,' he said. He didn't finish the sentence, but the movement noises in the background stopped as abruptly as if a tape had been switched off.

'Yes?' Aziz croaked.

'Hey.' The man spread his arms. 'Everybody makes mistakes. I made a mistake, once,' he added. 'And I'm sure that if I was to put in a good word for you with the widow bear and the orphan bear—'

'Yes?'

'And you guys sign a legally binding contract to cut them in on, say, ninety per cent of everything you make for the next forty years—'

'Yes?'

'Plus a small contribution, say five per cent, to the Arabian Nights Moonshine Coach Club social fund—'

'Yes?'

The man shrugged. It was an eloquent gesture. Louder and clearer than fifty-foot neon letters against a black background it said THIS COMMITS ME TO NOTHING BUT SO WHAT? 'Then,' he said, 'you guys gonna be so grateful to me, you might consider doing me a small favour.'

'Anything you say,' Aziz replied, in a voice so small that a bat would need a hearing aid to hear it. '*Padrone*,' he added.

'That's great,' said the man. 'Now, then. I gonna tell you a story.'

CHAPTER THIRTEEN

The air was foul with the stench of burning bone.

It's a distinctive smell; not perhaps overwhelmingly revolting in itself, but unbearable once you know what it is. You can get used to it, of course; human beings can get used to virtually anything, given plenty of time and no choice in the matter whatsoever. Fortunately, Ali Baba wasn't naturally squeamish, and he had the advantage of knowing that, although his drill turned so fast that the friction scorched the tooth as he drilled it, the patient never felt a thing because of the anaesthetic.

'There you are,' he said cheerfully. 'Quick rinse and we're done.'

Last patient of the day; no more drilling into people until eight o'clock tomorrow morning. A propos of nothing much, he wondered whether Akram the Terrible, his former great and worthy opponent, ever felt the same sense of deep, exhausted relief after a hard night's murdering. Wash off the blood and the bits of bone, change into nice comfy old clothes, make a nice hot cup of something and collapse into a friendly chair by the fire; what, after all, could be better than that? Apart, of course, from not having to get all bloody and covered in bits in the first place.

He had switched off the lights and was just about to lock up when a white delivery van pulled up outside. Mr Barbour? Yes, that's me. Delivery for you, if you'd just sign here. The driver handed him a crate about eighteen inches square, accepted his tip and drove away.

Ali Baba stood on the pavement for nearly a minute, feeling the weight of the box; then he unlocked the door and went back inside, locking up again afterwards. His heart was beating a little faster now, and he was beginning to sweat ever so slightly.

The museum authorities hadn't been best pleased when he'd called them up and asked for it back. He'd reminded them that it was only a loan, and pointed out that there had been a recent spate of thefts of similar objects. He mentioned in passing that he had a receipt. When they put the phone down on him, he rang straight back, ignored their claim that he'd got a wrong number and was now talking to NexDay Laundry Services, and demanded to speak to the Director. And so forth. Eventually they agreed to return it by armoured van, with Ali Baba paying the carriage charges. Then, having added (quite unnecessarily, in Ali Baba's opinion) that at least that meant one less card to send this Christmas, they rang off.

And here it was. He sighed and shook his head. If only the poor fools had realised what they'd actually got there, not all the bailiffs and court orders in the universe could ever have prised it away from them.

Yes. But. Bailiffs and court orders are one thing, but the greatest ever burglar in either of the two dimensions was something else entirely; and if Akram was still out there somewhere, plotting and scheming to find a way of nailing his ancient foe without transgressing the letter of his oath, then leaving this thing in the deepest vault of the most secure museum in the world was pretty much the same as laying it out on the pavement with a big flashing light on top to show him where to find it. It'd be criminal negligence of the most horrible and bloodcurdling variety to let it stay where it was. There could only be one safe place for it from now on, and that was under the loose floorboard in the store cupboard in Ali Baba's surgery.

'Blasted thing,' he muttered under his breath, as he carried it up the stairs. 'Wish I'd never pinched it in the first place.'

All loose floorboards are not the same. For a start, this one didn't creak. Nor could it be prised up with a crowbar and the back of a claw hammer. In fact, were a hostile power to drop a nuclear bomb on Southampton, the only thing guaranteed to be completely undamaged would be Ali Baba's loose floorboard. It'd still be loose, of course; exactly the same degree of looseness, not a thousandth of a millimetre tighter or wobblier.

Carefully – drop it and the consequences didn't bear thinking about – he lowered it into the hole and then stood back, hands on knees, to catch his breath and say the password. He did so, replaced the board and muttered the self-activating spell. Finally, he locked up and went home.

After he'd gone, the rogue tooth fairy that'd been hanging around the place all day in the hope of picking up sixpenny-worth of second-hand calcium clambered out of a half-empty pot of pink casting medium, looked around to make sure all was clear, and landed heavily on the loose floorboard. It wobbled, but it wouldn't budge.

'Bugger,' muttered Fang.

Three quarters of an hour later, she gave up the unequal struggle. During this time she'd snapped or blunted two dozen drill bits, broken a whole box of disposable scalpels and banged her own thumb with a two-pound lump hammer (don't ask what it was doing in among the tools of Ali Baba's trade, because unless you've got film star's teeth and will never need to go to a dentist again, you really don't want to know). There was no way of getting in without the password, and although she knew perfectly well what it was, having overhead Ali Baba setting it, she was just a fairy and couldn't say it loud enough. A pity; the contents of Ali Baba's improvised floor safe were worth more to her than all the molars ever pulled. If only she could get her hands on it, then she could name her price; including her old job back and sixpences enough to buy Newfoundland.

Nothing for it; she needed human help. But who?

Not a problem. She knew just the man. In fact, he was her landlord.

With a savage buzz she memorised the location of the loose board, checked the office waste-paper basket for teeth one last time, and flew home.

Aren't human beings wonderful?

Well, actually, no; but they do sometimes manage to achieve wonderful things, albeit for all the wrong reasons. One of their most remarkable abilities, which gained them the coveted Golden Straitjacket award for most gloriously dizzy instinctive behaviour five thousand years running in the prestigious Vicenza Dumb Animals Festival, is their exceptional knack of ignoring the most disturbingly bizarre circumstances simply by pretending they don't exist. No matter how radical the upheaval, as soon as the dust has settled a little and it's relatively safe outside the bunker, out they go again to weave their spiders' webs of apparent normality over whatever it is they don't want to come to terms with, until the web becomes as rigid and substantial as a coral reef.

Michelle, for example, found that if she went to work as usual, stayed on after hours doing overtime and then went straight on to meet friends for a drink or a movie, so that she

478

was almost never at home before midnight or after seven-thirty am, she could go hours at a time without thinking strange thoughts or feeling the naggingly persistent lure of the ring. It was like living on the slopes of an active volcano but without the views and the constant free hot water.

And then; well, you can only play chicken on the Great Road of Chaos for so long before you make a slight error of judgement. In Michelle's case, her mistake lay in stopping off for a bite to eat after an evening's rather self-conscious cheerleading for the office formation karaoke team. Perhaps it was the strain of having to put a brave face on Mr Pettingell from Claims singing *You Ain't Nothin' But A Hound Dog* in a Birmingham accent so broad you could have used it as a temporary bridge over the Mississippi that sapped her instinctive early warning systems; or perhaps it was just that her number was up.

'I'll have the . . .' She hesitated, and squinted at the illuminated menu above the counter. She'd originally intended to have the Treble Grand Slam Baconburger, large fries, regular guava shake; but a glance at the ten-times-life-size backlit transparency overhead made her doubt the wisdom of that decision. For one thing, it was too brightly coloured. Mother Nature reserves bright reds and yellows for warning livery for her more indigestible species, such as wasps and poison toadstools. The sight of the ketchup and relish in the illustration must have triggered an ancient survival mechanism. She had another look at the menu, searching for something there wasn't a picture of.

'I'll try the . . .' For a fleeting moment she was tempted by the Greenland Shark Nuggets 'n' Bar-B-Q Dip, but the moment passed. If God had intended people to eat sharks, as opposed to vice versa, he would have modified the respective blueprints accordingly.

The man behind the counter smiled patiently. 'Take your

time,' he said. 'Actually, I'd recommend the Chicken Danish Brunch.' There was, Heaven help us, a flicker of genuine, unfeigned enthusiasm in the poor man's eyes as he spoke. 'My personal favourite,' he added, 'for what that's worth.'

Michelle shrugged. 'So what's that got in it?' she asked.

The man straightened his back with – yes, dammit, with *pride* as he recited, 'It's a scrummy fillet of marinaded prime chicken, served traditional Danish-style in an open sandwich with choice of relish, all on a sesame seed bun.'

The speech went past Michelle like an InterCity train through a Saturdays-only backwoods station. 'I'm sorry?' she said. 'I missed that.'

'Okay. It's a scrummy—'

'Edited highlights, please.'

'No problem. Chicken, open sandwich, sesame seed bun.'

Michelle shook her head. It was noisy inside, noisy even for a Macfarlane's on a Friday night, and her ears were still ringing from Mr Sobieski from Accounts informing the world that ever since his baby left him, he'd found a new place to dwell. 'Say again, please,' she shouted back. 'Didn't quite catch . . .'

The man nodded and smiled. 'Sandwich,' he said. 'Open. Sesame . . .'

'Open sesame?'

('Two down. One to go.')

'Sesame seed bun.' Something strange had happened to the man's face. It was as if he was being used as a guinea pig by a blind acupuncturist. 'Guaranteed to make your taste-buds . . . Don't I know you?'

'I'm sorry?'

'You sound like someone I used to know.'

As he spoke, he saw that her purse was open on the counter, and there was her Visa card. Part of the shared heritage of thieves and lawyers is an ability to read upside down without even having to think about it: MICHELLE PARTRIDGE.

'Do I?'

'My imagination,' Akram replied; while he was saying the words, shutters came down in his eyes, like a snake's transparent eyelids. 'Do forgive me. Alternatively, the Saigon Ribs Surprise is very popular. There's a choice of dips, we've got Tangy Orange, Bar-B-Q, Byzantine Lemon . . .'

Her purse also contained a receipted gas bill, with her address. Akram's eyes lapped up the information like a cat drinking milk.

'I'll have that, please,' Michelle said quickly. 'Who did I remind you of?'

'Forget it, please,' Akram muttered. 'That was in another country, and besides, the sonofabitch is dead.'

'I beg your pardon?'

'Which dip? We got orange, barbeque, lemon . . .'

'Orange.'

'Coming right up. That'll be three pounds seventy-five, please.'

Now I know who he is, Michelle realised. He was in the waiting room, the day I—

'Your change,' said Akram. 'Enjoy your meal, have a nice day.'

'Thank you. I—'

The two girls behind her, who had been very patient so far, eased past and ordered hamburgers. She stood for a moment, at right angles to the queue, clutching her bag and trying to think.

Akram. *Akram the Terrible!* Here!

'Excuse me.' She elbowed one girl out of the way and stood heavily on the other's toe. 'Sorry,' she growled. 'Look, is your name Akram, by any chance?'

The man looked at her, and pointed at his lapel badge. It read: JOHN, ASST MGR.

481

'So sorry,' she whispered, and fled.

Of all the hamburger joints in all the towns in all the world, Akram reflected, as he locked up that night. Just when I was starting to get somewhere. Just when I was beginning to get some vague idea of what happiness might possibly be like. And now it's back to the old routine.

Just a minute, he reflected. Just because I've found Ali Baba's daughter (how come he's got a daughter, and what in buggery is she doing this side of the goddamn Line?) doesn't necessarily mean I've got to do anything about it. I can just ignore it. Forget I ever saw her. Take no notice.

I could indeed. And then, for an encore, I could hitch a ride on a flying pig and save myself the bus fare home. Get real, Akram.

Get *real* —

If only. Chance, he muttered to himself as he switched on the alarm, would be a bloody fine thing. He'd seen or read somewhere that humans had a proverb: Mankind cannot stand too much reality. As far as he was concerned, Mankind didn't know it was born.

When he got home, the tooth fairy was waiting for him. That, he reckoned, put the tin lid on it.

'Not now,' he said, as she fluttered down from the ceiling like a large moth, the sort that chews holes in chain-mail shirts.

'Yes, but listen . . .'

'I said not now.' He flumped into the armchair, kicked his shoes off, and put his hands behind his head. All other considerations beside, he'd had a long day, been on his feet for most of it, and he badly wanted to go to sleep. It occurred to him that on the other side of the Line, he never got as tired as this, even if he'd been in the saddle all day and out burgling and killing all night. In Story-book land, everyone has bound-less energy and extraordinary (by Real standards) stamina. In

482

Story-book land, people only keel over from exhaustion when the story demands that they say, 'I'm done for, you go on without me'; which is the hero's cue to pick up his worn-out colleague and carry him for two days across the desert.

'Listen!'

Akram turned, his hand partly raised as if to swat. 'Well?' he snapped. 'This had better be important. Anything less than world-shattering, and the only loose teeth around here are going to be your own.'

Tooth fairies are, of course, first-class narrators, and it took Fang less than thirty seconds to explain about her discovery. When she'd finished, Akram nodded slowly.

'Okay,' he said, 'so that is pretty world-shattering.'

'And?'

'And what?'

'And,' said Fang impatiently, 'as in, what are we waiting for? Come on, it's after midnight already.'

Akram held up his hand, as if he was God directing traffic. 'Not so fast,' he said. 'Admittedly, the obvious course of action would be to go immediately and steal this thing.'

'Right.'

'Ninety-nine out of a hundred villains would already be out of the door and halfway down the street by now. The hundredth would be hobbling along behind the other ninety-nine, cursing the day he got lumbered with a wooden leg.'

'*Right*. So why are we . . .?'

'But,' said Akram, 'you overlook one minor detail. I'm not a villain any more. I'm through with all that, remember? I'm a good guy now.'

'Don't be silly,' said the tooth fairy. 'What's got into you, anyway? If you've got some sort of hyper-subtle master plan . . .'

Akram shook his head. 'Nope,' he replied. 'Look, my fluttering friend, watch my lips. I am not interested. I don't do

483

that stuff any more. I mean it,' he added, as Fang made a vulgar noise implying disbelief. 'If I still wanted to nail Ali Baba, I've got an even better trick up my sleeve. I've found his daughter. I could put the snatch on her, demand that he release me from my promise, and then go scrag the fucker.' He paused for a moment. Without realising he was doing it, he'd taken such a tight grip on the arm of his chair that the wood was creaking. With an effort he let go. 'But I'm not going to,' he went on, putting his fingertips together and crossing his legs, as smoothly as a chat-show host. 'So, it was terribly sweet of you to think of me and if there's anything I can do that doesn't involve nutting people in the mouth so you can swipe their teeth, you just name it. But I'm not interested. You got that, or would you like me to tap it out on your head in Morse code with this teaspoon?'

At first, all Fang could do was stare at him, as if waiting for the practical joker to pull off the rubber Akram mask and say, 'Fooled you!' When it finally sank in that he was serious, the fairy couldn't trust herself to speak. She buzzed furiously to her shoebox, dived in and dragged the lid shut after her. Shortly afterwards, the flat was filled with the sound of a tiny person crying.

'Cut that out, will you?'

'Snf.'

'Look,' said Akram, raising the lid a few millimetres. 'I've brought you something, see? It's a left front incisor, I found it at work, a customer left it in a Triple Swiss Fondueburger. Don't you want it?'

The lid slammed.

'I'll leave it here for you,' said Akram, slightly shaken. 'For when you're a bit less overwrought. Look, it's still got most of its original plaque.'

From inside the box came a tiny voice telling him where he could put his lousy rotten tooth. The recommendation was biologically feasible, but not something you'd suggest to someone whose shoebox you were living in. Akram shrugged.

'If you don't want it,' he said, 'there's plenty that will. I'll put it under my pillow, and we'll see if it's still there in the morning.'

Nothing from the shoebox except bitter snuffling. Akram shrugged. Maybe she had a point, at that; but if she thought he was going to chuck away what might be his one and only chance to break out of the Story just to please a tiny gossamer-winged garbage collectress, she was deluding herself and that was all there was to it. It'd be like giving all your property to the poor, dressing up in sackcloth and wandering forth to preach to the birds just in order to get your picture on page seven of the *Assisi Evening Examiner*.

And anyway, he reassured himself, as he rolled into bed and switched off the light, virtue's its own reward, or so it says in the rule book. The better I am, the better I get. Turning down two opportunities for revenge in one day must mean I'm getting positively beatific. I bet that if I keep this up, I'll be so good I can sell my second-hand bathwater as beaujolais nouveau.

He fell asleep; his sleep lapsed into dreaming, and in his dream he was back across the Line and standing in front of the Fairy Godfather's desk with a terrified grin on his face and (since this was a dream) a schoolboy's cap on his head and an exercise book down the back of his trousers.

'So,' said the Godfather, 'you wanna be good?'

'Yes, *padrone*.'

'So you wanna be a hero?'

'Yes, *padrone*.'

'And you wanna nail that sonofabitch Ali Baba so good he'll wish he'll never be born again?'

And then Akram wanted terribly, terribly much to say *No, padrone* and he could feel himself straining the muscles of his brain as he tried to stop the other word, the one beginning with Y, squirming out through the gate of his teeth; but, since it was one of that sort of dream – I *knew* I shouldn't have finished off the two leftover Cheese Double Whammyburgers before we closed up, but isn't it a sin to let good food go to waste? – all he could do was stand back from himself and look the other way, and try not to listen—

'Yes, *padrone.*'

And now the Godfather is laughing; big man, big laugh. 'Your wish is my command,' he says. 'To hear is to obey. Rocco, you heard?'

'Yeah, boss.'

'So obey.'

'Yeah, boss.'

'But that's impossible,' Akram could hear himself protesting. 'If I'm the good guy and the hero, how come I can nail the creep Baba? I thought nailing people, I was through with all that.'

And a close-up of the Godfather's face; cigar clamped in corner of masonry jaw, black eyes burning. 'Hey,' he says softly, 'show some godamn respect. I mean, who's telling this story, you or me?'

Because it's a dream, one of that sort of dreams (all our cheeseburgers are made with a hundred per cent pure natural milk cheese; okay, it's industrial grade cheese, it's rolled out in huge fifty-metre sheets in a processing plant that's a dairy the way Greenwich Village is a village, but eat it late at night and you'll find out if it's real cheese or not) Akram finds he's no longer in the Godfather's study; he's standing behind a huge boulder in a cleft in a cliff-face, and it's dark, and there's a troop of horsemen riding in, he can hear their horses breathing and the soft tinkle of their mailshirts, the clink of their swords in their scabbards. He wants to run but he can't, and the leader of the troop rides up to the rock face, only a yard or so from where he's cowering and he says–

I know that voice!

—'Open sesame!' whereupon a door opens out of what looked for all the world like solid rock, and as it swings open on its hinges it creaks ever so slightly, and the leader of the troop rides past; and over his coat of mail he's wearing a white coat, and there's a scalpel, not a sword, by his side, which is why they call him Ali Baba the Terrible, leader of the Forty Dentists. And he looks up from writing *Open sesame* on his shirt-sleeve and through the space between door and door-frame, Akram can just see inside the cave, and it's stuffed full of gold – gold teeth, gold bridgework, gold dental plates, gold fillings prised out of the heads of screaming, dying men . . .

And of course, it makes sense, in a way; because surely stealing makes you a thief, even if it's thieves you steal from. On the other hand (but, since this is a dream, there's no actual contradiction; dream-logic is as flexible as a lawyer's promise) thieves are outlaws, and anything you do to a thief is perfectly fair; hell, you can *kill* thieves if you want to and still be as good as, well, gold (unfortunate simile, in the circumstances; all those *teeth* –) and so what, you don't get all hung up and conscience-stricken when you pour boiling water on an ants' nest, do you? And most of all, if you will go eating cheese last thing at night, what possible right have you got to complain if you have bad dreams?

Akram woke up.

'Fuck,' he said.

Stories grow, stories spread; and if you smuggle a story across the Line, don't go whining to the doctor when it starts frothing at the mouth and bites you.

'Fang.'

'Snfnottalkingtoyousnf.'

'Fang,' Akram repeated, 'get your coat. We're going out.'

CHAPTER FOURTEEN

J.F. Smith paused, his left foot on the top rung of the ladder, his right knee braced against the windowsill, and listened.

Far away, the railway hummed and growled, providing the nocturne's bass section. A little closer, the constant composite hum of traffic. Apart from that, nothing except the slow, regular pulse of his own heartbeat. Satisfied, J.F. Smith pulled down the sash, stuck his head in through the window and started to wriggle.

Destiny is a high-flown, rather romantic-sounding name for a whole host of factors outside one's own control that shape the course of one's life. Of these, where you happen to be born and who your parents are is perhaps the most important. J.F. Smith, for example, was born to follow one trade and one only. Anything else would have been as unthinkable as a teenage lion dropping in to the careers office asking if they had any openings for apprentice lambs. The fact that he'd actually been baptised John Fingers Smith came as no surprise to anybody who knew the family. They had been craftsmen in the burgling trade in Southampton ever since Henry V had strung up the first John Smith for stealing arrows from the quivers of the archers embarking for the Agincourt campaign.

The really remarkable thing about this great tradition was that, nearly six hundred years later, the Smith family still wasn't all that good at it; as witness the fact that John Fingers II, now in his fifty-second year, had just got out of prison for the seventh time, coincidentally on precisely the same day as Jason Fingers (19) and Damian (18) had started their first adult sentences in the same nick. The Governor, a man with a keen sense of tradition, had been keeping their great-grandfather's old cell ready and waiting for them ever since they were released from youth custody. It had their name on the door and everything.

As for this house; well, John Fingers could remember his father knocking it off in 1956 – he'd held the ladder for him, and it had been his momentary lapse of attention that had led to John Fingers I spending 1956–1960 in dear old B583. To judge by the paintwork, it was probably the very same sash as he was lifting now that had fallen on John Fingers I and held him pinned by the neck until the police arrived.

Having spent a few moments in silent contemplation, John Fingers II slithered through, landed in a heap and switched on his torch. In Dad's time, of course, this had still been a big private house, rather than a slightly down-market conversion into three flats. It was asking a bit much to expect to find any decent gear in a place like this; video, CD player, microwave, answering machine (except that they were now so cheap as to be scarcely worth the stealing) and maybe a few quid in loose cash if you were very lucky. You could forget silver, jewellery or works of art. Today's burglar, sad to say, is little more than a glorified furniture remover cum electrician.

Still, he told himself as he swung the torch round in a slow, careful arc, you never know. More for form's sake than anything else, he started pulling out the drawers and examining them for ring-boxes and jewellery cases.

(*'Well, don't just sit there, you moth-eaten excuse for a burglar alarm. Ring, damn you.'*

'I can't. I've got a loose wire.'

'Don't be ridiculous.'

'But I have, really. I've been waiting for her to notice it for weeks.'

'Oh. Of all the . . . Cordless screwdriver! Get your useless arse over here at the double!')

Hello, John Fingers II demanded of himself, what's this? He flipped open the lid of the little blue box, and sighed. Just a poxy little plain silver ring with a chip of glass stuck in it; you could buy half a dozen of these off a market stall, brand new and totally legit, for a tenner. Assuming you wanted one, let alone ten. On the other hand—

How *would* it look on the other hand?

With a shrug he lifted the ring out of the box and checked it for hallmarks. None. It wouldn't fit, of course; he could tell that without trying. It was a piece of cheap tat for the teenage market, probably less than five parts silver in any case. If I tried it on, it'd only get stuck.

No it wouldn't.

Yes it would.

'Armed police hold it right there move so much as the smallest hair on your bum and we'll blow you away!'

So it's true, a part of John Fingers II's brain noted with interest, extreme terror really does have an effect on the bowels and turn the knees to water. Why the hell is that? Bloody useless survival mechanism; not the evolutionary trait most likely to ensure the success of the species. He shuddered from head to toe, realising as he did so that he was breaking the embargo on movement. This only made matters worse.

'Move one millimetre and you'll go home in a plastic bag we have the building surrounded Nobby where's that SWAT team this

is a recorded— Oops, force of habit, damn.'

With infinite daring, John Fingers II frowned. Something funny here. For one thing, the voice seemed to be coming from inside his head.

Where were the searchlights?

Where, come to that, were the police?

'Hey,' he said aloud, 'what's going on here?'

'*Shuttup you another peep out of you and you're a dead man Nobby I want those snipers in here now.*'

There was something about the voice, definitely coming from inside him somewhere, that entirely failed to convince. There were no police. It was some kind of daft booby-trap.

The hell with it. Anybody who would have you believe that running away is a dying art should watch a member of the Smith family getting the hell out of residential property where they have no right to be. From unfreezing to shinning down the ladder and sprinting off down the back alley, the whole process took John Fingers II less than three minutes. If only Stanley Fingers III had been alive to see it, he'd have been proud.

The getaway car was parked just round the corner. He dived in, slammed the door and turned the key. Wouldn't start.

'No petrol.'

Who said that?

'I mean, what kind of pillock steals his getaway car from a garage forecourt? Next time, at the very least, look at the damn fuel indicator.'

Out of the car, slam the door, run for it. As he ran, he seemed to be able to hear his watch advising him to slow down, since a man of his age and weight was risking a coronary sprinting round the place like a twelve year old, it could feel his pulse against its strap and he was definitely overdoing it. Look, there's a bus, why don't you hop on that?

491

It was good advice, but John Fingers II chose to ignore it. Instead, he flopped down in a heap in a shop doorway, hyperventilating like an asthmatic extractor fan. A moment or so later, he looked up. There was a policeman standing over him. Oh . . .

'Here,' said the policeman, staring. 'You all right?'

'Urg,' replied John Fingers II.

'You gone a funny colour,' the policeman said. 'I'm going to call an ambulance.'

'No!' He managed to get hold of a lungful of air from somewhere. 'Don't do that. I was just going, anyhow.'

'Huh? Oh well, please yourself. Move along there. You got a home to go to?'

John Fingers II nodded. Some stray pellet of common sense lodged in his brain and told him to pretend to be drunk. 'Jus' going, offisher. Been out for a li'l drink. G'night.'

The policeman frowned and watched him stand up, stagger a little (not method acting; knees still water) and set off on an unsteady course down the street.

'Jesus!' muttered the watch. 'Close call or what? It was touch and go back there.'

Without a second thought, John Fingers II unstrapped his watch, dropped it on the ground and stepped on it. He imagined that as the glass went crunch under his heel, he heard a tiny thin scream.

'What d'you do that for, you bastard?' said a voice in his head.

John Fingers II stopped dead in his tracks. He had a heart-sinking feeling that the parking meter to his immediate left had just spoken to him; it was either that or the voice of conscience, and there were lots of reasons why it wasn't the latter. He swallowed hard and turned ninety degrees.

'You talking to me?' he asked the parking meter.

'Why don't you pick on someone your own size, you big

bully?' replied the parking meter. 'Never done you any harm, that watch, and you just stove its bleedin' head in. How'd you like it if some great big bastard came and stood on your head just 'cos you were trying to be friendly?'

In the circumstances, John Fingers II decided that a non-verbal response would be appropriate. Accordingly he unshipped his jemmy from the purpose-sewn inside pocket of his coat and dealt the parking meter three extremely sharp blows. Problem solved, apparently; no more voices inside his head. When he was satisfied that normality had been restored, he replaced the jemmy and walked on.

'You'll pay for that,' muttered a traffic light.

'We know where you live,' added the Belisha beacon.

'We know where your children go to school,' added a phone box. 'Or at least,' it added, 'we know where they used to go to school, before they burnt it down . . .'

'Burnt it *down*?'

'Well,' admitted the phone box, 'nothing was ever proved, but they've got a pretty good idea it was the Smith boys.'

'Hell's bells,' the Belisha beacon muttered. 'Whole family's a gang of hooligans, then.'

'Scum of the earth,' muttered a parked car. 'Ought to be run out of town, the lot of 'em.'

'*Hey!*' John Fingers II protested. There was a cold silence.

'Well?' said the clock over Gale & Sons, Jewellers (Estd. 1908. Robbed by the Smith family 1909, 1912, 1919, 1927, 1932 (twice), 1936, 1939, 1948, 1961, 1974 and 1977).

'What's going on? I mean, is this for real, or what?' John Fingers II wiped sweat off his forehead with the back of his hand. 'Are you things really – talking?'

'What if we are? You never heard a speaking clock before?'

'Yes, but . . .'

'Which reminds me. In 1948 your father nicked my ornamental bracket. I want it back.'

493

'Yes,' John Fingers II repeated, 'but how?'

Silence. 'You mean you don't know?' said the traffic light, incredulously.

'He doesn't know,' said the car.

'What a pillock!'

'They're all pillocks in that family,' commented the clock. 'When his great-grandad robbed this shop in 1912 . . .'

'Stan Smith who used to live in Inkerman Street?' queried the phone box. 'Thick as potato soup, that bugger was. I remember one time . . .'

'Shut *up*!' John Fingers II shrieked, and his voice rattled conspicuously in the empty street. 'That's better,' he added. 'You, the red square bugger. How come I can understand what you're saying?'

The things sniggered. It was only when John Fingers II got his jemmy out again and started patting it against the palm of his left hand that the phone box answered him.

'The ring, stupid,' it said. 'Silver ring, bit of glass stuck in it, you're wearing it right now.'

'Fine.' John Fingers II jerked open the phone box door, stepped inside and put both hands tightly round the cable connecting the cradle to the receiver. 'Now then, tell me all about it.'

Had John Fingers II been standing just inside the door of Ali Baba's surgery, instead of inside a phone box half a mile away, he'd have heard the singularly unpleasant and distressing shriek of a lock being picked. It was probably just as well that he wasn't, or he'd have been unable to sleep for a month.

Locks, when you think about it, have either a very nasty or a very nice life, depending on their mechanical orientation. Either they hunch rigidly in the doorframe with their wards gritted and think of England, or they go with the flow and relish every moment of it. Even the kinkiest lock, however – a triple-deadlocked Chubb, for example, or the Marquis de Ingersoll – could never pretend to enjoy being picked, even by a master cracksman with the most finely honed Swiss-made picklocks. All that Akram the Terrible knew about the art was what he'd learned from a quarter of an hour with a book from the mobile library. He could count himself lucky he wasn't wearing the ring, either.

'Right,' said Akram, 'we're in. Where did you say this safe is?'

'This way.' Fang fluttered through the dark air like a very cheap, damp firework. She couldn't exactly hear locks, but on some plane or other she was sensitive to the vibes in a way that no human could ever be; in the same way, perhaps, that horses are supposed to refuse to pass the place where a murder has happened. She had put it on record that she'd wanted to come in through the window.

'Just a minute,' Akram said, shortly afterwards. 'I may be being a bit thick here. I *hope* I'm being a bit thick, because if I find out you've brought me out here in the middle of the night to steal dental floss and denture moulding compound, I'm going to pull your wings off with a pair of rusty pliers.'

'Under the floorboards,' Fang snarled. 'It's his safe.'

Muttering something about a ruddy funny place to hide supposedly cosmos-overturning artefacts, Akram got down on his hands and knees, inserted his jemmy and pulled. Because Akram was tall, barrel-chested and very, very strong, the jemmy snapped.

'Ah,' he said. 'Right, I take your point. These floorboards aren't just to keep you from putting your foot through downstairs' ceiling, are they?'

Fang shook her head. 'If you'd been listening,' she said, 'you'd have realised that. Serves you right if you've pulled a muscle.'

'It's some sort of hex, isn't it? Magic, all that crap.'

'That's right.'

'And you know the key, don't you?'

'Yes.'

'And you're going to tell me what it is?'

'Possibly.'

'But first,' Akram sighed, 'you're going to rub my nose in it because I was rude and snotty and didn't listen when you told me all about it.'

'Of course not.' Fang scowled. 'That'd be childish. All you've got to say is the magic word.'

'If I knew the magic bloody word, I wouldn't be crawling to you, you overgrown gnat.'

'Not that magic word. *The* magic word.'

'Oh for crying out—' Akram paused. 'Please?'

'That's better. Actually,' she added, 'it's not that difficult to guess. In context, that is.'

A look of pain flitted across Akram's face. 'Oh come *on*,' he said. 'You're not trying to tell me—?'

Fang nodded.

'Really?'

'Really.'

'Dear God.' Akram rocked back on his heels and took a deep breath. 'Open seasame,' he said.

The floorboard slowly rose. Underneath it was a plain cardboard box, wrapped in brown paper and lashed up with Sellotape where it had recently been opened. Akram, however, could feel the intensity of the thing. It was as if a Mancunian who'd spent the last fifty years as a restaurant critic in Languedoc had wandered into a little café and unexpectedly found steak and kidney pudding, chips and peas on the menu. It was the kind of homesickness that makes you realise just how sickening home really is.

'Marvellous,' Akram muttered, making no move to touch the box. 'Now what the hell am I supposed to do?'

496

'Steal it.'

Akram nodded slowly. 'I have this depressing feeling you're right,' he replied.

'Why depressing?' the tooth fairy demanded. 'For pity's sake, if that's what I think it is, it's the single most valuable object in this whole solar system. God only knows what the Americans'd give you for it. Kansas, probably.'

'I know exactly what it is,' Akram replied. 'Look, let me try to explain. Does the expression *fairy-tale ending* mean anything to you?'

Fang nodded. 'Extreme good fortune, followed by a happy ending, happily ever after, C-in-a circle The Walt Disney Company, followed by a date.'

'Exactly.' Akram nodded emphatically. 'Things like this just don't happen in real life, agreed?'

'Well,' replied Fang uncertainly. 'Not often, anyway.'

'About as often as fourteen pigs playing aerial polo. In fairy-tales, however, it's the norm, right? Happens all the time.'

'So they tell me,' the tooth fairy said. 'Not that I'd know, having been stuck this side of the Line all my life. What of it?'

Akram sighed. 'All right,' he said. 'Now, just suppose you were flying down the street and you came across a huge luminous plastic spaceship with little green men running up and down the gangplank and *Alpha Centauri Spacecraft Corporation; Product of More Than One Constellation* stencilled on the side. Maybe you'd think, *Hey, what's this doing here?* And maybe you'd guess that the aliens had landed. Yes?'

'Conceivably,' Fang conceded. 'So?'

Akram pointed to the parcel. 'This thing's from the other side of the Line,' he said. 'So's the happy ending that comes with it. I've just *escaped* from there. When you've just broken out of Colditz and you're buying a train ticket to Geneva, you don't ask for a return. As far as I'm concerned, this has all been too easy. That thing's an obvious plant.'

497

'No it isn't,' Fang objected. 'If it was, it'd have leaves and a stalk and . . .'

'Be quiet. If I open that,' Akram continued, as much to himself as to Fang, 'it'll mean I'm back in the story. Every day for the rest of my life'll have a page number in the top left-hand corner.'

Fang bit her lip. Maybe the glamour of the parcel was starting to affect her, or maybe she was just curious. 'Open it,' she said. 'Go on. Just having a look won't commit you to anything.'

'Balls.'

'You know you want to really.'

'Go away.'

'Just a little peep,' whispered Fang, 'can't do any harm.'

'Drop dead,' Akram replied, opening his penknife and cutting the Sellotape. 'Opening this would be an awfully big mistake, you mark my words.'

Fang frowned. 'Don't you mean adventure?' she queried.

'As far as I'm concerned, it's the same thing.' He slit the last loop of tape, folded back the cardboard, reached in and lifted out a plain earthenware jar.

'I see,' said Fang after a moment's silence. 'A *potted* plant.'

Akram didn't reply. He was staring at the lid of the jar. I could open it, he told himself. And then, either whatever's in there will come out, or I'll go in, and in the long run it'll amount to the same thing. He screwed his eyes tight shut and said aloud, 'I wish this thing would go away.' When he opened them again, it was still there. Which meant that he didn't have any of the Godfather's three wishes left. Which meant he'd used them. Something, he told himself, like using the atomic bomb; at first it seems to solve all sorts of problems, and then, some time later, you begin to think that on balance it'd have been rather better if maybe you hadn't.

'Are you all right?' Fang asked uncomfortably. 'You don't

look very well. You've gone a very funny colour.'

'I'm not in the least surprised.'

'Sort of black and white.'

Akram laughed wretchedly. 'What the hell do you expect?' he said. 'My life has just changed. It's now got credits at the beginning and the end. Just when I thought—'

The jar twitched slightly in his hands, as if it was getting impatient. The sensation of movement against his skin made Akram shudder, and he seemed to reach a decision. Very swiftly, almost aggressively, like a man putting out a fire, he tried to stuff the jar back in its box. But the box was now too small.

'Think about it,' said Fang's voice, greatly to Fang's astonishment. 'The thing is here already. Right now, Ali Baba's got it. He knows you're this side of the Line. He knows you've sworn to kill him.'

'I gave him my word . . .'

'He knows,' the voice went on, 'that you've crossed the Line. When you cross the Line, you come out of character. If you're out of character, your word's about as valid as a Confederate banknote. He knows this.'

'But I've changed,' Akram protested. 'I'm good now.'

'This week,' the voice replied. 'Maybe even next week, too. Maybe the next fifty years; but there's no guarantee. He knows that, too. On this side of the Line, you have no character.'

'But I don't *want* . . .'

'He knows,' intoned the voice, 'exactly what he did to you, what he tried to do to you. He knows – *hey can I have my voice back, whoever the hell you are, nobody said you could use my* – bugger off, small fry. He knows exactly what he'd do if he was you. In fact, he will be you. And you will be him. You know that.'

'That's you talking, isn't it? You in the jar. Say "bottle of beer", go on, say it.'

499

'Open the jar, Akram.'

Akram stared at the jar. He could see the faint marks of the potter's wheel; he even fancied he could smell the distinctive smell of the palm-oil it had once contained. He knew precisely what was in the jar. He would not open the jar. When is a jar not a jar?

'When it's a door. Open the jar.'

'I refuse.'

'You can't. Remember?'

'I could take you back where you came from. Maybe there's money back on you.'

'Non-returnable. No deposit. Open the frigging jar, Akram, or it'll be the worse for you.'

'No,' said Akram, putting his hand on the lid. 'You will stay where you've been put. You can't come in here.'

Like a small guided missile Fang shot across the room. In her defence, it should be pointed out that she flew backwards, her legs and arms thrashing wildly; in any event, she smashed into Akram's hand, knocking the lid of the jar halfway across the room. Akram flailed wildly, trying to catch it; then he hurled himself over the mouth of the jar, but too late. A column of what could have been bees, or flies, or lumpy black smoke, curled upwards out of the jar, turning and twisting and buzzing, fending Akram off as if he was made of feathers. He swung at it wildly with a chair; the chair passed through the column and out the other side, and *then* smashed into matchwood.

'Bastard!' Fang yelled. 'Look, it wasn't me, I had nothing to do with—'

The smoke, flies, bees solidified, until they were a solid thing. The jar swelled up, until it was the size of a crouching man, maybe a little larger. The column stopped moving. It was a human shape. It stood opposite Akram, no more than six inches away from him. Akram stared at it; it was just like

500

looking in a mirror; or suppose you're standing between a whitewashed wall and a very bright light, and you look at your shadow.

'Go back,' he said, but his voice was thin and watery. 'Go back home.'

The thing, his other self, smiled. It was an exact likeness, except somehow dark, shadowy. Do you remember how Peter Pan came across the Line to retrieve his shadow, and all the trouble that caused?

The shadow reached out its hands and feet, and touched Akram, and joined him.

'I *am* home,' he said.

CHAPTER FIFTEEN

'I'm starving,' Akram said. 'Let's eat. I fancy Lebanese.'

'It's half past three in the morning,' Akram replied. 'In Southampton. If we're lucky, we might just find an unopened dustbin bag.'

Akram laughed. 'You always were a pessimistic bugger,' he said. 'Now, if my instincts are still working –' He stopped still, drawing his other half up sharply. 'This way,' he said, and darted off down the street, dragging Akram behind him like a large dog walking a small human.

Just around the corner there was a blaze of light and colour. Exotic music, strings and bells and cymbals, floated across on the languid night breeze. Over the door was a sign saying TRIPOLI RESTAURANT.

'Damn,' said Akram. 'Wouldn't you just know it. I seem to have come out without any money. I wonder, would you mind. . . ?'

Fang, snuggled inside Akram's jacket, peered out. She liked late-night catering establishments, bars, night clubs; because where you have drunken night owls, you have fights, and where you have fights, you run a good chance of picking up the odd dislodged tooth.

'You two,' she observed, 'remind me of something.'

'Really?'

Fang nodded. 'I got it,' she said. 'It's like when you've got a prisoner and a guard handcuffed together; you know, with the raincoat to cover the chains? Only,' she added, 'I'm not sure which of you's which.'

'He is.'

A waiter drifted forward and smiled.

'Hello,' Akram said. 'Table for three, please.'

The waiter nodded. 'If you'd like to come this way . . .'

'Or rather,' Akram amended, 'two. Actually, make that one.'

'As you like, sir. Please to follow me. Anything to drink before you order?'

'No, I mean yes.' Akram stood still for a moment, his eyes closed. 'That's, um, one tomato juice, one triple absinthe, no ice, and do you have any camel's milk?'

If the waiter was taken aback at all, he didn't show it. 'All in the same glass, sir? Or one after the other? Or. . . ?'

'Simultaneously, of course. Sorry, I mean, could I have those, er, simultaneously. Thank you.'

The waiter turned to walk back to the kitchen, hesitated and glanced surreptitiously back. An ordinary-looking sort of man, quite large, could easily be from the Old Country except that he sounded English. He was sitting at one of the side tables, and the candle-light seemed to be throwing a larger than usual shadow against the far wall. Occasionally his hand crept to his chest; indigestion? angina? None of the waiter's business. Neither was he interested in the fact that the man seemed to be holding an animated conversation with himself. When you're in the late-night catering business, the ones you watch are the ones who don't talk to themselves.

'This,' said Akram to his shadow, 'isn't going to work. I mean, listen to us, we can't agree on anything.'

'What, you mean like we're married or something? No, I take that back, we are at least talking to each other. By the way, you haven't introduced me. Who's the houri?'

'Tooth fairy,' Akram corrected. 'Shadow, Fang; Fang, Shadow. Better now?'

'Excuse me,' said Fang, 'but can I just get this straight? You're Akram and he's your shadow?'

'And vice versa. On the other side, it's the other way round. I think. Actually that's a gross simplification, but let's leave it at that for now.'

'So really,' Fang ground on, wishing she'd never raised the subject, 'you're both Akram. Is that right?'

'In a manner of speaking,' replied the image on the wall. 'To take the marriage simile one stage further; a happily married couple is two minds with but a single thought. We're one mind with two entirely different thoughts. Usually, at least.'

'Ah.' The tooth fairy nodded. 'Like a dual personality, sort of thing.'

The shadow shook its head. A split microsecond later, Akram's head moved too, with the result that a quarter of his camel's milk went down the front of his shirt. 'Schizophrenia, you mean? Not really. Schizophrenia is where the left hand knows perfectly well what the right hand is doing, and bitterly resents it. I prefer to think of us as two sides of the same coin. The yin and the yang. The positive and the negative charged particles, both circling the same neutron.'

'Except,' Akram interrupted sullenly, 'somehow he never has any money on him. And when he gets drunk at parties and starts making lewd suggestions to married women, I'm the one who gets thumped.'

'You exaggerate.'

'And,' Akram went on, 'the curious thing is, the one time in a hundred when the lewd suggestion leads to a result, it's always my turn to be the blasted shadow.'

'Ah.'

'And of course,' Akram continued, 'you don't get a shadow when the light's turned off. Marvellous.'

It's always embarrassing for third parties when couples argue in public, and Fang wished she could change the subject. 'I—' she said.

'I suppose it's the same for everyone,' Akram was saying, 'with the extremely important difference that they don't realise it. But I do. Ever since I was in that bloody jar, the time I found out I was in a story. I found out all sorts of things then that nobody else realises. Big mistake, that.'

'I agree,' said the shadow, nodding –

('For God's sake mind what you're doing!'

'Huh? Oh, sorry.')

'Glad you agree on something,' Fang replied. She noticed that whereas the shadow had finished its drink, Akram still had half of his left. He was wearing the other half. 'But I still don't see how you two came to, er, get together. I thought there was something quite other in that jar.'

'Such as what?'

'Well,' Fang replied defensively, 'the secret of absolute power. The, er, ultimate weapon. That's what Ali Baba seemed to think it was, anyway.'

'He was right,' the shadow replied smugly. 'You're looking at it.'

'You?'

'That's right. Well,' the shadow corrected, 'us. Together, we make the perfect combination. His skills of stealth, mayhem and cunning; my total lack of moral restraint. Who could ask for more?'

'What you find in the box,' Akram explained, 'depends on

who you are. If Ali Baba had opened it, he'd probably have found a fleet of nuclear submarines or a death ray or something. Me,' he added bitterly, 'I have to find him.'

The shadow bridled; a difficult thing to do in only two dimensions. 'The difference between me and a fleet of nuclear submarines,' he said with dignity, 'is that I cost less to run and I'm a damn sight easier to park. True, I can't stay underwater for up to five years at a time, but so what, nobody's perfect.'

'You can say that again.'

'I shall pretend I didn't hear that. Now then, I fancy the humus to start with, followed by the lamb with couscous and a bottle of the Riesling. It's all right about the alcohol,' he added. 'I don't have to drive home.'

Akram sighed. 'All right,' he said, 'I give in. Let's just get it over and done with as quickly as possible. I suppose I've got to kidnap the girl.'

'That's right. Splendid piece of detective work there, by the way. I'm glad to see you haven't forgotten everything I taught you.'

'Actually,' Akram pointed out, 'it was sheer luck. Anyway, we kidnap the girl—'

'Nice piece,' commented the shadow, 'if you like them long and bony. I'm told that sort keeps better, but I always trade mine in fairly quickly, so I can't actually vouch for it myself.'

'And then,' Akram continued with distaste, 'we let her go in return for Ali Baba releasing me from my oath. And then,' he added, 'I kill him.'

'Exactly. Won't that be fun?'

Akram shut his eyes. 'Won't it just,' he said.

The phone rang.

'Whoozit?' Ali Baba croaked into the receiver. The digital clock beside his bed seemed to leer mockingly at him, and its eyes read 04:59.

'Hister Harbour? Hit's Hisses Utchinson ere, he hum's harted hleeding hagain hand hoo haid hone hoo hif hat appened.'

'Could you just hold the line a moment, please?' Ali Baba put down the receiver and rubbed his eyes with the heels of his hands while the basic background information files of his brain gradually drifted back on line. Mrs Hutchinson. She's a patient, extraction, left upper molar, and yes, in a moment of surpassing folly I did say call me if there's any problems and gave her my home number. That reminds me, who am I and where the hell is this? Ah yes, now I remember.

'I'm very sorry to hear that, Mrs Hutchinson,' he replied, and the facility with which he did so without so much as batting an eye, crossing a finger or growing an extra six inches of nose goes to show that dentistry's dubious gain was the legal profession's palpable loss. 'First thing in the morning, or rather first thing later on this morning, if you could possibly drop by the surgery ...'

'Hut hoo hed, hif hit harts hleeding, hoo'd hum *himmediately.* Hoo hed ...'

I did, didn't I? I should be hanged, with my own tongue for a noose. 'Of course, I'll be right with you. Now, in the meantime, if you'll just mix up some ordinary table salt with some water ...'

Twenty minutes later, the phone rang again. Ali Baba was, of course, on his way to Mrs Hutchinson's; which is why Akram, taking a deep breath before stating his demands for Michelle's return, got the recorded message instead. He wilted slightly; even desperate extroverts feel just a bit self-conscious talking to answering machines. After a moment of being disconcerted, Akram cleared his throat.

The message went as follows:

'Hello, this is, um, me here, I'd just like to leave a

message. Er, ready? Well, here goes. Look, you pig-fucker, you ever want to see your daughter alive again, be at the entrance to— oh bugger, I can't read my own writing. No, not them, my reading glasses, the ones on the – thanks, now then, where were we? Entrance to Tesco's car park in Cinnamon Street, that's the Bishop Road entrance as you come in from the bypass, not the .. Sorry, just a tick. Yes? Oh. Oh, right. Sorry, that's not Tesco's, it's Safeways, at one thirty tomorrow, morning, and you'd better come alone or else, Okay? Right, er, well, oh God I hate talking into these things. Um. Bye.'

The second message was:

'Hello? Oh blast. Hello, it's me again. Did I say not to tell the Police or it'll be the worse for the girl? Well, um, that's it for now. Ciao.'

The third message was:

'Hello? Shit, where the hell can he have got to this time of night? Yes, it's me. Look, it's not Safeways, I looked it up and actually it's ASDA. Okay, it's the big supermarket on the corner of Cinnamon Street and Landau Way. Turn right at John Lewis and you can't miss it. Or else. Goodbye.'

Having played back the tape a couple of times and tried Michelle's number (answering machine) Ali Baba collected the sword and the gun, drove to his surgery and went to the store cupboard. Inside he found two hundred pairs of disposable rubber gloves, three large boxes of disposable forceps, five thousand doses of local anaesthetic, twenty tubs of impression material, a catering-size drum of instant coffee granules, an empty floor safe and an old-fashioned silver sixpence. He slumped, as if his backbone had just been repossessed by the finance company.

Wait a minute. The sixpence . . .

It goes without saying that all dentists' surgeries, sooner or later, get infested with tooth fairies. Dentists who find silver sixpences scattered about their premises therefore know the score and although the old-style djinn traps are now illegal (the details are a bit too grisly for print; suffice it to say that a fairy triggering one while foraging for teeth wouldn't have very long to reflect on the wisdom of being careful what you wish for) but pixie dust, Larsen traps and large, bad-tempered cats generally solve the problem sooner or later. Dentists, in short, know about tooth fairies, in the same way that farmers have a certain familiarity with the habits of rabbits, rooks and pigeons. They know, for instance, that in spite of the name, they don't just help themselves to teeth, in the same way that cat burglars will also take the occasional dog or pedigree hamster. A sixpence in the tea kitty or the bottom of the petty cash tin speaks for itself. On the other hand, very few tooth fairies go out tooled up with the hardware necessary to prise open safes. Let alone magical safes.

The logical conclusion therefore was that Akram had teamed up with a tooth fairy. Having run it past his mental panel of scrutineers, Ali Baba filed the fact in the back of his mind, and sat down in his own chair, wondering what to do next. The next thing he knew was the phone ringing; he looked up at the clock on the wall and saw that it was 7.45 am, start of a brand new working day.

It'd be wrong to call Ali Baba callous or uncaring; on the contrary, he had twenty-odd people coming to see him to be cured of excruciating pain, and he cared about each and everyone of them. He also cared about his daughter, very deeply indeed; but her appointment, so to speak, wasn't for another eighteen hours. He hoped she'd be all right, washed up, shaved as best he could with a disposable scalpel and his tiny mirror-on-a-stick, and buzzed for the first patient.

'First,' Akram said, lighting the paraffin lamp, 'I don't want you to be frightened.'

Michelle glowered at him. 'Really?' she said. 'Then I'd suggest you cancel the rest of the lessons and ask for your money back, because when it comes to not frightening people, you haven't got a clue.'

The corner of Akram's mouth twitched a little. 'You don't *seem* very frightened,' he said. 'Quite the opposite.'

'I'm absolutely bloody livid, if that's what you mean,' Michelle growled, tugging vainly at the ropes round her wrists. 'Doesn't mean I'm not frightened. You're the man in the burger joint, aren't you?'

Akram nodded. 'That's what I do for a living,' he said, with more than a hint of pride. 'They've recently made me the assistant manager.'

'I see,' Michelle replied. 'So creeping up on people and abducting them at knifepoint's just a hobby, is it? Other people seem to manage with bird-watching or flower-arranging.'

Akram looked hurt. 'Don't be like that,' he said. 'I tried to be as nice about it as I could.'

'Sure. *Could you possibly spare me a moment or I'll slit your throat.* I should have guessed then you weren't a real kidnapper.'

As she said the words, Michelle couldn't help feeling that situated as she was, bound hand and foot in a lock-up workshop somewhere with a knife-wielding six-foot-five stranger, her tone might usefully be a little bit less abrasive. There was something about the man, though, that entirely failed to terrify her. It wasn't that she didn't believe he would cut her throat, if whatever his strange motivation was

510

demanded it. It was just that he'd probably try and be as considerate and unthreatening about it as he could manage, and even at the moment of severing her jugular vein he'd be at pains to make it clear that he still respected her as a person. She knew all about the New Man; well, this was the New Villain. It intrigued her.

'You know perfectly well who I am,' Akram replied quietly. 'And I reckon you know why I'm doing this. I'm trying to keep everything nice and civilised, but really, you aren't making it any easier.'

'So sorry,' Michelle snapped. 'So what do you want to do, mix up some mulled wine and play Trivial Pursuit?'

'Play what?'

'Trivial Pursuit. It's a sort of game where you ask silly questions and move counters on a board.'

'Really?' Akram raised an eyebrow. 'Since my time, that. I've got chess and backgammon, if you're interested.'

'Get real, will you? I wouldn't play chess with you if you were the last man alive.'

'Quite,' Akram replied. 'If I was the last man alive, I'm sure we'd be far too busy foraging for food and hiding from packs of killer dogs and things. All right, then, what about canasta? Or mah jong?'

Michelle stared at him keenly. 'Are you trying to tell me,' she said, 'that you actually have a mah jong set in a *hideout*?'

'Why not?' Akram replied with a shrug. 'Look, I was kidnapping people when you were still ... Sorry, different timescale, but anyhow, you get the point. And the first thing you learn about the kidnapping business is, it can get very, very boring. So naturally I laid in a few games. I mean, I Spy's all right, but ...'

'Bet you haven't got Diplomacy.'

Akram shook his head. 'Not really suitable,' he said. 'I mean, the average kidnap ordeal lasts about one to three

511

weeks, which means the game'd just be getting interesting when it was time to go home. Actually, I remember the time I snatched the Grand Vizier's nephew and we started playing Racing Genie. Ten days that game lasted. The Grand Vizier paid up on day four, but we couldn't persuade the little brute to go home until he'd won. And you try deliberately losing Racing Genie without being embarrassingly obvious about it . . .'

'Racing Genie?'

Akram shook his head vigorously. 'No way,' he said. 'It's totally addictive, Racing Genie. You just get completely carried away.'

'Sounds interesting.'

'We haven't got time. I'm due to hand you over at half-one tomorrow morning.'

'Oh go on. At least show me the rules.'

'Well . . .'

'Please?'

Akram hesitated. As he did so it occurred to him to turn the lamp up a bit, but he decided against it. The dimmer the light, the fainter his shadow, and he felt more comfortable that way.

'Oh all right,' he said. 'But only for half an hour.'

'. . . And sixteen for a Wish, that makes ninety-four, doubled because you're on a Magic Carpet square in clubs repiqued, add two for his fez makes a hundred and ninety, which means I get four lamp points and you get another wish.'

'Yah!'

'Beginner's luck. Right, your go – Oh my God, will you look at the time?'

They looked up. The battered alarm clock sitting on an upended packing case read 12:57.

'Marvellous!' Akram sighed. 'We're going to be late for the bloody handover. Come on, get your coat.'

512

Michelle shook her head. 'We've got plenty of time,' she said. 'This time of night there'll be no traffic about, so if we cut down through Marchmain Street and under the underpass we can be there in fifteen minutes.'

'You reckon?'

'Easily,' Michelle replied, shaking the dice. 'Right, let's see. Hey, double four, that means I can have another mosque on Trebizond. Now then . . .'

Ali Baba waited until quarter to three; then it started to rain and he decided to go home. It wasn't that he was callous or uncaring; but he hadn't got much sleep the night before, either, and he had a very difficult root-fill job to do on Mrs Willoughby's lower back left molar in the morning. Having checked for the fifteenth time that he was in the right car park, he got in and drove home.

At half-past ten the phone rang.

'Sorry about that,' said Akram. 'We, er, lost track of time, and . . .'

'*We*?'

'We were playing Racing Genie,' Akram explained. 'In fact we still are, and – hey! I saw that, put it back – look, would it put you out dreadfuly if we postponed the handover till, say, Wednesday? Only I've got three back doubles in a row here, so if I can just get the full set of Utilities . . .'

'I quite understand,' replied Ali Baba icily. 'I mean, I'd hate to interrupt your game just to ransom my only daughter.'

'I – would you like a word with her? She's just here. It's your father.'

'Hello?'

'Michelle?' Ali Baba demanded. 'Is that you? Look, are you all right, because . . .'

'Fine, fine,' Michelle's voice replied. 'Listen, do you know this game? I mean, did they play it back in the Old Country,

513

or whatever you call it, because I've got major triples in all three Houses but no gryphon, and I was wondering if you could suggest . . .'

'You repique, naturally,' Ali Baba replied, 'which means Green has to go dummy and you can finesse on the last three tricks, leaving you just needing a double four for Home.' He paused, mentally playing back what he'd just said. 'So you're all right, then?'

'I am now,' Michelle replied. 'I was thinking about leading a blind shimmy to make four, but that's far better. It's a good game, this, isn't it?'

'I like it,' Ali Baba replied. 'Used to play quite a lot when I was your . . . well, once upon a time. In fact,' he couldn't resist adding, 'one year I made it to the finals of the Baghdad Open.'

'Really? Gosh!' Michelle said; and just for a moment, she sounded quite like a real daughter. 'And did you win?'

'Of course,' Ali Baba lied. 'All right, then, see you Wednesday.'

''Bye, then.'

''Bye.'

CHAPTER SIXTEEN

Midnight.

Actually, midnight isn't a particularly good time of day to go burgling. There are too many people still awake; three in the morning is far better, if slightly less dramatic. Of course, perhaps the best time of all to burgle a bank, office or other commercial premises is half past four on a Friday afternoon. Wander in with a clipboard and a trolley, ask the most junior-looking member of staff to sign in three places, and you can probably get help loading the stuff into the van.

Midnight is, however, more traditional, and tradition, as noted above, is ingrained into the genetic matrix of the Smith family. Somewhere at home, at the bottom of a wardrobe, John Fingers II still had a striped jersey, a black mask and a sack with SWAG embroidered on it in sampler-stitch.

It was tradition, in fact, that gave him pause for thought as he stood under the staff room window of the National Lombard Bank in Cinnamon Street, his right hand tightly clenched into a fist. He was about to try out a radically new and different technique, and the very novelty of it all was making his scalp itch. After all, screamed his genes, shinning up a drainpipe and busting a window was good enough for your father and his father before him, so it ought to be good enough for you. True, getting caught red-handed and spending most of their lives in the nick was good enough for them, too; but isn't that all part of the great rich tapestry of this thieving life?

No, muttered John Fingers II to himself, and added something about buggering it for a game of soldiers that would have made his great-great-grandfather turn in his grave, had he not died at a time when the bodies of criminals were used for medical research. (For the record, at that precise moment, on a back shelf in a dusty old cupboard somewhere in the University of Durham, a very old bottle of formaldehyde went *plop!*) If they'd had that attitude back in the Stone Age the wheel would never have been invented, and young Darren Fingers Smith would now be out trying to hotwire a motorised sled.

Here goes.

Directly above his head was a square box marked NEVA-SLEEP ALARM COMPANY. John Fingers II took a deep breath, slipped the ring on his finger and cleared his throat.

'Excuse me,' he whispered.

'Huh? Whoozat?'

'Excuse me,' said John Fingers, 'but would you mind switching yourself off?'

'You what?' grunted the alarm, sleepily.

'Switch yourself off,' John Fingers repeated. 'You see, I want to climb in through that window, and I don't want to set you off.'

'Get real,' replied the alarm. 'You think I was manufactured yesterday, or something? Bugger off before I ring the cops.'

John Fingers shook his head. 'I'm trying to be reasonable here,' he hissed back. 'Like, if you won't switch yourself off, it means I've got to climb up there and snip all your wires, which'll piss me off and hurt you, probably. And while I'm at it,' he added maliciously. 'I might just prise your box off and gum your works up good and proper. It'll take 'em weeks to get you straight again, and in the meantime you'll be going off every time somebody blows their nose in Winchester. It must be really embarrassing when that happens; you know, everybody stumping round in pyjamas at two in the morning trying to find the main cable, and of course it'll be you gets all the blame for their mistakes. They might even rip you out and get a new one.'

'Now steady on,' replied the alarm. 'There's no need to get nasty.'

'Whereas,' John Fingers continued smoothly, 'if you just switch yourself off now, I can leave you in peace and quiet and they'll blame some poor little clerk for forgetting to set you before locking up. You can see my point, can't you?'

The alarm considered for a moment. 'You won't say a word?'

'Cross my heart.'

'It's really unethical, you know. I could get disconnected for just talking to you.'

'You already did that,' John Fingers pointed out, 'so it's sheep and lamb time, anyhow. Tell you what, I'll just snip this wire here and then you'll know for certain how much it hurts, and then maybe . . .'

'All right,' the alarm snarled. 'But if anybody asks, I never seen you before in my life, right?'

'Right. I mean,' John Fingers added, 'even if I did say something, who the hell'd ever believe me?'

With the alarm off, John Fingers was able to take his time scaling the wall, and he made himself nice and comfortable on the window ledge before he jemmied the stay.

'By the way,' he asked the alarm. 'The CCTV camera.'

'What about it?'

'What's it called? I always think it's nice being on first name terms in business, don't you?'

'Zelda,' the alarm replied. 'Don't be fooled by her big round eye, though. She's a tough cookie.'

'Thanks. Be seeing you.'

The alarm, it turned out, was exaggerating.

'You really like it?' the camera asked. 'I mean really. You're not just saying it to please me?'

'Would I do a thing like that?' John Fingers replied. 'And what's more, it's not every camera that could get away with a mounting like that. I mean, black enamel square section tube, unless you've got the figure for it, you could look ridiculous. On you, though—'

Cameras can't smile; but they can open their diaphragms up to f3 and flutter their shutters. 'Glad to know there's some people who notice things,' it said pointedly. 'Of course, some people are so ignorant they wouldn't notice if a person turned up for work strapped to a length of four-by-two with red insulating tape.'

As he walked casually past the camera (which was far too busy admiring its reflection in the window to pay any attention to him) he quickly examined the space between the lines for relevant reading matter. Accordingly, when he came to the infra-red beam he was ready for it.

'Hi,' he said. 'Look, I've got a message for you.'

The beam narrowed suspiciously. 'You have?'

'From Zelda,' John Fingers replied. 'She said she's really sorry, she didn't mean it, and would it be at all possible to start over again?'

'Zelda said that?'

John Fingers nodded, hoping to hell he'd guessed right. 'I'm just the messenger,' he added, 'so don't blame me if . . .'

'Wow! She really said she was sorry?'

'That's right. Is there something between you guys, then?' he added innocently.

'There was,' replied the beam. 'Until a certain person made certain remarks about another person happening to pass the time of day with the fire extinguisher, even though he was just being polite, that's all. I mean, what kind of relationship have you got if you haven't got trust?'

'Absolutely,' John Fingers agreed. 'Anyway, that's the message, so if you'd just let me past . . .'

'What? Oh sure. Hey, you're *positive* she said she was sorry?'

'On my honour as a bur— I mean, service engineer. Cheers.'

'So long. And thank you.'

The further into the building he got, the easier it was. The hidden directional microphone ('Any friend of Zelda's is a friend of mine') was no problem at all, and all he had to do with the lock on the strongroom door was creep up to it and say 'Boo!', whereupon it curled up into a ball, retracting all its wards and letting the door swing open. As for the safe –

'Hello.'

''Lo.'

'It must be very boring,' John Fingers wheedled, 'being a safe.'

'You're not kidding.'

'Sitting in this horrible dark stuffy room all day, with the light off.'

'Yeah.'

'No one to talk to.'

'Well, there's the pressure-pad.'

'What press— You mean,' John Fingers corrected himself, 'the one by the door?'

'Nah,' replied the safe, 'the one under the steel grating, about six inches to the left of where you're stood.'

John Fingers shuffled unobtrusively to the right. 'Must be a real drag,' he said. 'And having to keep still all the time.'

'Huh?'

'With all that horrible dry scratchy money inside you. If I was you I'd be dying for a really good itch all the bloody time.'

You could almost hear the safe thinking. 'Now you come to mention it,' the safe said slowly, 'it's a right pain. Oooh, God, it's so itchy.'

'I bet,' John Fingers went on, 'there's times you just want to throw your door open and have a really good spit.'

'Yeah.'

'Well, then.'

'Huh?'

'Don't mind me.'

Safes are made of huge solid slabs of reinforced laminated sheet steel; or, to put it another way, they're thick. 'Yeah,' it said, 'why not, eh?'

'Go for it.'

'Yeah, right. Only, how do I get myself open?'

'You mean,' John Fingers said, shocked, 'they don't even let you open yourself? I mean, no time lock or anything?'

'Those cheapskates? Do me a favour.'

'We'll soon see about that. Come on, you tell me the combination and we'll have you open before you can say Open sesame.'

'Ta. Right, it's nine six four seven . . .'

Ten minutes later, John Fingers II hurled two black bin-liners full of currency notes into the back of the van, turned the key, thanked the engine for starting (politeness costs nothing, after all) and drove off hell for leather in the general direction of Bournemouth. He didn't even stop for red lights; all you had to do, he'd found, was shout, 'I'm a friend of Simon's,' and they turned green instantly. He had no idea how it worked,

520

but so what? The same was true of gravity and he had every confidence in that.

In the Bank, meanwhile, the safe yawned. With its seventy-millimetre-thick door hanging wide open, it had no choice in the matter, and it didn't actually care. It was thinking.

When it comes to the operation of their thought processes, safes are a bit like whales, elephants, trees and other huge, long-living, slow-moving creatures. They think slow, but they also think deep. And they remember.

The safe remembered. Something the human had said, some throwaway combination of words, meaningless unless you knew the background.

Open something . . .

Open . . .

It was on the tip of its tumbler . . .

Whatever the phrase was, it had heard it before – a very long time ago, in another place, ever so far away. The safe's steel mind mumbled away at the problem, like a toothless but invincibly patient man chewing toffee. Sooner or later, it would remember; and then it'd know.

Open . . .

For some reason, oil came into it somewhere, so the safe thought about oil for a while. Oil; yum. On a hot day, you can't beat a nice long drink of three-in-one, with maybe a sprinkling of Teflon to refresh the parts other lubricants can't reach. In the middle of winter, however, there's nothing to touch a good thick multigrade to keep the wet out and the rust away.

Open . . .

Thieves. Whatever the riddle was, it was something to do with thieves. The thought made the safe quiver slightly. Thieves do horrible things to safes; they drill holes in them and blow them up. *Hate* thieves.

And then it remembered.

521

Every alarm in the building suddenly went off.

'Hey!'

Scheherezade looked up. 'What is it?' she asked. 'Is something wrong?'

The Godfather nodded. 'What you think you're doing?' he demanded hoarsely. 'What is all this, a goddamn comedy?'

'I don't think so,' Scheherezade replied. 'It's not supposed to be.'

The Godfather stood up. 'You don't think so,' he mimicked unpleasantly. 'Then I ask you again, what you think you're doing? You gone crazy or something?'

'I don't think so,' Scheherezade said, 'I'm just turning the story round, that's all. Ali Baba is now Akram, and Akram is Ali Baba. What's wrong with that?'

'Nothing,' replied the Godfather impatiently. 'But all this sitting round playing games, it's not right. A man kidnaps your daughter, you hunt him down and you kill him. You don't go home and go to bed.'

Scheherezade shrugged. 'Why not?' she said. 'I mean, he's in no fit state to go hunting people down at this time of night. With a good night's sleep and a nice cooked breakfast inside him, he'll make a much better job of it.'

'But . . .' The Godfather waved his cigar in the air. 'And besides,' he added, 'what's all this with Akram and the girl playing Racing Genie till all hours? Where's it say in the story they do that? It's nonsense. How can the heroine be playing Racing Genie with the villain? Be reasonable.'

'But he's not the villain,' Scheherezade replied. 'He's the hero.'

'He is?' The Godfather scowled. 'Then who's the goddamn villain?'

'Ali Baba. I suppose,' Scheherezade added, frowning. 'Actually, I'm not sure. No, he can't be, can he? Except . . .'

'Well?'

Scheherezade realised that she was feeling cold, except that it was hot beside the fire. 'Let's just think about this,' she said, doing a marvellous job of keeping the panic out of her voice. 'We've turned the story round, okay? Akram is now Ali Baba, and he's found out the secret that makes him able to turn the tables on Ali Baba . . .'

'Who's now Akram, yes?'

'Just a minute, you'll get me all confused. He's turned the tables on Ali Baba and got hold of what Ali Baba values most in all the world—'

'You mean the girl.'

'Presumably,' said Scheherezade doubtfully. 'After all, she is his daughter. So what happens next is, Ali Baba tries to sneak up on Akram, and he hides in something – something like an oil-jar, let's say a packing-case or a milk-churn – and Akram realises what's going on and pours boiling water on him, and that's that. Freed from the threat of Ali Baba's vengeance, he lives happily ever after with the girl – that must be what's meant to happen, or else why are they getting on like a house on fire? Look—'

('And fifteen for a back treble makes forty-three, which means I can have another bazaar on Cairo. Your go.'

'Hey, double four! Oh damn, go to jail.'

'You could use your Lamp.'

'I don't want to use my Lamp. It's your go.')

'Hey.' The Godfather took a long pull on his cigar. 'Akram kills this girl's father, and you expect them to live happily ever after? You crazy or something?'

'Well . . . Perhaps he doesn't actually kill him, then. After all, he is the hero . . .'

'Precisely. And the hero kills the villain. What kinda mess you making of my story?'

Scheherezade bit her lip. 'It's all because of it being on the other side of the Line,' she said. 'It makes them all so difficult to control. They do things without me telling them to.'

'And another thing,' the Godfather snarled. 'You can't have a villain getting killed saving his only daughter from a kidnapper. That's crazy. That's hero stuff, except a hero wouldn't get killed. And that's not all,' he added, his scowl thickening. 'He ain't even trying to save the goddamn broad. Look—'

('All right, Sharon, who's first?'

'Well, Mr B, you've got Mr Peasemarsh for eight-fifteen, but Mrs Kidd's in the waiting room on spec, that abscess's flared up again, can you fit her in?'

'Hurting, is it?'

'Yes, Mr B.'

'Right, send her in and tell Mr Peasemarsh I won't be a jiffy.')

'You call that rescuing daughters,' sneered the Godfather, ''cos I don't.'

Scheherezade thought for a moment. 'I see what's happening,' she said. 'He's a hero, right?'

'But I thought you said—'

'Yes, but *deep down* he's a hero. And that's what heroes do. They sacrifice themselves for the good of others, because of duty and stuff. And because he's a doctor—'

'Dentist.'

'Okay, dentist, but the principle's the same. His first duty's to his patients, and because he's truly heroic . . .'

'It stinks,' the Godfather grunted. 'You let the whole goddamn thing get outa hand. It's all turning—' He paused, carefully selected the rudest word he could think of, and spat it at her. 'Real. I mean, what about Akram's shadow? What the hell does it think it's playing at?'

'He's turned the lights down,' Scheherezade pointed out. 'Clever,' she added. 'Makes his shadow too faint to be able to intervene.'

524

The Godfather leaned over, until his face was almost touching hers. 'Get it sorted out,' he growled, 'or you're dead. You understand me?'

After he had gone, Scheherezade sat quietly for a while, shivering a little and trying to get her mind clear. On the one hand, she recognised, he was absolutely right; the story was getting away from her, to such an extent that it had almost stopped being a story. It was frightening how easily it had happened. It had to be stopped, she could see that, or where would it all end? Next thing you'd know, they'd all be at it:

('Look! It fits!'

'Of course it fits, you idiot, it's a standard size four, D fitting. But that's not her. For God's sake, man, do you think I'd spend all evening dancing with something that looks like that?'

'But it fits, Your Majesty. And Your Majesty did say . . .')

Unthinkable. But, on the other hand, the story felt *right*. She didn't know why. She hadn't known why for some time, but that hadn't worried her too much. After all, she didn't know why the sun rose or why the rain fell, but she had a shrewd idea that they were supposed to do it.

On a notional third hand, if she didn't get it all back under control and doing what it was supposed to do, she was going to die.

She thought about it. She scribbled notes on the back of her hand. She drew little diagrams. She muttered things to herself such as 'Suppose this soap-dish here is Akram, and this hairbrush is the girl . . .'

It didn't help.

Just when she was on the point of giving the whole thing up as a bad job (and after all, why postpone the inevitable? Death and happiness ever after aren't so very different) it came to her, like the apple falling on Sir Isaac Newton's head.

Except; instead of an apple, suppose it had been a tiny scale model of a bomb?

And instead of Sir Isaac Newton, suppose it had been the Wright brothers?

John Fingers sat down on the floor of his lock-up garage and listened.

No distant sirens. No slamming of car doors, no clattering of big clumping police boots. Silence.

It had worked. Yippee!

A big, silly grin spread over his face like an oil slick as he opened his big canvas holdall and pulled out big handfuls of lovely crisp banknotes. Lovely, lovely money; tens, no, hundreds of thousands of pounds. It was hard to believe that there was this much money in the whole wide world.

Tradition demanded that he should heap it all up on the floor, roll on it, scoop up great handfuls of the stuff and pour it over his head like snow. Bugger tradition; he'd only get it dirty and leave traces of oil and dust on the notes which the forensic boys would use to put him in prison. Instead, he stacked it neatly in piles of ten thousand pounds each. It took a long, long time.

And then, at the very bottom of the bag, he found something he couldn't remember having taken from the safe. On the other hand, it hadn't been in the bag before, so it must have come from the safe. He picked it up, turned it over in his hands, and stared at it.

It was a box.

Well; more sort of a little jar, or urn. What the hell...?

Somebody's ashes, maybe? No, too heavy for that. He shook it. It rattled. He put it down quickly. He wasn't a superstitious man; ladders played too great a part in his life for him to have any hang-ups about walking under them and as far as he was concerned, black cats were only bad luck if you accidentally trod on them when walking stealthily through someone's kitchen at night. But there were definite bad vibes coming from this jar thing. He felt a strong urge to take the bloody thing, find a river, and throw it in.

Stupid! If it came from a safe, it stood to reason there was something valuable in it. A right fool he'd look if he chucked it on a skip and it turned out to be full of diamonds. But what *was* in it?

Only one way to find out. (Likewise, there's only one way to find out the answer to the question: 'What's it *really* like falling twenty-seven storeys onto a concrete floor?') He took a deep breath and opened the lid.

Inside was another jar, or urn. Identical, except slightly smaller. He opened it. Inside was another jar, or urn. Inside that, another. Inside that, another. All told, there were thirty-nine of them; and inside the thirty-ninth—

'Jesus!' John Fingers II jumped back as if he'd been bitten. There was something *alive* in the jar.

It was getting bigger, too. All the jars were getting bigger. He crouched in the corner, terrified, as all thirty-nine jars swelled up like balloons until they were the size of oil-drums.

There were *things* in all of them. Hell fire, he muttered to himself, what is this? Instant freeze-dried horror movie, just add boiling water?

'Boiling water?'

The voice came from inside one of the jars. Perhaps it was just the singular acoustic properties of sun-dried terracotta, but it sounded *awful*. John Fingers II gave a little scream and tried to back away, but some fool had left a wall lying about just where he wanted to back into. He slid down into a little heap.

A head appeared over the rim of one of the jars. First a purple turban, with a big red jewel in it; then a pair of burning coal-black eyes, a long thin nose, a thin moustache with twirly ends, a grinning mouth and a little pointy beard. Similar heads were popping up all over the place; thirty-nine of them. John

Fingers closed his eyes and hoped to God for all he was worth that this lot were in fact the police and he was just about to be arrested.

'Skip.'

'What?'

'Where the hell are we?'

'How the hell should I know? Hey, this place is weird!'

'How did we get here, then?'

'Search me. Last thing I knew, some bird was pulling my lid off and pouring boiling water all over me.'

'Hey, that's it! Maybe we died.'

'You feel dead, Hanif?'

'How the hell should I know? You think I got a season ticket or something?'

'Don't *feel* dead. I think you get all cold and stiff.'

'What, you mean like being cooped up in a jar for six hours?'

'Talking of which, why don't we all get out of these poxy jars?'

'Good thinking, Skip.'

'Hey, Skip, there's someone over there. Look, down in that corner, by the wall.'

'So there is . . . Hey, lads, look!'

'Isn't that. . . ?'

'Course it is! Wow, are we glad to see you! How the devil did you get here?'

John Fingers looked up, feeling like a lone rabbit facing thirty-nine oncoming lorries in the middle lane of a motorway. 'You talking to me?' he croaked.

'Course we are. Hey look, Skip, I mean Aziz, it's him!'

'Where'd you get those funny clothes?'

'He looks well on it, anyway. Hey, what's it like here? And where are we, anyhow?'

John Fingers inched away, slithering sideways along the

wall. 'Am I supposed to know you people?' he asked.

The one called Aziz looked at him strangely. 'Of course,' he said.

'Really? You sure you haven't mistaken me for someone else?'

Aziz grinned. 'Come off it, Skip,' he said.

CHAPTER SEVENTEEN

'And six means I get an extra muezzin on Aleppo, giving me three suits in baulk and two on the line, repiqued in green makes four thousand nine hundred and twenty-three, add ninety-three for the slam above the line makes six thousand and sixteen, plus four for his spurs makes six thousand and twenty, and it's on a double Carpet so that's twenty-four thousand and eighty, but I also get twenty for the finesse, making a grand total of twenty-five thousand and I *win*!'

'I hate you,' said Akram.

'I don't care,' Michelle replied happily, sweeping the pieces into her corner. 'And that makes forty-eight games to me and, oh dear, none to you, what a shame, never mind, mugs away, your go.'

'Don't want to play any more.'

'Your go.'

'This is a silly game.'

'Your *go*.'

'We have been playing this game,' Akram said, 'for eighty-four hours non-stop. Bloody fine kidnap this turned out to be.'

'You started it.'

'I think I'll call the police and give myself up.'

'Okay,' Michelle said, setting out the pieces. 'But we'll finish the set first. Your go.'

'You *sure* you haven't played this game before?'

'Course I'm sure. But I think I'm slowly getting the hang of it. Are you going to throw those dice, or are you waiting for tectonic shift to move them for you?'

'I've had enough of this game. Let's play Dragons' Teeth instead. You ever played Dragons' Teeth? You'd like it.'

'Throw,' Michelle growled sternly, 'the dice.'

'All right, all right . . . Oh balls, double one.'

'*Hah*!'

'I'd offer you money to go away,' Akram said, 'but I've only got a five pound note and some copper. Which reminds me,' he added. 'What happens to employees who stay away from work for four days without even phoning in to pretend they're ill?'

'Usually,' Michelle replied, 'they get the sack. Why?'

'Pity,' Akram said, 'I was just starting to like it a lot there. Did I happen to mention I got promoted to assistant manager?'

'Only about sixty million times. Pretty academic now, I'd have thought. Now then – oh wonderful, double four. Now, do I want the Emir's Palace, Samarkand? Might as well, I suppose.'

Akram cupped his chin between his hands. 'It was inevitable, I suppose,' he sighed. 'It's the bloody story catching up with me, I guess. You settle down, get a job, think you've escaped and then *wham*! there it is again, standing behind you breathing hot narrative down the back of your neck. Tell you what,' he added. 'I'll bet you. If you win this game, I'll let you go free. How does that sound?'

'Chicken. Admit it, you just can't take being beaten by a woman.'

Akram scowled. 'Woman be blowed. As far as I'm concerned, any life form whatsoever that beats me at Racing Genie by a margin of forty-eight to nil is probably pushing its luck. If I ask you nicely, can I concede the last two games?'

'No,' replied Michelle, 'I want to see you squirm.'

'How do you do that, exactly? I've always thought of it as basically wiggling your head about while trying to make your shoulder blades touch each other.'

'You'll find out soon enough. Now stop chattering and get on with the game.'

'What about your job, though? Won't they be wondering where you've got to?'

'I've been kidnapped,' Michelle replied. 'You don't have to go to work if you've been kidnapped. Ask Helen of Troy or anyone.'

'Or your father,' Akram persisted. 'I'll bet you he's worried sick.'

'No he isn't,' Michelle replied promptly. 'I phoned him when you went to the loo.'

'Oh. Right. And what did he say?'

'Never redouble on only two utilities unless you're finessing in baulk. He was right, too.'

'Hey, that's cheating.'

'No it isn't.'

'Yes it is.'

'No it isn't.'

Akram stood up. 'Do you think this is some sort of happy ending?' he speculated. 'I mean, *happily* at forty-eight to nil depends on which side of the board you happen to be, but *ever after* is starting to look like a definite possibility.'

'Sit down and throw the dice.'

Akram shook his head. 'No offence,' he said. 'I mean, it's been great fun, if perhaps a little one-sided, but I think I'll give it a bit of a rest for now. Do you realise,' he added, 'that my whole life is now in total ruins?'

'Oh come on. You'll get another job, I'm sure.'

'It's not that,' Akram replied. 'Just think, will you? For I don't know how long, probably since Time began, I used to go round in a sort of little loop of robbing, killing and getting scalded to death by that bastard Ali Baba. Fine. I escape from all that, and I come here, with the sole intention of catching him and torturing him to death. The bastard stymies me again. But that's fine, because for the first time in my lives I can see this little tiny ray of hope which says to me, *Akram, you don't have to do this kind of stuff any more*. And that's marvellous. I get a job, do something useful with my life, I don't have to be a villain or a hero. And then you come barging in—'

'All I wanted was a hamburger.'

'All I wanted was to be real. You come barging in, and all that goes out of the window, I'm back to where I was, but at least I've got a chance of getting my revenge on Ali Baba because I've got you. And now *that's* all stuffed up on me, because we've spent the last couple of days playing some damn kid's game, I couldn't kill you even if I wanted to, and your criminally negligent, stony-hearted excuse for a father isn't prepared to lift a finger to rescue you. Excuse me, I have to go and feed the phoenix.'

Michelle looked at him. 'You don't want to kill him any more, do you?'

'Of course I don't,' Akram snarled. 'What the bloody hell good would killing the feckless jerk do me? Absolute waste of everybody's time.'

'Then don't,' Michelle replied.

'What?'

'Don't kill him.' Michelle shrugged. 'Don't kill anybody. I know it sounds a bit strange at first, but you'll get used to it. They say the after-breakfast murder's the hardest one to give up. Once you've learned to do without that, you'll find kicking the habit entirely will be surprisingly easy.'

Akram gestured impatiently. 'You think it's that easy, you stupid bloody mortal? You really believe I can just . . .'

'Yes.'

Fang opened her eyes.

'Where . . . ?' she croaked.

A bright light, as hard and unfriendly as the headlights of an oncoming truck, hit her in the eyes. She started to wince away, but found she couldn't.

'Ah,' said a voice above her. 'You're awake.'

The reason she couldn't move, she discovered, was that she was tied up. Her memory was racing, like the wheels of a car stuck fast in mud. The last thing she could remember was a smell. Gas . . .

'This,' said the voice, 'isn't going to hurt a bit.'

Gas. A huge cache of teeth; and she'd been piling them up and wishing she'd brought the block and tackle, when suddenly there'd been this foul sweet smell, and then her arms and legs had stopped working.

'Not a bit. This is going to hurt a whole lot.'

She remembered. 'Aaaaagh!' she said.

She'd gone back to the dentist's surgery where they'd found the safe, because she'd been convinced there were teeth hidden around the place somewhere. And just as she'd found this mind-bending hoard, a light had blazed in her eyes and the gas had hit her and she'd realised that she'd been set up; Ali Baba had put out that great big stash of teeth as a decoy, and she'd flown straight in. She craned her neck to see what was holding her arms and legs. Dental floss.

'You certainly took your time coming back,' Ali Baba was saying. He was holding the drill in his right hand. 'For a while there, I thought I'd misjudged you. Now you've got two choices.'

534

'Eek.'

'Either,' he went on, switching on the drill, 'you can tell me where that bastard's holding my daughter, or else I'll fill you full of amalgam. What's it to be?'

'I'll talk.'

'You do that. While you still can.'

Another lesson learnt the hard way; never underestimate a dentist. As he unwound the dental floss, he explained that as soon as he'd opened the floorsafe and found the sixpence she'd left there, he'd known that the way to find Michelle was through her.

'I knew you'd come back for the teeth,' he said. 'It was just a matter of being patient. And now, here you are. You're being very sensible, by the way. You probably haven't seen the really big drill. It's thicker than you are. You wouldn't have liked it at all.'

She contemplated making a run for it; but that ceased to be a practical possibility when he took a great big lump of silicone impression material and moulded it round her foot, like an old-fashioned ball and chain. There'd be no chance of hobbling two steps together, let alone flying, with that stuck on the end of her leg.

'Did you ever see *Marathon Man*?' he was saying. 'No? Pity. It'd make scaring the living daylights out of you so much easier if we shared a common frame of reference. Never mind, I'll just have to do the best I can with crude physical violence.'

'I said I'll talk,' Fang squeaked, as he revved the drill. 'Please,' she added, as he slowly and ghoulishly counted out forty-six silver sixpences, explaining as he did so that he was old-fashioned enough to believe in payment in advance. 'I'll take you straight there, I promise.'

'I'm delighted to hear it. Well then, no time like the present. Just wait there a moment while I get a few things.'

He squished the ball of tacky silicone down onto the arm of

535

the chair, imprisoning her while he tucked the gun into the waistband of his trousers and wrapped the sword in a black bin-liner. 'You have no idea,' he said cheerfully, 'how much I'm looking forward to this. Which is strange,' he added, 'because ever since I arrived on this side of the Line I've tried my best not to inflict gratuitous pain and injury, and now here I am getting ready to slice your friend up as thin as Danish salami. I guess it's a case of the exception that proves the rule. Ready?'

It was insult spot-welded to injury for Ali Baba to mould the ball of sticky onto the bottom of his rear-view mirror, leaving Fang to dangle upside-down like some sort of horrible mascot, but she wasn't in any frame of mind to make anything of it. She was too busy feeling extremely ill.

'Which way?' he asked.

'Left,' Fang replied, 'then second on your right into Portland Avenue.'

'Thanks. The whole reason,' Ali Baba continued, 'why I went into dentistry once I arrived here was this horrid feeling of guilt, because of what I'd done; you know, the palm-oil jars and the boiling water. I assume you know about all that? Good. All right, I decided, now I'm here I'm going to devote the rest of my life to curing pain and alleviating suffering. Pretty noble sentiments, don't you think?'

'Uhg,' Fang replied, swaying crazily as Ali Baba swung the wheel for the right-hand turn. 'Carry on here for about half a mile, then left at the lights.'

'Thank you. The sad part of it is,' Ali Baba went on, 'that all that time, I was living in mortal terror of Akram showing up. And I mean really serious terror. You have no idea how much it costs in electricity when you sleep with the light on all the time. Strictly speaking, I ought to make him pay me for that. And then there's all the alarm systems and infra-red cameras and surveillance gear. None of it's cheap, you know.

536

And all that was because *I* was afraid of *him*. That's a bit of a joke, in the circumstances.'

'Left here. What are you going to do?'

'Kill him,' Ali Baba replied casually, indicating and waiting for a lorry to pass. 'As painfully as I sensibly can. I'm not going to bother with anything elaborate, of course, because once you start on that track you're virtually inviting the bastard to escape. Ye gods, though, I'm looking forward to this. I mean, we're talking very old scores indeed here. He's going to think boiling water was on the soppy side of humane.'

'Right. Um . . .'

'And dentistry,' Ali Baba went on, one hand on the wheel, 'gives you some fairly esoteric insights into the nature of pain, with specific reference,' he added, smiling dreamily, 'to agony.' He glanced up at the rear-view mirror, caught a glimpse of his reflection in it, and looked back at the road. 'And when I've finished with him,' he said, 'we must have a chat about you.'

John Fingers cleared his throat. Thirty-nine eager faces turned and looked at him.

'Right,' he said. 'Here's the plan.'

He wasn't sure why he'd said that. It seemed appropriate somehow, but he didn't actually have a plan, more a sort of rough pencil sketch, with lots of rubbing out and a shopping list on the other side. Maybe it was a case of the situation bringing out the best in him.

'Seaview Road,' he said. 'The industrial units. Now I want a nice clean job, in and out as quickly as possible, no messing around. Any questions?'

'Skip.'

'Yes?'

'What's an industrial unit?'

On the negative side, it had to be admitted, they were all

thick. You'd be hard put to it to find thirty-nine dozier people this side of a cryogenic vault. 'It's a sort of shed,' he explained.

'A shed?'

'That's right.'

'Who'd keep anything worth nicking in a shed?'

Patience, John Fingers muttered to himself. 'Not that sort of shed,' he replied. 'More a sort of – well, unit.'

'You mean a shed for keeping gold and jewels in?'

More patience. 'It's not actually gold and jewels we're after,' he said, 'more your sort of portable power tools and petty cash style of thing. I mean,' he added, as thirty-nine faces suddenly became as glazed as a row of cucumber frames, 'don't get me wrong, if we do happen across any gold and jewels it'll be a nice bonus. But what we're actually on the lookout for is electric drills, orbital sanders, arc-welding gear, anything we can get a few bob for down the car boot sale.'

He paused, and was immediately deluged in a flood of requests for footnotes. He held up his hand for silence.

'Let's keep it simple, shall we?' he said. 'If it's not nailed down, we pinch it. All right?'

Thirty-nine heads nodded. 'Right, Skip.'

'Then let's go.'

'Skip.'

'Oh for crying out— Yes?'

'Why can't we steal anything that's been nailed down? Is it a curse, or something?'

'No, it's just – yes, that's right, it's a curse. Can we go now, please?'

Why me, he reflected, as he backed the coach out into Merrivale Crescent. I was never cut out to be a gang leader. The Smiths have always been loners, single operators; mostly, he was realistic enough to admit, because of their almost supernatural knack of getting caught, but never mind.

Suddenly finding himself the leader of a gang of fanatically loyal, desperately eager to please, terminally stupid desperadoes wasn't quite what he'd had in mind when he woke up that morning; but it had been a pretty strange day in any case. A pretty strange week, come to that.

'Watch my offside front wing,' growled the coach.

'Shut up, you.'

Obviously it wasn't a coincidence. A less straightforward man would be trying to puzzle it all out at this point, but John Fingers wasn't like that. When things dropped on him from Heaven, he didn't stare up at the sky and demand an explanation; nor did he hold them up to the light or shake them to see if they rattled. No; he accepted them at face value, filed off the serial numbers where appropriate and, whenever possible, immediately sold them in pubs. In this instance Destiny had, for reasons best known to itself, endowed him with the ability to talk to consumer durables and a gang of thirty-nine semi-skilled assistants. John Fingers wasn't remotely interested in where they'd come from; not knowing where things came from was bred in the bone as far as he was concerned. Somewhere in the vastness of the Universe there was a lorry with a duff tailgate, from which all these wonders had tumbled into his lap. His role was to make the best of them he could. It was a way of life that seemed to work with video recorders, forty-piece canteens of cutlery, socket sets, wax cotton jackets, answering machines and all sorts of other things that came his way; no reason he could see why it shouldn't apply to miracles.

If he hadn't been so preoccupied with thoughts of this nature, he might have noticed that he was sharing Seaview Road with a big blue Volvo, which drew up round the corner as he parked the coach outside the entrance to the industrial estate and opened the doors.

'We're here,' he said. 'You two, Whatsyername and Thing,

see to the gates. The rest of you . . .'

Perhaps he should have been more explicit. Rashid and Yusuf, answering to the generic names he'd given to all his new-found followers, had seen to the gates by charging them with their heads. They evidently had very hard heads. Ah well, he told himself, at least it's got the gates open.

'Right, that'll have to do,' he said briskly. 'You lot, follow me.'

If they'd been wearing caps and carrying satchels, you'd have reckoned it was a school party. As they trooped through the mangled gates, furtive as an express train, inconspicuous as North America, the curtains of the darkness parted for a moment and a shadowy figure fell in behind them, followed them for a while, mumbled something into the top pocket of his coat and sneaked off into the shadows.

'This,' muttered Ali Baba, crouching in the doorway of Unit 13, 'is getting a little bit worrying.'

'You've noticed, at last.'

Ali Baba shook his head. 'That large party of idiots over there,' he whispered. 'I think I recognise them. Hang on, we can double-check this.' He counted up to forty and then nodded. 'What in hell's name are they doing here? And who's the new leader?'

'Does it matter?' Fang replied, her teeth chattering. 'Look, they've gone off down the other end of the estate. Let's get on with it and then you can let me go.'

'You think you're going to be let go? Really? That's that stuff, what's it called, optimism. Never could get the hang of it myself.'

It was at this point that Ali Baba felt the loss of King Solomon's ring. Most of the time he was glad, on balance, to be rid of it; having to stop and pass the time of day with every lock and thermostat and circuit-board you meet takes up such a lot of time, and generally speaking gets you absolutely nowhere. Just occasionally, though, it can be astonishingly helpful.

'You wouldn't happen to know,' he asked, 'exactly how one goes about shooting off a lock? It looks so easy in the films, but in real life I haven't a clue how to go about it.'

'Why not just try the handle?' Fang replied.

Ali Baba shrugged and, with the intention of showing what a silly suggestion that was, gave the door handle a half-hearted twist. The door opened.

'Good Lord,' he said. Then he kicked the door hard and charged in.

There are people who can simply blunder into difficult, dangerous situations and expect to be able to carry it off by trusting their instincts and riding their luck. They're the sort of people who also win lottery prizes with the first ticket they buy and attract the attention of off-duty Hollywood talent scouts at karaoke evenings at their local pubs. Unless you're one of these, playing the law of averages with a full Legal Aid certificate in your pocket, it's best to do it the other way and think things through carefully before kicking open doors and sprinting through. You never know what you're likely to find on the other side.

In Ali Baba's case, it turned out to be a very large, bad-tempered bird. His specialised knowledge meant that he was able to identify it as a phoenix, but unfortunately it didn't extend to what you do to mollify one when you're two feet away from it and looking down its throat. At least he was able to eliminate one possibility straight away. Saying, 'Now then, nice bird,' had no perceptible effect whatsoever.

'Ark!' screamed the phoenix, flapping its wings. 'Ark ark *graaaaoar*!'

Two and a half seconds later, Ali Baba was able to add drawing a gun and shooting at it to his definitive list of counterproductive ways to deal with an angry phoenix. He was just about to add falling flat on his face and cowering when Fang said, 'It's all right, he's with me.'

'Then what was all the shooting in aid of?' the phoenix grumbled. 'Daft bugger, he could do somebody an injury.'

Ali Baba looked up, puzzled. 'Tooth fairy?' he said.

'Yes?'

'What's going on? Why are you on my side all of a sudden?'

Fang grinned. 'That's three molars and a couple of upper front canines you owe me, Mister Dentist,' she replied. 'I may be small, but I'm not stupid. Would you like me to switch the light on? It'll be so much easier if we can all see what we're doing.'

A moment later, the light snapped on. The phoenix, dazzled, let out a pained squawk and huddled away into a corner, leaving Ali Baba face to face with Akram and Michelle.

'This is . . .' Akram began to say, but he got no further. This is where it starts getting complicated. Let's break it up into five phases.

As soon as he saw Akram, Ali Baba raised the gun, pointed it at Akram and said 'You bastard!' That's as far as he got, so we'll leave him for a moment and go back to Michelle.

She had started off with the intention of getting between Akram and her father, calming the situation down, getting a conversation going and then leaving them to it while she made a nice conciliatory cup of tea. Seeing Ali Baba raise the gun, however, she rapidly revised her plans and ducked behind Akram, saying, 'Eeek!' We'll leave her there for the time being, and turn to Akram.

Actually, Akram didn't do much, apart from starting to say 'This is . . .' and thinking better of it. Whatever he may have had in mind to do, the situation was radically altered by the light coming on. This meant that he now had a clear, sharply-defined shadow on the whitewashed wall behind him.

Finally, just to complete the picture, this was the precise moment when John Fingers opened the back door to Unit 13 and walked straight in, to find himself staring down the barrel of Ali Baba's gun.

One last thing. The electric kettle, which Michelle had put on a short while ago, now came to the boil and switched itself off. That's Phase One.

Phase Two began with Akram's shadow. It wasn't in the sunniest of moods to begin with, thanks to Akram's devious use of subdued lighting to keep it in its place. Suddenly restored, it snatched its chance, swept along the wall and went for Ali Baba's throat, dragging Akram along behind it like a very small child clinging to a huge kite on a windy day. Instinctively, Ali Baba swung round to face it and fired the gun. Dentistry and skill at arms are not mutually exclusive, but proficiency at one doesn't necessarily imply competence at the other. He missed badly. There was a scream.

For the phoenix, still recovering from its nasty experience with the light, a sudden loud noise in a confined space was the last straw. Rising like a startled pheasant (the comparison is only partially appropriate, because it was ten times bigger than the largest pheasant ever recorded) it rocketed towards the open door in a flurry of pounding wings, cannoned into Ali Baba and sent him spinning against the wall before hurtling away into the night in the general direction of the Isle of Wight.

John Fingers, wondering what the hell he'd just walked into, had meanwhile grabbed the kettle, as being the nearest remotely useful object to hand, with the intention of throwing boiling water in the face of the man who was pointing the gun at him. His principal mistake lay in not unplugging the kettle first. As it was, the kettle remained firmly tethered to the wall, ruining his aim. There was another scream.

That's Phase Two.

Phase Three kicks off with Ali Baba hitting the wall. The back of his head connected with the light switch, turning the light off. Akram's shadow immediately vanished. Akram himself, suddenly released, tripped over something – possibly a dead body – on the ground, lurched forward, slipped on the wet floor and went crashing into Ali Baba, hitting him in the solar plexus with his head. Feeling Ali Baba's fingers round his throat, he grabbed wildly for something to pull himself up by, found the wall and, quite by chance, switched the light on again. End of Phase Three.

The situation at the start of Phase Four, as revealed by the newly restored light, is as follows:

Ali Baba, backed up against the wall, is trying to strangle Akram; who in turn is doing his best to pull away and, rather less successfully, breathe. As if he didn't have enough to contend with, he's now further hampered in his movements by an extremely boisterous and single-minded shadow, which couldn't care less about breathing and is really only interested in inflicting mayhem on Ali Baba. Since Akram and his shadow only have the one pair of hands between them, this complicates matters no end. John Fingers, having contrived to soak himself from head to foot with boiling water from his own kettle, has fallen backwards over a small trestle table and knocked himself silly on the floor; in doing so dislodging a tooth, for which Fang is currently writing him out a receipt. Michelle is lying on the ground, not moving.

And ... action.

Akram, scrambling to get a foothold, kicks Ali Baba's gun across the floor. John Fingers, coming round and finding himself the apparent recipient of yet another unsolicited present from Destiny, grabs hold of it rather cack-handedly, presses the trigger, and sends a bullet neatly and fortuitously through the light-bulb. One immediate consequence of this is that Akram's shadow promptly vanishes, leaving Akram free to punch Ali

Baba scientifically on the point of the jaw, thereby knocking him out and simplifying the situation enormously in time for the beginning of Phase Five.

This is John Fingers' Phase, so it's appropriate to reflect that he has every reason to feel aggrieved and bewildered with the way things have been going. True, he's up one gun (Browning M1910 seven-shot automatic, he instinctively noticed, street value no more than £150, if that) and a solid silver sixpence; but he's been terrified, shot at or in the general direction of, facially edited to the extent of one upper front tooth, drenched in boiling water and stunned by a concrete floor. About the only part of him that doesn't hurt is his hair and he's standing, as far as he can tell, on a dead girl; not an agreeable situation for a man with seventeen previous convictions.

'Well,' said the gun. 'Don't just stand there.'

And a moment later, he wasn't; because Michelle, whose skull had been grazed by the second bullet, woke up under his left foot, wriggled and screamed. That, as far as John Fingers was concerned, was about as much as he could reasonably be expected to take. He neither knew nor cared what was going on, provided it carried on doing it without him. He started to back off, only to find that again there was a wall tiresomely in the way.

There was also, he was annoyed to discover, a man advancing on him with a large adjustable spanner (seven-eighths Bahco, nice bit of kit but still only a fiver, top whack, down the car boot sale) clutched in his large, powerful hand. Of course, he wasn't to know that the man was Akram the Terrible, but he didn't need an awful lot of background information to work out that the spanner wasn't intended to be used for tightening nuts, unless of course they were his.

'Stay where you are,' he said, pointing the gun at Michelle's head, 'or the girl . . .'

'Skip? You in there, Skip?' Aziz's voice, outside in the yard. Both men heard it, recognised it and felt an immediate surge of relief.

'Yes,' they said.

The phoenix rose into the night sky, wings whirring, tail streaming behind it like a Chinese New Year dragon. Its brain, roughly the size and density of a Land Rover engine, was disturbed by a whirlwind of conflicting messages, until it resembled nothing so much as a vigorously shaken snowstorm paperweight. A dominant theme was fear; bright lights, noises, bangs – far back in its profoundly confused genetic matrix there were pheasant genes, and the sound of gunfire acted directly on the wing muscles, bypassing the usual decision-making machinery entirely. Less urgent, but still influential, was the feeling that running away at the first hint of trouble was somehow conduct unbecoming, and any self-respecting fabulous beast would at least have hung around long enough to find out what was going on and whether the general trend of the narrative made it likely that it'd be needed. Having it away on its wingtips was more chicken than phoenix, it couldn't help thinking; and headless chicken at that. Without realising it, the giant bird halved its airspeed and let up a little on adrenaline production.

The mental debate moved up a gear, the main issue being revealed as self-preservation versus loyalty. The latter concept wasn't a familiar one; when phoenixes stand by their man, it's generally to make it easier to get their claws into his neck. On the other hand, they are honourable beasts, as befits their pedigree and status within the avian kingdom. It had responsibilities to Akram; it had sheltered under his roof and eaten his birdseed. This was, it felt, just the kind of situation where the advice of an older, wiser phoenix would have been extremely helpful. Since it was by definition the oldest and wisest phoenix around, however, as well as the youngest and doziest, it was on is own. Oh well.

'Bugger,' it said. It had slowed down so much that it either had to accelerate or turn.

Without really understanding why, it turned.

'Skip?'

Aziz was looking at two men. They were both tall, dark, lean, broad-shouldered, with curly black hair, pointed beards and regulation coal-black eyes. There the resemblance ended.

The problem was that neither of them actually looked very much like Akram, the way Aziz remembered him; except that, when it came to the crunch, he found he couldn't remember all that clearly what Akram did look like. Well yes, he was tall, dark, lean, broad, curly, pointed and coal-eyed. So were twenty-seven of the thirty-nine thieves. So, when the occasion demanded, was Douglas Fairbanks. Proves nothing. To make matters worse, they both sounded almost but not quite right, like Akram doing voice impressions with a handkerchief over his mouth. It wouldn't have mattered all that much if they hadn't both been ordering him to do contradictory things.

'Skip?' he repeated. 'Here, what's going—?'

He wasn't allowed to finish the question, because the air was suddenly full of the noise of sirens. The police, having heard no shots for over five minutes, had guessed that the combatants had sorted out their differences, and were moving in to arrest the survivors.

Being still relatively new to this side of the Line, Aziz didn't actually know about policemen and sirens and flashing blue lights, but his profession had given him a pretty good set of instincts; good enough to convince him that the men in blue uniforms streaming in through the mangled gates probably weren't autograph hunters. Reluctantly he decided that something had to be done and that he was still stuck with the horrible job of doing it.

'Come on,' he said, 'all of you. We'll sort it out later.'

'But . . .'

'But . . .'

'*Move!*' The authority in his own voice amazed him, and for one moment he firmly believed that *he* was Akram, and had been all along. Interesting though the theory was, however, this was neither the time nor the place. 'You lot,' he ordered a random selection of thieves, 'bring 'em all. Follow me.'

'Where to?'

It was a very good question, and Aziz hadn't the faintest idea what the answer was. So he drew his scimitar, yelled, 'Charge!' at the top of his voice, and ran out into the yard to see what would happen.

In the event, it all seemed to work out rather well. The blue guys who probably weren't autograph hunters started to run towards him, caught sight of the scimitar and appeared to think better of it, presumably remembering that they hadn't been formally introduced and not wishing to commit a social faux pas. This left Aziz with a clear run to the big fifty-seater coach they'd all come in. Since the rest of the lads were following him, also waving their scimitars and shouting, Aziz came to the conclusion that for once, the flow was worth going with. Just to be on the safe side he uttered a blood-curdling yell and brandished his sword even more flamboyantly, narrowly missing his own ear.

The moment when the last straggling thief scrambled aboard and pulled the door to after him was, however, the high water mark of the flow; after that, it started looking alarmingly like they were about to go with the ebb. The autograph-not-hunters had blocked off the exit from the yard with two white cars and were shouting things through megaphones. As far as Aziz could tell, what they were actually saying was, 'Ark wark fark argle wargle fargle,' but you didn't need a United Nations trained simultaneous translator in order to get the gist.

'We all here?' he demanded.

'Yeah, Skip, I mean Guv.'

'Anybody remember to bring the two scrappers? The girl and that bloke?'

'Yeah, Guv. Oh, and by the way.'

'What?'

'That bloke,' said Rustem, his face wallpapered from side to side with an idiot grin. 'I think it's Ali Baba.'

'Fine,' Aziz replied. 'Why am I not surprised? Fuck it, we'll sort it all out later. Right now—'

Right then, Ali Baba woke up.

He had been having a strange dream.

He dreamed that he was standing in front of the Godfather's desk. Directly in front of him, cigar-smoking and ominously looming, was the Godfather himself. Sitting beside him, rather less congruously, was a stout woman in a yashmak. She appeared to be knitting a pair of socks.

'Well?' said the Godfather.

Ali Baba blinked. 'Sorry,' he said. 'No offence and all that, but well what?'

'Your wishes,' the Godfather replied. 'You got three of them, remember.'

'Two,' the stout woman interrupted. 'He already used one.'

A pained expression flitted over the Godfather's face. 'You gotta excuse my wife,' he said icily. 'She ain't got no manners, she don't know how to behave in company. You got three wishes, and . . .'

'Two. Getting across the Line and becoming a dentist was one wish. That leaves two.'

'That wasn't a wish, that was a separate deal,' the Godfather snapped, restraining his rising annoyance King Canute-

549

fashion. 'For that he gave us the ring, remember? So three.'

'Two, because the stuff with the ring was just a cover. As soon as he was across we chucked it away.'

'Excuse me,' said Ali Baba. 'I hate to interrupt, but could I just get this absolutely straight in my mind? You want me to use my three wishes now?'

'Yeah.'

'Yes, but it's two.'

'Will you be quiet?'

'I can be as quiet as a tiny bloody mouse and it still won't alter the fact that it's two wishes, not three. The trouble with some people is . . .'

The Godfather banged his fist on the table, dislodging a small china paperweight inscribed *A Present From Palermo*. It fell to the floor, rolled a little way and then, disconcertingly, vanished. He stood up, leaned across the desk until his chin was no more than six inches from the tip of Ali Baba's nose, and smiled.

'You know what they say,' he said pleasantly, 'about having dinner in a Sicilian restaurant? How when you've finished they don't bring you a bill, but years later they come to you and ask you to do them a small favour? Well, Mister Baba, I hope you enjoyed your meal. Do we understand each other?'

'Absolutely,' Ali Baba replied, nodding enthusiastically. 'Consider your drift definitively caught. But what do you want me to wish for?'

The Godfather grinned. 'Any minute now,' he said, 'you gonna wake up. You gonna find yourself in a big yellow bus with thirty-nine thieves, Akram, your daughter and a guy called John Smith who I don't think you know. You shot at him, but you don't know him. All round this bus, you gonna find armed police. I think you might wanna wish you was out of there. Am I right?'

'That would certainly seem reasonable,' Ali Baba agreed,

'in the circumstances you describe. Please do go on.'

'And then,' the Godfather continued – he was so close now that Ali Baba could plainly see his rather second-rate bridge-work; somehow, that made him feel better. 'Then you gonna find that Akram's gotta sword, the thirty-nine thieves all got swords, John Smith's gotta gun, and you ain't got nothing except maybe the courage of your convictions. I figure maybe you gonna wish the ironmongery was a bit more evenly distributed.'

'Quite.'

'But,' the Godfather continued, 'that still ain't gonna solve all your problems, because until Akram's dead and all his men, and you and your daughter are far away where you're gonna prove very hard to catch, you won't never be sure they ain't gonna show up all over again. But on *that* side of the Line—' There was, Ali Baba observed, an infinity of disgust packed into the little word *that*. Significant, he felt. 'On *that* side of the Line, if you go killing guys all over the place, you gonna make yourself very conspicuous, and you don't want that. So I'm figuring, maybe you'll wanna come back here, where you belong, where all your friends are. After all,' he added, with an expansive gesture that entirely failed to inspire confidence, 'you only skipped out to escape from Akram and his boys, so if they're all dead, you can come home. Now, what could be better than wishing to come home?'

'Ah,' Ali Baba said. 'I see.'

'That's three,' said the stout woman. 'He's only got two.'

For a second or so, Ali Baba was convinced the Godfather was about to explode. It was gruesomely fascinating, watching him consciously, deliberately stopping himself from being angry. It was rather like watching a film of a fire in an oil refinery being played through the projector backwards. It'd be even more interesting to watch from five hundred yards away through a powerful telescope, of course, because then he

551

could concentrate properly without the distraction of extreme fear.

'He's got three,' the Godfather said. 'You got that?'

'Not that it matters much,' the woman went on, ignoring him, 'because you can easily run the first and third wish together and arrive at exactly the same result. I'd do that if I were you, and that'd put an end to all this silly bickering.'

'Good idea,' said the Godfather. He picked up a heavy marble ashtray in his left hand and squeezed it, reducing it to fine dust. 'Why don't we do just that?'

The phoenix banked, turned and dived. Far below there were lights, noises and scurrying humans. It fought down the instinctive rush of panic; it had already been a phoenix, a pheasant and a chicken. It had no desire to be a mouse as well.

It put its wings back, glided low, and accelerated, feet outstretched. There were eagles as well as pheasants in its ancestry, not to mention a whole host of large, featherless flying lizards with leather wings and huge pointed beaks. It was time to prove that it had inherited rather more from its forebears than a few sticks of old furniture and a broken clock.

Ali Baba woke up.

'I wish . . .' he said.

Claws extended, the phoenix swooped. There was a merry tinkling of glass as its talons caved in the side windows of the coach, and a dizzying, terrifying moment when it seemed that even those huge wings couldn't produce enough uplift to haul a Mercedes coach and forty-three human beings straight up into the air. That was, of course, perfectly natural. For a thousand generations, Mankind used to worry itself sick with the thought that come dawn tomorrow, the sun might not quite have the legs to rise and shine.

At ground level, the policeman with the megaphone stopped argle bargling in mid fargle and stood motionless for a while, his lower jaw nearly touching his bootlaces. Then, being a policeman and properly trained to deal with all possible contingencies, he ordered the coach to come back.

It didn't work.

With infinite regret, and blaming it all on the pernicious respect-dissipating effects of so-called community policing, he gave the order to open fire.

Or at least, he tried to. He got as far as 'Open', but before he could complete the command a passing tooth fairy darted into his mouth, neatly yanked out his dental plate, shoved a silver sixpence in its place and flew away. A split second later it flew back, hovered for a moment in front of the megaphone, and completed the sentence for him.

'Sesame,' it said.

Whereupon the sky opened.

CHAPTER EIGHTEEN

'Wait for it,' said the instructor. 'Let it come, let it come, let it come. Steady. And ... Now, plenty of forward allowance, and *let him have it*!'

This is a birth control clinic on the far side of the Line.

'Now let's just try that again, only this time follow the line, swing through and *keep it moving*.'

Six men with shotguns and a clay pigeon trap are standing in a field in the rain. They're learning the art of judging air speed and forward allowance, vital when shooting a moving target.

'The average stork,' the instructor continues, 'can reach speeds of up to forty miles an hour, with the wind behind it. That means that, at thirty-five yards, you need to be something like ten feet in front to be sure of a clean kill. Okay, everybody, let's try that one more time.'

This side of the Line, family planning means a Remington pump-action, a steady hand, a good eye and ten or twelve accurately placed stork decoys. In winter, when huge flocks of the dreaded birds turn south for the annual migration, the hills and valleys echo from dawn to dusk with the sound of aerial contraception.

The instructor beckons the next shooter to the stand, checks that the trap operator is ready, and shouts 'Pull!' The party gazes skywards, waiting for the next target to appear.

'Right,' mutters the instructor, 'here it comes. Now, remember . . . Oh my God!'

Instead of a three-inch disc of baked pitch, they're staring at a huge bird, with a wingspan of maybe fifty feet, wingtip to wingtip, holding in its claws what looks like a big red Mercedes bus. As the shadow of this monstrosity passes over them they stand rooted to the spot, unable to move.

'What the hell was that?'

'It's finally happened,' the instructor groans. 'The bastards have out-evolved us.'

'Did you see the *size* of that thing?'

'And the armour-plated cargo hold,' whispers an awestruck trainee. 'Oh God, it doesn't bear thinking about. What're we going to do?'

'Out of our hands now,' the instructor mutters. 'You boys stay here. I'm going to try and get a message through to Strategic Air Command.'

The phoenix, blissfully unaware that at that very moment nine F-111s of the 3085 Family Planning Squadron were on standby awaiting clearance to take off in search of it, lowered the coach to the ground as gently as it could, waggled its wingtips in salutation, and soared away. The sound of its giant wings faded into the distance. The cuckoo resumed its song. On the hillside opposite, a cow mooed.

Inside the coach, John Fingers levered himself up from behind the seats where he'd been cowering during the flight and rose unsteadily to his feet. His face was as white as a sheet in a soap-powder commercial and the hand with the gun in it shook disconcertingly.

'Okay,' he whimpered. 'This is a hijack, I want you to fly

this coach to Tripoli ...' He looked round, realised that there was nobody to hear him, and sat down heavily in the driver's seat.

Where was everybody?

A brief inspection revealed that the rear door of the coach was open. The bastards had gone and left him there. He was all alone.

Almost alone. On the back row of seats he found three slumped figures; two men and the girl. In spite of the phoenix's best endeavours there had been quite a sharp jolt on landing, and by the looks of it they'd been thrown forwards and knocked out cold by things falling off the luggage racks. John Fingers hesitated for a moment. On the one hand, he scarpers quickest who scarpers alone. On the other hand, when the going gets really tough, a boy's best friend is his hostage.

One of the men he recognised as the big, evil-looking bugger who'd been on the point of coming after him with a big spanner when the police intervened. The other one was the tall, slim sod who'd shot at him when he first wandered into Unit 13. Those two, he decided, would keep. The girl, however, was a different matter. The word HOSTAGE was practically tattooed on her forehead.

'You,' he said, prodding Michelle with the gun. 'On your feet.'

No good. She was out for the count. Damn, muttered John Fingers to himself, more heavy lifting. Having got her in a burglar's lift (basically the same as a fireman's lift, but not quite so humane) he staggered towards the open door and peered out, asking himself why his thirty-nine erstwhile henchmen had taken off so suddenly, without stopping to say goodbye or even steal his boots.

'Because of the fighters,' said the air-conditioning. 'Look, they're just coming back now.'

John Fingers frowned. 'What fighters?' he said.

'Those ones there.'

'What? Oh *those* . . .'

Sudden turns of speed, with or without heavy burdens slung over the right shoulder, ran in the Smith family. He was just able to make it down the coach steps and into the cover of a nearby pile of rocks when the nine fighter-bombers of the 3085th, squadron motto *Not tonight, Josephine*, screamed back over the skyline, hurtled straight at the coach, let fly with their full complement of air-to-surface missiles and pulled steeply away. The shock of the blast hit John Fingers like a hammer, sending him rolling down the escarpment into a clump of gorse. From where he was, he could actually feel the heat from the explosion on the back of his neck. He had the common sense to stay where he was until it had stopped raining shrapnel and debris; then he hauled himself upright, pulled gorse out of his hands and knees and looked round for his hostage.

He found her sitting up, wiping blood out of her eyes from a cut on her forehead. She opened her mouth to scream, but he showed her the gun and made shushing noises.

'On your feet,' he said, wishing he'd paid better attention to his mother when she'd tried to teach him elementary kidnapping. 'Shut up and do what you're told or I'll use this. Understand?'

'Who's *this*, the cat's mother?' muttered the gun, offended. He ignored it. Formal introductions would just have to wait until later.

Her eyes fixed on the gun, Michelle nodded. Something told her that it was going to take more than a steady nerve and a certain innate skill at board games to get her out of this one. Unlike her abduction by Akram, this all felt rather horribly real.

(Which was strange, bearing in mind where she was. Just over the brow of the hill, a cat was practising the violin, while

557

the dish was sulking because the spoon had forgotten to bring the sandwiches. But she wasn't to know that.)

'All right,' said John Fingers. 'Now start walking. And no funny business.'

'Spoilsport,' the gun grumbled. 'It's been ages since I last saw a really good custard pie fight.'

'Shut up, you.'

'Who, me?'

'Not you. It. Look, will everybody just shut up and get the hell out of here, before those bloody planes come back and blast us all to kingdom come?'

Had circumstances been different, Michelle would have liked to ask what planes, and how come he was talking to his gun? Actually, she had a strange feeling she knew the answer to the second question; and if the purpose of answers is to clear up mysteries, then it couldn't be more counterproductive if it tried. Something told her, however, that her captor wasn't in the mood. She started to walk.

Akram woke up.

It was dark. He was in a confined space. Something wet was dripping down the back of his neck.

Oh shit, not again! He drew in breath to scream, then hesitated. He could smell oil, but it wasn't the right sort. Not palm oil; something more in the SAE 20 super visco-static line, he fancied. Which was either a half-hearted attempt at updating the story and making it more accessible for modern audiences, or an indication that whatever he was in, at least it wasn't the familiar old smelly brown stuff.

Cue past life? Apparently not. Things were looking up.

Well, then. The last thing he could remember was being bundled onto a coach by Faisal and Hakim, with whom he intended to have a word on that subject when he saw them next. And then the coach had sort of taken off, and something had hit him on the top of his head.

Talking of which; what *was* this stuff dripping down his neck? If he could only get his arms to work, maybe he could find out.

Cheap Taiwanese arms, no good, pity they're not still under warranty. Legs? That's more like it. He pushed, until the top of his head came up against something solid that didn't want to get out of the way. Hmm. Interesting scenario, this.

Still no past life? No? Okay, fine. Let's try bringing the knees up and pushing outwards with the feet. Bloody uncomfortable, but no worse than a Jane Fonda workout routine.

Hello, Akram said to himself, I'm in a box. How jolly. Now then, what sort of box? Well, there's one obvious type, the kind with brass handles, satin lining and a flat lid. Now then, senses, best of order, please. Any satin? No, no satin. I think we can tentatively call that a good sign.

Maybe I'm still on the coach. There's no real reason to assume that I am, but let's pretend. If I'm still on the coach but I'm in a box . . . Cue schematic diagram of a typical coach. Ah yes, the bit under the windows where there's doors on the outside, where they store the suitcases. The luggage compartment. I could very easily be in that.

Why, for fuck's sake?

Yes, but just suppose I am. In that case, if I can wriggle round until my feet are touching the doors, and then give said doors a bloody hard kick, maybe I can open them. Anything's possible. Houdini, for example, did this sort of thing for a living.

His heels made contact with what could conceivably have been doors; a flat surface that flexed ever so slightly when he pressed against it. Time, he muttered to himself, to put the theory to the test. After all, what else is scientific enquiry of any sort other than a controlled version of bashing one's head against the Universe until something gives?

He drew his knees back and let fly. Something gave; he tried again, and the doors flew open. A few crab-like jerks and shuffles extricated him from the luggage compartment and landed him on the ground, where he lay for a moment, luxuriating in the rare, delicious sensation of having got something completely right for a change. Then he looked up.

Where the coach had been there was an untidy-looking jumble of tangled, fire-blackened metal. True, it had once been a coach, in the same way that homo sapiens was once a monkey or, more appropriately, Great Britain was once a leading exporter of manufactured goods. As far as he could see, all that was left of it was the luggage compartment he'd just wriggled out of, and a couple of skipfuls of twisted body panel. All in all, it had the same air of bewildered ruin that you'd expect from a short-sighted mugger who's just tried to rob Arnold Schwarzenegger.

Wow, said Akram to himself, whatever happened to that coach, I survived it. Lucky.

Not lucky. There isn't enough luck in the whole universe to save someone from destruction like that. Somebody must have saved me.

Shit. Somebody must *like* me.

Or else, more likely, somebody must hate me enough to believe that being blown to bits in an explosion would be tantamount to giving me a pardon and the freedom of the city. In any event, whoever they were, they don't seem to be around any more. Surprise, surprise.

Having dealt with these and similar issues, Akram scrambled to his feet, yelped with pain as cramp and a wide variety of pulled muscles made their presence felt, and tried to get his bearings. Not that he had much to go on; the landscape was about as familiar as downtown Ursa Minor Beta and slightly less hospitable. As far as the eye could see, provided that it could be bothered, there was nothing but scrub, rock and parched earth. There were a few low, demoralised-looking hills, some clumps of tired and thirsty-looking gorse, and the occasional pile of boulders. The most creative travel brochure writer living could just about get away with *totally unspoilt* and *well away from the normal tourist areas*, and would be forced to leave it at that.

'Gosh,' said Akram aloud, 'so this is where I end up when I'm being *lucky*. I can't wait to see where I land when I'm going through a bad patch.'

''Scuse me?'

The voice had come from behind one of the piles of rocks. Instinctively, Akram held still and turned his head in that direction.

'Hello?' he said.

'Hello yourself. Who're you, then?'

'Who wants to know?'

'Me,' said the voice, 'and actually I'm not really bothered about it, so if you don't want to tell me, then fuck you. Are you responsible for all this mess?'

'No,' Akram replied. 'Are you?'

'Do me a favour,' the voice said. There was a shuffling movement behind the rocks, and a unicorn trotted into view. It was the size of a small Shetland pony, rice-pudding coloured and chewing something in a half-interested manner. If its voice was anything to go by, it had either been born in south London or spent a long time there. There was a whisky-bottle cork on the end of its horn.

Akram stared at it, and his jaw dropped to such an extent that a passing ant could have used it as a staircase to get to his moustache. 'Oh hell,' he said eventually. 'I'm back, aren't I?'

'Don't ask me, mate. All depends,' it added, 'on where you just been. So, if this isn't your mess, whose is it?'

Akram shrugged. 'Don't ask me,' he said. 'Last thing I knew, I was in a coach being carried by a huge bird,

561

somewhere over Southampton. Then there's a bit I seem to have missed, after which I was wedged into the luggage compartment of that wreck over there. I was starting to think that perhaps things were getting a bit weird, but if I'm back in some blasted story. . .'

Something caught his eye and he stopped speaking. Poking out from under the crumpled chassis were a pair of small, elegant ladies' shoes, with brass buckles and buttons up the side. The unicorn was looking at them, too.

'I got you,' it said. 'You were in this house in, where was it you said? Southampton?'

'That's right,' Akram replied. 'Actually, it wasn't a house so much as a coach, but we'll let that slide for the moment. The obvious question's got to be, are there any tin men, lions, scarecrows, witches or yellow brick roads anywhere in these parts?'

'No.'

'Bright green cities? Munchkins? Insufferably cute nine-year-old girls from the American grain belt? Wizards?'

The unicorn shook its head. 'Never seen any,' it said. 'You reckon you might have come down in the wrong place?'

'Very possibly,' Akram replied, taking another look at the immediate vicinity and shuddering a little. 'Mind you, it'd take a pretty extreme set of circumstances for this to be the right place for anything. Has it got a name, by any chance?'

'Home,' the unicorn replied. 'That's what I call it, anyhow. And it may not be the garden of bloody Eden, but that still doesn't mean it's improved by having scrap metal scattered all over it. You planning to clear it up, or what?'

'Not really,' Akram said. 'You wouldn't happen to know whose shoes those are poking out from under there, would you?'

'Not got a clue, mate.' The unicorn thought for a moment, rubbing behind its ear with a raised foreleg. 'I'll tell you one thing, though. Last few weeks or so, everything's been up the pictures a bit. Things drifting in that don't fit, if you get my meaning. Like, a few hours before all this lot turned up, we had a bloke come through here wanting to know if I'd come across a ninety-foot-high beanstalk. Day before yesterday there was this bird drooping around asking if I'd seen her sheep. Two days before that, we had the King of Spain's daughter asking which way to the little nut tree. And now,' it added reproachfully, 'you. I think something's cocked up somewhere and they haven't yet sussed out how to fix it.' The unicorn hesitated, shuffled its hooves, looked the other way and cleared its throat. 'Talking of which,' it continued, with a trace of embarrassment, 'you haven't noticed any stray virgins wandering about the place, have you? It's not for me, you understand, it's for my friend. . .'

Akram and the unicorn looked at each other for a moment.

'The shoes,' they said in chorus.

'Not,' the unicorn added, as it braced itself against the remains of the coach and pushed, 'that they're what you'd call your typical virgin's footwear. Too much heel, for a start. Your typical virgin's more into the sensible, hard-wearing, value-for-money ranges. Those or slingbacks. Ready?'

'Ready.'

They heaved, and the charred bulk shifted. At the last moment Akram, rather to his own surprise, looked away.

'Well?' he said.

'Well,' the unicorn replied, ''tisn't a virgin, at any rate.'

'Oh,' said Akram. 'How on earth can you tell?'

'Because,' the unicorn answered, 'I don't think that sort of thing, you know, applies to suitcases. I mean, where little suitcases come from is either a department store or a mail order catalogue. Must be dead boring, being a suitcase.'

They examined the remains.

'Pretty extreme way of getting it to shut,' the unicorn said.

563

'Usually, just sitting on 'em does the trick.'

'Quite,' Akram replied, puzzled. What had a suitcase full of female clothing been doing on the coach, he asked himself. It wasn't Michelle's, as far as he could judge, and he reckoned he knew the thirty-nine thieves well enough by now to rule them out, too. Which left Ali Baba, the interloper he'd had the fight with, or somebody else he hadn't noticed. Or. . .

An icicle of guilt stabbed his heart. He'd forgotten. . .

'Fang!' he shouted. The unicorn looked at him.

'What?'

'Fang,' Akram repeated. 'My tooth fairy. Where the hell has she got to?'

No sooner had the words passed through the luggage carousel of his larynx than there was a flash of lightning, a shower of silver sparkles and a clap of melodious thunder; and—

Akram stared.

'Fang?'

The tall, slender, gorgeous creature standing before him smiled and nodded. 'You remembered,' she said. 'Eventually,' she added. 'I expect you're a terror for forgetting birthdays, too.'

At this point the unicorn whistled, stepped forward, sniffed at her embarrassingly, shook its mane in disappointment and walked pointedly away, leaving Fang blushing furiously. Akram, meanwhile, managed to get his lower jaw back into place and made a vague gesture to suggest that Fang had grown a bit since he'd last seen her. 'What happened to you, then?' he said.

'I crossed the Line, dumbo. Hey, I *like* it here, it's got all sorts of possibilities. An elf can, you know, really walk tall on this side.'

Akram frowned. 'Quite,' he said. 'But before that. The last I saw of you was when we were. . .'

'Why have you parked your bus on my suitcase?'

'*Your* suitcase?' Akram quickly stooped down. Sure enough, the sponge bag was full of . . . He zipped it up again, quickly.

'At last,' Fang was saying, 'I can cash that lot in. I got the address of a tooth broker over in the Emerald City who pays top dollar for quality stuff.'

'The last time I saw you,' Akram persevered, 'you were with that loser Baba. He captured you, right? And I didn't rescue you,' he added.

Fang shrugged. 'Actually, he's not so bad. Professionally, of course, he's a pretty useful contact. And anyway, it's me owes you the apology, since I did sort of lead him straight to where you were hiding out.'

'Ah.'

'But,' Fang went on, 'that's all right, too, because when the jet fighters from the family planning service blasted the coach to bits, I grabbed you and put you in the luggage compartment where I knew you'd be safe. That,' she added meaningfully, 'was before I knew you'd parked the damn thing on top of my suitcase.'

'That was *you*?'

Fang nodded. 'Talk about difficult,' she said, with feeling. 'Not you two; that blasted girl of yours. Must be because she's half-human. She took a real crack on the head when the bus landed; for a minute there I thought she'd had her chips.'

'Us two?'

'In the end I had to clap my hands and yell, "I *do* believe in mortals," at the top of my voice. You can't begin to imagine how conspicuous that makes you feel.'

'Us two?'

'Um.' Fang put her hands behind her back and looked away. 'Yup. You and the, er, dentist.'

'You mean to tell me you saved that *bastard*?'

Fang nodded. 'For you,' she said quickly. 'Last thing you'd

565

want, I'd have thought, is for him to slip through your fingers by dying before you could. . .'

'Oh, right,' Akram interrupted, scowling. 'I'm sure that's exactly how it was. And no teeth changed hands at any stage, needless to say.'

'No they didn't,' Fang replied angrily. 'Wasn't time, for one thing. You reckon it's easy grabbing hold of two grown men and shoving them in luggage holds in the time it takes for a jet fighter to fire a rocket? Try it sometime and see.'

'Luggage hold.'

'The other one,' Fang explained. 'On the other side of the coach.'

Akram nodded, and a smile started to seep through onto his face. 'So with any luck,' he said, 'the bugger might still be there. Unconscious.'

'No, he isn't.'

Akram whirled round, to see Ali Baba standing directly behind him. In one hand he had the gun, and in the other a galvanised iron bucket, from which steam was rising.

Cue past life.

CHAPTER NINETEEN

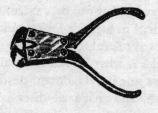

'Hello,' Akram said.

A wry smile shuffled across Ali Baba's face. 'To put it mildly,' he replied. 'Now then, let's get this over and done with before the water gets cold.'

Dragging his attention back from a particularly vivid reprise of a certain night at Farouk's in Samarkand (he never could remember her name and the flashback always petered out round about the fourth veil; even so, it was probably his favourite bit), Akram raised his hands slowly into the air.

'Where's Michelle?' he asked.

Ali Baba shrugged. 'Safe, I hope. I think she must have made a run for it, because the thief chap seemed to be looking for her when I crept up and bashed him. I'll go and look for her after I've dealt with you.'

'You feel that's necessary, do you?'

Ali Baba nodded. 'Since we're back on this side of the Line again, and since I have you defenceless and at my mercy, I think it might be a good idea. Now, are you going to hold still while I pour this lot over you, or do I have to kneecap you first?'

A series of lightning-fast calculations, involving the distance to the nearest cover, ditto between Ali Baba and himself, the probability (to three decimal places) of not getting shot if he made a break for it and sundry other relevant factors, flitted through Akram's mind. To give the program time to run, he temporised. 'Seems to me,' he said, 'you had all those that time I came to see you about my teeth. Why didn't you do it then?'

Ali Baba shrugged. 'That was over there,' he replied, 'here's here. Back flipside, I'm a peace-loving humanitarian dentist whose life is devoted to curing pain rather than inflicting it – which, I might add, is what I'd rather do, if it was up to me. But it isn't. On this side I'm the instant-dead-bandit-just-add-boiling-water man, and that's all there is to it. I guess a stereotype's gotta do what a stereotype's gotta do. By the way, if you think you can get out of it by keeping me talking till the water cools down, forget it, because I'd just as soon shoot you through the head as boil you. Ready?'

He raised the gun, and then lowered it again. 'Do you mind?' he said irritably. 'I'm trying to kill someone here.'

'Tough,' replied Fang, who was now standing directly in front of Akram. 'Go pick on someone your own size.'

Ali Baba made a few mental measurements. 'You, for instance,' he suggested. 'If you insist, I'm quite happy to blow you away too, because all I've got to do is clap and you'll come back to life. Nice try, all the same.' He frowned and looked down at the gun. 'Yes, all right, I'm being as quick as I can. Just try and be patient, will you?'

'I see you got the ring back, then.'

'Yes, and don't change the subject.' He put down the bucket and assumed a tidy two-handed grip on the gun. 'Like that? Left hand a bit further forward? God, you're fussy. And no, I don't give a damn if it does tickle.'

'It's all right, Fang,' said Akram. He was trying very, very hard not to look directly over Ali Baba's left shoulder. 'You stay out of this. It's a very brave thing you're doing, but. . .'

Fang was now also not looking in the same direction. 'All right,' she said. 'Well, so long. It was really nice knowing you. Thanks for the shoebox.'

'You're welcome. It was a pleasure.'

'On the count of three,' Ali Baba said, taking aim. 'Ready or not.'

A slight buzz of panic threatened to cloud Akram's mind but he fought it back. 'One last thing,' he said. 'That root fill you did for me.'

'Bit academic now.'

'I realise that. But I thought I'd mention it anyway. It's been giving me rather a lot of gyp lately.'

'It can't do,' Ali Baba said, his brow furrowing. 'I removed the nerve, there's nothing left in there to hurt. You must be imagining it.'

Akram shrugged. 'If only,' he said. 'But, like you say, that's neither here nor there. It's lucky for you I'll be dead in three seconds, isn't it? Otherwise you'd have had to go back in and sort it all out.'

'It was a perfectly good job,' Ali Baba retorted. 'I can't help it if you've got an unusually vivid imag—'

He didn't complete the word because, at that precise moment, Michelle crept up the last eighteen inches, grabbed the bucket and emptied it over his head. The gun, muttering something about if you want a job doing properly, fired two shots, but Ali Baba's hands were flailing wildly about, and all he managed to do was scare off the unicorn; which, after a perfunctory sniff at Michelle, was about to leave anyway.

'Kill him!' Fang shouted. 'Go on, get the gun, and—'

'No.' Akram, having relieved Ali Baba of the pistol, put on the safety and dropped it into his pocket. Since he didn't have the ring, he was spared the gun's views on recent events, which was probably just as well.

'Everybody finished?' said Michelle, standing in front of her father and folding her arms in what Akram mentally categorised as a what-time-do-you-call-this manner. 'Splendid. By the way,' she added, taking a long look at Fang, 'who's your girlfriend?'

Akram sighed, sat down on a rock and cupped his chin in his hands. 'It's a long story,' he said.

'Yeah,' muttered the Godfather unpleasantly. 'But not long enough.'

'Don't be so impatient,' replied his wife. 'You ain't seen nothing yet.'

'Aziz.'

'Yeah?'

'We've forgotten something.'

'Yeah? What?'

'The Skip, for one.'

'Or rather, two,' added a thief, using his fingers as a makeshift abacus. 'Akram and the new bloke.'

'Bugger,' Aziz said. 'There's always something, isn't there? Right, we'll have to go back.'

Even as he said it, a tiny voice perked up in the back of his mind and said *Why, exactly?* After all, a leader's job is to lead, not be fetched like a kiddie from playschool. 'When we've finished these,' he added.

Quite how there came to be an inn, miles off the beaten track in the middle of a thousand square miles of scrub, sand and rock, the thieves hadn't bothered to ask. For all they knew, it might be an exciting new form of virtual-reality mirage. If so, the virtual beer was nicely chilled and the virtual kebabs done to a turn. As for the dancing girls, they were virtually. . .

'No rush,' agreed Shamir, his mouth full of barbecued goat. 'In fact, we'd probably be better off waiting for him here. I mean, this is the obvious place to look for us. If we're all wandering around looking for each other it'll only make matters worse.'

'Especially since there's two of them now,' Hakim agreed.

'Good point.'

'Better than one,' added Rustem, sagely. 'Two heads, I mean.'

Aziz leant back in his chair and let his belt out a notch. 'Well,' he said, 'if we're going to be stuck here till they show up, we might as well have a drink and something to eat.'

'Another drink,' Hakim pointed out. 'And something else to eat.'

'Good idea, though. For all we know, it may be several days' march to the next mirage.'

Aziz nodded. 'We were lucky to find this joint,' he said. A little bell rang in his head as he said it, but he ignored it. 'Nice to have it to ourselves, as well.'

'It's always better if you come to these places out of season,' Faisal agreed. 'That way, you don't get the Germans hogging the pool.'

'What pool?'

'The swimming pool.'

Aziz frowned. 'What swim— Oh, right, I can see it now.' Funny, he couldn't help reflecting, could have sworn it wasn't there a moment ago. Maybe it was all a mirage after all. He pushed the idea around the plate of his mind like a piece of cold broccoli and decided to leave it. So it's a mirage; so what? At least it didn't have the Schmidt family from Düsseldorf sitting all round the edge of it in deck chairs. 'I could just fancy a quick dip in a minute,' he said. Assuming the water holds still long enough, added his subconscious. Then he cleared his mind of all such distractions, finished off his beer and waved to the waitress. 'Here, miss,' he said. 'I'd like a loaf of bread, jug of the house white, collected works of Omar Khayyam, a tree and what time do you get off work?'

John Fingers opened his eyes.

Usually when he woke up with a headache, the worst thing he had to worry about was where he'd left his trousers the night before. On this occasion he still had his trousers, but that constituted pretty much the whole of the credit side of the ledger. Just a small selection of the things he didn't have, on the other hand, were the gun, the ring, the girl and the faintest idea where he was. All in all, he'd have given a lot to be back in his nice familiar cell.

Self-pity was all very well; but fine notions jemmy no windows, as his old granny used to say. He sat up, rubbed the bump on the back of his head, and considered his position.

The bump was a pretty substantial clue, he reckoned. Obviously, while he'd been chasing about after that bloody girl, someone had crept up behind him and belted him one. He scribbled in *terrible vengeance* at the foot of his mental agenda, staggered to his feet and looked around.

'They went that way.' He was so used by now to disembodied voices that he'd gone twenty yards before it occurred to him that since (a) there were no electrical appliances visible in this awful wilderness and (b) he'd lost the ring anyway, he ought to be excused hearing voices, and it wasn't fair.

'Who's that?' he demanded.

'Down here.'

He looked down. Nothing but the dusty ground, his toecaps and his shadow.

A shadow. Not necessarily his.

'Huh?' he said.

It could, of course, be something to do with the bashing, and being out in the blazing desert sun without a hat; but that was almost certainly just wishful thinking. Either the light was playing silly buggers with him, or that wasn't his shadow.

'Please,' he moaned. 'Tell me it's all my imagination.'

'I can if you want me to,' replied the voice affably. 'I'd rather not if you don't mind, though. Call me old-fashioned, but I don't like lying to people I've only just met.'

'You're not my shadow, are you?'

'I am now.'

'Fine. Can I go home now, please?'

The shadow seemed to flicker slightly. 'You are home,' it said.

'Oh, really?' John Fingers toyed with the idea of jumping hard on the shadow's head but dismissed it. 'This is some bit of Southampton I never got around to seeing, is it? Easy enough to miss, a bloody great big desert. Probably sandwiched in between the docks and the new shopping precinct.'

'I'm so glad you've got a sense of humour,' replied the shadow cheerfully. 'I've got this feeling we're going to get along famously.'

John Fingers sighed, and sat down on a convenient tree-stump. Oh, his heart sighed within him, for the stately Victorian architecture, the vibrant atmosphere of the mess hall, the almost sensuous texture of the mailbag between his fingers and, when Old Mister Sun winked at him over the western horizon, the cool monastic solitude of dear old B583. In his time he'd said a great many harsh and unkind things about prison, but at that precise moment he'd have given all the magic silver rings in the universe to be back where you could tell the bad guys by their clothes and the locks didn't whisper things about you behind your back.

'I could run away,' he said aloud.

'You what?'

'I could wait till nightfall,' said John Fingers, 'when there's no sun and no shadows; then I could run away and you'd never have a clue where to find me.'

'Try it. See how far you'd get.'

Maybe, John Fingers theorised, it's only bluffing. After all, it's only a shadow. From what he could remember of his education, a shadow is basically nothing but an absence of light caused by one's body getting in the way of the sun; but he'd been parolled before they'd got to that part of the course, so he couldn't be certain. There was something in the voice inside his head that suggested otherwise.

'Want to try an experiment?'

'No,' John Fingers replied. 'We did those in science O level when I was in the Scrubs, we had to cut up frogs and things. And there was stuff with iron filings and magnets, too. No offence, but I don't think we've got time.'

'We'll try an experiment. Walk forwards. Go on, there's no catch. I'm going to stay here. If you walk away, I won't try and follow you.'

'Straight up?'

'On my word as a two-dimensional optical effect.'

'Okay.' John Fingers shrugged, grinned and remained rooted to the spot.

'Go on, then.'

'I'm trying.'

It was just, he couldn't help remembering, like when he'd been a kid and he and Ginger Bagworth used to play Ronnie and Reggie. An intrinsic part of every session was make-believe setting your opponent's feet in concrete and chucking him off the dock, and one time Ginger actually got hold of some quick-drying cement from somewhere and filled the cardboard box with it . . . Just like that, only several degrees of intensity worse.

'Now,' continued the voice smugly, 'let's go for a walk.'

Before he knew much more about it, John Fingers was marching briskly along at a smart pace, four miles per hour or so. Backwards. What really impressed him was the way he carefully walked round a tree-stump he hadn't even known was there.

'Satisfied?'

John Fingers took a deep breath. 'If I do exactly what you tell me,' he said, 'will you promise never to do anything like that again?'

'Maybe.'

'Fancy telling me how you do that?'

'Actually,' said the shadow, 'I could explain, but you wouldn't understand. If you hadn't spent all your time in those science classes trying to make dynamite, perhaps you could follow it, but it's too late now.'

'All right,' said John Fingers wearily. 'Now will you let go of me?'

'Sure.'

A moment later, he was on his face in the dust. Slowly, as if expecting his own teeth to bite him, he hauled himself to his feet and dusted himself off.

'So,' he sighed. 'What do you want me to do?'

'Excuse me,' Ali Baba said, his voice reverberating loudly, 'but would anybody mind if I took this bucket off my head?'

Akram nodded, realised that this wasn't much use in the circumstances and said, 'Fine, go ahead. You all right, by the way?' he added. 'I thought that water was supposed to be boiling hot.'

Ali Baba looked at him. 'It was,' he replied, 'once upon a time. But you kept me standing around chatting so long it went lukewarm. So, no ill effects. Thank you,' he added, puzzled, 'for asking. Why?'

'No reason,' Akram replied. 'I was just concerned, that's all.'

'Concerned?' Ali Baba narrowed his eyes, until his eyebrows looked like one continuous furry hedge. 'You're not supposed to be concerned. What's got into you?'

That, Akram realised, was a very good question; except that

it was more a case of what had left him. 'The shadow,' he murmured. 'Here, it's gone. I haven't got a shadow at all. Hey, can you see a shadow?'

'Now you mention it. . .'

'That explains it,' said Akram, grinning. 'Somehow or other I've managed to give the wretched thing the slip. It means—' He hesitated, his manner rather like that of a Greek philosopher who, halfway down the High Street with no bathrobe and the loofah still in his hand, is asked to explain exactly what useful purpose the shattering new concept he's just stumbled across is designed to achieve, other than getting the bathmat wet.

'Well?'

Akram shrugged. 'For a start,' he said, 'it means I don't have to kill you if I don't want to. Hell, I don't have to kill *anyone* if I don't want to. That's pretty remarkable, when you come to think of it.'

A small but irreverent noise from Fang indicated that she wasn't so sure. 'I don't get it,' she said. 'I go weeks at a time without killing anybody. Everywhere you look, there's people not killing anybody. Sure it's nice, but I wouldn't hold your breath waiting to be invited on chat shows.'

'You wouldn't understand,' Akram replied, pulling the clip out of the gun and drawing the round from the breech. 'As far as I'm concerned, it's bloody marvellous.'

'Odd you should mention it,' Ali Baba interrupted. He turned the bucket over, put it on the ground and sat on it. 'I think I must be feeling the same way. For instance, if someone were to bring me Akram's head on a platter right now, I'd probably ask them to take it away and fetch me a simple cheese salad instead.'

All four of them were silent. It was one of those peak-in-Darien moments, with Akram and Ali Baba being stout Cortes, and Michelle and Fang bringing up the rear, so to speak, unable to tell whether the boss is undergoing a deep spiritual experience, or has just remembered he'd forgotten to feed the goldfish before leaving Spain. When the inscrutability of it all got too much for her, Michelle cleared her throat and politely asked if someone would explain to her precisely what the hell was going on.

Ali Baba and Akram looked at each other.

'I don't think we're a hundred per cent sure,' Ali Baba said. 'All we do know is, your man here and I have been trying to kill each other since the Bible was still in copyright, and now we don't want to any more.' He glanced at Akram and raised an eyebrow. 'You agree with that?' he asked.

'Sure. It's a bit disconcerting,' Akram replied. 'On the one hand it's a really great feeling, like waking up and realising you haven't got to go to work ever again. On the other hand, there is this nagging question of what the hell we're going to do with the rest of our lives.'

'You want a suggestion?' said Fang crisply. 'Bearing in mind that between you, presumably, you know where there's this huge hoard of gold, silver and precious stones, guarded by a magic door to which you happen to know the password? Ho hum, it sure beats me. If I was in your shoes, I'd be absolutely flummoxed.'

'You mean,' said Ali Baba slowly, 'we split the treasure between us and go and sort of – do something with it? Rather than just fight over it, I mean?'

'The verb *to spend* keeps popping into my mind in this context,' Fang muttered, 'can't imagine why.'

'Could we, do you think?' Ali Baba asked uncertainly. 'It'd mean the end of the Story, for good and all. If there's no treasure, the whole thing falls to bits. No treasure, nothing to steal, nothing to fight about. Hey, that's neat.'

Fang nodded enthusiastically. 'Mind you,' she added, 'it wouldn't be fair to expect you boys to do all that spending by yourselves. I mean, that'd be one hell of a responsibility to saddle you with. I couldn't live with myself if I thought I'd lumbered you with a rotten job like that.'

'Many hands,' Michelle agreed, 'make light work. You can put me down for a share, too.'

A strange light glowed in Akram's eyes. 'This is remarkable,' he said. 'We could really fix the bloody Story good and proper, you know? I mean, I could spend my share on famine relief or helping refugees or something.'

'Or a free dental hospital,' Ali Baba added. 'Hey, wouldn't that be something?'

'You bet.'

Much more of this, Fang reckoned, and she'd need a paper bag, quickly. 'Hey,' she said, 'are you guys for real?'

'No,' Akram admitted, 'but we're working on it. Which reminds me; we'd have to find some way of getting the stuff back over the Line. If we stay here, it'll make itself into a brand new Story, and we'll be in just as much trouble as we are already. Any suggestions?'

'What about the ring?' Michelle put in. 'It must be good for something other than passing the time of day with household appliances.'

'Excuse me.'

'Not now,' replied Ali Baba, 'we're busy. I think she's got a point there. If we could find a way of—'

'Excuse me.'

'I said not now. All we'd have to do— Why are you all staring at me?'

'We were wondering,' Fang said quietly, 'who you keep saying *Not now* to.'

'What? Oh.' Ali Baba looked round. 'Actually,' he confessed, 'I'm not entirely sure.'

'Me.'

'I think it's coming from inside your pocket,' Ali Baba said.

'What, you mean the gun?'

'Could be.'

'No could be about it, you clown. Get me loaded quick, before—'

Before, it was just about to say, John Fingers and the thirty-nine thieves complete their classic encircling movement and have you completely surrounded. By then, however, it was too late, and so it didn't bother.

CHAPTER TWENTY

'Actually,' said Scheherezade, 'that wasn't supposed to happen.'

The Godfather gave her a long, cold look. 'Really,' he said. 'You amaze me.'

'I do?'

'I go to all the trouble,' the Godfather continued, 'of arranging for Baba and the big bad guy—'

'Akram.'

'Akram to cross the Line. I make it so they can fight each other. I got everything ready so we can start easing our way in over there.' He closed his eyes, and a look of great sadness crossed his face. 'And now you come to me and say, Look, I goofed, they've all come back. Honey, I'm disappointed. I expected better of you.'

Scheherezade squirmed a little. Only once or twice before had she heard the Godfather express himself so forcibly. Disappointed; judges used to put on little black hats to say more comforting things than that.

'I don't know how it could have happened,' she said

awkwardly. 'It's like they're making their own story. It's weird, I'm telling you.'

The Godfather's left eyebrow lifted a quarter of an inch. 'You don't say?'

'It's bizarre, it really is. Like, this realside thief John Fingers has sort of turned into Akram, Akram's acting more like the hero than the hero is himself, and now I got this Michelle person and a goddamn tooth fairy to fit in somehow.' She swallowed, aware that perhaps she wasn't making life any easier, or longer, for herself by dwelling in too much detail on the problems. 'But,' she said, heaping three tablespoons of positive vibes into her voice and stirring frantically, 'you just leave it with me and I know I'll have it sorted before you can say open. . .'

'No.' The Godfather lifted his head and blew a plume of cigar smoke at the ceiling. 'I had it up to here with these guys. Going off on a story of their own, they show me no respect. What can you do with such people? So, I figure it's time we cut our losses and move on.'

'You mean,' Scheherezade asked, 'leave them to their own devices? Let them get on with it?'

'No.' The Godfather shook his head and looked away. 'I mean kill them all.'

Scheherezade shuddered just a little. That'd be right, she muttered to herself. The Godfather didn't so much cut losses as hack, slash, slit and hew them. Not that he was a bad loser or anything; he was just the sort of person who, having bought a single ticket for the National Lottery and failed to win the jackpot, would have all the winners systematically kneecapped as a matter of course. Still, she reflected, rather them than me; although the two options are by no means mutually exclusive. The Godfather, she knew from long experience, didn't suffer fools gladly; with him it was more a case of being glad when fools suffered.

'Good idea,' she mumbled. 'You want me to, er, put Rocco onto it?'

'No.' The Godfather shook his head. 'He's got better things to do. You deal with it, okay?'

Scheherezade swallowed hard, difficult when her throat was suddenly dry. 'Me?' she said. Immediately she realised that that wasn't the most amazingly intelligent thing said in the history of the Universe by anybody ever. 'Gosh, thanks, I'd love to,' she added quickly, 'it's so kind of you to let me do it, that'll be a real treat.' But the damage was done; she had that extremely negative feeling you sometimes get when you're climbing stairs with a huge stack of plates in your arms, and just as you're at the top you put your foot on a place where a stair ought to be but isn't. It was at that moment that an idea, totally wild, extreme and unthinkable but at the same time the one and only logical course of action now open to her, started to peck tentatively at the inside of its shell. As soon as she became aware of it, she had to use every last milligram of self-control she had left to prevent it showing in her face.

'You got a problem with that?' the Godfather demanded.

'Absolutely not,' she replied.

'Skip.'

In a profession almost as ancient and even more honourable than his own, John Fingers reflected, they had a saying about never working with children and animals. Which category Aziz fell into, he wasn't quite certain, although he had a shrewd idea it was both.

'Well?' he grunted.

'Are we nearly there yet?'

John Fingers raised his eyes to Heaven. Hey, God, he muttered to himself, I wish you existed so I could hate you. 'How the hell would I know?' he growled. 'I keep telling you clowns, I've never been here before in my life. It's your weird bloody country or dimension or whatever it is. Also,' he remembered, 'it's your goddamn hideout. It's where you idiots *live*, for crying out loud. Surely you know how to find it by now.'

'No, Skip.'

Although he'd been convinced that his ability to be amazed by stupidity had already worn out through over-use, John Fingers was prepared to admit he was wrong. 'You *don't*?' he said. 'Why the hell not?'

'Because we always follow you, Skip. Because you're our leader.'

'But . . .' Some basic self-preservation instinct warned John Fingers that if he tried to argue the point, all that would happen would be that his top-joint-of-one-finger grip on reality would give way and his brain would probably implode, like a dying star. 'Okay,' he said. 'Ask the prisoners. I expect they know.'

'Okay, Skip. Skip.'

'Now what?'

'What'll we do if they don't?'

In moments of extreme stress, John Fingers found it helped to count up to ten. On this occasion, he got as far as two. 'Easy,' he replied. 'We just sit down right here, build a factory and start manufacturing prosthetic brains for people like you who don't have real ones. I have this feeling that we'd make an absolute bloody fortune in these parts.'

'Okay, Skip. I'll go and ask the prisoners.'

'You do that.'

When they'd found him wandering about in the desert, no more than a long gob and dust-clogged spit from death by dehydration and trying to hide from his own shadow, he'd assumed, more fool him, that things were looking up. When they'd hailed him as their lost leader and mentioned in passing that now he'd come back they could all go home to their secret

583

cave in the mountains, which just happened to be crammed from floor to roof with gold, silver and precious stones, he'd been deluded enough to take this as a stroke of good luck. If he'd had the sense he'd been born with, he now realised, he should have jumped into the mirage and drowned himself.

'Gift horses' mouths,' murmured his shadow under their mutual breath. John Fingers scowled.

'Listen,' he replied, 'I may not have found a way of getting shot of you yet, but it's only a matter of time. And when I do—'

'Promises, promises. As far as I can see, this is just the start of a beautiful friendship.'

'You'll keep,' John Fingers muttered darkly. 'Here, do *you* know where this bloody cave is we're supposed to be going to?'

'Of course I do.'

This time, John Fingers only just managed to get as far as one. 'Then why,' he snarled, 'don't you just take me there, you bastard of an optical bloody illusion?'

'Because,' replied the shadow smugly, 'the sun is in the west, and you're riding towards it. This means your shadow falls behind you. Now, if you were going east, it'd be no problem for me to lead the way. I'd have no alternative.'

'Fine.' John Fingers closed his eyes, but that didn't help much, either. 'And what direction is the cave in?'

'South.'

'Thank you ever so much.' With a petulant tug on the reins, John Fingers pulled his camel's head through ninety degrees. 'I'm terribly glad we've got that sorted out, aren't you?' By navigating a rather erratic route, he found he could drag his shadow along over some particularly jagged-looking rocks, but it didn't seem to mind.

'Skip.'

'*What?*'

Aziz blinked. 'Sorry,' he said, 'I was just going to ask why we suddenly started going this way.'

'Because that's where the cave is, moron.'

'Oh.' From Aziz's expression, you could tell that he honestly hadn't thought of that. 'That's all right then. Oh, and Skip.'

'Well?'

'Why were you talking to yourself just then?'

'Because it's the only way I'm likely to get a sensible conversation in this godforsaken bloody wilderness. Satisfied?'

Aziz nodded. 'Sure thing, Skip. I'll just go and tell the others. Oh yes, one last thing.'

'Speak just once more and it will be. Well?'

'The prisoners say the cave's due south, Skip.'

'What an absolutely staggering coincidence.'

'Yeah, I thought so too. Bye, Skip.'

'Drop dead. No, forget I said that. After all, what harm have the vultures ever done me? Here, do something useful for once and fetch over the prisoners.'

A short while and an imaginative medley of camel-cursing later, Ali Baba and Akram were escorted up the line of the caravan. They were roped back to back aboard one of the most peculiar-looking creatures John Fingers had ever seen while sober; imagine a giraffe with a collapsed compost-heap on its back, and you're halfway there. Given their circumstances, they had no right to be cheerful, as John Fingers lost no time in pointing out.

'On the contrary,' Akram replied. 'Haven't felt so optimistic in ages. Ask me why.'

'Look—'

'Go on. Humour me.'

Why not, John Fingers demanded of the residue of his soul, I've humoured every other loon in this hemisphere. 'All right,' he said. 'Why are you so bloody cheerful?'

Akram smiled; or at least, he tightened the muscles at the corners of his mouth, bringing about a half-moon-shaped contraction of his lips. John Fingers had the uneasy feeling it was a triumphant snarl in fancy dress.

'Because,' Akram said, 'I know what's going to happen next, and you don't. Isn't that right, Ali?'

Ali Baba nodded. At least he wasn't smiling; he had his lips drawn in under his teeth in a thin, tight line, the way people do when they're really trying for all their worth not to burst out laughing. 'Mphm,' he said.

'All right.' It had been John Fingers' intention not to let them see he was afraid, but that was rather like trying to convince a tankful of piranhas that they'd really prefer a nice salad. 'You tell me what's going on here, and I might just decide to let you two go. Not,' he added, as Akram beamed at him and Ali Baba failed completely to stifle a rather vulgar sniggering noise, 'that I'm worried or anything. I just thought it'd be more sensible if we try it the easy way first, if you get my meaning.'

Akram nodded enthusiastically. 'He wants to try it the easy way.' he said.

'Snngh!'

'You've got to admire the bugger's nerve, though,' Akram said. 'I mean, credit where it's due, at least he's consistent to the very last.'

'Tsshh!'

This was just a tiny bit more than John Fingers could stand. He pulled out the gun—

'Hi,' Ali Baba said. 'Oh, fine, fine, thanks. Yes, I know. No, you mustn't blame yourself. No, really, you've done everything you possibly can, it's not *your* fault if. . .'

'Shuttup!' John Fingers yelled, letting the gun drop from his hand as if it was red hot. 'Both of you,' he added. 'Aziz, pick up the gun. No, *not* like—'

There was a loud bang, followed by a rude word, then silence. Then Ali Baba cleared his throat.

'The gun asked me to tell you,' he said, 'that that was the last shot in its, what did you say that bit's called where you keep the spare bullets, its magazine, so if you don't mind it'd like to be excused duty for the rest of – for now, I mean. Also, I think your friend's just shot himself in the foot.'

'He's right, Skip. Hey, Skip, my foot hurts.'

'Also,' Ali Baba continued, 'your watch says it needs a new battery and your Swiss Army knife's quarrelled with your keys and would be grateful if it could go in your other pocket where it won't be obliged, I quote, to rub shoulders with the riff raff. Finally—'

'I don't want to know!' John Fingers shouted. Ali Baba shrugged.

'Sorry,' he said. 'I thought you said you wanted to know what's going on.'

For a moment John Fingers considered ordering Ali Baba to hand over the ring; then he thought, No, maybe not. 'You know perfectly well what I want,' he snapped. 'Come on, out with it or I'll have you buried up to your necks in sand and leave you here for the vultures.'

'Ah,' said Akram. 'So you don't need us to give you the password. Okay, anywhere here will do; maybe that dune over there...'

John Fingers gathered his right hand into a fist, took aim at the epicentre of Akram's smile and swung hard; in consequence of which he fell off his camel.

'A tip for you,' Akram said, leaning over as far as he could. 'When lashing out on camelback, it's vitally important to be absolutely sure you can reach the target. If you don't, you'll overbalance and fall off. Sounds easy enough, I know, but actually it takes years and years of practice.'

'A whole lifetime,' Ali Baba agreed.

'Or longer, in his case.'

'True. Very true. I hadn't thought of it in those terms, but. . .'

With very much the same air of disgusted weariness with which Oliver Hardy used to wipe custard pie out of his face, John Fingers hauled himself to his feet, dusted himself off and spat out a mouthful of desert. Then he asked the nearest thief to take the prisoners to the other end of the caravan and keep them there until they arrived. 'And then,' he added, 'bring me the other prisoners.'

'Sure thing, Skip.'

'My name,' said John Fingers, using up the last dregs of his dignity, 'is not Skip. Understood?'

'Sure thing, Akram.'

I could try and explain, John Fingers said to himself. And while I'm at it, I could try putting the sun out by spitting at it, but it'd only come back on my face. 'You,' he sighed. 'Tell me how you get back up on this thing.'

'Skip?'

'Don't worry, I could do with the walk. Just hurry up with those bloody prisoners.'

There were times when John Fingers was convinced that day would last for ever; but it's a long road that has no turning (the M25 is a good example) and eventually—

'Is that it?' he asked his shadow.

'That's it.'

He might well have hazarded a guess without the help of his two-dimensional guide. The bleak and barren landscape, the forbidding rampart of wind- and frost-eroded stone rearing up out of the flat desert, the great cleft riven into the cliff face, even the vultures wheeling insolently in the clear, cruel sky; with such unambiguous dollops of symbolism as these you didn't need signs saying THIS WAY TO THE SECRET CAVERN and LAST PETROL BEFORE THE BANDITS' LAIR to know what was coming next. It was as if Nature and Narrative had met up in the bar beforehand to discuss the design and decided that subtlety is for wimps.

'Skip.'

Sigh. 'Yes?'

'Are we nearly there yet?'

'Not quite,' John Fingers heard himself saying. 'I mean, that's it over there. Isn't it?'

Even as he spoke, a sickening feeling of déjà vu began to spread through him, making his flesh crawl. This place—

'You.'

'Me, Skip?'

'That big flat boulder over there. Can you see it?'

'I can see lots of boulders, Skip. Any particular one?'

'The black one,' said John Fingers. 'Nearest to us, with the thorn tree alongside. Isn't that where we put out the empties for the milkman?'

Sure enough, when Aziz and Hanif managed to drag the boulder a few inches clear and drop into the large dome-shaped cavern underneath, what did they find but a huge cache of empty bottles and a note, scrawled on a piece of charred vellum and reading: ONE HUNDRED AND TWENTY-SIX PINTS TODAY, PLEASE.

Fine, John Fingers muttered to himself, God only knows why I remember this horrible place so vividly, but I do. And, if my theory's right, that crack in the rock there is the letterbox, and you open the secret sliding door by waiting till the guard's back is turned and leaning on that small projecting rock there...

'Aziz.'

'Skip?'

'Just see if there's any post in the box, there's a good lad.'

For a moment it looked quite promising, as Aziz clambered out with his arms full of envelopes. Once they'd sorted out the junk mail, however, there was nothing left except a receipt from the lawn mower people and a dead lizard.

And then they were standing in front of a breathtaking curtain of sheer grey rock, extending upwards into the sky like the biggest, nastiest office block you ever saw, and John Fingers knew they'd arrived at the front gate. Something less like a gate you'd be hard put to imagine; all the king's horses, men and heavy artillery couldn't smash a hole in that lot, not in a million years. The only discordant notes were the door-knocker, a hundred feet above the ground and made of solid brass, and the little plaque saying *Beware Of The Dog*.

'What Dog?'

'Ah,' said Aziz, grinning. 'We haven't actually got a dog. We just put that there to frighten away burglars.'

'We get a lot of them, do we?'

'Burglars? Well, no; except us, of course, but we live here, so we don't count.' Aziz considered the point, obviously for the first time. 'Hey, it only goes to show how well the notice works, eh, Skip?'

John Fingers stood for a moment, staring upwards until he began to feel dizzy, and wondering what in hell's name he was doing there. Then he remembered; treasure. Ah yes, the treasure. According to these idiots, behind that massive slab of rock there was a very large jackpot indeed. When he'd tried to get specific details, the idiots had been a bit vague; call him prosaic if you like, but John Fingers didn't consider *inexhaustible* and *beyond the dreams of avarice* to be satisfactory terms of measurement. Going by the rough internal dimensions of the cavern which he'd finally managed to prise out of them, and taking a fairly arbitrary standard for the amount of gold bullion you could pile up in a square metre, he reckoned there was enough there to buy three fairly standard passenger airliners, and almost enough to pay the interest on public sector borrowing for an hour. That much.

The dreams of avarice, if avarice had eaten too much cheese the night before. John Fingers found his enthusiasm slowly seeping back.

'Fine,' he said. 'Anybody got the key?'

Aziz looked at him. 'There isn't a key, Skip,' he said. 'You've got to say the magic words.'

John Fingers made a small growling noise, like a tiny dog trying to pick a fight with a Charolais bull. 'And what are the magic words, then?' he asked.

'Stop kidding around, Skip,' Aziz replied. 'You're a great kidder, you are.'

'That's me all over,' John Fingers replied. 'Look, you lot stay here and don't move. I'm just going to, er, look at something.'

Having retreated to a respectable distance, John Fingers positioned himself carefully between the sun and the ground, and said, 'Well?'

'Well what?'

'Well,' he said impatiently, 'what's the bloody password?'

'You mean you don't know?' replied his shadow. 'Come off it. Everybody knows the password.'

'Then it must be a singularly useless password if everybody knows it. Except, it would seem, me.'

'Everybody,' the shadow explained, 'on your side of the Line. You probably learned it at your mother's knee; you know, when you were little and she told you stories.'

John Fingers' face hardened, indicating an extreme level of tact deficiency. 'Not me,' he replied, 'on account of my mother not telling me stories. Lies, yes. Like, I'd ask her, Mummy, why's my carrycot full of pretty beads and why mustn't I tell the lady at the till about them. Then, when I was three and a bit, we started Elementary Shoplifting and Mugging for the Under-Fives. Never any time for stories in our family. So what's the password?'

The shadow seemed taken aback. 'But you must know the story,' it said, bewilderment clogging its voice. 'Everybody knows the ... Except you, apparently. Bugger me, just my luck, we're going to have to do this the hard way. All right, watch the rock to your left.'

'Why?'

'Just shut up and do as you're told.'

John Fingers shrugged and looked.

'It's a rabbit,' he said.

'That's just to give you the idea,' the shadow said, as a silhouette rabbit waggled its ears at him from the cliff-face opposite. 'Now then, concentrate.'

'What? Oh I see, right. Two words. First word, door. Gate. Something like a gate. Something swinging, something opening, no, shorter, open. Open. Right, next word. Three, oh right, three syllables. Nasty smell, stink, lavatory, drains, like drains, sewers, cesspit, shorter, oh, right, cess. Open cess. Next syllable, sandwich, eating, sandwich filling, God I hate this game, I was always lousy at it when I was a kid, sandwich filling let's see, chicken tikka, no, prawn, tuna fish salad, cheese, ham, oh right. Open cess ham. Last syllable, finger pointing, finger pointing at me, me. Open cess ham me.'

'Again.'

'Open cess ham me. Hey, what a peculiar password.'

'*Again.*'

'Open *sesame*!'

Whereupon sesame opened.

CHAPTER TWENTY-ONE

'Hello, this is Michelle Partridge's answering machine, I'm sorry there's nobody here to take your call right now, so if you'll leave your name and *where the hell have you been*, we've been worried sick about you.'

What constitutes a telephone depends on which side of the Line you happen to be. Storyside, of course, they don't have the banana-shaped pieces of plastic we have here; instead, they use seer-stones, crystal balls, magic mirrors and similar gadgets, which work on pretty much the same principle but don't go wrong quite so often, and you don't have to pay the standing charges. Until recently, it was virtually impossible to patch into the Storyside network from Realside, and vice versa. With privatisation and the abolition of the BT monopoly, the advent of Mercury and the like, the situation has changed and, in theory at least, you can now gabble away across the Line to your heart's content. In practice, of course, it's not quite so simple; even so, it's still easier to ring Tom Thumb or the Seven Dwarves than, say, Los Angeles.

'Sorry,' Michelle replied. 'Look. . .'

'And speak up, will you? I can hardly hear you.'

'Sorry,' Michelle hissed, closing her hand around the small silver ring she'd just borrowed from her father. 'Look, I've got to whisper, I don't want anybody to hear me.'

'Then you're going the right way about it. I can't, for starters.'

'Anybody *here*. I'm a prisoner in a cave. I'm talking to you on a mirror.'

'A what? Hey, have we got a crossed line?'

'... *Kate Moss, Drew Barrymore, Naomi Campbell, Linda Evangelista, Demi Moore...*'

'It's this blasted mirror,' Michelle explained. 'Used to belong to a wicked stepmother; you know – mirror, mirror, on the wall, all that sort of thing? Anyway, why I'm calling is—'

'... *Julia Roberts, Yasmin Le Bon, Elizabeth Hurley...*'

'—Because I need you to do something up for me, quick as you can, and call me back. Okay? Probably won't take you five minutes; you can get the vacuum cleaner and the kitchen steps to do the heavy lifting.'

'I can try,' the answering machine replied. 'But listen, what do you mean, captured? And where exactly are you? I've been trying to get your number from the exchange but it doesn't seem to want to tell me.'

Michelle scowled. 'All right,' she said, 'I'll call you back. What I need you to do—'

'... *Jerry Hall, Helena Christensen, Kelly Klein, Isabella Rosellini...*'

'Is, get the big bottle of olive oil from the cupboard under the sink and a really large flowerpot, block up the drain hole in the bottom, get a saucer or a small plate or something—'

'... *Esther Rantzen, Judi Dench, Margaret Thatcher...*'

Michelle swore under her breath. 'It's no good,' she muttered, 'this stupid thing's on the blink again, I think somebody must have dropped it or banged it or something.

Look, I'll have to call you back.'

'Yes, but. . .'

The mirror went dead, leaving Michelle with a momentary feeling of great and frightening distance, such as one might expect at the end of a tantalisingly brief contact with the normal and everyday. Then she reflected that she'd just been asking her answering machine to get her Hoover to go through the kitchen cupboard, which put things back in perspective somewhat.

'Well?' Akram demanded.

'I got through,' she replied. 'I gave it half the message and then the mirror started playing up. I'll try again later if I get the chance; otherwise we'll just have to hope. . .' She was going to say, *hope the answering machine uses its initiative,* but that would be silly; rather like urging an invertebrate to put its back into it. 'We'll just have to hope,' she repeated, and as she did so, it occurred to her that that was sillier still, in context.

'It'll be all right,' said Ali Baba unexpectedly, holding out his hand for the ring. Michelle had given it to him before she stopped to ask herself why; after all, it was her ring, her aunt had left it to her. Or someone, an old woman she used to go and visit, had given it to her and she'd assumed it was the old woman's to give. So; did it belong to Ali Baba? Only because he'd stolen it from Akram, who'd himself stolen it from someone else, presumably now long since deceased in circumstances of extreme prejudice. She might have said something about this if she'd actually wanted the wretched thing; as it was, she didn't. You don't, after all, kick and scream and drum your heels on the floor and demand to have your ingrowing toenail put back when the chiropodist's just dug it out.

'Now then,' Ali Baba went on, slipping the ring on and closing his fist around it. 'Before we move on to phase two, how'd it be if we just think it through for a moment and make sure we know what it is we're supposed to be doing. For once in the history of the Universe, let's try and do something properly.'

Michelle and Akram nodded. Fang, who was sulking, went on facing the other way and pretending not to be able to hear them. That, as far as Ali Baba was concerned, was no bad thing. As befitted someone in his line of business he had particularly fine teeth, and he couldn't help feeling that smiling in the presence of a tooth fairy's a bit like sunbathing in full view of the vultures, lying on a big plate with a cruet beside you.

'As I see it,' Ali Baba said, 'it won't be long before our host comes back, unlocks the door and shoos us out to be executed or tortured or whatever. Probably tortured,' he added. 'I don't suppose he's brought us here and locked us up in the coal cellar just because he's starting a collection of trans-dimensional freaks. Now, when he shows up, we've got to get him to look in that peculiar mirror Michelle was talking to just now.' He stopped and turned to her. 'You think that thing's up to it? I mean, ordinary phone messages are one thing, but. . .'

'I've no idea,' Michelle replied. 'On the other hand, it's all we've got; I mean, if we want to be pessimistic and look on the dark side of it all, we really aren't spoilt for choice. Like, what if the machine at the other end isn't switched on, or it's engaged, or the men have just turned up to cut it off?'

'Maybe it'll scramble the bastard,' Akram growled. 'No bad thing if it does.'

Michelle looked at him. That last remark had sounded a little bit more in character; except that she'd never had much evidence of the blood-curdling villain side of him. Even as a kidnapper he'd been no more terrifying than, say, the average car park attendant or pizza delivery man; and since they'd been here, on what she'd come to believe was indeed the other side of this mysterious Line everybody was so fussed about, he'd been milder than a vegetarian biryani. Which was, of

596

course, no bad thing in general terms, she supposed. On the other hand, right now when a savage and ruthless killing machine might just come in quite handy, he'd apparently turned into the sort of bloke who'd have no hangups at all about staying home with the kids while his wife went out to work, and would probably be all sensitive and interested in colour schemes and wallpaper patterns. The expression 'shadow of his former self' crossed her mind fleetingly, until it was rounded up by the Taste Police and thrown out on its ear.

Ali Baba stood up. 'Seems to me,' he said, stifling a yawn, 'that all this is very true, but not really much help to us at the moment. I mean, yes, it's a bloody stupid idea in the first place and there's no way in the world it ought to work. On the other hand we are in horseshit stepped so far, et cetera; we might as well do something as sit around until we get our fat heads chopped off. Let's do it now, shall we? Get it over with.'

'All right,' Akram said. 'Here goes, then.'

To say that John Fingers, after half an hour in the thieves' treasury, was all open-mouthed with wonder would be an understatement. More precisely; if he'd been back in Southampton and standing on the dock at the Ferry terminal, he'd have been in grave danger of having cars drive in under his teeth and down his throat under the misapprehension that he was the ferry.

'I mean, *look* at it,' he said for the seventeenth time. 'Just *look*.'

Aziz and Hakim exchanged guilty looks. 'Yeah, well,' Aziz mumbled. 'We were meaning to get it tidied up, honest, but what with one thing and another there just wasn't time.'

Something about John Fingers' demeanour suggested that he wasn't listening. He opened the lid of a yard-long solid gold casket, gawped for a few seconds and let it drop. The valuation and unit pricing circuits in his brain had burnt out twenty minutes ago. The only problem was...

'How,' he said aloud, 'in buggery am I going to get this lot home?'

'We are home, Skip. At least,' Aziz amended, 'you said we were. Or I thought you said...'

And then, of course, there was the problem of converting it all into money. Some of John Fingers' best friends were receivers of stolen goods, but for this lot you wouldn't need a fence so much as the Great Wall of China. Even if you only released one per cent of it at a time, the market would flood so quickly that only a few bubbles on the surface would remain to mark where it had once been.

'Hey,' he said, sitting down on a coal-scuttle full of snooker-ball-sized cut rubies, 'where did you jokers get all this gear from? It's *amazing*. Makes Fort Knox look like a piggy-bank.'

Aziz shrugged helplessly. 'We had a good last quarter, Skip. According to the auditor's interim statement, takings rose by an encouraging twenty-seven point six four three per cent, whereas fixed overheads, interest on borrowing, bad debts and incidental non-recurring liabilities fell by seven point three nine two per cent as against the same quarter last year. Added to which the reduction in labour costs owing to Saheed falling off a roof and Massad sticking his foot in one of those horrible spiky trap things has resulted in a highly favourable cash reserves position, fuelling rumours of a record interim dividend once provision has been made for advance corporation tax, which we don't pay anyway 'cos we always chuck the collectors down a well.' Aziz paused to draw breath, and a thought struck him. 'You know all that as well as I do, Skip. Why did you ask?'

'Huh? Oh, don't mind me. Look, I want you to go into the nearest town and buy me a thousand camels.'

'Sure thing, Skip.'

John Fingers double-checked his mental arithmetic. 'Make

that fifteen hundred,' he said. 'Plus three thousand big panniers, two miles of rope and as much as you can get of whatever it is camels eat. Okay?'

'You got it, Skip.'

'Right. You still here?'

'Yes, Skip. That's how come you can talk to me.'

'Go away.'

'I'm on that right now, Skip. 'Bye.'

Alone with his thoughts, John Fingers began to work out ways and means. First, he'd sell just a little bit – this fire bucket full of diamonds, for example, or that breadbin of pearls – and use the money to buy a small uninhabited island somewhere; something remote and utterly godforsaken where nobody had ever bothered to go. Then he could pretend he'd discovered a really amazingly rich gold mine there, which'd explain where all this stuff came from. Security'd be a bit of a headache, of course; except that with what was in this tea-chest and the smaller of those two packing cases, he could buy a half dozen reconditioned submarines and still have change left over for a couple of squadrons of fighters. What it really boiled down to was, is there enough money in the whole wide world to buy all this stuff, even with generous discounts for cash and bulk purchases? Or was he going to have to pump countless billions of dollars of subsidies into the economies of the leading industrial nations just so that eventually they'd generate enough wealth to be able to afford to buy from him? Whatever; there were difficulties, sure enough, but even so he couldn't help feeling that it was a definite step up from stealing hubcaps and nicking the lightbulbs out of bus station waiting rooms.

Having resolved on a course of action and granted himself the luxury of two minutes unrestrained gloating, John Fingers allowed his mind to drift into the strange whirlpool of thoughts, impressions and memories that made up his recollections of what had happened since he burgled that flat and stole that weird ring. Having considered the position from a number of viewpoints and made of it what little sense he could, he came to the conclusion that his present situation was a bit like the very latest in jet passenger aircraft. He didn't have the remotest idea of how it all worked or why it was doing what it was doing, and there was an unpleasant feeling in the back of his mind that if it crashed, it was likely to crash big. On the other hand, it didn't look like he actually needed to know how it all worked, and it sure beat the shit out of walking. Provided he could get out of this place with even a half per cent of the dosh, he didn't give a stuff. Burglary, like the privatised electricity industry, is all about power without responsibility, and getting away with it.

Where the hell were those two clowns with the camels?

'... Michelle Pfeiffer, Sharon Stone, bzzZZZZwheeeshhhhZZZ-Zapcracklecrackle Princess Anne, Margaret Beckett...'

'Yes,' said Ali Baba, 'I'll admit, that was a flaw in my initial reasoning. I was rather counting on him coming down here, and since he hasn't I can see that getting him to look in the mirror may present certain difficulties. I'd like to point out,' he added, kicking over a three-legged stool, 'that since there's bugger all I can do about it, whingeing isn't going to help. If you're so bloody clever, you think of something.'

'I've thought of something.'

'Dad,' said Michelle quietly, 'calm down. This isn't like you at all.'

Ali Baba sagged, as if his spine had just been removed and replaced with rice pudding, and he slumped against a wall. 'Sorry,' he said. 'I'm not quite sure what's come over me. To tell you the truth, I haven't been feeling quite myself for a while now.'

'I know,' said Akram. 'You know why?'

'Well?'

'I think,' Akram said slowly, deliberately looking the other way, 'you're starting to turn into me. A bit,' he added. 'Sort of me, anyway. Ever since you turned up at that warehouse place, all guns and swords and adrenaline. It's just a thought,' he concluded, 'but maybe we're sort of changing places in the story.'

Michelle shook her head. 'Surely not,' she said. 'Because, hasn't the thief bloke become you, hence the other thieves thinking he's their boss? They can't all be you, surely. Or are you not so much a person, more a way of life?'

By way of reply, Akram sighed. 'Why is it,' he demanded, 'that all of a sudden everybody's asking me questions and expecting me to know the damn answer? Time was, all anybody ever said when I was around was "Help, guards!" and "Aaargh!" And that was only if they happened to wake up before—'

'I said,' Fang repeated, 'I've thought of something.'

The other three prisoners looked round. 'Hello,' said Akram, 'you still here?'

'Sesame,' replied Fang. 'That's what it's all about. You lot just wait here. Won't be long.'

She grabbed the mirror, smiled into it, and vanished.

'Hey,' said the Godfather, with an impatient gesture, 'you lost me.'

If only... 'Be patient, will you?' Scheherezade replied. 'We're just getting to the good bit now.'

'But all this with the fairy and the thief and sesame,' the Godfather protested. 'I don't understand. What's gonna happen next?'

His wife sighed. 'If you knew that,' she pointed out, 'there wouldn't be much point having a story, would there? This is all just a little bit of suspense. Perfectly legitimate narrative device. Most people,' she added, 'quite like it.'

The Godfather ignored her. 'And the camels,' he said. 'What's with the goddamn camels? What for does this John Fingers want all them?'

'To move the treasure, silly.' She paused for a moment before continuing. 'To move it out of the impregnable treasury, where nobody would ever have a chance of stealing it so long as the thieves were there even if they did know the password. . .' Longer pause. 'Out of there and then overland, in a long, straggly, probably inadequately guarded caravan en route to wherever he's going.'

'Hey!'

'Which,' Scheherezade ground on, 'is a curious decision, don't you think, bearing in mind that it'd probably only take a few good men – Rocco, say, and a couple of the others, to rob the caravan and make off with *all that money*. . .' Having hammered the point so far home that you could probably have tethered an elephant to it, she left it at that and smiled sweetly. 'That's why the camels,' she said. 'Shall I go on, or do you have, um, business to attend to?'

The Godfather stubbed out his cigar and stood up. 'Just wait there a second,' he said. 'I'll be right back.'

Meg Ryan Daryll Hannah IT'S ALL RIGHT IT'S ONLY ME *on second thoughts not Daryll Hannah this is getting difficult Jodie Foster?*

Eyebrow raised in bewilderment and disapproval, Ali Baba's receptionist tore the page off the fax machine, stared at it again, screwed it into a ball and dropped it into the waste-paper basket. For one fleeting instant she'd thought it might be a message from Mr Barbour, explaining where the hell he was and why he hadn't come in to work for a week. No such luck.

602

She shrugged, picked up the plant mister and sprayed the potted palm.

When she'd gone, the tooth fairy crawled out from under the fax machine, dusted herself off and looked around. There it was. Good.

The potted palm. There's one in every dentist's waiting room; a big, slightly lopsided, pointless-looking thing with flat, papery leaves and a general air of wishing it was somewhere else. It sits in a pot two sizes too small for its roots, and it's probably there just so that the room will contain one living thing more wretched-looking than the paying customers. Nobody knows where they all come from, although the chances are there's a big nursery somewhere outside Northampton that specialises in them, having seen a window in the market around about the time the bottom fell out of triffid-farming.

At least, you assume it's a palm of some sort; that's if you can be bothered. Of course, for all you know it might be an annual herbaceous tropical and subtropical plant with seeds used in various ways as food and yielding an oil used in salads and as a laxative.

Fang squared up to the plant and spat on her hands. Fine, she muttered to herself, I've done the easy bit; faxed myself across the Line without getting squashed, dissipated or lost in the switchboard. Now it starts to get a bit tricky.

No way her arms would go round the flowerpot; she'd have to get the other side of it and push.

And then, assuming that she found a way round the trifling matter of fitting a four-foot-high three-dimensional pot-plant into the paper feed of a fax machine and sending it to a magic mirror whose number she didn't actually know, that'd be the second easiest part done, leaving them to have a go at the difficult bit. And the difficult bit was going to be horribly difficult; in fact, the whole idea was so offputting that it was only the thought that they'd all be blown up, beheaded or converted into random molecules and dispersed long before they even got near the difficult bit that was keeping her going. Ah well. Here goes.

'... *Andie McDowell* OUCH! THAT HURT!'

'There,' said Fang, emerging breathless and bedraggled from the mirror. 'Here you go. What do you reckon to that, then?'

Ali Baba looked down. 'It's an aspidistra,' he said, 'how nice. What am I supposed to do with it?'

For a small portion of a second Fang was tempted to make a suggestion; since she was back to full human size, however, she decided it wouldn't be ladylike, and desisted.

'Not an aspidistra,' she panted. 'Look at the label.'

Akram picked out the little white plastic flag, read it and smiled. 'Neat,' he said. 'Absolutely no way it'll work, mind you, but a lovely piece of imaginative thinking.' He handed the plastic flag to Michelle, who read it and gave it back.

'So that's what a sesame plant looks like,' she said. 'Hang on, though. Are you seriously trying to suggest that if we put this thing against the door and say *open, sesame*...'

It was probably the most enjoyable four seconds of Fang's life so far. The tremendous feeling of smugness when the plant hopped out of its pot, waddled across on root-tip to the massive oak door and kicked it in was so utterly, orgasmically satisfying that she wouldn't have swapped it for every molar ever pulled. With her head held high, she walked over to the doorway and pushed the shattered remains of the door aside.

'Yes,' she said, with a little bow. 'Come on.'

CHAPTER TWENTY-TWO

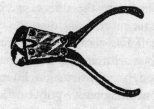

One camel is a bloody nuisance. By a mathematical paradox inexplicable except in the far dimensions of pure mathematics, fifteen hundred camels are a million times worse.

Buying fifteen hundred camels wasn't really a problem. Fortuitously, Aziz and his thirty-eight colleagues arrived in Baghdad just in time for the start of the annual camel fair, attended by livestock dealers from every corner of Central Asia, so all Aziz had to do was stand on an upturned jar, yell, 'We'll take the lot,' at the top of his voice, and start distributing money from the ten large sacks they'd brought with them for the purpose. The point at which the last camel-dealer had walked away, slightly lopsided from the weight of his purse and hugging himself with sheer delight, was the moment the problems began in earnest.

Take fifteen hundred camels, tie them together nose to tail with rope and point them at the city gates, and you have a spectacularly graphic illustration of Brownian motion in action; the only real difference being that Brown's justly celebrated particles don't bulldoze their way through crowded bazaars knocking over trestles and gobbling up the stock in trade of the fresh fruit stalls. Nor do they leave an evil-smelling brown trail behind them, sufficient to mulch all the roses in the continent of Asia. Nor, come to that, do they bite the market inspectors and commissioners of traffic, spit in the faces of the city wardens and wee all over the Emir's palanquin. Fortunately, at least as far as the thieves were concerned, the Palace Guard had far more sense than to get in the way of a thousand and a half foul-tempered ships of the desert and contented themselves with arresting any market traders who stayed still long enough for obstruction, littering the pavement and a variety of quite imaginative public order offences. Once the people had fled or been removed, there were far fewer obstacles for the camels to bump into, and the guards finally managed to shoo them out of the main gate by the cunning expedient of setting fire to the dried fruit warehouse.

From then on, it should have been quite straightforward; but it wasn't. Far from curbing their natural wanderlust, roping the camels together seemed to inspire them with a sense of purpose they would otherwise have lacked. Camels united, they seemed to say, can never be diverted. With a degree of precision you'd normally only expect from a regiment of soldiers or a top-flight flea-circus, the entire caravan took a sharp simultaneous left and headed off into the desert, in the general direction of Mongolia. Aziz, after water-skiing across the dunes behind the hindmost camel for half an hour or so, was on the point of cutting the rope and heading home with some fabrication about camels being temporarily out of stock and robbers waylaying them in a narrow pass somewhere when a wise thief suggested that they should try psychology.

It worked. As soon as the thieves galloped ahead of the procession and did everything they conceivably could to encourage them to follow the route they'd apparently chosen, all fifteen hundred of the loathsome beasts turned through a hundred and eighty degrees and started trudging back the way they'd just come. By dint of dragging on ropes, screaming abuse and trying with all their strength to pull their heads round, the thieves managed to keep the camels bang on course until they were safely penned up outside the entrance to their rocky fortress. Hence the old drovers' saying, supposedly first coined on this occasion, that if you lead a camel away from water, you can make him drink.

'Skip,' Aziz called out. 'Hey, *Skip*. We've got them. Do you want us to. . .?'

'He's not bloody well here,' Rustem interrupted, returning from a fruitless search of the cave. 'Buggered off somewhere with the prisoners, by the looks of it. Now what'll we do?'

Aziz shrugged. 'I think he wanted us to load up the treasure,' he said. He sighed. No rest for the wicked.

'What, all of it? There's bloody *tons* of the stuff.'

'Maybe that's why he wanted all these camels,' Aziz replied. 'Look, I don't know what he's playing at, and neither do you. Don't suppose we need to, either.' He peered up towards the roof of the treasury; it looked for all the world like the mouth of a chocolate-loving giant, all huge gold teeth. 'If we make a start now,' he said, 'we could be finished in a day or two.'

Rustem scowled. 'All right,' he said, 'but where's he taking it? And where is he, come to that?'

'Who knows?' Aziz replied, with a fatalistic shrug. 'Off enjoying himself, I s'pose.'

Aaaaaagh!

Whether he was falling or flying, flying or floating, floating or falling, John Fingers had no idea. Whatever it was, however, it was distinctly unpleasant, making him feel as if he was one of those newspaper photographs that turns out on close

607

inspection to be nothing but a pattern of black dots; only in three, or four, or maybe even five dimensions. All in all, it was even nastier than a trip to the dentist's, and he wished it would stop. Perhaps the most disconcerting part of the experience was the bland, bored speaking-clock-type voice he could hear in the back of his mind, endlessly bleating out lists of supermodels and famous actresses.

It had all started when the treasury door had burst open and his four prisoners had charged in waving weapons they'd found lying about in the corridors (that, as far as he could judge, was the thieves' idea of chic interior design; where you or I would have plaster ducks, they had crossed scimitars and whacking great curvy knives) and insisting that he look in a mirror. Assuming that he had dandruff or something and that they were trying to persuade him to change his brand of shampoo, he'd humoured them; whereupon this strange and extremely unpleasant falling/flying/floating business had started, and here he apparently was. He had the impression that the contents of his stomach were offstage in some sort of parallel universe; probably just as well, or he'd have a weightless cloud of half-digested ravioli to cope with as well as everything else.

If ever I get out of this—

And then he landed, with a spine-jarring thump, in what looked and smelled uncommonly like an outsize flower-pot; one of those big red terracotta numbers they stock in the grander sorts of garden centre for Japanese millionaires to pot their bonzai giant redwoods into. After a moment or so devoted to recovering from the fall and swearing, he squirmed round, got his fingers over the rim of the pot and looked out.

He was in a kitchen.

A *perfectly normal* kitchen, goddamnit; with worktops and cupboards and a cooker and a fridge and a washing machine and a dishwasher and a deep fat fryer and a blender and a telephone and a fax/answering machine and a tumble drier and an electric kettle—

A *familiar* perfectly normal kitchen, one he'd been in quite recently. That wasn't as much help as it might seem at first glance. In the course of his business he passed through a lot of kitchens, usually stealthily and by torchlight. After a while, though, they all start to look the same, whereas for some reason he distinctly remembered this one. Why?

Because, he realised, this is the flat where I stole that fucking sodding bloody ring, the one that caused all this. . .

As he looked round, he noticed that the kettle, standing on the worktop directly above his head, was just coming to the boil. It was balanced rather precariously on the edge; in fact, all it would take to dislodge it would be the disturbance caused by the steam charging about inside trying to find the exit. Our old friend Brownian motion, at it again.

He was in the act of reaching up to push it away or switch it off when he came to the conclusion that it was too late; the kettle had boiled, overbalanced and started to topple down onto him. A bloke could have a nasty accident—

Cue past life.

His boyhood. Playing tag in the dusty square. His father, coming home drunk. Stealing loose change from the jar by the fireside—

AND NOW—

Joining the gang of scruffy, good-for-nothing kids who were the despair and terror of the neighbourhood. Being the leader. Fighting the big, curly-haired boy, twice his size but slow and a coward at heart. The sheer pleasure of smelling fear on his opponent's breath (hang on a second) before hitting him, again and again and again, with the stone that'd happened to find his outstretched hand—

BANDIT, MURDERER, THIEF—

Feeling the warmth of someone else's blood on his skin; not

609

unpleasant, quite the opposite. Looking up, to see the awe, the terror, the *respect* in the faces of the other kids. Learning, then and there, that in the final analysis, respect is everything (now just a minute), no matter what you have to do in order to earn it—

VOTED FIFTEEN YEARS IN SUCCESSION—

Running. Being hunted. Hearing the breathing of the men who were chasing him, five yards or so away in the darkness. Feeling his own heart actually stop; and then the sickening wave of relief (I don't remember that) as they went away—

AKRAM THE TERRIBLE—

'Jesus flaming Christ!' John Fingers roared as the water hit him. 'You stupid bastards, that wasn't me! You've got the wrong—'

THIS WAS YOUR LIFE.

This is your life. . .

A young boy stands up in the middle of a ring of his peers. In his right hand he's holding a bloodstained stone. At his feet, a dead body. Nobody speaks.

'I. . .'

The boy closes his mouth again, and lets the stone drop. He notices that both his hands are red. The other boys start to back away.

'Akram,' one of them says, 'I think you've killed him.'

I am not Akram, my name is John Fingers Smith and I demand to see the British consul. 'I. . .'

Another boy snuggles back behind the shoulders of his fellows. 'It wasn't an accident,' he says, pointing. 'I saw him, he did it on purpose, I saw him do it.'

'I. . .' *You bastards, what have you done to my body, give me my body back or I'll wring your bloody necks.* 'Yes,' says the boy, 'I killed him. So what? Served him right.'

'Akram. . .'

There's no way, do you hear me, absolutely no way I'm going to stand for this, look, I've got rights, you just wait till London hears about this, you'll have Stormin' Norman and half a million tanks round your ears before you can say United Nations...

'Run!'

But...

'They're coming! Quick, Akram, run!'

But it wasn't me. I've been framed...

'Run!'

Men appear in the distance, shouting and waving their arms. The boy looks round wildly. He stiffens, like a deer hearing a twig break.

I'll get you for this, you scumbags. One of these days I'll be back and I'll bloody well get you...

The boy runs.

Fifteen hundred camels are a bloody nuisance. Fifteen hundred camels laden down with gold, silver, precious stones, lapis lazuli, freshwater pearls, works of art and limited edition collectors' commemorative porcelain statuettes are about as much aggravation as it's possible to get without standing in front of a registrar or minister of religion and saying, 'I do.'

'Yes,' repeated Hakim for the fifteenth time, 'but where are we actually going?'

Aziz, who'd been fending off this question with 'It's not far now', 'We're on the right road', 'Shut your face' and similar cunning evasions, finally broke down and admitted that he didn't know.

'You don't *know*?'

'That's what I just said, isn't it?' Aziz snapped. 'Weren't you listening, or are the holes in the side of your head just for ventilation?'

A man of many faults, Hakim did at least have the virtue of persistence; except that in his case, it wasn't a virtue. 'You

611

don't know,' he reiterated. 'We load up all that gold and jewels and stuff and piss off into the desert and you don't know where we're going.'

'Yes.'

'I see.' A look of indescribable deviousness dragged itself across Hakim's face, stopping in the foothills of his nose for a rest. It was probably just as well that Hakim had never played poker; his thoughts were so perfectly mirrored in his face that if he ever did sit down to a friendly game of five-card stud, he'd have lost all his money before the seal was broken on the deck. 'So Akram doesn't know either,' he continued. 'Where we're going, I mean.'

''Spose not. Why?'

'We're heading off into the wilderness with all the dosh, and Akram doesn't know where we are.'

'I said, yes. Now if you've...'

Slow, or rather glacier-like, on the uptake he might be; but when the penny finally dropped in Aziz's mind, it did so with quite devastating force. Reining in his mule, and doing his best to ignore the camel that was apparently trying to lick the wax off his eardrum, Aziz sat for a moment in a surmise so wild it'd have made stout Cortes look like a six-countries-in-four-days American tourist.

'Are you suggesting,' he muttered in a low voice, 'that we sort of, walk off with it?'

'Yes.'

'Good idea.'

Even as he said the words, Aziz was aware that he was guilty of an understatement on a par with referring to the First World War as a bit of a scrap. For years, a lifetime, far longer than any of them could remember, they'd been amassing this truly awesome hoard of pure wealth; and in all that time, nothing had ever been said about divvying up, sharing out or spending. The thought had never even crossed Aziz's mind before, for much the same reason that elderly people in wheelchairs don't try and cross the M6.

'Hang on, though,' objected a thief. 'What about when Akram finds out? He'll skin us alive.'

Hakim smirked. 'If he finds out,' he replied. 'And if he catches up with us. And if the thirty-nine of us are ready to hold still and let ourselves be skinned by the one of him. Think about it,' he urged. 'All that gold and stuff, it's wealth beyond the dreams of avarice. And a one-thirty-ninth share of wealth beyond the dreams of avarice is –' He paused, wrestling with the mental arithmetic. 'Wealth beyond the dreams of eating cheese last thing at night,' he concluded triumphantly. 'Or, put it another way, loads of treasure. Right, then; show of hands?'

Not, you might think, the most democratic way for a thieves' co-operative to vote in a country governed according to Islamic law; nevertheless, unanimous is unanimous. Admittedly, several of the voters were persuaded to join in the general hand-raising by the feel of sharp metal in the small of their backs; but friendly persuasion is what democracy's all about.

'Right,' said Hakim, 'that's settled, then. Soon as we reach the next oasis we'll have a share-out and work out what we're going to do about splitting up. That all right with everyone?'

'Okay,' murmured the Godfather, 'what's the plan?'

Scheherezade, shivering perhaps a trifle more than the slight desert breeze justified, nodded her head. 'Piece of cake, really,' she replied. 'We wait till they come past. Then I give the signal, you all jump out and scrag the lot of 'em. Then—'

'Jump outa what?'

That, as far as Scheherezade was concerned, was her cue. 'I've already thought of that,' she announced. 'You see that big row of empty jars standing there beside the road?'

The Godfather nodded. 'Hey,' he said, 'I think I'm way

613

ahead of you already. Rocco, Tony, you get the guys and go climb into those jars there. I'll come and join you in a minute.'

The Godfather's grey-suited companions, who had been expecting at least one nasty brush with bandits and the like, let go a sigh of relief. This, they felt, was rather more like it. By a curious chance, there were thirty-nine of them. By an even odder chance, Scheherezade had laid on a total of forty palm-oil jars.

'Okay,' observed the Godfather. 'Where you gonna hide, then?'

'Me?' Scheherezade went through a pantomime of thinking about it. 'How about behind the tea urn?' she suggested.

'What tea urn?'

By way of reply, Scheherezade pointed to a big old-fashioned hospital tea-trolley, on which was mounted an extra large capacity white enamel urn. Wisps of steam rose from the top of it. 'That's in case you boys get thirsty while you're waiting for the caravan to show,' she explained. 'I think of everything, don't I?'

'Yeah. You done good.' The Godfather stood up, took a deep breath and hoisted his substantial bulk into the fortieth jar, pulling the lid across after himself. His wife smiled; a long, detailed, intricate smirk that told its own story. Or stories.

Having satisfied herself that her husband and all his henchmen were in their jars and waiting patiently, she turned up the thermostat on the urn's electric element as far as it would go, until the water came to the boil. As the steam hissed furiously through the vents, she stopped to wonder what the exhilarating buzz she was feeling might be, and realised with joy that it was the Story, surging and expanding inside her brain, as vigorous, powerful and dangerous as the steam itself. Old stories burble and zizz like sleepy bees, lazy in the heat of the summer sun, until something wakes them up and stirs them into angry energy; at which point, woe betide anybody

who tries to restrain them in a confined space. That's
Brownian motion, folks; the more you heat the particles, the
faster they move and the harder they collide with each other.

She leaned forward and rapped with her knuckles on the
side of her husband's jar.

'Hey, you,' she said.

'You talking to me?'

'You bet I'm talking to you. You got three wishes,' she said.
'And one second to wish them in.'

'What you talking about, you dumb—?'

With a quick twist of the wrist, Scheherezade turned the
spigot.

Cue past life.

A young boy stands up in the middle of a ring of his peers—
Hey! What's going on here? You dumb bitch, you're spilling...

In his right hand he's holding a bloodstained stone.

'Akram,' says a boy to his left. 'You again. Didn't you just
leave?'

That crazy goddamn bitch – Ah, shit.

'Yes,' says the boy, 'I killed him. He didn't show no respect.
You gotta have respect, or else what you got?'

Hey! I got three wishes. I wish—

Men appear in the distance, shouting and waving their
arms. The boy looks round wildly. He stiffens, like a deer...

I wish I was outa this goddamn fuckin' jar!

'Run!'

The boy turns, shrugs. 'Which way?' he asks. His friends
look at him oddly.

'I think you went thattaway,' they say. 'If you get a move on,
you might just catch yourself up.'

After she'd dealt with the fortieth jar, there was about half a

615

pint of boiling water left. She used it to make herself a cup of instant coffee.

A few minutes later, a long procession of camels appeared on the horizon; about fifteen hundred of them, all loaded down with heavy burdens. Scheherezade stood up, brushed herself off, walked to the side of the road and stood there with her thumb raised.

'Hi, boys,' she called out. 'Going my way?'

The leader of the caravan hesitated. On the one hand, he wasn't sure that picking up hitch-hikers was appropriate for a gang of thieves on the run. On the other hand – Scheherezade adjusted her veil and hitched the hem of her skirt up another half inch, nearly causing Aziz to fall off his camel.

'Who're you?' he asked.

'Me?' Scheherezade's eyes twinkled perilously through her veil. 'I'm your fairy godmother. Now then, you're not going to stay on that mule and let a lady walk, are you?'

CHAPTER TWENTY-THREE

'Oh there you are,' said the receptionist. 'I was beginning to wonder where you'd got to.'

Ali Baba, sprawled on the ground with his head in his own waste-paper basket, looked up and grinned sheepishly. 'Sorry,' he said. 'Got a bit held up. Many waiting?'

The receptionist nodded. 'I managed to reschedule most of your appointments, but there's quite a few that insist on coming in every day on the offchance you might be back. Quite flattering, really, if you think about it.'

Ali Baba got to his feet, removed various bent paper-clips and knobs of dried chewing-gum from his hair, and glanced down as the fax machine printed out the inevitable confirmation slip. Instead of the usual details (sender, time etc) it read:

TRY THAT AGAIN AND I'LL ELECTROCUTE YOU

'Any messages?' he asked.

'On your desk. Oh, and a woman came in to see you. Personal matter, she said.'

Ali Baba described Michelle.

'No,' the receptionist replied. 'Isn't that Miss Partridge?'

'Oh, I forgot, she's a patient.' He shrugged. 'I take it she didn't leave a name.'

'Not a *proper* name,' the receptionist replied. 'Just said she was Yasmin, and you didn't give her the slip that easily. Strange girl. Funny clothes, like a lot of net curtains and brass teapot lids.'

'Oh. Her.'

Sloe-eyed Yasmin, she of the tiny waist and serrated tongue. He had hoped, really and truly fervently hoped, that he'd at least managed to give her the slip; apparently not so.

'Sharon.'

'Mmm?'

'What's a sloe look like?'

'I beg your pardon, Mr Barbour?'

'Sloe. You make gin out of them, I think.'

'Oh, *sloes*.' The receptionist considered for a moment; you could almost hear the filing-cabinet drawers of her mind swishing frictionless on their nylon bearings. 'Aren't they the small black things like cocktail olives? Sort of like undersized black grapes, I think. Why do you ask?'

'Oh, no reason. Look, I've just got to slip out for five minutes—'

'But you've just. . .'

'—So do what you can to rearrange the appointments and I'll be back—'

'Mr *Barbour*!'

'—Eventually.'

He typed a number into the fax machine, so fast that Sharon couldn't see what it was. She heard the ululating squeak of faxes shaking hands; then Mr Barbour stuck his hand into the paper feed, someone she couldn't see said, '*Scraping the bottom of the barrel what about Goldie Hawn?*' and he vanished. Then there was a brilliant white flash, a *zap!* and the smell of burning plastic.

'Mr *Barbour!*'

No reply. The machine chugged, beeped and fed out a slip saying:

I WARNED YOU

– and that was the last ever seen (so far) of Ali Baba this side of the Line.

Cue past life—

He'd just got to the bit where he'd been leaning over the last jar, peering in to see if the bandit it contained was substantially dead, and his lovely assistant Yasmin the sloe-eyed houri had tiptoed up behind him and cracked his skull with a two-pound hammer when the memory sequence suddenly froze and he fell out of it into what he recognised as the courtyard of his own house in Baghdad; the place, in fact, where his past life had just cut out, except that there were no oil jars, no boiled thieves and no Yasmin. An improvement, he couldn't help feeling.

'Oh well,' he said.

He rose, a little wobbly but largely intact. Somehow he'd contrived to burn his right hand, as if he'd touched a hot kettle. He wondered if he had anything to put on it.

'There you are,' said a girl's voice behind him. He turned quickly, then relaxed.

'Hello,' he said.

'Where have you been?' his daughter upbraided him. 'You've got a whole waiting room full of patients. Old Mrs Masood's been here since before nine. You're doing a root fill for her, remember.'

'Am I?' He thought about what Michelle had just said. 'I am? Oh *good*. Tell her I'll be right through, soon as I've found some Savlon—'

'Some what?'

He frowned. 'No Savlon? Pity. Never mind. I'll just wash up and I'll be there in a jiffy.'

Michelle shrugged and trotted back into the house. A little while later, he followed her. In the bathroom, or what served as a bathroom (he was going to have to get out of the habit of thinking in Realside terms) he scrubbed his hands and took a look in the mirror.

Snow White, it said.

'Correct,' he replied. Then he took it off the wall, smashed it, and disposed of the pieces tidily. What with one thing and another, he'd had enough junk faxes to last him a lifetime.

Ah well, he reflected as he dried his sore hand, it's nice to be back. So, quite possibly, he was still on the run. One of these days, for all he knew, a patient sitting in his chair would turn out to be Yasmin or John Fingers, and then it'd be time for another quick exit, yet one more fresh start in a strange new environment. It made him glad he'd taken the trouble to learn a trade that'd guarantee him a living wherever he went. Me and Doc Holliday, he said to himself; two dentists floating uncomfortably on the ebb tide of adventure. But, until the Story wound itself back to the beginning again, he had work to do, cavities to fill; a sort of purpose. A hero's gotta have a purpose, boy; it goes with the territory.

'Dad,' Michelle called, 'are you ready yet?'

'Ready as I'll ever be,' he replied. Then he finished drying his hands and went to work.

Cue past life.

Michelle landed awkwardly, narrowly avoiding banging her head on the huge flowerpot that someone had left lying about on the kitchen floor. When she looked in it, she found it was full of damp, dead burglar.

'Yuk,' she said.

The answering machine/fax chuntered at her and fed out the confirmation slip. It read:

AND STAY OUT

'A pleasure,' she replied. 'Well, guys, I'm back.'

No reply. She clicked her tongue. So her kitchen wasn't talking to her; offended, probably. It'd get over it. She glanced down at her hand; there was the ring on her finger, where it should be. It was, after all, her ring, given to her by Aunt Fatty on her deathbed.

She counted up to ten, and then smiled.

'Guys?' she said.

Still no reply. This puzzled her; earlier, she'd got the impression that her household goods were chattier than Parliament on a bad day. If they had sent her to Coventry, they wouldn't have expected her to stay there long enough to do more than have a stroll down the main street and a quick dash through the shopping centre.

'Hello? Is anybody there?'

Nothing. Not a vibe, good, bad or indifferent. The place was—

'Talk to me. Please.'

—Dead, deceased, in there with Queen Anne and John Cleese's parrot in the short-list for the prestigious Worthington Lifelessness Awards. When she opened the fridge door, a light came on to show that it wasn't just a power cut. She sat down on the edge of the table and burst into tears.

The ring. . .

Maybe it was the ring that had conked out. As quickly as she could, she hurried out onto the landing and prodded the call button for the lift.

621

'AllrightallrightI'mcomingasfastasIcan,' the lift muttered. 'SomepeoplenopatienceupanddownalldayexpecttheythinkIdo thisforthegoodofmyhealth.'

Michelle winced. 'Sorry,' she said, 'wrong number.' She returned to her flat and closed the door before the tears returned.

This is silly, she told herself, two sodden hankies and a large sheet of kitchen towel later. I'm sobbing my heart out because my blender won't talk to me any more. But that's crazy, because it means this whole stupid adventure is finally over, and I'm home.

Home.

Yes, well. Many years ago, she'd met a man who'd been captured by the Japanese during the last war. He'd survived Changi Gaol and the forced labour camps of the Burma railway, escaped, and tracked his way back through jungle, mountain and desert, until eventually he walked down a gangplank at Liverpool with his kitbag over his shoulder, took a train to London, and went home. But when he got there, he found that his house, his street, the entire neighbourhood had completely vanished, turned into a wilderness of bricks and rubble by a flying bomb in one of the last V2 raids of the war. And that, he had said, was what really got to him. He'd made the mistake, he later realised, of believing in the existence of happiness ever after, when he should have known that happy endings, like free lunches and rocking-horse shit, are not in fact as common as the fairy-tales would have you believe.

She stood up and looked around. Perfectly ordinary flat. Welcome to Reality; where there is only one ending, a dull and inescapable appointment with eternity, never happy by defini-tion. Until then, the story goes on, plotless and meandering, where Hope is a man who offers you sweets if you'll get into his car. Wonderful. It's great to be back.

Bleep, said the fax machine. *Susan Sarandon*.

622

No. Surely not. I couldn't.

But why not?

She picked the kettle up off the floor, filled it and switched it on. There was, she reminded herself, a dead body in her kitchen; another mess to clear up, and not something you could put off, like washing the dishes or ironing. Dead bodies don't come with Inhume By dates clearly printed on their foreheads, but she had an idea they had to be dealt with fairly quickly; and, this being reality, she was going to have to do either an awful lot of explaining or some extremely surreptitious digging. Oh bother.

She looked at the fax machine.

Looked at from another angle, it was a clear case of dual nationality. Although she'd lived all her life in Reality, she had now been given to understand that her father was in fact a native of Over There, where talking blenders are quite probably the norm, and boiled burglars so commonplace an occurrence that there's probably a little man with a cart who comes round three times a week to collect them and take them away.

The hell with it. Escapism is only futile and self-defeating if you can't actually escape. Closing her eyes, she jammed her right hand into the paper feed of the fax and—

'Hello,' said Ali Baba. 'What kept you?'

'Hey,' muttered Sadiq, his voice reverberating through the earthenware. 'Where did she get to?'

'Don't ask me,' replied Aziz. 'All she said to me was, Climb into those jars there, I'll be back in a minute. Seemed to me she knew what she was talking about, so I did like she told me. Always been a rule with me; if somebody who looks like they know what's going on tells me to do something, I do it.'

'Fair enough,' Sadiq said. 'Be nice to know what we're meant to be doing, though. Just for once.'

Aziz frowned. 'Would it?' he asked. 'Why?'

'Dunno. I just thought that maybe—'

Glug glug glug.

Cue past lives.

Scheherezade was alone.

'*Yippee!*' she said.

Because, Storyside, one thing you can never be is on your own. A character in a story has to be with other people, interacting with them, loving them, hating them, kissing them, killing them, rescuing them, robbing them, or else cease to exist. This side of the Line, the only person who can be alone is the storyteller.

She stood up and looked around. From this high point she could see for miles in every direction, and what she saw was nothing; or rather, nothing's understudy, sand. She was in some kind of desert. Ideal.

'Only I insist,' she said aloud, 'on a tap. And a fridge. And a deckchair and a beach umbrella.' Saying it that way made it sound like three wishes, not four; besides, it was her story so she was allowed to cheat.

There was a tap. And a fridge. And a deckchair and a beach umbrella.

'Hello,' said the fridge. 'What'll it be?'

'A turkey sandwich and a nice long cool drink,' Scheherezade replied without looking round. She turned the tap, and water started to gush out, rapidly filling the small hollow below the rock in whose shade the deckchair stood. 'Give me a shout when it's ready,' she added. 'I'll be over there by the pool.'

As she sipped her drink – the fridge had tried to fob her off with water but a quick rewrite had fixed all that – she reflected on what she'd achieved so far. The Godfather was gone; no more infiltration of Reality, no more wishes you can't refuse. Whatever story he was in now was welcome to him. As for Ali

Baba and the forty thieves, the story had served its purpose and could be left to carry on as before. Evermore, sesame would open, the thieves would die in their jars, rewind, go back to the beginning. It would be the same with all the stories now, except that there would have to be a few new ones. That would be no hardship. Neverland is big enough to accommodate anything; compared to it, Infinity's a studio flat in Hong Kong.

'Could I be a real nuisance,' she asked, 'and have a jar of barrier cream?'

(Her first major rewrite; the couplet now went—

A jar of barrier cream beneath the beach umbrella,

A glass of gin, a turkey sandwich and hold the Thou

– So maybe it didn't rhyme; so what?)

That wish being granted, Scheherezade leaned back in her deckchair, closed her eyes and lived happily ever after.

'Three quarter-pounders with cheese, three large fries, two regular kiwi fruit shakes, and a large tea.'

Akram opened his eyes. 'Sorry?' he said.

'Three quarter-pounders with cheese, three large fries, two regular kiwi fruit shakes, and a large tea.'

'Ah,' said Akram. 'So I did die, then.'

'Three quarter-poun— What did you just say?'

Akram looked the customer in the eyes and smiled enormously. 'I must be dead,' he said, 'or else how come I'm in heaven? Or are they doing day trips now?'

The customer took two steps back. 'Look,' she said, 'forget the order, I've changed my mind. Gosh, is that the time? I must be. . .'

'No,' Akram said quickly, 'don't go. Sorry, I was miles away. Right, three quarter-pounders.'

'With cheese. And three large fries, two regular kiwi fruit. . .'

'It'll be a pleasure,' Akram replied sincerely. 'Coming right up.'

He turned to get the order and found himself face to face with a dazzlingly beautiful girl with long, straight blonde hair under a baseball cap bearing the legend *Akram's Diner*. 'Fang?' he queried.

She nodded. 'And no, you're not dead,' she said. 'Come on, customer waiting.'

Later, during a brief lull, he took off his own baseball cap and read the words blazoned on it.

'You're wrong, you know,' he said. 'This *is* heaven. There may be another place of the same name somewhere that's all pink clouds and harp music, but I don't want to go there.'

Fang slit open a new sack of pre-sliced chips and dumped them in the fryer. 'You are not dead,' she insisted. 'And this is not heaven. It's just a small-time fast-food joint on the interface between the two sides of the Line. Only gets three stars in the Guide Dunlop.' She grinned. 'And in case you think that's good, most dustbins get four stars.'

Akram shrugged. 'That's all right,' he said. 'Gives me something to aim at. Fine afterlife it'd be without a sense of purpose.' He paused for a moment. 'Excuse me asking,' he said carefully, 'but, um, what are you doing here? Not,' he added quickly, 'that you don't deserve it or anything like that; I just thought that tooth fairies probably had a rather different sort of paradise, like an elephant's graveyard or a snooker-ball factory.'

'You haven't been listening, have you?' replied Fang indulgently. 'This is not the pudding, we're still on the main course. This is just where that dicky fax put us down after we zapped out of your old hideout. Recognise it yet?'

Akram looked round; it was sort of familiar, in a way. It was almost—

'Jim's,' he muttered. 'Jim's Diner. God, yes, I'd know it anywhere. Except that—'

Fang nodded. 'Now it's yours, apparently. You don't seem unduly upset by that.'

'Good Lord, no.' Akram cut open another bag of chips and dropped them into the boiling oil. Palm oil? Outside the back door, were there forty empty jars waiting for the delivery man to come and take them away? 'It's just such a strange coincidence. The happiest time of any of my lives was when I was assistant manager at that burger place, and now here I am with a burger place of my own. Is this some sort of witness relocation programme, or what?'

Fang shrugged. 'Maybe,' she said. 'That'd make some sort of sense, as far as I'm concerned. Otherwise it'd be one hell of a coincidence.'

'It would?' Akram looked at her. 'You mean, you always wanted to work in a fast-food joint too?'

'Don't be obtuse,' Fang replied, and kissed him. 'And if you dare count your teeth,' she added, once she'd let him go again, 'I'll be bitterly offended. Like you, I think I've retired from all that blood-and-bones stuff. About time, too.'

Akram let it all sink in while he served a couple of customers. After all, he told himself, why not? Perhaps there is such a thing as a happy ending after all, and this is it.

He hoped so. For you, a voice deep inside him muttered, the Story is over. He thought of all those POW escape movies, where at the very end the heroes come to a lonely frontier post in the snow-capped mountains, and suddenly they're in Switzerland. Now then, supposing this was meant to be Switzerland (have to tidy up a bit, give it a lick of paint first, maybe clean the windows) and suppose that, instead of going home and rejoining his regiment, he stayed here, for ever. Mountain air, nice people, good standard of living, all the melted cheese you can eat; there are worse places. Somewhere neutral, a hidden enclave halfway between still being in the adventure and living happily ever after; yes, he could really go for that. He'd been right first time, except for the death part. Formica-topped tables, vinyl-covered seats, a big greasy deep-fat fryer and a milk-shake machine. Heaven.

'This'll do me,' he said. 'I'm staying. What about you?'

Fang shrugged. 'All right,' she said. 'It sure beats the hell out of being four inches tall. Here's to Catering.'

Now then, where to end? The beginning would be the most logical place.

So; as the chips sizzle in the oil and the water simmers in the big enamel urn—

Cue future lives.

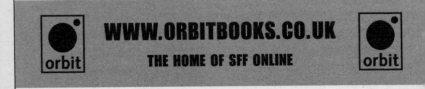